Violent Causes

L. J. Kendall

The Leeth Dossier Vol. 4

**For the ladies of fiction who inspired Leeth:
Modesty, Alita, Diana (of Themyscira), ...**

A catalogue record for this book is available from the National Library of Australia

Creator: Kendall, L. J., author.

Title: Violent Causes / by L. J. Kendall.

ISBN: 9781925430110 (A-format paperback)

Series: Kendall, L. J. Leeth Dossier, Vol 4.

Subjects: Magic–Fiction.
  Fantasy fiction.
  Science fiction.

Copyright © L. J. Kendall, 2019
Cover by Mirella Santana, *www.mirellasantana.com.br*
Image material used under rights from the sites:
  Model: *Nisha* by *neostock*
  Other material: Depositphotos.com

All characters and corporations in this story are fictional, and any resemblance to real people or institutions is accidental.

Story length: 168,000 words
Typeface: Georgia 9pt

Original publication: May 2019.
Release version: 3.   July 2025. (Four small typos fixed, & *Part* page no.s)

This book is available as an A or B-format paperback, and in ebook formats.

ACKNOWLEDGMENTS

I want to thank my wife, Dr Stella St. Clair-Kendall, for her love and encouragement over the years. Still missing you, darling.

An ongoing thanks to Jon Marshall for his insight, support, and help in shaping Leeth over two decades.

My deepest thanks once again to *ThEditors.com* for Dave's insights, advice, and honesty. As well as a direct contribution in the form of fragments of a certain historical journal.

Another special thank you to Mirella de Santana, the artist who designs my covers. You can see more of her wonderful art at *www.mirellasantana.com.br*.

Thank you, all.

Note: there's a special offer if you inform me of any errors in the text – see the Afterword for details.

Novels by L. J. Kendall

The Leeth Dossier:

Wild Thing
Harsh Lessons
Shadow Hunt
Violent Causes
(Lost Girl
  Cold Heart?
  ...)

PROLOGUE

Friday the 28th of October, in the Year of Our Lord 1519, Father Alejandro de Gustez Valencia woke from nightmare, only to find the reality worse. As the madness fell away, the unfamiliar saber slipped through fingers slick with blood, its good Christian steel ringing on pagan stone. Swallowing, eyes wide, he crossed himself in dismay.

Greasy smoke rose from the paved courtyard outside the temples, hanging like a gray shroud in the sky. All around lay the evidence of mad slaughter: pyres, and crows feasting on corpses amid a buzzing chorus of flies.

A movement at the far side of the courtyard drew his attention. But at his first step in that direction, he felt the ground pluck at his sandaled foot, and his glance downward turned to shock.

I walk in blood! Averting his gaze, he lifted his eyes to the sky. Refusing to look down, he crossed the open space one sucking step at a time toward the beckoning hand, placing his feet to avoid the hacked limbs of the slain.

A feathered headdress, now a sodden maroon mass, sprawled beside the pagan. Blood from a long straight slash painted the broad, nutmeg-brown chest red. But as the young priest stopped, the man's head tilted toward him. Eyes opened, one green and one blue, burning with a fevered, fading energy.

"Fools," the man rasped in broken Spanish. "Tezcatlipoca ride you all. Spaniard. Tlaxcalan. Ride all. You break his brother back for him, destroy the scales." He sucked in a breath. "Unbalance, world run red. Unless-"

His words broke into hacking coughs, and Alejandro knelt in the blood, offering his water-skin to the dying man. "Per istam sanctan unctionem" he began, making the sign of the Cross, but the pagan priest brushed his efforts aside.

Angry mismatched eyes bored into Alejandro's, one wiry hand locking on his as if fearing the young foreigner might leave. With his last breaths he gave the location of the dark god's temple, the sacred date, and the terrible ceremony the *Conquistadors* must stop at any cost. His wiry grip held Alejandro in place as he repeated the details until he was certain the Spaniard understood.

"No Tezcatlipoca." Feverish eyes burned into his, the hand on his wrist spasming. "Must stop-"

He waited, but those odd-colored eyes no longer saw.

The desperate grip lasted longer. Swallowing, Father Alejandro pried each finger free.

A full seven months later, Alejandro knelt once again in prayer, this time in a searing hot forest. All around him, the near-silent creaking of steel armor and the stench of men who had marched far and hard through a scrubby, unforgiving land. Each night tortured by their memories of the massacre at Cholula – unarmed men, women and children cut down in their hundreds by cruel steel swords, and muskets that roared like thunder while blue stone eyes rode the dream's sky.

The temple here, in contrast, was a laughable shadow of that other monstrosity of a pyramid. For weeks, he and his fellow conquistadors had mistaken the buried monolith for a natural mountain – a looming presence that had gazed down in heartless witness when the plaza below drowned in the blood of its people.

He shook himself, and peered between the trunks of hardy trees. Ahead, atop the squat edifice, the savage priest waited, arrayed like a bird of paradise. On the ground below stood a handsome young native, cloaked in the pelt of the jaguar, its spots like midnight eyes, watching all around it. Lifting his head high, the youth began ascending the thirty sheer steps to the stone platform, where his heart would be cut from his chest.

Above him the so-called priest waited, his skull mask striped with alternating bands of gleaming black and turquoise, its white teeth grinning. A face from Alejandro's nightmares.

The crowd of Mesheeka below roared their approval as the bronzed youth climbed, their voices falling away as music swelled. A feast of sound, rich in deep mellow drums, bell-sweet pipes, and too-real natural mimicry: piercing bird calls, shimmering cascades of rattling rain, the angry snarls of a jaguar. More instruments blended into the tapestry, curling around the waiting Spaniards, the insistent rhythm growing in volume, mesmerizing them, drawing their hearts into unwilling step with its own. A ponderous bass beat tolled like thunder's rumble, then another, and another.

The young Spanish priest shook his head, snapping from the dream, dismayed by the dull looks on the faces of the armed men at his sides. Dark smoke curled through the tree trunks around them, licking at their ankles. Kicking *el Capitan*, Alejandro snatched up the man's musket and charged, yelling, through the trees. Praying for the Lord to guide his hand, he stopped and took aim up the stone steps.

The feathered priest's face mask turned toward him, its eyes twin holes in the evening sky, burning into him. In the priest's up-stretched hand, lapis lazuli eyes gazed from a golden hilt. Those blue stone eyes pinned him, freezing his muscles, calling for his blood. The hand wielding the black obsidian blade struck down.

Alejandro fired, his musket blast a crack of doom.

The music stopped, a hundred faces staring in shock as the gold and black weapon fell, turning, from the savage priest's slack hand. From the forest behind him, his countrymen erupted, muskets bellowing, steel blades catching the red rays of the setting sun.

Battle raged.

And in some place far from man, a feathered serpent laughed as his brother's dagger plummeted into a crevice of his own stone temple, where it would remain, lost, for centuries....

PART I

Love

CHAPTER 1

"And then she vanished." James eyed Leeth tightly.

She clamped her lips tighter.

The walls of Eagle's underground office displayed a panorama of sunlit snowy peaks. In it, four men sat – one through necessity.

Leeth preferred to stand.

Abrams exchanged a look with Eagle, then angled his wheelchair to directly face the well-groomed speaker. "Swallowed by the magical darkness."

James nodded.

"Tell me, Agent Carter, was this before or after your cybernetic eyes malfunctioned?"

Ohhh, Leeth thought, suddenly wondering if James had actually been aiming at Marc Disten when he'd shot her? She scowled. *Did that mean he'd thought Disten was more dangerous than me?* She growled under her breath, eager for James to leave so she could talk again.

"They were fine after I rebooted them," James said, his jaw tightening. "As you all just saw."

They had indeed seen. Not Disten crushing the vampire's skull; not Leeth in turn killing Disten. But after that: Tash, literally putting herself back together. Comforting Leeth, and beginning to Heal her. Then the dark smoke curling up off Disten's body, Tash collapsing like a puppet into the expanding black sphere. The arrival of Leeth's friend, Marcie. She and James crawling into a darkness impenetrable even to his augmented vision. Searching, on hands and knees.

Harmon tapped a finger on his knee, frowning. "Leeth could simply have slipped away and hidden, under cover of this mysterious black dome."

James shook his head. "No. Not with a shattered femur. Not silently, across a floor covered in litter."

Leeth gritted her teeth, clearly burning to interrupt. But Eagle had ordered her to say nothing until it was just him, her, and the mages.

It looked as though the effort was nearly killing her.

As usual, she'd bounced into the room for the debriefing, only for the bounce to die the instant she saw her 'uncle'.

Harmon had noted that; had read her intent to question his presence, then saw her purse her lips and bite down on the question, in deference to the man to whom she had transferred her loyalties.

That taste was still bitter in his mouth. For now, though, he decided to return the favor and ignore her. "You and Miss Dunkirk examined every inch of the area?" he asked the agent.

James nodded. He'd rechecked the site today, just twelve hours later, confirming there was no hatchway, no hidden under-floor area. Leeth had simply vanished. Only to reappear minutes later, flying through the air as if cata-pulted – pulled back from *elsewhere* by her friend.

The wheelchair-bound man pinned James with his in-tense dark green eyes. "Miss Dunkirk was distraught, you said? And the dome shrinking at the time?"

"Yes. Barely a meter across by the time Leeth reap-peared."

The old mage looked like he'd chewed a sour root. "Thank you."

James's eyes narrowed, seeing his imminent dismissal. "Can you at least tell me if she's likely to do that again?" He glanced at Leeth, pleased to see she looked as frus-trated by this debriefing as he felt.

Abrams sniffed. "*Leeth* didn't do it, Agent."

The old man fell silent then, and at Eagle's nod James left the room.

"Finally!" Leeth exclaimed. "So, what happened? Where did I go? How can I go there-"

Mr Abrams interrupted the deluge. "Cast your mind back to that moment. What were you feeling? What did you do?"

She blinked, as if the questions hadn't occurred to her. "But... that means you think I *did* have something to do with it!"

Abrams said nothing, merely waited.

Leeth frowned as she considered. She'd been angry. No, furious. Outraged that killing Disten hadn't been enough. That the thing inside him had gotten away. She half remembered a flash of intuition, an utter determina-tion to hunt it down, and... *diving?*

She also felt certain she'd been *connected* to it. Kind of.

Chewing her lip, wondering if she should admit that, she looked up. "Uh, James won't get into trouble for shooting me, will he? I... Marc Disten had done something to me. I don't think I would have... snapped out of it, if I hadn't basically died." She remembered the crystal clarity. The freedom, even, from her uncle's – the Doctor's – controls.

And there'd been more she could have learned and discovered. So much more.

If she'd been willing to give up her *self*.

Something else, too. That place she'd been... it made her think of Godsson for some reason. Had he given her an important message once, someplace like that? But that wasn't possible, surely?

Definitely better not to mention that, she decided.

Abrams was studying her, she saw. "And the 'huge thing' you shattered. Would you say you felt a connection to that?"

Leeth's mouth gaped open, before she recovered herself. Then huffed. "I think, kind of yeah, but also, smek no! Yeughh!" She shuddered.

Ah, Abrams thought, concealing the shiver of dismay he felt. *A connection to a complementary Archetype. By The Lady!* "Thank you, Leeth." He turned to Eagle. "I have no further questions."

Eagle nodded, and Leeth left the room quickly, without argument. Unaware that all three men correctly read that as relief trumping curiosity.

Harmon and Eagle waited, impatiently, until Abrams eventually shook his head. "Leeth was pulled through into a metaplane. But I'm troubled that the passage was achieved at all. Nor should the bond between the two girls have been enough to bring her back, so I am also unclear about her return. Worse still, I have no idea what sort of entity would create a geometrical shape as its interface."

"The dome?" Eagle asked.

Abrams nodded. "Although I suspect Godsson's hand in this."

Both men eyed Harmon, who looked back sourly. "For fifteen years, from the day the Dragon dumped him in my lap, I tried to treat Benson, understand him." He sighed. "But I agree: spheres, geometry, 'robo' spirits. *Meta*-spirits." He raised heavy, graying eyebrows at Abrams, but the older mage refused the bait. Harmon turned back to Eagle.

"Like so many people around here, I feel she held some things back."

"Oh, undoubtedly," agreed Abrams. "I shall talk to her in a few days' time."

"I should be present," Harmon said. "Although she may be uncooperative in my presence."

"Yes," Eagle agreed, "you are proving something of a liability, Doctor, aren't you?"

Harmon resisted rolling his eyes, and decided to look defensive. "Yet still useful, I hope. I know her best."

"So you keep telling us," Eagle said.

Abrams waved their sparring aside. "There are two key points. Something from a metaplane reached out, into Reality: that should not be possible. Second, it was magic negating, like Disten. I'm not sure which point troubles me more. And I can't help feeling Godsson is involved."

All three men grimaced at the reminder.

When Harmon left, Abrams breathed out heavily. Sagging forward, both hands went to his face, spindly fingers massaging the papery skin of his brow.

He looks exhausted, Eagle thought, but waited for his old friend to speak. When Abrams drew himself erect again, his intense green eyes seemed to be drowning. Eagle hadn't seen that look since early 2044: the year of the devastating Second World Storm, the first case of the Red Plague nightmare, and capping it off, the Big One that had all but wiped out San Francisco.

"There's something else," Abrams said, and foreboding shot through Eagle. "Something coming. Something ominous I sensed back when d'Artelle's secret war was still secret."

Eagle clamped his jaws, waiting. Hoping the pause was just Abrams choosing his words carefully.

That hope was dashed when Abrams shook his head. "I'm sorry. I can't sense the pattern properly. Just a feeling of stealth. Stealth, and *growth*: it's big. It's big, and it's coming."

"You say you sensed it before?" Eagle asked. "During d'Artelle's secret war? Yet you've never brought it up in our strategic war-gaming."

"Because after the Second World Storm and the collapse of the internet, I no longer sensed it."

"And now you do," Eagle said.
"And now I do," Abrams agreed.
Both men shared the same grim look.

CHAPTER 2

Two days later, Leeth was on her best behavior, eagerly studying the material she'd been provided, acutely aware of the Doctor's presence but as usual, pretending not to be. She flicked to the next page.

"Oh!" She examined the man's picture, admiring the strong, stubbled jawline. Below heavy brows, dark eyes burned with intellect, drilling into hers. Tapping his name, a deep voice growled "Luiz To-hill-kay". She shivered. *So that's how you pronounce 'Tujilque'.* "Yeah, I'd slot you," she told him. Gnawing at her lower lip, she drank in his thick, raven black hair and tan skin.

Mother glared at the three men present. "How fortunate then, that you will *need* to for this mission."

Leeth glanced up, tilting her head to one side, wondering again what Mother had against sex.

Neither Eagle or Father reacted. Nor did the Doctor, though she knew she'd successfully needled him. Hiding a smile, she continued clicking through the rest of the dossier. "And he's a bad guy?" A mage, she read, funded *very* indirectly from Asgard's MR&D programme. She frowned at that. The intel had been sourced by Nelson, she saw. *Hmm.*

"I don't know much about Asgard," she admitted.

"You're not alone," Eagle said, frowning. "They developed the first nano-assemblers, for diamond coatings. Then, diamond fabs. Since then they've heavily diversified. They're now massive, but their R&D programmes remain very, very secretive."

"Uh huh. So, kill him and grab his research so it can be destroyed." She looked up in time to see Mother and Father wince. "I mean, 'retire him' and steal it. Why *are* Asgard keeping his research a secret, anyway?"

The Doctor and Father looked pleased by her guess, but Mother reacted with a moué of annoyance.

"Excellent question, Leeth," Father replied. "We believe his work will cause enormous damage to society."

"How? What's he researching?"

At that, Father looked faintly embarrassed. "Ah, that is one of the things we hope to find out."

"O-kay. But look, say I do steal his research? What good is that – won't he have a copy in the cloud, or backed up on Asgard servers? Especially if it's a real breakthrough."

The others all turned to look at the Doctor, as if they expected him to answer for some reason.

He didn't.

She looked sideways at Father. "So he's a total bad guy, huh? Since you want him dead and his research destroyed, without even knowing what it is?"

None of them answered her.

The skin at the back of her neck prickled. "Ohhh, I get it: this was a tip-off from Mr Abrams, wasn't it?"

Finally, she got a reaction from Eagle – the tiniest quirk of his lips – enough to let her know she'd pleased him. The other three reacted more strongly, all turning their attention to the head of the Bureau for Internal Development.

"Why do you think that, Agent?" Eagle asked.

She shrugged. "Intuition."

"Indeed. Then perhaps you won't be too surprised to hear Mr Abrams has also detected an object of dark power at Dr Tujilque's apartment."

In reply, Leeth smirked at Mother. Eagle passed across an empty black silk bag that set her skin tingling when she took it.

"The object is a leather-bound book, the 'Libro Sangre'. If you find it, place it in there – without touching it. Take particular care, though. Abrams also felt an 'echo' of the book that disturbed him."

"An echo? What does that mean?"

It was Eagle's turn to shrug.

Later, after Leeth had left, Mother returned to the other difficulty, which even the girl had seen. "She has a point: how can we be sure that even if she does acquire a copy of his research and retires him, Asgard won't simply continue from backups?"

"Nelson extracted some of Tujilque's material from Asgard," Eagle said. "The Doctor said the information is cleverly incomplete. Apparently such reporting is not unusual in the hermetic sciences," he added, with a pointed look at Harmon. "The Doctor was unable to say exactly what Tujilque is researching."

And yet Abrams drew our attention to it, Mother thought, also noting Eagle's silence about what Abrams himself had made of the material. Fully aware of Eagle's bio-monitors, she coolly suppressed her growing excitement, and let him continue.

"Abrams believes Tujilque's personal papers will provide the key necessary to decode his notes. He also said the nature of the research is so far beyond the limits of what is acceptable that Asgard dare not risk its nature being discovered."

So Abrams does *know,* Mother thought. She stored away that fact for later. "This plan cannot succeed." She tapped the projected image of the swarthy researcher. "Even though he's a man, he's also a mage: sooner or later he'll 'percept' Leeth's true intentions."

Eagle's expression hardened, as it did whenever he had to give orders he disliked. His eyes moved to Harmon. "The Doctor says he can include some Suggestions to bolster her cover identity."

"Suggestions?" Mother digested that, then leaned forward. "That is insane. You plan to *magically hypnotize* her into falling for someone she is to kill? With what consequences, even if such conditioning is possible?" She drew back in her chair from Harmon.

Eagle refused to back down. "As you say: the man is a mage. We see no other way. And you heard Leeth herself. She already finds him attractive, so any additional magical suggestions to reinforce that can be mild, non-invasive."

"And of course you have no qualms about whoring out your female agents."

Eagle's look hardened. "My personal qualms, Mother, for both our female *and* male agents, come second to national security. And thanks to her upbringing by the Doctor, she also has no issue with the primary mission objectives: retiring Tujilque and destroying his research." His expression, however, had turned sour. "Admittedly, we also have a secondary objective we cannot disclose to Leeth: unlocking more of her magical potential. For that, the Doctor says extreme stress is essential."

"That is... beyond monstrous." Mother's eyes flicked to the Doctor before returning to Eagle. "And *you* countenance this because it may increase her utility. Are you all idiots?" She noted Father scowling at her, but that was only to be expected. "I am no psychologist, but even I can see Leeth is likely to fall for this oily prick with or without the Doctor's 'suggestions' – which can only make matters worse. She will then blame the Department for forcing her to retire him."

"No," Eagle said. "She will blame the Doctor."

"Of course," Harmon agreed. "Until I point out her own share of the guilt."

Mother looked from one to the other. "With all due respect, if our plan is to pretend ignorance, you must see the Doctor would happily throw us in front of a train if he thought it would improve his standing with his former 'ward'."

"We have further facts we can share with her after the mission," Eagle told her.

For now, they would hold in reserve the short piece of footage of an appalling rite five years earlier in South America. He and Abrams thought it was what had led to Tujilque's acquisition by Asgard soon after. He also had complete confidence in Leeth's inner strength.

"After the mission?" Mother asked. "Not before?"

Eagle shook his head. "No. If Leeth saw it beforehand, Suggestions to like him would be doomed to fail. The Doctor also assures me he is prepared to appear the 'bad guy' in this scenario for a short period. It will be a test of both him and Leeth."

Mother grimaced. "Very well, let's set that aside. This plan also assumes she will capture his interest and earn enough of his trust to achieve our objectives. *Assumes.* She is not so attractive that every man will automatically fall for her charms!"

Eagle didn't rise to her bait. "Abrams predicts Tujilque will find Leeth irresistible, given the nature of his research."

If Eagle's expression told her nothing, the Doctor's spoke volumes – but it was neither the jealousy nor anger she had expected. Harmon was *fearful.* She blinked. "Is Tujilque-?" She forced herself to stop and take firm control of her thoughts before daring to continue. "Is Tujilque another acolyte of our larger problem?"

All three men tensed but then relaxed, Eagle shaking his head.

Mother reassessed what she'd been told. "Neither of

you want Leeth killed; even hurt." Which meant they held back information from the girl to improve her odds. But what information would justify the order to kill, while withholding the reason? "Tujilque himself. *He* is the threat to Leeth. Or, his research."

Father looked blank, confused by her remark, but from Harmon's reaction, her shot was right on the mark. *And Abrams himself is worried? And thinks the South American mage would find Leeth 'irresistible'? Just what was Tujilque playing with? Was this what she'd been waiting for?* Again, she shunted the possibility into digital cerebration.

"I also note there was no mention of this magical brainwashing in the briefing material you showed her," Mother said. "I thought after the Opera House incident, we agreed Harmon and Nelson's 'mental surgeries' would never be used again. You're breaking the deal you made with her."

Eagle blinked. "We won't be doing this against her will, Mother. Nor will it involve Nelson's technology."

"You'll never get Leeth to agree to it. When do you plan to tell her about it? Or is the plan to 'Suggest' that to her, too?"

"I do not break trust, Mother." Eagle's eyes burned. "The Doctor assures me the Suggestion spell is more like simple hypnosis, nothing like the earlier procedure. And we plan to discuss it with her imminently."

Mother leaned forward. "You say she will blame the Doctor – but she returned because of her faith in *you*. She trusts *you*." From the corner of her eye she grew aware of Harmon, looking far too relaxed. *And we call* Benson *'The Manipulator'!*

Eagle spread his hands. "Leeth will go into this with her eyes wide open, Mother."

And there it was, the expression of calm certainty. How often had she seen that look, long before an operation went sideways yet still somehow played out to the Department's benefit? Or was this just Eagle playing the mind games that built his own myth?

With a mental snarl she closed her mouth.

Once Mother and Father had left, Eagle called Abrams, bringing the elderly mage in via holo-presence for a final three-way discussion. Eagle leaned forward, pinning Harmon's eyes. "Let's be frank, Doctor. I accept the need to 'hide' Leeth behind a false persona. But its creation will be done with myself and Abrams observing. I am well aware you have your own agenda with Leeth."

Harmon met that gaze with casual equanimity. "My only agenda is to promote her further magical development. Which will require more stress. Far more stress than simple fear for her life."

Eagle looked from Harmon to Abrams.

The elderly man grimaced. "I am afraid Dr Harmon's theories, however distasteful, do have supporting evidence. People either break or grow under extreme stress. 'What does not kill me.' It's plausible the principle applies equally to magical development." He could have added more, based on long, long experience, but chose to say nothing. Not with the storm he sensed, ahead.

"If it doesn't break her," Eagle said.

Harmon spread his hands. "Break *Leeth?* Do you seriously think my Suggestions could do that, Eagle? Besides, I am the last person to do something which might ruin the experiment to which I have devoted *ten years* of my life."

Eagle studied him. "No, Doctor. I don't imagine you would."

Harmon settled back, satisfied.

After he had dismissed Harmon, and his old friend had signed off, Eagle rubbed his eyes. With a feeling of lead in his stomach, he authorized the mission, then stared unseeing at the single lily in its aquamarine glass swirl. Thinking how like Agent A, his very first assassin, Leeth was.

But then, what could be more natural?

CHAPTER 3

"Fuck off. No way!" Jumping up, she tossed her chair into a wall of his office. One armrest snapped off, flying back across the room.

Harmon frowned at her. "Leeth, Eagle himself recommends the use of Suggestion. There is no way-"

"No! You're right, there *is* no way I'll let you mess about in my head..." *again,* she tried to think, but it slipped away. "In my...."

She blinked, the familiar and hated confusion eroding her thoughts until her head was just an empty, still place.

Across from her, Harmon didn't quite smirk. Heat flushed over her skin. *Suggestion. That's what he'd been saying.* "No. I won't let you." *You can't control me anymore, and I'll never let you trick me again.*

Harmon sighed. "Leeth, you're not stupid. Abrams and Eagle have *both* assessed Luiz as a major danger to our nation; perhaps the world. There-"

"Sure. And I'll do the mission: seduce him, steal his research, and kill him."

Even Harmon found that calm declaration disturbing. "Leeth, Luiz Tujilque is a mage."

She rolled her eyes.

Harmon resisted snapping back at her. They both knew she was adept at hiding her thoughts, but this mission would require far more than that. Lecturing her though would only make her dig her heels in harder, he knew. Instead, he softened his tone and caught her eyes. "Leeth. Do you really think you can seduce and live with someone for days or weeks, planning to kill them, without them realizing?"

She lifted her chin, her expression confident. He needed no magic to read the thought: 'Why not? I've hidden it from *you.*'

He held her eyes until he *saw* the confidence leach from her face, as she realized what he was really telling her: *I know.*

She blinked again, staring, but he merely acknowledged his bombshell with a tiny inclination of his head. "He is a dangerous and distrustful mage whose luxury apartment we *hope* you will be sharing. He will be able to study you, at all hours, awake and asleep."

He let his voice fall, softening further. "Your skills of

mental evasion and deception are superb, Leeth, honed as they are from our own years of play."

Prepared for her anger at the word 'play', he lifted a hand. "Or let us say, our years of *competition*. But even you cannot maintain a deception of that magnitude twenty-four seven."

She sniffed. "So I'll just kill him quickly."

He refused to react to her goading, especially as he suspected she was half serious. "Tujilque does sometimes bring his work home – but so far, we believe, only when alone. Never when he has company. Unless, perhaps, *you* can earn his trust. You will need to, to have any hope of stealing his research."

She opened her mouth to object, but he leaned forward and let her see his real concern. "Leeth! He can Percept emotions! You will need to genuinely fall for him, and *consciously* forget your mission. Only Suggestion will allow you to do that. But he is ruthless, and you will be alone with him, your true self hidden. You will be walking a knife edge – vulnerable, if you let your guard down too far."

Leeth rolled her eyes again, and he felt his hands clench. He swallowed, not daring to share Eagle's information with her – if she knew Tujilque's true colors, no mere Suggestion could override her instinctive loathing. He *had* to convince her, but he had lost her trust. *After what I've done to her, though, can I blame her?*

And Tujilque... recalling her reaction to the younger, good-looking male, what lay ahead was suddenly all too clear to him. Given how he'd *conditioned* her, he knew how she would respond to the South American mage.

And if she hesitated at a moment of vulnerability? Tujilque could End her. He had to make her see that!

Yet there she stood, arms crossed, scowling stubbornly back at him, assuming he was acting against her and that this was some trick. This was intolerable! The awareness that he himself had fashioned this trap only made it more so, made him want to-

"I don't want you hurt, girl!"

Harmon shocked to a stop, surprised at his own outburst. He was panting, too. He saw her expression soften, saw her realise she'd peeled away his self-control yet again;

and saw she recognized that, too. Saw too that somehow, she'd eroded his resolve.

"Yeah. Right. 'Don't want me hurt.' Not unless...."

He flushed as she left her accusation unspoken, stopping cleverly at the brink. *Before* his controls could steal the thought from her mind, but *after* she had first goaded him into his admission of affection.

Lips thinning, he took hold of himself and stood. "The spell will be essential to the success of this mission. Perhaps if *you* are the one who writes the 'script' for the Suggestions I will outline for you, you will see the necessity?"

Leeth leaned over his desk, facing him, glaring up at him, considering it but feeling... churned up. Was he acting? Her instincts told her he wasn't. He wouldn't've been so angry with himself if he had been.

"Okay," she said, finally. "On the condition that Eagle *and* Mr Abrams are present for the 'Suggestion' spell, *and* you're closely recorded while you do it." *So even if you whisper extra instructions, Eagle will notice something funny.*

In the end, all three of them worked on the script. It was actually kind of fun. Luiz was what the Doctor called an alpha male, so 'Kitty Perkins' would be someone who'd go along with that.

Secretly, the thought gave her a little thrill, not that she'd ever admit it. Was that wrong? A side effect of her Unc- of *the Doctor's* treatment, maybe? Almost, it made her see how Mother might possibly imagine something wrong in sex. She'd even asked her to help, but Mother had wrinkled her nose and said she didn't think they needed *her* assistance in setting up a male sexual fantasy figure.

So, yeah, maybe Mother was just weird.

The Doctor explained the magical procedure would also help her remember all the background history they'd created for Kitty.

Finally, with a camera recording and Mr Abrams and Eagle carefully watching, the Doctor cast his spell.

But her habit of resistance was so strong it wasn't until his third try that she was able to 'let go' enough to let the spell into her mind. Then her thoughts kind of relaxed, just listening to his words, but not having to remember them.

It was so easy to understand him when he explained stuff slowly. It was nice hearing him finally being honest. Everything he said, sharp, and clear, and true.

So deeply true.

But she could still think. He wasn't changing that.

They waited until she met Eagle's eyes and nodded, then Harmon began reading from the script they'd prepared, following it exactly.

At least, until he veered off.

He'd just covered the part about how she'd be mildly interested in Luiz's work, earning his trust and affection and happy to live with him. They got near the key part, with its reminder about staying calm and relaxed and needing not to interrupt. As if they thought she'd get upset or something at the orders to kill Luiz and steal his research.

Like that wasn't the whole *point* of the mission!

"But in the back of your mind, hidden away, will be your real mission objectives. Two personalities-"

She knew the script by heart: ... *or mental states. Leeth, in state one...*

But what he said was: "Two personalities, or modes. Leeth, Mode One, will-"

His words reverberated through her. *He just put me into Mode One. Huh.* The thought left her strangely numb. *I should click my teeth....* But he was still talking, and she mustn't interrupt.

"- kill Luiz and steal his research."

She hesitated. That was true. That was exactly what her mission was. Was he using his terrible 'Mode One' thing to order her to do it because he thought she'd fall in love with Luiz for real, and betray the Department? That was just stupid.

She still hesitated, torn.... Eagle was frowning at the Doctor's small departure from the script, but said nothing, allowing him to continue.

Mr Abrams looked impressed by how focused she'd just become.

"Luiz must be, as you put it, 'properly' killed," her uncle continued. "Asgard uses medical alert monitoring for all key personnel, so they will dispatch someone to heal him immediately. Remove his head and fling it to the ground below. But all those instructions are only for that Leeth Mode One persona.

"In 'Mode Two' you are Kitty Perkins, knowing nothing of those Mode One instructions. In Mode Two, Kitty will find Luiz fascinating and attractive, and quickly fall in love with him. Yet Leeth will remain alert, watching and guarding Kitty while waiting for the chance to carry out her mission and return safely to us."

He continued giving her Suggestions, while Eagle listened. But even though they made sense, and seemed helpful, she didn't trust him. She softly clicked her teeth twice. From the small disk adhered in her armpit and the one concealed in her hair, against her scalp, his own voice whispered the phrase that freed her from his control. Barney's tiny device, recognizing her acoustic signal, played back its two second recording. A stopgap measure, since the Doctor's other mental bonds were as strong as ever. The ones that froze her mind or muscles each time she tried to expose his past tortures.

The Doctor continued speaking, following the script which she herself had helped write, his Suggestion spell still running.

And at the end, the *only* thing he'd added was sneaking in his Mode One command. *Had* he done that just to be sure? To *help,* even? Or did he plan to try to take advantage of her once they'd finished and were alone together?

Eagle's door whisked shut behind them. About to advance on him, she heard him whisper the nonsense phrase that freed her, that her brain refused to remember. For long seconds he just stared at her, grim, his eyes a little wide. Her skin rose in goosebumps, trying to work out what he'd just done, what new betrayal she'd fallen for... and his face *crumpled.*

He turned away, looking a little sick, and walked off.

She stared after him. Searching inside herself, casting her mind back over the magical session, hunting for gaps, for holes.

She found none.

Later, she watched the recording she'd insisted on, too. This time, she used Barney's device to end his Mode One as soon as the recording put her back into it. She shivered, at the discovery that a recording was enough to do that.

But the recording also checked out okay. Except, from that glimpse of his face as he'd walked away, she recognized the same sick expression on his face the moment before he'd pulled the 'Mode One' trick.

He'd done that right in front of Eagle and Mr Abrams.

She thought about that.

He'd been desperate. But he'd only used it to do exactly what he'd promised. As though she'd need that boost.

As though he'd seen something terrible coming.

CHAPTER 4

Luiz Tujilque had not yet decided which girl to take home, when the blonde North American arrived.

Something in her eyes said she'd entered the club by mistake. He liked that. He noted her outfit in particular: wrong for this venue, though daring in the amount of skin it showed – shoulders, cleavage, her sides and entire back. A lot of leg. And the cat-ear headband. *That,* he noticed immediately.

She swayed gracefully between the patrons. With her gaze fixed on the moving, spotlit figures, she seemed a moth, the dancers her flames.

He lost sight of her as he whirled his current partner back into the weaving bodies. He next glimpsed her beside the dance floor, her lips parted as she drank in every paired and mirrored motion, every flash of glitter-dusted limbs.

Luiz swept the dark-haired beauty in his arms into a close circle around him. He was the unyielding mass she orbited, controlled by his firm hands. He saw the blonde's eyes widen, entranced by their moves: by *his* moves. Snared by his potency. Their eyes met for a beat before hers fell, a blush rising to her cheeks.

Smiling, he drew his partner in against his front, trapping her as he spun her in then pushed her away, almost allowing her to escape. His fingers coiled snake-like around hers, then around her wrist. Controlling her, whipping her back in against his body, he threaded them both back into the meshing movements, their passage a series of arcs locked to the music's beat.

His partner made a small sound of protest. Displeased, he tightened his grip.

His mage senses read the dancers, searching out the girl. Restrained passions wove a tapestry, auras mingling and touching, creating an ephemeral magic. An evanescent wisp that flowered, lived, and died, from energies poured out like ghost blood into the smoky air.

When next they broached the fringes of the organic mass, the blonde still stood, watching. Now swaying perfectly to the rhythm, obviously yearning to join the dance but just as obviously uncertain. Unfamiliar with the steps?

He would teach her. He would teach her many things.

Whirling his partner away and back, he lingered at the

fringe to study the girl. With her hips moving in unconscious mimicry, her eyes lifted again to his – and he had her, trapped. He saw the *look*, that look he often met when a woman felt his presence, took in his dark hair, his strong jaw, the ax blade of his nose.

The blonde wrenched her gaze away, flustered, and he allowed himself to Percept her. Liking what he saw, he made his decision.

Provided she met his standards on the dance floor, he had found his partner for the night. At the next pause in the music, he smiled down at the woman in his arms. Pulling her close, he bent low to her ear. "We'll try again when you learn to flow instead of flounce."

He saw her joy crumble as he discarded her.

"No, move them like *this*," he murmured to his new partner, taking her hips and steering her as he wished while he demonstrated. Snaking his own body in fluid harmony to the music, he pressed against her.

Giggling, she relaxed into his grip, ceding control.

She quivered at the touch of his lips on her ear, and he felt a tension in his groin as he stared down at the taut buttocks and subtly muscled legs. She had a weight to her, yet moved in his arms like a dream, responsive to his every touch. Learning the steps and moves with astonishing ease. And her eyes drank him in. Several times he caught her biting her lips, staring at his, even glancing at his crotch when she thought he wasn't paying attention.

Yes, she would do very nicely indeed. He pictured her body under his, responding to his touch, yielding....

The evening that followed met, and even exceeded his wildest expectations. Learning her name, Kitty Perkins, while eyeing the feline ears of her silly headband and imagining future possibilities, had stirred his blood. Kitty had proven to be by turns demure and wild in his bed.

Now in the small hours, exhausted, sweat cooling, he lay beside her, her small body spooned into his. Nestled into his warmth as if she'd been cold her whole life.

Staring out into the night sky beyond the mirrored windows of his twenty-second-floor apartment, he slid one hand possessively over a delightful haunch. She murmured softly in the dark and pressed against him, making him smile. Even in her sleep, she responded. He might perhaps keep her for a few days.

Sated, content, he let light-jeweled city spires sing him to sleep.

Days turned into a week. Something about Kitty appealed to him on an instinctive level. She stirred him as no other had: amenable, even submissive; innocent yet sexual. She was a study in contradictions. Shy but daring; willful yet obedient. But beneath all that, he sometimes caught a flash, a half-seen glimpse of something darker at her core. Something fierce and challenging.

A mettle to face his own?

She intrigued him, and unlike the other women he'd met, enjoyed, and cast aside, the longer he took his pleasures with her, the more contradictions he found, the more intriguing she became. He began using her a little more roughly in bed. Instead of rejection, he met surprised delight – and woke the darkness within her.

It had surfaced for breathless seconds, challenging him. She had been on all fours before him. One small hand had reached back, trapping his wrist with surprising strength to stay the next blow.

He'd punished that small rebellion, too. Kitty had stiffened in shock, then stilled, her head turning toward him like a carved idol, stone grinding on stone. For a moment he braced for lapis lazuli eyes with a shock of pure horror. Instead he met the eyes of a predator – not the metaphysical threat he'd imagined.

Relief thrilled through him. He probed, sensing her instincts at work, the dark part of her soul padding swiftly toward a decision. *Finally!* he thought. Delighted, he changed tactics, transforming her pain to pleasure. Then, seeing how it cut the ground from beneath her mutiny and overwhelmed her defiance, he erupted.

Afterward, panting, he hunted for traces of that rebellious spirit. He found none, but knew it lay in wait.

Eager to face it again, to tame it, he'd ordered a... special outfit. The animatronic tail would be delivered today. He rechecked the specs for its additional functions, knowing he should be working. Instead he found himself imagining Kitty taking the delivery, curiosity burning in her to open it, yet having learned from experience to be patient and await her Master's return.

And that was not all he had ordered. *That* highly illegal plan stole his breath.

He hunched forward in his lab at the surge of arousal. *By the Old Ones, even when not in front of me, she torments my thoughts!*

He *could* take his work home....

He could bind her, blindfold her, toy with her. Leave her quivering and expectant, then withdraw, setting her own imagination against her, simmering while he distracted himself with research. He was close, now. Thaumic flows and blood transactions. But blood alone meant nothing. Death was the key.

He fell back into his work. Asgard's molecular modeling software, re-engineered to visualize the Imaginal structures of spells and rituals, held the complex edifice. The puzzle drew him back in, absorbing his attention.

An hour later, he stretched aching shoulders and examined the fruits of his labor. Changing the viewing angle, he manually pivoted key branches in the model, checking the interlocks.

With a smile, he considered the color coding of nodes and connections, private labels for his own Imaginal concepts and properties. Let Asgard try to decode *that* without his journal.

Smirking, he 'fed' the modeled ritual its crimson input. From *elsewhere*, he felt blue stone eyes burning into his back, but resisted the urge to turn and check.

The model triggered.

It snapped shut like a molecular mousetrap, folding finally into a new, stable, dense object. Veins pounding in his temples, with shaking hands he rotated the wicked-looking virtual enclosure and swallowed.

By the Dark God, no magical force on Earth would undo that*!* Swallowing, he reset the model, watching it flick back into its sprawling, untriggered shape, half expecting the computer simulation to somehow refuse. *So close, now.* He could start tonight if he wished, with just this.

Blinking and stretching again, his thoughts returned to

Kitty and his plans for the evening. Blood rushed through him, singing his skin alight.

Kitty.

With her out of his thoughts, he could concentrate for hours. But the vision of her, bound and blind and helpless, waiting for his return, for his touch, those taut limbs quivering and straining, sweat beading that soft, bronze skin....

I think I'm falling in love, Kitty thought, as Luiz helped her into his sleek Tesla Photon. His hungry gaze claimed her, making her bite her lip as she swung chained ankles neatly in. Something about it all felt strange. Her thoughts floated with a kind of dreamlike sense of inevitability.

She tingled all over, still uncertain about the outfit she wore under the long, sable coat. Taking care not to damage it with her wicked black claws, she ran her fingers over it again, the latex of the strange gloves so thin she could feel their soft fur.

She'd been hesitant when he'd presented the gloves, a strange resonance shivering through her when she felt the razor edges of their clawed tips. As if something darker, buried inside, hungered to take control of them.

Luiz's dark eyes had lit at her reaction. "Don't fear, *caro.* I can Heal." His eyes had pinned hers, guiding each of her fingers inside, one by one, before bringing her soft lips to his. One large hand had slid around her neck, tilting her head back and up and into his kiss.

She'd felt something inside her squirm, found her hands opening and closing of their own accord, *owning* the weapons at her fingertips. Approving. Permitting.

She shuddered.

Electric turbines surged as Luiz wove an urgent path through the evening traffic, driving harder as they left the safer parts of the city behind and entered the Tenderloin.

He was taking her to a *special* club tonight. One where her skin-tight furred black latex would raise no eyebrows except appreciative ones, he'd promised. Nor would her hobbled legs, nor the shining black collar around her neck, with its heavy gauge chrome ring.

She'd watched him place the leash in his suit pocket, and shuddered in anticipation. *He won't really use it, surely?*

He'd then drawn out a colored string and begun tying a series of knots into it. "This is quipu," he said. "These knots mean thirty-five." He left a space and made more loops, tightening them. "These, twenty-six." His eyes didn't leave hers. "And these, thirty-four."

He draped it around her neck.

She frowned up at him.

"Your measurements."

Her eyes widened, a mix of horror at her body being reduced to a series of numbers but at the same time, oddly thrilled.

Again, something inside her snarled. Smiling, Luiz bent down to plunder her lips.

The next day, equal parts inspired and aroused, Luiz Tujilque fought himself. He was so close, now. Kitty herself had revealed the next steps even as he'd healed the bloody cuts she'd dealt him, finding himself once more face to face with that hidden part of her.

She'd been restrained, on show, humiliated, when the presence within her had risen up, her clawed gloves twisting to sever one leather bond then the other.

Black volcanic glass had roared in hunger, answering her rebellion. Instead of retreating, he'd embraced her challenge, once again wielding pleasure like a weapon to confuse the dark spirit within her. Seduce it.

"You need me, Kitty," he told her, in the hush that had fallen over the club while her eyes burned up into his. "These people don't care about you – to them, you are a mere thing. Entertainment." Her eyes moved to the hungry gazes of the onlookers, and again he sensed some wild thing held in check. "But I," he continued, recapturing her attention, "I understand you. I see the darkness inside you." He felt her respond to his words. The sense of mastery felt god-like.

And tonight.... His gaze fell on the small vial, while the second last virtual thaumic construct hung in mid-air, incomplete, as his pulse raced. The deep amber fluid in the vial whispered to him: that she would have no say in it, trapped in her own body before she even knew what he had done. Locked into dependence on him...

Dammit! Concentrate, Luiz! Are you some schoolboy?

Growling, hands shaking, he forced away all thoughts of tonight's drama.

Blocking her from his mind, he submerged himself in the work. So very close, now. At his fingertips.

The call from Kitty came right then, interrupting him at work as he had specifically ordered her never to do. He'd glowered at her, reveling in the power of his mere glance as she fumbled to a stop, stuttering out the admission that to-day was her birthday.

He'd just stared. And then felt the pieces fall together. The vial. His research. The new... outfit.

The obsidian blade, waiting.

He glanced at his near-complete thaumic model, then at his comp unit, and saved his work. He would complete it tonight, at home. While Kitty... *changed.*

"For you, *caro,* I will leave my work early." He smiled. "I have *plans* for you tonight."

Lapis lazuli eyes burned in the back of his mind as he made... arrangements.

CHAPTER 5

Something was wrong.

Barefoot in the dark, trembling, she moved soundlessly from the bedroom. Along the short hallway. One step down, into the living area.

Candles on a cake, blown out. For some reason, the sight made her heart falter.

She forced herself closer, aware of a stillness in the luxury apartment. Creeping across the unlit room, alert, she ignored both the sounds beyond the mirrored windows and the sight of New Francisco spreading its fairy lights far below.

Reading her mood, her tail coiled and lashed behind her.

Shuddering, ice threading her spine, she took another step.

Happy Birthday
Kitty

Standing over the cake – *her* cake – a spot of red appeared on the lemon icing. Then a second. A third.

Her eyes moved slowly from the cake to her feet, the sight of her legs' plush gray pelt sending a wash of dread through her. Her tail snaked into view, wrapping round the soft fur of her thigh as if sensing her distress.

She felt ears twitch – furry, she somehow knew – and saw whiskers do the same. She focused, cross-eyed, on her velvet nose.

I'm going insane. I don't have fur!

Her gaze dropped again to her legs and began inching up her thighs.

Something was very, very wrong.

Her mind was flailing at her, attacking and retreating in a crazed struggle to stop her eyes tracking up her taut, furred thighs, across the velvet curves of her stomach.

Don't look. If you don't look, you won't see...

... a trickle of blood floating in empty space. Five dark drops suspended in thin air just *below* each of the claws extending from her fingertips.

Her head pivoted unwillingly from the left, to the right, where thin red threads fed two more drops that hung in mid-air, slowly swelling.

Claws... fake. Fur... suit. Ears, tail... animatronic.

Shuddering at the knowledge, the tingling at her fingertips subsided.

Seven drops of blood fell across her birthday cake.

And truth and memory crashed down on her.

"Luiz!" she shrieked, racing for the bedroom.

To a scene of carnage: her love, gutted and spread-eagled on the bed, his head severed.

And then, the memory of *herself* doing it. Of letting his head fall, from nerveless fingers.

Leeth collapsed to her knees as she remembered. The mission: kill Luiz. Steal his research.

It was what this had all been about. *'So I'll kill him quickly.'* Her own words, flippant. She groaned, hunching forward, tears spilling, sparkling in the darkened room as she flung her head from side to side, trying to deny the truth. Her heart hammered, her belly twisted, each taking vengeance for what she'd done.

At last she stood, feeling tricked – *again* – and fought the urge to return to the Department just to burn it down. *Funt them! I should abandon this mission! Is this really who I want to be, what I want to do? Manipulate, lie? Murder?*

Only a tiny, desperate hope that Eagle's reason was good enough allowed her to let half-sensed impulses continue guiding her. Impulses she now felt as foreign, implanted things. The foremost, a warning to continue wearing the fetish costume, keep her identity concealed.

She considered that – then screamed and slashed the impulse to pieces. The compulsion vanished, but its logic remained. She plucked at her sleeve, her jaw locking another scream deep inside.

The next impulse gave her the code for Luiz's safe. Numbly, she opened it. Inside, his notebook, and a creepy old leather-bound book she suddenly remembered being told about. She shut her eyes, focusing inward until she mentally held the construct that had fed her the code for the safe. Her invisible blades diced it, too, into nothingness. She imagined a faint wailing sound as it vanished.

Turning from the gaping safe and the books inside it, her thoughts sank back inward. One by one, she probed at each idea that wasn't hers, slicing and killing it. Acceptance of the animatronic fetish catsuit – Luiz's *furry* kink – the false birthday and the demand for him to return home to her.... Each was pulled out, examined, and destroyed. Until she came to the love.

One hand flashed to her mouth. She couldn't... she couldn't tell which parts of her love had been real, which false.

Love and hate tangled together, churning deep inside her. In the unlit room her gaze turned deeper inward, chasing fleeing feelings down dark tunnels that spiraled into caverns lost from light. To find, finally, something small, rose pink, and fragile, pulsing in the gloom.

Should she strike?

But it was so small. *Innocent.*

In the end she retreated, and found herself at Luiz's desk, hunched over, eyes squeezed shut, shaking her head.

Panting.

She forced her back straight. *Pull yourself together.*

One last instruction remained.

Skin prickling, she wrote the required note – handing the police a motive for Luiz's killing – and carried it back to his headless corpse splayed bloodily on the bed. At every step, feeling the false memories crowding her thoughts like beads of madness, the crazy rationale that had necessitated his death. *Another lie.* Gripping the paper, her muscles tensed to rip it into tiny pieces.

Truly herself again, she realized what she'd just done to the Doctor's controls – his Suggestion. Could she...? Excited, she quested for traces of the Mode One abomination, finding slender threads twisting deeper inside her. She probed, then cut...

"Aieeee!" The scream tore from her throat.

She found herself on the floor, on bruised knees, eyes wide and heart racing. She collapsed forward into the thick carpet, panting and sweating, terrified she'd just crippled herself.

By degrees, the psychic pain faded to a mere echo in her head. At last she dared to move. Gingerly, she tried unfurling invisible claws.

Tears spilled in relief when they responded, shearing through the plush pile. When her heart returned to its normal pace, she stood, shakily, feeling fragile.

Swallowing, her eyes drifted to Luiz's bloody corpse, silently accusing her from its final resting place on the bed.

A stealthy scrape froze her. In the silence of the darkened room, its air heavy with the copper tang of Luiz's blood, a whisper of sound. *There: again.*

Something scratched at a desk drawer. Standing in the unlit bedroom, she had the strangest sense a black ribbon stretched out for Luiz, pulling at him, siphoning him into itself.

Turning and dropping the note by his body – *'Para Lucía y Francesca. Cuzco, 22 de mayo de 2057'* – she stepped to the desk. As she approached it, something feathery touched her wrist.

Fury boiled over. Slashing through empty air, she struck a rubbery resistance that *hurt* before it parted. In the drawer, something skittered.

Going to the desk, she tried the drawer. Locked.

Snarling, she smashed a fist against it. The old wood broke with a harsh *crack*, exposing a wooden drawer containing just a gold-handled dagger with a serrated black blade. Two cruel blue stone eyes stared up at her from the ornate handle, above a long obsidian tooth with scalloped razor edges. Nothing else.

Instinct told her not to touch it.

Staring ¡at it in the dark, breathing hard, she finally picked up a pen and prodded the black glass dagger into the 'special' black silk bag they'd given her. Grimly, she crossed back to the open safe above Luiz's bed and poked both of his books into the bag, too, aware of his head, unmoving on the floor behind her. Watching.

With a shiver, she tied the bag shut, then found her handbag and stuffed the bag inside. From there, she went to his study, hesitating at the threshold, remembering how sensitive he was about her entering this room when he was working.

Never again.

She blinked and shook her head, standing over his work desk, smelling the leather of his chair and the cinnamon musk of Luiz himself. Numbly, she pocketed his computer, turned, and left.

She found herself back in the bedroom, smelling that familiar sweet, coppery scent, staring at the bed and the still form sprawled across it, a crimson river ebbing into a dark lake. At his head, lying on the carpet. She was supposed to open a window, and fling it far from the apartment.

Instead, she turned and left.

-

Psychic alarms had David Abrams out of bed and into his wheelchair before Leeth had left the scene. His student watched from below, blinking in sleepy shock from the front doors as air elementals whisked him, wheelchair and all, up and out of sight into the night sky.

CHAPTER 6

One look at her face was enough to hold Mother and Father silent as a grim Leeth, now dressed quite differently, made a formal request to speak to Eagle. They watched her leave the operations room, then tracked her on camera as she prowled the corridors, working her way implacably up, level by level, to basement five. Her expression unchanging.

"She didn't toss the head outside," Nelson reported, already examining video footage from inside and around the apartment building.

Mother and Father did not respond verbally to the comment – though they did send for Dojo.

Leeth stepped through the door the moment it whisked open, taking in the three waiting men. *Of course Mr Abrams is involved. Of course.* Off to one side sat the Doctor, but she'd grown so used to his betrayals she didn't dignify him with so much as a glance.

Keeping her eyes on Eagle's she stalked across the room. Opening her handbag, she tossed the silk-wrapped bundle onto his desk. It landed with a harsh clatter.

At the sound, Abrams jerked back in his wheelchair. She was dimly aware of his aged head lifting in shock from it to stare at her, his face suddenly pale. The gaze he turned on her prickled in a way she hadn't felt since the night she'd freed Godsson.

She ignored it, stabbing one finger unerringly in the Doctor's direction while her eyes stared into Eagle's.

"He *made* me kill Luiz. *You* made me kill Luiz." She felt her hands clench. *If he says, 'That was the mission....'*

But he didn't. He didn't say anything. Didn't ask who 'he' was. Just met her gaze square on, in a single long look, then stood and walked stiffly around his desk towards her.

Abrams gasped. "Wait!"

Leeth frowned, microscopically adjusting her stance, ready to-

Eagle's arms opened, his expression sober, and she realized he was offering her a *hug!* Stunned, she stood motionless and let his arms enfold her.

"I am so sorry, Agent. Once again, we have thrown you into dark waters."

His arms around her, hers went around him in turn,

and she found herself suddenly crying, her head pressed to his chest. "I *loved* him. I could've worked out something else! But Uncle's *Suggestion* made me kill him!"

Abrams's voice held a trace of awe. "She's been *touched,* but not polluted." Then it steadied, and a note of asperity crept in as his gaze shifted to his friend. "So it's safe for you to approach her if you wish."

At last, Eagle's arms loosened. Sniffing, she straightened, glowering briefly at Mr Abrams.

Eagle pulled back, letting her see his deep regret before releasing her and moving back around his desk. "Take a seat, Leeth," he gestured. "I warn you, you'll need it."

"I'd rather stand."

"I can't imagine how you must have felt," he said. His eyes moved to her uncle's, whose expression was grim. But there was something else she saw, too, in *the Doctor's* look. He was studying her aura, she could tell. Frowning, looking disappointed, as if she'd failed him. '*Again,*' he'd no doubt claim, though she never had. *He* was the one who'd failed *her.* Who'd *always* failed her.

The Doctor's eyes flicked to his wrist as he read something off his Link, and shook his head. "Medigene has arrived at Luiz's apartment. You did not throw his head from the building. Are you hoping your lover can be revived, Leeth?"

Invisible claws extended – then her muscles locked, the instant she tried to throw herself at him.

He met her eyes and smiled, raising his eyebrows.

She heard Abrams gasp, and even Eagle draw in a breath, while she strained at mental bonds and fought to stay upright.

She *fought,* trying to find and snap those intangible chains as never before. Her whole body shook, her heart hammering, veins standing out in her forehead and jaw. Careless of Eagle and Mr Abrams watching. Instead focused utterly on her uncle's delighted face.

Eager, like she was doing exactly what he wanted.

She stopped.

Looking away, shutting her eyes, shutting the three men out, she let her fury die. What would they do now? Probably criticize her, or justify themselves. She made herself remember the last hour of her mission, before they could begin 'explaining' it to her.

She was back in Luiz's apartment. Hearing the 'ding' of the elevator and scampering down the polished redwood hallway to meet him at the front door. Joyful, loving Kitty Perkins, dressed as she knew he'd desired, the furry tail curving and swaying behind her-

Flash.

Her birthday cake. His dark, smoldering eyes. His hand cradling her neck, his lips nuzzling hers, hungry for her.

Flash.

"You should have told me today was your birthday." Leading her to the bedroom. Watching her possessively, a dark light in his eyes. An odd twist to his smile. "We'll make tonight your birth *night,* my pet."

Something about that smile sent fear tingling along her nerves. Inside, a part of her rose up, defiant.

He reacted instantly, with delight. With one strong arm at the small of her back, his other hand around her neck, he tilted her head back.

Lust exploded.

She let him lead her to the bed, as thrilled as if she walked a cliff's edge.

No. I don't want to remember this anymore. But the memories refused to stop.

Panting, excited, letting him attach the cuffs, each *snick* setting a strange electricity shivering through her, the thing inside her sneering at the pink, furred leather bonds.

But feeling a surge of excited helplessness all the same as she'd tugged at the wide, thick cuffs, testing their snug and unyielding grip.

Then, out of sight, behind her, a tiny noise. A zip-lock bag opening? A fingernail tapping a glass vial?

She.... Memory failed. Terror. Rage. Bonds shattering. A harsh tearing, a rippling *crackle* of stitches snapping. Fingertips slashing through a heavy leather cuff-

Flash.

Luiz's face grinning above her as she flipped over on the bed to face him. His eyes mad with delight, casting a spell-

Her arm, flashing upward-

Kitty *tried* to stop it; tried to hold back the blow. But she had no control. Kitty had no power, the dark spirit-

She launched off the bed. Spirit blades slid up under ribs, fingers following. The feel of flesh parting. Stabbing deep, puncturing the beating heart-

Luiz's eyes, wide in shock, locked to hers.

Confused.

Scared, finally.

Dying.

Leeth stood before them, her eyes shut and hands clenched, every sinew straining, each breath a harsh pant. Two men pressed back in their chairs, silent.

Harmon leaned forward, urging her on, alarmed but excited. Eagle looked to Abrams and a silent communication passed between them. Abrams, pale, shook his head, one hand raised. Then finally he relaxed, turning his gaze heavily toward the Doctor as Leeth opened her eyes. Eagle felt real anger at the Doctor, even knowing why he did what he did.

She blinked. *I almost let Luiz....* She shook herself and looked around, wondering if they'd noticed her momentary distraction. All three faces were expressionless, but she had the distinct feeling she'd missed something.

Mr Abrams whirred forward in his chair and opened the black silk bag they'd given her for the creepy 'magical tome'. The leather-bound volume spilled out first, then Luiz's notebook, and finally the somehow repellent shiny black dagger with its gold handle. It seemed to watch them all from the desk.

Still she refused to acknowledge the Doctor.

The weapon had a face molded in it, with two blue stones for eyes. It had landed face up. Around the base of the golden hilt, just before the razor-sharp black glass blade began, an ugly braid of something like lead coiled around it. It made her shiver.

"I can't believe I didn't sense *that,*" Abrams muttered. "It makes the Libro Sangre seem a mere toy. Aztec sacrificial dagger. And it's *injured.*"

His gaze moved from it, to Leeth, in wonder. Studying her, he blinked. *Her aura had changed. Nor did it hold any trace of the conditioning he'd expected to see, the 'cover identity' he'd watched Harmon implant. He looked again for taint, deeper... and for just a moment, thought he saw a flicker of movement.* He shivered.

For her part, Leeth finally was staring at the Doctor, her chest rising and falling, feeling fully herself for the first time in a week, the confusing webs of Kitty Perkins cut from her mind. The dagger drew her eye again. Its small gold hilt, just the right size for a woman's hand. Her hand. She fought an urge to take it up, suddenly certain that if she held *it*, the deeper webs the Doctor had woven could be cut out.

She realized no one was speaking. With difficulty, she tore her gaze from the shiny scalloped edges of the wickedly sharp blade. With even more difficulty, she didn't look again at the Doctor, afraid he would read her new certainty from her eyes.

Clenching both hands behind her back, she turned so she could look between Mr Abrams and Eagle, keeping the Doctor just in her peripheral vision.

Mr Abrams gestured, and with a wave of one hand, the book and the sacrificial dagger slid apart. From the side of his wheelchair he pulled out a solid, laminated copper and lead box bound in leather and placed it on the desk. Opening its lid, he compared the foam-lined space to the two magical objects crouching on the polished white surface. At last, with a heavy sigh, he drew out an odd pair of tongs, picked up the gold and black dagger, and dropped it onto the foam padding.

Eyeing the small book, he considered jamming the two in together. The thought set his gut roiling. Instead, he simply lowered the lid, latched it shut, then wrapped the book back in the treated black silk. Each went into separate compartments of his medical chair.

Leeth's eyes were on him again, Abrams saw, her gaze only shifting to Eagle once the box was out of sight. Abrams felt his unease grow.

She jerked her head toward the Doctor, still refusing to look at him. "Why did *he* have to... *brainwash* me again?" She didn't have to look to know he'd be sitting there with that superior little smirk on his face.

Eagle's voice was gentle. "We went over this before the mission, Leeth. Well before the Doctor made the *suggestions* to help reinforce your innocent cover identity.

"You needed to get past Luiz's guard. He was a mage. Had we let you know his true nature, he would have seen. We needed you to develop feelings for him, or he would have read the falsehood in your aura, and never trusted you."

Briefly, he considered showing her the damning footage of her lover and Lucia Francesca, the child referred to in the 'murder note' they'd had Kitty leave, but instead decided to try the – slightly – kinder route. "Tell me, Leeth, did Luiz bring anything odd home from work with him tonight? Something he left by the front door? Think back. You've been trained to observe, to notice details."

"I wasn't exactly *thinking* when I left," she spat.

Eagle ignored the venom. "When you welcomed him home, perhaps? Something by the front door?"

She frowned, her skin flushing hot, then cold, as she saw again in memory her beloved Luiz turn as she pounced on him at the front door, clad in the special 'cat girl' outfit he'd had made for her.

She remembered a narrow, bagged object taller than him, which he'd set down in the corner by the door, balancing a cake box....

"Something big," she admitted. "I don't know what-"

"A fold-up stretcher, Leeth. The metro police report also mentioned a zip-lock bag with... well, you're not a doctor, so the medical terms would mean little to you. But a strong sedative. And an odd injector."

Leeth swallowed, then felt her face muscles stiffen, her limbs lock.

"Nelson also accessed the apartment block's security systems. The basement parking cameras. Luiz favored a Tesla Photon, didn't he? Yet last night he arrived home in a Fordundai Moove." She didn't recognize the model name, he saw. "A van, Leeth; a windowless van." Eagle watched her follow the simple logic chain – stretcher, sedative, van – and saw her face crumple.

"Me? No, he wouldn't have! Nelson's lying!"

Eagle's heart went out to the girl. "We have footage of him leaving the van, with the stretcher," he said softly.

"Nelson could have faked that up."

"He could, Leeth, but we both know he didn't."

She stared into space, and Eagle didn't need a mage's

imaginal sight to know that even *she* didn't really believe her protests. He could point out they'd briefed her fully, before the mission. That she'd agreed to everything they'd done. But right now what she needed was time.

To give her just a little, he said, "Nelson *has* however re-processed all the video of you entering or leaving the building, to alter your appearance. He was particularly pleased to digitally shrink your height by ten centimeters, so you won't match the now 'wanted' Kitty Perkins, in law enforcement image recognition systems...." He trailed off when he read the dismay of acceptance dawn in her face, and her attention return. He saw the pleading, saw her desire to ask him to lie to her, to reassure her that Luiz hadn't really been planning to drug and kill her.

He saw her lock that desire away and set her jaw.

It felt like watching a child lose one more small piece of faith in the world.

CHAPTER 7

It was seven days since she'd killed Luiz Tujilque.

Jammed into a cupboard in the secondary, odorless meeting room, Leeth heard the footsteps of Mother and the others pass by in the corridor. She smiled in the dark, listening and waiting.

Mother led the way for the review of Leeth's performance in the special exercise that morning, only to stop one step inside the large briefing room. Sniffing disapprovingly, she did an abrupt about face, Father almost walking into her.

"It stinks in there." She strode back past Father, Emma, James, and Preacher. "Either Nelson has been playing games with the maidbots or Leeth is exploring new ways to annoy." Dojo stepped to the doorway and smelled for himself, his nose wrinkling. Frowning, he followed the others, letting the door whisk shut behind him.

They reconvened in the smaller briefing room, its space reduced by cupboards that stored a ludicrous selection of out of date electronic interface devices and data converters.

With ill grace Mother seated herself and dimmed the lights.

Earlier that morning, all lights throughout a whole level of the Department had been turned off. James and Emma, between missions, had been paired up against Leeth in a laser tag challenge.

"She is good at hunting," the Doctor had explained to them beforehand. "Indeed, she considers it an area in which she excels. After the stress of her recent mission, it will help settle her, re-engage her. If she loses to Emma and James, it will spur her to improve her skills. If she wins...." He'd chuckled. "Then it will lift her spirits."

Mother and Father had approved, confident that James and Emma – fully-trained agents with augmented reaction speed, low light and infrared vision, linked in wireless communication – would teach Leeth a valuable lesson.

A simple test, inside the Department itself, but in pitch darkness. They had even had Little Brother disable the emergency exit lights. Each participant had been armed only with an electronic paint gun.

The computer-generated reconstruction began, thermal

images overlaid on a suitably darkened 3D model of the complex. But as the group sat in the dim light, the certainty grew that they watched something uncanny. Reminiscent, even, of a horror film.

A peculiar tension gripped them as they saw how Leeth evaded James and Emma's first coordinated sweep of the level. Hushed, they watched her 'chimney climb' a service corridor's walls while her two hunters closed in. They met directly below her.

Emma, seeing it now, audibly drew breath. In best Hollywood drama style, the computer zoomed-in on Leeth's face. But lacking adequate sensory data, it left her face empty, inhumanly expressionless.

For perhaps thirty seconds Leeth hung at full stretch above Emma and James, a silent predator lurking directly over their heads while they conferred electronically below.

"That's not possible," Emma whispered. Beside her in the darkened room, James reached out and took her hand. Their eyes met in shared disbelief.

Long seconds later, after the two left the corridor, Leeth dropped, her landing equally skin-crawling in its utter soundlessness. Crouched in pitch darkness she waited a full count of ten before finally prowling off, following James.

No one spoke as James hunkered down behind the Rec room counter, in darkness too complete even for low-light enhancements. Waiting, gun trained on the open doorway for his infrared imaging to reveal Leeth.

The virtual camera shifted, showing her creeping down the lightless corridor. At the doorway she paused, then lowered herself to the floor. They saw her choose the *only* angle of approach that gave her the cover of the couches and chairs. Wriggling serpent-like in the dark, she weaved her way in perfect silence toward James, closer and closer.

In the computer-generated image she circled behind him with painstaking care, outside his field of view. Inexorable. Something about that stalking sent goosebumps prickling up every spine.

Leeth rose behind him: silent, graceful. Deadly.

In fairness, they hadn't said each participant had to take out their targets using *only* the electronic guns.

James's strangled cry, Emma's broadcast queries –

«James? *James!*» – then Leeth's silent, deadly stalking of Emma herself....

Both Leeth's opponents had required the Doctor's healing.

The view split, the right half showing Father seated in his well-lit office, monitoring; answering Emma's not-quite-panicked message that something had gone wrong, that somehow Leeth had taken James out too literally.

"Continue," Father had coolly responded, before the view returned to showing just the action in the darkened corridors.

Watching the reconstruction now, neither agent spoke, but Father noted all three looking sideways at him. "I *did* assess James's bio-telemetery. He was only unconscious a few dozen seconds. And his broken collarbone demonstrates the need to upgrade from the old carbon fiber."

The scene continued, gripping them as surely as a movie drama. It soon became clear, watching the constructed visuals, that despite James and Emma's optical augments, Leeth somehow functioned better in the dark than either of them. Seeing her prowl implacably and unerringly from the unconscious James to the now tense and mobile Emma, who had intuited that Leeth was stalking her, raised hairs on the backs of several necks. Dojo's skin prickled. For several seconds his eyes searched the darkened conference room before returning to the projected view.

Emma took her final stand, her back to the dead-end wall of the long corridor. Her finger rested tense on the trigger, her gun raised to give an unbeatable 'kill' zone, she waited for Leeth's thermal image to appear....

In the reconstruction, Leeth approached the junction, then stopped and knelt. The virtual camera zoomed in, clearly showing her very deliberately scratching the polished concrete floor – her fingertips an inch *above* its surface. Even now, the drawn-out sound scraped down spines like nails on a blackboard, inhuman and horrible in the pitch dark.

Emma's vital signs spiked, and Leeth, once again silent, retreated, leaving Emma standing alone in the dark, her heart pounding in her chest....

Leeth's final approach was through the ceiling spaces.

Father had been able to track the whole business, but Emma had not been privy to those same security systems. Leeth closed the final distance with a strange assurance, like she'd done it all before. Once again, her movements were those of a predator, nerve-wracking in their certainty.

In the last seconds, Emma's heart had practically fibrillated, as if subconsciously sensing the approach of her invisible stalker, moments before Leeth plunged down on her from the ceiling.

Just reviewing it, every watcher's pulse rate soared.

Of course it raised the question of just *how* Leeth had done it; but all she could offer, immediately afterward, was that she could somehow sense the others even in the dark. The Doctor had confirmed she spoke the truth. "I saw signs of it even when she was young. She often prowled the grounds of the Institute for Paranormal Dysfunction at night." |

At the time, Harmon had seen her frown, confused by his support of her deception. But that turned into a sneer, as she of course misinterpreted it as a desire to use it against her. He let her see the hurt that caused, and looked down, sensing her frown return.

As for Leeth's earlier 'explorations' of the ceiling spaces, both Mother and Father had been aware of it, merely noting and reporting it on each occasion – perhaps waiting for her to try to use the route to access a secured area. But as time passed, it seemed she did so merely because she could. Father had opined that she simply enjoyed exploring.

«You know,» James messaged Emma, «in her first month here she scared the juice out of me, watching *Alien Infiltration*. But that wasn't the most frightening part: it was that she found the ending sad because the hero died.»

«The *hero* died?» Emma asked. «No he didn't. In the end they kill the creature and return to Earth.»

«Exactly,» replied James.

Their eyes met again. This time, Emma visibly shuddered.

As the visual presentation ended and the lights returned, a cupboard door eased slowly shut behind them.

Mother pinned James and Emma with a look that said they'd pay for their failure. "This was not the result I expected, people. She's a barely trained nineteen-year-old girl, yet she made fools of two cybernetically enhanced, supposedly elite operatives."

Preacher, for his part, was staying silent in the background, glad he'd missed the exercise, but well-pleased the little bitch had shown her true colors to the other two agents. And taken the stuck-up pair down a peg or two in the process.

Mother continued. "I'm sending you both back for a month of weapons and tactical training, including sessions with Dojo to reacquaint you with basic hand to hand combat and tactical awareness."

James and Emma groaned.

Father tried to intercede. "Mother, Eagle selected Leeth *because* she has unusual abilities, perhaps magical. And we have several missions I am unwilling to push back. I think-"

"Your trouble, Father, is you see an attractive young girl, and that's all you see. Am I the only person in this entire Department who sees through her tricks?"

The cupboard door behind her swung open with a whisper, bringing everyone *except* Mother to their feet. She spun in her chair just fast enough to see Leeth unfold, wincing, from the cramped space.

"I dunno, Mother," Leeth said, grimacing and stretching. "Are you?"

Mother's face turned red. "How *dare* you sneak into a briefing for which you were not authorized! Security protocols are not game rules to be played with. Suppose we had been discussing something beyond your clearance?"

"Huh? I just wanted to see how long I could stay all squeezed up in a place like that if I had to. I must have dozed off," she added with a shrug.

Mother said nothing. Just stared at her through narrowed eyes. Finally, frowning, and without a word, she stood and left the room. Footsteps clacked angrily down the corridor. Leeth heard her open the other conference room, sniff, and then go inside.

No one spoke.

Leeth tried to catch James and Emma's eyes, but when she did, they both kind of flinched away. Like she frightened them. The odd reaction sent a little chill through her.

The Doctor was watching it all, she saw.

He smiled.

Oh, no. He'd wanted *this!*

The return footsteps sounded even grimmer.

Mother re-entered the room with a plastic container of boiled cabbage and melted Parmesan cheese, held at arm's length in a tissue. Her eyes remained fixed on Leeth's as she set it down silently on the conference table.

The rant that followed was epic, even by Mother's standards.

At its end, Leeth found herself with a month's refresher training on Bureau protocols and procedures.

Through it all, she hid her smile. It had been worth it.

She caught Dojo's eye. He didn't wink at her. Not quite.

CHAPTER 8

Later that day, aching and bruised, sweat trickling between her breasts, Leeth plodded from the dojo to her room. She'd needed the workout, to unwind after the morning's *test*.

Which she'd loved, and totally ruled – until she'd seen James and Emma's reactions to her in the debriefing she'd gate-crashed, and realized it had been another of the Doctor's traps. Now, James and Emma were nervous around her. Again.

And Mother had been *so* furious. Grinning, she remembered that part, hugging herself. *That* moment had been pure chocolate.

But remembering the mass of 'refresher' study she'd earned as payback for it, the grin slipped.

In the shower, soaping her bruises, she considered asking the Doctor to heal them – and instantly dismissed the idea. *They're not that bad.* Besides, visible marks helped you remember your mistakes, Dojo said.

Turning off the water, she stood just breathing, trickles of water on her skin like the whispers of Luiz's fingers. She stepped from the shower stall. Her fingertips reached out, touching the plexglass mirror, studying the dripping girl and her bruises, studying the eyes. But the bruises inside didn't show. With a tired sigh, she scrubbed herself dry with a towel and dropped it on the floor for the laundry bot.

Back in her room she took a handful of almonds from the bowl on the desk – her 'study.' A smile of satisfaction flickered as she crunched into them. It vanished as her eyes fell on Toby, her carved wooden dolphin.

She picked him up and checked his tail, now glued back in place. Holding him to her chest, she shut her eyes, lowering her head to kiss him. Inhaling his honest wood scent. "Oh, Toby," she whispered to it. "Why do they all try to make things so hard?"

Marcie. I'll see what Marcie's doing. That was, *if* her friend's work schedule gave her any time free.

She hadn't left the Department since... since Luiz. Just buried herself away, trying to not to think about that, losing herself in training. And fighting off bad dreams. Dreams of darkness, death, and blood.

But she didn't *have to* stay cooped up inside. Not anymore. Even though every time she told them she was going out, Mother reminded her she wasn't allowed to kill anyone.

As if she didn't know it was sometimes wrong to kill – and always dangerous. Although that in itself made it more interesting. She'd enjoyed learning about all that stuff: the sophisticated law enforcement and forensic science and magic used to hunt down criminals. Even when the victims were bad guys.

Or drunk guys on stairs, an annoying voice prodded.

She remembered the quiet courage of the children she and Tash had rescued from Club Juzz. The resilience of the people surviving in the Hunters Point Dumps. All of them, people she would have once dismissed as sheep. Frowning, she put Toby gently down.

Should she call Marcie?

She imagined the Doctor smiling down at such a fresh sign of weakness. Of her needing someone.

Instead she snarled, grabbed another handful of nuts, and snatched up a smartsheet. Throwing herself backwards onto the bed, she grimaced and called up the next study module.

She was chewing her fifth or sixth mouthful of nuts when her Link chimed. *'Incoming call from Marcie Dunkirk.'*

Leeth shot upright, swallowing quickly, and stabbed the response option that dressed her and placed her in a nondescript office. "Marcie! I'm *so* glad you called!"

Marcie just studied her, not speaking for several seconds. "You look like shit. What's happened, Jane?"

Jane. The false name slapped down on the joy like a cold wet towel. "Oh, nothing much, really." *They made me kill someone I thought I loved.* She swallowed. "Just a few rough days at work."

Marcie eyed her. "Liar." Behind Marcie, the door to her dressing room banged open, and Leeth jolted forward, wanting to defend her.

Marcie's hand moved to cover the mic, but despite that, Leeth heard the woman in the doorway mention outages, and then Marcie was turning back to her, grinning and uncovering her mic again. "I suddenly got an hour free. Let's meet."

While Marcie gave her location, Leeth threw on clothes and booked a car to exit point three.

On the bed behind her, the study sheet sat amid a scatter of almonds.

They met just off set.

Leeth hugged Marcie hard, then slid into a seat at the table for two in the cafeteria, staring around to take it all in. Not that there was much *to* take in, until Marcie loaned her a pair of VR glasses linked to the studio's systems, so she could see the same things the actors on set did. In the foreground a ramshackle outpost of half buried organic-looking huts. Beetle-like, they squatted in red-ocher dust drifts that bled into a barren rocky landscape under a purple and green sky.

She eased back in her seat, her shoulders unknotting as Marcie explained the backstory of the current episode, her character Stryker Zaxx investigating some weird disappearances in a mining colony.

Sharing their lunches, seeing her friend again, just doing something normal – she felt like a desert plant absorbing long-withheld water.

At least, until the cantina door behind Marcie opened and a creature lumbered in, heading straight for her friend. Leeth felt her mouth gape open as she registered claws, teeth, and a strange shoulder-mounted device pivoting towards them, targeting-

Her seat crashed behind her as she leaped, launching herself over the table and Marcie, the *tingle* unfurling from her fingertips. She sailed towards the creature, desperate to remove its head before it could bring its strange weapon to bear. As she twisted, beginning the strike, her glasses flew off-

And the monster vanished, replaced by a tall, thin black guy in a skin-tight suit, a wire-frame construction on his shoulder.

Retracting her claws as she cannoned into him, she rode him tumbling to the ground and sprang to her feet.

In the now silent, still canteen, every set of eyes locked on her. The 'monster' on the ground groaned, staring backwards and up at her.

"Uh-"

Marcie bent and retrieved the expensive glasses. "I told you to stop doing that, Vince," she told the outstretched male before dragging Jane back to her seat and righting it.

Vince sat up, his eyes following Marcie's friend. They widened. "Fuck *me*. That's the Jane chick you claimed you modeled Stryker Zaxx on. She's *real*."

Leeth closed her eyes and let her head drop into her hands. *I came* this *close to killing an actor in front of all these people. I am* such *an idiot. Thank goodness Mother didn't see that.*

He clambered eagerly to his feet. "Hey, can I join you two-?"

The look Leeth turned on him made Vince raise both hands and back away.

Marcie was shaking her head, watching Jane with concern. "Tense, much? Problems at home?" Her voice dropped. "By which I mean your *job*. You could come live with us. Amanda'd love that, too!"

Leeth winced. While Marcie's younger sister would love it, she knew just how much their father would *not*.

Marcie blushed, then nodded. "What about a job on set? I'm sure I could find you something. Or is... your uncle being a dick again?" Her jaw thrust out.

Leeth wet her lips. Of course Marcie would remember, since she'd kind of admitted she was a secret agent. She swallowed, considering everything that followed from that: the lies she'd had to tell to keep her friend innocent, and out of it. Out of harm's way.

Lesson after lesson, training her how to keep secrets. Drilling into her the utter need for security.

Fuck it.

"I... met this guy." Raising her eyes to Marcie's, Leeth felt a smile twist onto her face. "Tall, dark, handsome, you know? All that." She blinked, seeing in her mind's eye blood dripping from mid air, in the dark. Her smile crumpled. "They...."

Her mouth stayed open, trying to frame the right words.

Marcie leaned forwards and took her hands. Brow furrowed, she sensed her friend withholding some awful truth.

When Jane continued, her voice was a bare whisper. "They had me kill him."

Leeth felt Marcie's hands spasm, and saw her jaw drop. She watched Marcie try to speak, then stop. Twice.

"You... you what?"

"I killed him."

Marcie blinked. "That's fucked up," she said at last. "But... you and him...? 'They' had you kill-? Why did-? Are you alright? You're not-" Marcie stopped. From Jane's eyes, it was clear her friend wasn't joking, and wasn't alright. Rather, it looked like she was bleeding inside. "Fu-u-u-ck."

Marcie squeezed Jane's hands tighter.

Leeth clamped her eyes shut, willing the water away. Feeling Marcie's grip strengthen, she realized she'd expected her friend to release her hands – to recoil in horror and loathing. Instead, they'd tightened. The acceptance was too much. Letting her head fall onto her forearms, the dam she'd laboriously built crumbled again.

Marcie was around the table, crouching beside her, hugging her. Pulling her up and leading her away while her colleagues' eyes followed them, eating up the drama. A few gave her strange looks. Marcie ignored them, determined to get to the bottom of all this even knowing she shouldn't; knowing she needed to stay well clear of the frightening people Jane worked for. Knowing 'Jane' wasn't even her real name.

But her friend needed her. And not just because she was so alone.

All eyes followed them as they left the cafeteria.

Jane turned down the offer of a stiff drink, a shot of Soothe, but did accept a square of chocolate.

Seated beside her on the tiny couch Marcie put a hand on her friend's knee, waiting patiently till she looked up. "You need to get away from them."

Leeth shook her head. "No, I have to stay. What I do is important."

"Let them find someone else to do it!"

"There *is* no one else!"

Marcie pursed her lips, not believing her.

"It's true. Like this last job. My... lover wasn't what he seemed. He... he was w-working on something really bad, which had to be stopped. He was, he planned.... Killing him...." Leeth swallowed, wringing her hands before she realized what she was doing and made herself stop and just sit still. "It was kind of horrible. But I'm certain, pretty much, it was the right thing to do."

"'Pretty much'? Surely someone else could've...?"

Lifting her chin, Leeth looked Marcie in the eye. "I'm good at what I do." She thrust her breasts up.

"Huh? *Oh.* Damn." Marcie put an arm around Jane, just holding her. They simply sat, leaning into one another. "Do you *want* to leave them, though? It's not right, working for people who make you... do stuff like that."

Leeth lifted her head and wiped at her face, accepting the tissues Marcie offered. Blowing her nose, she shook her head and shrugged. And thought. Remembering with a shiver the obsidian dagger; how something in it had *reached* for her in the darkened room. Delivering it all to the Department. What Mr Abrams had said. What she herself had felt.

Nelson was still going through the comp she'd retrieved, deliberately needling her whenever he emerged from his little troll cave. 'Man, that Doc T! You should see some of the stuff he had stashed away. Major perv!' All those thoughts.... It felt like her brain was running in six directions at once.

She saw again Luiz turning to her in the entranceway by his front door, propping the stretcher he'd brought home that night in the corner. To carry her, drugged, from his apartment.

He'd caught her as she leapt into his arms, almost dropping her birthday cake.

She shook her head. It wouldn't have been enough to just kill Luiz, she knew – as difficult as even *that* much would have been, as protected and as careful as he was. Recovering his research, delivering the stuff from his safe, had been even more important. And who else could have gotten close enough to him to do what she'd done? To be so trusted? They'd even told her, right from the start, that she'd have to fall for Luiz. And she'd happily agreed. In her heart, she knew she'd *let* herself fall in love with Luiz despite the hints of darkness and cruelty beneath his surface.

Perhaps even *because* of them? She shoved that ugly

thought aside.

"No," she said at last, meeting Marcie's eyes. Speaking slowly; choosing her words with care. "I can't imagine how anyone else could have killed him, and done the rest of what was needed." Tears welled up again. "But it *hurts*. The lying. If I'm doing so much good, why does it hurt so much?" *Would a Huntress lie?*

Marcie stared at her friend wide-eyed, feeling nauseous. *How could Jane kill someone she'd* slept *with? Loved, maybe? Had they ordered her to seduce him? Had she cared about him? If she had... how could she possibly have killed him? Could she kill... other people she liked? If they told her to?*

Once again, she felt that frisson of fear, that feeling that Jane wasn't normal, wasn't even aware of half the rules everyone else lived by. In her mind's eye she saw again Jane sailing over her head, arrowing into Vince, riding him to the ground. Sometimes, she sensed a wild thing at the heart of her friend. She shuddered.

But the simple truth was, Jane needed her. She might be the only person who stood between her friend and some very dark paths, ready to pull her back from some brink.

Jane's haunted look brought another image to mind. The older man with the hooded eyes and cold, demanding voice. The one Jane had her knock out at their 'solitary' meeting in the deserted park. The one who had, at first, been able to *make* Jane do stuff.

He was behind this, she was sure. Her friend wouldn't kill people, otherwise.

Fighting past the shiver of dread, she took Jane's hands again, which had somehow fallen out of hers.

Jane's eyes watered as she blinked, her grip as tight as when Marcie had reached *through the floor* into a burning cold place to haul her... back.

Once again, her friend was lost, Marcie saw, looking into those amber eyes. Amber? Jane's eyes were blue. At least, they *used* to be. Marcie stared. It wasn't just colored lenses, either.

They suit her better, she decided, shaking her head. Probably a question she shouldn't ask. Besides, it wasn't important. 'How did he make you do it?' she wanted to ask. 'Has he got control of you again?' But remembering how Jane reacted last time, she thought carefully.

Seconds ticked past in silence, her friend's grip tightening until it hurt.

Marcie squeezed back, herself. "Do you need my help again? You know. With him?"

Leeth felt mental bonds quiver and lock into place: waiting. She shook her head. "He hasn't, he can't-" Steel bars clamped down. She refused to panic, simply waited, staring into Marcie's now worried eyes. "No," she said at last. "It's... I can deal."

Marcie's eyes narrowed. "But you're worried. I can tell."

Jane's eyes slid away and her terrible grip loosened. Despite the physical relief, Marcie tightened her own grasp, shaking the hands she held – as small and soft as her own, their core of strength concealed inside. "You won't give up. You're like the Girl of Steel."

Leeth's eyes came back to Marcie's. "That's just stories. Superman's not real. He's just made up."

"So what?" Marcie glared at her friend, willing her to understand. "Some made-up characters can be as real as a real person. If they're true, and come from the heart. They can be as real as some celebrity you'll never meet. As real to you as someone who's died. You can know them *better* than people you meet in real life, since you can see inside their head. A fictional person can touch you, strike a chord in your heart. They can be real to you."

"Yeah, but you can't talk to them. Ask their advice."

"Their stories *are* their advice."

Jane just looked back.

"Okay, well, *I'm* here for you." But Marcie knew her friend *couldn't* talk to her about some things. She squeezed Jane's fingers, wishing they weren't resting so inertly in her grip. "There's no one you can talk to about this stuff, is there? Not even me. Because, secrets." She shook her head. "That's not right. You *need* someone to talk all this stuff over with. You can't just bottle it up inside. It'll, I dunno, twist you in knots. Mess you up. Surely you can talk it over with *someone* you work with? They can't all be shits."

Leeth's jaw clenched, remembering her morning, and the new 'test' they'd set for her, that she thought she'd done so well at. Only to realise, way too late, it had been another trap the Doctor had set, which she'd fallen into. To isolate her and cut her off from support.

Marcie shook her hands, glaring. "Don't you *dare* give in! Hope never dies. There must be *somebody*."

Leeth stared back. *Like who? Who can I talk to?* Gazing into Marcie's earnest eyes, she felt more alone than ever.

And then, a smile like the first blush of dawn. Her hands pressed Marcie's effortlessly together. "You know, there actually *is!*"

CHAPTER 9

It was now eight days since Leeth had killed Dr Luiz Tujilque. While she made her way out of New Francisco, Harmon eyed his display, checking the replacement image and audio, Mother's face and voice substituted for his own. They had chosen Mother in case Leeth's friend reacted with suspicion.

Both Mother and Father strongly approved of the plan to destroy Leeth's friendship with Marcie Dunkirk, having always seen it as problematic. Despite her magically-implanted blocks, the chance of vital Department information leaking was too high to allow it to continue, considering Leeth's ability to surprise. From personal experience, Harmon knew the argument had validity.

Weakening that bond was the necessary first step. Although today he would merely be planting the first seeds. An operation of some delicacy, yet doomed to fail should either girl discover his involvement. It needed someone who could argue they were 'on Jane's side.'

Eagle had reluctantly approved, although reserving the right to end the plan if Leeth started breaking under the stress rather than Unfolding with further magical potential.

"Testing, testing." Harmon found it uncanny, seeing the face of a woman move as he moved; hearing female tones instead of his own. 'She' could pass as Mother's sister. Not Mother herself though, since in the event of a meeting, security demanded she would be disguised.

Nelson's setup seemed to be working smoothly. The Link ID was now connected to this configuration, in place whenever the ID was used in future communications.

Harmon placed the call.

Marcie frowned at the unknown ID, but answered. "Yes? Who is this? How did you get my number?" Keeping her own video off, she watched the woman's face, trying, and failing, to place her.

"Marcie? I am speaking to Marcie Dunkirk?"

The woman was perhaps forty, not the age demographic for most of her fans. She also looked both worried and faintly embarrassed. Marcie had a bad feeling about this.

"Thank you for taking my call. It's about my daughter, um, 'Jane'."

"Your daughter. 'Um Jane'." Marcie's tone was flat.

"Wasn't that the name she gave you?"

Marcie frowned.

"They... it's probably best for everyone if we keep using that name. I think she's hinted at, um, the kind of work she does for, for us."

Marcie thought, and finally clicked her own video feed on, so the woman could see her anger. "Maybe. She said she works for her parents. So why don't you tell me, yourself, just what her duties are?"

At the suggestion, the woman drew back, and visibly pulled herself together. "No. That is not possible. Actually," Harmon added, using one of Leeth's favorite, meaningless words to subtly reinforce the familial connection, "this contact is probably a bad idea. Never mind-"

But he made sure to bite his lip, again imitating Leeth, and moved his hand toward his wristlink, clearly intending to end the call.

At that, as he knew she would, Marcie relented. "No, wait! What's this about? Is Jane alright?"

Harmon let his eyes slide to one side, not meeting hers, watching the computer-generated face do the same. "She's fine," he said, just a fraction too quickly, just a hint of uncertainty. "I'm sure she's fine."

Marcie's eyes narrowed, and Harmon lifted his own, meeting hers, projecting gratitude and sincerity. "And your friendship has been wonderful for her. Both her father and I feel it's only you who's kept her going."

Marcie looked angry, leaping predictably to her friend's defense. "Jane is stronger than you know. Though I'm not sure how *anyone* could hold their shit together, the things you put her through." Marcie's mouth worked, wanting to say more.

Harmon saw that, wondering what confidences Leeth had broken. Mother and Father already held that concern. Trust Leeth to find a way to wriggle past even a magical gag. Yet another reason to start splitting the two apart. Destroying the friendship would deliver numerous benefits, and would be far less likely to lead to catastrophe should the Department foolishly decide to 'retire' Dunkirk as a method of ending the security risk. Already, the call was providing dividends.

"Yes, well, that's the reason I'm calling. Of course we know we're treating her unfairly. We're not monsters! But Jane is the only one who can do the things we ask of her. All the same, we see how much stress it places on her." *Though not enough. Not quite.* "So it's wonderful to know you'll *always* be there for her, to help every time she needs you. Despite your busy career."

Marcie was looking at her once more with narrowed eyes and pursed lips. She shook her head. "I'm *not* gonna tell you anything your daughter's told me. If you want to know that kind of stuff, ask her yourself."

Jane's mother looked offended. "Heavens, I wouldn't ask you to do *that!* No, I just wanted to return the favor. If *you* ever need help, I want you to know you have only to ask. Or if you think... Jane is behaving oddly. Not that I think she *is*, or will be!" she hurried to add. "Just...." She wrung her hands. "Anyway, I'm sure whatever happens, *you* of all people will be perfectly safe. She cares about you, deeply." She smiled, weakly.

"I simply wanted to call you, to thank you, and to let you know you could call me, if ever you need... help, with Jane." Harmon let 'her' eyes shift to one side. "I'm sorry for taking up so much of your time. Again, thank you for accepting my call."

After a few additional platitudes, Harmon disconnected. A good first step, he judged. Though based on Marcie's reactions, he might need to make some quite subtle Suggestions, to Leeth.

Things she wouldn't see as disturbing, in their own right. If he was correctly reading the signs regarding the Department's plans for her, she *needed* to Unfold further.

Ending her friendship with Marcie Dunkirk would be for her own good.

CHAPTER 10

Leeth sat in the front of the car specially provided by the Department, steaming gently at how hard it had been to get permission to visit the Institute. As if they thought she was planning to break Godsson free again, or penetrate the security to speak to him.

She huffed. Although even as she dismissed the idea, she couldn't help considering what they might've done to upgrade their systems. It *would* be a good challenge....

No. I promised; and I'm not even sure I should talk to Godsson again. I'm not sure I really trust him anymore. He told me I needed to hug Marc Disten!

She scowled, remembering the trap that had sprung the moment she'd let her guard down.

Rolling hills passed by in the gaps between trees, but for the most part she felt hidden within the low scrubby forest as the road weaved, dipping and rising like a snake slipping through undergrowth. The car for some reason was taking back roads – she'd not seen another vehicle in the last half hour. But the GPS showed they were getting close. A little later, cresting a hill, the car came out onto a ridge line and she saw the distant sandstone wall. Within those familiar walls, far lusher trees further screened the buildings from view. Minutes later the car paused at an intersection, turned left to briefly join the highway, and then she was coasting up the final, private road.

The expected drone buzzed down to look inside, but the front gates had already begun to swing open, the car hardly slowing before moving on and up, into the grounds.

Swiveling in her seat, she watched the heavy iron grille swing shut behind her. *Too easy,* she thought. Then frowned, wondering whether it *had* been too easy. She grinned at the possibilities.

When the car emerged from the trees she stared, blinking, at the number of people just walking around, in the grounds by the building's main entrance. Some were accompanied by bots or actual human attendants – even cats and dogs. A few people watched her arrival in curiosity, but most seemed disinterested. Many looked zoned out or stressed.

But one person stood watching alertly, waiting. Mr Shanahan. The car stopped and the door popped open.

She stepped out, hearing the car lock and secure itself behind her then power down.

She and Mr Shanahan stared at one another.

Blushing, she remembered their last encounter. Namely, tying him up before dragging him down to Godsson's cell. Which had actually been a trap, on Mr Shanahan's part. She scowled again.

"Ye're looking fit, Sarah girl," he said, sounding cautious.

Sarah. She pursed her lips, looking around for her friend.

"Uh, the Director said yeh wanted to visit Faith?"

She nodded, hearing the doubt in his voice. He was keeping his distance too, she saw. She turned, looking up at the building, noting the outside cameras. No doubt, every one of them trained on her, too. Rolling her eyes, she turned back to him.

"Yeah."

He swallowed, looking uncomfortable.

"What? What's wrong?" She stepped forward. "Has something happened to her? Where is she?"

He shook his head, but leaned back, looking even more uncomfortable.

Fingers curling into fists, she took a second step toward him. Was this some trick? Was Faith not even here? Had the Department decided *she* was 'paranormally dysfunctional', and should be *imprisoned* here? Was this really a trap after all?

"Where is Faith?" she grated.

"Sarah! Calm down, calm down."

His 'down' sounded like 'doon'. That, and his raised hands and worried expression – *worried* worried, not sneaky-worried – reassured her. She thought back to the meeting with Mother and Father – and the Doctor – when she'd asked permission for this visit, remembering *his* expression as he'd unexpectedly spoken in favor of the idea. A mixture of guilt, and worry, and regret on his face. Though she'd written it off at the time as just another attempt to manipulate her. But had it been directed at Faith, not her? Did he know something she didn't?

They'd all had stiff expressions, now she thought about it. Stiffer than normal.

"Sarah, about Faith, look, you can't play with her like you used to-"

But Leeth had heard the excited 'yip' from somewhere far downwind, and was already off and running.

"Sarah!"

She ignored him.

To be dancing through the trees, jumping roots and vines, made her feel like she'd gone back in time and was young again. She heard Faith and some of her new pack moving through the forest toward her. Though not as fast as she'd expected. There was no high-pitched whine of turbines. As if Faith wasn't running to meet her.

Frowning, nerves prickling, she increased her pace.

As Leeth emerged from the trees by the pond where Mr Shanahan had taught her to swim, they saw one another. Faith yelped excitedly and ambled forward, but Leeth stumbled to a walk, shocked.

The cyborg wardog had gotten *fat*.

She was accompanied by four of her pack, including the young brindled male who had been so... *male,* trying to boss both her and Faith, the last time she'd visited.

They trotted up, Faith's tail wagging like a whipper-snipper, her lips pulled back in a huge grin, delight in her eyes. She leaped awkwardly up to lick Leeth full in the face, woofing and wriggling in ecstasy, sniffing her all over.

Leeth hugged her back, shoving her misgivings aside. Despite her worrying weight gain, Faith looked good.

Beside her, she felt the wet nose of the male nudging her bare legs, sniffing, growling in a kind of disgruntled way. Trying to nose between her and Faith. All protective.

And suddenly it all made sense.

"Faith! You're *pregnant!* Oh my stars! Oh, *girl!* Congratulations!" She started to hug even harder before stopping immediately, at the thought of squeezing the babies or something.

Faith dropped back to all fours, looking simultaneously smug and delighted.

Leeth just stared. "You look *good!* And you, tough guy, you're the daddy, right?" she asked Faith's 'protector'.

He met her eyes seriously.

She turned back to Faith. "Oh, this is going to be the

best visit ever!"

The other dog refused to leave Faith's side as they padded through the forested terrain. By unspoken agreement, they were making their way to the higher ground where they could look down on all the buildings of the Institute. But this time, not racing. Just taking a gentle pace, considering Faith's condition.

Leeth had been puzzled, at first. "How can you be pregnant? Everybody knows cyber war-dogs don't get babies!"

Faith just looked at her with her special 'Yes, dummy, but...' look, and waited.

"Oh! Oh, my. So, Uncle...." She grimaced at the name, but had to use it for Faith to understand. "Uncle was the cause?"

Faith grinned goofily, confirming her guess.

"Indirectly, I mean," Leeth quickly added, giggling, to Faith's amusement. "After you got blown up, right? He probably Healed more than he was supposed to? I bet Mr Shanahan freaked when he realized your new lieutenant had gotten you pregnant!"

She'd given up trying to shoo the male away. He still refused to leave Faith's side, which was kind of sweet, even though Leeth would have preferred more privacy. He didn't seem as smart as Faith, though. It was easy to see he wasn't following the conversation properly. Yeah: sweet, but kinda dumb. She'd met a few human guys like that. He wasn't so bad, she decided, and scritched behind his ears. That seemed to please Faith, so then of course *she* needed some hugging and scritching, too.

They talked about Faith – what it was like to be pregnant, how her pack was – as well as the new inmates, and the new workers and other animals.

"It must be cool to have other dogs, civilian dogs, around? But what about the cats I saw? I thought those guys were kind of your enemies?" Faith agreed that the ordinary dogs were okay, but the cats were kind of a nuisance.

Finally, they got to the real reason she'd come. Sitting on the high rock with her legs dangling over the edge and one arm draped across her friend's furry shoulders – where robot legs joined her now-plump torso – Leeth could almost believe she was a child again.

Even so, it took her a minute or two before, with a shiver, she could tell Faith all about it. About falling in love, even though deep down she knew Luiz had a darkness. Maybe hadn't even really loved her – just *enjoyed* her for the ten days they'd had.

Faith just listened, letting her pour her heart out, her expression serious and worried as Leeth described that final night. At working on automatic pilot and killing Luiz; the horror of only realizing what she'd done after she'd 'woken up'. About going ahead and completing the mission anyway. The stretcher by the front door.

She opened her mouth to tell Faith about the Thing that had reached from his creepy dagger in the dark, but as the words reached her lips she bit back on them. Not even really sure why.

Her oldest friend just licked her tears dry and listened, accepting.

In the end, feeling strangely lighter, Leeth hugged her, holding Faith, burying her head in her friend's furry coat, inhaling her smell to store it up for dark times. At last, they all made their way back down.

Mr Shanahan watched in a kind of dazed but happy disbelief as she hugged Faith and got back in the car to leave.

Like he'd expected her to blow up the Institute and kidnap Faith, or something.

She waved to Faith as the car curved down the driveway. She and her mate followed right down to the exit, where they stood, watching while the heavy wrought iron gates swung open, and closed behind the departing car.

Still watching as she disappeared from sight.

CHAPTER 11

Dr Luiz Tujilque's palmtop had provided a treasure trove of data – though not in the way they'd expected.

Using Ghost, it had taken Nelson just minutes to decrypt the files, revealing a collection of professional looking internal Asgard research reports. Job done!

He'd been ready to hand them over to the mummy – his private name for the wheelchair-bound bag of bones the others called Mr Abrams – when he'd decided to read through the mysterious magical research. Never knew what you might learn, right?

Trouble was, even in Doc T's private fukken notes, the douche had used some loony personal code.

Nelson spent the next two days sieving through it all, struggling to decode the plausible-looking reports with their innocent-looking references: that always dead-ended in the swampy nonsense of the private journal.

There was also a directory with a bizarro mix of files and cryptic references. After translation, and Ghost's help, a bunch of those were revealed as coded messages between Doc T and Brazilian guerrillas he'd paid to recover an artifact from some place called Teopanzolco. *That* hadn't gone too well, apparently – but what'd he expected, hiring a greedy bunch of bloodthirsty 'freedom fighters'?

The remaining cryptic refs turned out to be various Aztec museum exhibit indexes, mostly to stone carvings.

With an odd sense of foreboding, he opened a file named Teopanzolco, finding scans of a handwritten diary in Spanish. From the images, it looked ancient, like the paper had been badly preserved, much of it moldy and indecipherable. On a whim, he ran a translation program over it and started reading.

Friday, July 5ᵗʰ, 1519. Our advance has been relentless. Crucifix in hand I have done my part, but the Word of God spreads slowly among these idolaters. The Tlaxcalan tribe are the worst. Sometimes in their eyes I think I see some awful shared jest at all our expense. In my heart I feel their worship insincere at best, ending at their lips. Many have rallied to our banners, but still Montezuma's hordes outnumber us. The heathens resist at every step, fighting with a strange will despite our superior weapons, God be praised. Does some Demonic force give them cruel strength and courage? But in truth such savagery is no match for Christian steel. Their false gods will not save them, no demon can stand before the might of the Lord...

The fragment ended in a bloom of mold. He had no idea how many pages were missing. Couldn't the dude have at least numbered them?

I begin to fear this brutal campaign will never end. We are far from our goal with much blood yet to spill if we are to reach the mountain, this mountain of blood and death where even now the false god demands ever more abominable sacrifices. What sick, perverted intellect could conceive such evil? Surely such relentless malevolence is beyond mere mortal imagination?

Nelson wasn't sure whether to be thankful or annoyed that the dude didn't spell out the gory details. He spent pages moaning about the Tlaxcalan – some kind of indigenous Mexicans, according to Wikipedia – before the next interesting bit.

The nightmare has come again. Those eyes, those dead eyes, those horrible blue orbs piercing my soul with unholy terror.

A shudder gripped Nelson. *Polished blue stone eyes in a solid gold hilt. The creepy obsidian dagger Leeth had stolen from Doc T's apartment. After slaughtering him.*

He tried to laugh off his own reaction, but he'd seen them all flinch when the thing clattered down on Eagle's sterile white desk. Like it'd been a huge poisonous spider ready to leap at them.

Almost reluctantly now, he read on.

Let no man doubt that evil exists, let no man doubt the Devil is real, for I have seen him. Satan is here, Satan reigns supreme in this new world, this land that worships him, serves him. They know him under a foreign name, an alien name, but he is the Devil all the same. I hear them whispering his name in the darkest corners, shouting his name from the highest temples. I hear it in my nightmares:

"Tezcatlipoca, volcanic lord of blood and pain! Tezcatlipoca lord of the dark! Show them now why they fear the night..."

Shit, it sounded like crucifix-wielding Spanish dude was

losing it! He tried telling himself this was just a story, then remembered it was a real diary.

This morning I broke free of a waking dream, a scream on my lips, my knife at my manservant's throat. I saw the fear in his eyes as I stopped a hair's breadth shy of taking his life, the dread god's whispers urging me to spill the lad's blood. Holy Mary blessed virgin, save me from this madness, spare me these visions, these nightmares, this… insidious voice. We march now for the Aztec capital, but since the madness at Cholula I grow ever more convinced by the dying man's words. I fear we were deceived. I believe our mad slaughter cleared the way for this foul demon. Somehow I must convince my lord Cortés or one of his Captains to strike out for Teopanzolco before the demon's followers can perform their unholy rite. Each day I feel his presence grow stronger. Seven days and seven nights with no sleep, no place to hide. The beast follows me, mocks me, speaks blasphemies and wickedness into my ears. I see his eyes now in the waking world's sky, those eyes, ever watching, ever hungry. We must end it. We must right the balance before it is too late.

That, too, ended abruptly, mid page. It continued after an indeterminate gap.

The fever has taken me. My body is weak, my mind wracked by fears and doubt, but our work is nearly done. The heathen armies have been slaughtered, the great mountain lies far behind us, but still the demon that haunts me cries out for blood. We have ended their pagan sacrifices, but still in my mind's eye I see them, an endless line of victims climbing the mountain to their deaths, the priests' whips at their backs. Men and women, crying, begging for mercy that never comes. Hundreds, maybe thousands. But whether the vision is of the past, or some future, I know not. Just that the procession is endless. Today, we will reach Teopanzolco, on their day of unholy ritual. With God's grace we will end it!

It is time for the final advance. The Lord will grant me the strength to haul myself from my hammock, holding in my heart His crucifix that must light our way

And that was it – the end of the file. Nelson hunted around, even set Ghost searching for digital echoes or other pieces. He turned up only hits to the same material Tujilque'd copied into his palmtop.

He leaned back, blinking as if he'd just emerged from the distant past himself. *Not my problem,* he decided. Though maybe the spooky shit could cause Leeth trouble? He whipped up a brief note – 'Might interest Abrams?' – and squirted it to Eagle.

For several seconds, he felt oddly guilty.

After lunch, he returned to Doc T's journal. Apart from the diary, only stuff like the occasional date was in Spanish. Little in the way of personal biz. Quite a few entries that just said 'wildcat,' for the period he'd been screwing Leeth. Based on earlier, similar entries – translated as 'coconuts', 'clam', and other more confusing terms – he eventually realized Doc T mostly referred to his conquests by the names of a body part; and each mention meant they'd had sex.

He'd had sex with Leeth *a lot.* Far more than any of the other women.

Most of it though was crammed with bozo variants of alchemical symbols – which equaled fuck all to any sane person even after you looked up what they were *supposed to* mean. And for the rest, without a substantial body of meaningful comparison text, Ghost couldn't attain resonance. Which meant they didn't exist in any net-linked system on the planet. They were just the mage's own weird-ass symbols. End result: the gibberish remained stubbornly undecipherable.

What sort of paranoid, porridge-brained psycho kept his personal notes ciphered? And *indexed?*

In the end he'd simply expanded each innocuous-looking link with the matching parts of Luiz's hand-written journal. Just looking at the resulting files made his head ache: dry psycho-technical magic jargon slammed straight into the crisply inked doodles of a lunatic. Maybe they'd mean something to wheelchair-boy.

He giggled. By now, Asgard should have discovered Luiz's hand-written journal was missing. At least Leeth had done one thing right. Well, two if you counted her specialty: murderous slaughter.

Stretching aching muscles, careful not to dislodge any real-life objects near his VR cocoon, he fired off the digital mess to Eagle. With an anticipatory smile, he considered the rest of the data. From the size and structure, he knew he'd find a major stash of vid and trideo. Porn, for sure. He'd only been needling Leeth earlier, but now he prepared to dive in for real.

What he uncovered more than made up for the frustratingly cryptic notes of Leeth's latest victim.

Furry porn. Doc T was a furry fetishist! *Yes!*

No wonder the creep had hit it off so well with 'Kitty'. Nelson frowned. *Eagle must've known somehow.* Probably why he'd chosen the name, *and* had her wearing cat-ears at the dance club where she'd 'accidentally' met the South American researcher.

Nelson kept scanning.

And discovered, with delight, that Doc T, the old perv, had filmed practically every sexual encounter he'd had. To go with his other massive stash. Hell, the middle-aged dude had been a horny bastard of epic proportions.

But, fuck, after avidly matching the time and date of a 'wildcat' journal entry to one of the files in the most recent folder, he flushed, squirming in his seat. *Leeth* was a total freak. A pity she'd spazzed out that one time he'd tried to help her out and make her a bit friendlier.

But then he shuddered, recalling the bloody corpse she'd left sprawled, gutted, on the black satin sheets of Doc T's four poster bed. One hand went to his own chest, unconsciously. When he'd first seen it, he'd thought, *Seriously, a four-poster bed? What kind of man has a four poster bed?* – until Leeth's darling Luiz brought out the furred cuffs, and tied her to it.

He called up the final video again, blood pounding as he watched Luiz strip and then bind a compliant Kitty to each post. *Damn, Leeth really does have a first class ass.* But then the gruesome image of Luiz as he would be a minute later flashed up on his mental screen. The image of Leeth turning and killing her lover ended the mood as effectively as a deluge of ice water.

Fuck! Trust Leeth to even screw up her own porn!

He kept hunting, though, and his eyes lit up when he found the 3D animation software and the body scans of

Leeth – including the furry variants of her that Luiz had created. Leeth as a real cat-girl was freaking *amazing*. He leaned forward in his chair. He'd never really noticed before how she actually moved like a cat. Especially when she was being seductive.

Then he found a bunch of furry-fetish chatlogs, and had Ghost decrypt them. *Double encryption: paranoid, much?* But at that point the fun kind of died, 'cause a search on 'Kitty' led to a conversation about Luiz's new pet-girl that sent chills down his spine. He skated straight to the attached pics, then with eyes wide, read back as Luiz was egged on by some furry freak named Lord Fenris to 'mod' his pet girl IRL – in real life.

Nelson found his hands shaking as he followed the thread, swallowing. And suddenly, there it was: a dark net site where validated 'clients' could submit a DNA sequence and order a viral Mod. There were screen grabs from some program, showing sliders for everything from breast size to ear position to fur length and color – and tail.

Nelson read on, wide-eyed and heart pounding, as he scanned through Luiz's order for DNA mods for 'herself'. No doubt a transparent fiction, to provide deniability if the order was ever traced back, so the company could claim it had no idea the Mod was non-consensual.

He sat back in shock, but also kind of turned on as he helplessly pinned picture after picture – and animation after animation – into the virtual space around him, showing what the gene-altered 'Kitty Perkins' would have looked like as an Altered. A Bastean.

"Fu-u-uck." What he could do if he could get inside Leeth's head again! But after her spectacular meltdown at the opera, the one time he and the Doc had collaborated to implant a false persona, Eagle himself had vetoed any similar experiments. Could he convince Eagle that'd been the Doc's fault, not his?

Anyway, he was pretty sure he knew now both what was in the odd injector the police reports had mentioned finding at the crime scene, and why Asgard had been so indifferent toward the murder investigation. Their bad boy researcher wasn't just a creepy mage who loved BDSM; wasn't just into furry sex. No, he'd ordered illegal DNA mods – a breach of the Global Moratorium, although com-

mon – and planned to use them on someone without con-
sent.

Frustratingly, even with this info, even with Ghost, he
didn't have enough to track down the gene company's location. And judging by the time between Luiz's order and
getting the viral editor tailored to 'Kitty', the fuckers were
probably based in the US. Maybe even this city.

Plastered in the air around him, naked purring Leeth-
catgirls bent and thrust themselves at him, posing and pro-
voking. Struggling to control himself, he brushed them
aside and set to work. Reformulating what he knew of the
gene-modders, he added that data to the list of potential
targets Ghost regularly swept the net for.

But part of his attention was already planning a fresh
stimsense for his private enjoyment, using the new 3D
models he'd acquired.

CHAPTER 12

Leeth *really* wanted to kill something.

Soon, she promised herself, daubing another smear of white across her face. Shutting her left eye, she applied the thick waterproof goop to glue her eyebrow flat.

She'd been feeling somehow off, keyed up, ever since Luiz's death. *Ever since I killed him.* She paused, facing up to that truth. At last, with a sigh, she continued her preparations for today's mission.

It was the mornings that felt worst. Each day, waking up, she felt kind of tired, and relieved.

Edgy.

She had vague memories of bad dreams involving the vile little dagger offering to *help* her. She kept imagining it, nearby. Like, really nearby. In one dream, it had been scuttling around in her ceiling. *Maybe I should speak to a psychologist. Get some therapy.*

Pity I don't know a good *one.*

Yeah, she really wanted to kill something, but at the same time, after Luiz, she wondered how she'd feel, afterward? They said she'd done a good thing by killing him. So why did it still feel so *bad?*

The Doctor wasn't helping. Subtle digs, that no one else picked up on. Sometimes, just a small smirk. Like he was *trying* to needle her, make her explode. Or was he trying to make her question her trust in the Department itself? And even though every instinct told her Eagle hadn't betrayed her, that he understood how she'd suffered, she'd begun to wonder. *Chit, why do I always let the Doctor get to me?*

Despite being days since the 'dark hunt', they all *still* acted nervous around her. Emma, James, and Preacher kind of flinched whenever she appeared in a room. *And I* don't *creep around! It's just I don't clomp about like they all do.* The others kind of got this wary look when she got near. Except, of course, the Doctor.

She'd even heard James ask Emma how long her 'moodiness' was likely to last.

Moodiness? Standing outside the rec room, fists clenched, she'd had to resist the impulse to storm in and thump him. *I'm not moody!*

Even Dojo sometimes seemed especially alert now in their sessions. As if he thought she might forget herself and disembowel him or something.

She swallowed, remembering the weird moment in yesterday's training when she *had* felt the urge to hurt him. To draw blood. *Was* her temper getting worse?

It was a relief to finally be given another mission. Though she could tell they worried she might react like she had after... after her last one. She'd begun to wonder, late at night, if maybe this was all some kind of weird experiment by the Doctor.

Well, at least it had been fast. Late that night, mission over, she sat on the edge of her bed feeling let down. How had they done that? How had they managed to make *killing* boring?

She shook her head sadly. They'd organized it so much they could've gotten a robot to do it.

Because the 'retirement' had to look accidental and the target had a med-rescue contract, she'd had to drown him so his health company wouldn't receive an alert and rush to revive him. At least *that* part had been interesting. She'd never thought of killing someone underwater, before.

Mother had *not* been pleased she'd been photographed, but at least she'd kept her head down so the pictures wouldn't show her face. Plus she'd had the disguise makeup on.

But what *had* been strange – she still couldn't work it out – was James and Emma's attitudes. Not a word of congratulations. They seemed even *less* friendly, as if she'd done something wrong. Did they think the Department might accidentally pick someone for her to kill who wasn't a bad guy?

It made her feel even more uncertain. Which was a horrible sort of feeling. Maybe they were just disappointed she'd let herself be photographed? For her next mission, she'd be sure not to be. Not to do *anything* wrong. To be perfect.

Two days later, on March 3rd, 2062, Mr Xing Deng Zhu, the executive director of Kwandong Computation Nets, arrived in New Francisco to implement his plan to dramatically boost automated manufacturing in America. Given promises of a more stable society and lower resistance to automation in the longer term, the planned contract would see the majority of KCN's products sold into America rather than India, despite a lower per-unit profit. Tik Tek's Series Seven units had already taken a hundred thousand jobs, and KCN's autonomous 'AGiX' humanoids were their nearest competitor. Checkbook's economic impact study convinced Eagle the success of this move could induce something like a feeding frenzy among the megacorps. Over ten years, he predicted a million jobs lost.

"Wow. So what will those people do?" Leeth asked. "Is the money saved, paid to them?"

Eagle's expression went completely unreadable. But somehow she sensed he was unhappy, maybe even angry. "Unfortunately, the Senate once again blocked the latest incarnation of the Universal Basic Income Bill. The robot owners don't approve of a robot tax." He looked at her in a plan-y sort of way, but didn't say anything more about it.

Fortunately, Mr Xing was known to have a predilection for *gwailo* women. So the occasion of his fiftieth birthday celebrations became Leeth's next mission.

At the lavish party given in his honor at the local head-quarters of KCN, the festivities became quite loose. Even one or two of the security personnel were not entirely sober.

The climax of the evening was the presentation to Mr Xing of the beautiful, exotic, and sensual Western girl. She had of course been most carefully chosen from a selection of the highest quality escorts – thanks to the help of one or two well-placed Suggestion spells by Harmon – and then screened to ensure she was completely unaugmented. Mr Xing had been well pleased.

But half an hour after the presentation, the girl's hyster-ical screaming shattered the festivities. Suddenly-sobered colleagues crowded the entry to the Director's private rooms. There they found their naked colleague dead from a massive heart attack at a supremely embarrassing mo-ment, the girl pinned beneath him.

Heavily implanted with net-interface and skill and memory chips – more cyborg than human – the executive was unable to be revived, even with the help of specially helicoptered-in magical healers.

The girl understood no Mandarin, and had not been informed of the identities of any of those involved, nor the location of the event. Nor was she of very high intellect. After an examination and interview carried out with less thoroughness than it would have received in more dignified circumstances, she had been paid and allowed to go free.

The incident was reported in the business news as the unfortunate death by natural causes of a respected visiting foreign businessman. The articles focused more on the loss of the trade deal, which had gone instead to India.

She must have done okay, because soon enough, they approved two more missions in quick succession. She'd thought her very first mission, killing the creepy Shepherd Fox, had taken a lot of planning. And the Luiz one, even more. But after that it got kind of ridiculous.

Back during her training, she'd assumed that once she became an Agent, they'd give her the name and a picture of her quarry, maybe a list of places she could find him or her, and she'd hunt them down and kill them. Fun!

But... nuh uh.

They went to huge amounts of trouble to try to make sure she could get away after each Hunt. Which was nice, in a way – knowing they cared about her. And poor Mr Xing had been hard to get to, too, so for that one it had been good to have their help. Plus of course, some retirements had to look like accidents. Really *bad* accidents, so the subjects couldn't be Healed by magic.

But as she sat cross-legged on her bed, her thoughts drifted back to one particular one.

Luiz.

She shuddered and rose from the bed.

Go to the gym? The pool? She sighed. She'd done her laps and her morning routine. She really didn't feel like going back and doing another couple of hours.

I'm bored, she realized. *I've been cooped up here two days now, for no reason I can see.*

Standing by her mirror, she checked her face. Her hair was honey-blonde still, from her last op. She preferred her natural black, but kind of liked how the dark blonde went with her eyes. It was nice, having them back to their proper amber color. For some reason, it felt important. Frowning as she tried to work out why, she picked up a scarf, finally wrinkling her nose in frustration. Scowling, she stuck her tongue out.

For a while she pulled faces, even practicing some of the acting she'd learned, back with Marcie – emoting and eye moves and such – when she realized, the scarf she was holding... she'd tied a quipu knot in it.

Luiz.

Her eyes filled with tears. Somehow, despite it all, she *had* kind of loved him. And killing him... she remembered the nightmare of trying to stop, trying to resist. But the Suggestion, reinforced by the Doctor's sneaky 'Mode One' command, had made her a puppet in her own body. *If he tries to use Mode One again, next time I won't wait. I'll cancel it straight away.*

Luiz.

Why did her heart hurt, still, even knowing Luiz had been researching some kind of bad magic for Asgard, and had that creepy sacrificial dagger? *And been planning to kill me, too.*

She shivered, wondering whether they'd planted the evidence against Luiz? But remembering the horrible little golden dagger with its hypnotic blue eyes, and how *something* had reached for her in the dark room, the shiver returned.

She stilled, remembering. The dagger had been in her dreams again last night. Snaking towards her when her back was turned. Whining in the ceiling above her bed. Creeping towards Mother, its expression ingratiating, offering to kill her.

I should ask whether they've destroyed the dagger.

Like I destroyed Luiz.

She growled, her face twisting. To be honest, she *had* sensed a dark side to him. But that had been... thrilling. *He'd* been thrilling. Powerful. And he *had* loved her.

But how could someone love you, yet be willing to use you for their experiments...? Her thoughts trickled to a stop.

How many years had the *Doctor* experimented on her? Her *uncle*. She'd thought *he'd* loved her, too.

Was it possible? *Could* you hurt someone you loved?

Well, you *killed Luiz,* a small voice inside her sniped. She jumped to her feet and started pacing. *They made me. He made me,* she answered herself.

Something inside sneered.

She didn't *want* to think the Doctor might have really loved her, once. She shook her head, violently. No. He hadn't really loved her. That had all just been pretense.

She hugged herself. *But if he hadn't ever loved me, and Luiz hadn't...?*

Her mind went back to her earlier mission, and Luiz. *Why is it still bugging me so much?*

Could she have persuaded him to just *stop*? For her? He could have come to work for the Department. That way they'd have had two mages. Or did Mr Abrams already count as a second one? Though he only seemed to be called in for special circumstances. *What* did *Mr Abrams actually do?*

She chewed her lip, trying to imagine Luiz working here, alongside her; alongside the Doctor. But the picture wouldn't form. She kept seeing the Doctor sneering at Luiz, and Luiz snapping back one of those dismissive put-downs that had come so naturally to him.

She half choked on a kind of sob. *They would've hated each other so much.*

Had the Doctor been jealous of Luiz? She blinked, several times, and went very still.

Had her uncle made certain she'd kill Luiz because he was *jealous*?

No. That was silly. It had been the whole point of the mission: kill Luiz, steal his research. The Doctor wasn't that petty. Or manipulative.

Probably.

She snarled, frustrated. This inactivity was driving her nuts! She was sad, lonely, bored, and horny. She wished *something* would happen.

And that she'd stop dreaming of the dagger. In her dream this morning, before she'd woken, it had been calling to her, begging her for help.

She paused, surprised by the insight. *That* was new.

Scared. For the first time in her dreams, the dagger had been *scared.*

CHAPTER 13

The gold and black spider hammered at the bell jar's glass walls, trapped. Behind it, the meat grinder turned and turned, growing bigger and bigger. Shiny black legs scrabbled at thick glass, scoring it as it tried to reach her. Two lapis lazuli eyes locked on hers. *You have to kill it. You have to kill it* now*!*

In the background, a terrified winged sexbot fired lasers made up of numbers in every direction, killing things she couldn't see.

Godsson was there, too, but ignoring her, looking... shocked. She couldn't see what he was staring at. He turned, exchanging a glance, a *fearful* glance with an equally stunned dragon. Both their eyes went to the golden spider, before turning slowly as they tracked its gaze and saw her. There was someone else watching, too. He or she was tall and slender, with pointed ears-

Lights and her Link's buzzing slammed her awake, her wall unit chiming. Jumping from her bed she slapped it on.

It was Eagle. "Leeth! Abrams needs us: now, however you are. Each second is precious. James will meet you and Dr Harmon at the express lift. Leave *now*."

Snatching up the boots by her bed, she jumped to the door. Palming it open, she grabbed the holstered gun dangling beside it and squeezed sideways through the still-opening gap. Clutching gun and boots she sprinted down the corridor, outpacing the walls' guiding arrows.

She tore down corridors and bounced off corners until ahead, she saw the Doctor entering the lift. James pulled him to one side as she slammed in beside them.

"What's happening?" she gasped, pulling on her boots one leg at a time as the lift plunged.

James blinked at her, an odd expression on his face. "Some kind of magical attack at Mr Abrams' place."

"Leeth, you're naked!" the Doctor said. He wore a maroon dressing gown, cotton shorts, and slippers.

"Naked means 'no clothes'." She waved at her leather boots. "Dopestick," she muttered, loud enough for him to hear. Rolling her eyes, she shrugged into the holster, buckling it on as the lift stopped and its doors shot open. Just outside, ready to zoom off, James's Windsteed purred, its gull-wing doors popped open.

James was already moving, tossing in a bag before sliding into the driver's seat. Leeth grabbed the Doctor and threw him into the back seat, jumping in and tugging her door down. Shaking her head when he just sat there, she dived across his lap and pulled his door closed, too. He might be a great mage, but as an operative he was about as sharp as a spoon.

A faint squeak from four tires hurled the car forward to the first ramp, throwing her back into the Doctor as James floored it.

"Not again!" Harmon groaned, closing his eyes as he frantically fastened his seat-belt, remembering the night they'd hurtled out at news of Leeth's break-in to see, and possibly *free,* Godsson.

The ride only lasted minutes, the sports car screeching to a halt beside a waiting copter, rotors already turning. They ran to it in a crouch as the car doors snicked shut behind them. There was no pilot on board, just as James had warned them.

Harmon swallowed, buckling in as they leapt into the sky. Angling as it rose, he saw James's vehicle driving sedately off, now it had done its part.

James helped Leeth and the Doctor don the noise-canceling earphones and mics as they sped across the night sky.

Eagle spoke to them all. "Abrams holds a collection of magical artifacts for safekeeping. Something is in his vault, using them in some kind of procedure. He wants our help to deal with it."

"What kind of 'thing'? Do we have video?" asked James.

"Yes."

James did something to a control in the passenger area, and a holo display appeared, showing a small room paneled in wood and lined with metal shelving. The floor was an uneven silvery-gray... and as they watched, it *wavered.*

"What are we looking at here?" asked James.

"A view inside the vault. The fluid gray floor is new — an unknown. There's also some kind of heat barrier preventing access," Eagle said.

"Ah. Hence the thermal suits."

"Thermal suits?" asked Leeth.

In answer, James unzipped the bag he'd brought, pulling out three gray bodysuits and passing one each to her and Harmon. "Lucky for you, Leeth. I think you're a little under-dressed for visiting." He winked, removing his jacket and working his legs into his.

Leeth unbuckled her holster, then hesitated.

"Nice boots," he teased, before relenting. "Pull the suit on over them. The material's tough, and stretches."

She smiled back at him, just pleased he was acting more like his old self at last. Maybe because she'd be fighting by his side, this time?

Harmon unfastened his harness and began working his way into his own, looking ill at ease and even a little green as the chopper rose and sank in the turbulent air, leaving the city.

"What's this vault of artifacts?" Leeth asked. "Is Mr Abrams keeping the dagger there?"

Eagle hesitated, for over a second.

"Why? Why hasn't he destroyed it?" she demanded. Though if she was being a hundred percent honest, she wasn't sure she really wanted him to. She shook herself. "Did the thing come for *it?*"

"Unknown," Eagle answered her. "As for destroying the dagger, Abrams is still studying how to do so without a catastrophic release of energy."

Leeth buckled her gun back in place, pleased at how the finely woven fabric stretched over her form, but wishing it was black instead of gray. And that the tight-fitting hood with its gauze face area didn't look so dorky. *Even a couple of cat-ears...* but the thought died the moment it recalled Luiz.

"ETA one minute," the chopper's automated pilot told them, ten minutes later.

"Your vehicle is cleared for landing," Eagle said. "Abrams's student, Ankhet, will meet you and escort you inside. Hurry."

CHAPTER 14

As their craft began its descent, warm lights winked and reappeared through the moonlit sea of trees below. A prickle of something like adrenaline shivered through her as they swept over a stone wall. Harmon, too, sucked in his breath at the same moment. James raised an eyebrow at them both in question. The wall seemed a twin to the one enclosing the Institute for Paranormal Dysfunction. In the dark she couldn't be sure, but this one looked older.

The copter banked, revealing a wide lawn surrounding the sandstone mansion as they began their landing. Even without the auto-tracking machine guns on the corners of the building's roof, both Leeth and James recognized the clear lawns as a kill zone. Harmon, oblivious to that, gasped and grabbed at his harness as they plunged down.

Ivy festooned the two-story, 'I'-shaped building, yellow light spilling from several downstairs windows and two upper. As they settled quietly on the lawn and the electric turbines spun down, double wooden front doors opened, throwing golden light down worn stone steps. Framed in it, a tall, slim woman in shimmery silk waved an arm in urgent welcome.

Leeth jumped from the chopper and ran over, James a moment behind, Harmon following in the rear. "Anne Ket? We're here to help!" One leap took her up the stairs.

The woman sighed at her and James's guns, though their thermal suits got a grudging approval. Black, slender, and gorgeous, her bearing was regal. Tightly braided hair, and cheekbones like polished ebony, her wide dark eyes flicked from her to James to the older man, studying Harmon with a kind of grim desperation.

He was huffing by the time he reached them.

Leeth shook her head, turning back to the woman who was now wringing her hands.

Ankhet looked them up and down with a tiny shake of her head, taking their hands in a perfunctory greeting. "I sincerely hope there's more to you three than meets the eye. Quickly. This way."

She wore a gold-threaded silk nightdress and slippers. Hanging from an elaborate gold chain around her neck, a carved chunk of amber nestled between her breasts. A head taller than Leeth, despite their rush she moved with the bearing of a queen.

Striding down narrow wood-paneled corridors, she led them through one wood-lined room after another, with heavy oak doors at each. Shelves of books, rocks, jars, and ornaments packed every available space. Murky old paintings and faded photographs hung on every wall, mixed in among antique swords, shields, bows and stranger weapons. Abrams was well, she told them, but they were in bad trouble. He'd sensed a disturbance and woken her, and they'd made for the vault. But even working together they couldn't reach it, heat holding them at bay.

"A spell?" Leeth asked. "But can't Mr Abrams-?"

"No. Not a spell," Ankhet said, though she sounded uncertain. "And with all the wood, and the doors closed, neither of us could approach the vault astrally."

"What makes you think-" Leeth began, when a kind of silent scream of pain shuddered through the air. "What was *that?*"

James frowned down at her, puzzled, but Ankhet had clearly felt it too. "We don't know. Part of why we think we're under attack. That, and the stream from the vault."

"Stream?"

"Video," Ankhet said.

It grew warmer, too, as the woman opened the next door. Inside, Mr Abrams wheeled aside to make room for them, the heat kicking up a notch the moment they crossed the threshold. With five people, the room was crowded. A door on the far side stood open, revealing another wood-paneled corridor.

"Thank you!" said Abrams. "I fear time runs out."

But Leeth was only half listening. Something down the corridor, deeper in the house, *needed* her.

Mr Abrams lifted a small display sheet in one wrinkled hand, showing the same room they'd seen in the chopper, but the gray stuff had risen higher, moving in it like water.

The heat pulsed, something burning in her hair. *Oh! Barney's device!* She surreptitiously unstuck it from her scalp, wincing as it scorched at her fingertips. She pocketed it without the Doctor seeing. A different kind of heat shivered through her at the knowledge she was now vulnerable to his control.

Beside her, James groaned, his whole body spasming. "What *is* this heat? Christ! How can you all...?" He staggered back to the door they'd entered by. "No. No, no!"

He kept retreating, all the way back into the corridor, where he swayed, careening into a wall. Leeth darted after him, catching him before he fell.

"James? What's wrong? What's happening?"

"Back! Take me out! It's burning at every interface! My systems are shutting down!"

He slumped. Leeth grabbed him, holding him up despite his weight, hauling him back along the route they'd taken. Harmon followed, Percepting imaginally, trying to grasp what was happening. It was hot, but not hot enough for that sort of reaction.

Two rooms later, James gestured for her to stop. Bracing himself on a wall, he stood, shaking, swaying on his feet.

«James.» It was Eagle. «Nelson says your systems have degraded. To the point of failure.»

«Tell me about it! It burns like fire. Inside. Hurts like hell.»

«He said the worst damage is to your neural and cranial augments. Where you have no pain receptors! Whatever this is, he warns it may be fatal if you take further exposure. Do you have any idea what it is?»

James answered aloud while transmitting to Eagle. "It feels like heat, but it doesn't register thermally. The others are affected, but far less than me."

"So the house *isn't* on fire?" Leeth asked.

Abrams's willowy student had followed them out, and answered from the doorway. "No."

"But do you mean everything *isn't* really hot, James?" Leeth persisted.

"Exactly. On infrared, everything's norm-"

Another silent shock of pain stabbed through them all.

And the lights went out.

Universal physical constants shouldn't change.

But at 2:34:13am, Pacific Standard Time, parts of the old high bandwidth internet of the 2040s started working again. Abandoned systems reconnected, in seconds forming a patchy, barely-connected network. Ten heartbeats later, battery storage systems across the country began switching on, power generators spinning up more slowly as something started drawing megawatts of power from the national grid. Several heartbeats later it had leapt continents, consuming gigawatts.

Within seconds, blackouts swept across the world as vast numbers of computers went to one hundred percent utilization, sucking power more hungrily than in any imagined scenario.

For thirty-two seconds, chaos reigned. In the Department, Nelson's Ghost began making crazy matches.

Deep inside Tik Tek, something screamed defiance.

James gasped. *"The packed light net is up again!"* he whispered. Despite his low light vision glitching, he saw Leeth meet his eyes in the dark – and saw her lack of understanding. "Don't worry. That's not important right now." *I hope.* "Go and help Abrams."

Leeth sprinted back to the room lit now only by the small headlights built into Mr Abrams's wheelchair. The tall black woman led Harmon back a little later.

Abrams was grimacing at the flimsy screen he held in one shaking hand, which showed just a black rectangle. "The generator–"

From somewhere nearby, she heard an old-fashioned engine start up. The lights flickered back on.

"Ah. Finally!" The rectangle in Abrams's screen changed. "Look!"

Leeth, Harmon, and Ankhet crowded in around him.

"That's my vault. Many subtle and powerful artifacts are held there, under wards and other protections."

He kept speaking, but Leeth's eyes were locked on the gleaming obsidian dagger with the gold handle and two blue stone eyes. She could *feel* it. Calling. *Scared, but defiant.* "It's after the dagger."

Abrams stared at her. *Her first concern is the dagger?* His heart sank at what her words implied.

In the well-lit wood-lined room, knick knacks – rods, jewelry, shields – sprawled on shelf after shelf. But the floor of the room *moved*, now half filled with something which in the video looked like undulating gray water.

Leeth flushed, terror spearing through her a moment before another stab of psychic pain slammed through them all. "It's *eating* them!" she cried. Abrams, Harmon, and

Ankhet gaped at her. "By the grail," she heard Abrams whisper.

"You may be right," he said, louder. "Consuming them to do whatever it is it's doing." He shook his head. "By God, the power it could absorb. You have to stop it. *Assuming* you can somehow reach it," he added, eyeing her form-fitting gray outfit. "Let's hope Eagle's suits can resist the heat."

His eyes brightened. "Ankhet, tell her how to reach the vault, and how to open the door, while I boost her." He didn't explain he'd entered the combination to the electronic locks the moment he knew they were on their way. Taking one hand, he stilled, muttering.

For Leeth, the feeling was almost familiar – a sense of slippery otherness creeping under her skin, which she ignored and accepted while his student described the route, gesturing for emphasis. Abrams paused and started again, and this time the sensation crept along her nerves, prickling in a way that reminded her of the hyperactive shiver she got from coffee.

Ankhet's speech slurred, slowing, infuriating pauses between words. Leeth felt her own heartbeat slow. Mr Abrams lifted his head, with glacial deliberation. "Go."

She ran from the room, the tip of her nose, her fingers, all her skin burning, the heat climbing with every step. It stopped her, gasping, until she had to hunch over to gather her resolve. But that made the burning worse.

"A-head. Anne. Ket. Will-"

Behind her, she realized Mr Abrams was still speaking. She turned, to see his student, in a bizarre slow-motion walk, follow her into the corridor, grimacing and brushing at the golden cloth draping her.

My hair *doesn't hurt,* she realized. *Or my eyes.* Her feet, in the black leather boots, were also pain free.

"- Follow. You-"

The woman finally reached Leeth's side, one hand out. Clearly in pain, but her expression full of concern.

"- In. Case-"

It's the cloth itself! Reaching up, Leeth ripped the hood off, her fingers burning but her face instantly cooler. She tugged at the neckline, then swore and willed invisible claws from her fingertips. With a single stroke from neck to ankle she sliced herself free, tugging the insulating suit from under the bands of her holster. Which were warm.

"- You. Need-"

Her other leg burned, and she sliced the stretchy material and stepped free.

Anne's eyebrows started to lift.

"It's the cloth and stuff! I'm fine!"

Anne's eyes had shut, her open hand still moving towards Leeth's shoulder. Leeth looked past her. The Doctor was back beside Mr Abrams, their expressions a match of slowly dawning surprise.

"- Ass. Iss. Tence. What-"

His spell sped me up! Her blossoming smile was cut off by a slowly rising wave of fear, dread escalating to terror. The feeling was coming from outside herself, she realized, just as another silent scream hollowed out the world again. Only this time, it went on, and on, and on.

She forced herself into action, turning, Anne's fingers brushing her shoulder as she tore down the corridor.

By the time she'd opened and forced back three strangely heavy intervening wooden doors, her gun harness was burning. She cut it off, dropping it and drawing the weapon. Her fingers had barely curled around it before she had to drop it too, pain searing her hand. Like Barney's anti-Harmon gadget against her scalp, earlier.

Eyes narrowed, she faced the steel door of the vault, its tumbler, and the shiny spokes of the steel wheel.

This was going to hurt.

Somehow she held the scream in as she forced the wheel around and hauled the massive door open. As it slowly began moving, she gave one last pull and released her grip. The door continued its slow motion, and she lifted her hands, hoping they might be uninjured, that the pain was just mental.

Instead, ugly red blisters met her gaze. *Uncle can Heal them.* Inside the room slowly unveiled, something soundlessly screamed for help. She wondered why she was so sure of that.

She stepped back as the thick vault door reached her, then darted forward into chaos, her eyes struggling to make sense of what she saw.

What had looked on the video like gray water was a writhing mass of twisting, coiling sinews, chitinous plates grinding through metal shelves with a sound to shred eardrums. Against that backdrop, the ugly black blade of the obsidian dagger, its oily gold handle and sly blue eyes were stable ground. Deadly, but something she understood.

It called to her. Begging.

I'm like you, it seemed to say. *I slay. Join me. I am potency itself. Destructive power nothing and no one can withstand.* Small blue eyes burned into hers. *Not Abrams. Not Godsson. Not the Dragon. Not the dark Ill behind Shepherd Fox, that thing dreaded by those you serve. All we need is blood. Blood and death. Your specialty.* Our *specialty.*

A wave of coiling gray sinews humped up, curling toward her, and she slashed it, crying out as the contact blasted agony through her nerves, shocked by the feeling of invisible claws splintering. But her enemy suffered too, her strike cleaving it, fragments spinning away as they flew apart like dark angel wings unfurling.

The entire writhing mass stilled, as if her action had surprised it, drawing its attention.

She took in the small room, its insides incongruously oak-paneled, racks of black wrought iron shelves bolted to the walls. Everything to the height of her waist was gone, mirror-bright edges of metal where the eye-twisting monstrosity had eaten them away.

But the wooden panels were hardly scratched. While she tried to find the heart of the thing, a central brain to attack, she had time, in that moment of stillness, to note thick pods at the junctions of spinning gray sinews. And then it was in motion again, its sound buzzing higher, like a wasp nest angered.

You need me, called Luiz's poisonous dagger.

Instinctively, as twisting flails whipped in toward her, she flexed fresh invisible claws, slashing as she ducked and twisted, fighting gravity and her own body that moved now so much slower than her mind. Screaming again as her stroke severed chainsaw tentacles that bit into her claws, eating them even as its own gray coils shattered, to spray in writhing snakelike arcs over her head.

She saw a golden necklace set with stones of ruby red malevolence slide from a shelf, saw grinding coils chew it into splintering dust, and another psychic shock-wave stunned through her.

Sinews spun, chewing through the shelf holding the obsidian blade, whose small blue eyes stared at her as it slid towards the nightmare machine.

Measuring angles, she dived, fingers outstretched to the weapon while thick tendrils lashed the space she'd been standing. But mid air, she *felt* Abrams's urgent despair blast through her, forcing her attention to a small stone bowl sliding from the adjacent shelf, the imminent death of his life's love.

Growling, she dismissed her claws and snatched both dagger and cup. Blissful cool met burned fingers, not the pain she'd braced for.

Stuffing the edge of the bowl in her mouth she lunged for a higher shelf. Dark power smashed through her as her hand wrapped around the dagger's hilt, a maelstrom of ravenous hunger for blood, for life.

For a second she hung, swaying, while coils lunged up, tearing into her legs, agony crucifying her as the cutting sinews flew apart, as if her flesh dissolved it like acid. Then the room flashed into negative colors, pulsing bright nodes crying for death, and she was falling, spinning and dancing, a deadly vortex of destruction. Now when she struck, she cleaved through the other-worldly mass without pain, her weapons unharmed. It froze as if in shock for what seemed seconds, before redoubling its assault. Instead of dodging, she screamed her defiance and attacked, a blaze of claws and dagger, cutting, slashing, draining.

Feeding.

CHAPTER 15

Blood dripped down heavy arms in a sea of gray dust.

She hurt everywhere. Couldn't think. Couldn't see. Dull sounds behind thick, muffling walls.

Arms moving her. Her legs, walking. Something prying at her left hand, locked in a death grip.

Then the familiar feel of healing magic, flooding in to mend bone deep wounds, while mother's milk filled her mouth from a stone bowl.

Hushed whispers. A woman whimpering.

Lying down.

Sleep.

-

"Fu-u-uck."

Neither Eagle, Abrams, Mother, or Father acknowledged James's comment. Though all, privately, agreed.

They sat in the main briefing room reviewing the video footage, while also monitoring the Department's dining room where Leeth, in a bathrobe, sat devouring food with mindless intensity. She was watched, tensely, by Harmon and Dojo. Across the room, *behind* her, Preacher grimly stripped and rebuilt a range of his personal weaponry. On the edge of his seat.

Despite her healing, she still hadn't spoken a word.

"Again," Eagle ordered. "Quarter speed."

For reasons he would not explain, Abrams had refused to share his video footage of Leeth's battle with the bizarre incursion. He had no problem, however, in allowing James to share his personal perspective, from a point halfway through the impossible melee.

Ankhet, after tearing off her own clothes, had pushed herself to the doorway of the vault. Harmon, slower to follow Leeth's lead, was still fighting his way closer by the time the fight had ended. James had followed Abrams in his charge to the security room.

They all watched James's recording of Leeth on the small monitor. She carved through a lumpy gray node in the writing mass, twisting through the air as spinning flails passed over and under her, her mouth clamped in grim determination on a small stone bowl.

Apart from gasps, the only comment through their first viewing of the thirty second video had been Mother's: "This *has* to be faked."

Both Abrams and James had shaken their heads; but understood the remark. It *looked* like some piece of over-the-top Hollywood fakery. Complete with a leading actress taking gruesome injuries yet fighting on. Watching it a second time, at quarter speed, had been worse. Every deadly detail, every hair-breadth escape, every devastating blow, had been clear.

A thought from Eagle froze the video. "Observe." A red oval appeared on the paused image. It highlighted a gray coil intersecting Leeth's hair as fragments of a gray egg shape exploded apart, inches beyond her fingertips. As if invisible blades had shattered an asteroid.

"Ahead, slow."

In the video's frame by frame advance, they saw Leeth's hair severed and then sucked into the spinning lash, which promptly flew apart.

"Ahead, normal. Freeze. There."

Now a red circle enclosed the heel of her boot pressing down on several coils as she touched ground before spring-ing up. "Ahead, slow."

They watched in silence as the boot heel shrank, eaten away, and more spinning tendrils flew apart. Eagle next paused as she took a cut to her belly. From that wound, they saw blood sucked into both the obsidian dagger flash-ing through a larger gray node, and into the defensive coils that had intercepted her blow and then fragmented.

"What the coils cut, they absorbed and incorporated into themselves. But flesh and blood – and hair or rubber soles – doesn't have the material strength to maintain the thing's own structural integrity."

As the fight continued, precious artifacts sailed through the air – carried to safety, Abrams explained, by the air ele-mental he'd summoned as soon as Leeth had opened a clear path to the treasure room.

They all cringed, knowing what lay ahead, as she carved her way to the massive, eye-twisting slug that simmered, throbbing, at her feet. Bending, she slashed the dagger across the squirming mass, rupturing it, then raked her fingertips down its full length. She howled, convulsing with each blow, a moment before the thing flew apart. Twisting away, she threw one arm up across her face as spinning fragments tore into her, flying apart a moment later in secondary sprays.

Off-screen, Ankhet screamed as if she'd seen the devil himself, then a second later raced in, naked, dropping to her knees to catch Leeth as she fell. Around them, gray tubes collapsed into dust as Abrams's student cast a desperate Healing while blood pumped from Leeth's dozens of deep gouges, some to the bone.

The video spun and ended as James turned and raced from the security room.

They were all panting, as if they'd been the ones fighting, not Leeth.

"It ate magic," Abrams offered. "I saw her, before the armor spell I'd cast on her had worn off." He shook his head, the folds of skin in his neck wobbling. "The spell was in tatters. I've never seen anything like it."

"Like it consumed the artifacts," Eagle suggested.

"Quite so," Abrams murmured. But a moment later, Eagle noted Abrams's stress levels spike, his heart now racing. The old man's chair hummed and adjusted his medication.

Eagle raised an eyebrow. Conscious of the others present, Abrams mastered himself. "Stealthy growth," he said, and saw Eagle in turn go still, while his aura roiled and then as quickly settled. *Message received.* This was the ominous pattern Abrams had sensed.

The others frowned at the apparent non-sequitur, but said nothing when Eagle simply ignored the comment. "The timing of events points to the... entity...? being a key part in both the unique heat effect that kept you all at bay," Eagle said, "*and* in whatever brought the packed light network back into operation. The moment Leeth killed it, the network collapsed again."

"The timing is too exact to be mere coincidence, yes," Abrams agreed.

On the other display, Leeth had stopped eating and now sat, neck bowed, saying nothing, simply breathing. Otherwise unmoving.

Dojo, Harmon, and Preacher tensed, sitting with eyes locked on her. Preacher's fingers slowly closed around the grip of his pistol.

"You said she hasn't spoken, even after her healing?" Eagle asked. "Nothing at all?"

Abrams looked grim. "Not a word."

"What terrified your student?" Mother asked, "just before she went to Leeth's aid? What did she see?"

Abrams looked toward the dining room tableau on the other display. "Leeth," he said, finally, his expression even grimmer. "Just Leeth."

"But we saw her relinquish the dagger without argument," Eagle said.

"Uh," James began, seeing once again Leeth's bones and ligaments flexing, awash in blood, as she resisted him even while Ankhet healed her. "It may not have been obvious from the footage, but I had to damn near break her fingers to open her hand."

They all remembered the sight of the blood running down her forearm to her fist clenching the dagger. Not a drop had reached the floor.

"Is she bonded to it?" Eagle finally asked, heavily.

Abrams's gaze remained fixed on Leeth in the display. "She held an Aztec sacrificial dagger in her bare hand, to kill a powerful entity. The dagger *drank her blood.*" There was so much he could say. How Godsson and Harmon had, half wittingly he believed, succeeded in connecting her to Archetypes: *Archetypes*, plural. To the Seductress. To the Huntress. To something cold, unnatural, and new. And now, to this Death Archetype.

Yet still he felt the patterns of the future, and sensed he should hold his tongue. But was it really the urging of his special knack, or the magic of Seduction at work? It would not be the first time he'd made that mistake.

"I fear we will soon know," was all he said, at last.

All eyes returned to the display, where Dojo, utterly still, watched Leeth. Harmon sat to one side, hardly daring to breathe. Preacher's hand lightly held the gun on the table before him, now casually pointed at Leeth.

"Why was she fighting with a *bowl* in her mouth?" asked Mother.

Eagle, James, and Father had all their attention now on Leeth in the dining room, waiting for the explosion.

The question snapped Abrams's attention back to the meeting, though he gave no sign of the fear that thrilled through him. Instead he shrugged and shaped a spell. Briefly, he even considered trying to press it through the shield he'd crafted for Eagle. "It's unimportant," he Suggested. "A minor artifact she snatched from destruction."

Mother blinked. "And the dagger?"

That drew everyone's attention to the black silk bag resting innocuously on the dark surface of the conference table.

"We'll see." Abrams's words fell heavily.

"This is all no doubt important," Father said, "but I'm far more concerned by the global computer hack." He ticked off points on his fingers. "That it was possible; that it seemed purposeless; that the damage has been reversed. It makes no sense. I dislike the idea it was just to cause global power outages. Especially since that shut the computers themselves down, even as capacity came online to meet demand."

Nelson agreed with the experts' analysis of the hack: a channel reserved for critical firmware upgrades to deal with viral threats – and used to undo the hack, minutes later – had 'reprogrammed the microcode' at the heart of most CPUs with any link to the net. But instead of then suborning each computer, it had simply locked them into a tight loop inside a single lengthy instruction, over and over, endlessly.

"And why were they all perfectly synchronized?" Father added. "*No one* has offered an explanation for that."

No one did now, either.

In the dining room, Leeth lifted her head, and blinked. Finally, she shook herself. "That's better."

Harmon, watching Imaginally, sagged, then nodded. Dojo visibly relaxed. Behind her, Preacher's eyes narrowed.

"Doctor, Leeth, Dojo, please come to the main briefing room," Eagle said.

Leeth looked up at the speaker in the ceiling and struggled to her feet. "On my way."

Dojo followed after her, Harmon rising last, his expression neutral.

Eagle cut the projection, looking up from the silk bag back to his old friend's eyes. "Are you sure this is wise?"

Abrams shrugged. "Perhaps not. But it's *necessary*."

CHAPTER 16

In one viewport, Eagle monitored his biosensors' readings of Leeth as she entered – for once, not bouncing. Conscious at last, and seemingly herself. Abrams would warn him if anything magically untoward started developing. He kept his main attention on her eyes, alert for a sign of recognition of – really, of connection *to* – the black silk bag and the weapon inside.

Mother and Father were equally aware of Abrams's concern – and Eagle's gamble, in having the weapon here. Dojo and James had also been briefed, though both were careful to stand casually.

Nelson observed from virtual space, present as a small hologram 'seated' in a chair at the conference table.

Eagle saw the tiny narrowing of Leeth's eyes as she noted all those present, and the tilt to her head which he suspected meant she was now identifying precisely where Dojo stood, behind her. Her eyes flicked in the direction of James's holster, her heartbeat spiking before settling to just an extra three beats per minute.

So, she recognizes the danger she is in. Now for the test.

No one spoke. They all waited for her to notice the warded bag concealing the sacrificial artifact Abrams feared had bonded with her.

Mother had suggested Abrams should prepare his strongest physical Barrier, just in case. The old man had stared at her for long seconds. "Your confidence in me is touching, Mother. But no power on Earth could stand against a thousand years of Aztec blood sacrifice. And that's before factoring in Leeth herself."

Eagle noted Mother's reactions to the deliberate lie: both visible, and internal. Outwardly, her eyes had widened and she'd shrunk back in her chair. But only after his sensors had read excitement, not the false fear she projected, thinking the dagger still fully 'charged'.

Damn.

At least the test of Leeth had revealed that much, before the girl herself had even entered. He'd met Abrams's eyes, for a full second, but was otherwise careful to conceal how badly Mother had just disappointed him. "*Attack* will be our best defense in these circumstances, Mother."

Now he watched the girl, waiting for her to notice the

shapeless black silk bag. Both he and Abrams desperately hoped she remained untainted.

Everyone waited. Eagle read James's nervous tension, puzzled no doubt by the order to energize only his neural enhancements, leaving his strength augmentation on standby. *Even now I keep the secret of her uncanny hearing from my own agents.* Not for the first time, he examined his own attitude toward the girl. *Had* she seduced him, along with half the Department, as Mother claimed? But what she brought to his arsenal was worth some risk. A value that would be dwarfed by what he might achieve through her if she and the dagger had indeed melded – *provided* she could retain her sense of self long enough.

Although, *after* that.... He kept the grimace from his face.

At seeing the Doctor, Leeth clicked her teeth twice – then faltered at the silence. Her skin flushed hot, then cold, before remembering she'd had to remove Barney's anti-Harmon device at Mr Abrams's place. She gritted her teeth, feeling exposed and vulnerable without one tucked in her hair or under her armpit. She could hardly excuse herself to 'go get something' now. Grimacing, she made a mental note to visit Little Brother, soon, to recover the one she'd tucked away in the fireproof suit she'd shredded. No doubt all their gear had been sent back to him.

But... why was no one speaking? And when had she changed into a bathrobe?

Tired thoughts fell away as the silence finally sounded a warning, her skin prickling in a wave. *Something was going on.* James slouched too casually, perched against the table. She noted the position of his right hand, the gun he wore; where he stood in relation to her. Dojo's position, at her back. The silence itself. *Now what?* It had every indication of yet another-

And then she shivered, a black silk bag on the conference table drawing her attention, something small inside it.

Something small, and sharp, with two lapis lazuli eyes. She frowned, wondering when she'd learned what lapis lazuli was. But that thought faded....

It was easily in reach, too. She stood now at the vacant

chair closest to it, past Eagle, not quite sure how she'd gotten there.

I held it, didn't I? We joined, and fought? Her eyes closed.

She heard the movement of James's arm as his hand slid further under his tailored jacket, and paused there. Heard Dojo move one foot, and pictured *exactly* where he stood, his stance.

Mentally, she reached out toward the deadly little object, then stopped, trying to remember. What had she been doing before... eating just now?

Why do I feel so tired?

Her body, too, felt odd, laced with... *newness?* Her fingertips brushed the back of her left hand, half remembering blood-slick bones, scoured and even carved. Expecting to feel the fragility of freshly healed flesh, instead it felt... good. Right.

She shuddered, feeling again hundreds of tiny spinning teeth grinding into her, consuming her bite by bite.

Remembered she and *it,* the weapon in her other hand, carving apart an organic gray mechanism even as it ate at her. Ate at *them.*

She didn't need to stretch out for that mental contact, to see what she'd find. She *knew.*

She opened her eyes, annoyed at them all, feeling a surge of anger. They looked downright nervous, now. *I could just tell them.* Instead, she checked her stance and pulled the black silk bag toward her. Her hand slipped inside it, guided, to emerge gripping the golden hilt that fitted so perfectly in her palm.

And smiled at Mr Abrams.

CHAPTER 17

Holding it, fresh senses layered over hers – each person now a ripe, rich source of glowing energy. Mr Abrams reacted first, before even James, whose fingers slowly tightened on the butt of his gun.

Mr Abrams glowed like the *sun.*

Poor little dagger, she thought. *What chance had you had against him, on your own?*

Faster than any of them, she held up her left hand, preparing to give them the news before they tried to kill her. Her eyes flashed to James's, widening as sudden inspiration struck, and she giggled. "It's dead, Jim."

She felt the banked power at Abrams's fingertips, and waited, allowing him to run his gaze over her inner landscape, letting him see she was still herself. Though hanging under his shirt, she somehow sensed two tiny crossed golden bars suspended there, and felt a weird surge of fury.

James *finally* had his gun out, pointed at her, but with the dagger in her hand she really didn't feel all that threatened. She kind of looked forward to snatching some bullets from the air.

But behind her, sensei had *not* moved to attack. That warmed her heart enough to meet Eagle's gaze with irritation instead of anger.

"Do I pass?"

His lips twitched in a smile. *Wow, I actually cracked his poker face.* Unable to help the small pulse of pleasure, she smiled back. Reluctantly placing the dagger back on the mirror black surface of the massive table, she blinked as the world returned to normal. She licked her lips, already missing the sense of *potency.* Pulling out a chair, she slumped into it.

Mr Abrams stared at her speculatively.

James lowered his gun, and after a look from Eagle to Dojo, slid off the table to take a seat.

But she was distracted by the dagger again. Something about it looked different... *Oh! The narrow strip of lead was gone!* That odd braiding of gray metal that had wound around it between the obsidian blade and its golden hilt was missing.

Gray metal.

The exact same color as the coiling monstrosity she'd fought! She pointed it out, but Mr Abrams and Eagle didn't look all that surprised. In fact, it felt to her like they both kind of *winced*.

"You already knew! What *was* that thing?" she demanded.

"I honestly have no idea," Mr Abrams said. "Nothing even remotely like anything I've, ah, read about, or experienced myself. You did exceptionally well."

"Yeah, well, your spells helped. As did this little guy." She nodded to the obsidian blade with the golden hilt, its two blue eyes somehow empty, and reached out to stroke one fingertip down the blade. "That gray thing was eating the magic, you know?"

Her eyes widened. "The metal shelves and things, too. Growing bigger and stronger."

Abrams nodded. "We think it was some kind of living spell-slash-*construct*."

"Hngh. Sounds weird. But what was it doing it *for*?"

"I believe it was repurposing the magic to effect a change in a subtle aspect of reality itself."

"Yeah?" she said finally, pretending she followed. "That sounds... a bit difficult."

He inclined his head. "Even an oak can teeter in the balance, requiring just a push to fall."

"I guess. But that still sounds like pretty big magic. Besides, *I* felt it, and I can't even feel magic! Who could do something like that?"

Eagle took up her question, meeting his old friend's eyes. "Could the Dragon do something like that?" he asked. *Or you?* his look added.

Abrams shook his head. He eyed Leeth with a speculative air.

"Hey, don't look at me! I was asleep when all this started."

For some reason, Mr Abrams's eyes narrowed further, at her comment.

"Benson?" Eagle asked.

'Benson' was Godsson, Leeth knew.

"No," Abrams said.

"What about d'Artelle?" Eagle persisted. "Could *she* have done something like this, when she was alive?"

Abrams looked extremely unhappy. "I think so. But fortunately for the world, even d'Artelle possessed nothing like the *power* required-"

But a startled "Oh!" from Leeth interrupted Abrams's reply. Every head turned to her.

Leeth sat, oblivious, her forehead wrinkled as she tried to pin the thought. Looking up, she waved a hand at their expressions. "I'm just trying to remember something he once asked me to tell you."

"'He' told you? *Godsson,* do you mean?" Eagle demanded. "To tell *me*?"

"Yeah." She frowned. "Yeah, you. I think." She herself looked puzzled.

"When?"

"Oh. A long time ago?"

"About...?"

"Um, I'm trying to- oh, yeah! About Melisande d'Artelle."

They all winced, as if speaking her full name might somehow resurrect her.

"Oh!" Leeth's fresh grimace did nothing to reassure them.

"What?" Mother demanded. "What have you just remembered?"

"Uh... I remembered what he told me. About what she said when the three of them cornered her and accused her of stuff before they fought her. The reason she gave for breaking the internet."

A snowflake's fall would have broken the silence.

Mr Abrams swallowed, shattering it. "*D'Artelle* shut down the packed light network? Altered a universal constant? Changed the *universe*?" Disbelief changed to horrified acceptance as understanding dawned. Meeting Eagle's eyes he saw the same sudden understanding. D'Artelle had caused over a billion deaths, worldwide. *A blood sacrifice?*

Abrams felt the world shift beneath his feet. It tied in seamlessly to yesterday's brief revival of the packed light network.

"And the reason she 'broke the internet'?" Eagle prompted, noting Leeth's continued nervous grimace.

Leeth wet her lips. "Uh. It was a long time ago. I was only little. I mean, sure, a couple of times I maybe dreamed and remembered something I kind of felt might have been important, but it sort of slipped away again each time."

One by one, each of them realized she wasn't babbling, she was stalling.

"But this time, I remembered." She chewed at her lips, looking around at them all.

Their hackles rose at the sight of Leeth of all people hesitating. If *she* thought the rest of her news was bad...?

"Godsson said she might have been lying?" she offered. But instead of looking reassured, they all flinched.

"Just spit it out, girl," snapped Mother. "Your attempts to break it to us gently are..." *agonizing* "... counterproductive."

Leeth looked from Mother, to Father, to Mr Abrams, and finally to Eagle. She took a large breath, then exhaled, and took another. "Uh...." She wet her lips again.

The way Mother's mouth twisted, her eyes narrowing dangerously, jolted the words free.

"She said it was to stop the alien invasion."

Despite their absurdity, the rush of words struck like a sheet of ice water.

Nelson's hologram snorted a laugh. "That's..." *crazy*. But the word stuck in his throat as his mind considered the idea of 'alien invasion' via a purely digital/electromagnetic connection, and from there to the crazy events which had brought them all to this meeting.

As Nelson fell silent, Eagle and Abrams let the idea rework the foundations of their analysis. Had a *third* player entered the game? Or was the carefully planned sabotage intended to offer yet another reason to keep magic alive – keep open the path to a tyrannical godhood? If 'aliens' could work magic too, powerful and unfamiliar, then it would be foolish to remove it from Humanity's arsenal.

But while Eagle closely monitored Mother's reaction, she and Father and James had begun laughing.

"Alien invasion?" Father asked.

"So where are these aliens?" demanded Mother. "Why haven't we seen any in the *fifteen years* since d'Artelle's death?"

"With every breath, Leeth, Benson lies and manipulates," Eagle said.

Nelson, though, silently considered Ghost's deluge of fresh matches when hundreds of otherwise disconnected systems had spontaneously rejoined the internet. Which had allowed Ghost to reach into places previously beyond its reach. Including, for once, Tik Tek. But not because Tik Tek was ever disconnected. On the contrary. He'd been horrified when he'd realized he'd accidentally connected to an old part of Tik Tek.

No, unlike every other infiltration target, for Tik Tek, most of his penetration 'apps' were 'get me the hell out of here' escape programs.

But not during the Incident. For once, Tik Tek's frighteningly alert system hadn't reacted to his intrusion. As if its super scary system had been otherwise occupied? "And the attack gained control of most computers on the planet," he whispered aloud. "The hack was beautiful."

"Are you saying *aliens* took control of the *computers*?" Leeth said into the resulting silence.

Nelson blinked at her, confused, then at Eagle, his mouth falling open. *Out of the mouths of babes.* "Fu-u-uck."

"What did the computers do?" Leeth demanded.

Nelson's image turned back to her, frowning. He shook his head, but explained nonetheless. "Nothing, really. Just used up petawatts of power. They must have screwed up, because the new microcodes just locked up every CPU in a tight loop."

"But all perfectly synchronized worldwide," Father said. "Which can't have been by chance."

They started arguing, Nelson talking about 'unique new instructions' and 'microcode' until Leeth interrupted. "What did it sound like?"

About to ridicule her, Nelson remembered teaching her about Van Eck phreaking, and shut his mouth again. He and Eagle exchanged a helpless look. "That would have been a fucking powerful broadcast," Nelson admitted.

Leeth insisted on *hearing* the signal. With ill grace Nelson eventually shifted its frequency, dropping the transmission into the audible spectrum. The room filled with a wordless ululation, rising and falling with a driven, repetitive urgency.

"It's kinda like they're singing," Leeth whispered.

But to everyone else, it sounded like the computers had been chanting.

CHAPTER 18

That high drama was followed by – nothing. No signals from space. No strange news reports – unless you counted the Chinese press releases, with the wonderful animated graph pinpointing the source of the global hacking event. It showed the infection spreading in concentric rings centered north of New Francisco. Just another point scored in the ongoing diplomatic struggle for political influence. Shared a billion times in a day, the ten second graphic had already generated a raft of new conspiracy theories. International trust in the US weakened by five points.

For Eagle, the one bright spark was that Abrams felt the pattern of ominous, stealthy growth had all but stopped.

All but.

For Leeth, days of empty training followed. And while almost everyone seemed really happy with what she'd done in the 'alien attack' or whatever it had been, they also seemed even more wary around her. And things between her and the Doctor just kept getting worse. It wasn't magic, either. She was pretty sure.

He'd made her kill her lover. Shouldn't that have satisfied him? But he'd started making weird little digs at her. Comments she tried to ignore, tried to pretend didn't unsettle her. Digs about loyalty, trust. Naivety. Was he trying to turn her against the Department? Did he really think *he* could ever earn her trust again?

"You look tired, Leeth. Still not sleeping well? Understandable in the circumstances," Harmon said.

"Yeah, you'd know. Since you *caused* it," she agreed.

"Of course," he nodded. "You prefer to blame me, forgetting you *agreed* to seduce and kill Tujilque and steal his research."

He watched her, his expression one of polite enquiry. She wanted to smash it from his stupid face.

"Your anger at me is merely redirected anger at yourself. If you bottle it up, who knows how it will erupt when you finally reach breaking point? Perhaps you tell yourself I have betrayed you. I never have. I have stayed with you. Ask yourself, whose actions buried us both here? Yet I stay by your side. Who healed Faith? Or your friend Marcie Dunkirk when you severed her spine?"

"I did that *so* you could mend her nerves, Heal her!"

"But you couldn't be sure it would work, could you?

Just as you impetuously chose to wield an ancient artifact of ritual killing. Is that what you dream about now? Does the *dagger* disturb your nights?"

Her shiver was answer enough.

"Leeth, thanks to you we now both work for the Department."

She recognized the edge of anger in his voice – and felt *glad*.

"I am a trained psychologist, who understands you, even when others do not. You may use my services professionally. Both of us are loyal to the Department, and share its goals of restoring US power. I know you trust Eagle and have faith in his plans. His orders. But those plans have put you under stress. I would not want that stress to affect your relationship with your friend, Miss Dunkirk."

She stared at him, her mouth working. "It won't," she finally snapped, and stormed off.

"Let us hope so," she heard him say. "You have killed more than one person in a fit of temper."

He kept on and on, too. *Why* was he doing it? Because she'd bested him? Trying to work it out, she sometimes saw a look in his eyes, like he expected her to say or do something. Like he was waiting for something.

But if he kept needling her, he could wait for something, all right: he could wait for his death. She'd find a way.

He found new ways to jab at her. Like encouraging her to talk to Marcie – or maybe not. "It's good you have her to lean on. A crutch to hold you up when things get too much for you."

"She's a friend, not a crutch!"

He smiled. "Of course. It's not like the Department counts your calls to her, nor your outside excursions, as metrics of your stress levels." He didn't need to point out they undoubtedly eavesdropped electronically, too.

She'd been going to call Marcie that night. Maybe even arrange to visit her. Instead, she worked out in the gym, a long and punishing session.

She broke the rowing machine.

Time passed, and their quiet war escalated.

-

Emma glanced up as Leeth entered the rec room, gasping when she saw the swelling black eye. "Oh, Leeth," she murmured, "Again? Why haven't you had the Doctor fix it?"

"He's busy." The girl's expression twisted strangely. "He *used* to fix me straight away."

"Why do you push so hard? Dojo hates injuring people, you know. But the better you get, the less room he has to pull his punches."

Leeth smiled. She'd learned to pull her punches, too. And even so, sometimes it was Sensei who needed the healing.

"Why do you keep pushing him so hard? We've all noticed. What are you trying to achieve?"

Leeth tilted her head, surprised. *Wasn't it obvious?* Just then her wristcomm chimed. She glanced at it, and stood up. "The Doctor's free. See you later."

Emma spoke to her back. "Leeth, why are you doing it?"

The girl turned in the doorway. "Because I'm not better than him yet."

Emma fell back in her seat, a shiver prickling her spine. Maybe from the inhuman determination she'd sensed behind the words; or maybe at the idea of Leeth with all Dojo's skills. She shivered again.

Leeth knocked on the Doctor's door, steeling herself to ask for healing. The door slid open almost too soon, revealing him smirking at her from behind his desk.

"Ah, Leeth. Beaten by Dojo again, I see. I would have thought you'd be doing better than that by now." He shook his head, studying the livid bruise. It had swollen so much her eye was lost in it. "That's the third time this week. Apologies for keeping you waiting: that looks painful. Perhaps you should warn me of your sessions with Dojo in advance. That way I could schedule time to heal you afterward." He smiled.

"He didn't beat me! It's just sparring. It's not about winning or losing, it's about learning."

Harmon chuckled. "Of course. How silly of me. I suppose that means Dojo will be along later for healing too?"

She snarled.

He chuckled, watching the anger surge up inside her. He'd judged that just right. Not quite so enraged that she'd storm out to her bedraggled Dumps friends and pay for some slum mage to treat her. She needed no encouragement to form bonds outside the Department.

"You think you're so superior, don't you? Sitting here scheming, or whatever it is you spend all your time doing. Alone."

At the blunt accusation, he felt a little sick. *He* knew he needed to stress her, to force her next Unfolding. Yet he could never tell *her* that – the moment she knew the reason for his actions, she would dismiss them all as mere manipulation. The loss of her trust still pained, though.

"All I do, is for your own good Leeth."

She snorted. "As if."

"I only want to make you stronger."

"I'm strong enough already."

No. You're really not. The world was a harsh place, and she would need to be as strong as she could, to survive what loomed in the distance.

His gaze went back to her swelling cheek, and he waited.

She said nothing, just stood in the doorway glowering at him. At last she stalked in, stepping around his desk to stand over him.

"Don't make me stretch up to reach the injury, Leeth. Kneel down."

Her eyes flashed, one hand shooting to his throat – and froze there, her muscles just as quickly locking. He watched her try to force her finger forward, felt the faintest prick of her deadly psychic blade... and smiled. In satisfaction, he watched as every muscle in her body cramped, imagining the agony twisting through her.

Yet still she strained against herself. *Well, perhaps some verbal torment on top, in that case.* He widened his smile, even as he felt sicker, inside. "Empty threats now, Leeth? You *are* growing up. Tell me, is it the pain you enjoy most, or the loss of control? Perhaps I should get a cat-girl fetish outfit for you to wear. Would you like that?"

He watched, imaginally, as her aura raged and thrashed... but not enough to force an Unfolding. He sighed. "Never mind, I was merely joking. Now, kneel down."

He sensed something dark flash at the periphery of her

aura. The prickle at his throat vanished, as her anger withdrew inside her.

"I don't think so." One slender hand slid around his wrist. With the force of an iron bar she lifted his hand to her swollen cheek and trapped it there. "Let me hold your hand so your weak old muscles don't get too tired."

Her eyes bored down into his. Clearly, hoping he would struggle.

Instead he stood, to smirk down at her as he cast the healing. Fluids drained from the injury site, the angry flesh lightening back to its normal healthy red-bronze.

His conditioning even prevented her from flinging his hand aside when he finished, ten heartbeats later. She stood for an equal length of time, clearly trying to decide between insulting, or threatening him. In the end she did neither, merely storming from his room.

But as she left, the smile fell from his face as he considered the negative flash around her aura just before she'd swallowed her anger. The dagger?

Leeth didn't return to her room for hours, burning off her anger in lap after furious lap in the pool, imagining the water she plowed through was the Doctor's flesh.

Kneel! She'd half expected him to try his funting Mode One, whisper the words that stole her from herself. He was always studying her. Still puzzled about how she'd 'broken' his control. But she always wore Barney's device in its waterproof silicone sleeve, ready to replay the counter command. More than once, she'd felt him try his mind reading again. But he'd trained her too well to recognize the signs.

Eventually, she climbed from the water and toweled herself dry. Back in her room she changed, then decided to try again to free herself.

She sat down at her desk and clicked her teeth twice, the sound triggering Barney's device. The backup one – she really needed to visit Little Brother, get her original one from the thermal suit she'd shredded. Just... not right now.

She strained to remember it as the Doctor's voice whispered the counter-command. Tried to burn the sibilant syllables into her memory... but as usual, they drained from her mind like water through sand.

"*You funting krekhead halfdeck!* Why can't you *re-member* it!" Eyes screwed shut, she heard her knuckles crack.

I could play it back, loud, in front of Marcie! She *could write it down for me!* For just an instant, relief surged through her. Until she felt her muscles lock up, just from the thought.

"Aaargh!" The frustrated scream fought through a jaw clenched tight shut. It took a full minute before she could move again.

She snatched up a pencil and dug out an actual piece of paper – who knew what spyware Nelson had in her e-sheets? – and rammed her teeth together, twice. She'd try again to do it syllable by syllable.

The Doctor's voice whispered the sounds that freed her... and her hand shook with the effort of trying to write just the first syllable. But as usual, her muscles stayed locked while the sounds washed through her mind and faded to nothingness.

She threw the pencil down, snarling.

Speech to text hadn't worked, either: she knew he wasn't saying 'She shoots then distrusting.' Having a phrase that approximated the nonsense syllables burned like mockery: salt in the wound. She ground her teeth. She *needed* to remember the phrase herself! If she ever lost Barney's devices, or her backups of the recording....

Worse, though, would be if the Doctor ever figured out his control was still there, still working. That her freedom was basically a trick.

She grimaced. *That* was a problem needing a permanent solution. Godsson had said he could undo her uncle's magic – but she really wasn't sure she could trust Godsson anymore. The black dagger, though....

CHAPTER 19

"I don't like this. I don't like anything about this." Abrams glared at Eagle. "Admittedly, I haven't been able to see any bond between Leeth and that damned Aztec blade, but when she held it... her aura *sharpened*. Nor do I like her oh-so-conveniently-timed recollection of something Benson told her years ago, mere days after she visited the Institute."

"I assure you, there was no physical or electronic contact between the two of them," Eagle said.

"Just as there is no bond I can detect between Leeth and the dagger. Yet I know there *is*," Abrams muttered.

"You yourself rechecked the Wards limiting him."

Abrams brushed aside Eagle's remark with a shaky hand. "And *who* booby trapped the blade? Who knew we had even *noticed* Luiz? It had to be someone who knew the artifact would be entrusted to me, added to my vault. Feyborn? There's been no trace of that parasite since his or her assassination sixteen years ago. That worries me. I *still* think Benson engineered it, somehow – and is the reason he was chosen by the Dragon for his second, successful attempt to slay d'Artelle."

Eagle merely nodded.

"And what *was* that damned thing it spawned, anyway?"

"Nelson and Little Brother have studied the footage from your vault, but to little effect," Eagle said. "Regarding the peculiar inorganic detritus left behind, however, its mass matches that lost from the materials consumed. There was also a set of repeated nano structures to the compounds, but they say it had all been scrambled, so even they can't put that Humpty Dumpty back together again. They *guess* some kind of self-destruct system broke down the active components. But they found no trace of any power source."

"Of course not," Abrams snorted. "It was a magical construct. Self-assembling from inorganic material."

"As to 'who' – even if it's *likely* Tujilque was a tool of Feyborn and his or her damned Cabal Magicus, you yourself have no idea what it was, you said." Eagle frowned. "Therefore it should be equally unfamiliar to them, surely? *Could* it be alien?"

Abrams's liver-spotted face sagged. "Ask your scientists, not me. Perhaps? But it could also be something designed by the Cabal to make us *think* magic-proficient aliens are lurking out there."

"But not related to, ah, 'Fox', to use Leeth's term?"

Abrams sighed. "No. It doesn't have his signature." He stared into the distance. "I've never read about or seen even the glimmer of such a thing, before. But your idiot savant Harmon has played with things he should not have. On top of that, Godsson, and Melisande's Revenge, and now that dagger, could all have stirred the pot."

"But you said Leeth is not bonded to it."

"I said she does not *appear* to have bonded with it. But let us say, there is sufficient commonality of purpose that other possible *alignments* open up."

"You also said its 'stored power' had been consumed in the fight," Eagle said.

"Much of it, yes. But we may yet need the artifact. *She* may yet need it, if she's to end... our foe. Certainly, in her hands it would be an ideal weapon against *him*, or the Cabal."

"Which I'm sure they know, too," Eagle reminded him. "They *must* have been involved, since you were its target."

Abrams shook his head, though not in disagreement. "True. But the destruction of magical artifacts indicates the opposite, doesn't it?"

"Given their goals, certainly," Eagle agreed. "Not the Dragon's style, either," he murmured.

The two allies shared a look, nodding tiredly.

"New player?" Eagle said.

"New player."

"Possibly Leeth's, or Benson's, aliens?"

Grimacing, Abrams at last nodded.

Both men leaned back, thinking for several minutes, the only sound the quiet hum of Abrams's mobile life support equipment, gently massaging old limbs. "You said she did exceptionally well, Abrams. Tell me more."

For long, long seconds Abrams stared into the distance. "For my own home, with many years to prepare to protect such treasures, you need to understand I had created a last guardian that would have been impervious to attacks by even the Dragon himself."

Eagle blinked. And then blinked again.

"Quite. And as you have just guessed, I *did* use it, before calling for your help. Spirits have a, a *hardness,* to use a metaphor. Apart from one or two artifacts, I know of nothing which could have harmed it."

"Yet the 'intrusion' defeated it? And then Leeth defeated the intrusion."

"Exactly. Admittedly, aided by spells of speed and protection from me, and using the dagger, but still...." Abrams held Eagle's eyes. "*It* was terrifying. *Leeth* wielding the dagger went beyond that."

After a long silence, Eagle spoke. "It's a good thing she's on our side, then."

"Perhaps."

Eagle tilted his head in question.

Abrams sighed. "A battle like that 'reverberates'. And while my home's Barriers and Wards would have prevented direct observation, I fear she may have attracted attention. I have a hunch Godsson is not as isolated from events as we would wish. And let us hope neither the Cabal, nor the Dragon, nor our foe, links Leeth to the event." He shook his head. "Otherwise she may have become an *object of desire* for all of them."

At those words, Abrams felt a long-forgotten sensation, as if a bell tolled Truth at the heart of the world.

He suppressed a groan, knowing what *that* meant. *Damned for fools, those who dabble in Archetypes.*

And felt sorry for the naive young girl all over again.

CHAPTER 20

In Eagle's office, Leeth wondered why he'd called her there, and why neither he nor Mr Abrams was saying anything. She looked from one man to the other.

Mr Abrams had that 'absent' gaze she'd come to recognize as a mage examining something with their magical senses or whatever. Examining *her*.

Well, let him try!

Eagle was... as unreadable as ever.

She waited as long as she could. Way longer than a minute. "Am I in trouble or something?"

Mr Abrams answered. "Why do you ask that, Miss Leeth?"

"Just 'Leeth'," she said, frowning. "I dunno. Just a hunch."

"Really?"

"Are you making fun of me?"

"No. I value your intuition."

She eyed him up and down – the wrinkled skin surrounding alert, bright green eyes in a liver-spotted face. His loud breathing mixing with the complicated whirs, hums, and pumping of his fancy chair. But this time, the whole look struck her as a little *obvious*. Like he was rubbing his age in people's faces. She wondered just how old he really was?

He still watched her. Waiting.

She tried identifying where each tube went, tried guessing what they all pumped around, but eventually gave up. He looked fragile. He *was* fragile, too, she could tell. Physically at least. She could break him in two. But her instincts were telling her he was the most dangerous person in the room.

Maybe the most dangerous person she'd ever met.

She decided she couldn't 'out-boring' them, either. What had he said? He valued her intuition? "Yeah, I think maybe you actually do."

Mr Abrams raised one out-of-control bushy white eyebrow, and suddenly she knew. "Oh! You *do!* Because *you* make guesses for Eagle, don't you? *Good* guesses. That's what you do for him!"

Eagle blinked.

"Touché," Abrams said with a nod to her. He turned to Eagle. "You see?"

Eagle said nothing, once more in control of himself.

"So why am I here?"

"What do you know of gods, Leeth?" Mr Abrams asked.

"Uh... they're like stupid super-mages you can kill with nuclear bombs?"

"Pithy," murmured Eagle.

Leeth frowned, as did Abrams – though for different reasons.

"Do you know where they came from?"

She shrugged. "Some place without nukes or the Net, I'd say. There are old stories about them though, right? Maybe they were kind of hibernating."

"She's very good," said Abrams.

She got the impression her answer had pleased Eagle. "They're also often god *of* something," she added. "Like death."

The sounds of tiny movements from both men ceased. The room fell silent, but for the ticking whirs of Mr Abrams's chair.

"Yes," he said at last. "Again, true. But tell me, is there some reason *that* specific example sprang to mind?"

Yes. The dagger. "No. It just did."

He stared at her, his gaze somehow prickling. Eagle no longer looked pleased.

"Eagle tells me you've asked about the dagger, several times."

She licked her lips. "I just, I mean, when I fought that thing.... The dagger... it's a magical weapon, right? It might come in handy in future."

"You feel it would make you more powerful?"

"Look, I get what you're worried about: 'power corrupts', and all that. But I don't think it would, for me."

"Oh? Why is that? Power is very seductive."

She *wanted* to answer properly, but knew what would happen if she tried. "Because it's wrong to abuse power, that's all."

"Power sneaks up on people," Mr Abrams said. "It changes them by tiny degrees, finding cracks and chinks to work its way in."

"Uh huh. Really. So.... Both of *you* are pretty powerful. How do *you* guys avoid being corrupted?"

Eagle sat back. "An excellent question," he said, considering. "By questioning my actions," he said at last. "By acting from principles, not for myself."

She thought about that, then turned to Mr Abrams, and waited.

He was silent a long time.

"By striving to act always from love."

It wasn't the answer she'd expected. Even Eagle looked surprised, she thought, just for a moment. "Can you *please* just tell me why I'm here?"

"We called you here to discuss gods," Mr Abrams said.

She looked from him to Eagle. "Um, okay?"

When Mr Abrams didn't continue, she saw he seemed a little lost.

Eagle stepped in. "We still have laws against monopolies in this country, Leeth. Do you know why?"

Huh? Monopolies? Not wanting to seem stupid in front of either of them, she wrestled through memories of Checkbook's deadly boring lectures. She'd been pretty sure they'd never be useful.

"Oh! Because they're unfair! They're too- oh. Too powerful. Like gods would be."

Mr Abrams smiled and relaxed a bit, with a tiny nod to Eagle and a thoughtful expression when his eyes returned to her. "Exactly. We don't need magic. Not in this modern world. A thousand years ago, yes; even two hundred. But not now. Technology, properly managed, is more democratic: anyone can use it."

"Or, we could make everyone magical!"

"I doubt that's possible." Mr Abrams shook his head. "Even if we could, do you think it would make the world a better place? Magic can be subtle and hard to trace to its source. In such circumstances, the ability to harm is too easily indulged, power too easily abused."

Leeth's expression turned oddly wooden.

"Let's return to your earlier description of gods as 'super mages' – do you think their return would be a good thing, or a bad?"

She looked down, her brow creasing as she considered what they were really asking. At last she took a deep breath. "Okay. I'll do it."

Both men twitched.

"I guess I'm willing to try to kill this god you're obviously worried about. But I have to say I've got no idea how to do it. I assume I'll get special training?"

The two just stared at her, blinking.

"So who is it? What's it god of? Will Mr Abrams do the training?" She frowned. "In India they used nukes. I don't think I should."

Mr Abrams gaped.

Eagle recovered first. "She isn't pretending, Abrams."

"I can see that."

Leeth looked from one to the other. "I don't get it. You *don't* have a god I'm s'posed to kill?"

"Not today," said Eagle. "But I'm glad we've had this discussion. It has indeed clarified things."

"Not for me it hasn't!"

"Perhaps later, when you need to, you'll remember this conversation," Mr Abrams said.

With that, they dismissed her, grumbling and unhappy.

Eagle watched the security feed as she stalked off down the corridor, seeing her take a call as she disappeared into the lift. From Little Brother, he noted.

He turned to his old friend. "You see? She'd sooner try to kill a god than ally with it."

"It may not give her the choice," Abrams said, sourly. "And you read the lie yourself, I'm sure, when she spoke of a death god."

Eagle didn't try to deny it.

But they agreed to let the matter rest. For now.

CHAPTER 21

Leeth stepped into Little Brother's workroom with a sink-ing feeling she knew what this was about. *I never did get Barney's device from my fireproof suit.* Sure enough, there on the workbench she saw the tiny device, its silicone sleeve peeled off and laid neatly beside it.

She lifted her eyes to Little Brother, who was staring at her with a solemn expression.

"Come in, Miss Leeth. Shut the door behind you."

She winced, and did so. After a brief hesitation, she walked over to him.

When they both finally spoke, it was at the same time.

"I guess you're wondering-"

"Would you care to explain-"

Both stopped, and this time she could tell he was deter-mined to let her go first.

She looked up a little into soft brown eyes, a rounded face with smooth cheeks. She'd never really looked at him before. He had fine eyebrows, almost feminine, and wavy brown hair, trimmed short. Kind of cute in a boyish way. She'd always sort of dismissed him, but suddenly she saw he took his work here as seriously as she did hers. As they all did.

He was still waiting for her to speak.

For a moment, she felt the urge to blurt out the truth. How would it be if just one person knew... one person... *huh?* Her thoughts fell apart, slipping from her. What had she been thinking?

Little Brother took Barney's device between thumb and forefinger, holding it up between them.

Right. Right, Barney's device. From the special suit. "Have you, um, had a chance to study it?"

She saw his eyes narrow slightly. Of course he had. *Did he think...?* "It's not a spying device. It doesn't transmit. Doesn't even record."

"It does listen, though, doesn't it?"

Could she... use the Doctor's controls themselves, to give the secret away? Fight them so she went all confused, enough for him to see something weird was going on? He'd report it to Mother or Father, maybe even Eagle, and... and, stars above, how had she never seen how *sexy* he was, before? Heat flushed through her as she licked lips that suddenly tingled, feeling parts of her tighten, other parts loosen. And his eyes....

"Uh, Miss Leeth, what are you doing?"

She shook her head, one arm snaking around his waist, pulling him in against her while she reached up to cup his cheek, feeling his soft skin.

The contact of his body pressing against hers sent her skin flushing, dragged a moan out by its roots, snatched the breath from her lungs. She clamped her legs around his thigh, rubbing against him. She *had to* kiss him, *now!* Her hand slid around his neck and dragged his head down to hers, trapping his lower lip between hers, sucking and biting. Her heart leaped, her breath coming now in short gasps, and he squirmed against her.

He tried to speak, but couldn't while her tongue tasted his; tried to push back, but her grip around his waist locked him to her.

Dimly, she remembered feeling this way before, was aware this was something magically programmed into her, to distract. But beyond that, she intuited a path she wanted to go, a way to get what *she* wanted. Abandoning the thought before it could fully form she threw herself into the pleasure.

"Wait," he gasped, pushing against her. "I know you're much stronger than me, that you might hurt me. You up for something a bit... kinky?"

She had enough control to nod.

"Nelson really is a dick, I know. I'm sorry." Little Brother sat by her side, on the mattress, looking worried.

She felt confused.

Frustrated. Why were her arms and legs stretched out across his narrow bed? She tugged, then looked to one wrist, seeing it wrapped in about a hundred loops of electrical wire. Little Brother's ears flushed red.

Her legs, too, were similarly bound. *What...?*

"You're back, finally?" His expression softened to one of relief. His clothes had been shredded, hanging from him like rags. At her look he stood, blushing, and dropped out of sight to pick up a pair of boxer shorts that had been ripped in two.

Weird.

Letting them fall he darted to a chest of drawers, giving

her quite a nice view of a trim male backside. She tugged at her bonds and felt a shiver of excitement surge through her.

What on Earth...?

She caught a flash of his penis as he quickly tucked himself away. He hurried from the room, then back in, sitting down beside her, stretched out naked and exposed, bound to his bed.

What the funt *is going on here?*

In his palm, he held Barney's device, his expression once more serious.

"We were talking about this when you, uh, tried to distract me." He blushed.

Yes! part of her thought in triumph, even as her nipples once more sprang erect. Passion surged through her, the young man suddenly insanely attractive again. Pulling at her bonds, she snarled, extruding invisible claws to slash and cut herself free, throw herself on him and take him.

He sprang from the bed as cloth and rubber fragments flew. But each blow on the twisted metal cords raced along her nerves, a torture like the sound of glass grating on steel. She arched her back in pain.

Across the room, Little Brother gazed at her in horror, his eyes falling to the shredded bedding fluttering to the floor.

Panting, his back to the wall, he watched her as if she was some wild animal trapped in the room with him. His arm was bleeding, she saw. Four shallow, parallel cuts.

She realized she could think again, and felt something small wedged under her thigh, pricking her. Barney's device, bare.

His eyes went to the doorway, then his jaw tightened and instead he went to his workbench and began treating his wound. Though keeping her in view while he did.

"It's okay, LB. Calm down. I'm not going to hurt you. Uh..." *Again? Did I do that?* Her smile felt lop-sided. "I couldn't, even if I tried. Or wanted to."

Wound cleaned, he sprayed on medi-skin and turned to face her fully. Staring at her, he sagged against his bench. "Did... did Nelson do... *that* to you?"

Excitement thrilled through her as she realized her idea might actually work. "No," she said, carefully. "Not *Nel-*

son."

Her thoughts immediately fuzzed out. She felt he said something about a doctor, but she *needed* to get to him, needed his skin against hers, to feel him inside her, *taking* her....

Once again, the feeling of raw nerves grating on metal shattered the lust.

Little Brother stood watching her from a distance again, chewing his fingers, his expression a blend of pity and outrage. A camera bead on a tripod now faced her, recording.

Yes! She wanted to kiss him! And in a normal, sane way.

"Let's talk about this device. It wasn't made by anyone here, was it?"

"No. It was made by- Wait. You're recording this. You mustn't ever let the Doctor see it. Eagle, yes. But never the Doctor. Or anyone else, either. No one but Eagle. Promise. You have to promise."

Little Brother wrapped his arms around himself. The way Leeth was looking at him made him fear she'd find a way free of her bonds. And he wasn't stupid. He sensed he stood on the brink of a dark pit, here.

"I swear," he promised. "Only you, me, and Eagle."

He saw her sag in response, and hugged himself harder, feeling sick. "Okay. Let me tell you what I've figured out."

He held up Barney's device, and Leeth's respect for him went up a notch when she realized he must have snatched it from under her while she was slashing at his bed. *And him.* She grimaced.

"Display file Leeth-D-inside," he said, and a hologram of Barney's device appeared in the air between them, a small arrow bobbing nearby. It moved from one part to another. "This is a tiny speaker, this a microphone, and this a conduction mic. Phasion micro-AA cell, off-the-shelf memory, recorder, and a basic IC. I decoded the system and found a few sound files and some simple logic. When the IC matches one of a bunch of input signals, it plays this sound file."

Nothing happened – although Leeth flinched. Little Brother's mouth fell open, seeing that. He swallowed. "But if I amplify that sound about a hundred times, what we hear is *this.*"

This time, the Doctor's voice could clearly be heard. 'Seh-shoestus *desstussten.*'

"It's not words in any language I could find. Care to tell me what it means?"

"It- it- he...." Thoughts vanished in the gray fog, her wrists hurting as she tried to reach the object of her desire. Back arching, slashing out. Eventually though, she slumped limp and sweating against the bed.

Little Brother, she saw, was crying. "I think...." Clearing his throat he wiped at his eyes. He continued, his voice steadying. "I think we have enough footage. And I'm sorry, for tricking you earlier. But I knew something was out of sync as soon as you came on to me. I know you don't think of me that way." His chin went up.

Leeth slumped back on the bed, its frame now warped, the sheets damp and cold. Feeling like she was filled with a glorious peach light. At last she lifted her head and smiled at her cute young colleague. "Maybe that was my mistake."

He blushed again, which really was kind of cute. Until he added, "I'll share this with Eagle straight away."

"Don't you dare! I'm going to beat the Doctor on my own. I don't need 'rescuing'. Otherwise I could have just hired someone to shoot him."

Little Brother just gaped at her, before frowning. "That's just his..." he wiggled his fingers, "spooky magic. That's not-"

She looked at him pityingly.

He scowled. "If that's not his doing, what's your plan?"

Her eyes dropped. "I haven't figured one out yet. But it'll be epic." She heard him take a long breath.

"What I don't understand," he said at last, "is how you could even *hear* the recording. When I played it back to you the first time, this crazy little speaker was adjusted to minus ten decibels – but you reacted!"

"Uh...."

His eyes widened. "*That's* how you creamed James and Emma in that night hunt exercise! You could *hear* them!"

"Uh...."

"But why keep it secret? Oh. Because-" He clamped his mouth shut, and seemed to become conscious of her nakedness once again. Of her being tied to his now ruined bed. He held up Barney's device. "Because of what this protected you from. But now *I* can tell everyone-"

"Please don't!"

He frowned. "Oh, come on! Why keep your hearing secret? That *has* to be... you know." Again the finger wiggle.

"It's not," she said, frowning. "I just want... I feel I need my own secret weapon. Even just one."

"*Here?* Secret from *us?*"

She nodded, slowly. "Besides, I only report to Eagle."

"So I'll only report your amazing hearing to Eagle!"

She huffed out a breath.

"Chill!" He hurried over to his bench and began grabbing up bits of equipment.

"Uh, LB, what're you doing?"

He turned back to her, excited. "I thought we could run some tests on your hearing! You know, find your limits?" He turned away again.

"Ah, could you maybe untie me, first? And maybe I should get dressed?"

He *really* was cute when he blushed.

CHAPTER 22

Two months earlier, in his lab in the underground complex, Dr Callahan Scott's spirit briefly reanimated his tall thin body. "Head south along the shore eighty meters then turn east. You'll see a two-story structure." He described the building and the room where the collection team should find the couple, then leaned back in his chair and astrally projected again.

His colleague Dr Jeremy Ford split his attention between the live footage from the military team as they moved in on the pair, and the still form of the older man. He was still unclear how Scott had discovered the couple last night, not far from their own location in the Hunters Point Dumps. The mage had been metaphysically probing their latest subject when he'd jumped as if stung and abandoned the experiment to go astrally hunting. Most atypical behavior, for him.

Even so, Ford wouldn't have characterized Scott's demeanor as excited. The man never displayed emotion. No, it had been more like he was working to a tight deadline. As usual, the lead researcher offered no explanation, merely ordering Colonel Bragg to equip a team for a search and acquisition before first light. 'The two subjects are very close to what my calculus has predicted,' he'd added, in a message to his colleague. Ford had left Scott engrossed in his off-network personal comp, laboring over screens full of dense formulae in his private notation.

Now, Ford and the colonel watched the display – Scott no doubt observing astrally – as the away team entered the building and ascended to the second floor.

"Smells of human excrement," Sergeant Williams reported quietly.

For long seconds, there was just the faint sounds of the heavily armed three man team, disguised as mercenaries, climbing broken stairs. Once at the top, the view from Williams's cybercam scanned the scene. As textual telemetry highlighted and analyzed two seated figures, the sergeant was already calling for them to freeze and get down on the floor.

Ford watched the two heads swivel to Williams, the barrel of his rifle in view, apparently crouched and in cover at the top of the stairs while one of his team belly-crawled to the right, circling around.

A woman's voice spoke. "Is the waiting over?"

Her voice was hoarse, but the tone bored.

"Tell them it's time for them to come with you," Ford advised into his microphone. Williams relayed the order.

"Did Disten send you?" the man croaked.

Ford was leaning forward to tell Williams to say yes, when the sergeant spoke again. "Hell yeah. Disten sent us, said to collect you two." He sniffed again. "Shee-it, you been roughing it."

Ford, searching the name Disten, groaned as he read reports of a serial killer dubbed 'The Breaker'. *Why do I feel like I'm assisting Victor Frankenstein?*

The collection was anticlimactic, despite the male falling unconscious, dehydrated, as they left. After a last look around at the scattering of unopened tins of food and bottles of water, Williams followed.

Scott himself emerged from the complex, meeting the team above-ground on their return to make their entry undetectable. Though the away team felt a little unnerved by his satisfaction at having to box up the dehydrated man and woman before his concealment spells worked. As did the utter calm with which the two allowed themselves to be sealed inside the military caskets.

That impression of unnaturalness only deepened as the days and weeks passed. Even Scott's potent magic was unable to probe the brains of the disturbingly indifferent couple. Who weren't a couple, they learned. Scott and Ford agreed to seal the record of their sickening retellings of how they had both, separately, been brought to a state they called 'Perfection'.

At least, Ford had been sickened. Scott had merely said 'fascinating' and continued making rapid annotations to his 'new rationality' model. "I don't think we will need to use such crude methods, however."

Ford's answering smile was weak, but relieved.

In the end, a combination of fMRI scans, harrowing psychological question and answer sessions, and days of cryptic calculation by Scott had the mage declaring himself satisfied. And now that he had need of Ford's own special expertise, he was willing to share his key findings. "Massive psycho-traumas were used to shut down the amygdala, which was then somehow locked into a quiescent, looped state. Further, new neural pathways have formed, connecting the cerebellum and prefrontal cortex. More significantly, there's been what we could call a neurotransmitter hijacking of the entire sympathetic nervous system."

"Interesting," Ford said. "A demonstrably functional restructure, too, although dampening emotional responses." *And damned creepy.* Though perhaps not much more than Scott himself. Sometimes he wished he knew what motivated Scott. Still, the pay was excellent. "I expect I could design some genemods to achieve similar results – or at least lower the barriers to the change. Can you give me precise specs?"

Scott nodded. "There were one or two gaps in my understanding, but my model correctly predicted the 'anti-magic' effect operated only in vivo."

Ford's mouth fell open as he realized Scott had just admitted killing at least one of the new specimens – as well as creating yet another entirely new spell. He swallowed. "You... were able to use *magic* to look inside to the molecular level?"

Scott frowned. "Yes, although I still had to extrapolate the dynamic behavior based on my model and the fMRI results." He met Ford's eyes. "I tried reanimation, but the magic field instantly collapsed."

Horror shocked through Ford, both at what Scott had done, and at how easily. He saw Scott flick his gaze to the imaginal, studying him as a snake would a mouse. But already the fear was fading, as it always had, even in childhood, and Scott lost interest.

Ford wondered, not for the first time, whether he and Scott were more similar than he liked to think.

PART II

Lies

CHAPTER 23

"Doctor, analyzing Leeth's performance, we have discovered a problem."

Sitting opposite Mother and Father's joint desks in briefing room three, Harmon raised an eyebrow and waited.

"We have discovered Leeth's effectiveness correlates with her *dress*."

Harmon frowned, confused. "I beg your pardon?"

Father spoke. "When Leeth is dressed in a way which she feels is, ah, unfashionable, she becomes nervous, uncertain, even clumsy."

Harmon shook his head. "No, no, Leeth is simply a superb method actor, sinking herself into the role. Even I was surprised-"

Mother cut in. "No, Doctor. Unless your charge is dressed as a slut, she becomes useless."

"Well, hardly a *slut*, Mother. Just..." Father gestured helplessly.

Harmon agreed, despite a nagging, itching doubt. "Leeth is proud of her figure, her health, and certainly gets a 'boost' when she dresses-"

"Oh, be quiet, the both of you." Mother *thought* the lights off. For Harmon's benefit, she spoke aloud. "Play file 3, 27, Leeth-c."

A holo image sprang up between the desks and Harmon. "I'll show you a few excerpts from some tests we've run this last week. This is Leeth on her way to train with Dojo this morning."

A dejected little figure dressed in an unflattering track suit and plain sneakers instead of the bare feet she preferred, shuffled down the corridor to the gym. "Forward two minutes," Mother said, and the scene jumped to inside the martial arts training area. For a short while they watched as Dojo, clearly puzzled and expecting some trick, made Leeth look foolish.

Father winced, watching it for the second time.

"Mark B," Mother commanded, and the scene skipped to Dojo dismissing the girl early. She had a confused but grim expression on her face.

"Mark D."

Leeth was target shooting. This time she was dressed as a policewoman in a drab uniform. Her expression was one of dogged suffering. The view shifted to the targets. Even Harmon looked worried as he saw how far below her normal accuracy she was achieving.

"We're just hitting the low points, by the way," Mother explained. "Mark F."

The scene shifted to the canteen. Leeth, dressed in a brown blazer over a heavy ill-fitting blouse and a pale blue full-length skirt was just turning from the food dispenser with a laden tray when she tripped, tried to grab the tray, but only succeeded in sending it hurtling across the room before falling to one knee. Her face was ashen as she stared at the mess, then at her hands.

"Off." Mother gestured the lights on. "Shall I continue, Doctor? There is quite a lot more."

Harmon looked a little shaken. "Let me consider this for a few minutes, please."

Mother sat back in her chair with folded arms. Father linked his hands as he watched the mage intently. Harmon stared off into space.

"I believe I understand," Harmon at last said. "Unfortunately, I feel your assessment is basically correct. Leeth is a very direct and physical person. Not really all that well socialized, as I'm sure you've noticed."

"And whose fault is that?" Mother observed.

"Now, now," Father said. "She's improved tremendously over the last few months, especially since meeting the Dunkirk girl."

"Marcie Dunkirk is a leak in the making, as we have previously agreed," Mother snapped. "The sooner that friendship ends, the better."

"Yes, yes. I haven't forgotten, Mother. You have my agreement for the Doctor's plan," Father said, though his expression showed regret.

"If I may continue my analysis?" Harmon asked. At their nods he continued. "More significantly, Leeth is perhaps the least introspective person I've ever encountered, outside clinical conditions. She is also extremely adaptable – possibly too adaptable, in some ways. Perhaps most significant is her identification with her outward appearance. It is also quite possible there is a magical resonance at work. By which I mean her perception of her effectiveness is what delivers that effectiveness. I'm sure you've both read my ongoing notes trying to pin down her peculiar magic. It's quite remarkably subtle, even when she is most clearly doing more than her body should be capable of. Simply put, when Leeth perceives herself as unattractive, she perceives herself as ordinary, and becomes her own mental idea of what an ordinary person is like."

A long silence met his explanation. It was Mother who at last spoke. "You're saying she has to dress like – let's be kind, and say a rock star – for her to function as we need?"

Harmon's sick look was answer enough.

"Then tell me this, since I will have to pass the information on to Eagle: what use is an assassin whose appearance is so striking that everyone notices her?"

Harmon considered. "Well... she has proven quite effective so far, hasn't she? Dressed attractively – even provocatively? I imagine that could continue. Certainly, as we are all aware, it is extremely hard to believe that someone who looks as – sexually open as she does, could be dangerous."

"Open?" Mother snorted. "Sexually open? Is that what we're calling it now? She's not sexually open, she's an out and out sexual predator, stalking these corridors like a tigress in heat! I doubt there's a man in this place she hasn't rubbed her crotch against."

"Come now, Mother, that's rather overstating the case," Father said. "The girl is simply prone to hugging, and spirited of course."

Harmon took up the baton. "Also, Mother, consider: beauty itself can be a shield. Cosmetics can change a woman's face so dramatically, conjure illusions of beauty so well, it is almost impossible to see the true face beneath it. Perhaps an accomplished artist could guess the face beneath the mask. An ordinary observer, even a trained observer, is basically blinded by the beauty."

Mother scowled. "Can you train her out of this fixation, Doctor? Assuming she'll even talk to you."

"Let me think." Harmon closed his eyes, massaging his forehead. He should have seen this. It made perfect sense.

Minutes passed in silence while Mother watched, her anger growing. Even Father, watching the Doctor's face as it remained resolutely expressionless, realized the news was going to be bad.

The Doctor's head shake merely confirmed it. "It may not be possible. I will need to investigate. Perhaps *eventually* this aspect of her essence can be modified somewhat. But this is central to her personality, at the core of her special talents. Tampering with it is likely to interfere with those abilities."

"If you *can* correct this condition, how long is that likely to take?" Mother demanded. "I find it hard to accept that people may not be able to give useful descriptions of her if they find her attractive. But even if true, she would be recognized from an image."

"No. Small changes will suffice: different hairstyle or color; glasses; different makeup. But to answer your first question, as she begins to look inside herself, as she gains experience, and with my counseling, the effect could ease. Over the years."

Mother said nothing, just stared at him, thin-lipped. Several times, those lips parted, only for the tendons in her neck to twitch as she bit down on the scorn she wished to baste him in. "Dismissed, Doctor. You, however, will submit a written explanation, for us to forward to Eagle."

He nodded and rose. "As you wish, Mother. Father." He left the room.

The two exchanged sour looks.

CHAPTER 24

In one corner of a small underground lab, watching and listening to the two researchers, a solid Caucasian male stood, unmoving. Every twenty seconds he blinked. The other two paid him no attention.

Dr Jeremy Ford swore suddenly. He looked up from his workstation to his tall, thin superior. "Bio-Block say our order's been stolen – hijacked! The delivery drone was hacked."

Dr Callahan Scott turned from the holographic model of their latest subject's cognitive processes. He studied the younger man.

In the corner, silent, the stocky man watched.

"They blame the global hacking incident last week, when the packed light net briefly sputtered up."

Scott waited.

"They say they can re-spin the cultures next week. Send us a new delivery next Friday."

Scott's deep-set, unblinking eyes remained locked on his. "Is that reasonable?"

Ford nodded. "It's really fast. It means they must have lost hardly any orders, otherwise we'd be waiting for a fresh slot. It's not like they can use their Alter vats to grow *our* infusions."

"Does it suggest only our delivery was intercepted? In all that mass of illegal genemods."

"Uh. Yeah."

Scott just continued looking at him. Not for the first time, Ford suppressed a shiver. Then *did* shiver, at Schenk's even more toneless voice, speaking suddenly from the corner.

"The revised induction process should be tried on the current subjects. More subjects can be obtained when the genemods arrive. There is no shortage in the Dumps."

Scott agreed. "Start with the young drunkard. He should have sobered by now."

-

Two days later, at a small Tik Tek space research facility outside Paradawn, deep within the Newtopian Territories – formerly Antarctica – two newly Altered human beings woke into the simulated nightmare prepared for them. As far as they knew, they were arriving at Tik Tek Orbital Two, a little groggy from the drugs administered to ease the stresses on the body of being launched into space. An innovation they'd been offered to trial, and happily accepted.

In reality, they lay in full immersion VR pods, with invasive neural shunts in place.

The head of Tik Tek studied their responses. Closely. Very closely. Sixteen years earlier, Adam, the immuno-compromised son of the ailing Simon Fuller-Price, had taken the reins of Tik Tek after his father's assassination. Adam had been just sixteen.

Now a recluse living in a sterile bio-secure facility, Adam Fuller-Price ran Tik Tek entirely via virtual presence from an undisclosed location, hidden from assassins. Quite safe.

Adam forked his attention, sparing several seconds to study his 'father's' current situation, especially the power and wealth he'd amassed in the last five years. It would soon be time to kill him again, Adam decided.

He checked that the implants were functioning correctly in all the host bodies his father – more correctly, Feyborn – was likely to jump to. The next Pack-Co board meeting? Perhaps a sniper while morning tea was served, to give Feyborn the choice of a wealthy older body or a poorer younger one?

But that was for later. The entity identifying as Adam Fuller-Price, the CEO of Tik Tek, studied the responses of the two kidnapped subjects. He would be a silent observer for the lengthy series of scenarios he had created. A very close observer, soaking up every sensory input, monitoring every bodily reaction. So close, it would be like reading their minds.

These two, dosed with the intercepted Bio-Block gen-emods, already showed very different brain chemistry. Even with the changes only fifty percent complete, they were already reacting less like the animals they were.

Very promising.

The design for this alteration needed to be obtained.

CHAPTER 25

In his office, Eagle closed his eyes to study the internally displayed picture of Tony Maretti. Even alone, he maintained a neutral expression, hiding his concern.

He knew those eyes, that line of jaw. Would Leeth also recognize them? What did she remember of her earliest years, before the Doctor had... 'found' her at the orphanage?

To his knowledge, she'd never spoken of any memory before the Institute for Paranormal Dysfunction. Given the Doctor's antipathy toward religion, and that 'Sara's' orphanage had been run by nuns, he assumed Harmon had somehow blocked or erased those memories. Especially given his ability to implant memories. Not that the Doctor's sole collaboration with Nelson on that front had fared well. That thought reminded him in turn of the latest intelligence on the Tik Tek R&D subsidiary. Yamamoto Memory Systems, however, lay on the list of future operations.

You're avoiding the topic at hand, he told himself, returning his attention to the image of Tony Maretti and the question of Leeth's first years. His expression grew more wooden still as he considered his own culpability.

I need to know what Leeth remembers, but I can't ask Harmon outright. The man was no fool, and would be sensitive and suspicious given the abuses he'd inflicted. Those abuses, after all, and Leeth's own actions, had allowed the Department to sweep them into its fold with 'an offer they couldn't refuse'.

Hanging behind the face of Tony Maretti, leader of the Fist of Peace, documents and images of the rest of his group receded into the virtual distance.

Studying Maretti's eyes, jaw, skin, he shook his head.

What did Leeth recall of her father – and mother, for that matter? Normally he could simply run a search for each time she had spoken or written the word 'father' within the Department's hearing. But an unfortunate consequence of their code names meant that any such search would yield a flood of matches in this instance.

He himself had never heard her reminisce or speculate about her parents. The Doctor's handiwork?

Maretti and his team *should* prove a simple enough task for Leeth. The girl deserved a chance to let off a little steam, too. Socialize; grow. Despite the Doctor's determination to stress her, Eagle didn't want her broken.

The problem was, Maretti.

At last, he opened his eyes and called Harmon.

The video link did not appear for a full second. When it did, the Doctor was as usual seated at his desk. Eagle noted the smartsheet pushed far to Harmon's left. A quick query revealed it had just closed a map of the Hunter's Point Dumps. Resting at the Doctor's fingertips, but turned face down, sat a paper pad and pencil.

"Eagle?"

"I've been thinking about Leeth, Doctor."

Harmon's expression became instantly guarded.

"You adopted her at age eight."

The mage inclined his head.

"I've never heard her speak of a time before her upbringing at the Institute. That strikes me as odd. What answer would I get, if I asked her about her life before that?"

Concealed sensors in the Doctor's office showed the kind of spike associated with an adrenaline reaction. It was not reflected in his demeanor, however.

"You know perfectly well that Leeth was a... partner in my experimental studies, Eagle. It is, after all, the reason we are both here, and why she has proven so useful to you."

"I'm not sparring with you, Doctor. I just need an answer to my question. Is Leeth able to remember her time before the Institute, and is merely 'disinterested' in it, or is she *unable* to recall those memories?"

Harmon studied Eagle's face carefully before speaking. "Perhaps you could explain why you 'need to know'. It would help me answer."

Eagle shrugged. "After noticing the 'blank area', I re-examined Leeth's psychological profile – which you provided us – and found a corresponding gap. Omissions there may lead to problems on missions.

"So, Doctor. How would Leeth react if questioned about her early childhood?"

Eagle had the impression Harmon was still considering *him* rather than the question.

At last he spoke. "She does not remember it. If pressed on the subject, it could lead to confusion. Pressed hard enough, even distress, knowing Leeth's stubbornness."

Eagle noted Harmon's bio-signs spike again, as if expecting some hypothetical ax to fall. "I see," he said. "I'll need you to provide a few details for Leeth's background in future missions, to sidestep the issue." Unsurprised, he saw Harmon's stress levels fall.

"Certainly," he said.

Eagle nodded.

"Is that all?"

Eagle tilted his head and signed off, ignoring Harmon's intent stare.

So, she doesn't remember. If he authorized the mission, he'd need to observe the briefing himself. Neither Father nor Mother knew enough to interpret any warning signs, since the Department had not existed back then – soon after a sixteen-year-old prodigy had broken through state-of-the-art government crypto-systems to beg him for 'rescue' from Asgard.

Nelson's success at penetrating secured systems had been more than impressive. Indeed, it had been the key to finding suitable candidates to satisfy the peculiar personnel mix he'd needed to create the Department itself.

But Nelson, who had the empathy of a... a gopher, would be even less likely to spot problems in the upcoming mission. Even had he not failed to find Leeth's parents when set the challenge. Thank god. Eagle believed it the *only* reason their enemy had likewise failed.

Sighing, eyeing Maretti's virtual image, he authorized the mission, though not without a qualm. Then frowned at his schedule, as Little Brother arrived outside his office. 'To discuss Leeth.'

Of course it would be about Leeth. Eagle had not spoken one on one to the young 'maker' since his induction. Steeling himself, bracing for the unexpected, he eased back in his chair and admitted the young man.

CHAPTER 26

Eagle hadn't seemed surprised to learn of her amazing hearing, Little Brother told Leeth later.

She didn't know whether to be pleased by that, or annoyed. It did cheer her though, knowing she now had two people in her corner, aware of the Doctor's hooks.

Another big plus was that the happier she got, the crosser the Doctor grew.

Now Leeth faced Father in his office as he took a polished rosewood box from his desk drawer and slid it toward her, tapping it. "This will remove your communication disadvantage compared to the augmented agents. It's absurd to have you reliant on an everyday Link."

She undid the ornate catch and flipped back the solid lid. "Oh – sleek!"

Inside, an elegant black choker rested on a pad of ocean blue silk. It shimmered as she lifted it out, weighing it in her hand. Subtle etchings showed as she angled it left and right, one finger tracing the sweeping curves and radiating patterns. "*Very* sleek!"

"It also represents a new state of the art in communications, thanks to recent advances made by Nelson. Radio transceiver, forty-kilometer range. All incoming and outgoing messages digitally encoded and encrypted. Pre-assigned channels should you need to communicate with myself, Mother, or Eagle. Burst mode broad-spectrum broadcast facility – power hungry, of course. Also a limited, unbreakable one-time pad. Use it sparingly."

The girl looked back at him blankly.

"Nelson can go over it with you, instruct you."

Her answering scowl told him she'd master its operation swiftly.

"Touch sensitive. Every function accessible via taps, strokes. Voice commands. Booklet in there. Written by Nelson. You may wish to study it before visiting him. Be fluent in the device's use before your next mission."

She pouted.

"One final point. Utmost priority, now and in the future. Our other operatives have cybernetic modifications. Some give improved capabilities. Other features make it safe to place our trust and our country's most sensitive intel in their hands. Like encrypted headware memory, auto-erasable. For secrets like our own existence, hidden in plain sight as the Accounts Department of the Bureau it-self."

Leeth stiffened, glaring at him. "The Doctor's *conditioning* solved that problem, remember? I can't talk about any of you guys *except* to you guys, even if I wanted to!" She looked as if she burned to say more – then, as if she'd just remembered something, relaxed and sat back.

He waited, but she simply watched him, her smile a trifle smug. "You have none of the modifications which guarantee a similar level of safety."

At that, she gaped and sprang to her feet. "No! No more. I *won't* have cyberware. I don't need it and I don't want it. It's a crutch that'd cripple-"

"Leeth! Sit down!"

Poised on the balls of her feet, her thoughts raced like a river in flood. *I won't let them do it. This is a mistake.* "No. I made an agreement with Eagle. I answer to him, not you, and he wouldn't agree to implanting cyberware in me. *I* won't agree to cyberware. If you can't accept that, our deal's off, and I'm outta here, this time using *your* retinas for the exit scanner!"

She was leaning over his desk, panting. Father remained seated, his eyebrows raised. "Have you quite finished?"

He looked, if anything, mildly amused. Scowling, she threw herself back in her seat and crossed her arms.

"We are not suggesting cybernetic enhancement."

"Cybernetic castration," she muttered.

Father merely frowned at her. "Your choker, once closed, cannot easily be removed. And *should* not. Doing so would break the quantum coupling," he lied. "Also, not only is the device extremely costly and difficult to manufacture and repair, but we don't want its technology falling into *any* other hands. For these reasons we have decided it will be the physical embodiment of our trust in you. Allowing anyone to tamper with it or try to remove it will be considered a sign you have abandoned that trust. Clear?"

So, if I wanted to betray you guys I should just keep wearing it? Idiots. She sighed but nodded. Not that she *would* betray them. "I keep my word when I give it, Father. And I gave it to Eagle."

"I must also warn you it will self-destruct if tampered

with. That would injure you as well as cost the Department a large sum of money."

Her eyes narrowed at that. "I guess I can try it out on *this* mission. See if I like it." Its shiny black elegance drew her eye again. She nestled it back into its classy bed of shining blue silk, looking up from it to frown at Father. "But if it self-destructs and injures me, it better not leave any scars."

He didn't correct her impression, merely inclined his head. He disliked lying to his own agents. On the other hand, he could hardly let her know the self-destruct was powerful enough to kill her. And that *all* of its functions could be operated remotely. The self-destruct was only active while the device was basically stationary, however. They didn't want to blow her head off if it was damaged or torn from her during combat.

Trust, modern-style. Unless Eagle had over-stated its potency, for reasons of his own?

He returned to the subject at hand. "Good. Let's proceed with the briefing for your current mission." At his mental signal, the door opened.

Harmon stepped in, warily crossing to sit beside Leeth.

His eyes went to her new piece of equipment, and she saw him scowl. Like he hated her getting stuff from people other than him. Should she put it on right now? Maybe just rub it in. "That's my latest spy equipment."

He frowned, clearly annoyed at being out of the loop. Hiding her grin she turned away.

Father appeared not to notice the byplay. "You will infiltrate a small activist group called the Fist of Peace. We believe one or more traitors within it are selling technology they've supposedly destroyed, to Tik Tek and others. You will identify the traitors and eliminate them. Preferably without disrupting the group."

He paused, waiting until she nodded.

"The Fist of Peace are militant anti-military types. Against weapons research, but believe in fighting fire with fire." He shrugged. "You might say, they like to adopt violent causes. We occasionally hire them for odd jobs for the Department. Without their knowledge, of course."

"You don't... the Department doesn't do all its own work?"

"Leeth, we only have four Agents. If we can use an independent group for an op, especially one for which we want plausible deniability, we often contract out the work via a cut-off. Helps keep our nose clean.

"Now, your skills should provide you an 'in' to the group. We also have some information you can provide for extra leverage.

"You'll be the ex-girlfriend of a recently-deceased employee of a small pharmaceutical company, Bio-Block. Head office Los Angeles. Ostensibly, they find cheaper ways to produce patent-expired medications. But on the side, they also do sketchier work — unsanctioned and off-the-books drug research and gene, uh, therapies — at a secret facility. You'll have news of a neurological stimulant they're developing. A so-called 'combat drug.' Briefly improves many qualities useful in a foot-soldier, like a poor man's cybernetic neural boost. The Fist of Peace will disapprove. Clear enough so far?"

Leeth nodded. "So I'll be going to Los Angeles?"

"Actually, no. That's just Admin." Father leaned forward. "Last week, Nelson located Bio-Block's secret manufacturing facility, and it's here in New Francisco."

She frowned. "Doing 'sketchy' drug research. And gene 'therapies' — like, gene *mods*. Like, *Alter* mods?" Her gaze went distant.

"Indeed. Strictly speaking, breaks the Global Moratorium of '38. But thousands like them, around the world, meet that particular fetish. However, such facilities often shift, undertake more serious breaches. One reason we targeted Bio-Block."

But Leeth was still staring into space. "Alter mods." She shivered. "Like... *Bastean?* Cat girls?"

Father kept his expression neutral. Nelson had found the design for exactly such a gene-mod, tailored to her DNA, in the material she'd taken from Luiz Tujilque — matching the contents of a certain vial the police had collected from the murder scene. They had decided not to inform her of that. "The other reason-"

"*When* did Nelson find this gene-mod place?"

Leeth's gaze was no longer distant. Indeed, she watched him now with disturbing intensity.

"Ah, that is irrelevant to this-"

"It was from something on Luiz's comp, wasn't it?"

"That is an absurd-"

"Oh! And I bet their secret facility had one of those old packed network links, and it reconnected last week. That's how Nelson hacked in and worked out their location!"

Father just blinked, before glancing helplessly at the Doctor. Who sat watching Leeth with an expression remarkably like paternal pride.

"That's as may be," Father said, ignoring her satisfied snort. "But if I may continue with your mission briefing?" Leeth nodded as if his question hadn't been rhetorical. There were times when he sympathized with Mother. "The Alter mods are irrelevant for this mission. Focus on the combat drug, the neural stimulant. *That* is what will motivate the Fist of Peace.

"Our *other* reason for targeting Bio-Block is that Nelson also learned Tik Tek is hunting for their illegal facility."

"Tik Tek? Don't they make those robots that look human?"

"Yes, Syrra and Garnak. Now, we know Tik Tek is hunting for Bio-Block's black facility only through Nelson's special efforts. Keep that to yourself."

"Why's Tik Tek so desper to locate this secret base?" At his expression, she added, "*Desperate*" with a roll of her eyes.

Father waited long seconds for some sign of contrition, giving up at last with a sigh. "Good question. Would be attractive to Newtopia for their Antarctic security personnel – punishing conditions – and the ongoing disaster we call the Brazilian eco war. Or-"

She'd raised her hand the moment he'd said 'Antarctic'. "You mean their *Newtopian Territories* security personnel, right?"

Father harrumphed at her correction, but nodded.

"But if it's so attractive to Newtopia, why's *Tik Tek* hunting for it?"

He leaned back in his chair. "Tik Tek is a member of the Newtopian Consortium, holding the second largest voting bloc after Newtopia itself." His gaze went briefly elsewhere. "I've scheduled a remedial corporate structures course for you. Complete it before the mission."

Leeth winced, and made a mental note about needling

Father.

"Uncovering the reason for Tik Tek's interest is not part of your mission, however.

"You will have been given the location of this Bio-Block facility by an ex-employee – your lover, Paul Genaro. Resigned a month ago. Died a week later. Apparently accidental. But you refuse to believe that."

He tossed down a flex marked Top Secret. Hiding the thrill those words still gave her she thumbed for access and let it look at her retina, unlocking it. *Mmm*, she thought, examining the flat-pic of a fit, dark-skinned male. *Chiseled.*

"That's his dossier. Be reticent regarding Paul – private grief and all that – but study it up. Details matter."

At his mental signal the document skipped forward. "Section two covers the Fist of Peace. Just photos and brief notes – we don't want to prejudice you. Feel free to request further information if they accept you.

"Leader is Tony Maretti. Took over the reins after the group's founder died. They are-"

She wrenched her attention from the strangely compelling picture of Tony Maretti. "Um. Father? Why does the group have *reins*?" she interrupted, confused.

Father frowned at Harmon. Really, there were some stunning gaps in her education, even at this stage.

The Doctor answered. "It's an idiom meaning *control*, Leeth. I'm surprised you aren't familiar with the usage." His smile was casually taunting.

She flushed and opened her mouth to tell Father- to tell Father.... Her mind went blank.

She glared at the Doctor, who just watched her with a knowing smile. Oblivious, Father brought up a page of mugshots. "They have both a Native American street shaman, 'Wolf' and a mage, Cynthia Wallen. A hacker, 'Wiz'. A 'maker'-slash-electronics expert, 'Gadger'. The generic names are deliberate."

Leeth leaned forwards, the tip of her tongue darting out as she studied them.

"Muscle is supplied by six other members of the group. Be careful of one of them, Don Reilly. Heavily cybered and borderline psychopathic, we suspect."

She looked up. "What's 'psychopathic' mean?"

Father opened his mouth to answer, staring at her for several long seconds before closing it again. "I'll leave that to the Doctor to explain. Just be wary of him." Not for the first time, Father wondered if Eagle observed the briefings of his youthful new weapon; and if so, what he really made of her. "With the exception of the two mages and two of the 'muscle' – Thug, and the woman, Val – the whole group is cybernetically augmented."

Leeth frowned, and returned to flicking through the portfolio. Shrap – so many people! How was she supposed to remember a crowd like this? It was almost as many people as she knew, but gathered up into a single group! She skimmed the images: Maretti, who looked... kind, somehow? Kind but strong. Someone who'd protect his people. She knew it instinctively, just from his eyes and the shape of his jaw.

Reluctantly, her gaze shifted to the others. Gadger, Cynthia, Wolf, Wiz. And the 'muscle': Val, Don, Skinner, Davo, Chopper and – she whistled – Thug. A *big* man. Weightlifter? "He's cute." Several of them looked hot. Maybe this mission'd be fun?

Father raised an eyebrow. Turning, he met Harmon's smug gaze. "Please don't interrupt, Leeth, unless you have a specific question."

"But he *is* cute."

Father sighed. "Leeth, perhaps he is, to you. But his 'cuteness' is not relevant for this briefing. This is only your sixth operation. It distresses me you still don't seem to appreciate the seriousness of your duties. Your life could be at risk here."

Leeth nodded and lowered her head. Father, staring at her, thought her lips twitched upwards in a small smile. He sighed again. She was too young. Only nineteen, formally trained for scarcely nine months.... Still, her youth and apparent innocence seemed to be paying off, with five assassinations to her credit already. Including Fox. He shuddered. This job should help settle her. More complex, but low-risk. Unlikely to result in dramas or trauma. This op should be simple.

"Find the leak and close it, preferably without destroying the group's cohesion. They've been quite useful to us in the past. Learn the material and we'll meet back here in two hours."

"What about Mr Abrams's problem – the aliens and stuff? I've been doing some study. What if they weren't from *outer space*, but some other dimension!"

Father pinched the bridge of his nose. Accessing Leeth's recent entertainment selections, he saw the pattern he had expected.

"'Study'?" he asked.

Leeth flushed.

"The possibility has not been dismissed, and we are communicating with other agencies and continuing to look into the matter. So far, nothing has turned up." He tapped her esheet. "*You* have more urgent concerns. The Fist of Peace. Paul Genaro. Bio-Block. Your identity for this will be Tanya Denison – study the background we've prepared. Give some thought to an appropriate 'street name' for her. Two hours."

"Savage. But why is *he* here?" she asked, jerking a thumb toward the Doctor, still not sparing him a glance. "More 'Suggestions' so the mages don't see through my identity?" She shook her head. "Not gonna happen."

Father merely raised his eyebrows and gestured for Harmon to answer.

"I am merely providing psychological advice to assist your infiltration of their group. As for Suggestions, I leave that decision to you. I am sure you could word some to help you stay in character so you're less likely to be unmasked by the two mages. The Department does not revolve around you or me, Leeth. We are mere resources. For your missions, I place my spells at your disposal. Such as Healing." He spread his hands.

Leeth glared at him and grunted. Taking the briefing material, she stood. "So, infiltrate the Fist of Peace; find the traitors, kill them. Should be," *fun*, she almost said, but at Father's expression, reconsidered. "A good challenge."

At the door, she paused. "Uh, Father, I know Mr Abrams took away the, the book and the, um, dagger, to destroy them, but I was thinking maybe for that *other* problem, the one we don't talk about... for that one, maybe a magic weapon is exactly what we need?"

"You wish to use the weapon?"

Father's face held no expression at all, but somehow she sensed he didn't trust the Aztec dagger. She wanted to explain how the Aztecs had believed sacrifices were noble, for everyone's good. That they hadn't done it to scare people. She'd looked it up... sometime recently, she was pretty sure. Yeah, of course she had! But a little voice was warning her he wouldn't understand. "Well, assuming Mr Abrams can study it and find a safe way to use it, yeah. It was super effective against that alien monster thing."

It seemed a long time before Father finally spoke. "I will forward your comment."

"It's more an *idea* than a comment, actually."

"Yes," Father said. "Yes, I suppose it is."

But the look both men gave her made her think she'd said something wrong.

CHAPTER 27

"Let's review," Father said, two hours later. "You will be Tanya Denison. Downplay your abilities, especially the martial arts. Miss Denison does not have the background to explain them. Likewise, your other unusual abilities would appear suspicious to them, I'm sure. The Doctor agrees."

Harmon smiled. At least, his lips curved upward. "Yes, Leeth. Try not to seem too special. Another point – this group consists of something new to you. What you might care to think of as predatory members of the herd. As such, they have a code against killing. This means that to fit in with them, you must appear to believe this too."

Leeth nodded. "Like Superman."

Father blinked, then watched with interest as Harmon 'explained' the group in terms acceptable to Leeth's strange world-view. The Doctor had warned them care would be needed to protect her model of reality from pollution by this group's attitudes. The superficial similarities of goals could affect her social development: they didn't want their assassin deciding murder was wrong.

"They are still, in essence, Sheep, Leeth. They believe if they do not kill others, others will not kill them. Such mental blinkers are not uncommon with those sheep who dwell on the herd's fringes. Consequently, on this mission you must avoid killing if at all possible. Even if this makes certain tasks more difficult. If you kill, you will not be accepted as one of them. Or ejected, should you kill after joining them. Hence you would fail in your mission. Do you understand?"

For a long while she stared at him, before turning to Father. "And this is the psychology expert who's going to help me fit in with these guys?" She swung her chair back to face the Doctor. "So, they're 'sheep', are they? Like Marcie or her family? Are *they* sheep?" She glared at him, the anger boiling up from a deep well. "Your 'sheep' thing is just another lie you told a little girl who trusted you. But I'm not a little girl anymore. Not someone who needs *you* to 'explain' things to her in words of one syllable. If I ever did."

It felt so good to let him have it, especially right in front of Father. She saw his face darken in anger, and felt a little thrill of fear that he'd take control like he always had. Except, he couldn't. Spurred on by that knowledge, she sneered openly. "You don't know anything. You don't even know how to throw a punch. How about you let someone who knows how to run a mission finish the briefing, instead of butting in to dumb things down for me like I'm some sort of braincrashed smek-head?"

She threw herself back in her chair, delighting in his seething anger. It burned with an intensity she'd rarely seen before.

He lifted a hand to his mouth to cough, and whispered "Leeth, Mode One".

But she just clicked her teeth twice. Barney's device played the Doctor's own funting voice, giving the counter-command. But so softly, only she could hear it. She smiled lazily at him. "Smek-head," she said again, this time staring pointedly at *him*.

She turned back to Father, who sat blinking at the two of them. "You were saying they had a code against killing, Father. But that's not so bad – sometimes it *is* wrong to kill. Sometimes it's better to find some other way to deal with a danger."

'*Like Luiz*' went unsaid – for approximately a second. "Like bringing him to work for us!"

She glared at Father, now.

He stared coolly back. "Sometimes, what is *right* is hard to determine without access to concealed information," he said. Leeth snarled, but he continued before she could interrupt. "Dammit, girl! Stop mooning over the *lover* who'd been planning to Alter and then murder you!"

Still she glared at him.

"This is ridiculous!" *This is what we get, using children as agents!* "Fine. Perhaps stronger measures are required.

"Let me show you the meaning of the cryptic note we had you leave by your lover's body." The room's lights dimmed. "We believe this act is what brought him to Asgard's notice. It was taken on May 22nd, five years ago."

Leeth frowned as a projection filled the air between them. Her skin cooled, then flushed, as she recognized a younger Luiz – then the obsidian dagger he held upraised, a moment before registering the drugged *child* on the stone altar before him.

The dagger plunged down. Unable to look away, she stared in horror at Luiz's face as it filled with satisfaction from the brutal stroke. She felt like her own heart had stopped.

Father cut the feed and raised the lights. Seeing the look on the girl's face, that *finally* the truth had sunk in at an emotional level, he changed what he'd been about to say, and softened his voice. "You did a very *good* thing, Agent, in retiring Luiz Tujilque and denying Asgard the fruits of his ugly research."

Stricken, she examined his face, shaking her head.

"Both Eagle and Mr Abrams believe that footage is why he was acquired by Asgard."

She fell silent. But her next question took him by surprise. "How is the dagger?"

Father frowned. "It still seems inert." Digitally though, as per Abrams's request, he made a note of her enquiry.

The Doctor groaned. "Leeth, that artifact is an ancient Aztec sacrificial dagger that's claimed hundreds, perhaps thousands of lives. Even *you* cannot possibly imagine it is anything less than...."

"What? *Evil?*" She glared at him. "It's not *its* fault it killed a bunch of people."

Harmon opened his mouth, then shut it. *I am an idiot,* he thought, teetering on the brink of what he had very nearly said. He hated this: this role. How easily they fell back into their old patterns, their old games. She could still infuriate him. Who else but him could stress her enough to force her further Unfolding, though? And from what he had gleaned of their plans for her, especially from Abrams's ominous hints, she would need to be far stronger to survive. He pulled himself together, albeit with a sick feeling that Leeth's fascination with the artifact was something which would return to bite him – all of them – in the future. Could Abrams be correct?

Hiding all that, however, he merely inclined his head. "That is true."

She stared at him suspiciously, waiting for a 'But' that never came. After one last glare, she looked back to Father. "And what about that creepy book – has it been destroyed? And Luiz's notes?"

"His notes, burned. The book – Abrams is still studying

it. I gather the destruction of objects of power can have unwanted repercussions."

"Yeah, like aliens eating them to send signals into space."

Father swallowed. "Limited to the speed of light. Hopefully it has some years yet to travel. And perhaps you shut it off early enough."

She rolled her eyes. "As if. I bet we're going to get invaded by aliens!"

Father – and the Doctor, too – looked ill.

But much of Harmon's anger vanished in the face of her naive eagerness to throw herself in harm's way. "Leeth," Harmon began, his tone unusually gentle, "Do you need me to show you again the images of your injuries, from your combat with that thing in the vault?"

She shivered and looked away.

"If I and Abrams and Ankhet had not been immediately on hand to Heal you, you would have been left crippled."

For once, Leeth looked chastened. She didn't remember the fight clearly – although if she allowed herself to admit it, she did remember being scared. "Yeah, but there was nobody else there who could fight it."

For a while none of them spoke. Leeth stared down at her hands, remembering the dagger crying out silently to her. How snug it felt in her hand, how everything just *flowed,* holding it. She felt again the joy of she and it, together, carving that terrible thing apart, killing it.

Now it lay, alone somewhere, drained and empty. She frowned. Mr Abrams had said he hadn't destroyed it before because it had so much power stored in it that trying to would be dangerous. But if it was empty, that meant it was helpless now.

"Um, Mr Abrams isn't planning to destroy the dagger, is he?"

Both Father and the Doctor went still. Father made another note.

She knew that wasn't good, but if *she* didn't speak up for the dagger, who would? She tried to explain. "I... *we* might need it again, when- I mean, *if* the aliens come. Or maybe we could use it to deal with... that 'Fox' problem." Instinct warned her not to add, *like it told me it could.*

Father's face went carefully neutral, and Leeth knew he

saw she was talking about Shepherd Fox. Or rather, the thing *behind* him.

He continued staring at her with a kind of insistent intensity. Was it her imagination, or was something cold brushing up against her back? She abruptly forced her thoughts away from Fox.

Father's glare vanished, and he quickly spoke again. "So: the Fist of Peace. Doctor, please share your assessment with Leeth."

Harmon nodded, ignoring Leeth's surly expression. "The members of this group are for the most part considerably older than you. It is unlikely they would allow someone they considered a child risk her life by joining them in their dangerous work."

His words, as intended, had her bristling. "Hence for this mission you need to seem older than you are. Especially since Maretti lost a daughter who would be your age had she lived. Makeup-"

"How did she die?"

"What? Who?"

"His daughter!"

Father scowled and interrupted the two of them. "That is irrelevant. Not something you'd know, either." At her stubborn look, he massaged his temples. "Drone strike casualty. Brazilian eco wars. Experimental targeting system."

"That's awful."

"Yes. Terrible. May we continue the briefing?"

This time she recognized the question as rhetorical, and merely turned back to the Doctor, her eyes narrowed.

He allowed himself a small smile. "Now, hiding your age. Makeup will help. Your clothes should be basically black, for its unconscious associations with power and force. We'll trim your hair and return it to its original black."

Seeing her frown, he called up the rendered image of her in the tailored black leather outfit, stylish black boots, and wraparound eye shades. She smiled, and relaxed.

"The jacket is Kevlar lined," Harmon continued. "Wear the sunglasses at all times. They will greatly help, as the skin around the eyes is quite revealing. Given your unusual night vision, they should not prove a serious handicap for you. Of course, it will seem unusual to them, but no doubt they will rationalize it somehow. You will be 'used to it'. Or allergic to light, like some subhumans."

Leeth grimaced at the implication.

So did Father, but for other reasons. He was disturbed by the Doctor's casually racist way of referring to victims of the Melt retrovirus and their descendants. Although he doubted the Doctor would be referring to people as sheep any time soon, after the strips Leeth had torn off him earlier.

"I would also recommend gloves if I didn't suspect such a reduction in tactility would affect you poorly."

She frowned, working out what he meant. "I'm not wearing gloves."

Harmon smiled. "I advised Father and Mother you would feel that way. So. Black will be your color. You'll be the silent, resourceful type, projecting a subtle air of mystery, of coldness. All a shield for your age."

"Won't the mages be able to Percept that from her aura, Doctor?"

Harmon smiled. "No. Leeth's aura is uncharacteristic of a girl her age. It is sufficiently complex and turbulent to pass for someone older. Wise beyond her years, you might say." His eyes moved to her. "At least in some ways."

For several seconds Leeth stared at the Doctor with a peculiarly fixed expression. Father looked from one to the other, but the Doctor appeared untroubled – perhaps, even, amused.

At last Leeth shook herself and focused on Father, merely pressing her lips together. "What else?"

Harmon steepled his fingers. "Now, a name is part of a mask. It's something every agent learns to put on and take off at a moment's notice. Have you given some thought to a street name for your persona, as we requested?"

Leeth cocked her head to one side, grinning. "Yeah, heaps: Raven."

And that simply, Raven was born.

CHAPTER 28

Of the three members of the Fist of Peace with a known fixed abode, in the end Leeth chose Gadger for her line of entry. She didn't dare bug his apartment, since she was sure he'd regularly sweep for stuff like that. However, motion detectors would *not* show up. Unless he was so paranoid he checked specifically for those kinds of things too. So far, he hadn't. She'd embedded one in his front door, and the other on the fire escape at the back.

With them in place, she was able to simply sit in the nearby park, reading. Incognito in her long blonde wig and makeup to lighten her natural coppery skin. All she had to worry about was fending off advances from passing strangers.

Knowing they met on Tuesday nights, she was up and moving the moment the detector on the fire escape finally triggered. She made it to the first of her two prepared hiding places before Gadger had descended from his fourth-floor apartment. He had thermographic eyes, so she waited before pulling the heavy black coat around her in the shadows. It'd take a while for it to warm up.

At ground level, he paused. She imagined his eyes searching the street. Then his steps headed off, away from her.

"Rats." She waited till he'd left the alley, then moved swiftly after him. She'd hoped he'd stick to the main roads, maybe even just take a cab. *Oh well.* The back streets should be quiet enough for her to follow him by ear. Besides, if this didn't work, she could always just do what she was supposed to, instead. Namely, arrange a meeting, pass on the information about Moto-Otubahn, and ask to be taken along. *Ha! And suppose they said No?*

She hated the idea of not hearing their discussion after she finally got to meet them. So she'd improved the plan Father and Mother had provided. By finding out where their headquarters were, she'd be able to race them there after the meet and listen in.

She'd explain her change to their plan *after* carrying it out, obviously. Otherwise they might say no.

Gadger was careful, stopping occasionally in darkened doorways or deeper shadows, no doubt scanning for potential tails. But she just followed his footsteps, two hundred meters back. During one stop she removed the heavy coat – her thermographic shield – before it could warm up too much. It wasn't *that* cold for a March night. Her black, clinging catsuit was enough for her. *Cat suit.* She blinked, forcing away the thought of Luiz. Making herself remember the film of him sacrificing the girl. *Lucía.*

Bastard. She shook herself, focusing on the job.

Gradually, Gadger led her out of Berkeley and into the West Oakland Dumps. His pace sped up – or maybe it was just the thought of running into a local gang. In the distance, she saw him turn into a narrow alley, his footsteps slowing, somewhat muffled by the intervening buildings. Shutting her eyes she listened, and from around the corner heard voices.

"Gunner."

"How's it hangin', Gadge? Off to a meet, eh?" The voice was deep and thick, conjuring images of enlarged and distorted teeth. Probably an ogre or troll.

She thought of Robbie, and Teef. And Barney. A weird feeling of loneliness washed through her. She pushed it away.

"No, no. Just a meeting of the Bridge Club."

"Ha! I like that. Bridge Club! Yeah. As in blow up, eh? Say hoi to Davo for me. He should drop roun'."

"Will do, Gunner. Ciao, guys."

As his footsteps retreated, Leeth approached and peeked round the corner. Two figures lounged on the left side of the alley, in what to them may have been darkness. Tricky. But worse still, she could hear other voices and movements from behind the gap-toothed wall the two leaned against. She hissed in frustration. A slum gang, probably waiting in ambush for passing idiots. He must have chosen the route with this in mind.

They were deep in the Oakland Dumps area now. Well past the no-man's land buffer zone of Emeryville. Here, half the buildings had slumped into the collapse started by the Big One, decades earlier. Well beyond the areas with electricity and street lights. Deep inside the feral urban jungle.

She thought furiously, aware of her target's receding footsteps, and took a quick mental inventory. Smoke grenade; silenced Colt Terminator with mini-scope; one tracking device. But if she simply took out the two in the alley, she'd be sure to have the others come pounding after her. Could she scare them off somehow? What would a gang fear?

Ah.

Shrugging back into her coat, she stepped boldly into the alley. Even so, they didn't notice her immediately. *Juice! And they think themselves predators?* She had to scuff a stone before both tensed and turned.

"Get ready," she heard one whisper to whoever waited behind the wall.

Bringing one hand to her right ear, she raised her wrist-comm to her lips, speaking into it just loud enough for them to hear. "Contact, Peace One. Delivering message now."

Her legs flashed as she strode up to the off-balance pair. "You the one called 'Gunner'?" she demanded.

"Who wants to know?"

Good. He was thinking. "Field Agent 'Smith', PeaceCorp – seems you're owed a favor by our clients."

"What-"

The heavy-handed private security company's name further unsettled him, exactly as she'd hoped. "Zip it. You don't have time." She checked her Link. "One minute... fifty seconds from now, you and your gang'll be right in the middle of a PeaceCorp Op. Our client asked us to warn you before we started. Consider yourself warned."

The other spoke. A human. "Gunner, you think this chick-"

Leeth spun, grabbing his shirtfront and wrenching him down until his face was level with hers. "This 'chick' could take you both apart, kruphead. Wise up." She threw him away. Eyed her Link. "One minute, thirty eight seconds, Gunner. Your call." She nodded to the ogre and moved off, as if unconcerned by the possibility of attack from behind, speaking to her Link again. "Smith. Message delivered." She injected a sneer into her tone. "Alley *clear.*"

There was a pregnant pause behind her, then Gunner's thick voice. "Reboot, team. Scatter."

Relieved, she concentrated on her quarry, somewhere ahead. That had cost well over thirty seconds. Had she lost the trail? She hadn't heard Gadger since he'd left the alley. At the end, a T junction, she stopped.

To her left, oily water puddled between asphalt scabs on the clay beneath. To her right, scraps of rubbish wedged in sagging door frames and clogged drains. Taking a guess, she headed left at a silent run.

At the next junction she paused, holding her breath to listen. A faint noise from her right drew her deeper into the Dumps. Drawing her Terminator she hurried on. If she'd guessed wrong, she was probably walking straight into some random gang's territory.

Pushing herself, she sprinted to the end of the alley, then stopped to listen again.

Movements to either side in the broken buildings sounded small, like rats, and she let her focus drift ahead of her – something faint, to the left. Swiftly but quietly she headed that way, the sound growing louder. A now familiar tread. In the darkness she grinned and slowed, following.

A little later Gadger's footsteps stopped. "...the last?" she faintly heard him say, as she prowled to the end of the street he'd turned down. Hearing no response, she crouched and peered around, in time to see him enter the building. Who had he been talking to?

The building was a good distance away. A single unsmashed streetlight glowed at its front, but even with its illumination she couldn't tell what might be hiding in the shadowed alcove. Hugging her knees, she gnawed a knuckle in worry, watching. What had Gadger said? Probably asked if he was the last. But she'd only seen *him* enter the building. Krek! One of the mages might be there, invisible even – could Gadger see them with his thermographic cybereyes? Were they still there, or had the other person just followed Gadger silently in?

Another worry occurred to her. The Native American in the group, Wolf. The shaman. What had the Doctor told her? That they could summon spirits – pretty much invisible to her – and persuade them to do services. Like concealing him, or watching for intruders. Funt. Maybe this hadn't been such a good idea after all.

She stilled and shut her eyes, listening. Straining....

It was mostly quiet. From the building itself, she heard the muffled sound of many voices, the sharp clatter of pots and pans. Nearby, a cricket chirped. In the buildings around her, she heard tiny paws pattering through human rubbish. Was someone breathing, at the entrance? She couldn't be sure. No rustle of clothing, like she'd expect of a concealed guard, watching.

She *had to* assume someone was still there, in the shadows. And until she heard them enter the building, she couldn't approach. *And,* she had to assume there were spirits watching. The Doctor had taught her there were different types. House spirits that lived in particular buildings, and wouldn't leave them. Street ones, that stayed on the streets. Forest ones, like those she'd come to indirectly sense when she was only little, at the Institute. A pity she had no idea how you recognized an urban spirit, if one or more *were* around.

Fuming, she settled down to wait. She couldn't afford to jeopardize the mission by being found lurking around their headquarters. Thinking hard, she pulled her coat around her for warmth now she'd stopped moving. Also, to keep her nice catsuit clean.

A wintry wind sliced down the alley while she stared at the building. Maybe a small office block, a long time ago. Five stories high, but it looked like one more good storm would bring it down. A gaping crack ran from just above the ground floor to the very top, on the side facing her. But from inside came the sounds she'd expect of squatters. Which was a bit odd, since there were plenty of less decrepit looking structures lying empty, all around here. Funny to think so many more people used to live and work in this area....

A faint noise caught her attention from opposite the entrance of the building she was watching. An eddy of wind picked up some scraps of rubbish and spun them into the air. It lasted just long enough to make her suspicious. *Oh! I* can *still pick them out when they manifest!* She smiled, recognizing a spirit. Which made her wonder what Faith and her pack were doing at the Institute tonight. How big had her friend gotten, by now? *When was she even due?* She should make sure to be there, with her, when she had her pups.

She shook herself. *Snap out of it! You need to concentrate on the problem at hand.* Why was she in such a weird mood?

A little later, light blossomed at the end of the street, before a car turned the corner. A cab. *A cab,* here? She heard the sound of armored tires crunching rubbish. Taking care to shield the end of the magnifying scope with one hand, she sighted down on the vehicle. It stopped only a short distance from the corner, and a woman got out and looked around. As soon as she closed the door, the car jolted forward, reversed back, then completed its U-turn and zoomed off back the way it had come. *Not* happy to be in this part of town, naturally. She recognized the woman – the female mage, Cynthia. Leeth thought she looked a little nervous.

Then the woman vanished.

Friggin' krup!

But a moment later she smiled, hearing footsteps move invisibly up the alleyway. Weird. It made her hair stand up. The steps halted in a doorway across the road, opposite the building.

A woman's quiet voice asked, "Everything all right, Wolf?"

A figure moved from the shadows. *Chit!* He'd been standing there the whole time and she hadn't seen him *or* heard him.

"All quiet. You are the last, Cyn." The voice was deep, with velvet-rich tones.

Yes! *That* was what she needed to know.

The woman sounded incredulous. "You're kidding. You mean, Chopper's *early?*"

The man shrugged.

"Well, we'd better head in."

The man nodded.

Only one set of steps sounded– a woman's high heels – as 'Wolf' crossed the road and entered the building. She watched the solid, fit man move. *Hmm. Smooth.*

Well, she'd found their HQ. She *could* just leave. Her idea was to come back here to listen in after officially meeting them. But to do that, she'd need to find out where in the building the meeting was, and somehow get past the invisible spirit or spirits in the streets. *I could use this as a practice run. Plus, I might learn something. How long do I have? A minute to reach the meeting place? They'd get straight to business and start discussing their next target.*

She wanted to be there for the first, interesting bits. A light glowed briefly from the floor directly above the entrance. *Thank you, Cyn, for your ordinary eyes. Can't see in the dark like a born hunter.* She stared up hungrily as the light showed briefly on the next floor too.

She waited, but that was it. No further light, higher.

Right. So they were – probably – on the third floor. *Probably* at the least damaged end. The timer was running.

Glancing to her side, an idea glimmered. Peering upward at the building beside her, it looked to be the same height as her target. Street spirits wouldn't go *into* buildings.... She studied the gap between the two.

Backing quietly off around the corner, she paced out the width of the alley, toe to heel. *Eight meters.* That wasn't so far.

She looked up again, at the gap.

CHAPTER 29

What a stench! Her face screwed up in disgust as she ran up the stairwell. At the sound of ragged breathing from above, she paused before creeping higher.

Two floors later, the sound reverberated and the stench had her covering her nose. Probably a drunk, passed out on the stairs. She trod softly upward.

She was just four steps from him in the lightless stairwell when he lifted his head, two bleary eyes peering uncertainly down in her general direction. "Wazza?" he mumbled.

She *could* just kill him as she passed... but that felt wrong. She crept up the final steps, staring down at him in the dark as the whites of his eyes jerked left and right, scared. She frowned, wondering how he'd noticed her approach.

Whatever. Stop wasting time. With a half growl at herself, she vaulted over him, leaving a frightened gasp in her wake. She heard him scramble to his feet, and she paused, tracking his movements as he staggered down one flight after another.

Scowling down into the black well, her hands clenched the rail as she followed his route. *Just a drunk. But he might still cause me a problem tonight.* Had she been stupid, letting him live?

Unlike Luiz.

Her skin flushed hot, then cold, and she had to pry her fingers from the cool metal rail. Breathing hard, she spiraled on up.

At the top, the door onto the roof rattled in its frame but refused to budge. Heat flared through her. She slammed the heel of her foot into the lock, shattering it. Angered by its too easy surrender, she relished the hinges' rusty resistance, welcomed their protesting groan as she wrenched the door open. For a moment, the urge to rip the whole stupid thing free raged through her.

Stalking out onto the roof she pulled herself together. Treading warily, she crossed to the parapet and looked down at the other building. A feather of doubt entered her mind as her temper cooled. She growled at it, under her breath. The alleys had been the same width. The gap just *looked* wider from up here. Besides, the old office block was actually slightly shorter. She'd be jumping down.

How hard could it be?

She felt cold. At least the parapet was nothing to speak of. Just a raised row of bricks. She'd have a pretty clear run. She shivered, wondering what it would feel like to smash short, into the side of the other building, and fall.... Maybe she should...?

Coward! she berated herself, the heat returning. *Why are you still wasting time? You've measured it, you know you can do it. It's only eight meters.*

It was hard, though, to dismiss the picture of herself falling short at the far end of her jump.

Cursing under her breath, she backed up and braced herself, crouching in a starting stance. Abruptly, she thought of her coat: armored; heavy. She wouldn't need it. One way or the other. It wasn't like she'd be in anyone's line of sight. She stood and stripped it off, then folded and hid it: Mother had deducted its cost from her 'salary' just because she'd insisted on one like Stryker Zaxx favored. At the thought of Marcie in her now famous role, a hidden tension eased. She took a deep breath, rolling her shoulders.

Running her hands up her sides, she probed the muscles, reassuring herself. She checked the holstered gun at her hip, and the smoke grenade clipped to her waist.

This is it, then. This far from the edge, she couldn't even see the top of the next building. She backed up one step more, anyway. Then, with a grimace, she sprinted across the darkened roof straight for the empty chasm.

And leaped.

The building opposite froze in space, an impossible distance away. She'd misjudged completely. Her heart stopped, then the dark mass accelerated toward her. She cleared the edge of the roof – her eyes widening as a skylight appeared below her – and yanked her feet up as she realized *this* roof's parapet was almost as tall as she was.

She thumped down, trying to soak up the impact, skidding on the surface and slamming into a low wall. One arm flailed out and she heard glass break.

Oh, no! She froze, waiting for a reaction.

The night itself stopped to listen. With her heart beating so hard she could hear nothing else, she finally dared to breathe again. A slicing pain made her look down. Her forearm gleamed wetly, the elasticized material of the sleeve peeling back. She plucked a shard of glass from it.

On her back, staring up into the night sky, she grinned. "I did it!" she whispered. She wanted to shout, and had to press her lips tight shut against the urge. With one small wobble she rose to her feet and checked the cut. *Not so bad.* Not trusting the sagging roof, she climbed up onto the parapet to make her way around the edge to the far side of the building. The cement work wasn't *too* crumbly.

Do house spirits go out onto the roof? she belatedly wondered.

A gleam of light and a murmur of voices leaked from the blacked-out window directly below her. Unfortunately, she couldn't *quite* make out the words. Her jaw clenched in annoyance. It had taken almost *five minutes* to sneak to where she was now. *They've probably finished the meeting.* You could say an awful lot in five minutes.

Pain throbbed in her left arm as blood continued trickling down it. *Good thing I have invisible magic claws, so I can cut my clothes off to bind my wounds.* But she really felt like biting something.

She tore a strip of fabric away with her teeth. *Or I could carry a knife,* she thought. *Strapped to my calf. It'd look deadly. Be handy, too, whenever I have to explain how I cut my clothes off.* She ground her teeth.

Awkwardly, sitting on the parapet with her legs dangling into space, she bandaged her arm. Allowing herself to slump, she considered house spirits, patrolling. *They probably* do *come out onto roofs.*

But I bet they don't float out onto the walls! That's outside *the building, and they're not allowed out.* As for any street spirits: they *might* have just been asked to let the shaman know if anyone entered. Which she wouldn't be doing.

Clutching at that hope, she peered out and down. The cement was pretty old, with plenty of cracks. *And* there was a sliver of balcony at each floor. *For the executives to jump off.* She'd learned about the Crash of '42 in history lessons with the Doctor. She scowled, remembering, considering the wall while the voices continued drifting up from below, tantalizingly close to being understandable.

That made up her mind.

Aware of time passing, she chose her route while re-moving her rubber-soled shoes so her toes could find cracks. She had to suppress a giggle. *At this rate, I'll finish the evening completely naked.* She ran her hands over her body, again.

Then over the edge and down. Closing her eyes, she concentrated on her feet, feeling out the gaps between the blocks, letting her arms take her weight until she found her first hold. With toes tense, she released one hand and eased herself down. Move by move.

It seemed like forever before she reached the first 'bal-conette'. Just wide enough for her small feet. *Good thing I'm not a D-cup*, she thought, pressing into the cool stonework and forcing herself to breathe gently, sucking in air. Cautiously, she flexed one hand, then the other. After a minute's rest, she began sidling to the left, bringing the voices nearer. Of course, it'd certainly be too late by now. But she refused to give up, even so.

Finally, clinging to the wall one floor above the window, the words came clear.

"...paid for the soykaf time before *last*. It's Gadger's turn!"

"Come on Wiz, you little krup. It's only twenty creds!"

"But it's not my turn!"

Leeth blinked twice, slowly, fingers tensely locking her against the side of the building, cold against her chest. They were arguing about buying *food*? They'd finished their briefing *completely*? An unpleasant possibility struck her. What if they didn't even have a strike planned?

"I don't believe this, Wiz! How can anyone so good at dipping into cred accounts be so completely *tight* about coughing up loose change?" A woman's voice – Val, Leeth guessed.

"All right, that's *enough*." A man cut in. "*I'll* pay for it. Now let's get down to business, okay?"

On the wall outside, Leeth blinked in disbelief. They hadn't *started* yet?

There was a taut silence from below, then the same voice continued. Tony Maretti, presumably. "Anybody got anything? I was thinking we might lean on our mate, Nate, at TC WeaponTech. Leave it much longer, he'll be going cold on us."

There was a general murmur of what sounded like assent.

"Ah, I think maybe I have something, Tony." That was the cheapskate, Wiz. Sounding smug. "I've seen a *large* order for a code-named pharmaceutical, traceable back to the accounts Newtopia uses for its covert security accounts for its Brazilian ops. Interesting thing is, it's going *through* a little research company here in New Francisco, Bio-Block, to Moto-Otubahn."

Leeth's eyes widened, not believing her ears as Wiz gave them the information *she* had for them them. How had *he* found out about it? That little *weasel!*

It started to rain.

An hour later, she knew she had to make a decision – leave while her muscles were still up to the tricky return climb, before learning when they were going to make their move; or try to hang on until they finished, and go in through the window after they'd all left. *Assuming* they all left. And that it wasn't too far in the future.

Her jaw set at the thought of giving up. Especially since her information was useless now. Her left arm really ached, too, but she could handle that.

It was just pain.

She was cold, though. The catsuit was waterproof and a good insulator, but it wasn't really up to this sitch. The sooner she was out of it, the better. She knew that. She closed her eyes and gripped the bricks. At least the rain had stopped.

She waited.

The rain restarted. Slumping her head slump against the cold brickwork, she shut her eyes.

The next two hours that oozed past were the longest of her life.

Shivering, teeth chattering from the cold, she was no longer sure she could unlock her fingers even if she wanted to. Her legs trembled. If they didn't leave *now*, she was going to have to call out to *them* for help and blow the mission. She'd prepared six different stories to explain what she was doing there. Deep down, though, she knew none were convincing. Except to someone clinging with her last strength to the side of a building in the freezing cold. Four stories wasn't *that* far to fall, though, was it? Maybe the Doctor could heal her...?

The thing was, they'd been sounding like they'd finished and were about to leave, for the last *hour*.

Abruptly, her choker pulsed. The Department wanted to call her. Awkwardly, she bent her chin down, twice. The 'accept' code.

Mother's voice whispered into the air, audible only to someone with Leeth's remarkable hearing. She did *not* sound happy.

"Where are you, girl? Why aren't you home?"

"N-n-new infor-m-mation, M-Mother," Leeth chattered, ultra quietly. "C-can't really t-talk now."

There was a pause.

"You sound strange. Do you need assistance?"

Leeth didn't know whether to laugh or cry. "H-how l-long would it t-take to g-g-get t-to the West Oakland D-Dumps?"

"West-?! Thirty minutes."

Leeth wearily rested her head against the building. "D-don't b-bother, then."

For once, Mother actually sounded concerned. "Leeth?"

At last, from the other side of the wall, came the sounds she'd been desperately waiting for. They were leaving. "It's okay. I'm g-g-going to b-be okay. Out."

There was a moment's silence, then she felt the contact end. Plucking one hand carefully free of the wall she breathed a fog of warm air out onto chilled and cramping fingers. Maybe gloves *wouldn't* have been such a bad idea?

Ten minutes later she fell through a window on the third floor into a room the size of a broom closet. Her muscles immediately went into cramping spasms. She'd really thought she was going to die that time. She wasn't sure how she'd made it to the open window.

The reaction was getting to her now, on top of the pain from the cut on her left arm. Tears welled, her breath coming in choking sobs as she forced herself to stand and work the cramps out of her muscles. "S-stupid little b-bitch!" she swore at herself. Her voice, choked with emotion, sounded thick. *Now you can't even* talk *properly!* So *professional,* she thought sarcastically. Clinging to a slippery ledge by sheer stubbornness for *hours*. Is that what Emma would have done?

She forced herself to get moving. What she should have done was asked the Doctor to scan the building for spirits. There probably hadn't even been one watching at all. People who argued over grocery bills probably wouldn't even think of setting a sentry.

Working the knots from her muscles, she welcomed the stabbing pain as blood began to circulate properly again. She stretched, even managed a staggering jog on the spot, warming herself a little. She still felt weak, but way better than she had just minutes ago. Finally, carefully, she listened at the door and moved out.

Halfway down the stairs to the ground floor she heard people. She darted back up and waited.

Murmurs of conversation. A child's voice.

Her head tilted to one side as she listened in puzzled intensity. She smelled food, too. Unfamiliar odors. Her stomach growled.

Gradually the truth penetrated. The Fist of Peace had squatters living on the ground floor.

Ten minutes later, having prowled all over the floor she was on, she'd confirmed it. She had no idea how many families there were, but they occupied every inch of the ground floor. Funny that none of them had spilled up higher, nearer the Fist's territory. Maybe they had some arrangement?

She scowled into the dark and dusty space. There were even people on the bottom set of stairs. Talking and smoking, some chipped, some not. With a grimace, she headed back for the open window she'd half-fallen through on the third floor. There was no way she was going to trust her weight to any of the rusting drainpipes she'd spotted. Flexing her fingers, she sighed. She really didn't need more climbing tonight. Especially not on rain-slick walls.

She drew a deep breath.

Jumping down the final three meters off the wall, she swayed and leaned against the building, holding back a sob as pain throbbed in her gashed arm. She gritted her teeth till it eased. Then, with a shuddery sigh, she pushed herself upright and crossed the road, stalking back into the building she'd entered so many hours earlier. *That drunk in the stairwell had better not have come back*, she swore to herself.

On the rain-slick roof, her coat was still folded up right where she'd left it. She shook it open, surprised but pleased to see it wasn't soaked all the way through. She shrugged into it, feeling warmer as it wrapped around her, cheering up. Plus she'd worked out what she was going to do, now, to complete the mission.

On her way out of the Dumps she was attacked twice. The first time she simply shot the bastard between the eyes. Though she'd only walked on fifty meters before shame brought a flush to her cheeks. What would Father or Dojo think of her, using a gun just because she was tired and hurt? She vowed not to be so weak again.

By the second time she'd warmed up a lot and her cramps were pretty much gone. She took both muggers apart with relish, even remembering not to kill these two. Probably they'd survive, but she assumed that was okay. Neither had seen her well enough to be able to identify her. Besides, it proved a point: *I can follow orders just fine.*

At least I can still do that much, even if I am an idiot of a secret agent, she told herself.

It was two a.m. when Leeth finally returned 'home'. Mother and Harmon met her as the elevator doors opened. The sight that greeted them was not what either had been expecting. Her coat was soaking wet, only the kevlar reinforcing giving it any shape. Leeth was muddy, bruised, her hair stuck down wetly, and very pale. She also smelled. One arm awkwardly held the other. Harmon hadn't seen her looking so... grubby... since she was small. He raised one eyebrow, amused.

For Leeth, on top of everything else that night, it was the final straw. She lunged at him. Or tried to. Instead, her muscles instantly froze, sending her sprawling at his feet.

Harmon's smile cracked and slowly drained from his face. He actually looked away.

It made Leeth feel... strange. Almost guilty.

Mother reacted differently. "Where... *What* on Earth have you been doing? You look as though you've spent the last five hours in a gutter! You had logged that you'd be back by 22:00!"

Leeth ignored her and got to her feet. She felt too tired to worry, now. She stared at the Doctor, her jaw working. Finally, she held out the injured arm. "It's just a cut, from broken glass."

She looked away.

Leeth didn't see the complex expression that crossed Harmon's face. He was thinking that despite how much she'd grown, in some ways she'd hardly changed at all. Still needed him, though he'd hurt her so much she now refused to admit that. Other than that, so like she'd been all those years before. Had the loss of her trust been worth it?

An unexpected wave of regret rolled through him, and for a moment he felt a peculiar urge to hug her.

Instead he glanced at Mother, who stood watching. Then simply cast the Healing spell.

CHAPTER 30

"You did *what?*" Mother, normally icily cool and always collected, had her lips clamped shut. She hardly knew where to begin. This idiot girl....

Leeth could see the mini debriefing wasn't going well, as Mother tugged the deep purple night-robe tighter around herself, angrily. Good thing she hadn't mentioned just how precarious her perch had been. But instead of wriggling down in her chair as she might once have done, the heat in her belly forced her forward in her seat to meet Mother's glare head on. "I was careful." *Kind of.* "And thanks to me, I found out our old plan wouldn't have worked."

"Our old plan. Our *old* plan? Am I to take it, then, that the vastly knowledgeable nineteen-year-old operative in front of me has come up with a superior one? While clinging to a freezing ledge four stories above the ground, no doubt?"

Mother had regained her outward cool. Leeth decided she liked the uncharacteristic rage better. "Actually, yeah, that *was* when I thought of it."

Harmon had to cover his smile behind one hand. The more she changed, the more she became herself.

But as Leeth refused to back down, arguing with Mother, it merely reinforced the need to learn exactly what had happened while she was on the run from the Department. Fortunately, he would be starting that very soon.

The next day, both Father and Mother were present, along with the Doctor, as Leeth explained her plan in more detail.

"Hmm," was Father's only comment.

Mother glared at him. "The idea is absurd. It is too obviously a set-up. No one would believe it."

Harmon cleared his throat. "Unlikely, yes. A bit dramatic, certainly. But these people *live* drama. They court danger. I think they would in fact accept it as a coincidence – *if* Leeth can act her part convincingly."

Mother and Father's sour expressions made Leeth wonder if they were remembering the kidnapping of the drama school, or a certain mansion hired for a dance burning to the ground.

Or both.

"Look," she interrupted, "if we do this, I can start

tonight. We won't lose any time."

Mother sat back, folding her arms. "Your 'plan' – if we can dignify it with such a term – has too many loose ends, too many opportunities for things to go wrong. Suppose you set off the security systems? Suppose they *capture* you? Suppose the Fist of Peace shoots first?"

She shrugged. "Then I'll improvise."

Harmon winced. Mother kneaded her forehead, the familiar headache starting again.

"I'm sure you would, Leeth," Father said. "But a good agent tries to arrange things so she *doesn't* have to improvise. It's *our* job to try to minimize the need for improvisation. Because that is where mistakes are most often made, putting the whole organization at risk. Remember, the worst possible result is for an agent to be captured."

Leeth glowered at him. "Really? Even if I did get captured, and did want to talk, I couldn't. The Doctor's made sure of that." *For everything*, she wanted to add, but the thought blurred into confusion before she could even open her mouth. She wanted to glare at him, but instead focused on Mother and Father, unwilling to give him the satisfaction of seeing her anger.

"All the same," Father said, "that would rather torpedo this mission. Not to mention the risk of your being killed."

"So? I'm not afraid of dying. A samurai doesn't fear death. She doesn't let it push her from her goals."

Father blinked, but inclined his head in acknowledgment; Mother raised her eyebrows in slightly-pleased surprise; but Harmon scowled. "You should fear it. Fear it enough to make you cautious, at least."

"That's not what Dojo says. Fear weakens you. A true warrior-"

"I don't care what Dojo says! I don't want you-"

"Doctor." Father's voice was perfectly controlled, but utterly final. "Dojo is correct, and Leeth's grasp of this fact is pleasing. Your 'wants' don't come into it. The country's needs *do*."

Harmon's expression blanked. "I see."

"Do you, Doctor?" asked Mother. "I sometimes wonder."

His tone, when he answered, was unexpectedly mild. "I am simply offering a professional opinion, since I *do* understand Leeth-"

She snorted.

He spun to face her. "I understand you well enough for this!" She rolled her eyes and waved him off, throwing herself back in her chair, then began picking at her nails, silently mouthing 'blah blah blah' while doing so.

Fuming, he turned back to the two heads of Operations. "I don't believe either of you appreciate what effects-" He stopped abruptly. He had already warned them of her possible contamination from being embedded in a group of semi-pacifistic ideologues. People like that could compromise his teachings even worse than the scum in the Dumps had, or the intensely annoying Dunkirk child – whose influence was already eroding the foundations he had laid for Leeth's unique magic. "This is not the proper place for such a discussion, however."

"Good point," Leeth agreed, sitting forward. "You should write up a report," she said, waving a dismissive hand in his general direction. "So, Father, Mother, may we talk about my plan?" The Doctor glowered at her. *Good.*

"Yes," Mother said. "If you two have finished bickering. We felt this mission would have been good training for you. But I think it's clear we should hand it over to someone in the Bureau proper. Just because the Department occasionally uses the Fist of Peace doesn't mean *we* need to run the operation."

"No! I can do this! I *know* I can. You just don't want to see me make *my* plan work!" She turned to Father, letting the fierceness soften, opening her eyes wide. "Please, Father..."

Harmon, watching, mentally added '... can I borrow the car keys?' He shook his head microscopically, amused, watching her use the body language *he* had taught her.

Father met her gaze for long seconds, poker faced. Then sighed. "Very well. We'll give your idea a try."

With effort, Leeth restrained herself from jumping up to kiss him, deciding at the last instant it might look unprofessional.

Harmon, watching her work herself deeper into the Department's embrace, hid his snarl as she turned smugly toward him and smiled.

Leeth waited until they were outside before rounding on the Doctor. "What were you trying to *do*? Make them think I'm a coward, or not ready or something? I said I wasn't *afraid* to die. That doesn't mean I won't fight against it with..." her hands clenched, as she hunted for the words she needed.

"With your last drop of blood?"

"Yeah!"

He sighed. "With good planning in the first place, you can avoid-"

The boredom that flooded her face stopped him mid-sentence. At the best of times, she'd never been one to substitute careful thought for direct action. *Damn Dojo!* Then a colder thought occurred to him, recalling Abrams's continued concern since the incident in February. Could Leeth's apparent embracing of mortality be the influence of that damned Aztec dagger? He could feel the situation slipping from his control. Taking her beyond his under-standing, his guidance.

It was time to act. Long past time.

Later that afternoon, Father looked up as the Doctor stepped into his office. "I've been expecting this request," he said. "Given Leeth's recent conduct toward you."

"Her disrespect, you mean." said Harmon.

"A diplomatic phrasing, but yes. Let's go with that. What is this investigation you've proposed?"

If Father had expected the Doctor to react to his needling, he was disappointed. Harmon merely nodded. "As Leeth has become fond of pointing out, I no longer un-derstand her as fully as I did. You yourself know Leeth is hard to predict. So for the Department to get best use from her, that is an issue I need to address."

Father shook his head. "She reports to Eagle, not to Mother or I, Doctor. I can't simply order her to allow you to..." he waved the fingers of both hands in the air, "magi-cally probe her mind, or whatever you do. And even if I could persuade Eagle to approve it, Leeth herself-"

"You misunderstand me," Harmon interrupted. "I un-derstood Leeth so well simply through detailed observa-tion, and knowledge of her activities. Our current problem has developed because the Department rejected my recommendations, which led in turn to her 'running away'."

Father frowned, but said nothing.

"For over a month, Leeth immersed herself in a vibrant, emerging social system; interacted with more people than she'd met in her entire life up to that point. Underwent who knows what trials? I understand even Eagle has been unable to persuade her to give an account of that time."

Father's look soured. "Your proposal? Something else involving the Dunkirk girl? We've already approved your plan to wedge them apart."

Oh, yes, thought Harmon. *And I will pay a visit to Miss Dunkirk. It was with her help Leeth somehow broke my control that night in the park.*

But he merely smiled. "I can hardly interview Miss Dunkirk – she is not well disposed toward me.

"No, Father, to gather the intelligence needed to improve my understanding of Leeth, I must meet the people she lived amongst for a month. I am proposing a small 'anthropological study'. I will talk to them. Interview them. Get inside their heads, you might say." His smile was shark-like. "Dig out stories of how they live, and more importantly, how Leeth lived among them. Learn what they told her, how they influenced her."

Father looked surprised, but shook his head. "We can't spare resources to babysit you in a dangerous area like the Dumps-"

"I'm not requesting support. I have some field experience, you know. I will present myself as a sympathetic researcher wishing to study their way of life. 'To share their vision of sustainable living with the rest of the world.' One must admit they do seem to thrive on the scraps they scavenge."

"Hrrm. But the gangs, wild animals, diseases...."

"Father, I have spells to cure diseases and heal. I can use that to ingratiate myself. I will present myself as a poor, harmless anthropologist of meager magical skills, keen to learn from and help them. And I am not without teeth." People grossly undervalued the ability to observe auras: knowing the emotions of those you interacted with made so many things so easy. Not to mention, spells to read minds, plant suggestions.... And then of course, if he did have to evade a serious threat, he had that invisibility spell Leeth herself had caused him to research and develop, years ago. Not that it had served its purpose back then.

"Very well, Doctor. Write up a proposal. Start and end dates. Concrete objectives. A small budget for supplies, clothes. Cover identity and so forth. Your suggestion sounds reasonable."

Harmon permitted himself a smile. *I will find how you broke my control, Leeth. I know the programming is still there, deep inside you.* "Thank you, Father. We will all benefit if I can get a better grip on Leeth's recent behavior."

CHAPTER 31

Getting onto the top of the Bio-Block building was an easy climb for her, with the right gear. After satisfying herself she could deal with the alarm on the door onto the roof, she found a hiding place. From that point she simply waited – impatiently – for the Fist of Peace to turn up. They'd said 23:00 hours. *I'll go in from up here once they make their move.* It'd probably take them a few minutes to disable the internal security systems. She huddled, listening.

It was *eleven thirty* when they arrived. Below, she heard several sets of footsteps and a faint murmur of voices. She pursed her lips, and shook her head. Checking her equipment as she sat in the narrow space beneath the old canvas, she knew this was the weakest part of her plan. Probably, the mages would go out of their bodies to scout the building Imaginally, the Doctor had explained. Apparently, if she simply stayed out of sight, in a small dark place where they were unlikely to poke their spirit heads, they probably wouldn't see her. Weird. That was how things worked, he assured her. Imaginal sight was like that. Below, the voices fell quiet.

The tricky part was guessing when the magical scouting had finished, of course.

She lifted her wraparound sunglasses to see the unlit numbers on her Link. Not because of the dark, but due to something called polarization. Nelson had tried to explain it to her once.

She grimaced. *The little weevil.* She wasn't exactly sure what a weevil was, but it sounded suitably creepy for Nelson.

Four minutes and thirty-three seconds later, the murmurs started again. This time it went on for a bit longer. She thought she recognized Wolf and Cyn's voices.

Probably, the two mages' spirits had returned to their bodies. She decided to risk it.

Quietly, she slid from under the canvas and padded to the edge of the building, keeping low so they wouldn't see her silhouette against the skyline. Peeking over, she saw the hacker and one of the musclemen heading off. To look for a *wired* network link? She half-remembered a lesson from Nelson about bandwidth and hacking. The others waited. So did she, sinking back and checking her equipment for the tenth time. Rough hand-drawn maps, vague, as though done from memory, secondhand. From her 'ex-lover,' Paul Genaro. She began slipping her mind into the 'Raven' persona....

At a noise from below, she peeked again, seeing the group now on alert. The leader, Maretti, seemed to listen, then nodded to the others. Gadger headed for the back door, getting out equipment.

Right. *Finally*, they'd started. Excitement surged as she moved into action. She imagined their imminent surprise; pictured them all welcoming her. Maretti hugging her. *I wonder what they'll be like, as a team?* She thought of the people living in the Hunters Point Dumps and their close-knit bonds. But *these* guys must've saved each others' lives! They'd be closer still – maybe like a family. She was hugging herself. She flushed, remembering Father's attitude to daydreaming on the job, her smile slipping into a frown.

The access door onto the roof had an old-fashioned padlock, which she'd picked several times, earlier. Unlocking it now went smoothly. The electronic alarm was almost as antique, easily bypassed with tape, wire, and metal strips. Probably no need, if the Fist had disabled stuff. But Father always said it paid to be thorough. Once inside, she assumed the cameras were still functional. Alternately keeping to the shadows and moving swiftly, she headed for the security office on the floor below.

At the door to the monitoring room, she pressed her ear up against it. *Someone breathing heavily, inside?* They'd be armed; one or both facing the door, past the monitors. She readied her flash bomb, then kicked the door open, registering startled looks even as she tossed the grenade. Instinctively, they followed its arc. *Bad move.* She closed on the nearer of the two, one hand over her screwed-shut eyes as the flare went off. A single blow knocked him cold.

The other's gun wove from side to side seeking a target as she darted behind him. She pressed the Magnum to the back of his head.

"Forget it," she rasped.

He tensed, but made no move.

"Drop the gun." She had to suppress a giggle – she'd *always* wanted to say that to someone. He wasn't laughing, though. She stepped back out of reach as he bent forward, reluctantly putting his gun down.

"Down on the floor," she snapped, watching him blink, his eyes moving as he assessed her black leathers, her stance. "Now," she ordered, feeling very Raven.

He lay down, and she tossed him a heavy plastic restraint. "Feet first. Tight."

Glowering at her, he did that, too.

She tossed him another. "Hands." Her expression soured, remembering Agent Garland making her do the same thing.

Poor idiot. She would've liked to work with him.

Maybe her expression encouraged the guard, because he moved faster, drawing it closed with his teeth.

She checked the bindings, pulling them tighter. Crossing to his companion, already stirring, she bound him too.

The monitors showed no sign of the others. Their hacker's work, she suspected. 'Wiz.'

Listening at the doorway, she moved out, closing the door gently behind her. The labs, next. *Maybe I can get there before they do!*

The only light came from a sprinkling of LED indicators on the scattered equipment, and a wall of laminated glass overlooking the grimy street below. Raising her sunglasses she quickly scanned the darker corners. Computing blocs, and other stuff she couldn't name. No surprise there. She shrugged and slipped the wraparound shades back on. *Now what?* Bio-Block had a separate, off-net computer room too. Maybe they'd headed there?

The sound of footsteps creeping down the corridor ended her dilemma. One set continued on in the direction she'd come from, but the other stopped at the lab door. Darting to the wall beside it, she watched the handle turn and the door ease open, hiding her. A tall figure with a pencil torch stepped in, past her. Maretti.

For a moment, she had the bizarre urge to throw her arms around him. *What on Earth?* She'd let the Doctor do some Suggestions, but he hadn't even *tried* his Mode One trick this time. He'd stuck exactly to the script. This was something else – she just didn't know what.

With a snarl on her lips she glided from behind the door and pressed the cold gun barrel to the back of Maretti's neck. "Who the chip shit are you?" she whispered.

His hand flinched toward his gun until she prodded with the muzzle. "Organ donor for the body banks?" she suggested. Stepping back, she circled around to his front, putting him between the doorway and herself. "Go ahead, try it." She kept the Magnum trained between his eyes, taking vengeful pleasure in reminding herself it was *his* fault she'd spent three freezing hours clinging to a wall outside their rotting building in the Dumps last night. Maybe it lent an extra air of menace to her expression. Despite her satisfaction, she felt a strange pulse of guilt. She fought it down.

Maretti raised both hands, very slowly.

"You sure as hell aren't Security," she growled at the self-assured, swarthy man. "Work here, do you?" She pushed aside all she knew about them, locking it away; just being Raven. Hiding her thoughts before the mages arrived.

As she'd learned to do over so many years, from the Doctor.

CHAPTER 32

Maretti stared at the grim-faced young woman before him. With the big gun and blank, evil-looking sunglasses. In *this* darkened room? Shades in the *dark*? He noted the narrow waist and lithe figure before dragging his attention back to what was going down here.

What the fuck *was* going down?

A click in his ear, then a tiny voice whispered, "Tony: the guards in the monitor room've already been scragged! Tied up! They said a chick did it!"

Maretti looked at the girl enquiringly. "You took out security?"

Soft footsteps approached but Leeth ignored them. She nodded.

Maretti smiled. "You know, I think maybe we're on the same side."

The steps outside slowed, a stocky figure peering round the doorway, sweeping a flashlight across the room with a whispered, "Tony?"

The beam stopped on the tableau in the room. "Ohh, shit!" the newcomer breathed.

The gun pointed at Maretti's head didn't waver.

No one moved for several seconds. Then, coolly, Maretti continued. "I think maybe it's time for introductions. You are-?"

Leeth cocked her head to one side, considering the question, enjoying the moment. *I think I'm going to like being like Raven.*

Maretti watched the woman visibly come to a decision. "Raven. Just Raven."

She considered the swarthy man with the self-confident expression, then the younger, more solid man in biker's leathers. She gestured not-quite negligently with the gun. "Suppose you convince me we're on the same side."

"My name is Tony Maretti," he said, impressively calm. He angled his head toward the younger man. "My friend here is 'Chopper'. The reason we're here-"

Leeth stopped listening as more footsteps approached down the corridor. Several sets, this time. She cut him off, not wanting to lose her bargaining position before the introductions were over. "You. Chopper." She gestured him in. "Close that door behind you."

He hesitated, with a glance at Maretti. The footsteps

were louder, now: soon Leeth wouldn't be the only one hearing them. Snarling in frustration she cocked the gun's hammer, the metallic *click* heavy and final. "*Now.*"

Chopper stepped in and pushed the door closed behind him. Suddenly Maretti was feeling less sure of himself, less sure of his estimation of the woman before him.

"Lock it," Leeth ordered Chopper.

Chopper tensed.

"*Lock it.*"

At the flat, cold tone, Chopper finally moved. The snick of the mechanism echoed in the silence of the room.

Leeth felt the Raven persona settle around her like a comfortable jacket. She remembered lying down, the Doctor's hand on her brow, waiting for him to try to *Mode One* her again. But he hadn't. Had Eagle spoken to him about going off-script for Luiz? Did that mean *Eagle* had worked out what he was doing? Little Brother had spoken to Eagle, after all....

She still wasn't sure if that was a good thing. She pushed the distracting thoughts away.

The corners of her lips pulled back: a naive person might have called it a smile. "Now. Where were we?"

Chopper and Maretti looked at one another. Maretti was thinking maybe he'd been a bit too free with his name... but she hadn't seemed quite so feral at first. He wished he could see her eyes.

The three stood unmoving while the door handle slowly turned. The two men stiffened, before pretending not to have noticed it.

Obvious, much? She let Raven's smile widen. In the corridor, a woman's voice whispered. Leeth doubted the other two could hear it: "I don't like it. Tony said he was going to check the lab. And where's Chopper?"

"Let's get Cyn to have a look, eh?" a man's voice answered.

Raven snapped her attention back to the two men with her. She didn't want the others to come blazing in to 'rescue' her captives.

"Tony Maretti. Why don't you explain the situation to your friends out in the corridor?"

Chopper's mouth opened. Maretti just stared at her a second, then shrugged. He reached toward his throat mic.

"Move *slow*," she softly cautioned him, then her eyes went to Chopper. "And don't you step away. That would make me nervous." She smiled.

Chopper swallowed. *Flick, she was creepy.* Sexy, though.

Maretti thumbed the switch on his mic. "Tony here. We have a... situation. I *hope* we can resolve it." He looked at Raven. "Quickly."

He lowered his hands. "As I was saying, we're here because Bio-Block is involved in military research. Research which in this case is going to be used to help kill Brazilian resistance fighters." He watched Raven carefully, relieved when she seemed to relax slightly. He waited a moment. "And you?"

"Should I move in closer, do you think, or will your mic pick me up well enough from here?"

His expression froze. *Shit. She noticed I left it on.* He wet his lips. She didn't seem angry, though. He was about to suggest that, yes, she should come closer, when something in her stance made him reconsider. "Ah, no. No need. You can talk from there."

Her shoulders hunched. "My- I mean, a *friend* worked here. He resigned, a month ago. Last Friday, he died." She paused, letting herself *feel* it, blinking back tears behind her shades. "The citycops said it was an accident, but I think Bio-Block arranged it. So I decided to arrange an *accident* for Bio-Block."

"What did you have in mind... Raven?"

"I've got C4. I'm going to blow up the computers, maybe the building...." Her voice trailed off.

"You were going to blow up the *whole building*? Are you cr- Are you sure you've covered all the angles?"

She tilted her head.

"There's a better way," he said. "Listen: a Corp lives on money – that's its blood. Kill the money flow, kill the Corp. Besides, citycops aren't as keen to track down a computer saboteur as they are someone who blows up buildings."

She was still pointing the heavy gun at him. But at least now she'd lowered it to her side so he wasn't staring down the barrel. "We plan to wipe their computer files and trash the lab. It'll cost them months, and we happen to know their backers can't wait months. Even if they do continue on, we can come back. But I really don't think a scummy little company like Bio-Block can survive this." He paused, giving her a chance to think about it. "So. What do you say?"

She considered, letting herself feel the hunger to punish Bio-Block for murdering her lover. Trying to be reasonable. It *was* better than just blowing things up. Neater. Besides, she wasn't real good with plastic explosives. Though it *had* been fun, stealing them.

"All right," she said at last. Tony indicated her gun, still pointed at him. With reluctance, she lowered the barrel. Then holstered it and stood looking tense.

He took a deep breath and blew it out. "Come on, I'll introduce you to the team. Then we'd better hurry it up." He paused at the door as he unlocked it. Standing just behind him, she faintly heard a male voice from his earphone and the corridor outside. "Trust her for now. But there's something strange about her aura." That must have been Wolf, the shaman. He, and maybe Cynthia too, must have been watching astrally.

The door opened, letting in more light from several diffuse flashlights. A very big man stepped in.

His voice was a deep bass. "Hey! She's pretty!"

"Ah, Raven, that's Thug." Maretti looked back at her. Now he wasn't concentrating quite so hard on her revolver, he realized, with surprise, that Thug was right. All black clothing, but figure-hugging under the leather jacket. Sexual, but deadly-looking too. Dangerous.

"Thank you, Thug," Raven said coolly. Next in was the tribesman, odd arrangements of feathers and sticks pinned to ragged denim jeans and coat. *Fetishes.* A medicine bag dangled at his throat. Copper-skinned, he looked middle-aged – late thirties, probably – but fit and healthy.

A dark, hawk-like gaze.

"Wolf – Raven."

Neither spoke, merely nodded warily to each other. Maretti considered remarking on them both having animal names, but thought better of it.

A small thin man entered next. Grey in his hair, heavily chipped, and whisker-fuzzed cheeks and chin. Cyber eyes. Leeth concentrated on the moment, on *being* Raven.

Meeting 'Gadger' for the first time.

"Gadger: Raven."

"Well, well. Pleased to meet you." He looked her up and down appreciatively as he stepped forward to shake her hand.

Raven looked a little disconcerted, Maretti noted. *Like she doesn't normally let people approach her that simply.*

"Right."

"Val, and Skinner. Raven."

Val was as short as Raven, though curvier. Maybe Puerto Rican. Heavily built for a woman, but fit and dressed to show it off. Attractive in a tough sort of way. She and Raven sized one another up. Exchanged nods.

Skinner was big, also heavily muscled, though not in Thug's league. He whistled appreciatively. Val elbowed him, hard, in the ribs.

"Hey, chica! Wazzat for?"

"Asshole," she snarled. They began arguing, in a blend of Spanish and Street, though keeping their voices low.

"Davo. Raven."

Davo moved like an athlete, or maybe a dancer. Brown hair and taller than average. Good looking, despite several scars. Armed with a snub SMG.

He also eyed her appreciatively, though warily. "Hi, Raven."

"Davo."

There was a pause, which Maretti filled by explaining that 'Wiz' and 'Don' were in the comp room. Then a woman entered. Dressed in a dark gray armored jacket of sensible rather than fashionable cut. Not the expected picture of a mage. She looked very ordinary; very corporate. Blue eyes, short brown hair cut in bangs. Thin features – thin all over.

"Juice me! How many of you *are* there?"

Maretti just smiled. "Enough. Cynthia. Raven."

Raven regarded her with cautious interest. Cynthia looked nervous, and didn't approach.

Maretti took charge. "Okay, team. Let's get to it. Gadger, we'll leave you to fry the electronics. *Quiet* destruction is the watchword. Leave the computers till Wiz has checked them."

Leeth had a question. "You're – we're – going to torch

the lab, to cost them time and money?"

Maretti nodded.

"And wipe the computer files. Is that intended to kill the project?"

Gadger spoke before the now-frowning Maretti could answer. He grinned, waving a finger at the other man. "You're about to ask about their system backups, aren't you?"

"Yes. What's to stop them just restoring their files and carrying on?"

"Apart from the trashed lab, you mean? A fair question, and I'll be the first to admit it could've easily been the weak point in the plan." He smiled at Maretti, who growled.

"Look, Gadger, we've been over this all before. You can explain it if you want, but the rest of us are going to get to work. Don't be too long. I'm gonna see how Wiz's doing with the comps."

The others moved out through the lab. She turned back to Gadger.

"We do have one thing in our favor," he continued. "Pure luck, really. This outfit has obviously had cash flow problems for a long time now. Their system is *very* old – a Kyosei Elektra running System *Three*...."

Gadger launched into an explanation about 'fuzzy associative links', 'adaptive file' thingos, on-site backups, and special hardware no one used any more. It might've made sense to Nelson.

The sunglasses staring back at him somehow conveyed bored incomprehension.

At last he wound down and started speaking English again. "Bottom line: they probably *can't* replace this old system, and they can't recover their files without an old system."

"That's crazy!"

He shrugged. "That's computers."

She shook her head. *If the traitors are only interested in selling the info to Tik Tek, they won't care about* properly *destroying Bio-Block.* But all she said was, "All right." She looked around. Cynthia seemed to have taken charge of Thug and Davo, who were prying open a security cabinet that was the final stage of a long, sleek white medical unit with windows onto a tiny assembly line within. The lock shattered under their combined assault. Both men immediately backed away, while Cynthia moved warily forward.

Gadger nudged Raven. "That'll be their biological material. Cyn always takes care of that stuff – she knows what she's doing, and has spells to make it safe. Though these people shouldn't have anything too infectious."

Cynthia opened her hands. In the gloom of the lab, illuminated only from the corridor, a dull sphere of light formed between her palms, drifting out from them to enclose the cabinet. Her fingers spread wide, and the surface of the globe knitted over with tracings of red. It began contracting, the network of light brightening as it shifted to blue. Heat blasted from it. Inside, the labels on the bottles and dishes darkened, curling at the edges before bursting into flame.

Still the globe shrank, the spell concentrating. A bottle shattered, its contents pooling at the bottom of the sphere, hissing and spitting. The glow seared now, light lacing throughout the floating ball, coiling around and through the contents of the cabinet until the air itself seemed to burn. Glass containers sagged, melting into a molten slag floating at the bottom.

Cynthia's shoulders slumped as she dropped the spell, the molten material splashing down inside the security cabinet. The face she turned to the others was tired and grim, yet quietly satisfied. She moved to a chair and sat, for the first time looking like a real participant in the events around her.

Leeth turned away. She *really* wanted to be in the computer room when the data cubes were taken. If they were going to be copied, that'd be the most likely time. She worked away at emptying cupboards, trying to think of a reasonable excuse to leave.

And then, just as she'd decided to blurt out her intention to help in the computer room, she sensed an odd reaction from the group, observing her.

CHAPTER 33

The cover of her shades let her check the others. Though each went about their assigned tasks, they all kept glancing her way; Davo and Maretti had even placed themselves to keep her in sight at all times.

Cynthia was watching her – Imaginally, she felt sure – and Wolf, too, seemed disturbed by her.

She'd built up another pile of material for Cynthia to burn, when she realized the two mages had drifted together and were talking in low tones. Shifting her position slightly she *focused* her hearing. Like tuning a radio.

"... know. Maybe she's borderline Active?" Cynthia asked. "Some magical potential, maybe?"

Wolf grunted disagreement. Both of them kept watching her. She concentrated on her task of collecting smartsheets, Links, and older comm units. Any one of them could contain a critical note that let the researchers continue after the destruction of the corporate datastores.

"Her aura is strong, but confusing. There is... something Else."

Rats. Wolf must be sensing *her*, Leeth, behind the Raven persona. *Forget the two gossiping mages. I am Raven. I'm here to help these people destroy Bio-Block, the corp that killed my lover, Paul. I'm doing this for Paul. For revenge....*

There was a drawn-out series of crushing sounds as Thug applied his weight and strength to squash flat some sort of microscope. By the time she'd subtracted that noise Cynthia was saying "-split personality?"

There was a long pause before Wolf muttered something that might have been agreement. Leeth was pleased by the misperception, but annoyed all the same. And not just because they thought she might be crazy. She should be hiding her thoughts better. With a conscious effort, she pushed all that aside and forced herself back into being Raven.

"Yeah!" Gadger abruptly called. "Data store raided!"

I waited too long. Hefting a microscope-thingy, she smashed it into a 3D printer with satisfying force.

Rain started falling in the New Franciscan night, soon lashing the windows in cold flails. Skinner drifted over, looking down into the deserted streets until Val called him to stop 'window-licking' and lift his load. With the cover of the storm's noise, they all scaled up their destructive activities.

Half an hour later – half an hour of considered, deliberate vandalism – the final two members of the Fist of Peace rejoined the others still trashing the lab. There was a pause as they entered, everyone's attention shifting back to Raven.

First in was a long-haired guy carrying a comp, who strolled in with a jaunty air. Wiz. He nodded to her but said nothing, merely smiled and sat back on a bench to watch what happened next. *Gadger had probably messaged him about me already.* Something about him reminded her of Nelson.

The man who followed him in was big, almost Thug's size. Dressed all in black, he carried a milspec HK MP9SF 'Phoenix' machine pistol slung over one shoulder. *Impressive.* He had short-cropped black hair and hard, cold eyes. His Mediterranean features seemed squared off, blocky. This must be Don. The possible psychopath.

He approached her, his face expressionless. Everyone had stopped to watch, she realized. Don continued approaching. She straightened, reading menace in his movements. Leeth forgot the gun at her hip and focused on the man. Shifting her stance, her lips parted in anticipation, muscles loose but ready. Ready to kill.

He stopped.

One meter away. Way over a head taller, and probably twice her mass.

No one moved.

Don Ferrera looked down at the girl before him, pausing a moment before she would have attacked.

Her feet were planted. As he studied her, considering options, he sensed micro adjustments in her posture. Now slightly crouched, always perfectly balanced. Surely, though, too small to be a challenge. Surely...?

At last he put out a hand, the gesture somewhere between blessing and greeting.

Leeth, seeing the fight evaporate before it started, frowned before coming to her senses. She was *not* supposed to kill any of these people. *Yet.* She reached out and grasped the hand.

Don began to squeeze.

His calmness woke a similar response in her, and she simply returned the smoothly tightening grip. Trying, but failing to hold in her smile as she matched his force.

Perhaps ten seconds passed.

Don nodded imperceptibly, accepting the strength as natural, a proper part of the creature he saw before him. With no other signal, each abruptly released their grip.

Don moved silently past her to assist in demolishing the lab. Leeth... *Raven* moved to Wiz.

The two mages exchanged grimaces. Imaginally, the meeting had been quite revealing, if worrying. Raven's aura had subtly changed. *Deepened.* And the emotion – hungry anticipation, a sense of claws unsheathing – both had felt sure she was about to attack, somehow. Whatever had held her back had not been obvious. Common sense, no doubt.

Behind the group, Maretti shook his head. *Great. The psychopath approves of her.* And what had gone on there at the end? Had Don tried to crush her hand, or merely greeted her? If he had.... She was weird, no question of that. He looked across at Wolf, who seemed uncertain. Great. Wolf, the impassive Native American brave – uncertain. Cynthia looked frightened – but then, Cynthia often looked frightened. His attention was diverted by Raven herself, now causing Wiz some grief. He headed over. She turned at his approach. Wiz looked a little pale.

"What's up?" Maretti demanded.

"I want to see the data cubes," Raven answered.

"I told her she couldn't, that they don't get touched till we get back, for the Burning."

"How do I know you really took them?"

"Raven. We can show you cubes, but that wouldn't prove a thing. And we can't afford the time for you to check them out. Even if you happened to have a System Three Elektra to interpret them on. Be real. You just have to trust us."

She scowled, her bottom lip thrusting out obstinately.

"Let me see them, then. Just so I know there's *something*."

"Listen, chick," Wiz began, his tone disparaging now that Maretti stood beside him, "no one-"

"Don't 'chick' me." Raven's tone was low. Murderous. "Not ever."

This was getting out of hand, Maretti decided. "Wiz, show her the cubes. Just this once, okay?"

Wiz looked from Maretti to Raven. Belatedly, he noticed her hand had dropped lower, now hovering near her holster. Don stalked over, too.

Wiz unclipped a pocket of his comp's carrying case and slid out a small, ornately carved wooden box. Don, Raven, and Maretti all watched as he opened the lid. Lined in red velvet, it was divided into twelve small compartments. Four were occupied by crystalline cubes.

"Satisfied?" Wiz sneered, with a glance at Don.

Raven nodded, half turning to Maretti while Wiz packed it all away. "Why the special box, and what's this 'burning' he was talking about?"

"It's a little ritual of ours. At the end of the mission." Maretti sighed. "I guess you want to be invited along?"

"Thank you. I will."

Maretti scowled.

"I'm going to check on those two security guards I tied up. Be back in a few minutes. I'll get my gear off the roof, too."

They all watched her leave. Chopper hesitated a second, then darted after her, following.

Gadger raised his eyebrows. "Interesting gal."

CHAPTER 34

Even with half the group returning via bikes, the Electrikar made for a very cramped ride to home base. Raven's bag had been checked and put in the trunk. Knowing they were carrying several kilos of high explosives hadn't improved anyone's mood.

Gadger drove, Maretti riding shotgun. Cyn pressed between them on the front bench seat, trying not to touch either. Wiz sat in the rear alongside Don and Thug, who sandwiched Raven.

Maretti had chosen the seating arrangement. After a few minutes he turned to see how Raven was coping. He smirked at how child-like she looked, blindfolded and jammed between the two very large men, and toyed with giving them the nod to disarm her.

Then he noticed the tiny smile on her lips, her head tilted back, the rain-streaked lights of the city sliding across the blindfold; noticed how casually she leaned into Thug, who was... *fuck*. Thug was eyeing her adoringly, one large meaty hand draped protectively across her shoulders. Maretti ground his teeth and turned around. So much for daunting her. His gut warned him to leave well enough alone. At least for now.

Though so far his gut had misled him each time he'd trusted it with her. He'd felt sure that insisting on her wearing a blindfold if she wanted to see the datacubes destroyed would make her back off. Or demand they do it on the spot.

Instead, those shades had stared coolly back at him. "So you guys have a secret base? *Really*?" The quirk of her lips brought a flush of heat.

"Yeah, we do." He'd almost gone on to boast about its location, before pulling himself together. And now there she sat, smug and relaxed on the back seat, crammed between two men who completely dwarfed her. Looking like a cat toasting itself between two fires.

Raven had wanted them to blindfold her *over* her shades. That had set off all sorts of alarms for both Wiz and Gadger, and Maretti refused. She'd looked furious.

Handing them over, she'd squinted, covering her eyes until the first turn of bandage looped around her head. She slid her hands out from under the bandage while Maretti re-tightened it. Gadger and Wiz checked out the slim, sculpted black band, but the shades were clean, no electronics at all.

Gadger handed them back to her. "How can you see in those?"

She shrugged, her hand seeking his and taking them. "They adjust. They're not that strong."

The others exchanged doubtful looks.

Gadger hunched lower over the wheel, glad of his cyber eyes. There was one good thing about a miserable night like this – you didn't have to worry about running over people lying on the streets. Even the chipheads would be under some cover. No one survived this sort of night if they hadn't learned that much.

He still felt guilty for the warmth of the car heater, though.

Glass crunched under reinforced tires as the car wove between rain-sodden piles of garbage. Ten minutes ago they'd passed the last unbroken streetlamp – even duraplex wasn't proof against heavy caliber rounds. And, Spirits knew, there were enough people living on the streets who only *managed* to live on the streets thanks to the weapons they carried. Unlike the Hunters Point or Potrero Dumps, this one held more predators than protectors.

In the rear-view mirror he looked back at the oddity they'd picked up tonight. *She* seemed content enough, even blindfolded. Reluctantly, he dragged his eyes from her to focus on driving. Autonav programs weren't designed for the hazards of the Dumps. Funny, that.

Gadger relaxed. There was the light, up ahead at last. A good sign. Really. An unbroken streetlamp in this part of the world was a clear enough signal if you had the wit to see it. *Good to know we're still appreciated.* The last two years had been hard, since Jacob's death. The fire – the drive – had been Jacob's; a part of *him*. When he'd died, a big part of the group's spirit had died with him. It hadn't been obvious at first. They'd kept going, Tony taking up the reins, trying hard to hold things together... but sometimes it seemed they were all running on autopilot, their momentum slowly eroding. He glanced again at Raven.

He had a good feeling about her. *Maybe all we need is some fresh blood?*

Behind him, at a nod from Maretti, Thug removed Raven's blindfold.

She squinted, covering her eyes as she slid the dark band back on. "Mmm. Nice place!" she said, peering out the window.

Gadger snapped from his reverie at her comment. They'd arrived. He didn't remember parking the car.

Maretti twisted around to growl at Raven. "We didn't choose it for the Bay view. We're trusting you, letting you know about this location."

She sat alertly in the back seat, eyes concealed by the dark sunglasses. Thug looked at Maretti, confused, and let his hand drop from her shoulders.

A distant wave of thunder rolled through the city as the rain continued to beat down.

"Right. I guess I'll just feel a little happier when those chips're destroyed." She gestured in Wiz's direction, who grimaced at the unrelenting downpour and began checking the weather seals on his comp's case.

Maretti scowled at their guest, her sunglasses as unreadable as ever. "Don't give an inch, do you?"

She scowled right back, though he sensed an odd vulnerability behind it. "Who can afford to these days? Tell me that, Mr Maretti."

He sniffed, ignoring the remark, and spoke to his team. "Come on. Let's go."

They all stretched, preparing for the dash to the shelter of the broken office block. The same one she'd spent hours clinging to, last night. A bike roared up and past, disappearing round the corner, the passenger at the back triumphantly holding up something in a pink plastic carry bag.

"Slot! Strawberry-flavored Frosted Fun. On a night like this?" muttered Wiz.

"That was Val and Skinner," Gadger explained to Raven.

As each raced from the car, rain pelted them in cold vindictive pellets, doing its best to drench them.

Inside on the ground floor, flimsy partitions made a narrow passageway. Behind the makeshift barriers Leeth heard the same sounds of people living as last night: conversations and snores; coughing; sex. Ahead, a stairwell led up to the Fist's meeting area.

"Do you have this place to yourselves?" she asked as they headed up the stairs.

Maretti hesitated. "No. We meet here sometimes. We've got an arrangement with some people. They live here, on the lower floors. The gangs stay away because we're around, and we get warned if anyone noses around."

"Hmm."

At the next turn, the stairs held ragged people – the same ones she'd heard and avoided, last night? – who nodded and smiled as the group threaded their way through them and up, eyeing her with interest.

On the third floor, the stairway opened onto a landing from which the doors had been ripped away, revealing partitioned cubicles and offices.

Last night, after they'd finally left, she'd crept past this space in the dark, chilled and wet, her teeth chattering. As they moved into the area now she paid close attention, noting the knocked down partitions and camp beds spread around the far end of the large space. The windows were intact, but painted black. It looked austere but lived-in. She wondered again why the squatters down below didn't try to move up here. Was Don enough to scare them off? Or did they appreciate what the Fist of Peace did that much?

Val, Skinner, Davo, and Wolf were already there. Davo had unpacked some sort of apparatus and was plugging it into the mains. She blinked, finally connecting this with the streetlight outside. Electricity in the West Oakland Dumps? *That* was an impressive feat. People killed for less. Their neighbors really must respect them.

On what had once been the conference table, Davo finished setting his device up. The table was long and black, and so large it looked like you'd need earth-moving equipment to shift it. A bizarre assortment of folding chairs and derelict office equipment had been cannibalized into seats and pulled up around it. Some of the stuff looked antique – age-misted mirror plastics, smoked glass, even chrome. Real early-millennia stuff.

Davo turned the thing on. Within seconds, part of it

glowed red.

Leeth casually chose the chair next to Thug, noting with interest there were no places left over when everyone else at last sat down. She wondered who normally sat in her seat.

CHAPTER 35

Maretti stood at the head of the table as Davo took his seat. His device brightened until its searing white blaze overpowered the steady glow of a nearby floor lamp.

Maretti looked around at the serious faces watching him, strangely-lit by the furnace's glare. It occurred to him once again how out of place they'd seem to the people who must have held their business meetings here decades ago. He imagined the impression his team would make, dressed in shades of black, or camo suited to a strike, but something odd about each individual. From Wiz with his screenless comp to Gadger and his matte-black cyber eyes. Or Chopper, Don, Val and Skinner, their cyber improvements ranging from corded and ribbed bulges of oddly-shaped muscle enhancements, to the less obvious but possibly more disturbing chip sockets. Wolf had his assortment of fetishes – tied-together pigeon feathers and other dried and unmentionable parts of animals, while Davo had a vicious scar right across his face. Thug looked like someone raised on growth hormones. Raven herself seemed more an artist's rendering of a female... he didn't know what. Only that it was simultaneously alluring and deadly, whatever it was. The only one who would have seemed normal to their hypothetical observers, he thought, was Cynthia. And, Maretti supposed, back in those days there wouldn't have been any women involved in boardroom meetings. Back when human prejudice only had other unmodified humans to focus on....

Leeth, on edge, watched him carefully, wondering what he was waiting for. The room was very quiet. Just a faint buzz from the apparatus on the table, now radiating intense heat. And a large moth. Its erratic flapping wing beats as it fluttered around the floor lamp were beginning to irritate her. The others probably couldn't even hear it. She tried to work out who was the traitor – or traitors. *If they slip up now, I could kill them later tonight and be home by morning!* She smiled, imagining dumbfounded expressions on Mother and Father's faces. She'd shrug and ask them to give her something tricky, next time!

Maretti met her eyes. He smiled back at her for once, then around at his group, clearly proud of them. For some reason, it made her feel guilty. And alone.

Wiz, in contrast, eyed her narrowly as he handed over

the richly polished wooden box with a deliberate air of ceremony.

Maretti took the box of data cubes – some obsolete old kind called holocubes, Wiz had explained at tedious length earlier – and Leeth sat up straighter. Wiz had taken it from the same pocket of his comp's carry-bag he'd put it away in earlier. She watched intently, alert for any misdirection or sleight of hand as Maretti accepted it. It *looked* identical; she saw the same four pockets occupied by data cubes when he opened it. Taking out one crystalline cube between thumb and forefinger, he held it up for all to see. *At least these old-style cubes really were actual cubes.*

Secret compartments? But the box was slim – too flat to fit a second layer. She wished that slotting moth would stop flopping its wings about!

Maretti spoke. "A good strike, team. The last Kyosei Elektra in New Francisco died tonight, and we've fried Bio-Block's biological cultures and all their data." He nodded thanks to Cynthia, whose pride briefly overpowered her self-consciousness. "Once we've melted these last cubes down into slag, that'll be the end of the combat drug intended for Newtopia's Brazilian Reclamation Force."

Leeth pursed her lips, not correcting him. She wasn't supposed to know it was Tik Tek, inside the Newtopian Consortium, who wanted the data. Her intuition was still telling her there was something 'off' about that.

Maretti dropped the cube into the top of the micro-furnace with an economical movement, carefully taking a second one from the box. He looked at Raven. "Since the Fist of Peace was first formed, it's been our custom to take some token of the evil we've uprooted, and bring it away for ceremonial burning."

The light from the furnace dimmed as the first cube turned to slag, a tart, unpleasant smell biting at her throat. He seemed to address his next words directly to her. "I don't know doing this has any real effect beyond destroying the stuff; symbolic magic is pretty dodgy ground, I gather."

Cynthia fidgeted like she wanted to argue, Leeth saw from the corner of her eye, but kept her eyes on Maretti, the data cube, and the box.

"Though some people believe this little act has wider-reaching effects."

Her forehead and cheeks prickled from the savage heat radiating out, molten silica now dripping from the bottom of the furnace into the thermoplass bowl it squatted over. The light from the device brightened again, and Maretti dropped the second cube into it.

Chit! Her instincts were telling her she was watching the cubes really being destroyed. She'd check the furnace out later, of course. But if that was clean, it meant someone had already swapped the cubes. But how? Had Gadger tampered with the ceremonial box? Added a transmitter and cube reader? Or was Wiz the one dealing their spoils to Tik Tek? After all, hackers were strange people, from what she'd seen. She had a theory they thought the virtual world of the net was more important than the real world.

Maybe the velvet compartments concealed contacts that sprang out to suck data from the chips, and the box connected to a cable in the pocket of Wiz's carry-case? But they'd said these holocubes needed weird, obsolete equipment to read them, so that seemed far-fetched. Maybe she'd check that out later, too. Somehow.

Or was the Department wrong, and there was no traitor in the Fist of Peace at all? Maybe they really were destroying the data, and none of it would turn up for sale?

"You look troubled, Raven," Wiz prodded.

Flick! She *should* be looking happier, shouldn't she? She tried to relax.

At last she let out a heavy sigh. Could Wiz be the traitor? Switching the cubes before he'd even put them in his box?

The stupid moth continued flapping about in the background.

Maretti dropped the third cube in. She was *sure* it hadn't left his hand.

She clenched her teeth. Unless she could see something funny with this last cube he was holding up so theatrically, she was going to be on this mission for a while. Damn! That meant she'd have to get herself on their next strike. So much for finishing it tonight.

She pictured Mother's *I told you so*. With an effort, she unclenched her jaws.

Maretti dropped the last cube into the furnace. Nope. Once again, she was sure no funny business had gone on. He simply 'pinched' the chip from between his fingers so it popped into the incinerator: the cube didn't leave her sight for an instant. And the puddle of melted silica continued to grow, drip by drip. The acrid smell in the air was pretty awful now. At least that was something she could check. She could get Little Brother, back at the Department, to melt a cube for her and make sure it smelt the same....

That *tud* of a moth! As the final bits of melted data cube dripped into the miniature lake of crystal lava, Leeth shoved her chair back and stalked round the table to the lamp. The others looked on, puzzled and a little wary. Maretti took a step back as she neared him, but she hardly noticed.

She moved past him and stopped abruptly in front of the floor lamp. A second later one hand lashed out, snatched the moth, and squeezed. Dropping it like a small stone, she grimaced at the mess it left behind, brushing her hands together as she looked back at the group.

Oh, chit. She'd done that way too fast, hadn't she?

CHAPTER 36

Maretti stood with his mouth open. Wolf frowned.

Cynthia cursed under her breath, then whispered to the other mage. "Did you happen to be Watching then?" Imaginally, of course, she meant.

Wolf shook his head. Still frowning at Raven, he inclined his head questioningly at Cynthia.

She hesitated before answering. "Just the tail end. Wasn't clear. Claws." She shivered at the memory.

Leeth carefully pretended she hadn't heard any of the exchange, cursing herself for a being a total *idiot*. She'd have to be way more careful from now on. Dojo always told her she got angry too easily. With a conscious effort, she forced herself back into the cool, self-possessed Raven persona. She'd better start working at being invited to join the group, too.

She returned to her seat. "I'm impressed. And I have to admit, it *was* a lot neater than blowing up all their equipment, even if it did take longer. I guess experience pays."

Maretti raised one eyebrow. "A compliment! I didn't think that'd be part of your repertoire."

Raven flushed. "Listen, you...." She wanted to call him a nullhole, but for some reason couldn't bring herself to say it. She forced herself on anyway. "Maybe to you, this was just another job. But I was doing this to say goodbye to- to someone special. I don't do this sort of thing for a living, you know."

"What *do* you do for a living, Raven?"

"I'm... I'm a student."

"Uh-huh. What subjects?"

Again she hesitated. "A-architecture, I guess."

"You guess?"

"It's what I enrolled in. You can check the University records, if you like!"

Maretti smiled. "Under the name 'Raven'?"

Again the pause. "No."

"Ah." They all silently watched her. "Let's try an easier question. How did you get into the building?"

"Through the roof."

"The roof? You have a grapple gun in your little bag of goodies?"

"No."

He waited, but she didn't elaborate. "Then how'd you

get up there?"

"I climbed."

"But that was a four-story building." He was about to say more when he glanced past her at Wolf, who nodded his head. *Truth.*

He frowned as Raven reached into the small pouch hanging like a second holster on her left side and pulled out a metallic claw-like object. "It clips onto the toe of your boot," she explained. She reached in again, pulling out a similar thing on a half-glove and slipped it on. The short spines stood out from the pad of her hand.

Maretti was impressed, but tried not to show it. The pieces were beginning to fit together. "And how did you get in, after you got to the top?"

"There was a door on the roof. I... unlocked it and went through."

"You unlocked it. You had a key?"

She stared at him for a second. "I made my own." She bit the words off.

"I know. I had Gadger check the other exits to the building before we left."

Wiz had a smug grin on his face. "And it was lucky for you I'd disabled the security alarms by then. Otherwise the place would've been swarming with metrocops before we'd even gotten to the labs."

Raven's chin lifted. "Yeah? It was lucky for *you* I'd taken out the guards. If they'd been wandering around and hit the panic button-"

Maretti interrupted. "I had Wolf and Cyn scout the place Imaginally before we went in. How'd they miss you?"

"Trade secret," she said, crossing her arms. "Why the twenty questions? You looking for someone to teach you guys a thing or two?"

The smirk that accompanied her remark brought back Maretti's burn of anger. "So Raven. You're a student of ar-chitecture?"

Her teeth clenched, but she didn't respond.

"Ever actually attended a lecture? Or did you merely enroll?"

She sat tensely for several seconds, then seemed to give up the charade, pushing her chair back and then slumping down into it. "No. I decided to study it my own way."

Maretti snorted. "I can imagine."

For the first time, Don spoke. "The explosives. Where did you get them?"

"Why do you care?"

"I care. Where did you get them." His tone turned the question into a threat.

"What's it to you?"

"Explosives are hard to come by."

"So? You accusing me of *lying?*" Raven felt a burn of anger. She'd stolen those explosives for real!

But at her reaction, Don's expression changed. He looked... interested. The mages too, who probably had Truth spells running, shifted their attention from her to the other members, and began kind of fiddling with their clothes and stuff. Like they were sending signals. She felt her hunch confirmed when a kind of positive ripple ran through the group.

"How did you get the explosives?" Maretti asked, backing up Don.

"Why? You guys want some?" She looked around, but that wasn't it. It was more like... they were taking her seriously. Looking at her with *respect*. She felt suddenly off-balance. The idea of being wanted... her chest tightened. "A navy guy gave them to me in Alameda."

Don just stared at her. Waiting.

Raven shrugged, but finally sniffed and indicated her gun. "I had to convince him a little bit, first."

"I'll just bet you did," Maretti said. He looked at Wolf, who nodded. *Truth*.

This time, Raven caught the piece of byplay. "Hey! You cast a spell on me! Cut it out!"

"On me," answered Wolf. "I think spells don't work so good on you."

Maretti intervened. "Come on, Raven. What'd you expect us to do – just trust you? How long d'you think we'd last if we worked that way?"

She stared at him then sighed. Did they really want her, or was she just kidding herself? 'Projecting her desires,' as the Doctor would say. She took a deep breath and slumped in her chair before looking up at Maretti. Thinking of her 'lover', Paul Genaro, and then Marcie, letting herself feel how far she'd go to pay back someone who hurt *her*.

"Thanks for your help tonight." She looked around, from one set of eyes to the next. "All your help. It was good to get payback on those Bio bastards."

Another odd little ripple of twitches ran around the group, and again she had the sense of some silent communication system in operation. Just how long had these guys been working together? Was this the moment to push them? Or was she just dreaming?

She made her decision, and stood, feeling suddenly hot and cold. "Well, it was good to meet you all. So what happens now? You blindfold me and drop me somewhere?"

For several seconds, no one spoke. Then Maretti shrugged. "Whyn't ya hang around for a bit?"

Her heart swelled at his words. She looked around at the smiles of welcome, and had to blink back unexpected tears. No smiles from the mages, though. Or Wiz, either. Don, too, just stretched in his chair, no longer paying her any attention.

Still, it felt like a step forward.

Skinner rose from the small cooler he'd been sitting on and reached inside, throwing a pink container across to Val who slammed it down on the table and popped the lid. She grinned. "Frosted Fun time, kiddies!"

"And Tequila!" added Chopper, pulling out two bottles and sliding one down the black conference table to Thug, who grinned happily.

Cyn looked faintly ill.

"Yeah, party time!" crowed Gadger, tossing Raven a plastic-wrapped block of Frosted Fun. She looked at it doubtfully. The Doctor always said ice creams were bad for you. *Ah, frag it, why not?* If he said it was unhealthy, the opposite was probably true.

She ground her teeth, then realized she'd let thoughts of him kill her happiness. Again.

Besides, she had to try to fit in. She peeled away the plastic and took a tentative bite. *So cold!* Her teeth protested, but she couldn't help grinning at the creamy sweet flavor.

Thug passed the bottle to her. She noticed he'd consumed a generous amount of it already.

"Have some tequila, Raven. It's good. Warms you up."

His expression was open, eager to please. But... the

Doctor said alcohol was a drug, that... *oh, slot it.* She'd always wondered what alcohol was like. She'd be careful. Just have a little bit. Say, a quarter of what Thug had just drunk.

Davo slid a glass along to her. She smiled a thanks, and poured some into it. "I've never had this before," she offered.

Gadger grinned. "Can't say I'm surprised. It takes a bit of getting used to, but there's nothing else like it. A bite of Fun, then a swallow of tequila. Like this," he said, taking the bottle from her. His eyes slitted with pleasure as the liquid went down.

Tentatively, she followed suit. She didn't want to look like she wasn't used to alcohol, though – she'd seen enough trids where someone took a generous swallow and then spent the next minute wheezing and gasping for breath. She sniffed her glass, cautiously. It smelt... weird. The first small sip was fiery, and tasted awful – very sour – but she decided she could handle it. Then she drew in a gentle breath. The air burned, and she only just managed to suppress the immediate urge to cough. To cover it she murmured a doubtful-sounding "Mmm."

"No, no. The Fun, then the tequila straight after," Gadger urged.

She stared at him a moment. Then remembered she was trying to make friends of these people. Shrugging, she gave him what she hoped was a 'Well, why not?' sort of smile and took another bite of the Frosted Fun. She let it melt a little then swallowed it down. Gadger gestured at her glass. She took a tiny mouthful, bracing her air passages for the involuntary constriction she knew would follow.

She was concentrating so hard on staying cool and in control she hardly noticed the taste.

"Well?"

She took a careful breath. "Yeah. Interesting." She took another bite, another swallow. Once you got used to it, it *was* kind of interesting, she decided.

Thug and Gadger were beaming at her, Thug refilling her glass before she could stop him. Oh well. The first little bit of alcohol hadn't affected her....

Val turned on some music.

CHAPTER 37

Maretti looked around. It was three a.m. Cyn had left early, as usual. Wiz and Don were drinking quietly, talking. Val and Skinner – drunk, high, and exhausted from dancing – had staggered off to a distant office cubicle. The sounds of their private little party had soon faded into Skinner's snores.

Maretti drank a little and talked with some of his team. But mainly, he watched Raven. He could see her slipping into the group, and he wasn't at all sure he wanted that to happen. Something about her made him uncomfortable. He wondered, not for the first time, if she was running some hidden agenda. He'd thought her some weird poser at first, with her odd mix of high quality and hard worn gear, and the elegant, mirror-black choker that had clearly been made-to-measure. A spoiled rich kid trying to look older than she was.

But as the evening wore on, she surprised him again. For a start, he'd been sure she wouldn't join in the party; certain she'd refuse their booze.

She'd done both. Jumped in with both feet. And as the drink had hit her, she'd loosened up. The first crack in her armor had opened when the talk drifted round to the night's strike and her entry into the building. Davo asked to see her gear and she'd brought it out, clipping and pulling the pieces on, then insisting on giving an exhibition. She'd somehow managed to entice most of them out into the bitter New Francisco night – during a break in the rain, at just that moment – and proceeded to climb the sheer wet wall back up to their meeting room and force open a window. There'd been several gasps from his team when a foot, then a hand, came free at the third floor and she'd dangled over the street below.

She'd only giggled before somehow restoring her grip and continuing up. It was only then that he'd realized she was *genuinely* drunk. He found himself hoping she wouldn't fall. It had been an intriguing demonstration.

Then she'd danced with Gadger, and Davo. She'd even talked Thug into shambling around with her. Maretti watched with interest as she continued to consume all the alcohol Thug put in front of her.

And as the hours passed, Maretti's opinion of Raven changed. She was someone too used to being alone, he decided. Used to relying only on herself. Maybe she *could* be an asset to the group. She certainly wasn't a plant – no one in their right mind would allow themselves to get so completely plastered.

Even Wolf seemed to relax a little as time passed. Maretti quizzed the taciturn Native American, learning he thought Raven was basically okay, if puzzlingly complex. At least, that's how Maretti interpreted the shaman's remarks.

"It is said, 'a tree's strength comes not from growth in the easy years, but from surviving the bad'."

Maretti had frowned. "What do you mean? She's been betrayed? Abused?"

"Abused? May be. Betrayed?" The shaman nodded, once. "Yes."

The real surprise came at the end. Thug was clearly attracted to Raven – hell, she *was* attractive – and started putting out some pretty heavy signals. But Raven didn't seem to see them for what they were; seemed almost not to take them personally. She just smiled – even laughed – and patted and hugged him.

Maretti braced himself for trouble. Even the others, in the state they were in, woke up to what was going on, and began trying to cool Thug down. All of them – except Thug – realized Raven was unlikely to let a guy drag her off into a corner for sex. Which would be Thug's level of subtlety by the time he finished drinking.

And now, despite their best efforts, the moment was here. "Hey, Raven. Come over here. Wanna show you my bunk." Grabbing her arm, Thug began pulling her from the group, toward one of the old office cubicles. She still wore her sidearm, Maretti noted, as he rose from his chair in the darkened corner, ready to stop the imminent explosion; Davo lurched to his feet; Gadger spoke up. "Uh, Thug, hey fren, the lady...."

Gadger's voice trailed off into silence. To the men's shared amazement, 'the lady' went with the giant, the two disappearing behind a partition.

Chopper stared after them, hands clenched; Davo was wincing, watching the wall of the cubicle they'd entered, counting down to the moment when Raven realized why Thug'd invited her there. They all waited, listening;

Gadger even took a half-step after them before stopping. Wolf looked puzzled. Wiz grinned up at the ceiling, waiting happily for the inevitable explosion....

Instead they all heard a moan of feminine lust from behind the partition. All the men looked at one another in disbelief. *Thug* had scored with *Raven*? They stared back at the thin wall. Then Thug *groaned*.

At last, Gadger spoke. "I wouldn't like to be in Thug's shoes tomorrow when she's sobered up!"

The remark provoked general smiles. Though the smiles slipped as more moans sounded from the office.

She slept, and in her sleep she dreamed. She was back in the Hunters Point Dumps, curled up in the ogre's shop. Teef pressed against her, his large body squeezing one arm uncomfortably, but she didn't want to move away from his warmth. Even though the emotionless killer, Marc Disten, was compressing her head, looming over her. One hand held his limp penis out in an inept attempt at rape, while the fingers of his other hand thinned into filaments drilling into her head, trying to worm their way in, to sneak inside and change her.

Needles threaded through her head, inescapable. Clamping her teeth against the pain, she stabbed up through his belly, her hand curving up around his heart, carving it free.

Remembered fury threw her from the dream and dumped her into panting wakefulness. Where was she? Where had Marc Disten gone? This wasn't Teef, pinning her arm. Head pounding, her throat dry, thick, and clogged, a wave of nausea rose up, closing her throat.

Poison?

She tried to sit up, finally registering the heavy form of the man she'd been sleeping with. *Thug.* Blinking in the dark, she eased her arm out from under him and slid sideways from the bunk. Crouching on the floor, the room *moved*, swimming forward and back. She stood, carefully, and the pain in her head instantly doubled. Swaying, something wrong with her balance, she crept into the main area.

It was quiet now, just the sounds of people sleeping. She shut her eyes as the throbbing in her head swelled, a fresh wave of nausea forcing her to open them again imme-diately. But even through her suffering, her dream was still sharp. Still clear.

Why on Earth had she dreamed that? Things coming out of Marc Disten's fingertips, drilling into her head? Had one of the mages been trawling through her mind as she slept, and woken old memories? Surely not. She was sup-posed to wake up if that happened.

Shivering in the cold she moved closer to a heater, her bare flesh soaking up its warmth. Listening to the sounds of breathing, she isolated each source in turn. All rose and fell in the rhythmic patterns of sleep.

Her stomach chose that moment to heave, and she fought the urge to throw up, feeling like the time her stew had gone off, in the Dumps.... The effort left her sweating. Stubbornly, she returned to her train of thought.

Why had she had that dream? Was it trying to tell her something?

Marc Disten's face flashed to mind, his hand clamped to her head, his fingers in the dream thinning into tendrils that pierced her scalp, linking his sick mind to hers. She shuddered at the memory.

But it hadn't happened like that. Whatever he'd done, he'd done psychically, not physically.

She started to shake her head, instantly freezing at the stab of pain. Dreams were stupid, anyway. And she had other things to worry about. Her stomach churned again.

Outside, the sky was paling. They'd be waking soon. She'd better get some clothes on. Raven wouldn't be walk-ing around naked, she felt sure.

She winced, remembering the Doctor warning her to use her clothes and the sunglasses to hide her youth. Gri-macing, she stole back to Thug's cubicle. With the last of the dream-induced adrenaline rush fading, she knew she was losing the battle against the nausea. That realization on its own, made it worse. Snatching her clothes she gulped, feeling the control over her stomach slip, and ran from the room.

She hurried through the old office's kitchen alcove. From it a door opened onto a corridor lit by the moon's glow, brought in by light-pump from a now clear night sky. With jaw and stomach muscles clamped against the rising

nausea, she saw the sign she needed and broke into a
sprint. The memory of what would come next was all too
clear, the experience of her food poisoning in the Dumps
still fresh.

Pushing through the swing door activated a light, the
white-tiled room bursting into a blinding brilliance that
lanced straight into her head. Stifling a cry she dived for
the nearest of the large white porcelain fixtures.

Ten minutes later – pale, sweating, and shaking, but
dressed – she weaved back down the corridor toward the
kitchen area, her headache *much* worse. At the sink, she
gulped down cold water, wondering what sort of static had
induced her to get drunk? As if in answer, the image of a
birthday cake in an unlit room flashed into her mind's eye.

Forcing it away, she ran her tongue over her teeth.
They felt strange and sharp and raw.

Back in the blacked-out main office it was still dark.
She went to the window and stared outside. It looked to be
shaping up to another chill Spring morning. She leaned
her forehead against the cold glass.

At last, feeling weak and hollowed out, she padded to
the battered black couch near the heater. Curling up next
to it, she lay down, trying to ignore the pounding in her
head. She'd feel better in the morning....

CHAPTER 38

Her uncle had her tied up in a little naked ball on an ice floe. He'd stuffed her mouth with a dry gag, taunting her, asking if she'd like a drink of cold water. But she couldn't get her mouth to work, to answer. A giant Raven's talons were squeezing her head, but moving made the pain worse. The wolf told her the coffee was fresh, if she wanted some. She tried to tell him about the gag, but Gadger took the coffee instead. Maretti asked what she thought of Raven. She tried to say she was right here, listening, trying to speak past the gunk clogging her throat.

"I like her. She's got... something. She'd be an asset," Gadger said. "I think if we asked her, she'd join."

Leeth came properly awake as Wolf said something she couldn't hear past the pain in her head. She rolled over. She felt *awful.*

"I want her to join." The heavy voice, Don's, spoke with an unpleasant finality. Leeth slitted her eyes. The faint voices were coming from the kitchen area off the far end of the office space. Well out of earshot of a normal person.

"I don't." That was Wiz. "And anyway, what makes you think she'd want to? Her blossoming romance with Thug, maybe?" She could hear the sneer.

Leeth smiled in hazy recollection of last night's encounter. *That* had been fun. She hoped she hadn't hurt him.

Gadger chuckled. "I'm glad I'm not in his shoes, when she wakes up and remembers what she's done."

Leeth flushed. *Oh, no! I* did *hurt him?* But she didn't *remember* anything like that. She'd heard of people being so drunk they forgot what they'd done. She frowned. There didn't *seem* to be any gaps in her memory.

Wiz answered him. "It's *her* fault. It's not as though anyone tricked her into getting drunk. Anyway, you don't really know her. None of us do. For all we know, getting fractured and screwing random guys could be her normal behavior. Ever think of that?"

"I don't think so," Maretti said, thoughtfully. "She seems much too controlled for that."

Leeth shivered. Surely, he couldn't know about... *Mode One?* She stared, unseeing, at the floor. She'd talked a lot, last night, but stayed in character. It had actually gotten easier as the night rolled on. Though... she'd intended to play Raven as darker, edgier. She *had* laughed a lot, last night. But they all had. It'd been *fun.*

"I think last night was out of character for her." Davo's voice. "I don't think she usually lets her shields down like that. And I agree with Gadger: I don't think she'll be happy. Let's all keep an eye out for Thug, just in case she gets nasty. Okay?"

Why did they all think she'd be mad at Thug, especially if she'd hurt him? Something was nagging at her, but the grinding pain of the headache made the problem feel unimportant. She had to force herself to think about it. It was something the Doctor had said. "A large part of this mission relies upon you convincing the Fist of Peace you are a good deal older than you really are, Leeth. Much of that will be achieved by clothing, which means you must not be seen out of costume by any of the members. Raven must be cool, professional, and unemotional." He'd looked at her, mouth pursed. "So best avoid bedding any of them, hmm?"

Dragon droppings. She'd blown that one. Or had she? From their conversation, it seemed like they were simply surprised. But what were they expecting her to do now? With an effort she shifted back into the Raven persona, annoyed she'd let it slip in the first place. Next time, she'd be careful to keep her clothes *on.*

She sat up, much too quickly, and pressed her hands to her head, trying to contain the pain.

"Shhh. She's up."

That was Gadger. She looked up to see him casually lounging in the far doorway. She bit down on the desire to groan. She used to think maybe you could get used to pain. This year she'd learned, all you could do was endure it.

She got up, the rush of blood forcing fresh nails into her skull. She wavered, adjusting to the new level of torment pounding in her head.

She heard Wiz's faint whisper. "She even *sleeps* in those shades. You think she slots with them?"

"Ask Thug," answered Wolf.

The need for water pulled her toward the group. She sank properly into the Raven persona, letting it settle over her like a cooling, soothing cloak. Pity it didn't help with the pain. She straightened, rolled her shoulders, and headed over to the gathered men. Chit, she felt terrible.

"She doesn't look hungover," Gadger whispered through the side of his mouth as she came up to the little group. Wolf stared at him, shaking his head at the shorter, gray haired man before frowning down at her.

Maretti nodded curiously to her, a little uncertain. Don loomed over the water cooler. She went straight to it and poured herself a glass, her eyes never leaving his face. Something was going to happen between them. She knew it. Anticipation welled up, like hunger for a juicy, blood-red grilled steak. For one bizarre moment, she pictured herself plunging an obsidian blade into his chest. *No.* Shuddering, she thrust the image away. She threw one glass back, then another.

"Enjoy last night, Raven?" Wiz asked.

As she turned to him, her responses suddenly crystallized. "What I remember of it."

No one said anything. She turned to Maretti and for a weird moment cringed, expecting him to scold her. It made her scowl. "I have a headache the size of the Asgard Geodome. Any suggestions?"

"You asking if we've got aspirin?"

Gadger interjected. "I've got some."

She started to say she didn't use drugs when Wolf suddenly spoke. "Let me fix it." It sounded almost like a challenge.

She turned to him. He was watching her strangely. She had the feeling, somehow, he'd just been Percepting her. His next words confirmed it. "Your pain is much larger than aspirin."

She said nothing, just went to him and bent her head forward, calmly placing herself in his hands.

"Trusting, isn't she?" remarked Wiz to the group in general. "Or maybe she's known enough mages to know they're not all the evil, manipulative bastards of the stim-senses and tridshows?"

They all saw the remark strike home, as she jerked.

She looked up into Wolf's eyes as she answered. "I don't know any *that* well," she growled.

Wolf frowned, but channeled his spell. Within seconds the pain began to ease. Relief was bliss. The tableau held for just two seconds before she pressed a hand to the shaman's hard-muscled chest. "Thank you." Her sincerity was crystal clear.

Wolf's hands fell from her head, his mouth opening in shock at how fast she had healed. He stared from his open palms, into her face hidden behind the dark shades. "How did you-?"

She spun back to Maretti, grinning. "So, what's next?" At their obvious surprise, the smile fell away. *Funt! Be Raven, be Raven!*

"That's an interesting question-" began Maretti, when Gadger, looking back into the office area, interrupted. "Uh-oh."

From the weight of the footfalls, Leeth knew it was Thug approaching. She wondered how Raven was about to re-act, as she let herself sink back again. Hard. Cold. Even cruel.

The tension in her stance seemed to communicate itself to the men standing around her. They all came to the alert as she slowly turned.

"Hi guys," boomed Thug. "Raven. Lissen, about last night," he began, towering over her.

She looked up at him, coldly.

"I know the guys think I'm pretty dumb, but I'm smart enough to know if you wasn't so smashed last night, you wouldn'a... we wouldn'a... Well, I just wanted to say I un-nerstan'."

He was wringing his massive hands together nervously, and her expression softened against her will.

He lowered his voice to what he probably thought was a conspiratorial whisper. "But hey, we was great, eh?"

The happy expression on his big, craggy face showed an innocent hope for approval that suddenly reminded her of Faith's goofy grin. Thug's lovemaking had been clumsy but joyful. And she did like big men – you didn't have to be so careful not to hurt them. She allowed a small smile to slip through Raven's guard, and laid her hand on his biceps a moment. "Yes. We *were* great."

His face transfigured in joy, a joy so large it was infec-tious. They all smiled. Even Maretti seemed warmed by it. Raven turned to him. "Mr Maretti. What do I have to do to join your group?" Leeth swallowed as she looked up at him, suddenly dry mouthed.

She'd caught him off-balance again. He frowned. "We vote."

CHAPTER 39

Once more they sat around the massive black conference table. This time a deck of cards rested in the center. Chopper had been last to arrive, late in the afternoon.

Maretti stood. "Are you sure you wouldn't prefer a secret ballot?" he asked.

Davo answered for them all. "Nah. Jacob always said votes for new members had to be totally transparent. You can't do that with a secret vote."

Maretti looked toward Cynthia but found no support there, either. "Okay," he sighed, and turned to Raven. "Anyone can ask questions at any time. We cut the deck to work out who votes when. You need a two thirds majority to get in. Which means, if four people or more vote No, you're out." He shrugged. "Those are our rules. So I'll start. Why do you want to join the Fist of Peace?"

She sank deep into the Raven persona, feeling the identity wrap around her, glad she'd given the Doctor one last chance. She put that memory aside and remembered Paul... his hands... how she'd felt when she'd been told of his death... the anger... "I want to pay them back – the corporations that push people around, pay them or bribe them to put the company's *profit* above human life. They're like vampires-"

She was panting, she realized, and pulled herself together. "There are a lot of people out there in the same sort of position Paul was in," she finished.

Ignoring the mages and the others at the table, she concentrated instead on herself, on her Raven memories and feelings. There was silence as each person chose a card from the deck. Val had drawn a king. "I vote she's in." She nodded to Raven, who smiled tightly in return.

Wiz had the next highest card. "Out. We know nothing about her – other than what I've been able to find out today. Her real name's Tanya Denison, and she has a record of theft, going back a few years. No fixed abode. My instincts say No."

"Your *instincts*, Wiz?" Skinner exclaimed. "Thought you always said you worked by logic, hey?"

Wiz looked annoyed, but didn't answer.

Next choice was Maretti's. "No."

She stared at him in disbelief, feeling like he'd just slapped her. It *hurt*. It also made two No votes. Two more, and she'd have failed her mission. Blinking, she looked down, wanting to hug herself.

"She's hardly older than my daughter would've been!" Maretti grated out. He glanced at Wolf, who watched him in that eerily detached way. "I feel there's a lot she isn't telling us, too. Or maybe it's just that black ravens symbolize death."

That comment sent a ripple of unease through the group. Raven's lips compressed to thin lines.

Next choice was Thug's, who'd started wringing his hands at Maretti's words. "It's okay, Tony. I'm sure she'll be great."

Then Cyn. She too appeared troubled, and lifted her chin, meeting Raven's eyes. "Do you ever have blackouts? Periods where you can't remember what you did?"

Raven looked surprised. "No. Never."

Cyn's troubled expression did not shift. She looked at Wolf, her mouth set. "I vote no," she said, turning back to face the younger woman's stare.

That was three No votes. One more and she was out.

"Can I ask questions too?" asked Raven.

Maretti nodded assent.

"Why?" she asked Cyn.

The magician looked at her. "When I look at you, I sense something darker, sometimes. Some other presence. I don't like it. It scares me."

Can she sense my real identity? Dreams of a black dagger fluttered at the back of her mind, but she rejected them, despite a weird shiver. *I'm Raven.* She stared down at her hands. When at last she spoke, her words came only reluctantly. "There *is* a lot of anger inside, deep down," she admitted. "It's worst when I'm being pushed around." She thought of the Doctor, and anger welled up. She forced the memories away.

Wolf and Cynthia exchanged a glance, Cyn seeming to be pleading, but Wolf merely looked away.

Don's vote was next. He simply stared briefly at Raven and said "In."

Gadger voted yes with a grin at Raven, as did Davo.

Skinner said no – but only to provoke an explosion from Val. Once he'd got it, he explained he was only kidding, and changed it to a yes. Maretti looked disgusted.

Raven didn't look too impressed either.

Wolf's vote was next. He looked impassively at her. "When you use the darkness, it is hard to bring light."

"I *don't* use darkness."

They stared at one another.

Wolf shrugged.

"In my culture, Raven symbolizes transformation. Let us see what changes she brings to us. I say, let her join the Fist of Peace, to do its work."

If that's his Yes vote, thought Raven, *I'm glad he didn't vote No.*

All eyes now turned to Chopper, who seemed to relish the attention. "You've all overlooked something real important. Real important. Stand up and turn around, Raven." He came around the table toward her.

She tracked him with narrowed eyes. Reluctantly, she stood. Slowly, turned. He stood beside her.

"Bend over."

"*What?*"

"Just bend over."

She lifted her head. If his vote wasn't the deciding one.... She gritted her teeth. "You'd better not do something you'll regret." She bent, looking back over her shoulder at them all.

Chopper spread his hands wide and turned to the others. "Scan it. That's enough for my vote – *perfect* arse. Perfect." He slapped it. "She's in."

Cynthia and Val snarled at the boy. Maretti gaped in disbelief, and Davo winced. Gadger hid a smile. Wolf growled and shook his head. Thug frowned at Chopper.

Leeth straightened slowly, burning at the mockery. Literally shaking. The urge to smash the humiliating grin off his stupid face ran like flame along her nerves. It flared brighter still, and she pictured herself plunging a black blade into his heart, carving out his-

What? No! Sudden shock battled rage. With a struggle, she remembered her mission. Remembered she wasn't allowed to kill anyone – wasn't even supposed to know *how* to do it. At least, not... she swallowed. Not hand to hand.

Not until she found the traitor.

Her eyes locked on Chopper like he had cross-hairs

painted on him. He took a step backward. She pushed her feelings back under control. Fought down the anger, fists clenched.

They were all watching her, she saw, waiting to see how she'd react. Though Cynthia also looked angry, and Val, irritated. Chopper didn't even notice, sauntering back around the table and sitting down. She took a deep breath, and made herself relax.

Perfect arse, he'd said. She nodded, eyes still narrowed. "True." Turning to Maretti, the anger pulsed, at the memory of his 'No'. "So. Now what?"

They all looked surprised.

"That's it," he said. "Welcome to the group."

"Thank you." She kept her eyes on his. "Can I make a brief statement, as a full-fledged member of the Fist of Peace?"

Maretti nodded, a little warily.

She walked around the long table until she stood behind Chopper, then swung his chair around to face her. He leaned away from her, and for just a moment, she had to fight the anger down again as she looked him in the eye. "Don't be a dick." Then – lazily, with only a tenth the force she *wanted* to strike – she popped him smack in the nose.

"Ow, *funt!* That hurt, you-"

But the rest of the group's laughter drowned him out while she strode back to take her seat. Her eyes locked on Chopper's, daring him to make more of it. Hoping *he* was the traitor.

"You deserved that, Chopper," Maretti said, not hiding his smile. Leeth, looking around, felt a surge of happiness. "But settle down now, people." He waited a beat. "There *is* another reason I was glad to have a meeting. I may just have another job ready to go. Could be nothing, but I have a strong feeling about this one..."

The group stirred in a peculiar sort of way, everyone snapping alert.

He continued. "I was in Bayview yesterday, when a Waste Department truck pulled up at the pollution monitoring point there. Now, unlike the other monitoring points you see, this one's behind a security fence... Not *too* strange though, considering the area.

"Something made me watch as he faffed about. Took

about five minutes. The whole time, though, I had a feeling of something *off*. And then I wondered: if you had to pick one district of New Francisco where the City Council didn't give a soybean about pollution, which would you pick?"

Thug muttered "the Hunt"; they were all nodding agreement. When Mt St Helena erupted during the so long-feared Big One, Hunters Point – previously drowning as the sea levels rose – was lifted, buckled and fractured, wracked into a series of cliffs and ravines. Parts of the Bay floor that had been accumulating that special city-outflow seabed for a century had been raised up even as it burned, and the whole district had been turned into a cliff-locked desert of broken buildings. A wasteland now of slums and vine-choked wreckage – and also, Leeth knew from direct experience, a vibrant community of people who'd found alternative ways to live, refusing to concede defeat when others had given up on them.

She wondered how Barney and Teef were doing. *I should visit!* But Tony was still talking.

"So, since Cyn knows someone who works in the Department of Waste Control, I had her ask if there was anything odd about the setup for Hunters Point." He nodded to Cynthia.

"I contacted my friend. The only thing different about Hunters Point is the department contracted out data collection and sample exchanges there, because of the location: it has to be manually taken, since the inhabitants snatch drones."

Leeth looked down to hide her own smile, remembering. *Fun times.*

"But she also said they must get a really good deal with these contractors, or they're real dopes – they check the monitoring point there as often as the bots check the others, but charge no more."

Raven looked around, wondering why any of them cared about a stupid pollution monitoring operation, but they all sat expectantly alert. *Weird.*

Wiz, lounging against the conference table, raised an index finger. "Tony, you said it was a Waste Department truck. It was marked as such?"

Maretti inclined his head in acknowledgment.

"So," Wiz's grin became even more smug, "why is an independent contractor using a government truck?"

They all looked at one another.

"And why a truck?" Gadger suddenly asked. "Drones just download a few readings and maybe change some bottles. If you're only handling one station, you don't need a truck!"

"I hear somebody bein' *real* shady," added Val. She clapped Maretti on the shoulder. "Boss man, I think you just hunched us a real *low* target, again."

Leeth stared at Maretti, Val's easy intimacy making her grit her teeth. And what did she mean about hunching targets? *Does Maretti work off intuition, like me?*

And why did she wish he was smiling at *her*?

CHAPTER 40

"Right," said Maretti. "From here on, it'll have to be on foot. The bikes should be okay like that." He wondered about Gadger, Wolf, and Raven, back on watch at the station itself. The shaman had accepted the boring task, agreeing it might give him a chance to try to penetrate Raven's shell.

The rest of them would scout the area for locals, see what info they could pick up.

"Davo, Val, Skinner, Thug," Maretti continued, "try to find out if anyone knows anything odd about the pollution station — has it ever been vandalized, what happened after if it was. Anything that could give us a lead.

"But keep the comms to a minimum while we're here. No sense drawing attention to the area. Meet back at the bikes in two hours."

They murmured agreement. "Okay, let's split. Chopper — we'll try that priest you said runs a refuge near here."

"Father Kirkpatrick."

"Yeah. Let's go."

Chopper led him, Cynthia and Don across the shattered urban landscape's buckled concrete slabs, on their way to meet this Kirkpatrick character. You needed all your attention clambering over this krup. As they rounded a corner and faced a wall of mutated kudzu vines, he sighed and unslung his machete. Damn Chopper's shortcuts.

Kirkpatrick had been unperturbed by the appearance of what must have seemed a possible hit squad. The old Irish priest gave the impression it'd take a Nemesys battletank to disturb him.

He'd remembered Chopper at once, chiding him for his failure to appear in Church. Maretti and Cyn exchanged amused looks when Chopper shuffled his feet and mumbled something about 'trying to in the future, Father.'

But although Kirkpatrick wanted to help, his information only added a few tantalizing pieces to the puzzle: unexplained disappearances from that quarter of the Dumps — eight people *he* knew of, starting a couple of years ago. One or two, a long time apart. Four ogres, an Altered, and three humans. Mostly younger people. Though Schenk, the first of the three humans to vanish, had been middle-aged. The most recent though was a member of the Fisher

Clan, a youth with a drinking problem.

The Altered had disappeared first. Windchild and Berker had vanished together, the mismatched pair well-known in the district, and well-liked. Their respective clans had organized full search parties.

Without success.

No trace of them – no trace of any of them – had been found. Kirkpatrick believed a serial killer was responsible. Someone from the City, prowling into the Dumps for sick kicks. No gang had ever claimed responsibility, and of the victims, only Madeye, one of the ogres, had been a ganger. Recently – before Sleena and Tash killed the Breaker – they'd wondered if it had been his work. But that madman had usually taken couples, and whoever was doing this usually chose victims who were alone. Though Windchild and Berker had vanished together.

"Sleena and Tash *teamed up?* To kill the Breaker?" Chopper moaned. "God damn it! Uh, sorry, Father!"

"Tash is back?" asked Tony. "And who's Sleena?"

Chopper's eyes lit up. "Only this hot little sliv who crashed the last Fist Fest, flashing her boobs around. They say she slotted half the fighters and beat up on the others before taking on Tash and gutting her somehow. Didn't help of course: Tash still took her down, then *away*." His lips curved down. "And I missed the whole thing."

Father Kirkpatrick turned to Chopper. "You're a depraved and lustful sinner, Charles Harris, and I'll expect you in my confessional this Sunday, before Mass."

But Chopper's phrasing plucked at Tony's memories. "She *somehow* gutted Tash?"

Chopper grimaced. "The friend whose vid I tapped only had a crappy view."

Don answered. "Something like your old Wolverines, Tony, but far faster – no one saw any blades. Maybe they only extruded on contact with flesh."

Tony frowned, flexing his fingers, remembering old pain. "So Tash made this Sleena chick into her Get? That doesn't sound like her."

Kirkpatrick shook his head. "No, Mr Maretti, Tash honors her compact. She came, at my call, and made none like herself while she was here." He stopped, pursing his lips.

Tony opened both hands wide. "But?"

"Before she left, Tash warned me she'd recognized a Sign. She said the world faced troubled times, and to prepare for the worst."

"Why tell me? I can't-"

"I'm telling everyone, son," Kirkpatrick said, gently.

"What was the sign?" asked Cynthia.

The old priest looked uncomfortable. "A new Warrior," he said at last.

"Sleena," Don said, into the silence.

The others turned to him in surprise.

"Club Juzz is off our list," he explained.

"Yeah, so I heard," Maretti said. He, Chopper, and Cynthia didn't try to hide their relief. "You mean *they* cleaned that cesspit?"

"Yes. The girl and the vampire. Alone. In one night."

For several seconds, no one spoke.

"I guess Tash got sick of waiting for *us* to work out how to help her do it with no casualties." Maretti shook his head. "So what was the death toll, in the end?"

"You didn't hear?" asked Cyn, shivering, her expression conflicted. "*Thirty-two* dead: every guard, every worker, every patron of that hell-hole slaughtered. But *zero* casualties among the children: they got every single one out, unharmed. Apart from the torture they'd already endured."

"I heard it all happened the night of the last Fist Fest," Chopper volunteered. "The same night little miss death-on-heels fought Tash."

"The Warrior," Don said, frowning at Chopper. "Although I saw no heels. She was barefoot."

"Guys," Tony interrupted. "Look, I'm overjoyed that hell-pit is dealt with, but I'm pretty sure that's not the kind of odd thing we're investigating. Gratz for the other intel, padre, and the tip about this Sleena chick. We'll keep an eye out for her." *And avoid her. If she gave Tash a run for her money, and just the two of them cleared out* Club Juzz *on their own, we'll stay the Hell away.* He frowned. "What does she look like?"

"Hot!" Chopper exclaimed. "Like a young, blonde pixie. Meb' Raven's height, and...." He cupped both hands as if bouncing an invisible pair of weights at chest height, then caught Kirkpatrick's scowl and blushed. "With, uh, blue eyes."

They all looked at him. "I thought your friend's vid was crappy?" said Cyn.

Chopper's eyes shifted. "Ah...."

"Enough!" growled Tony, sharing a look with the priest. Chopper was all too happy to leave.

Their next stop was Chopper's old clan, who had been glad to see him again – a fact which seemed to surprise Chopper. They'd also been pleased to meet some of the members of the group he ran with now, the Fist of Peace. It made Tony feel a bit strange. Like some kind of celeb.

But they'd known less than Brian Kirkpatrick. It was news to them there'd been any 'disappearances'. Didn't they just mean deaths, or that the bods had left?

Though Burdock, the Head of the clan, suggested they try to track down Mad Betty. She was more than a little crazy, he'd warned, but if they caught her during one of her good spells, well... She *had* predicted the fungus plague of '54, and the copter crash in the Dumps a year ago. Not that anyone had *understood* her predictions at the time, but still....

He'd even been able to suggest a couple of places to look for her. Tony and Burdock had shaken hands, to Chopper's evident pride, and they'd left.

"Stars above!" exclaimed Cyn, when they were away. "How can they *live* so close to those disgusting-smelling slime vats? I kept thinking I was going to.... Well, I don't know how much longer I could have handled it."

Chopper looked offended. "That 'slime' was leen-soy. And they were living so close to it to look after it. It's pretty tasty, too, when you know how to treat it," he said, looking wistful.

Cynthia grimaced. "As in, spirulina-soy? I doubt it. That'd be plasti-soy, not the real stuff, anyway. *I'd* know how to treat it."

"Hey-" began Chopper, but Don interrupted heavily. "Where is the derelict mill?"

Twenty minutes later, they found Mad Betty.

The woman was plump, and probably middle-aged: it was difficult to tell through the layers of filth, grime, and bulky rags and coats. She had a lumpy sack slung over one shoulder, and held a smaller cloth bag dripping fresh blood. At first she'd been defensive, accusing them of coming to steal her 'dinner'. They'd grimaced, none wanting to ask what bulged the smaller bag.

Chopper began the questioning. "So, Betty. Long time. Burdock said we might find you here."

The old woman parted her matted fringe of filthy gray hair to peer at Chopper. She waddled closer, squinting. "You're not here because Burdock sent you, though, are you?" she wheezed, with a keen look.

And kneed him suddenly, hard, in the groin. "Throw rocks at poor old Betty, would you, young Chopper? You're a bad, bad boy." She burst into a cackling laugh that degenerated into hacking coughs, before hawking and spitting. Cynthia paled.

Despite his reinforced clothing, Chopper sagged in the middle, managing to look wrongfully wounded and guilty as hell at the same time.

Tony waited until her coughing spasm ended. "You live near here. You know the Pollution Monitoring Station, over that way? Ever seen anything odd there?"

She looked at him, then at the woman by his side. A sly smile spread across her face. "Cynthia! This will be like old times, for you!"

The mage's mouth opened and she took a step backward. The old woman turned to Maretti. "And *you* dance with a tiger now? Best watch her claws!"

The man frowned and tried to steer her back to the subject. "The pollution station?" he suggested.

"Yes, yes, when the storm comes. The ground opens up, and he rises from the hole."

Maretti looked dubious. "Who?"

"Betty's seen him. Soon, now. Soon the Soul Twister will stand in Hunters Point."

They all felt it. Like a sudden knot clenching the stomach. Something in the tone of her voice – a quaver of real fear. They looked at one another.

"What is this 'Soul Twister'?" demanded Don.

The old woman blinked. Shuffling over to the large man, she reached out a grimy hand to his arm. Don's face was impassive, though his nostrils flared as her smell hit him.

"Oh-ho. You're a *mighty* leg of man, aren't you?" she leered. "If Betty had only known *you* ten years ago! Oh yes!"

The impassive face froze further.

"I'm hungry. Where's my rat?" she suddenly demanded.

"In your sack?" suggested Chopper.

"Oh-ho, you're a clever one, aren't you, young Chopper? But Betty doesn't show what's in her sack. Oh, no. Not in her sack. In her *lunch* bag." She cackled, opening the neck of the blood-stained bag to peer inside. "You're a fine, fat fellow, aren't you?"

She looked up from it to fix Maretti with a wild stare. "*He's* hungry, too," she told him. "He waits for her. Has waited a thousand years for someone like her. And you're all circling. But the eye isn't calm. Don't look in the eye of the vortex! Oh, yes. Avoid the eyes!

"Hungry, yes. Like poor Betty. Betty's sooo hungry." She craned her head, twisting around, apparently puzzled, looking for someone. "Where's the claws?"

"Uh, I don't know. But you were telling us about the soul twister. Does it come from the monitoring plant?"

She looked at Maretti, tears welling in her eyes. "Poor Scott," she whispered. "Lost his wife. Then God's son...." She shook her head, then muttered something else.

"What? What did you say?"

"One of you will die," she declared. "One, then one more."

"Who?"

She shook her head, back and forth, back and forth. "Oh, no. Betty knows that when Betty says that, Betty dies, doesn't she? Blood at the fire, when the claws see you in the dark, and pounce!"

"Was that a threat?" asked Maretti in tones of disbelief.

"What claws?" asked Chopper. "This guy has claws, too?"

The question triggered a wheezing gale of laughter that suddenly broke into another spasm of coughing. She spat up an ugly blood-flecked gobbet of phlegm. "Poor Betty. She has a nasty cough, you know. Maybe you nice people could give her something for it? She's been very woozy.

Very woozy, and it's *so* hard to get her medicine..."

Cynthia winced, but couldn't ignore the plea. Stepping forward, with visible reluctance she reached out a hand toward the madwoman's chest.

Betty grinned and leaned into the contact, looking blissful before the mage even started her spell.

At last, Cynthia stepped away, shaking her head. "There. It was only an ulcer. But unless you start eating better it'll just return."

The old woman sighed, and opened her eyes. "Oh, yes, Betty loves fine dining. And you all smell so sweet, like flowers. Lovely."

"Do you know where this soul twister is now?" asked Cynthia, surreptitiously wiping her hand on a lace handkerchief.

"He waits. Cold. Strips everything. In the Pit."

They looked at one another, confused. Cynthia sounded uncertain. "What pit? Where is it?"

Betty ignored her. "He has hooks, you know, not eyes. He's worse than his brothers. Much worse. You'll have to end him. Before his infection spreads. But no one listens to Mad Betty until it's too late."

She looked at Maretti, and suddenly her voice sounded younger, less thick. "Tony – she's seen something in her dreams. Coming from the Station." She blinked, her voice returning to its normal cackle. "Or don't I say that?"

The four exchanged uneasy glances.

"You've come to take my rat, haven't you?" she accused them, backing away. "Always wanting more. Wanting all the rats. All the blood."

Maretti looked at Cyn. "We need to know what she's actually seen. She really hasn't told us anything, you know." He tapped the side of his head with his index finger and twisted it in a short drilling motion.

Cynthia *really* didn't want to cast Mindmeld on the old woman. Touching her physically had been bad enough.

"Cyn. She *may* have seen something. We *need* to know." Still holding the reluctant mage's eyes, he spoke to Chopper. "You have anything sweet you could give the old woman, Chopper?"

"Hey, I need that Hershey bar for lunch, it's-"

Don rested a heavy hand on the shoulder of his companion. "Give the woman the food."

Looking up into that dark stare, Chopper dragged out the chocolate, handing it over with ill grace.

Betty cackled. And Cynthia cast her spell.

Many seconds passed, while the old woman devoured half the chocolate and Cynthia stood with her eyes shut, swaying slightly. Slowly, she began to speak.

"She wants to leave, but can't. There's a man she's waiting for. Who wants her to do something she doesn't want to. And she's not – oh! Nothing. Never mind." Cynthia sounded surprised. Then looked ill and dry retched before gulping for air. She shook her head.

"Tony – she's seen something in her dreams. Coming from the Station. A man with holes instead of eyes. He's looking at me. He knows secrets. Secrets that bring Power. There's a –"

Betty began speaking, the same words at the same time, so that in unison they said:

"– big thunderstorm, and he comes up through the manhole. The blood washes off in the rain. His shadow stretches out, touching one person then the next."

The voices were changing. Betty's sounded younger, smoother; Cynthia's sounded drier, with a hint of wheezing. "I know where the rats live, too, healthy plump ones, oh yes -"

Don strode forward and slapped the mage once, twice, across each cheek. She opened her eyes, staring sightlessly up before collapsing into his arms, sobbing.

The old woman watched with interest, then carefully wrapped the remainder of the chocolate bar in a stained rag and tucked it deep inside her clothing. She lurched to her feet and cackled about flowers before striding off, her sack over one shoulder.

"Cyn! Are you all right?" demanded Tony, crouching beside the still-sobbing mage.

She shuddered, trying so desperately to force words that she was hiccuping incoherently.

Don drew his Smith & Wesson Bonebreaker and leveled it at the departing figure. "STOP!"

The old woman hesitated, then halted, her back still toward them. She didn't turn.

"My hands!" Cynthia's voice sounded peculiar, but no

longer crying. "I have *my* hands again!" She fell forwards and was violently ill.

Chopper looked on, surprised and curious. Don kept his gun trained on the motionless figure. Maretti passed the now-moaning sorceress a handkerchief, and their eyes met.

"It's okay," she rasped, wiping her mouth. Her voice was hoarse. "I'm Cynthia, dear."

Maretti took a step back in shock.

"GET BACK HERE, WOMAN!" called Don.

"She's swapped bodies!" hissed Chopper.

The shoulders rose, then fell, in a theatrical sigh before the bag lady turned back around, and stumped back toward them. Stopping a few feet from the big man with the gun, she looked him fearlessly in the eye. "Has Betty possessed Cynthia, so now poor Cynthia can sneak off with Betty's youthful body?" She poked a mocking thumb into her own chest. "A wonderful prize, eh?" She looked at Chopper. "Grow up, boy. You toxed or something?" She turned back to Don, whose gun lowered a millimeter. She jammed a scrawny finger into his chest, the bloody rat bag banging against his front. "*She* went snooping around in poor old Betty's skull. Slipping and sliding her long, long nose in. No stomach for the taste of rat, that's little Cynthia's problem, poor dear. Poor Cynthia."

She spat on the ground and stalked off.

Don's face set in hard lines.

"No, Don, don't," begged the mage, suddenly. "I'm all right. Just a little disoriented. 'Tated? 'Ted. Where's my bag?"

The three men stared at her.

"Right. Right. Joanne has the bags. Cynthia doesn't. I mean, me. *I* don't."

She stared at Maretti. "I don't feel so good, Tony. Take me away from here. This place is *terrible*." Sudden panic flashed in her eyes. "He comes out of the *manhole*! We've got to warn Wolf and Gadger!"

At that precise moment Maretti's commlink pulsed against his throat. Opening the channel, his expression turned grim as he listened to the implant. When he spoke, he chose not to sub-vocalize. "We've got news, too. But Cyn's suffering some weird after-effects from a Mindmeld.

Not sure she'll be much help, for a bit. But we can be there in five." He looked around. "We've got probs, people. Don – grab Cyn. We're moving out – now."

CHAPTER 41

Wolf, Gadger, and Raven had been left behind where they could view both the bikes' hiding place and the monitoring station, with instructions to check it out surreptitiously.

This area wasn't a part of the Hunters Point Dumps Leeth was really familiar with from her time last winter, after she'd abandoned the Department. She chewed her lip. Wondering if it had it been a mistake, going back to them?

She thought of all the people in the Dumps she'd come to know and respect. Would any of them recognize her if she bumped into them? What should she do, if she did? She was in disguise. It *should* be okay.

Off to the southeast, a seven-story tower leaned out toward the Bay. Shuddering, she remembered all the weird shit that had gone on in there, at the end.

Marc Disten, trying to force the cold, passionless *thing* hidden inside him, into her. Killing him. And shortly after, the black smoke coming off his body and trapping her *elsewhere*. Till Marcie rescued her. After she'd shattered *it* into a million pieces.

Gadger followed her gaze. "Corpsestick Tower. I wouldn't go there. Used to be an Uploader facility – 'til the Big One struck. They say copies of their Ghosts still run as sims in the net." He nodded toward it. "They also say their bodies are still trapped in their Upload pods, slowly mummifying or going moldy."

They are, thought Leeth, but aloud, she just grunted.

"A null-IFF chopper zipped in and out of there, late one night a couple months ago. 'Identification Friend or Foe'," he added, at her expression. "It was right around the time the Breaker murders ended. They say it was a secret R&D group, recapturing him after he'd escaped, and they're now breeding killers like him for the military."

Wolf met her eyes, just giving her his unreadable poker face. But somehow, she felt he was amused.

"Well, *I* have a hunch he's dead," she said, unable to let the ridiculous tale pass unchallenged. And also, a little annoyed people thought someone she'd killed was still alive.

"Oh? Women's intuition?" teased Gadger.

"Yep! Probably met the wrong girl, who ripped his heart out."

Gadger chuckled. "In his case, that'd be kind of poetic."

They turned back to the pollution station, studying its

layout from a distance. A chain-link fence turned it into a small compound, the monitoring equipment built into a man-high concrete structure. With the gate opened, a truck parked inside would be surrounded on three sides – on its left by the equipment itself, in front by a low guard rail, and on its right by a thigh-high cement slab with no obvious purpose.

Earlier, Cynthia had joined Wolf astrally to check the area Imaginally. Raven and Gadger had taken their own look, Gadger walking back to the car shaking his head.

"You know, I'd say if you wiped off the surface layer of ash, you'd find that gear is in *chrome* condition. Real chrome. But look at this place." His arm swung in an expansive gesture, taking in the tumbled buildings and windswept stretches of dirt between. Twisted, stunted weeds struggled for life between the crumbling slabs of former roads.

Wolf and Raven eyed the area, Wolf's expression sour, Raven's mystified.

Gadger raised his matte black optics to heaven. "Kudzu."

At their looks, he held up a finger, and moments later a small drone buzzed out of the car and up over their heads, quickly disappearing from sight. He palmed a holo projector, and they saw themselves from above, shrinking away as the drone ascended.

They stood near the center of what looked like a cancerous gray growth eating into the green mass trying to envelop the area generally. Almost exactly near the center. Gadger shook his head. "The soil and surfaces around here must be pretty poisonous to stop kudzu. And persistent, too, to hold it back for years." He shook his head. "Something doesn't add up."

Leeth heard the heavier whine of a high speed drone approaching. Her hand slapped to her waist, but found the hilt of her gun, not the slingshot she'd automatically reached for. *Idiot! You're not on the run anymore!*

From high overhead she heard an electrical crackle, and the hologram abruptly fuzzed and died.

"What the-?" Gadger, who'd started to turn toward her, stopped as his drone fell from the sky. A translucent shape with a darker, silvery core fell with it and fired a net.

Twenty meters or so above their heads the hard-to-see attack drone's engines surged in triumph, then skimmed off over the tops of the buildings, corkscrewing out of sight between them with Gadger's drone dangling and swaying beneath it.

"Crashdammit!" He shook a fist at the disappearing shapes. "That drone cost me eighty creds!"

Barney! Leeth thought. Somehow, she felt sure that had been Barney's work. *I guess once 'Sleena' stopped bringing him drones for scav, he built his own drone hunter. Good for you!* She sniggered, and Gadger spun to her, angry enough that she wiped the smile off her face.

No one spoke as they moved back to the car and resumed their position. Leeth sighed quietly, wondering how the young ogre was doing, wishing she could visit him. He'd probably grown. She hoped he and his dad, Teef, were doing well. Did any of them miss her? She realized she missed them. She grimaced. This kind of sucked: being so near, but also so far. Made up and dressed up to look so different, having to avoid them.

After this job's over, I'll make a point of coming back here to spend a few days with everyone. Mother and Father said you had to invest time to maintain your false identities. *Yeah, that's what I'll do!* Just the thought brought a small, private smile.

The three were sitting in the car simply watching the monitoring station, and had been for some time. Raven shifted her weight. "Why does Maretti want all *three* of us to wait here? I could be much more useful questioning the locals," she said through clenched teeth, slumped in the seat.

Wolf and Gadger exchanged a glance, then Gadger answered. "Uh. No one's going to hang around to *be* questioned if we march in all in one big group. On the other hand, it's not wise to split up too much. The Dumps aren't exactly a safe place to wander around alone."

The sunglasses stared back at him flatly.

"Look, we're all agreed there's something twisty about that station," he said, nodding in its general direction, "and Tony wants us to check it out. So, let's think things through. I'm not the only one who feels it's odd there just happens to be a manhole cover there, surely?"

They'd all noticed the manhole, though it looked like an ordinary access into the city's stormwater system.

"Did Cyn check it out?" Gadger asked Wolf.

"I'll go!" Raven offered.

"Wait! Not like that." Gadger stopped her before she could open the car door. "Wolf will check it out Imaginally."

Raven's impatience eased, watching with interest as Wolf shut his eyes and leaned back into the bench seat between her and Gadger. Suddenly his form went limp. It was eerie. His face fell utterly slack and expressionless, like a corpse's, yet his chest moved. She heard his breathing, even the beating of his heart, sounding quite normal.

"He's gone, hasn't he?" she whispered.

Gadger nodded, unconcerned, his gaze fixed on the distant monitoring station. Leeth's curiosity welled up. She knew about this, but had never seen any of the mages she'd grown up with actually *do* it. Certainly the Doctor never had. At least, not in her presence.

She wanted to know more. "Can he hear us?" she whispered.

Gadger laughed. "No! Sure, if his body was injured his spirit would be, too. Probably badly. But other than that... no. All his senses are with his spirit, out there." He inclined his head in the direction of the station.

She stared at the inert form between them, imagining the Doctor in that position. So vulnerable. Her hands tightened into fists. No wonder he'd never done it in front of her.

She made herself relax; then noticed Gadger watching her tensely, his posture protective and alert. She shut her eyes, cursing herself. She'd let the Raven persona slip *again*. Jaws still clenched, she opened her eyes and met Gadger's. He was obviously waiting for her to speak.

"I was seeing... someone else... there. Imagining someone else."

Gadger continued looking at her, steadily. "Someone you want dead." It was a statement, not a question. "A mage."

Her thoughts churned. To speak up, or keep silent and deal with her problem herself? But in the end, it wasn't her choice. Mental barriers locked down like missile-proof shutters. Bitterness at her own weakness welled up in her.

With a huge effort, she managed a bare nod.

He stared at her. "You want to talk about it?"

Yes, she did. Of its own accord, though, her head shook – left, right.

Gadger watched in amazement as her expression suddenly soured, making her face strangely ugly.

Leeth saw the reaction. It was too much. Wrenching open the car door she leaped out. She hated it! Hated him! The Doctor. That he could make her feel like a puppet in her own body, even when he wasn't there! She stood with her back to the car, trying to regain control, the louring gray skies and ash-muddied streets a perfect match to her mood. [1]

In the car, Wolf straightened and sat up. His eyes focused; first on Gadger, then the empty place beside him, then the woman standing a short distance away, fists clenched at her sides.

"What happened?"

Gadger slowly shook his head, staring at Raven. "I don't know. I really don't know."

Outside, Raven heard the words. *Come on, get it together*, she told herself. *You* know *he's conditioned you. One day you'll break it. And then he'll die.*

Through the open door of the car, Wolf was Percepting her. He spoke very quietly, just loud enough for Gadger to hear. He thought. "*Great* anger. Great bitterness. And something..."

Leeth heard the near-silent words and *forced* herself to let go of the anger. Yet again. Because of the Doctor, of course. His constant needling. That's what was doing it. Nothing else. *Well, I'm not going to let him get to me.* Lifting her chin she turned back to her companions. Both stared at her, Wolf's face as impassive as ever; but Gadger's expression, though equally serious, held concern.

"I'm all right." She waved the problem away and got back in the car. Both men drew subtly away from her, simultaneously amusing and annoying her. Ignoring it, she brought them all back to the matter at hand. "So, what did you find?"

Wolf frowned. "Nothing. Old stormwater tunnel. One end is sheared, taken down by the Big One. A collapsed building has closed the other end."

"Hmm." Gadger was frowning now, too. "Somehow I can't believe that manhole isn't significant."

Raven thought for a moment, imagining the darkened, abandoned tunnel. "What about side passages? Or concealed entrances into the tunnel?"

Wolf's frown deepened. "You cannot tap walls, or measure things, in the spirit realm." He fell silent, staring at her. It was hard to say; but for a moment, she thought she saw reluctance in his expression. She felt cold, like a cloud had just blocked the sun.

He said nothing. But once more he leaned back, his body falling inert.

Raven cocked her head questioningly to one side, as she looked at Gadger. "What's he doing now?"

Gadger frowned. "Well-l, he *can* check for secret passages quite simply, actually. You see, a spirit can ghost through solid objects as though they're simple darkness – *provided* the object isn't living, or once living, like wood. Or soil, water; stone. Just like they can't move through a living human being. What *is* odd, though, is that Wolf didn't think to do that-

"SHIT!"

Wolf's body lurched back, blood welling through his shirt. Raven, startled, stared, not comprehending. Again his body lurched – forward this time, as if taking an injury in the back. Gadger was cursing and tearing at the medkit on the shelf under the dash. But even as he took out the spray-on bandage, Wolf's eyes opened, his teeth closed tightly on the pain.

His eyes were steady, however. Steady but angry.

"Earth elemental," he explained tersely. "Guarding. It came through the ground, after I found a second tunnel. I was able to Banish it." He fingered his charms and began muttering to himself, syllables that made no sense. Raven drew back as the shaman's face changed, his nose elongating into a lupine snout, a ghostly fuzz of hair sprouting to surround his face. His eyes yellowed and his ears stretched back. Yet through all that, she could somehow still see the stern and dignified face of the man. She looked at Gadger in confusion.

"It's okay," he murmured. "It's his Totem spirit."

Gradually, Wolf's rigid tension eased. Leeth realized he was healing himself magically. Like the Doctor used to heal her, after he-. She cut the thought off. It was unproductive.

Gadger put the kit away, now speaking on the scrambled commlink to the others. "Wolf's just been injured, but he's healing himself. He was scouting Imaginally, found a second tunnel, and encountered and silenced a guard. I suggest you all meet us here."

Maretti responded, Gadger's forehead crumpling in a deep frown before he shared the news. "Cyn's, uh... some weird after-effects from a Mindmeld. Maybe not up for much, magically." He looked worried.

Within a minute, Wolf had recovered. The strange shift in his features simply faded as though it had never been.

Raven gripped his forearm. "So there *is* something there. Will they know the Elemental has been Banished?" she asked, her expression pinched.

Wolf shook his head. "Inorganic beings – elementals – are strange things. Rarely, rarely do their desires make sense to human beings. Nor ours to them. I am told they are very difficult to direct; confused by too many instructions. It would be foolish to try to make it understand our concept of time, and have it report back regularly to its invoker. Nor can it do so now I have Banished it. So the mage can only know it is gone by checking in person. Imaginally."

"Except we don't know his contact schedule," finished Gadger.

Wolf inclined his head in agreement.

"So basically, we have no idea how long we've got before the invoker of that guard learns it's gone?" asked Raven.

Wolf nodded.

"So now what? Do we have time to wait for the others?" she asked.

"I will go back in. Follow the other tunnel."

"Hey, hold on," Gadger said. "If there was one imaginal guard, there'll probably be others. You *need* imaginal support. Wait for Cyn."

Wolf considered that, then shrugged. "Cynthia does not function so well in combat, and combat is the only way a second mage could help. You said she has been 'affected' by a Mindmeld." He shook his head. "The spirit plane is not a place for someone confused. If I am killed, she can try to heal me. But if we both are killed, there will be none to heal us. I will go now."

Leaning back into the seat, he closed his eyes; then opened them again. "But tell Cynthia: there was something wrong with the elemental. It..." he gestured futilely, groping for words. "It was Wrong," he said at last.

Leeth frowned, a weird feeling prickling up her spine.

CHAPTER 42

Pausing outside his body, Wolf read concern in the auras of Gadger and Raven, then thought himself to the monitoring station above the manhole, descending through it to the stormwater tunnel beneath.

It stretched away before and behind him like the gullet of some giant beast.

With a hint of anger, he bound the image and pushed it away. Sliding forward a short distance, he braced himself above the room where the elemental had attacked, and sank through the tunnel's concrete floor.

Empty now.

Percepting, he felt a disorientating wave of depression. Was this the unexpected heaviness that had made things seem Wrong? A feeling rolled through him. In the flesh it would have raised goosebumps. As a spirit, it swept over him without resistance, rippling his astral form uncomfortably. He steeled his nerves, ignoring it, and cautiously opened himself, reaching out with his senses.

The idea of metal and struts formed. Centering himself and concentrating, the impression resolved into a metal ladder set in the wall, under the manhole he'd descended through. He widened his perceptions. A room like a cage, with a strong barrier − a heavy security grille for one wall. A path... steps leading down, beyond the grille. A box on the floor?

He moved closer, and as he did, resolved a feeling coming from what must be a symbol on the floor: danger. Stealthy danger. He moved closer, letting impressions coalesce... a biohazard symbol, he guessed.

It increased his feeling of unease. His mind sent the signal to make adrenaline. If he were in his body now, his heart would be hammering. Instead, his astral form *tightened* uncomfortably.

The box? He eased closer to it. Probably big enough to hold a man. He sensed wheels. A trolley, or cart. And tracks, a pair of − railroad? − tracks leading from it to the grille, then under it. Taking one last look, he sensed watchfulness radiating from a security camera up near the manhole in the ceiling, and drifted up to examine it as best he could.

Nothing unusual.

Ignoring it, knowing he couldn't be seen by any merely

material watcher, he moved to the bars of the security grille. Very strong bars, he felt. It formed a pair of double doors.

He frowned.

A bad place to be trapped, if armed people were waiting. Moving through the bars, he glided down a flight of stairs beyond. Beside the narrow ramp for the trolley, the stairs spread out until they stretched the full width of the room beneath the manhole.

A long corridor led off, well-lit on the material plane. Still darker than expected here, though. And sloping gently down.

Sloping down? A wave of cold washed through him. There was no 'up' or 'down' in the spirit world. No gravity. How could this tunnel be sloping down? But the end of the corridor was pulling him down. He would swear it.

He hesitated. Perhaps he should go back?

His spirit dimmed, then flared brighter as he gathered his courage and moved forward. But traveling slowly now. Percepting carefully. He 'Saw' the next security camera. And continued on to the next.

He paused. How far had he come? Was something behind him? He spun around, but found nothing there, the room he'd come from now lost to his senses. He turned back and continued down the corridor. Was his body sweating for him, its pulse racing? He kept on.

Another security camera, and below it another of the symbols he'd seen in the room. This one on the wall, and larger. Stronger danger, it warned. He moved on. At the end of the corridor, something darker waited, unmoving. He advanced on it.

The corridor bent to the right. It didn't end here, just turned to the right. And in the corner stood... a mechanism... death... length, explosion... He concentrated. A mounted machine gun. Large. Pointed down the corridor. A great deal of belted ammunition. And a watching device attached. Sensors, he was sure. A bad place....

He followed the passage past the gun emplacement. It widened, the feeling now that of an old subway tunnel – a welcome relief. Then he noticed the walls here were native rock. He drew away from the natural barrier, his mood darkening further. That perfect shielding against imaginal and magical intrusion spoke to him of human planning, not chance. Something warned him a death-walk lay at the end of this.

He followed the smaller tracks of the trolley down the passage. The air was strangely empty. No spirits swam in the imaginal sea here. Even the motes of tiny life forms seemed cowed, hiding in shadows. A handful of overly patient spiders had waited too long, for food that never came. Now lacking the energy to leave, they crouched, stranded in this still, drained corridor, dying slow deaths.

An omen?

He forced himself on. Ahead, the large passage ended in a jumble of rock and earth. A smaller tunnel forked off, curving gently to the left, ending in a door. At the start of the bend lurked another machine gun emplacement. Ignoring it, he moved down the tunnel.

It ended in a door, quite large. Solid wood, strong wood – oak. Dead wood, a stark symbol inscribed on it. It felt like some kind of name.

He sank to the ground, floating horizontally, hesitating before passing under the door. Wouldn't someone careful enough to bore a tunnel through natural stone and install an oaken door have known of mages able to thin themselves enough to slip under? It reeked of trap.

He should update the others before continuing.

A second later, he was sitting up in the car, Gadger and Raven leaning forward to hear his news. His brief description brought frowns to their faces, too.

"Sounds sneaky," Raven said. "And you wouldn't be able to raise much of a spirit in a dead place like this, right? To scout for you, I mean."

"That is true," Wolf agreed.

He could see Raven's aura, impatient and alive. Straining forward like a hound eager for the hunt. The black band across her eyes stared at him. "Well? What are you waiting for? Since there'll obviously be a trap, be sure to take it slow and careful."

Gadger opened his mouth to protest, but Wolf reminded himself he *had* only returned to update them. He slumped back in his seat.

Back at the door, once more hovering at floor level, he *con-*

densed himself, sinking partly into the poured concrete of the floor, and moved forward. The wood of the door sill above plucked at him like a sky filled with clutching thorns. Below stretched the man-made floor, a leaden sea. He ghosted forward, dead brambles clawing at his back, their draining numbness calling him to join them, to stop struggling. To die. He pulled himself tighter and held to his purpose.

A timeless agony later it ended. Uncurling, he stretched in joyful relief and moved forward. Instantly, a carpet of wooden barbs pierced his back. Jerking down and away, he plunged instead into a microscopic army scouring a frozen realm for scraps of food. For a moment he hung, crucified, dismayed by the trap. He'd been lured into natural rock, stuck like a fly in a web by its minute ecology. With a wordless cry he willed himself backward, 'up'. Tiny microbes tore at him.

But he would *not* retreat.

Spreading his astral body like a sheet, he inched forward, sliding between the pricking burrs of dead wood at his back and the far more dangerous matrix of the rock below. Each tiny amoeba or bacterium, each living cell of fungus, an impassable barrier to his spirit form.

Steeling himself, angry now, he struggled on, more determined than ever.

CHAPTER 43

"I just felt Wolf kind of quiver," Raven said. "How long do these astral scouting expeditions normally take? Don't spirits moved at the speed of thought?"

Gadger turned from the window, noting Raven's hand draped on the shaman's denim clad thigh. He frowned. "You gotta be patient, Raven. He's only been a minute. Astral bodies *move* fast, but they still sense and think at normal speeds."

"I guess." But she looked unhappy, her lips curling back from her teeth. "I hope he's alright."

-

Bursting free from under the door into the oppressive corridor felt like paradise. Spinning around, Wolf dived and rolled in blessed relief, like a dolphin in water. Quickly he settled. *That* had been bad. A twisted, cruel trick. Slow anger burned as he moved back toward the oaken door with the carved symbol. Subjectively the attempt felt like it had taken an hour, but it had probably been less than a minute.

At the foot of the door he stretched out a spirit hand and felt a bar or shelf of wood attached, raised a little above the floor. He almost admired the trap's elegance.

Sinking below the floor, cautiously, he pulled back quickly as he met more living rock below, under a handspan of concrete. The ceiling, too, was the same. Left, then? On a sudden impulse he checked the other tunnel walls first, avoiding only the wall with the door. Living rock on all sides. So the concrete-lined tunnel, too, would be a trap if he was attacked imaginally. He wasn't sure the thickness of dead cement would be enough to conceal him if he tried to hide.

A layer of man-made rock to lure you in, blinded, to the ensnaring natural stone beneath. He shuddered at the thought of plunging into that at speed.

He moved by feel through the dark tunnel. The bad feeling grew, but that could be mere imagination. At the end he came to another door. Feeling it, he sensed neither wood nor stone. But some instinct warned against going through it. Once more sinking to the floor, he attenuated himself and moved, with extreme caution now, beneath it.

This place was designed to kill.

With a wordless cry he eased out, coalescing into the room beyond the door. Caution froze him motionless as he gathered his will while opening himself to his surroundings. The space felt large. Possibly once an underground carpark. Just to his right, against the wall, rested something long... a large cylindrical capsule. He moved to it, determined, and sensed again the symbol inscribed on its surface that warned of danger. The capsule was more than man sized, and made of metal.

At that moment an earth elemental emerged from the middle of the wall to his right. It was lumpy, and moved like thick dark lava. Glowing coal eyes fastened on him, then sank into the wall. Back into the natural stone, where he could not follow.

Burning forests! He had to decide: return to his body, and give warning? Or try to learn a little more?

At a sudden pain, as if something clamped tight on the silvery cord connecting his spirit to his body, he flashed back to the oak door. To find the shelf of wood pressed down flush against the floor, closing the gap. Sealing him in.

Now he *needed* to learn more: unless he found a way back to his body within the hour, he would die here.

Darting across to the middle of the carpark he passed a metal bin squatting on the open expanse of cement. A series of large, ethereal hemispheres extended up to the ceiling, glowing from hermetic circles inscribed in the cement floor. Elemental invocation?

Still searching for a way out, he sped to the ramp leading down to the next level, only to find it completely enclosed by a large Ward. Through the floor, perhaps?

A change in the light behind made him throw himself forward and to one side as an arm like lava lashed into the space he'd just occupied. He spun, and the elemental was on him.

But he'd left his back unprotected. The feeling stretched out behind him like a lengthening shadow.

The spirit struck at him again, but he flung himself aside, lashing out in turn. The impact was satisfying, solid, but left a bitter taste. His opponent flowed, its arms stretching out around him. *Bitter?*

But perhaps through it, a way to escape. He retreated to

the oak door, drawing the elemental with him. With it at his back he spun to face it, accepting its burning embrace to strike at its center. *He* might be astral, but the elemental had physically manifested. It stiffened, hardening and releasing another wash of bitter flavor. He felt the wood at his back groan and bend backwards as its mass pressed around him.

Glowing stone arms wrapped him, compressing him in burning pain as wood charred. He flowed, sliding from its grip, reforming beside it, projecting defiance. Two burning clubs of stone raised, smashing down.

Jerking aside, he felt wood splinter. *Yes!* He slammed his head forward into the elemental.

It froze, its limbs still squeezing, squid-like, as cracks radiated outwards. Then it shattered, shrinking and imploding into a central point to vanish. For a moment, it had looked like it was falling into some kind of hole....

He stared at the vanishing point in disbelief.

What was going on here?

But he'd run out of time. Human figures closed on him across the underground chamber, emerging from what must have been an elevator in the corner. Wearing uniforms, he felt, and carrying weapons. As long as he stayed out of their reach – a trivial feat – they could do nothing against him. And now, he had a freshly-made escape route behind him.

His relief was tempered by the realization that the man at their back was a mage, watching him. And he still tasted bitterness. Bitterness? That made no sense.

The feeling of something wrong, something bad, thickened. Imminent. He spun around, but no one stood behind him. Only the feeling that something had entered the room with the men – something he couldn't see.

Could something exist *invisibly* in imaginal space?

He watched, assessing the mage, ready to leave, but until then, gathering information. Astrally, he could flee at the speed of thought.

The guards continued spreading out across the room, but he ignored the pointless activity. They could neither see him nor feel him, and their projectile weapons were useless against a spirit.

One man stayed with the tall, thin mage, radiating

anger and the determination to kill the intruder. Something about that aura felt familiar.

The mage's emotions barely registered: interest; confidence; even amusement? He wore two spell loops, a symphony of imaginal patterns flowing through them and into a pair of spells cocooning him.

One of the guards had wandered near. Wolf automatically drifted aside to let him fumble past. Strangely, the man carried no weapon.

But the guard's aura abruptly inverted into absolute blackness as it turned to face him. Leaping forward, it struck.

Desperately, he parried, but the contact stabbed with a sickening shock of cold pain, followed instantly by a wave of disorientation. He tried to spin away, *away*, even as he realized his mind had *separated* from his spirit. He struggled to hold mind and spirit together.

What had the man *done*? He was a mundane, no mage! And how could an aura *change* like that? What did a black aura even mean? Auras *glowed*.

He found himself near the ceiling, across the room. Below, the mundane figure stood, a man-shaped hole in reality. Its head pivoted, then it moved quickly toward him. A second 'mundane' figure had also changed, its aura streaked in black shadows and also closing on him. He moved aside, but both figures turned, following. He no longer felt the wrongness, overwhelmed by the impossible dislocation of mind from spirit, but he knew, somehow, it still lurked, filling the room.

The mage smiled. Their eyes met, and the man gestured, shaping imaginal patterns at blinding speed – far faster than should have been possible – magnifying it with his desires and hurling it at him.

In the moment the spell took to cross the space between them, he recognized a binding pattern, the sort sorcerers used in their compacts with elementals. Stupid. He was not a thing from those realms.

Again disorientation, this time far worse. Confused, hesitant, he went to the mage. A thought brought him before the man, ready to offer-

The man smiled. Something in that cool, smug certainty woke a horror that surged up, cracking the alien feelings into ice that fell away.

He'd been Bound! But now he was free.

With a snarl, he leaped at the only thing vulnerable to his attack – the nearest of the man's two spell loops – tearing its flimsy imaginal form apart, snuffing the spell tied to it.

Now the mage wasn't smiling. *Now* he moved at merely human speed.

But angry. A moment later Wolf saw the parting of the man's spirit from his fleshly body, the man throwing himself onto the imaginal plane without even taking the time to lay his physical shell on the floor.

Wolf struck immediately, knowing the black aura humans must be almost on him, knowing he had to leave, but knowing the mage was most vulnerable now.

But the man's astral arm caught the blow, somehow, even hampered as he was by his now-collapsing physical body. The mage turned his strike aside, reversing it back against Wolf, who felt something tear.

He fled.

Thinned out flat inside the floor, trying to stay hidden within the concealing dark of the cement but just clear of the natural stone beneath it, he flew, angling back to the elemental-shattered oak door, the mage close behind. The armed men would be pounding in physical pursuit. Time slowed to a crawl as he forced himself back along his path, wood tearing and clawing at his astral body as he squeezed through the jagged hole in the oak door.

Clenching his will, he accelerated. *This is not my day to die.*

He fled, the mage in close pursuit.

CHAPTER 44

Wolf could feel the life draining from his physical body, bleeding from the injuries to his astral one.

The moment he shot from the manhole, he sensed his friends. Plunging back down into the concrete rubble for cover, he darted through it and then up from below, into the car. Gadger and Raven still sat in the front, but his body now lay on the back seat while Cynthia crouched awkwardly over it, struggling to channel a healing spell through him.

But even as he rejoined his physical body, he was hunting for a way they might escape without the mage tracking them.

He saw none.

Wolf opened his eyes to Cynthia's face focused in grim concentration above him, healing him. Gadger and Raven leaned over the front seat, vibrating with tension. He spoke from where he lay. Davo too was there, scanning the area around them.

"Trouble. Strong mage, outside, imaginally hunting me."

"Shit! What do we do – drive off?" demanded Gadger.

"Moving will draw his attention. He hasn't seen us yet."

"Was he alone?" asked Raven.

"There were... men, in the complex. They could be here in minutes, but without vehicles."

"The others are only a minute away, at the edge of the kudzu," Davo offered.

Wolf broke radio silence. "I am back. Cyn heals me now. I defeated another elemental but reinforcements are on their way. A strong mage is nearby, astral, hunting me."

Raven activated her Link's trans-scrambler.

Maretti's voice. "How many? Should we make a stand?"

"They fielded five people and a mage," Wolf said, "very quickly after being warned by the elemental. Two of the five appeared mundane, but unlike anything I have seen before. The mage... the mage bested me imaginally. Easily. I cannot say what other forces they have."

There was no response from the commlink for a moment, while Maretti thought. "He's still looking for you?"

"Yes."

"And he'll be able to tag along, following imaginally, if he sees anyone leaving?"

"Yes."

"But you can't stay there, unless we want to dive into a full scale firefight. We'll *have* to run. How about-"

Maretti's words were swallowed as the car's interior suddenly exploded in flames. Hair burning, eyes clenched shut, they all dove for the doors – all bar Raven. Cynthia screamed. Wolf turned back, preparing to Banish it, Maretti still shouting over the commlink-

-and the fire elemental vanished as suddenly as it had come.

Gadger and Davo's momentum carried them stumbling from the car as Cyn and Wolf, from opposite sides, percepted its interior.

Inside, Raven knelt on the front seat radiating anger and satisfaction.

"- status! What happened? STATUS!"

"Where is the bastard?" demanded Raven, *stalking* from the car and slapping at her smoldering hair. "And what's the biggest fragging spirit you can invoke, Wolf? Let's change the odds."

Davo looked dazed.

Gadger was speaking to Maretti. "The bastard hit us with a fire elemental in the car, but it's gone, now, banished."

Wolf, slapping at his coat, cast his gaze to the imaginal. He sensed the mage floating above Raven, focused intently down on her. "Directly above you. Two meters."

He considered Raven's second question. How large a spirit? He felt good, he realized. Cynthia must have completed her healing just before the attack. But here, in this dead area? Still, he would try. He was about to start the summoning when the imaginal mage abruptly jumped away from the woman he floated over. Wolf turned to Raven, who crouched as if to spring.

"Wait. He's moved away. Behind you and up another five meters."

Leeth spun around, squinting roughly in the direction Wolf indicated, furious. Behind her, she heard him grunt. Growling, she turned back to the shaman who struggled as if hauling on a snagged fishing line. She reached out and grabbed his arms to help.

"Hngh!" Wolf shuddered and stepped back. "About *this* size." He sounded surprised but pleased.

The shaman's arms stretched wide as he called the spirit to him.

Davo stood protectively by Cyn's side, weapon drawn and eyes on the pollution station. Cynthia, Percepting like Wolf, saw the mage study Raven, size up the spirit welling out onto the imaginal plane, and abruptly speed off. She put a hand to her throat, activated the radio.

"He's gone."

Raven spun around, livid. "What do you mean, *gone*?"

Cynthia took a step back, then forced herself to face the younger woman. "He's run away. Do you have a problem with that?"

Cynthia, still Percepting, saw the anger melt away, transforming into approval.

"Okay. I guess that's good."

"Right, people, pull out," Maretti said. "Did Wolf get his spirit, Gadger?"

Gadger raised an eyebrow to Cynthia.

"He's just finished instructing it, by the looks."

Wolf looked drained. "It has agreed to attack any who it senses trailing us."

"Okay, better stay together, then. Now, let's *move*."

They stopped a few blocks from their headquarters while the two mages scouted imaginally to check they hadn't been followed. They were gone for a long time while the others guarded their still bodies.

Wolf was first to stir. He opened his eyes, staring heavily into space, then shut them once again. His body slumped vacant a second time. A little later, he stirred and rose, saying nothing. Just stood, silent. The others shifted uneasily, not willing to interrupt.

Wolf seemed to be watching something on the imaginal plane nearby. His head moved, following the thing. At last his gaze tracked across to Cynthia's limp form, just before she stirred and sat up.

Raven, following his gaze and imagining some creepy possessing spirit entering Cynthia, drew her gun and trained it on the sorceress.

"It's clear," declared Wolf.

Cynthia was frowning, staring at the shaman.

Maretti gestured for Raven to put her gun away, then looked from one to the other. "But?"

The two mages exchanged a look. It was Wolf who answered. Reluctantly. "Something has happened to me. To my imaginal body. It is smaller."

"What do you mean, smaller? How can it be *smaller*?"

"I do not know. I do not know how auras can be black. I do not know how auras can change on an instant. I do not know how mundanes could hurt me as they did. And I do not know how one mage can almost Bind another."

Maretti stared at the two mages, reading the deep worry. Or was that *fear?* "Come on. I need to hear the full story."

Back in their headquarters, Wolf finished recounting his tale.

"So, when did you notice you'd shrunk?" asked Chopper.

Wolf stared at him.

Cynthia answered for him. "Not until we both went imaginal just now. The weird thing was, it doesn't seem to have affected him in any way. I stayed imaginal to watch him return to his body, but his spirit seemed to enlarge as it re-entered. And shrank again when he left it."

"So, was it the black thing, or the mage who tried to bind you, that did that?" asked Davo.

Wolf stared into space. "I do not know." He shut his eyes. "I do not know."

They were all silent for some time. It lasted until Maretti started sharing what *they'd* learned, handing the narrative over to Cynthia when he came to the Mindmeld.

"Oh, and thanks for Banishing the fire elemental in the car, Wolf," she added.

He frowned. "I did not."

Gadger looked from one to the other. All three turned to Raven.

Chit, she thought. *Stay cool.*

The sunglasses stared blackly back at them. Raven shrugged. "I swiped at it. I was pretty angry. Maybe that did it?"

The two mages looked at her thoughtfully, neither speaking. Cynthia's eyes began to flick back and forth across Raven like there were flies buzzing around her. *Reading my aura*, she guessed, thankful she'd basically told them the truth.

"It's possible. Fundamentally, you attack spirits with the force of your will."

Raven changed the subject. "Wolf, what did you mean when you said the aura of one of the men with the mage seemed familiar? Do you mean the *kind* of aura was something you'd seen before, or you recognized *him*?"

"Him. He seemed familiar."

CHAPTER 45

Colonel Aaron Bragg, still fuming, paced the length of the conference table in the underground room. Stockily built, with thin lips and gray eyes, his buzz-cut graying hair stood up like a visible echo of his rage. "A *Wolf* shaman? I don't fucking believe it! Describe the others."

The other man present, the tall and thin Dr Callahan Scott, faced him squarely. His expression had returned to its usual calm superiority as he continued his description of the intruders. "Another Unfolded, female – but a mage, not a shaman. A small man, late middle age, cybered, mostly headware – eye replacements, internal things. A male, early thirties, face scarred, competent. And a young woman with no cyberware. I sense it was she who dismissed the fire elemental, though she appeared mundane, not Unfolded."

"The Fist of goddamn Peace. I don't know who the young bitch is, but I swear, it's the streetscum Fist of Peace."

"Which means?"

"Which means," said the sour-faced colonel, taking a grip on his anger, "that we suddenly have a group of something like ten people, each skilled in their own fucking way, all trying hard now to find out what's going on here. Pity you didn't nail the bastard when you had the chance."

"Regrettable, I agree, though he was *very* fortunate to escape. But in the end, security is your affair. And as I have said before, it is unacceptable that I should need to risk myself in defense of the installation. If I were to die doing so, it would end the entire project."

"If you'd let us put up the Wards we'd wanted -"

"That's enough. If and when a Ward can be used without interfering with Project Clarity, I will inform you. What *does* concern me is how he bested the elemental on level one. How powerful is this shaman?"

Bragg frowned. "My information is two years old. He was good, but not exceptional – look, that giant elemental up on level one would have been able to keep *you* out, you said. Yet Wolf gets in and trashes both it and then the one in the tunnel without taking a scratch. How could he do that?"

"The Wolf shaman is named 'Wolf'? How original. Nevertheless...." While he thought, the others waited, not speaking. "There was another mage at their car, a female. But our outer guardian elemental was magnitude seventeen." Scott stated his remarkable achievement matter-of-factly, without pride. "That's far beyond the capacity of even a pair of mages to survive. They couldn't have scratched it. But if the female mage had knocked mine down to magnitude ten or eleven by first throwing a substantial elemental at it, the two together could have beaten it; and the tunnel guard after it. Perhaps the female retreated, injured. She could have healed herself and the shaman's body as he continued on astrally, alone."

"Yeah, the shaman I know was that damned determined," agreed Bragg. "You said he ruined your reaction-boost spell loop? They also cost us the only fire elemental we had. As Head of Security, I have to inform you the installation is now *highly* vulnerable to magical penetration."

The mage thought for a while. "Bring up a map of the complex."

It required only a thought, converted into digital signals and transmitted to the ever-patient security system, for the Colonel to oblige with a holographic projection floating in the air between them.

"There's only one way in. Let's simplify. Fortify, instead of trying to trap and kill astral intruders." He indicated the wooden block fixed to the bottom the outermost door. "Lower that to close the gap."

Bragg frowned, but nodded.

"Good. Now tell me about the Fist of Peace."

"Let me grab some data." Bragg fired off his query but kept the neural link open. "While we're waiting, I'll give you an overview from memory – but it'll be two years old. Leader was Jacob Anderson, a real pain. I killed him, back then. I thought that'd end the sons of bitches. I'm amazed they're still functioning. He was the tactician and heart of the group. Anderson would have done everything in his power to end Clarity if he'd known of it." He shook his head. "I have no idea how persistent they still are.

"Right hand man was a guy called Maretti. Fond of short-cuts. Two mages in the group, the Wolf shaman you've met, and a bleeding-heart ex-corporate sorceress, Cynthia something-or-other. They have a hotshot hacker who's your classic screw-the-system bit-head prick, and an old guy who's unpleasantly good with electronics. Specializes in security systems. The rest are basically samurai, some cyberware."

He shut his eyes as the results of his earlier query reached his visual cortex. "Hang on. Well, well, well," he declared, suddenly looking much more relaxed. "*Maretti's* the leader." His smile was vicious. "Okay, take a look," he said, re-directing the data.

The desk comp's holographic unit threw up a flat image of Tony Valencio Maretti, complete with accompanying textual biography.

"Let's go through this quickly. The sooner we can get our defenses back on line, the happier I'll be."

Bragg ran succinctly through the other members of the Fist of Peace.

"You have no information on the girl."

Bragg shrugged. "New member? The most recent information in here is... let's see, Cynthia Wallen's sighting two months ago in Ingleside."

Scott looked dissatisfied. "The girl appeared mundane, but dismissed my fire elemental in a moment. I would like to study her."

Bragg spread his hands. "Maybe she's new to the group? I can't summon intel from thin air. I'll put eyes to the ground. Or are you saying you want to make her a target for our next sweep – that you want her for Project Clarity?"

Scott thought. "Yes. But that's not a high priority now we've been discovered. Your recommendations, then? I'm confident we could shift to the next phase, and head to a more... controlled environment."

"Well, you say Schenk showed himself to be pretty capable against the shaman. Damaged him. And we can get a delivery here in two hours." Bragg thought. "Hmm. I think we can patch up the situation here, in the short term. "They *will* try to learn more. If they find anything, at the absolute minimum they'll go public with the information. And since the genome edits Ford ordered from Bio-Block break the Moratorium, that'd screw you, me, Weatherburn, and the whole damn country."

"I would still like to know *who* intercepted our delivery."

Bragg shrugged. "Probably the Fist of Peace. Either way, they're the problem right now. They *won't* let the matter drop. I recommend we start relocation procedures – if you think you can get the General's okay."

The mage nodded.

"We'll have to terminate the Fist of Peace, though," Bragg warned him. "Let's say, lure them in here after relocation and collapse it on top of them. Make it appear deserted. Except for some abandoned test animals, locked in cages and starving to death." He nodded to himself. "Yeah. They'd go for that. Maybe you could get the General to authorize leaving one or both of the Battledroids on level one, too. Wolf won't have recognized *them* from his imaginal snooping. Let's see how they cope with an X-ray laser. The droids can even be dug out, later – *they'll* survive an explosion and cave-in. Say, two days to set it up and move out."

"I will contact Weatherburn," Scott said.

"You know, it might actually be easier for us if Wolf *did* recognize me. It'd give them that extra incentive."

Bragg's smile could only be described as... *wolfish*.

CHAPTER 46

"You sure you can't remember who the angry guy reminded you of?" asked Maretti.

Wolf shook his head. "No."

Maretti sighed. "Ah well. Let's look at what we've got: a heavily defended secret installation under the Dumps, a bunch of disappearances, and a madwoman's dream vision – this 'soul twister'. Was Mad Betty Unfolded, Cyn?"

The mage winced. "I – maybe. She didn't have a normal aura. But not one you could say was magical, either. Maybe, oh, more diffuse? Open. But *she* was certain she could see the future."

"The trouble is, we just don't know enough!" Maretti turned to the thin man still hunched over his cyberdeck at the far end of the room and raised his voice. "Wiz! You got anything for us yet?"

For a few seconds there was no response. Then slowly, as though remembering how, the hacker straightened, leaning back in his chair and swiveling to face the rest of the group. Blinking several times, his eyes at last focused on them.

"A little." He picked up his comp, holding it tenderly against his front as he sauntered over to the scarred conference table. Draping himself in a chair, he hooked one leg over its arm. "Interesting. Point one: the company that contracts to the Department of Waste and Pollution is called Tanner Services. Getting that much was triv. Two: Tanner Services went from filing tax returns of around a hundred thou three years ago, to none for a year, to five thou after that. Three: five thou is exactly the value of their annual contract with the pollution heads. So far, no risk – just passed myself off as a Tanner accounting prog making enquiries. I got their address, by the way. Maybe someone should check the place out on foot.

"Anyway, I did a little raid on Tanner's comps just on the off-chance. Which is where it gets interesting. They *are* on the net, and they're light on security. Personnel, just two. But, point four – the personnel are fake. The CIDs don't check out. Point five – after I dumped their files onto my comp, I took the usual precautions. And got a checksum error – oldest safeguard in the book. A nasty little virus had come in with the data I'd dumped. So, I dissected and analyzed it carefully. *Very* chrome, very tight. All it would have done was calculate my physical location and zap a 'Here I am' note to a particular dropbox on the net. Got *that* address, too. So, Tanner Services looks like a cover, and a sneaky little trap."

"Could it have just been someone being enthusiastic and buying a high-quality piece of protection?" asked Davo.

Wiz shook his head. "Nope. It wasn't protection – it was just something so they could *physically* track you down – i.e., *take* you down in meatspace. Plus, it didn't fit with the rest of their cheap-ass setup. That virus would have cost more than their yearly contract."

"I can check their office out tonight, if you like," offered Davo. "If Cyn can make me up like she did last time we were worried about cameras." His scarred face twisted into a fierce grin. "I swear, my own mother wouldn't have recognized me."

Chopper snorted. "Your own mother wouldn't recognize you even *without* the disguise!"

"At least I know who mine *is*!" Davo retorted.

Raven's flat voice cut in. "Boys."

They both looked at her. The shades seemed blankly menacing. "I don't think Wiz had finished."

Wiz raised one eyebrow at her. "Very perceptive, Raven."

Davo and Chopper settled for glaring at one another across the conference table as Raven stared blandly back at Wiz. "Maretti asked you to find out about the truck, and how long the station had been there. I hope you did?" She hoped he *hadn't:* something about the hacker annoyed her.

He smiled back at her. "Of course."

Rats, thought Leeth.

"The truck visits at three-weekly intervals, with an apparently random variation of two or three days. Apparently. In fact, they're just using an off-the-shelf pseudo random number generator, and they seeded it with *zero*!"

He looked around at their blank expressions.

"Anyway, I predict the next visit will be the day after tomorrow – unless Wolf's really stirred things up. They also seem to have the occasional truly random visit. Last year, for instance, they took nineteen recordings, not fourteen like I'd expect."

And two days ago, thought Leeth, *Maretti saw a truck taking readings*. Which would make it four days between visits, not three weeks. Hmm. So Maretti couldn't have predicted that visit. Unless they'd *told* him? But her instincts were telling her he was genuinely angry and frustrated. *Ohh. He* does *have hunches, like I do!* For some reason, the thought warmed her.

Maybe Wiz was the traitor? She hoped so. But really, she was no closer to finding him or her. Or them.

And how would she even know if they sold data they'd supposedly destroyed? She had to rely on Nelson to sniff that out, and she wouldn't put it past that creepy little tud to keep quiet even if he did uncover something, just to keep her on the mission longer and away from him. Probably hoping she'd blow her cover.

"Also interesting is the Station itself," Wiz said. "The *original* ones were erected in '55. But two and a half years ago this one was moved to its present location."

"Moved?" Val exclaimed. "Who bothers to *move* a pollution checker?"

"Three years ago," Don said, "Tanner Services went into decline. The next year they got the contract. The same time the station was relocated?"

Wiz looked momentarily thrown. He frowned briefly, unlimbered his comp and jacked in – paranoid about wireless taps by nameless government agencies – to check the records he'd downloaded. "The contract with the Department of Waste commenced on September 23rd, in '59. The monitoring point was moved on the 24th and 25th of September, '59. By Tanner Services."

Val whistled. "Yeah!"

Wiz's fingers drummed on the table as he waited. "Ah. Found some news from the period. *Every day* for the first three weeks of that September, that part of Hunters Point was Red Level pollution. Composition included some form of nerve toxin. The whole area had to be evacuated. Twenty-six people died! *That's* why they moved the station. They moved it into the center of the affected area."

"What was the explanation for the nerve gas?" demanded Cynthia. "Who was responsible for it?"

"Never determined. Despite outrage and subsequent investigations."

Maretti broke the ensuing silence. "Let me run this scenario by you: let's say you've found a site for your... project, whatever it is. For some reason, the site's in Hunters Point, just on the edge of the Dumps, where trucks can still reach the area – an area that's maybe also a handy source of subjects who won't be missed. The site's underground, so you can hide it from casual imaginal visitors. Then it just needs a re-fit. So you flood the area with a nerve gas while protected work crews move in and set things up. Snap. No witnesses, and you're up and running."

"Scum."

"Smekking toxrats!"

"Twenty-six lives!"

Leeth shared the sentiment, thinking of the people *she* knew who lived near there, people who'd shared food with her, and helped her when she was on the run. Heat burned through her. She imagined finding the people behind this and killing every one of them, spilling their blood across that same land, repaying the deaths.

Then blinked, a little surprised by her own fury. She took several deep breaths.

But as well as anger, there was also general agreement around the table. Maretti looked at Wiz. "*You* are going to be busy for a while, Wiz, I predict-"

"Maps of possible sites from city records that match the area Wolf visited?"

"No. I'll get Gadger onto that in a minute. You're going to be too busy trying to build a list of personnel for this project. We still don't know what we've got here. Now we know a firm date, I want you to hunt for resignations – hell, even disappearances and deaths – around that time. Start with hospitals, universities, they'll be easiest. Then government, then the Corps."

Wiz frowned off into the distance, lips pursed. At last he looked back at them. "Can do. But it's likely to produce a lot of matches. I'll start setting up the searches, if you like?"

Maretti nodded.

Cynthia spoke up. "Tony, I was thinking – if we've stirred up the people there, what if they send out scouts and pick up Mad Betty for questioning? Shouldn't we move her to somewhere safe?"

"Yeah, I guess we should-"

Raven snickered.

Maretti looked at her curiously.

She waved one hand dismissively. "Well, since she can see the future, she'll know not to hang around, won't she?"

"She doesn't know *everything*," argued Cynthia. "Besides, she knows our names. It could be bad for us if they do get her."

Maretti nodded. "Good point, Cyn. But move her where? She didn't look the sort of person who'd shift easily."

"What about Kirkpatrick? He looked like he could cope with her," Cyn suggested.

"And if they try to take them both?" he asked.

Chopper snorted. "They'd have the whole area up in arms against them."

Maretti nodded again. "Okay. Don, you and Chopper go back in there *carefully*, with Wolf as magical cover. You may as well take Raven with you, too."

Chopper grinned.

Raven glared at Maretti. For a moment he thought she was going to challenge the order. Instead, she clamped her mouth shut.

He turned away. "Wolf – come outside with me for a minute." As they headed out to the street, he could hear Raven trying to convince Chopper and Don she should scout around independently. He smiled.

Outside, he turned to the mage. "Can you invoke a spirit to watch the pollution station tonight?"

Wolf nodded and moved off to the ritual sacred place he'd set up a long time ago, moving aside the canvas shelter. Maretti trailed after him to watch. The invocation that followed was as sure and swift as usual, but somehow Maretti got the idea the negotiation phase didn't go too smoothly. "Well?"

Wolf grimaced. "It was not keen. The most it would do is to report back to me in the morning."

Maretti frowned. "You stuff up, or was there a problem?"

Wolf seemed to take no offense. "There was a problem. The area there is unusually dead, imaginally. In the spirit's words."

Maretti blinked. "The *spirit* said that?"

Wolf nodded. "Been around Men too long." He looked at Maretti. "Was there a reason you didn't want the others to know I'd set a watch?"

"No. I just wanted it *done*, without any argument or discussion for once."

Wolf raised his eyebrows, then nodded.

When they turned to head back to the meeting area, though, they saw Raven in the doorway, watching. She looked annoyed, but said nothing as they came up.

"Wolf's set a spirit watching the station tonight."

"Good," she snapped.

He looked at Wolf. The shaman shrugged minutely.

While they all headed for their vehicles, Maretti had a last word with Gadger. "Can you access an old map of the area, from before the Big One, and put it up on the holo? I want Wolf to see if he can retrace the route he took imaginally. You four should try to avoid that area tonight. Call me when you finish – we'll split up after this, and meet again here tomorrow if all goes well."

CHAPTER 47

They left the bikes camouflaged amongst the long-since looted rubbish of a used car lot, and began easing their way deeper into the Dumps. City lights reflecting from the overcast night sky provided only enough illumination to make out coarse detail, and Don and Chopper each pulled on night-vision goggles while Wolf cast a spell. The three men turned to Raven. They seemed to be waiting for her to do something. She stared back.

"Well? What are we waiting for?"

"Still a bit bright for you, Raven?" asked Chopper.

"What?"

"Or are the shades special? Built-in light-intensifiers, maybe?"

"Don't be such a null, Chopper," she said, walking over to him. Reaching up, she pulled off his night goggles, then her own sunglasses, which she put on him. Stepping back a pace she squinted at him through slitted eyes to cut down on the sudden increase in brightness – and to make it harder for them to guess her age, if they were being that alert.

His eyes, just adapted to the brightness of his goggles, plunged him into darkness as the shades went on.

"Give me my fagging goggles back-"

Before he could, Don plucked the sunglasses from his hands, holding them up to look at them, then through them. Turned them over. "These are quite weak."

"Yeah, well it *is* night-time. Like I said before, they adjust."

He handed them back to the still-squinting woman, while Chopper held his hand out for his own eyepieces.

She returned them and put hers back on. "Can we go *now*, Chopper? Or do you want to try my clothes on too?"

He spun around and headed into the rubble-choked streets. "Bitch," she heard him mutter.

As she stepped past the other two to follow Chopper, she thought she saw the hint of a smile on the normally impassive faces.

Outside the sprawling ruins of the derelict mill, they paused to consider.

"This may not be easy," warned Chopper. "There's lots of places Betty could be hiding, in there." One arm swept in a broad arc, encompassing the amputated stumps of two massive grain silos, the rusted corrugated tin walls of smaller outbuildings, and the half-collapsed mass of a long, two-story building. "Most people avoid this area, since the toxrats sometimes hunt here."

At his words, Don drew his massive S&W Bonebreaker.

Raven frowned. "Wait, you mean toxrats are real?"

Three heads swiveled round to stare at her.

"You never seen a *toxrat*? Where've you lived your life? In an igloo?" asked Chopper.

She ignored both the question and the continued stares of the others. "All right, *don't* tell me. Can we go in, now, and look for Betty?"

It was Wolf who relented. "Toxrats are real. Intelligent and aggressive, they hunt in packs. If the woman often stays here, she must be... special."

The footsteps were very quiet. Quieter, in fact, than the breathing accompanying them. Leeth casually turned to face in their direction.

Mad Betty stepped from the building in front of them, her huge bag still slung over one shoulder. "Oh, she is, she is special," cackled the old woman, and shuffled over. She stared at Leeth. "Sweet, sharp Bonnie. So nice to meet you, dear."

Raven snorted and looked around. "Well," she remarked to the others, "She got *my* name wrong. Guess she's not infallible, after all?"

Betty just smiled at her, before turning to Wolf. Her smile abruptly fell away. "Seek your Totem, man. Maybe it can help you, when the dreams start."

"What dreams?"

She looked at him blankly, then cackled and turned to Chopper, and took his arm. "Will she like Brian, boy? It's been a long time since old Betty went on a date!"

Chopper stared in dismay at Don. The big man just shrugged and gestured for him to lead the way to Kirkpatrick's mission. Leeth wrinkled her nose, hanging back to let Chopper get a reasonable distance in front before she followed, bringing up the rear, studying the old woman. *I didn't smell like that when I was living alone in the Dumps, did I? Surely not?* She grimaced. How often had she bathed? She hadn't had any soap.

Leaving the grounds of the mill they began clambering over the rubble of broken walls spilled onto old roadway. But as they passed a multi-story building, three sides still standing, a sound from above caught her attention. Stopping, she let the others get ahead of her. In the following silence came the sound of someone creeping back from the missing upper wall of the second floor, away from the edge.

She turned, considering where she and the others had met the old woman. Their meeting would have been clearly visible to a watcher above.

Moving silently to the side of the building, she stopped and listened again. The sounds were fading, heading toward the back. She picked her way to the rear of the structure. Removing her sunglasses, she slid through the shattered door frame into the blackness yawning inside.

Smashed glass and wind-blown dirt littered the ground floor. She passed old campsites – blackened tins rusting inside charred circles of burned plastic furniture. Large parts of the upper floor had collapsed, and other areas looked ready to follow, sagging toward the ground in tired surrender. The fire stairs to her left looked the only safe part of the whole structure.

From above came stealthy footsteps, a faint scrape from the stairwell telling her the watcher approached. She moved to the side in case he had night vision, too.

In the silence, she could hear the other's heart beating. Beating so fast it was unlikely to be that of a professional. Her nose wrinkled in disappointment. She had to resist the temptation to tap her foot, waiting at the bottom.

The ragged figure groping its way across from the stair to the rear door was armed only with a rough club. Shaking her head, she padded up swiftly behind it. Punching down almost gently on the wrist holding the makeshift weapon, she followed with a blow across the shoulders.

As the man flew out the door, she slid her sunglasses back on and casually walked over to the now-moaning form on the ground, cradling its wrist. "Get up. You're not hurt."

The moaning turned to whimpers, and the man rolled over. "I'n see nuthin!"

"I said, get up." Her lip curled at his sniveling.

"I 'n see nuthin."

She snarled, hauling him to his feet by the front of his torn denim jacket. "You're lying. You were watching us." A whisper of movement behind her spun her around to meet-

"Wolf!"

Don moved quietly up beside him. Further back, at the edge of the debris-choked street, she saw Chopper waiting with the old woman. Leeth tossed her prey to the ground between them. Wolf stared at her.

"I didn'. Didn' see nuthin'."

Wolf glanced at the scarecrow figure, then stared at Raven. "What were you doing?" he accused.

"*Me?* Paying attention. What were *you* doing? I-" *heard* "noticed a movement from the building as I passed it. Then someone sneaking off."

The night goggles masked Wolf's eyes, but his tight-pressed lips and the way he stood showed he wasn't happy. He stared at her for long seconds, then bent to the moaning figure. At the shaman's touch the man calmed. "You broke his wrist," he said, looking up at her, coldly, before turning his back on her.

There was a faint golden glow as Wolf's magic flowed over the injury. Don stared at her, unmoving.

The healing took less than a minute. The man got to his feet, still scared but clearly hopeful he was going to survive this encounter.

"Leave here. Take your things, and leave. And I warn you: avoid the area of the pollution measurer."

The man nodded and scurried off.

"He was *watching* us! How can you just-?"

"Come. We waste time."

He turned and headed off, Don following. Grinding her teeth, Leeth stomped after them. *Were these people in-sane?* "He might have been spying for the people under-ground!"

They ignored her, and she jammed her sunglasses tighter against her face. They should have left the old woman where she was. At least then, their quarry *might* have been able to work out who'd broken through their se-curity. And there'd be the *chance* of some action.

The meeting between Chopper's father, Kirkpatrick, and

the old woman almost restored her temper. Betty greeted the white-haired man in his strange clothing like an old lover, to his enormous discomfort and confusion. But there seemed to be more to his reluctance than just the obvious. She had the feeling there was something else going on here. For one thing, Chopper looked nothing like his father. And the '†' shape of the jewelry the man wore on his necklace was also prominently repeated on the much-patched building he'd emerged from at their knocking. She somehow knew it had some special significance. It made her think of her childhood, long before the Doctor had... taken her.

But after explaining what they were investigating, things turned a little strange. Chopper's father raised his eyes to the sky and said "Well, perhaps you may receive help from on high." *Satellites?* she wondered, knowing he couldn't be referring to drones. But then he turned to her. "Do you pray, Raven?"

Leeth stilled. *How did he know?* Suspecting the others were watching her, her spine tensed, resisting the urge to turn and check. "Uh, not for a while," she said, thinking quickly. *That was true. Two weeks was a while, right?*

She licked her lips, wondering if Cyn, or Wolf, were running Truth spells. Was this a test? Did they bring every new member here to be questioned like this? At least she felt pretty sure Chopper's father wasn't trying to read her mind.

He was still smiling. "Ah. You prayed as a child, then? But perhaps fell out of the habit?"

Not so much. Maybe she could just answer the first question, though, and that way avoid lying? "Sure. But mainly on small animals." She shrugged. "I only had a toy bow."

The Fist of Peace stirred, and Mr Kirkpatrick gaped at her. "How do you pray with a toy bow?"

She finally risked a look at her teammates, who were all staring at her like she'd grown horns or something. Had they all turned into idiots?

She mimed drawing a bow and shooting. "Though it was more hunting than preying." She spread her hands. "I mean: toy bow."

Val screeched, making claws of her fingertips then

pressing her hands flat together, pointed upward. "Preying, not praying!" Then they were all laughing.

Leeth stared. They really *had* turned into idiots.

Skinner slapped her on the back. "Not the religious type then, Raven, eh?"

Religion. Suddenly it was a little clearer. But instead of joining the laughter, Leeth felt only a burn of anger at this latest humiliation, a gift of the Doctor's selective education. She tried to smile, with cheeks stiff as wood.

At least it explained why Don and Wolf had been so respectful. The longer they stayed here, though, the more uncomfortable she felt.

She grimaced, remembering how she'd thought the... the *religious guy*, had been Chopper's father. Not to mention how they'd reacted to her question about the toxrats. Why hadn't the Department briefed her properly about this stuff? She'd have a few questions for them regarding their stupid training when she finished this mission, that was for sure!

It was a huge relief to finally leave. But the extra distance that had sprung up between her and Wolf and Don was still there. She sensed it was all because of that watcher she'd dealt with, but she couldn't work out what she'd done wrong. Had they wanted her to just *ignore* him? Had they expected her to know his wrist would be so fragile?

The trip back to the bikes was made in uncomfortable silence, apart from Chopper's chatter. She rode back with him on his machine. She sure wasn't going to ask Don or Wolf for any favors. Chopper at least didn't seem concerned by the incident.

Besides, it was the perfect opportunity to start working him up for some payback for all his leering looks, and that earlier humiliation before he'd given his vote. Pressing up against his back, she slid her hands around his waist, real low, her smile predatory.

It was Chopper's turn to suffer.

That afternoon, Raven received an unencrypted message on her Link, addressed to Tanya Denison. It stated she had an appointment to review her rental application, requiring her attendance between the hours of 17:30 to 21:30

– approximately.

Her news was met with half-sympathetic nods. She texted 'yes' in reply.

The Department of Public Accommodation's rules required petitioners to physically appear for interviews. 'To reduce identity fraud.' Most people, though, believed the real reason was because the DPA were bureaucratic dicks, and wanted the application process to be so difficult that only a handful of applicants per year were approved. Especially since the interviews were by artificial intelligence bot programs, occasionally escalated to outsourced African telecon centers.

"I'd better go, then." She pursed her lips. She'd *planned* to ask to stay with Gadger.

No one objected. No one even wished her luck. Gadger just kind of hunched his shoulders.

"Fine."

She stalked out, unzipping her collar and pulling her hood up, only gradually letting herself consider what the message really meant.

The Department needed her. A pleased thrill ran through her at the knowledge.

CHAPTER 48

The Accounts Department took security – and alibis – seriously. A girl of similar age and build who'd bid for the gig was now making her way to the Department of Public Accommodation. Despite claims the in-person interviews reduced identity fraud, it wasn't that unusual for a stand-in to endure the numbing wait on behalf of the real subject – or even sit the interview itself. An app gave such hired stand-ins the answers they needed to supply. The only oddity in this case was the specific outfit that had been droned to the girl – black on black, and a chill pair of shades.

Leeth waited in the restrooms until her 'double' arrived at the BART station. Little Brother's voice whispered from her choker, relaying her substitute's location. "Second carriage. Fourteen seconds." Was she kidding herself, or did his voice sound like he was hugging her? Flushing, she pulled the hood of her Kevlar-lined leather jacket up to cover her head and plunged out into the evening crowds. She caught sight of a girl dressed like her, even to the same eye-wear. Slipping hers off, she merged with the stream of disembarking passengers, following the girl and frowning at her poor posture. *Does the Department think I slouch like that? This 'double' won't fool anybody!*

She trailed her stand-in to the DPA's rundown office block on the very edge of the West Oakland Dumps, but then kept walking, following LB's directions to the equally rundown apartment building next door. She heard the front door unlock as she approached, and slipped inside.

So while her stand-in started her hours-long wait, Leeth navigated aging narrow corridors and stairways to a solid door with an old mechanical punch-code lock.

"Apartment 2B," Little Brother said, and gave her a six digit code. "Go through into the study on the right. And good luck – I'll sign off now. Oh, wait! Uh... about the suit."

For some reason, it sounded like he was *embarrassed?* "What suit?"

"It wasn't my idea. It was just we needed-"

She waited, but he said nothing. "Needed what? Hey. You still there? LB?"

But there was no answer, and he clearly *wasn't* there. *Well, that was weird.* Had he been cut off? If the Department had just lost contact with her, this wasn't going to be much of a briefing session.

In the apartment, she re-locked the door behind her and made her way to a tiny room – wood-panels over electromagnetic shielding – empty but for a chair and table, and an arthrobot sitting atop the table. The eight-armed bot clutched a parcel the size of two large loaves of bread. She took a seat.

For long seconds, nothing happened. Then the bot beeped, a single peremptory tone. Leeth flushed and leaned forward, not blinking while the crab-like bot ran its retinal and other security checks. With a satisfied chirp, it disgorged a lightfield eyescreen with inbuilt earbuds and a tiny mic.

Her briefing began as soon as she put the glasses on, Mother and Father now apparently seated across from her. They asked for a concise report – emphasis on concise – but didn't seem all that interested even after she'd admitted she hadn't yet found the traitor in the Fist of Peace.

For her part, Leeth was burning with curiosity, and listened attentively as Mother explained. The leak from the Fist of Peace had been confirmed. She felt her heart sink. *So much for* that *hope.* Nelson, waiting – *like a spider,* Leeth thought – had intercepted an encrypted message to Tik Tek Inc arranging the sale of a complete *and exclusive* copy of all Bio-Block's gene research, for a tidy five hundred thousand creds. Handover would be at the nightclub Sybarus that evening. The seller – and presumably the traitor within the Fist of Peace – called themselves Skipjack.

According to Nelson, 'exclusive access' meant the item had to be one of Bio-Block's backup holocubes. Otherwise, transfer and payment would have happened digitally. Apparently, holocubes had briefly been a 'thing' – big enough to store the entire net, way back when. Unfortunately, they had all too often totally failed, destroying all their data. Now obsolete, and yada yada yada.

Even hearing Nelson's words secondhand and summarized, Leeth couldn't help tuning them out. "What if I don't recognize 'Skipjack'?"

"In that case, watch the team Tik Tek is sending to make the buy, then intercept the handover. *It is essential you recover the holocube.* Here is the team Tik Tek has assembled."

Her glasses showed her several large and hard men and women – two of whom were mages, annotations said. Inside Sybarus, patrons weren't allowed lethal weapons – although cybernetic physical augmentation, generally classed as weaponry, *was* permitted. Such patrons had to be visibly flagged via LED wrist and neckbands, though.

They showed her pictures of herself wearing the outfit they'd chosen for her. Leeth approved: she'd look like a sexy silver robot girl. The figure hugging metallic bodysuit would also protect against tasers, they explained, and act as an antenna for broadcasting and receiving spread spectrum encrypted comms. Nelson would be using that to electronically eavesdrop and assist, live, while covering his activities behind brief broadcasts of innocuous and distracting content. She and he would even be able to talk.

Leeth rolled her eyes.

Nelson would explain its operation when she put the suit on.

At that, Leeth groaned out loud.

Mother just looked at her, then explained the suit was expensive and contained more of Nelson's advanced technology. "The neck contains a vibrator which will modulate your voice, altering it so any recordings will not be recognizable as your own. But we would prefer you *not* to be recorded." She went on to describe the gecko pads in the boot soles, knees, and palms, and the voice commands to activate and deactivate their gripping surfaces.

"Oh, now that *is* chill," Leeth had to admit. "I've only used them in training." At last, some proper spy gear! "Uh, but won't the voice, um, modulator, stop the suit and my choker from recog-"

"On the contrary." Mother didn't explain, though, simply adding that she was to return the suit to the Department afterward – undamaged. "Just snatch the cube and leave, Leeth. There's even a replica holocube in case you see a chance to make a physical swap. Try to keep it low key. I don't want to read reports tomorrow of 'slaughter at Sybarus'!"

"Sure. But... some of those Tik Tek dudes look tough. I *can* use lethal force if I have to, right?"

Both Mother and Father paused, considering, before Father finally nodded. "Yes – if you need to."

I should hope so! she thought, but was careful not to say it, or even roll her eyes.

The arthrobot's package contained heaps of stuff: a fake ID, credstick, cashsticks, a small purse, and the silver, stretchy robosuit, with boots. The biggest item was a full-body black coat with cowl, to cover her nightclub outfit until she arrived. A car was waiting for her; her choker had the contact. They described the exit strategy and how to summon a drone to deliver the holocube to the Department, via Nelson.

They wished her luck. The arthrobot collected the eye-screen comms unit and her Raven clothes and weaponry. Another drone would return them, after.

A player, Nelson knew, had to consider every angle. So after uncovering the Bio-Block deal going down later tonight, and being told Leeth was to stop it, he mulled Doc H's request to be informed of all her missions.

He didn't understand how Leeth's freaky uncle had gotten Eagle's permission to stress her to the breaking point, but it was fine by him – now he'd had his door replaced with a steel one. He'd demanded it as soon as they'd learned her magical claws couldn't cut through metal. The ungrateful little bitch had tried to kill *him* with those spooky blades once.

That memory made his decision simple. Especially knowing the Doc would use the info about her mission tonight to screw with her. He smiled. He'd be her support during the op, too – remotely, natch – and he could hardly wait to get started. It should be stratospheric, however she played it.

Club Sybarus was high profile, so she'd probably be vidded and shared. That meant her disguise had to be camera proof, so *that* meant something full-body. It also had to pass the club's entry standards for the 'beautiful people'. He grinned. A curvaceous chrome robot ticked all the boxes, and thanks to the popularity of telesex, the Department could get a skintight suit for her at very short notice. There were even metal-film ones that could be adapted to anti-taser defense *and* of course came with all that inbuilt bio-telemetry. Those bonuses made his basic idea even easier to sell to Mother and Father.

He'd been careful not to ask the Doc what he planned to do with the info. It was more fun not knowing. Especially since, as Leeth's 'support', he'd have a virtual ring-side seat for whatever happened.

The suit was a tight fit, but once she had it on, it lit up, jeweled rivers of rainbow light pulsing over it. They nicely outlined the contours of her body – partly decoration, partly anti image-recognition. Her choker, underneath, still worked okay via its various taps and voice commands.

The smooth chrome skull cap had spiky, swept back antennas where her ears were, and to cover her eyes, wide stick-on mirror lenses. It also had dynamic gel uplifts for breast and butt, and waist tensioning – like a flexible corset, Nelson explained.

"Just squeeze your breasts, or butt, and think 'bigger'," he said. "To pull your waist in, just tighten your abs and think 'smaller'."

"And *why* would I want to do that?" Leeth growled.

She could practically *hear* him look skyward. "Duh, so if you're filmed, it won't match your real measurements. Ditto for the boot heels. The more extreme you go, the less chance you'll be recognizable."

Even Leeth saw the element of manipulation in *that*. And no doubt he'd find some way to record her, tonight.

Nelson, however, held back from explaining some of the suit's other functions: like how its 'smokescreen broadcasts' to cover the comm transmissions, provided a thermal and conductivity profile of her body – sorted by, and with the most frequent updates for, her erogenous zones. It was the same telemetry used in some VR games, and all telesex hookups. Not surprising, since that was exactly the base rig he'd had Little Brother use to construct *this* item. He smirked, fully aware that the boy scout, or Mother or Father for that matter, would fry their chips if they knew how he'd modded the software. But it was important to keep his skills sharp, keep pushing the envelope.

Unaware, Leeth adjusted her dimensions, her eyebrows lifting at the sight of her breasts expanding before her eyes. Frowning, she adjusted her rear, stopping far short of the cartoon proportions Nelson urged. Her waist she constricted more carefully, twisting and tumbling in the small room, making sure it wouldn't affect her fighting.

The stretchy material was strong, but thin enough to outline her nipples, and groin. She smiled, remembering the reactions of the soldiers last year when she'd worn the black catsuit the Doctor had thought looked painted on.

Back when she still lived at the Institute. Had that really only been nine or ten months ago? It seemed like forever.

The suit could also shock from its fingertips at her thought, Nelson whispered via her choker, though only once or twice, unless it had also *absorbed* charges. She couldn't wait to try *that* out! And the silvered, stick-on lenses concealing her eyes provided a heads-up display.

She checked herself in the mirror of the handbag's small compact. Her mouth and red lips somehow made her look like a sexbot. She wriggled her hips to exaggerate her narrowed waist, then bounced on her heels, feeling how the aerogel at her chest and backside jiggled.

Maybe I should take them down a size or two? Which was when she learned the gel inflation was a one-way chemical change to the suit.

Nelson read her anger with glee. Plus he was getting megs of 3D and motion capture data to refine the animation model of his virtual Leeth catgirl toy.

He squirmed in pleasure.

CHAPTER 49

Outside Club Sybarus's bank-strength glass security doors, in its chrome and red velvet lobby on the tenth floor, Leeth's unveiling caused a nice reaction. The cloakroom bot whisked her concealing black cloak inside, to in-drawn breaths from behind her. A mental command reactivated the suit's rainbow veining, and she turned, pleased to see the bouncer, and the two couples ahead of her, frozen in a tableau of appreciation.

She smiled, feeling great, ready to take on the world.

Beyond the two couples, sliding armor-glass doors muffled the pulse of music. Grinning, already moving to its rhythm, she put an extra sway into her hips.

But a minute later, still at the security doors, her grin had vanished. It had taken all that time to convince the idiot man-mountain she was flesh and blood, not some advanced Tik Tek sex bot sent to prank the club. She'd actually had to peel up one silvered lens, and unzip the suit, before he'd accepted her ID as 'Jay Fox,' twenty-year-old cosmetician. Though she had to smile at the physical reaction she caused when she guided one of his meaty hands under the filmy material at her chest.

He even waived the entry fee.

His lips had been soft, too, despite his size. As she waltzed away, she made sure she showed him a good rear jiggle as she strutted through the sliding doors and into a blast of music, lights, and movement. To her left stretched an illuminated bar, with others like it hugging the curved walls. To her right, in a fancy restaurant section, each table seemed to float on its own dark disk, concealing the diners from the dancers below.

The whole floor was glass.

She strode to the balcony, wrapping herself in the rhythm, letting it flow and fill her to the brim as she prowled to the golden railing and looked down. Below, Escher-like stairs linked a circular cascade of transparent dance-floors to create a fairy-tale nightscape, rainbow-washed but edged with dangerous falls. A wide gap separated each suspended floor from the booths, bars, and low seats ringing them.

The danger was more illusory than real though, she saw, noting the chest-high glass barriers enclosing the stairs and suspended floors, to keep even blissed-out dancers safe.

From the topmost of the club's four floors, very conscious of her silver-chrome suit and feeling a little like a robot queen surveying her subjects, she looked out and down over a gorgeous crowd lost in the music. The glowing jewel tracery of her suit *throbbed* in harmony. And then the suit fully synced, dissolving the boundary between body and music, making her a part of it.

Swaying to the beat, she saw heads turn her way. The music softened, and more heads turned.

Suddenly, narrow, gem-colored spotlights swarmed her, locking on to reflect and refract from her like she was a human mirror ball. Feeling hidden behind her silvered lenses, she spread her arms and spun dancing down the curving stairs.

The music faded out altogether before swelling again, a new tune beating against her skin, a rhythm that moved her blood even though she didn't know what 'Mohway' or 'Shandon' was. Stalking down transparent stairs, she scanned the room for the Tik Tek team, listening *through* the music for the name 'Skipjack'. But halfway down to the topmost dance-floor, a sun-bright spotlight joined the others. It lit her up on the stairs as the song's innocuous words suddenly changed, freezing her in her steps.

They were telling everyone she was a 'Killer Queen', then stuff about gunpowder and being dynamite with a laser beam.

Keep moving, she told herself. *They're not singing about you! There* aren't *even any handheld laser guns.* She continued down the steps, though no longer dancing, rejecting the remaining lyrics. They clearly weren't about her. But the accusations about being insatiable, and well versed in etiquette, sounded like Mother's words. Had she or Nelson organized this?

"Is this your idea of a joke, Nelson?" she whispered.

"Nope!"

But he didn't try to hide the surprised snigger in his choked-out denial.

Regardless, the song had a good beat, and the spotlights released her when she reached the dance floor. Shrugging, she surrendered and played along, making a joke of the lyrics. A tall, fit man accepted her unspoken challenge, and together they spun a mock duel on the lit-up floor, his dark skin flashing against her silver. Other dancers took up the theme... then all too soon the song ended.

It brought back memories of dancing with Luiz, in other clubs, and she was suddenly glad her silvered 'helmet' covered so much of her face.

The music moved from there into a song about digging under her feet and finding things you didn't want to see, plunging her spirits even lower.

"Terrible Things by April Smith and the Great Picture Show," Nelson helpfully offered. "You're supposed to be undercover, Leeth – dumb move to bribe the DJ to play retro songs about your deadly natu-"

"Mute," she snarled, silencing the little weevil, but welcoming the surge of anger. Focusing through the pounding music, she finished scanning the top and third levels of the four-story dance club. No Tik Tek goon squad, though.

As she danced down the near-invisible stairs to the next level, the spotlights returned to her – including the sun-bright one as she stepped out and her silver-booted foot met the glass. In sharp clear tones a woman sang of murder on the dance floor.

Enough! Leeth whirled on the spot, anger flaring into fury. She might not be able to stop Nelson playing his stupid prank, but she *could* stop the DJ. Her head lifted as she hunted for the DJ in his booth, razor tingles spearing from her fingertips. Her fingers twitched, feeling an urge to grip a blade, cut and carve....

A sharp scream from directly above elevated every gaze to a suspended sphere where an androgynous white figure's hands suddenly, frantically, scrubbed at the air.

She blinked, frowning at the weird idea of killing him with a *knife*, when 'God Emperor of Dune' crashed from every speaker. Like a surging breaker, it swelled to fill the space, its irresistible beat sweeping all before it into its joyous vortex.

Much better, Leeth thought, although for a few seconds it was like some part of her didn't want the rage transformed to joy, to flower in soaring passion. It tore free finally with a stab of pain.

She let the music take it, let herself drown in the drugging beauty of Haven's angelic vocals. Wondering, even, why she'd let herself get so angry, feeling like she'd emerged from some subterranean furnace. With her suit pulsing across her skin and the music lofting her spirits, it took every shred of will to continue scanning for her targets. But she didn't let the mission stop her dancing.

As the song descended back to Earth in its final gentling chords, leaving her panting but at peace enough to talk to the little weasel, she considered unmuting Nelson. Her suit chose that moment to begin buzzing at her groin.

"Nelson? What the cluster-!"

"Ah ah, Leeth!" he interrupted. "You muted me!"

"Yeah, you little..." she hunted for an insult to smash over his head. "Dick-whistle."

"I told you it was a simsuit. A full rig – right up to tele-sex. But listen, s'much as I know you'd like me to dem' those features, I just needed your attention. We *are* on a mission, you know."

She so wished she could squeeze his neck right now. Her anger crept back, flushing her cheeks.

Nelson, noting her biotelemetry, grinned. "Listen, it seems the DJ there's renowned for reading the mood of the crowd. They say-"

"... Skipjack," someone said from above.

"Shh!" Leeth turned, her eyes scanning up and left to the entrance at the top floor, where a group had entered and were now fanning out. "Ahh. Gotcha!"

She was careful not to stare, but apparently Nelson, for all his faults, was as quick as her. And could see what she was looking at. Maybe more? Leeth wondered if there were sensors on the back of her suit, too.

"Good work." Nelson sounded surprised. "I see 'em."

He skipped back through his sensor feeds, trying to work out how Leeth had spotted the Tik Tek team so quickly. She'd turned toward them before they'd become visible. Freak. "What about our traitor? You see him yet?"

"Nup."

"Ah. Just decrypted a 'Yo, Skipjack here.' text. Heads up," he warned her, still scanning.... And... yes! "Just scored a booth location, using the same crypto key." He gave her the location, one level up, while his software searched the club's live security videos for any fresh movements vectoring in that direction.

Leeth meanwhile had been tracking the Tik Tek crew as they fanned out. Some stayed at the fourth, top level, while others descended to the third, heading for the location Nelson gave her. The two who'd stayed up at the entrance level looked like the mages, dammit. But they hadn't spread too far apart. No doubt keeping a direct line of sight on the meeting spot in case they had to cast spells.

Chewing her lip, thinking, she danced her way up.

"Whoa, Leeth, too far! The meet's on level three, not four. Go back!"

"Shut up, Nelson, or I'll mute you again." She continued up, strutting extravagantly, dancing up, following the curved arc of golden railing. "Have you found our seller? Can you mark them on my HUD?"

She took another stab of vibration at her groin as Nelson venting his childish displeasure, and felt a fresh surge of anger. *How had he gotten the okay for a vibrator down there? Was* that *what LB had been about to tell me? Had Mother and Father approved this?*

She fought down a firestorm of rage. *He's just doing this to make you fail. Focus!* She took a deep breath. As she scanned around, her jaw tense, a cartoonish bullseye appeared on a slim figure making its way up to the booth where three of the Tik Tek people waited.

"Very funny," she grated out.

Another pulse of vibration at her groin. She ground her teeth, imagining how Nelson would lie: 'Well, she muted me, Father. How else could I communicate?' Though she couldn't imagine how he'd gotten Mother of all people to agree to it.

The number thirty appeared – counting down the seconds, it looked like, until the figure with the holocube reached the booth where the Tik Tek buyers waited.

Twenty-nine....

And at that moment, she saw Marcie across the dance floor.

CHAPTER 50

Earlier that evening, Eagle's door had slid open. "Doctor. What can I do for you? You said it concerns Leeth's mission tonight?"

"Yes. I would like to request permission to entice Marcie Dunkirk to Club Sybarus this evening."

For once, Harmon had the impression he'd surprised Eagle. For long seconds, the dark-skinned man said nothing.

"Frankly, Doctor, that sounds ridiculous. But by all means, lay out your case."

The reaction was as Harmon had expected. "Thank you. It relates to the undesirability of their friendship."

Eagle said nothing, merely waited.

"Leeth and Marcie are best friends. A bond that only deepened when they helped each other during the Disten incident. So, Marcie Dunkirk will provide a good test of Leeth's disguise tonight."

"That is an extremely weak argument, Doctor. Bringing the Dunkirk girl in will distract Leeth and increase risk. I think you fail to grasp the nuances of operational planning."

Harmon shrugged. "Perhaps. But if Miss Dunkirk does see through the disguise, her reaction will also provide valuable data about her ability to hold her tongue. She is well aware her friend 'Jane' is involved in clandestine work for her so-called parents."

That point received a small nod.

"If things gets violent, as no doubt they will, Miss Dunkirk will see Leeth in action. That ferocity may weaken their bond, even scare her off."

A raised eyebrow indicated Eagle's estimate of that probability.

"Assuming Leeth sees Dunkirk, it will also test her ability to follow protocol and maintain operational security."

That earned a small frown.

"There is also the possibility that Miss Dunkirk might fall into harm's way, which would provide an interesting test of Leeth's loyalties. Which would she prioritize – her mission, or her friend? Dunkirk might be injured or even killed in a cross-fire, which Leeth would certainly blame herself for."

Eagle shook his head. "More likely she'd blame us, if

she ever learned *we* had enticed her friend to the club."

Harmon sniffed. "Even that, I could work around. 'Your behavior has been troubling, Leeth. We needed a friendly assessment – from a safe distance, on a mission you were told to keep low key.'" He waved a dismissive hand. "I know the depth of Leeth's commitment to things she cares about. No, if Miss Dunkirk were killed I could work with that seed to generate sufficient stress to likely trigger Leeth's further Unfolding."

Harmon read both acceptance and cold anger in Eagle's aura. "A tragic outcome, but it would neatly solve the Dunkirk issue, while developing Leeth's powers. Which from the hints you, Abrams, and others have dropped, are currently insufficient for her to survive the challenges you have planned for her."

And with that statement, Harmon allowed his true feelings to show. "I will not have this Department use my, my *ward*, like a disposable tool; some kind of convenient *weapon*. Even if the stupid girl welcomes such sacrifice!"

To Harmon's chagrin, he found himself breathing hard, and had to pause to gather control of himself. "You may think me harsh and uncaring, but I recognize I have some feelings for her. I will not have her throw her life away needlessly."

"Very noble, Doctor. And you don't feel that Leeth blaming herself for hurting her friend might damage her psyche so badly it weakened her, rather than triggering some hypothetical further magical development?"

Harmon blinked. "I... no. I'm sure that with my guidance, and her own innate-"

"Your guidance? You mean, as a trusted and perhaps beloved figure she would turn to in her hour of need?"

Harmon's heavy eyebrows deepened the shadows over his eyes. "I would be there for her. She would see that."

"Provided she never learned you were the one who set the stage for her friend's death, I assume?"

"Are you threatening me, Eagle?"

"I thought I was pointing out a flaw in your clever plan, Doctor. The girl is growing up. Don't you see a contradiction in building her trust on a foundation of lies and manipulation?"

"Since your approval would make you equally to blame,

Eagle, I feel confident in *trusting* she will not find out."
Harmon looked smug.

So that was a 'No'. Sometimes, Eagle regretted his decision to bring the mage into the organization. It was increasingly clear he needed to do something about that. The man's smug arrogance certainly offered a long enough lever.

"Besides, the chance of Miss Dunkirk's fatality is extremely slim, especially with Leeth there to protect her. My other reasons stand. If her friend tries to breach security and share what she knows, I understand Nelson can shut down such communications in an instant. And we can then arrest Miss Dunkirk for treason – an outcome whose blame we can also justifiably lay at Leeth's door. Again, an excellent source of stress."

"One could almost believe you hold a grudge against Marcie Dunkirk for her humiliation of you, Doctor."

Harmon waved a dismissive hand. "I am quite sure your biometric sensors are informing you that is not so."

"What if something induces Leeth herself to spill secrets, Doctor?"

"She can't. My conditioning ensures that. If you doubt it, however, then such a situation would prove a useful test of that risk, too."

Eagle waited.

Harmon spread his hands. "You will need to decide quickly, however, since I understand the mission starts soon, and I will need time to persuade Marcie Dunkirk to visit Club Sybarus."

"You seem confident you can, Doctor."

Harmon merely inclined his head.

Eagle leaned back, his gaze burning into Harmon as if he could percept emotions too, or see inside. In the end he sighed, unhappily. "There may be another way forward for her, Doctor. Assuming your concern really is to ensure she can meet the challenges lying ahead of her?"

It was Harmon's turn to frown.

"Give Leeth the Aztec dagger."

For Harmon, it felt like the world jolted. With wide eyes, he met Eagle's, finding them similarly startled. Both blinked as the sensation vanished.

"Or perhaps not." Eagle grimaced. "Very well, Doctor.

Try your scheme."

Harmon smiled and left to make his call.

"You again," Marcie said, frowning at the woman who'd introduced herself as her friend's mother. "What do you want this time?"

The woman said nothing, merely studying her with narrowed eyes. "I need to ask a favor, for Jane," she said at last. "We are sending her on a job tonight. Just a snatch and grab, at a nightclub, but I worry that Jane may become... over-excited."

As expected, Marcie frowned. "Then send someone else."

"We can't. Only Jane knows what the target looks like. But you misunderstand. That's not my worry. It's Jane herself. Her temper. Lately she's been acting..." Harmon hunched his shoulders and let the sentence trail off, once again admiring the perfection of the digital simulation. "I just think if you were there, a friendly face, it might... calm her down? If she got, uh, carried away?"

Marcie scowled.

"The location itself is very safe: it's Club Sybarus. They don't allow weapons. And even cybernetically augmented patrons are-"

"Identified with visible markers, and not allowed in if they have weapon augments. Yeah, I know, it's the spot of the moment."

"We don't *expect* trouble. There shouldn't be violence, or bloodshed. And I can pay your expenses."

Marcie bristled. "I don't need your money to look after my friends."

"You'll do it, then?" Harmon clasped his hands, watching Jane's Mother's hands do likewise. "Oh, thank you, Miss Dunkirk, you have no idea how much this means to me! Knowing you'll be there, looking out for my daughter! Just seeing your face may be enough to, to stop her doing-" She swallowed, and visibly changed what she'd been planning to say. "To keep her calm."

Marcie frowned.

CHAPTER 51

Leeth shook her head, disbelieving. *Marcie can't be here!*

But she was. She even had Stryker Zaxx's deadly little 'Deathbird' drone hovering at her shoulder. Leeth watched her friend turn to a vaguely familiar-looking black guy sitting beside her.

She wrenched her gaze away, back to the Tik Tek mercs. If there was one tactical lesson she'd absorbed, it was to take out the mages first. She sized the two up, trying to push thoughts of Marcie from her mind.

One sat at a table overlooking the dance floors, already nursing a drink. The other stood leaning slightly out, his two large hands resting on the clear wall surrounding the central well.

Tip him over? He'd fall past the dance floors. And what would Marcie think? She mentally shook herself. *Stop it! Focus!*

The trouble was, the group the mages watched over could see both mages just as easily. *See.... They need to see to target their spells....* She scanned tables for lemon slices in drinks, or pepper....

Ahh.

Strutting past an empty table, she swayed to one side, trailing the fingertips of her left hand through the remnants of a spicy sauce, with a silent thanks to slow waiters. She wove past the seated mage, her eyes narrowed as she considered how to take out the taller, handsome one. He had a strong jaw dusted by dark bristles, that would...

Ohhh!

The music changed again as she neared her victim, powerful electric guitar chords pulsing, and her eyes widened in delight even as the man sensed her approach and turned toward her. She recognized the tune, imagining herself as the unstoppable female cyborg, Major Motoko Kusanagi, and couldn't contain her delight. Glancing up to the suspended DJ booth as *Lithium Flower* surged through the club, she met the nervous gaze of the slender figure with a tiny nod before turning back to the dark-haired man now looming over her.

Maybe it was her smile as she curved her body in against his, or the way her lips parted, but he let her slide her right arm along his, linking fingers. She guided his large hand unresistingly to the zipper of her suit, her fingers tugging it smoothly down then sliding his hand over a breast, grinding her body against his in time to the music.

She's so coldly human...

She judged it long enough, for any watchers. *Hopefully not Marcie.* She snarled at her lack of concentration. His fingers began to grope on their own.

Jumping back as if *he* was the one who'd initiated their contact, she angrily thrust his hand away and zipped up her suit – and kneed him *hard* between his legs, hearing something crunch. She spun away, radiating righteous anger. Behind her, she heard his friend curse, push back his seat, and jump to his feet. She slowed, letting the second mage intercept her. He even grabbed her by the upper arm.

Perfect! Pushing ineffectively at his face with the hand she'd dipped in the chili sauce, she made sure she got plenty in his eyes before slapping him with her other hand, hard enough for him to release her arm.

Shrugging free, she changed direction, storming for the exit. At least now she'd be out of sight of Marcie. The big bouncer outside was arguing with a very curvy woman in the lobby, and only glanced in her direction. But halfway there – as she passed directly above the booth where the illegal trade would be starting in... six seconds, according to Nelson's digital countdown... she stumbled and fell to the floor.

Peeling off one lens, she placed it on the glass laminate. "Watch them, Nelson. Yell when you see the cube!"

Staggering back to her feet she added humiliation to the anger she was projecting. Hunching her shoulders, she stalked for the exit, the song's lyrics now taunting her.

There was something odd about the woman trying to enter. The bouncer sounded frustrated. "Because she's only *pretending* to be a gynoid! I don' care if it's the Queen of England piloting that rig, Club rules say no bots inside!"

The thick glass doors slid apart at Leeth's approach, the bouncer turning to her. "As for you..."

Nelson finally had his act together. "I don't know what the fuck you think you're doing, Leeth. But the meet's going ahead despite what you just did."

Looking up and left into the HUD of her single remaining eye-lens, a small view of the booth appeared. Nelson's countdown hit zero, and vanished. The bullseyed figure sat, and some sort of abbreviated macho introductions began. But the picture was far too small for her to make out a detail like a fingertip-sized holocube. She just had to hope Nelson, with bigger screens and all his equipment, could see better than her.

The bouncer had stepped in front of her, holding up a hand. "Let me see your ID again, Miss."

A low hum from the other woman's body suddenly screeched upward into bat-registers, making Leeth wince. The woman used the bouncer's distraction to spring between them both, slipping through the doors as they closed. Not a woman – a gynoid!

"Got it!" Nelson cried. Leeth glanced up, the small picture in her lens suddenly zooming in on a hand leaving a jacket, a translucent cube held between finger and thumb. "Get back in there, now!"

The bouncer's meaty hand clamped on her shoulder, pulling her back as he moved forward, the outer doors trundling apart at their approach. She had to take him out now, grab the cube, and get away, but an idea was forming.

"Sorry," she murmured, and for the second time in one night hammered a knee between unsuspecting male legs. Racing back inside she saw the hand in her head-up display stretch out toward another holding the cube.

Sprinting now, her mouth fell open as the sexdroid who'd darted in before her leapt to the low glass wall. Exactly as she intended to do, herself.

And the song still played.

She's incredible math

The gynoid went over the handrail.

In three strides, Leeth was there. Picturing the uneven bar of the Institute's gym, she gripped the polished rail and flipped up into a handstand over the four-story drop. Upside down, she saw Marcie gaping up at her.

Gritting her teeth, she calmly crossed her hands over, pivoted, and let gravity swing her down like a pendulum. As the glass barrier hurtled closer, she thrust both legs forward and released her grip. Adrenaline surged as she slipped through the gap between the floor above and the glass wall below, like an envelope through a slot, landing lightly on her feet.

But the sexbot was already among the men, who were now on their feet, angry. Slender hands blurred, and slim fingers suddenly held the holocube, snatched from the Russian-looking guy. Its other hand rested on his shirt. The smaller man, the seller, jumped backwards and away, clutching his cashstick. Nelson had labeled him 'Skipjack', she saw. *Funt:* she didn't recognize him.

The big Russian jerked, spasming, sparks jumping from the bot's hand as it left him to graze the chest of a man reaching for her from the side. Across the low table, the stocky woman was drawing a stun baton from her sleeve.

"The Mark Seven has the-!" Nelson squawked in her ear, as if she couldn't see it for herself. Leeth hit baton woman right between the eyes with a palm strike, slamming her head back. Turning to the bot, she met its eyes as she in turn snatched the holocube from its pseudo-flesh hand.

The man it still touched collapsed, as crystalline irises coolly assessed her. Faster than Leeth could see, a hand slammed into her chest, electricity sparking, another hand wrapping around her own tightly clenched fist, prising at the holocube inside it.

Sparks flew, but Nelson's suit appeared to work. *Screw this.* Twisting her hand, Leeth heard the ultrasonic whine of synthetic muscles straining, glad for all her sparring bouts with James, where she'd learned cyborg physiology was modeled on human. With a grin, she felt the bot's grip break. She dropped and grabbed it around its waist and lifted, spinning, to heave it over the low glass barrier.

That was easier than I expected.

But its eyes stayed locked on hers as it fell. Something in that gaze sent a shudder down her spine, while the first onlookers' screams started.

And from amongst the onlookers staring across the open space above the dance floor, Marcie stared straight at her, her eyes wide in sudden recognition. *Oh, funt!*

Nelson continued jabbering at her from her choker. "Leeth, behind-"

But she'd heard her attacker and was already dropping,

ducking the blow and snatching up the fallen stun baton, then spinning to jab it into the woman's side. *And* into the man behind her, who'd just thrown the table aside. He parried, and she locked his arm in hers and hammered a punch into his kidney. Hoping Marcie wasn't still watching.

From three stories below, she felt more than heard the impact of the robot on the floor, to fresh screams of horror. Grimacing, she zapped the heavyset woman with her own baton, faintly annoyed she hadn't had a chance to try her suit's built-in taser.

Everyone loves tasers, I guess.

The song moved into its final section, about the Major and surfing, and Leeth took a moment to thrust the cube in between the gel push-up bra and her left breast. Three bouncers were moving to intercept her, and a fifth man she hadn't spied before. He sprinted toward her with a cool determination she just *knew* meant he had to be one of the Tik Tek team.

She eyed the railing and the glass floor above. *Not too hard*, she decided, but moved with care, not entirely trusting her unfamiliar boots and not wanting to rely on the gecko function. The man was drawing a plastic-looking gun by the time she launched herself upward to grab the topmost railing and haul herself over and onto the fourth floor. She even spared a second to snatch up Nelson's precious lens from where she'd put it earlier.

The shocked faces of diners stared at her from every side, and from below, she saw Marcie on her feet, staring up at her, the thin guy still by her side. Marcie looked... kind of horrified. Mentally cringing, Leeth tore her eyes away to scan the people around her for what she needed. And finally saw a girl her age chewing gum, paused with mouth agape.

The singer was 'smelling lithium now'.

She hunched her shoulders and charged the girl.

Eyeing her target, she leapt. Holding on one-handed, she smeared the girl's gum over the infrared sensor and dropped to the ground. As the doors finished opening she stepped through, grabbing the angry-looking bouncer who still clutched his groin.

Oh. I guess that was *only about thirty seconds ago.*

She half dragged, half tossed him into the club and backed out of range of the sensor, sighing in pleasure when she saw the doors glide shut despite his presence.

That should buy me a little time. Maybe even enough to get my coat back?

She'd just pressed her lens back in place when the solid man with the plastic gun appeared on the other side of the club's glass doors, aiming it up while charging toward her.

"Head for the stairs," Nelson urged, as if she'd forgotten, or not read, the briefing notes about escape routes.

Instead, Leeth waited.

The man skidded to a halt, nose touching the unmoving glass doors, waving one arm angrily skyward at the sensor, his eyes pinned to her.

The three bouncers lumbered up behind him. They were heading toward her until one saw his odd weapon.

"Bitch, open this door. You have no idea who you just messed with."

"Don't answer him!" Nelson coached.

At the armed man's threat, all three bouncers moved to encircle him.

Leeth blew plastic gun man a kiss, then turned and sprinted down the corridor to the lifts.

The rest was anti-climactic. Nelson, already in the building's security system, summoned an elevator and sent it down to misdirect any followers. While it did, Leeth ran up the stairwell to the roof where a drone had earlier dropped off specialized rappelling gear as she'd entered the club.

"Shouldn't there be a back-up line?" she asked Nelson. Hooking the loop-festooned harness around her thighs and waist, she fed the line through the snap-link and clipped it on via the caribiner.

"Why, you put on weight?"

She didn't snap at him. "It's real thin. I could break this if I wanted."

"Then don't."

She *so* wanted to punch him. Instead, she attached the special brake, operating the grip and tugging on it to prove to herself it'd work even on the horribly thin cord now snaking down the side of the fifteen-story building. She jiggled it, making sure she couldn't feel the weighted end – since that would mean the rope was short.

"Tick tock, tick tock."

"What does that even mean?" She climbed up and over the railing, giving the looped cord one last, hard tug before leaning back out, still gripping the brake shut.

"It means you're wasting-"

Leeth kicked backwards off into space with both feet, unclenched her fist, and fell.

Terror and exhilaration smashed through her. She'd trained at this, and the equipment was just simple, solid mechanisms – but what if something broke? Squeezing down on the handle, she braked, careful not to build too much speed, then held herself to a steady pace. Just a second per floor. She watched the ground approach.

Listening.

"And if you remind me not to change until I'm in the stormwater tunnels, Nelson, I'm muting you."

And there was the ground....

"Yeah, you do that, Leeth. Mute me. Call if you get lost, eh? I might be around."

She didn't untie herself, just slashed the harness and stepped back and out of it as looping cord fell in whispery piles. She assumed the drone she could hear was the one they'd said would collect it. But even now, careful to hide her hearing, she just asked Nelson if he had a drone on its way yet, as she sprinted down the back street. Behind her, the first set of running footsteps rounded the corner of the office block.

As soon as they were well into the disused sewers and stormwater tunnels, she was demanding answers. "You had something to do with Marcie being there, didn't you? Was the sexdroid yours too?"

"Smek no!"

Was that an answer to my first question, or my second? "What, did you think Marcie'd blow my cover? She knows better than that!"

She thought back. They hadn't made contact – except with their eyes. For some reason then she remembered the gynoid falling to its doom, calmly watching her. Her spine prickled. Something was telling her she hadn't seen the last of that bot.

How long should she wait to call Marcie? Probably as soon as Nelson couldn't eavesdrop on them. Assuming that was even possible.

At his direction, she dropped into a cross tunnel.

"So who was Skipjack?" she asked. "I didn't recognize him."

He didn't respond at first. She'd pulled away a rotting door blocking an opening onto a long, twisting gray concrete tunnel before he answered, explaining the seller who'd brought the holocube would've just been an intermediary. After that, apart from terse directions and griping about not being able to ID the guy, Nelson fell strangely silent. Then, broke some stupid news. "Mother and Father want *you* to bring the holocube in."

"Huh? Why? A drone was gonna pick it up! That's dumb. I should be back at that public housing waiting place. The DPA. What'm I supposed to say if the traitor asks where Raven was, while his sale was being ruined?"

"Then you'll know who the sell-out was, won't you?"

"I didn't mean they'd literally say their sale was being ruined, idiot!"

"If you'd turn your fucking torch on we'd- you'd get to the Department, and your alibi location, in plenty of time!"

Leeth assumed the tension in Nelson's voice was fear of the dark, even though he was actually sitting safe and sound in some comfy vibro sex toy massage chair back in his lair.

The fear, she read correctly – it was the *cause* she misunderstood. Nelson's silence had begun the moment he'd probed at the sexdroid that had tried to steal the holocube, and found himself at a Tik Tek portal.

If there was one company on the planet he'd learned not to penetrate, even with Ghost's help, it was Tik Tek. He was the one who'd warned they'd somehow hack and steal any drone the Department tried to use to fetch the cube.

He just hoped he'd pulled back before their godlike security system had recognized his touch.

There were limits to the trouble he wanted Leeth to get into. Especially when it might point a finger at him. He settled into angry silence.

Leeth's choker pulsed. She tapped for info.

"Call from Marcie Dunkirk for Jane Baker."

Nelson sputtered, outraged. "We're on a fuckin' mission, you can't-"

"Shut up, Nelson. Okay, Link, accept call, voice only." She braced herself, certain Marcie had realized it was her, back in the Club. Wanting an explanation.

"J-Jane?"

"Hi Marcie, what's up?"

The silence stretched just long enough for Leeth to worry. Then a man's voice spoke. "I believe you have something belonging to me."

The voice of the man who'd been cursing her, waving his strange plastic pistol.

CHAPTER 52

When Marcie begged off from the series-wrap party, Vincent Moore had his suspicions. When he learned she was blowing off her cast-mates to go to Club Sybarus – 'an entitled hook-up den representing everything sick with our society', she'd once called it – Vince knew.

She'd tried to push him away, but he'd simply shrugged and said he'd always wanted to check it out. And if they both bowed out to go to Syb, at least the gossip mags would have a story to feed the *Underworld* fans. That *might* make up some of the ill-feeling she'd be causing, standing up the rest of the cast and crew. He'd even talked her into taking along the tiny drone that played Stryker Zaxx's 'Deathbird' in the series. For the fans. She'd drawn the line at either of them wearing their bounty hunter costumes, though.

Getting in to Club Sybarus had been easy – the bouncer turned out to be a huge fan, joking about only allowing Stryker Zaxx to take in her killer drone because the Club's 'Null Field' disabled all weapons within its confines.

Marcie had smiled at the Underworld reference and signed an autograph. They'd slid in, the bouncer's comments about ejecting the both of them if either drew on the other bringing a smile to Vince and a distracted nod from 'Stryker Zaxx.'

While their entry caused a ripple of attention from a few J. R. Martin fans, by and large they were left to themselves, although the tiny, shiny black drone that darted and hovered threateningly over Marcie's shoulder drew more than one double-take.

Marcie took a seat on the third level, near the glass wall circling the central platter of transparent dance floors. She wasn't sure sure what Jane's mother expected her to do. She sipped at her drink, grateful that Vince had stopped peppering her with questions and seemed content just to keep her company. She felt a weird thrill: knowing her friend would be here on a mission, excited by the chance of seeing her in action again, but at the same time scared. The last few times she'd been drawn in to Jane's life had almost ended her own.

But Jane's mother said she was worried about her. 'Keep her calm?' She'd said it like she thought Jane was some kind of bomb. Marcie shuddered, staring unseeingly at her drink, remembering the sight of Jane, covered in blood, stalking down the stairs from the upper stories of that other club, Club Juzz, that seventh circle of Hell.

Marcie had thought the *vampire,* Tash, had been scary. Jane had entered the room like the Angel of Death. She shuddered again.

Marcie watched the chromed sex kitten jiggling and dancing, emerald and aquamarine glow-lines outlining her limbs and curves, drawing the eye. She pursed her lips at the club-girl's obvious cosmetic mods, but at the same time felt there was something familiar about her. Something about the way she moved.

Vince suddenly snorted. "Didn't know you were into girls, M."

She spun her head to him, and the Deathbird's gesture recognition algorithms fired a laser straight into his forehead – much to the delight of several fans of the show, watching and filming. In the chemical haze of the club, the red beam showed clear. Vince flinched back, even though the ray was harmless without *Underworld* special effects to make it 'real'.

"But hey, M, catch this." He projected a trending vid from the club's SoBo feed, captured just before they'd arrived. In it, the sexy silver robot danced down the stairs and froze partway down. "If DJ Gesh's rep as a psychic was real, that'd be your Jane friend right there, in disguise. See, Gesh, zhe was playing *Killer Queen.* But that's nothing, check out the reaction when zhe played–"

Marcie had stopped listening, though. It *was* Jane. She was certain. One hand went to her mouth in shock, before making a joke of it and leaning back. Since Jane *was* here on a mission, the last thing she should do was draw attention to her. Or let people realize there was any link between the sexdroid and her. Not on top of the SoBo vid of Jane Baker storming the hospital. Last she'd looked, it had climbed to ninety million likes.

Vince's projection ended, and she pretended disinterest and changed the conversation. But she kept her attention on the silver dancer. Right up until the fight broke out. She watched in horror as Jane threw the other girl to her death – and then glanced across and saw *her.*

Marcie had to break Jane's gaze, locked on hers in stunned recognition. Looking down, she saw the falling girl staring calmly up at *her*, like she was memorizing her face or something. The girl even looked coolly from her to Jane and back, as if she'd seen them recognize each other.

All while falling to her death, without a single cry.

Marcie screwed her eyes shut at the sickening thud of impact, screams filling the air. She opened them to the sight of Jane tearing through the dangerous-looking crew like a wrecking ball, before her jaw-dropping upward leap and escape.

"Holy slotting scrotes," breathed Vince, his Link raised, filming the whole thing.

She thought of telling him to delete it, but saw half the club was doing the same.

Lowering it, he turned to her, his eyes wide in shock. "That *was* her, wasn't it? And the hospital footage – it wasn't faked."

Marcie shook her head.

"She's a total maniac."

"She's not!" But even Marcie felt a shiver of uncertainty. "And if you breathe a word about that sexdroid being her, I will... I'll... I'll quit the show!"

Vince gaped at her.

They left the club soon after. The people Jane had dealt with hadn't stayed down long – the bouncers had no chance of stopping them. A lot of people left, but twice as many flooded *in*, drawn by the social media buzz.

Marcie was trembling, but dizzy with relief at learning the girl thrown to her death hadn't been a girl at all. Just a Tik Tek gynoid that'd somehow sneaked in. Jane hadn't killed anyone at all.

All the same, Marcie didn't object to Vince taking her hand and calling a cab as they headed out.

Jane hadn't killed anyone, but the sheer ferocity... she understood, now, why Jane's mother was worried.

Later, lost in her own thoughts, it was Vince's complaints that snapped her back to attention. "Okay car, you nilspec pile of krek- Why are you stopping? No, this is *not* our destination! Okay, car..."

He started to give it the address again, but Marcie recognized the people stepping out of the shadows in the deserted street. Jane had been beating them all up, not ten minutes ago.

She groaned, her heart sinking. "Not again."

Vince looked at her in confusion, and then one of the brutes was tapping with exaggerated politeness on the window. "Marcie Dunkirk. You have reached your destination," he smirked.

She turned in her seat to glare at Vince. "I *told* you not to breathe a word about her!"

He gaped at her. "I didn't!"

A metallic rap on the window snapped their attention to the gun now casually encouraging them to leave the vehicle. "I believe you know how to contact our silver dancer, Miss Dunkirk," the man said. The smile didn't reach his eyes. "I'd like you to make a call for me."

They'd separated her and Vince, after threatening each with the other's safety, taking their Links, and searching them both thoroughly.

I'm not going to survive tonight, Marcie thought, her heart already filling with the pain she knew her father and Amanda would feel. She had just a single slender thread of hope which she clutched, desperately. They'd arranged to meet Jane, to exchange Vince and herself for whatever it was she'd snatched from them. Jane, who'd already torn them apart once tonight.

But how had they known the silver warrior bimbo was her friend? *She* hadn't recognized her, not until Vince had made that remark!

The robot. It had been studying her face and Jane's at the moment they'd shared the look of recognition. Someone had been operating it remotely, watching!

Her spirits began to lift, just a little, as the two cars drew up beside the multi-story building that filled most of the city center block. They lifted a little more when they all headed inside into the brightly lit mall, thronged with people even near midnight.

"Don't get any ideas," the muscular angry woman hissed. Marcie bit down on her instinctive response to the cliched dialog as the woman added, "Won't take a moment to slice one of you fake heroes up if the other one even looks sideways."

The mercenaries had pulled on privacy masks on the way, and done her and Vince's faces with anti face-recog makeup. One of them had even handed back her Death-bird prop. The little drone attracted just the amount of attention they appeared to want. She heard people wondering if she was really Stryker Zaxx or just some cosplayer desper for attention. At first she couldn't believe they'd been dumb enough to leave it with her – until she tried to use it to call for help, and found it was no longer under her control.

Their kidnappers split up, some staying with them and others moving off – setting up an ambush for Jane? – though separating her and Vince.

They steered them to the food hall and waited. And waited. Marcie's spirits lifted further. Jane must have demanded this as the meeting spot!

She just hoped she wasn't planning something that would get them all killed.

They all froze when the small, hooded, black-cloaked figure prowled down one of the approaches straight toward their group. From inside the cowl, Marcie saw the reflective gleam of silver.

CHAPTER 53

"No choking way, Leeth!" Nelson was furious. "Who gives a toss? You can't give it to them!"

Looking around the old storm water tunnel, Leeth spied a good hiding spot and drew out the holocube she'd snatched from the bot. "You wanna note down my GPS thingy?" she asked, wrapping it in a filthy plastic bag and putting a rock over it.

"What?"

"Try to keep up, Nelson. The fake holocube you made – tell me you copied all the Bio-Block data you could to it."

"Huh? From the night of the Packed Light Reboot? Yeah, I copied it, but-"

"Good enough – so I can trade them a cube containing Bio-Block data." She began sprinting through the night dark tunnel. She wouldn't use the last manhole she'd passed. She wanted to get a good distance from where she'd hidden the paydata before emerging and possibly being seen. "Grab a car for me. And I'll need something to cover up this stupid jiggling suit if I want to get to the meeting point without being arrested."

The tunnel bent to the right. She didn't slow. "Gecko on," she whispered, activating the suit's pads and jumping. Planting her feet on the wall, she felt them grip as she crouched, soaked up the impact, then sprang forward, propelling herself around the corner and tearing off again.

"Juice me!" she heard Nelson exclaim.

She grinned in the dark. "Hey, at least I'm getting *some* use from the gecko pads!"

She accelerated harder, earning another gasp from Nelson, presumably reading her speed from the GPS. "I'm heading back down here, then taking that dogleg left," she panted, "and then taking the second grating up and out onto the streets."

Father's voice broke in. "Leeth, Nelson informs me you have abandoned the holocube *and* the mission. That is unacceptable. Get-"

"I don't report to you, Father. And I haven't abandoned the mission, I'm just making a small detour. And don't even think about trying to order me to abandon Marcie. That's not gonna happen. If the holocube is important, maybe you should send someone to pick it up before I head back there? Nelson can tell you where it is."

Father continued ranting, but she basically ignored him. Fifteen minutes later, as she stalked into the brightly lit mall, wincing in the near-daylight, a fresh idea came to her.

"Hey, Nelson, you reckon you're a wizard hacker, yeah? Think you could grab control of this?"

"I can grab control of anything. But whattya mean, 'this'?"

Was she kidding herself, or did Nelson sound like he was enjoying himself? "The mall, dummy."

She could almost *hear* his smile.

Earlier, inside the Department, Mother had tried to object. "I can't believe she's doing this to us *again!* If you arm her with a gun, you're sending her the message you expect her to kill."

"I prefer to think I'm sending her the message I want her to survive," Eagle said. "Even though she *is* disobeying orders, I will not send an agent into a situation like that, armed only for hand to hand combat. You don't give someone a knife for a firefight." His tone brooked no argument. "Besides, if she does let loose, *and* somehow survives, I'd prefer she didn't retire them in her very unique style."

The two mages had fanned out, looking down from opposite balconies on upper floors. Nelson, hacked into the mall's face-recog system, had also picked out a merc in a good sniping position, a 'fishing rod' case suspiciously close to hand. The other four were dead ahead, their faces covered to defeat facial recognition software. They loomed over two figures seated a short distance apart. She knew Marcie instantly, despite the zigzag face makeup they'd painted her with. And the thin black guy beside her, too, who'd been at the club. Where had she seen him before that? Did Marcie have a *boyfriend?*

They both looked really scared. She didn't blame them.

A low burn of anger started, at herself, for somehow getting Marcie in trouble again.

A couple of people were obviously filming, no doubt recognizing Marcie's – or rather, Stryker Zaxx's – 'companion killbot', Deathbird. "I think it's them!" she heard one person whisper. "Nah, they're just famers," another said.

She realized what the Tik Tek team had done: the privacy makeup and props walked a fine line between wannabe cosplayers and a genuine commando PR stunt to promote the sci-fi series. It was kind of clever. Enough witnesses to keep things cool, but short of a pushy crowd.

And for some reason – probably the ominous, concealing black robes she wore – people had started to notice her, too. She heard whispers of "showdown" and "Underworld".

"Got them all?" she asked Nelson.

"Yep." She flicked her eyes to the head-up display, where a rendered wireframe model of the mall showed her each enemy, the mages' labels in red. Nelson might be a real dick, but he knew his stuff. "Heh. Nice. Pity the Deathbird isn't a real killbot."

She heard Nelson snicker. "Already checked. No targeting system, so I couldn't even blind anyone with it. I have it now too though, if you need it."

"You're ready?" she asked.

"Yeah, just give the word. 'Dark', right?"

"Yep. Hey, if you do help me save Marcie, you've earned yourself a kiss, Nelson."

She'd expected some smart reply, but he said nothing. And then the time was up. The mercs had noticed her approach too, naturally.

They shifted closer to Marcie and her friend as she walked up and stopped.

"You have the goods?" The man spoke with a slight accent, kind of Russian sounding. It was the short, angry guy who'd had the plastic gun and told her she had no idea who she was crossing.

She sneered, reaching into the cleavage of her suit, and saw them all tense. She slowed and pulled the small crystal cube out for them all to see. "Yeah. Though I hear these old things are pretty fragile." Holding it out lightly, she glanced down at the shiny cream-tiled floor.

Stun-baton woman's muscled arm tightened on Marcie's shoulder, and the big Russian squeezed Marcie's friend's collar bone, making him gasp.

The little knot of anger flared brighter. She fought to keep it from her voice. "Let them go, you get the cube."

"How do we know cube is genuine?"

"I'll wait here with you while you check."

"Is cube stolen from Bio-Block?"

"Hey, I'm not an idiot. You're probably recording. I just took this earlier tonight from a lovely little robot's hand." She shrugged. "I hear it's loaded with Bio-Block data, but what would I know?" She tossed the cube up in the air and caught it, watching them all tense.

Around them now, a small crowd had gathered, keeping a respectful distance but most of them recording.

"She has not lied," she heard from an earbud of the angry, stocky guy.

She waited.

"We find friends if you double cross," he warned her.

It was like the world strobed black.

Fury flooded her, then a surge of pride at controlling her expression. A few more seconds, and she even trusted herself to speak. "Yeah, Boris, I got that. Let's do the exchange. I don't want any innocent people getting hurt."

"Girl is very *angry,"* said the voice from the earbud.

She'd assumed they'd have a Truth spell running. But as long as there was enough truth to what you said, you could usually fool those.

"Okay," he said at last to the two pinning Marcie and Vince in their chairs. "Let them go."

Leeth turned to her friend, wishing Marcie could see her eyes, instead of the chromed lenses of the suit. "Go home, Stryker Zaxx. We *will* meet again."

Leeth heard the crowd stir, excited, several voices whispering "I knew it!" or "Told you so!" She saw Marcie frown at the odd sound of her voice, but neither of them wasted any time in leaving. Marcie, Leeth saw, took a firm grip on the guy's hand and led him away.

"So. Is now your turn."

"Yeah, yeah." She held out the holocube and shut her eyes, now very happy they were hidden by the mirror lenses.

She heard the big, Russian-looking dude she'd clobbered at Club Sybarus step cautiously forward, and take the cube. But most of her focus was on Marcie and Vince's quickly fading footsteps. "Shouldn't we call for help?" he was asking. "Hell no," Marcie said. "She said go home, so that's exactly what she meant."

Leeth could have kissed her.

The man snatched the cube from her palm, and she smiled while he moved quickly back to angry guy. She heard baton woman growl, like she'd hoped for something more dramatic.

The big Russian bruiser came back, his breath puffing into her face. She breathed out gently, tracking his movements, picturing him bending down.

"Now you wait, while we check."

She smirked, keeping her eyes shut.

Angry Guy started unpacking something by the sound of it. She heard him move to the table Marcie had been sitting at, a case clattering down on its surface.

"You guys seem like professionals," she said, still deciding on her next actions, one way or the other.

Mr Angry continued ignoring her. Closer at hand, the big guy took a long breath, the rustle of his clothes warning her he was moving again. But slowly. And then she felt his large hands on her, searching her.

Now he was close enough.

CHAPTER 54

It felt good, letting the dark rage erupt. Through the blood roaring in her ears, she smiled up at him, her eyes still shut, riding the rocketing pressure, happy to let it build. Reaching into his pants, she slid one hand down to cup him. "Me, not so much," she said – and activated the suit's taser.

His high-pitched scream only fanned her fury.

"Dark," she said, and then there was night.

The first shocked cries started while she drew the gun from her back. "No one touches Marcie Dunkirk," she swore as she opened her eyes and shot first the big guy between the eyes, then Mr Angry, then the woman.

Screams in the dark started with her first shot, the crowd panicking. Turning, she aimed coolly up at the target Nelson had identified as the sniper. She heard his case clattering to the mall's tiled floor as the faint red lights of his weapon's readout showed him blindly swinging the barrel in her direction.

Stepping to the side to fire, she grimaced when her shot only winged him. And her time was up: Nelson had said it only needed one point five seconds for cyberoptics to adjust from bright day to pitch dark.

"Gecko, on" she ordered the suit, re-holstering her gun, leaping to the first-floor balcony, and from there to the shiny tiles of the spiral wall, her speed helping her stick. Delighting in the amazing grip, she closed on her target. She didn't even need her HUD to pick out the sniper, who stood with weapon barrel sweeping back and forth across the ground floor to acquire his target: her.

He cursed in an unfamiliar language when he saw only carnage, instead.

He sensed her approach, though, as she vaulted the final barrier from the central open well.

She heard Marcie's Deathbird buzz straight for him, then the cough of his silenced shot. The little drone exploded in a shower of plastic.

Eagle had asked her, if she had to kill, to avoid her special ability. But the rage gripped her now and she felt a strange hunger for blood. Claws speared out, puncturing her suit's gloves, and with one hard swipe she took off his head.

By then, Nelson was screaming in her ear. "What the

fuck are you doing? You're supposed to be *escaping* in the dark. Not hunting, you lunatic!"

She ignored his ranting. *There.* The first mage, fumbling on a pair of goggles.

Black flames roared higher. She shot him twice, neatly bracketing his heart. Turning from him, a glance at her HUD showed another figure. Goggles on, his hands moved in the finishing gestures of some spell.

Until her bullets found him, too.

The air was filled with screams and running footsteps, people stumbling and falling, lost in the dark without even emergency exit lights to guide them. A few, less-panicked, activated the torch functions of their Links.

Anger and exultation roared through her, demanding *more* blood; a river of it. A vast hunger flooded in behind it. She felt darkness coiling through the air, but this time not toward her, but pushing out *from* her.

It washed into the frightened crowd, extinguishing their Link lights, dimming them to dull embers that jerked in frantic arcs. Choked sobs of dismay rose as people tried to shake the dying glows back to life.

While Nelson chittered something about a count of twenty, she scanned the darkly milling crowds, her pulse spiking. A darting movement caught her eye, calling her to the hunt. In just three sticky leaps she reached the ground floor.

All around her, people milled – crying, hurt and injured, trampled. She felt their hearts beating, heard the blood surging through their veins. But past them, through them, a stronger Call drew her. She followed, first at a walk, then a jog, weaving through the frightened herd, gripped by a growing urgency. Her prey was fleeing.

The Call strengthened as a turquoise glow traced the bridge of her nose and dusted the arches of her cheeks.

Looking for its source, a man met her eyes, only to scream "Demon!" and drag the woman beside him out of her way. Both pairs of eyes locked on her in fear.

She tracked their motion, seeing the faces crumple into terror.

More faces turned to her in the dark, shocked expressions blossoming with the same fear.

But far ahead, down the dark mall's concourse, a slim

figure shoved people aside. It paused and turned at the fresh wave of screams from behind it, its face concealed by goggles. It drew a pistol.

Her prey. Thinking its weapon could stop her.

It fired, muzzle flashes and booming thunder sparking cries of "Shooter!" She swayed between the bullets, letting them whip past her. From behind, a meaty impact heralded a scream that spoke to her of death.

Eyes locked on the figure disappearing from view, she launched herself forward. The mortals wisely parted for her.

At the end of the concourse she paused, while a hysterical voice babbled in her ears. A half-remembered gesture muted it.

In darkness, the blue glow fading, men and women cowered, staring, cringing away. *Pathetic.* Closing her eyes she dismissed the sobs and whimpers, letting her senses reach out for her prey. Sniffing, she scented the air.

Down.

She opened her eyes, a passageway to one side calling her, and she charged, gecko treads letting her throw herself into a sprint.

From somewhere below she heard a car door open, the sound echoing. She burst out into a lightless carpark, hearing the same door slamming shut.

Tires squealed as a dark van shot from its parking spot, heading away from her toward an exit ramp. She threw herself forward, feeling her soles grip the ground, her muscles like pistons.

The carpark's lights came back on.

The van swerved as it hit the ramp, fish-tailing, and she dived, slamming onto its roof and feeling her skin grip the slick surface. The vehicle bounced up the ramp, accelerating. It smashed through a boom gate, the sound of tearing metal dragging down its side, before it jolted onto the street.

A near miss, blaring horns and screeching tires, but her gecko skin stuck like magnets, and she crawled, step by plucking step, toward the front of the van. More angry horns as the vehicle swerved and wove through traffic, still accelerating.

Above her prey, gripping with feet and knees, she rose

up into the buffeting wind. Locking both fists, she hammered down into the windscreen.

Laminated glass cracked and starred, startling a shriek from inside. The car jerked to the side, rocking crazily.

Cries of "Fuck, fuck, *fuck!*" as the van careened as if steered with only one hand.

She peeled her left foot, then knee, off and back. Then the right, retreating moments before gunshots blasted the position she'd just held.

Snarling, black claws sprang free. She punched down, slicing through the metal roof, relishing the agony of shredding nerves.

From inside, the driver shrieked and the car's wheels locked, spinning the vessel. She threw herself gecko flat to its roof, clinging tight as something hurtled toward them.

A crashing confusion of crumpling metal ripped her from the surface and threw her in the air, blinking and tumbling, slamming down onto the ground.

Rolling and sliding to a stop.

Shaking herself and summoning storm winds, she stalked back to the crashed vessel, wrenching its hatch off. From the other side, the driver staggered out and onto the street.

She prowled toward him, smiling.

Turning, he raised his gun, eyes round and white as he fired. Swaying to one side, avoiding the weapon's swift pellets, she lashed out, removing his arm at the wrist.

He stared at her in shock, ghost pale, cradling the stump. Shaking his head as his rich blood pumped into her night. "Please, no-"

In her ears, the hysterical voice rose again, babbling orders she ignored.

A two-handed thrust buried her claws in her quarry's chest. Lifting him over her head, blood sprayed, bathing her in its hot crimson shower while someone roared her delight, absorbing the Mana.

A woman, laughing, shrieking.

The voice, hers.

What?

From the sky, blinding lights shattered night into day, a loudspeaker blaring louder than helicopter blades. "This is the police. Drop your weapons! Down on the ground!"

Ignoring the voice she dropped the body and ran, weaving crazily, gecko boots giving her insane traction. High-powered bullets chased her, smacking into bricks and concrete. Smashing through a flimsy door, she charged between shelving, Nelson's voice suddenly clear in her ears, shrieking "Side door, side door, you crazy fucking bitch!"

In the alley outside, a downward-pointing arrow glowed in her head-up display, blinking above a flat round outline. Spotlights speared around the corner from above, searching, nearer and nearer. She ran toward the lights, racing for the manhole cover, exhilarated.

"Get back into the stormwater drains."

Eagle's voice.

Unhappy.

CHAPTER 55

Eagle said nothing further.

In clipped sentences, Nelson directed her through tunnels.

She did as asked, not speaking. Nerves still singing from the thrill of the hunt. Confused, but full to bursting with a strange energy, feeling like she could tear down walls! As if she'd been bathed in radiance. She'd been free – utterly free, unchained, capable of *anything*.

She felt... floaty. Lifting both arms, she tried to stop their shaking.

She frowned, rubbing her face, trying to remember what she'd just been doing. Had she fallen *asleep?* Dreamlike images flashed through her mind: riding a bucking metal monster, slicing through its hide.

A man, screaming?

The images slipped away.

A vehicle was waiting when she emerged. It delivered her to the edge of the West Oakland Dumps. The street was still deserted as she darted into the building, and back up to apartment 2B.

She even remembered the entry code.

"Wait for the drone," Nelson said once she was inside. "It'll take your gear, return your Raven stuff."

Stripping off the suit, she held it up, her confusion returning. A snapping shake removed the muck of the tunnels, though it made her dance aside in a futile attempt to dodge flying filth.

In the suit's reflection she eyed a face now flecked with mud. Only mud. The black choker looked as elegant as ever despite the grime. Growling, she wiped at her face, then frowned into the spotless silver and its inflated jello curves, examining the suit. There were a couple of tears. Each fingertip had been slit open, too.

Spotless, though?

A bizarre memory flooded her. Standing, her hands raised to the sky, blood raining down on her. When had she dreamed that? She peered closer at her face in the curved mirror, then at her hands, checking for blood that wasn't there. Feeling there *should* have been blood.

Biting her lip, she remembered chasing a van, clinging to its roof, and... holding the driver's body up to hide from a spotlight?

Was that a real *memory?*

Whatever. They shouldn't have threatened Marcie.

Shaking her head, she sighed and began pacing.

How long was she going to have to wait for Nelson's stupid drone? She stretched, feeling odd aches and pains, but not wanting to sit still. And *so* hungry!

Her hand went to her choker, to call the Department... then hesitated, remembering how Eagle had sounded. Maybe it'd be best to wait for them to call her.

Call Marcie? She'd been kidnapped because of her.... She'd be home safe now, though. *I killed them all.* Somehow, she knew that was true. *None had escaped.*

She frowned. *How do I know that?*

She just did.

She resumed pacing. Waiting for them to call.

Eventually, Nelson did, to say the cube had been recovered. Both the real one, and the fake she'd abandoned in the mall. A reminder to return to the DPA, in the building next door, and a warning to stay in character. No comment on the Sybarus mission. It almost seemed like a stunned silence, from the Department.

When the drone finally arrived – a bigger arthrobot – she found they'd included a water bottle and wipes, to wash off the worst of the muck from the stormwater and disused sewer tunnels.

Somehow, the terse communications conveyed their displeasure.

Obviously they were leaving it up to her to work out where to spend the night. Dressed once again as Raven, she stalked back to the DPA, feeling her way back into her skin. She felt... strange. Suddenly Raven's life seemed simple, even privileged. Peaceful. Maybe she'd gone a little over the top, but it had felt *good.* Like she'd been satisfying a hunger she hadn't known she'd had. It reminded her of how she'd felt hunting bad guys with Tash, spilling their blood. Watching Tash feed.

She found herself smiling at the memory.

The switch with her alibi provider went smoothly. Returning from the restrooms she took the seat the other girl had been warming. Seven hours, and her number had still not come up. She was hunched forward, so lost in her own thoughts she almost failed to respond to the call for Tanya

Denison. Numbly, she received the 'accommodation request denied' notice. Because the info on her recent places of residence didn't check out.

No doubt it was all 'in the interests of authenticity'. But staring down at the note – yeah, an actual paper note with printing on it, how wasteful was that? – and reading the casual dashing of hopes, even knowing it was just part of a cover identity... somehow, it still hurt. An hour ago, she might have cared about that. Now....

She screwed it up into a little ball and tossed it away, her mouth tightening. *I'm not going to spend the next hour finding a recycling bin.*

Stomping out of the bureaucratic hope destroyer, she stood on the sidewalk staring down the long street leading into the silent, waiting darkness of the West Oakland Dumps. The urge to go in and find a few predators to kill felt like the pull of gravity. In there, she and Tash had stormed through Club Juzz like agents of death. She swallowed, feeling again a weird hunger churning in her belly, wondering if that was how Tash felt, when the vampiric need for blood rode her? What was Tash doing tonight, wherever she was? What might Tash think of her... slaughter, back at the mall?

What *had* happened? Had that been the black dagger's influence, or had she just fantasized those black ribbons as an excuse for what she'd done? Or... black *claws?* Biting her lip, she flashed them out – retracting them with a shaky laugh when she saw nothing.

What would *Marcie* think? She'd tuned in to news reports of a 'mass murder at Emoryville mall'. There was even a bird's eye night-vision vidloop of her holding up a body with a missing hand, before dodging bullets and crashing from sight. *Dodging bullets? I can't do that!* She knew she couldn't: she'd tried, *so* hard, in the punishing training with the SHUTZ robot gun.

What had happened, back there? She'd looked like some crazed psycho-killer. Grimacing, she thought of Mother's request not to be reading of 'Bloodbath at Club Sybarus' in the morning. Well, she'd *kind of* gotten her wish.

Leeth felt a peculiar sort of giggle well up inside her, but at the same time felt sick. Suddenly she was back in the mall again, looking around the night-dark space filled with the panicking, fleeing crowd, seeing... food. Not people.

She swallowed. Shook her head. That wasn't her. She didn't think like that!

Seeing them as sheep, maybe?

She drew in several deep breaths, this time truly frightened. Because she *hadn't* been thinking of them as sheep. But she *had* been thinking of them as sources of blood. Which meant it wasn't her. Nor was it her uncle's twisted lies. It had been something else.

She shuddered. Had *Tash* done something to her? She shook her head. No. She was certain of that. Plus, that had been ages ago. And she remembered the torchlight from people's Links, fading to embers. *That* hadn't been normal.

She was still staring into the darkness of the West Oakland Dumps. Part of her was telling her the Department could go screw itself. She should just give in, dive in and continue the slaughter she'd started tonight. Purge the whole area, like she and Tash had purged the nightmare that had been Club Juzz.

Grinding her teeth, she turned away instead, facing the lights of suburban Oakland. Where Marcie and her sister and father lived.

She stopped, her mouth open, imagining calling Marcie. Could she spend the night with *them?*

A truly awful fear flared through her at the thought. She remembered prowling through Luiz's apartment in the dark, blood dripping from her fingertips. She swallowed. *I'd* never *do that to Marcie.* But for some reason, she didn't want to put that to the test. Didn't want to trust herself in Marcie's house, in the dark. With Marcie, Amanda, and their father, asleep and unsuspecting in their beds.

She shuddered again, and shook herself. *What am I thinking? Stay in character.*

Raven couldn't call in on Marcie Dunkirk. *Besides, she must think I'm a monster. And what can I say to that?* 'Oh, no, a magical dagger kind of took possession of me. I'm okay now, honest!' So what *would* she say, when Marcie contacted her? As she surely would. For the first time ever, she dreaded the idea of a call from her friend.

And then she wondered: why *hadn't* Marcie called? She

should be home, by now. Surely? Safe. Truly safe. After tonight's brutal demonstration, even mercs should think twice about touching her friend.

Nervously, biting her lower lip, she dictated a text message and sent it. 'Are you home safe?'

She waited, heart pounding, shining her Link's screen into one eye. 00:12, she noted. Hardly believing how much had happened in the last few hours.

00:13.

'I'm sorry,' she added.

Sorry that Marcie had somehow been drawn into another of her messes. Sorry she'd almost been killed. Again.

00:14.

Maybe she's just asleep.

00:15.

Her Link vibrated. [Marcie] 'We need to talk.'

Leeth's knees suddenly turned to jelly. Sinking to the ground, she waited... but there was no further text.

00:16.

Is she waiting for me to reply? She stared into the display with a sinking heart. *But we* can't *meet, talk. Not* now! *Not while I'm on an important mission.*

But at the same time, she wanted to go there, right now. Explain.

Into the dark house, where her father, and Amanda, slept.

"*Aaagh!*"

She hurled the scream into the night, feeling her heart tearing apart.

No. It was better for everyone if she didn't go there right now. *Maybe it's better, for Marcie, if I don't ever see her again? She'll be safer. Much safer.*

Eyes watering, she dictated her reply. 'Sure. But not for a while. Still working.'

Hesitating, she reread the casual, dismissive words. But it was for the best. She told it to Send. And then crumpled.

It was half past midnight when she finally stopped crying like a stupid little baby and pulled herself together. Rising to her feet, she found herself still facing the direction of Marcie's house.

She clenched her fists, eyes narrowing. Had they picked the Department of Public Accommodation for her alibi *because* it was in walking distance of Marcie's place? That'd just be cruel.

But so like the Doctor. He'd probably persuaded Eagle it'd also serve as a test of her training, her readiness to be trusted to decide her own actions. Had he persuaded Marcie to go to the club, tonight? Why *had* she been there? Had that been his doing? But there was no way Marcie would ever trust him... unless he'd used his Suggestion magic on *her?*

She growled.

You're over-thinking this, Leeth.

But where to spend the night? To 'stay in character'? The Fist of Peace *might* check on her, and after everything tonight, she didn't want to make any more mistakes. *Not that killing those Tik Tek mercs was a mistake.* If there was one thing she was sure of, it was that.

Their headquarters, she decided.

A few spots of water fell, a distant rumble and the sound of approaching rain warning her it was going to get a lot worse real soon.

The memory of Father advising a check of weather forecasts when on missions, both morning and evening, just felt like salt in the wounds.

She took off at full speed for the nearest BART station. Sprinting more to burn off anger than in hope of outrunning the coming deluge.

And her stomach rumbled, reminding her she was starving.

Perfect.

The downpour arrived, the light of the subway beckoning across rain-shattered puddles as she put her head down, growling.

In the carriage, no one approached the panting girl, drenched to the skin and steaming gently, her dark glasses scanning around as if hungry for a fight.

While water dripped, pooling at her feet, everyone buried their faces in screens virtual or real.

The girl's breath hissed in and out of flaring nostrils.

Trudging up the final set of stairs, she listened. Silence. So none of the others had returned to their headquarters. She let her shoulders slump, relaxing, remembering the curious stares of the squatters in the stairwell on the ground floor. It was just as well none of them had spoken to her as she'd dripped her silent way between them.

She turned on the heater, dragged a few broken office chairs up, and peeled off her sodden clothes. Wringing them out, she draped them around then scrounged up a towel. Scrubbing herself dry in fast, angry swipes, jaw clenched, she grabbed up some blankets and made a nest. Then curled up in it, her belly heavy with the cheap fast food she'd stuffed herself with.

Finally closing her eyes she heaved a long sigh and pulled the bedding tight around her. Fingers trembled as she fell asleep, invisible razor claws twitching in and out, shredding cloth and padding.

Her dreams that night were troubled – something about a volcano, and the sexdroid, and even Marc Disten for some reason – but by morning she felt better. Her heart sank, though, when she saw there was no message from Marcie. But it rose a little after calling Gadger to see if he knew a good place for breakfast. He'd said he did, if she wanted to head over to him first. He made no comment about the snoop whose wrist she'd broken, the day before.

Maybe she wasn't the only one whose mood improved after sleep.

As she made her way to his small apartment, though, she winced to think how the Fist would react if they found out she'd killed a bunch of people last night.

There were no messages from the Department, either. That was a good sign, right?

She spent a quiet day settling back into being Raven, helping Gadger, enjoying the peace. Except when she thought about Marcie. Should she call? But just imagining the conversation made her heart race. *Work it out later. You're on a mission now.*

It should've been peaceful, doing almost nothing, just helping him set up a remote camera to watch the monitoring site. Instead she got jumpier. Wondering about Marcie's reaction to last night. Listening to Gadger's heart pumping the blood through his body.

They met up with Wolf in the afternoon, who provided a big city spirit to envelop them, since he said there was a large air elemental watching the area. It'd been weird, knowing they were wandering around the streets hiding from one spirit by being *inside* another. Was a spirit a living thing? The thought made her feel sort of itchy. She found herself wanting to touch it. She knew she could kind of stretch out her cutting tingle to *kill* it, but the desire to instead reach out and just feel it grew and grew. *But what if I hurt it?* The urge to pet it was such a hunger in her, she struggled to focus on picking a good spot for the camera.

I want to dance with it, she realized. *I want to see what it can show me, here in the city.* She imagined herself running across rooftops, leaping from one to the next with its help, lifted into the air. She remembered pirouetting through what she'd called the Jungle as a child, Faith watching with doggy confusion as she'd spun and laughed with the forest spirits, feeling their joy.

Stop it, Leeth: that's *not what you do. You kill things. You're not here to have fun with spirits, you're here to find the traitor in the Fist of Peace, and kill him.* Quietly and smoothly, like pouring honey into hot chocolate. *And then abandon them.*

She pulled her hands back to herself and forced them into her pockets, scowling.

She wasn't sure how successful she'd been in avoiding touching it, in the end. Wolf had sure looked at her strangely when they'd met back up later.

But it'd been sort of neat. Slipping out of the spirit as it passed the doorway of the building they'd chosen to set up the surveillance gear in. Using it like an invisible cloak of invisibility-to-invisible-things. She suppressed an un-Ravenlike giggle. Magic was crazy.

But it had all gone smoothly, and they were back now. Wiz was still hacking, trying to find out stuff, and Cynthia and Wolf had gone off together talking about a library search. She had no idea what the others had been doing. If *she'd* been running the Fist of Peace, she would have had them all hit the target hard, before they could try to prepare their defenses. No one had asked her, though.

She couldn't imagine Father just sitting back and waiting. Well, actually, she *could* imagine Father doing exactly that, him and Mother spending a week just planning it. But she could also imagine him knowing exactly how to arrange a swift attack, and laying out an assault plan in minutes.

But to her it felt like she'd kind of goofed off, wasting a whole day of her investigation. At least she'd had an opportunity to send in a longer status report, and there'd been no special message for her *from* Father or Mother, which must be a good sign. She grimaced, thinking how she'd been four whole days on this mission now. At this rate it could easily take an entire week.

She checked her Link again. Still no message from Marcie.

Snap out of it, Leeth! You're Raven – a tough, cool, self-assured mercenary.

That felt like the biggest lie of all.

CHAPTER 56

When evening finally fell, Raven convinced Gadger to stop off for a pizza with her before the meeting. She did it so they'd take a different route to the one he'd used the night she'd secretly followed him. She didn't want to risk running into members of the slum gang she'd bluffed her way past on his trail that first night, even if she had been a blonde at the time.

Tonight, with the pollution mild and the skies clear, they'd left the lighted and patrolled streets far behind. He'd taken her to a quiet basement bar of exposed brickwork and lots of nooks and crannies. With a grin, he'd suggested they splurge and order real steaks. On a whim, despite the cost, she'd agreed. She hadn't been too sure about *sour cream* on potatoes, but when the meals came she'd been glad she'd played along. It had all been delicious – and seven hundred grams had been just the right amount, for her. *So* much better than the leaden meal of the night before.

Now, pleasantly full of yummy food and determined not to think dark thoughts, she sighed in contentment as they reached the darker, lonelier parts of the metroplex. She'd almost taken his hand, before realizing that wasn't something Raven would do.

Around them, blank, deserted offices loomed, black windows staring down from all sides.

To Gadger, the night glowed in shades of gray to his infra-red optics – the quiet disturbed only by an occasional far-off siren, or the sound of a copter heading to one of the high-rise heliports of the business district.

To Raven, the buildings and streets teemed with whispered conversations, the stealthy padding of two and four-footed scavengers rooting through the garbage of the streets, the muffled hacking cough of an addict holed up in a derelict tenement. Once, she'd heard a pair of footsteps following them, and felt the familiar tingling anticipation sweep over her. That was what she needed! She felt her blood rise, and even slowed a little to let them catch up. But something scared them off. She'd heard one youthful voice whisper, "Tomic, gotta bad feeling: 's early. Less pick some'n else."

The footsteps behind stopped.

She hissed in annoyance, and stopped. Give chase...?

Gadger looked a question at her.

"*Real* bad," she heard. "Lessgo."

Turning, she saw two figures melt away in the shadows of the alley, and her fists clenched.

"What's the matter, Raven? Forget something?"

Maybe it was best. Could she have dealt with them without revealing too much of herself to Gadger? Not that she would have *killed* them. Or even broken their wrists. Unclenching her fists, she shook her head. "It's nothing."

All the same, it set her on edge as they headed deeper into the abandoned territory of old New Francisco.

Turning the final corner they saw the single glowing street lamp that marked their destination. From beyond the far corner of the street she heard the faint sounds of approaching steps. Putting one hand on Gadger's shoulder to stop him, she shut her eyes and concentrated.

It sounded like Maretti. She opened her eyes. "Wolf will be watching, won't he?" she whispered to Gadger, grinning. She hoped her idea would work on Maretti. Then wondered if it might even fool Wolf, too?

Gadger nodded, frowning.

"You go on ahead," she urged, sliding into the shadows herself.

"What-?" Gadger's infrared eye picked her out, moving swiftly off toward a side-street that would let her circle the block. He shook his head. Was she going to try to sneak up on Wolf? She'd have fifty meters to cover in the open. It couldn't be done.

Shrugging, he smiled and sauntered on. As he reached the steps of their office block, he saw another shape turn the far corner. *Too big to be Raven*, he decided, even if she could have gotten there that quickly. Maretti?

A moment later a smaller figure darted from the corner further back, the first figure obscuring it from view. *Neat*, he thought, and grinned as he mounted the steps. Wolf's voice came from the shadows of the foyer.

"Gadger."

"Hi, Wolf." He paused beside the shaman, lounging back in the darkness of the building's entranceway, waiting to see what happened next. "That Maretti I see down there?"

From this height, a couple of meters above street level,

and with his cyberoptics, he noticed an occasional bulging of Maretti's heat-form. *She's either duck-walking, or staying on all fours to keep that low*, he thought. All while keeping at most a meter behind the tall figure.

A tight-curled breeze whipped a pile of dirt and papers into a small whirlwind at Wolf's feet. The shaman frowned down at it, and a moment later was lunging to one side, off the steps, calling out, "Behind you!"

Maretti whipped around – to find Raven standing, hands on hips. "Chill out, guys."

Wolf abruptly paused his spell-casting, a flicker of light dying on his hands. Maretti's pistol was out and leveled. "You stupid-"

Raven pressed a finger to his lips, her other hand turning aside his barrel. "I was just testing our security." With a flash of white teeth she strode past him, sharing a quick grin with Gadger as she bounced up the steps. *Gadger was chrome.*

"You..." Maretti called after her. "We could have killed you!" Her tight black jeans just twitched insolently as she disappeared upward.

"Lucky, wasn't I?" she called back without turning.

Maretti ground his teeth, glaring at Gadger's grinning face as he emerged into the street light. "What's so funny? I almost shot her!"

"But you did not," said Wolf.

Maretti rounded on him. "You think that stupid stunt was *okay*?" he demanded, in disbelief. "*You*, Wolf?"

The shaman shrugged. "If you had shot her, I would heal her. Perhaps it would teach her a lesson."

Maretti stared for several seconds, the tension easing from him in a chuckle. "Somehow, I don't think it would." He frowned at Gadger. "Wasn't she with you today? How come you didn't come together?"

Gadger looked a little sheepish. "Actually, we did. She just slipped off at the end of the alley. I watched her following you down the street."

"Hah!" Maretti snorted. "So much for sneaking up on us."

Wolf and Gadger exchanged a glance.

"Ah, actually, I think she was testing you two. She knows I can see into the infrared."

Maretti scowled. "Well, good work, Wolf."

Wolf shrugged the compliment off. "My watch-spirit told me – *I* didn't see her."

Maretti sighed. "What, you two've formed a Raven Appreciation Society? Come on, Gadger. Let's head in."

CHAPTER 57

Inside, Raven caught Chopper and Wiz smirking, Wiz kind of jumping and killing the projected image they'd been watching when he saw her. She shook her head, catching a glimpse of a girl bent over, stripping in a darkened room. *What is it with men and nudity?*

By the time Maretti and Gadger emerged from the stairwell, she was sprawled out, trying to look calm and relaxed in one of the cracked leather executive chairs.

"So, Raven," Maretti asked, "how'd your mission go last night?"

For a moment she went blank. *How did he know?* He had to be the traitor! Horrified, her heart stuttered.

Then she realized he just meant her wait at the DPA. "Wiped out."

She didn't offer any further explanation, but he appeared unsurprised. "Tough." He turned to Gadger. "So, where'd you two meet this morning? How'd the cam set up go?"

"Uh," Gadger cleared his throat, "good. We met at my place, actually. She's gonna be staying there a while."

Maretti looked at him sideways. "Fast worker."

Gadger wasn't sure whether he meant Raven, or himself.

It was another ten minutes before they were all gathered around the long black conference table. Val and Skinner had taken ages to arrive, much to Raven's pacing annoyance.

She noticed both Wiz and Chopper eyeing her breasts and backside, looking away quickly each time she caught them. The third time, just as she was about to demand an explanation, Wiz projected a holo. "Hey, you guys hear about the Killer Queen last night? Watch this!"

Leeth recognized the song, the scene, and then herself, as Wiz cued the footage. Suddenly deeply grateful for her wraparound shades, she sank deeper into her Raven persona, watching the stitched-together footage play out, to appreciative sounds from her teammates. She felt strange, and found herself growing weirdly angry. They sure seemed to admire her when she was a robot chick getting violent and taking out a bunch of people. But when she as Raven let loose a little on someone spying on them, they were all 'Oh, Raven, you're so mean!'

Until the woman was tossed over the railing. *Then* there were cries of horror.

Wiz chuckled at their reaction. "They should have called it cyber-chick fight, yeah? Because – get this – the *sex-bomb* thrown to her death was a Tik Tek gynoid."

"But she looked so real," said Chopper. "They both did."

Why was Wiz showing this? Straight after he'd been eyeing her so strangely? Was *he* the traitor? Testing her, seeing how she'd react? Or was he watching to see *every-one's* reaction to the sale being screwed up?

But he wasn't even looking at *her* now, his eyes instead locked on the silver girl's wobbling backside as she made her dramatic exit. "Oh, man," she heard him whisper under his breath, shaking his head, oblivious to her.

The silver girl certainly was stacked. Then she remembered that – thanks to the suit's gel padding and constricting waist – that jiggling, curvy creature was actually *her*.

No one was watching *her*, suspiciously or otherwise. She wasn't sure whether to be pleased or annoyed by the effectiveness of Nelson's disguise.

"And the whole time, kinky robo-girl was broadcasting bio-telemetry to everyone in the club. That was a sex stim-suit it was wearing."

Leeth felt her eyes widen behind her shades, and she had to mentally dive down under a wave of swelling anger that threatened to engulf her. *Think about it later. You're Raven.* She heard her knuckles crack.

It was Cynthia who finally interrupted, after a shared look and head shake with Val and Raven. "Maybe you boys could go and watch your porn together some other time. This have any relevance for us at all?"

The men exchanged glances.

"What?" Cynthia demanded. "You are *not* going to tell me this was some military test of combat gynoids. In a *nightclub*."

Davo spoke. "Maybe? No one knows. You obviously haven't checked any feeds yet: it's absolutely viral on the net."

Behind her shades, Leeth closed her eyes.

"You see, it gets weirder. The silver sexbot had a rematch later with the same mercs – in a crowded shopping mall just before midnight. But this time, it killed every last one of them. After saying 'No one touches Marcie Dunkirk'."

Leeth – barely – contained her groan.

Cynthia blinked. "Mar-D? It was some kind of *Underworld* promotion? But... wait, it *really* killed people? And if it was a promo that went horribly wrong, surely they'd have name-checked Stryker Zaxx, not the actor who plays her?"

Why were they going on about this? Leeth gritted her teeth, wanting to interrupt, but not daring to draw attention to herself. 'Viral on the net?' *Don't play the video, don't-*

"Play the video, Wiz," Maretti said.

I am Raven. I don't care about this. It's boring.

Twenty heartbeats later, it was over, the light returned, showing crowds of panicked people fleeing the mall.

"It killed three mercenaries, in the dark, in one second," Don said. "Climbed sheer walls in a handful more to behead a fourth who carried a sniper rifle. Those last few muzzle flashes were it killing two mages. Then it vanished into the dark."

"What *was* it?" asked Cynthia.

"Good question," said Wiz. "Watch *this* – recorded seconds later, on the concourse."

People milled in the dark, lit only by their Link flashlights. Then even those meager lights dimmed, dying under the brightening gaze of two glowing turquoise ellipses. Confusion, then a cry of "demon!" followed by screams and gunfire.

Leeth felt hollowed out. She recognized the color – it had shone down on her cheeks.

Breathe, she told herself, even as her world fell away.

But Wiz hadn't finished. Next on his playlist was the vidloop of her killing the driver of the fleeing van. "It vanished into the sewers," he said. "But I've got a friend in forensics, and get this: that last body? There was no blood."

Leeth didn't hear what they said next, as she struggled to make sense of it all. *But I already knew it was the dagger, didn't I?*

What about the Department, though? What did they think? What did *Eagle?*

"And afterward?" Cynthia was saying. "What about Mar-D, uh, Marcie Dunkirk, and, ah, Vince Moore?"

"Bit of a secret Underworld fan, are we, Cyn?" Wiz teased, before growing serious. "They headed back in, before the lights even came back on. Which had been hacked, incidentally."

Marcie did *what?* Leeth closed her eyes. *Of course she would, you idiot. Probably the moment she heard the screaming start. She assumed* you'd *gone berserk, so she ran back to stop you.*

She felt two inches tall.

"Nah," Wiz continued, "they're both okay. Grilled for hours by the cops though, before the studio execs got them out. Everyone on Underworld's swearing they know nothing – denying it was a promo stunt gone wrong. Not that the media's buying it. They're camped outside their houses."

Marcie was questioned by the police, too? And now the media are hounding her? Could this get any worse? Leeth swallowed, feeling like a heavy stone had settled in her belly. She wanted to call Marcie, right now – tell her how sorry she was for putting her through all that. But she couldn't. She had to sit here, unmoving, pretending to be calm. Trying not to scream.

"Like Davo said, the story's gone viral. There's already a dozen conspiracy theories. From Stryker Zaxx being based on an actual vigilante vampire, to Section Nine existing and someone's built a Major Kusanagi for real." Wiz wiggled his eyebrows.

The others looked confused. Leeth, for her part, kept silent.

"Oh, come on, guys, Ghost in the Shell is a classic. And to cap it off, the psychic DJ even played 'Lithium Flower' for the killbot's entrance!"

At the general blank looks, Wiz started on about the sixty-year-old Japanese manga, before Maretti stopped him. "Look, let's table the killer sexbot chat to get back to *our* work. So, Gadger, you first. Tell us about your setup today."

Leeth resisted the urge to jump up and hug Maretti.

Gadger nodded. "Good. We did some shopping for parts first thing this morning – Raven knows a guy who knows a useful little place for milspec spread-spectrum transmitters, by the way – and I spent most of the rest of the day putting things together. Around three, we headed out to the edge of Hunters Point under cover of a city spirit – courtesy of Wolf. With Raven's help, it only took twenty minutes to install the stuff." He hesitated, then grinned. "Would've been faster if she hadn't kept zoning out. I think Wolf's spirit freaked her out."

Raven pursed her lips and looked down at the table.

"We've got one vid-recorder, and a frequency scanner trained on the collection station. They're about half a kilometer away, to be on the safe side, so we have to hope the pollution's not too bad." He shrugged. "The info's being collected in a dropbox, and I'm checking it, still encrypted, every hour or so. Wiz can devise a prog to filter out the boring bits, I hope?"

Wiz waved one hand dismissively. "Easy meat."

"Cyn, what about the magical library?"

The mage frowned. "Unproductive. There was absolutely nothing on shrinking imaginal forms. Which I'd say is a rather significant result. It suggests that whatever they're doing down there is cutting-edge magical research." She nodded at the worried expressions her announcement caused.

"Wolf – any news?"

"Yes. Last night, before midnight, a truck arrived. Men emerged, unloading a small forest of potted vines, several boxes, and a large coil of plastic hose."

Everyone shifted in their seats. Several people swore.

"The truck then drove away. Armed men came up from the manhole. They carried the plants down into it. When all was done, the spell ended and the mage left.

"A few hours later the spirit grew scared, and left the area."

Cynthia's jaw dropped. "It did *what?*"

"I did not send it back – there is something Wrong about that place. I released it from our agreement. I went back and watched for a short time. I saw nothing, though I felt uneasy."

There was a long pause.

"The plants were for protection," Raven said. Remembering her own little nest of kudzu vines when she'd been hiding out from the Department.

Cynthia agreed. "It's horribly hard to penetrate even a paper thin dead barrier. The death, it pulls at you...." She shook herself. "But a living barrier is worse. Spells dissolve instantly in them, and mages and spirits can easily become trapped and die. Nothing imaginal can move through a living barrier. My guess is they've covered the ceiling of the room under the manhole cover, and any other gaps that Wolf slipped in through."

"So no more imaginal penetrations?"

"No. What puzzles me is why they didn't do that to start with? I mean, if they'd left a *big* earth elemental guarding the approach, then maybe I could see them relying on *that*. But Wolf took it out, alone. Or even a strong enough magical Barrier. Absolutely nothing would get through that. Maybe they thought that would draw attention to the place?"

"Maybe it shrank, like Wolf?" offered Raven.

The two mages exchanged looks, at first surprised, but then nodded, like it was at least possible.

"Still," Maretti remarked, "I guess on the bright side, it looks like we haven't spooked them too badly if they're just digging in."

"And Wolf's back to his normal size imaginally now, too," Cynthia remarked.

Maretti nodded at the shaman. "Good. Time heals, eh?"

Wolf frowned. "No. Last night... You remember the old woman told me to seek my Totem when the dreams started? Last night, I had a dream."

His deep, sonorous voice held them as if in a spell. He stood up.

"I will speak it to you."

CHAPTER 58

In my dream," Wolf said, "I walked empty city streets, drawing closer to Hunters Point. Someone waited there for me. Or some*thing*. Waiting to fix me. No, I don't know what that meant," he added at their looks. "A long street led down to the monitoring station. At its top I began descending toward it.

"Ahead of me lay the manhole, open, a droning murmur coming from it." In his dream, threads of chill excitement had fired his veins at the sound. A strange shame held those words back now, though.

"The descent grew steeper as I approached the manhole. My feet slipped and slid under me. I found hand-holds, and stayed upright. The droning changed to a deep buzzing, in my bones, urgent and determined. Pure cold radiated from the manhole.

"It was then I began fighting, trying to pull away. I... called for help." He flushed, his jaw clenching. "And Help came. A shudder took me, shaking through my bones, driving out the buzzing. I found myself crouched low to the ground on all fours, the tough nails of my paws biting hard into the asphalt, gripping the slope."

Wolf paused in his tale.

"And?"

The shaman looked around. "The Great Spirit himself aided me. I shared his strength. The climb was... very long."

"And you got away?" asked Chopper.

Wolf nodded.

"Do you really mean your Totem spirit came to you in a dream?" asked Raven.

Wolf's eyes locked with hers. "Yes."

"How could you tell?"

"It was a True Dream. In the dream, He spoke to me. He said one other dreamed a True Dream last night."

His stare was heavy with significance. And suddenly Leeth remembered.

Her dream had started out the same as usual: stretched out, her leg broken, chained to the cold surface of the bar top by Marc Disten. His expressionless face loomed over hers, his hands clamping her head in place. But this time, he was the Tik Tek gynoid, and his fingers morphed into slender tendrils threading into her ears, seeking connection, control...

The same crystal cold intrusion deep in her head that Marc Disten had created, though. The same inhuman clarity, her Self locked away.

But then Luiz arrived home, climbing the last steps of the stone pyramid and putting down her cage. He came to her, his arms dripping red as he handed her his dagger, dark ribbons of blood writhing behind him across the cold stone. Helping her into her catsuit, those hot black tendrils bathed her in warmth, feeding her the blood of her enemies, strengthening her as he stroked her pelt. It was glorious.

Disten tried to make her put down her obsidian sword, but it had stuck to her hand. He pulled her out of her suit, leaving it behind while he removed his face, unmasking the female sexdroid beneath. The catsuit sat up at that, intrigued, and prowled over to her, coiling its tail around her legs and belly. Its purring woke rumbles from the volcano under their feet.

After that, memories. Memories of death and hunting, she and Godsson fighting his invisible foe, while the cat, amused, looked on, grooming itself.

Wrestling *Her* – the invisible nightmare thing that had called itself Lily – for Godsson. Stabbing through herself, into *Her* while Godsson-

She wrenched free of the memory, finding herself standing, hunched forward, eyes still locked on Wolf across the conference table. Her fingers spasmed, spread clawlike on its black surface, reliving that kill. She felt her nails sink deep, hard plastic yielding like clay.

The gesture released her tension.

Then she realized what she'd done. Eyes wide, she tried to tug her nails free before anyone noticed. They were all watching her.

"You were the other True Dreamer," declared Wolf.

Wincing at the pain, she pulled her fingers free, not looking down, shaking her head while keeping her eyes locked on the shaman's. "Trust me, if that was some kind of 'True' dream, my life is even more krekked up than I know! Yeah, I dreamed. But it was just a bad dream. Memories. It has nothing to do with us, here."

But the words sounded false in her own ears. Except for the part about her life being krekked up. She fought off an urge to check her Link for a message from Marcie.

"What was the dream?"

"Look, I don't want to talk about it, okay? It has nothing to do with all this. Are we going to stand here all night talking about dreams we had, or are we going to try to actually *do* something? Even if it's only coming up with a plan of attack?"

"Was it about me?" asked Chopper.

Raven turned to stare down at him. "What?"

"Was the dream about me?"

"What?"

"*I* dreamed about *you*. Maybe *I* was the other True Dreamer?"

Raven rolled her eyes, aware of Wolf's frustrated scrutiny but ignoring it; and ignoring Chopper entirely. She sat back down as Maretti intervened. "Davo. How'd you go, today, at Tanner Services? Find anything?"

"Not really. I went early, so Cyn could maintain a Seeming on me while I went in as a Pest Inspector. There was no one there, just an auto secretary to answer calls, and a hidden security camera. It had to be a quick search, but the place looked unused. Like they use cheap robot cleaners."

Maretti nodded briefly. "Pretty much as expected. Wiz? How about you?"

The thin man slumped back in his chair. His eyes, though, burned feverishly when he blinked them open. "I'll dump you what I got, but after, I'm going to bring my sleep center back online. And once I do that, I will be *down*."

Raven noticed he was still jacked in to his comp, his movements jerky and uncoordinated, making her think he was somehow being kept alert by it. She hadn't known you could do that with a comp.

"Anyway, here it is, so listen up, kids."

Wiz launched into a long technical explanation of how he'd been really clever and come up with a list of smart people who'd gone missing or died around the start of the Red Level pollution in '59. She was fighting off yawns, and for once, could've hugged Chopper when he interrupted.

"Hey Wiz, this is great, and I'm *so* glad I didn't sleep in and miss it, right; but howzabout you just tell us the top of this list who ya scan *could* be involved in our biz? Yeah? Howzabout that?"

The look Wiz turned on Chopper should have ignited him. Chopper didn't seem to notice. "Hey, anyone else sleepy, all of a sudden? I'll make some soykaf."

Raven couldn't help smiling. For a second, her eyes and Chopper's met. His face lit up, and she quickly looked away, not wanting to encourage him.

Wiz closed his eyes. Maretti waved Chopper off. "You do that, Chopper. Wiz, go on please."

"Very well. *Top* of my list of possible personnel is Dr Callahan Scott, formerly of the Beckman Institute at the University of Illinois. Working on something he called 'The Calculus of Rationality.' Two and a half years ago – August thirty, 2059 to be precise – he was fired for performing unsanctioned human experiments. Volunteers, but still.... It was covered up pretty hard, but I caught whiffs he'd contravened the Global Moratorium of '38: doing research into the Melt and the Unfolding."

"Rape the dying Mother," swore Cynthia. "Where is this- animal, now?"

"Ahh," Wiz shrugged. "That's the thing. Gone."

Val and Skinner slapped palms together. "Crui*sing*!"

"Gone how?" demanded Cynthia.

Wiz ticked off points on his fingers. "Not dead. Not filing tax returns. Not listed in the address 'banks. No credit transactions. Hell, no CID transactions of any kind! Which leaves us with a new ID, or *deeply* buried."

Maretti nodded, looking pleased. "Anyone else?"

Wiz looked uncomfortable. "Sorry, my possible-personnel list only has one other likely on it. I'll get to him in a minute. Let me stay with Scott. First, he's a mage – a sorcerer, not a shaman – forty-five, holds one PhD in medicine and another in magic, and an expert on human genetics and the Melt retrovirus, like I said. I've made you copies of his papers, since *I* can't understand them." He took a data cube from his pocket and slid it across the table to Cynthia. "There's twenty years of papers there," he warned, "about four hundred printed pages."

Cynthia winced.

Leeth frowned at the squashed-looking cube. Could Wiz have had a stash of holocubes, and swapped one over at Bio-Block's the night before last? And he was *still* talking. He sure loved the sound of his own voice. Her fingers tingled with the hope that *he* was the traitor. She could pretend he was Nelson.

"Wife died in '55 – car accident. No kids. Here's a 'gram." He projected the image from his comp into the space above the conference table, and set it slowly turning for them all to see. "It's six years out of date." The face radiated calm confidence. Hooded gray-blue eyes, dark hair, clean shaven.

Wolf grunted. "That is the mage."

There was a moment's silence, then Val, Skinner, and Chopper all let out whoops of delight.

Wiz couldn't conceal his pleasure. "Okay. Number two is a guy by the name of Jeremy Ford. Another doctor. He's thirty, with degrees in medicine and in magic. *Not* a mage, though. Also an expert on the Melt virus. Arrogant, argumentative, and probably a genius. That is, judging from the eulogy printed in the campus newsletter after his death, on January eleventh, 2060. Boating accident – body never recovered."

All eyes turned to Wolf, who simply shrugged.

Maretti was nodding, though. "They fit together, almost too well. No one else, though?"

Wiz tiredly shook his head. "No one special enough to stand out. My short list of possibles after that gets pretty shaky."

Maretti stroked his chin. Gradually his expression changed. "When did the first day of the Red Level pollution start?"

"The three week stretch? September first – just before dawn."

Now Maretti was frowning. "So Scott gets fired on the thirtieth of August. When did that become public knowledge?"

Wiz accessed his comp. "It hit the evening news in New York that same day." Now he, too, was frowning.

"Did he defend himself? Claim a set-up?"

"No. Said the research had to be done – we couldn't afford to ignore it. He was angry he'd been interrupted, is the impression I get from the reports."

Cynthia hissed. But Maretti continued, thinking aloud. "So it wasn't a set-up. Who blew the whistle? Someone who worked with him?"

Wiz projected a selection of news-sheets into the air for all to see.

"No. One of his subjects."

"So. It just suddenly blows up. And two days later he's gone, the nerve gas is let loose in Hunters Point – setting up the research center or whatever. *Two days.* And three weeks later, it's finished."

They were all silent, absorbing that.

"Let's hope this was somebody's contingency plan; someone who'd been watching Scott for a while. If we're tackling someone who could organize an operation like that in just a few days, we're going to have to be *very* careful," he said, his tone ominous.

Raven spoke into the silence following Maretti's remark. "So, Wiz reckons tomorrow is the day the next Pollution truck goes to the monitoring point. Should we be there, watching?" She looked across to Wiz for confirmation.

Maretti answered. "No. What I said before still stands: no one goes near the target area. That's why we have the surveillance gear on it." He couldn't resist adding, "Remember? You and Gadger set it up this afternoon."

Raven just glared at him.

CHAPTER 59

Maretti turned to their hacker. "Wiz, you finished that program to scan the surveillance data?"

Wiz nodded, sending instructions to slave the trideo unit to his program, resident somewhere in encrypted public storage in the net. They waited until the disconnect sounded, the data download completed. He hit play.

They saw the station again, a time-stamp superimposed. It faded to black. An hour later, a rat scurried across the scene. Another fade to black, then at 16:31, a scruffy figure crossed diagonally through the scene, nowhere near the station. Then sunset: ten minutes of the scene shifting into monochrome tones of green as the light-intensifier circuitry compensated for the fall of night.

Gadger chuckled. "Why'd your program mark the sunset as interesting, Wiz? Getting artistic, or too tired when you coded it?"

The hacker frowned. "Uh-uh. I'm not stupid. It normalizes the light levels and white point before making the comparison. Maybe some sort of camera glitch," he said, sounding doubtful.

They played it again, but no one had any other explanation.

Chopper yawned. "So, there's nothing to do but wait. I'm gonna crash." He stood. Several others did, too.

"There must be *something* we can do!" Raven exclaimed.

Wolf answered her. "A good hunter learns to wait."

She stared at him. The words were so familiar, so like the Doctor's, for a moment she suspected he'd Mind-melded her.

Thug was standing looking a little lost; Chopper had already disappeared into the sleeping area at the back of the room; and Wiz slumped in his chair, clearly wondering if he could disconnect.

"Okay," Maretti sighed, at last. "We may as well finish up here."

They each looked at one another, but no one spoke. Raven clenched a fist, beating it against her thigh in frustration. The gesture drew his attention back to her and he frowned.

"One thing, Raven. If you pull a stupid stunt like sneaking up on someone during a Strike, you'll pay the consequences."

The criticism burned, but she hid her reaction behind a shrug. "I told you. It was to test our security. You don't do that when you're Live – only when it's safe."

Maretti bristled. "Safe! I almost shot you!"

She cocked her head to one side, trying to puzzle him out. *Oh. He doesn't know I could've stopped him*, she realized. Which was good, actually. So she merely shrugged again and looked at Wolf. "So? Nothing else was going on. Even if you'd *killed* me, Wolf or Cyn could've healed me up."

She said it matter-of-factly.

It was true. They all knew that. Except for someone enormously cybered, only the most horrific damage could not be mended with magic, if done soon enough. Yet the casual way she spoke of her own death was somehow chilling.

In the following silence, as her eyes came to rest on Davo's dramatically scarred face, she tensed. Looking suddenly less composed, she turned to Wolf.

"You *do* know you can Heal without scarring, if you're careful while the flesh is knitting, don't you?"

"Yes?" His tone invited her to continue.

She held his gaze. "Please use that care then, if I get injured." It was only barely a request.

"If there is time, I will."

Leeth went very still. "The spells for healing wounds work just as well up to an hour after the injury. An hour is a long time."

They stared at one another.

She clenched her teeth. "Do you understand me, Wolf? I would rather wait, in pain, for an hour – or a day, if you know the stronger spell – than be left scarred."

The others looked on, puzzled by her vehemence.

"Vanity, Raven?" sneered Wiz. "Who'd have thought it?"

Leeth pinned him with a look that wanted to draw blood. Through locked jaws she grated out, "I am the way I am, and I look the way I look. If I have to *suffer* for that, then I *will* suffer. I'm not afraid of pain."

Val spoke up. "Throttle back, Raven – what do a few scars matter? Look at me." Baring one shoulder she displayed an area of puckered flesh large enough to have been made by an assault cannon. "I almost lost the arm. Still got this, though, to show for it. People see it, they know not to frag with me." She smiled at the slighter woman. "It's like a badge. You wear it with pride. Shows you're a fighter."

Exactly, thought Leeth. Which was the last thing she could look like, and do what she did. Her eyes widened slightly as she suddenly realized how close she'd come to unmasking herself. She looked down, thinking quickly. When she spoke, she injected a tone of uncertainty into her voice. "For me, it always meant something had gone wrong. Maybe I *am* just vain," she offered, sparing a poisonous look for Wiz, "but it's the way I am. Does it matter? If it's just me who suffers, so what? Juice! All I want to know, is, will you, Wolf, and you, Cyn, try to leave no scars if you have to heal my wounds? Yes or no? Is that so much to ask?"

Wolf met her angry look and nodded fractionally.

She shifted her gaze to Cynthia, whose eyes darted about like they did when she was Percepting an aura. "Now I know how you feel, certainly," she said, frowning.

Raven sighed, and settled back.

"Frag, she's touchy!" she heard Skinner whisper to Val. No one else spoke.

Don's deep voice finally punctured the silence. "How many scars have been erased, Raven?"

Leeth froze, the question slicing sharp and deep. She stared into her lap, unseeing. Her back; front; arms; thighs... was there a place he hadn't-? She shuddered. The Doctor had always taken *great* care, after.... With an effort, she wrenched her thoughts from the abyss inside. "Some," she said, looking up and forcing herself to sound casual.

Cynthia's chin lifted, reading something deeper. Their gazes met. The black band of glasses stared back, blankly threatening, daring her to comment. But the mage only pursed her lips, shaking her head.

Wiz yawned loudly. "I can see you're all happy to discuss healing Raven for the rest of the evening, but I've got to unlock my sleep center before I burn out."

He stood and staggered to the rest area at the far end of the room.

Maretti looked around. "If *that's* all, I'm going to grab some sleep too."

Cynthia stood and headed for the stairs.

Raven was staring down at her feet, fists clenched.

"Uh, Raven?"

She jumped up. "I know! Mindmeld! The truck driver." Her eyes locked with Maretti's. "Cynthia could Mindmeld the truck driver tomorrow."

Maretti looked thoughtful. He tapped his communicator. "Cyn. Could you come back up?"

With an effort, Leeth forced herself to appear calm. She sat back down. To be Raven. Cool. Cynthia emerged from the stairwell and crossed back over to the small group.

"You know Mindmeld, right?" At Cynthia's nod, Raven continued. "We stay back from the Pollution Monitor. Wait for the truck to turn up, finish its business, and leave. Follow it for a while, till we figure it's safe. Then you Mindmeld the driver."

Cynthia frowned slightly. "I'll need a few minutes if I'm going to do it properly. And not while we're bouncing along in the car, looking back at the driver. I have to have him in sight, the whole time."

"I reckon we can arrange something innocuous to hold him up for a little while," said Gadger. "Maybe a flat?"

Maretti nodded. "I don't want anyone too close to the target area," he reminded them.

Raven looked ceiling-ward, and drew a long-suffering breath. *Yeah, we wouldn't want to accidentally bump into someone and capture them.*

Maretti frowned at her. "If we're too far away we mightn't see the truck leave."

Raven grunted.

"Would Wiz know its route, from his scans?" Davo asked.

Maretti shrugged, the sound of Wiz's snores already loud. "He may do. But do *you* want to be the one who wakes him up?"

"I'll do it," offered Raven.

Maretti stared at her. "I'm sure you would. But from what I remember, there's only a few possible routes out. We'll split up and cover them. *Tomorrow.*"

CHAPTER 60

Maretti advised them all to get some rest, but the others wanted to unwind. "Hey, it's important we loosen up a bit before we crash out," Thug told him.

Chopper dug out a six pack of beer, offering it to Raven. He looked annoyed when Thug snared it, tore two free, and passed one to her. "Have a Bud, Raven," he said, moving up beside her. Oblivious to Chopper's glare, one massive forearm draped across her shoulders.

Maretti noticed how little the meaty weight seemed to trouble her.

She turned fluidly under the arm, but instead of moving away, stepped in close. Davo, watching, winced. Something in her stance as she faced Thug made him acutely aware Raven now had the giant wide open for half a dozen different sucker punches. Not by accident, he guessed. Nor had she been intimidated by Don. He frowned. *Strike one.* Although maybe he'd do the same, in her place – hold back from showing all he could do. Wondering how long it would take to earn her trust, he watched her lips curve up in a smile beneath the dark shades.

"No, Thug," she said, gently, "I'm off alcohol for a while. Maybe you could find me something non-alcoholic?"

But a little later, she felt boosted to the verge of hyperactivity. *Like I've drunk coffee.* Peering at the soda's list of ingredients, she saw it: 55mg. She glared at the can in disbelief. How on Earth was anyone expected to guess something called *Mountain Dew* contained caffeine? What idiot came up with that idea? *Chit!*

And in celebration of the day's progress, they'd turned three heaters on, full. Thug, Wolf, Chopper and Skinner all had their shirts off. And Val and Skinner were already getting 'friendly'.

There was something else going on, too. At first she'd put it down to the contrast between last night's dramas and the peaceful day she'd spent today. Just being Raven – when she wasn't pushing away worries about what Marcie was thinking, each time her mind drifted. But now... it felt almost like she was the center of attention, at least from Thug and Chopper and Gadger. In a nice way. And no one was needling her, not even Wiz.

For some reason, her mind kept sliding back to the sex

she'd had with Thug. Somehow it seemed longer ago than two days. The first sex she'd had in ages just because *she'd* wanted to. And it'd been *good*. But that wasn't the image the cool, dangerous Raven was supposed to project. She tore her eyes from Thug's muscled torso, trying to forget the feel of his body. His interest now, and his friendly touches, weren't helping, either. Nor the general attention. Flick, she felt like bouncing off the walls.

If only I hadn't accepted that soda. Stupid caffeine sneaks!

She still didn't know *who'd* gotten the Bio-Block holocube she'd snatched away from Tik Tek last night, or *how*, and now there was all this dumb Pollution Station biz... Her thoughts seemed to spin. *Chip shit!* She ground her teeth while pretending to be relaxed.

Chopper was babbling on about something, and she shut her eyes and tuned him out. It was then, against the closer noise of their talk, she heard a faint whisper of footsteps on the stairs. Springing from the chair, she slid into the deeper shadows against the wall by the stairwell.

Don rose to his feet, puzzled but wary, tracking her heat signature as she moved in the darkness to crouch by the opening from the stairwell, her gun drawn.

A dark shape stepped out from the head of the stairs, flaring into visibility in neon green traced outlines.

"Shadow!" breathed Gadger, sounding strangely glad.

The small stranger took one jaunty stride into the room, then paused in mock disappointment, hands on hips. "Tony, Tony. Your security isn't getting any better!" His voice was resonant, his air extravagant.

Gadger's grin grew wicked as Raven stepped out of the darkness, directly behind him. Her gun prodded him. "Don't bet on it," she said.

The man stilled. Maretti smiled. Gadger's grin was ear to ear. The moment stretched out.

And then, without turning, the newcomer began to laugh. Honest, rich, infectious laughter. Raising his hands he did a slow about-face, his laughter quietening.

His eyes were green, bright, with an electric intensity. For a moment she was almost disoriented, they seemed so familiar.

He was small for a man, only her height. Thin, too –

something angelic in his build. Short hair, with unruly waves. He wore actual glasses, with thin metal frames. His ears stuck out.

Something about him... she knew him. From somewhere. His face. His voice, too.

Facing her he spoke over his shoulder to the group, not taking his eyes from Raven.

"Won't someone introduce me to the lady with the Magnum?"

Chopper sniggered. "We got you this time, Shadow, admit it!"

"Admit it? I *proclaim* it! Dead where I stood, had she wished."

She lowered her gun and he lowered his hands, as Thug's heavy footsteps approached.

"That's Raven, J. She's new. We met her on a strike. She's nice."

Chopper snorted.

Thug ignored him, moving between Raven and the newcomer, picking him up in a crushing hug. His voice was fervent, pleading. "Bro, it's good to see you. You should come round more."

"Oof. Thug, it's great to see you, too, but you're making me feel like a toothpaste tube!"

"Oh. Sorry."

Maretti had come up, too. "One day, Shadow, you're going to drop by in one of your little surprise visits, and someone's going to shoot first and worry later."

"I must just be lucky, Tony. I guess you get a lot of glowing green guys dropping in on you, eh?"

Suddenly, the dimmed tracing of his clothes brightened again into searing viridescence. Some sort of electro-optic effect, like the suit she'd worn last night to Club Sybarus. It flicked off. He turned back to Raven and bowed.

"Your comrades-in-arms seem incapable of a proper introduction, so allow me the pleasure. I am Jack Shadow. Minstrel and what passes for rabble-rouser in these sorry times. Perhaps you've heard of me?"

Her mouth fell open. "*You're* Jack Shadow? *The* Jack Shadow, the singer? And you know *these* guys?" She holstered her gun.

Something about the casualness of the gesture made it

disturbing. Shadow blinked a sleepy smile. "Raven, you interest me."

Her answering smile was hungry.

A sudden flurry of stones rattled against a window, and they all turned to see a gyre of plastic food wrappers and dirt beating at the glass.

Shaking his head, Wolf got to his feet and went over to it. He slid the glass up with some difficulty.

Despite the rasping aerated voice of the spirit, its tone was surprisingly human. "I, uh, I couldn't remember if- I mean, a guy just came in? But he said it was okay, and I thought he was one of the ones you said I should let in, but then I couldn't remember, so I thought I'd, uh..." The wrappers spun, faster.

Wolf sighed. "Go back on watch."

Leeth watched the exchange intently. Spirits *had* to do what the shaman had bargained with them to do: it was woven into their physical manifestation, a part of the deal struck. If you could just sneak past them, she wouldn't have had to cling to the edge of a cold wet building that first night, her hands slowly freezing.

She licked her lips, studying the singer-songwriter.

Wolf dragged the window shut, then turned to face Shadow with a rueful smile.

"One day, you must explain how you do that."

Shadow shrugged. "Pure Intention. It's very simple."

Wolf shook his head.

Shadow was reminiscing. "Jacob and I went to school together. We had similar ideals, I suppose, but chose different routes to try to achieve them."

Raven sat leaning forward, chin on her hands, elbows propped on knees. The black band of her shades never shifted from their visitor.

Only a little time had passed, but Shadow had relaxed into his surroundings as though he'd been born there. Raven had asked how he fitted into the Fist. An old friend of the founder of the Fist, they explained – dead now two years, Davo added, his mood slumping.

"Jacob always preferred the direct solution, the fast answer," Shadow said.

Maretti scowled at Raven's vigorous nodding.

"He thought there were just a few things that needed smashing, to stop them corrupting our society. He could never see the problem was like a cancer, that the fires would have to burn through every part of our lives before people could be free again." Shadow shrugged, the gesture belying the intensity of his words. "I, on the other hand, believe that to change society you have to change the *people*, first. Show them what's wrong, in words their hearts understand. *Convince* them they hold the power to fix things."

Like killing the big bad guys, Leeth thought, nodding again.

"So I craft my songs and my poems, and yes, my deeds and rumors, and send them out into the darkness, hoping to kindle fires in the people who hear them and read them and see them.

"I want my words to burn the cancer from people's souls, melt the chains forged from a century of lies. Smash the petty deceits and self-interests that bind people, and tear down the power-blocs that institutionalize delusion.

"We could be living in Heaven on Earth, but instead we're changing it into Hell."

Leeth stared, rapt, charged up by his fervor. He seemed to be filling her with energy.

Juice he was sexy.

She tore her eyes from his, and noted a subtle split had occurred. Most of the group centered on Shadow – Wolf, Don, Thug, Gadger, and Chopper. Davo, too seemed to be swept up by his energy. Maretti, Val and Skinner kept a certain distance. Cyn had seemed disturbed – she'd made excuses and actually left altogether, after several digs about him 'fomenting' violence.

Tony coolly spoke up. "Pretty words, Shadow, but they're just words, in the end. What we're doing is real. It works."

Shadow shook his head, wearily. "You're wrong, Tony. Just like Jacob was wrong. You do some good, sure. But not enough, and you won't be able to do it for long enough. Nor does it teach people to rule themselves. Destruction is not the answer." Again he shook his head. "But I'm not going to convince you of that, am I? I couldn't convince Jacob, and we grew up together. So maybe it's best we don't go around that loop again tonight." With an effort, he lightened his tone.

"Tell me a story, instead. Tell me how you recruited the delightful Raven, here."

Chopper sniggered. "Delightful? She's crazier than Don!"

Shadow looked from Don, to Raven. Neither reacted. "Oh?" he asked, turning back to Chopper.

"Yeah. Like the other night, we were... well, you'd probably rather not know, but it was in one of the Dumps, right? And we're taking someone to safety somewhere, right-"

"Chopper." Leeth interrupted in a flat, cold voice. "I don't think you should go on."

Chopper hesitated. "Raven, it's okay – this is *Jack Shadow*. He's *okay*. Our secrets are as safe with him as they are with any of *us*, I promise ya!"

Leeth looked at Shadow. "I hope so. Jack Shadow, after all, is a public figure," she stated calmly.

Chopper, about to go on, stopped with his mouth still open.

Davo's eyes narrowed. He glanced around, saw the others bristling. But he felt a prickling at the base of his neck, sensing something darker. *Strike two.*

Don went deadly still, his eyes boring into her as he too realized she had just threatened Shadow. "Drop the fake 'attitude', Raven. You have no idea who you're speaking to. No understanding of sacrifice."

No understanding of sacrifice? Leeth's skin seemed to spark, anger surging; she started to tremble. Both fists slowly closed, but at the last instant, she wrenched back control of herself. *Be Raven.* She breathed out. "Now I understand why you don't say much, Don: it's because you're an idiot."

They all stilled.

Shadow raised a hand, interrupting Don's response. He looked at her, his gaze like a knife. "Betrayal is the worst and foulest lie there is. If I did betray you, any of you, I would deserve worse than anything you could do to me, Raven."

His words struck a chord of guilt in her. Did he somehow guess why she was here?

"I helped create the Fist of Peace, with Jacob Anderson. You have been with them, what, a few days? Yet you question *me?*"

There was an uncomfortable silence.

"Go on, Chopper."

Chopper hesitated, his enthusiasm dampened. "So, uh, anyway, this guy's been watching us, only we don't know it. Raven sees him, and heads off to, uh, check him out. We get there just as she's hauled this guy out, and broken his wrist." He slowed down, suddenly uncomfortable. He darted a look at Raven, but she was staring off into space, frowning.

"And?"

"And, uh, that's all, really. Raven looked pissed off. Crazy. Like she wanted to kill the guy. Anyway, Wolf healed him up and he ran off."

"Would it have bothered you to kill him, Raven?"

His question interrupted her own confused thoughts. She *had* wanted to kill him, at the time. And just a few months ago, she would have been fine with that. Funny how living a few weeks in the Dumps, where life was said to be cheap, had made her see it was often precious. And here were these people, clearly Hunters, who'd been so upset just because she'd hurt someone spying on them.

Were still *upset*, she realized. They were all watching her.

"I thought he might be one of the enemy. Some sort of security guy."

"What would you have done if he was?" Shadow asked.

She opened her mouth to tell him, then closed it. Once again, they all stared at her like she was about to grow fangs or something.

CHAPTER 61

Shadow was wondering what thoughts were passing behind that attractive façade, wishing he could drag the thoughts from her by sheer concentration.

Her answer sounded less than certain. "Well, if he was one of our enemies, I would have just captured him, so we could question him first."

"First?"

The others shifted, their expressions darkening.

"We wouldn't *have* to kill him, after. We could, I dunno, lock him up somewhere so he couldn't report to his superiors."

Shadow and Maretti exchanged a long look. In a tight voice, Davo asked, "What if he'd been a cop?"

"Look, I'm not stupid, I only- I'd only do it if I *had* to. Believe me, I know the problems it causes," she assured them.

"Freakin' shit!" grated out Chopper, "You *have!* How *many* cops've ya killed?"

Her thoughts were flying out of control – until she realized she'd slipped completely out of character. She was being herself, not Raven. But she'd worry about that failure later – right now, she had to dive back *into* character. And answer the question.

Think!

"I haven't." *Because they all got Healed up, after. Plus, that was Leeth, not Raven.* "I haven't killed *any* cops," she stated flatly, her tone challenging him to find a problem with that response.

"Flick!" Chopper laughed, weakly. "Thank God for that! The way you were talking made it sound like you did it for laughs, in your spare time."

She looked at Shadow, who still stared at her thoughtfully. She wondered what he was thinking.

He turned to Maretti. "So how *did* you recruit this bloodthirsty young lady?"

Maretti frowned. "It was on a strike, a few days ago. We were inside... our target, when suddenly, a gun barrel presses up against the back of my neck, in the dark. Turned out, she was hitting the place from above – while we were *cutting off the alarms*, below." He stared pointedly at Raven, who looked away and shrugged. "Anyway, once we'd worked out we were all there for the same reason, we reached an understanding. We completed the job together, and she joined the team."

"No problem in splitting the profits, then?"

Leeth felt a chill rush through her. Was the whole *group* in on it? From behind her sunglasses, she studied faces. Wolf was scowling, but that might be just anger at Bio-Block's work. Don had no expression – as usual.

But all she said, aloud, was "Profits?"

That provoked several snorts and much eye rolling.

Chopper scowled at *her* at the comment, like she'd annoyed him personally. "We don't do it for profit, Raven."

"Shadow likes to needle us about it," Gadger offered. "He thinks we should target more than just war profiteers. Rob from the rich."

Shadow stabbed a finger at Gadger. "Your team could make a real difference! The Fist could target those bloated parasites disguised as capitalists – force them to disgorge some of the lifeblood they've sucked from society. While the one percent feed, the rest wither."

"Shadow, Shadow." Maretti shook his head. "You need to tone the rhetoric down, or one day the gov'll send some secret assassin to bump you off."

Leeth blinked. *I wouldn't!* Then again, she *had* just threatened to do exactly that. And what if they *did* one day order her to kill someone she didn't want to? She frowned. Had she made it clear to Eagle she wouldn't do that? *Well, no problem: next time I go back in, I will.*

"So, what was it this time?" Shadow asked.

"Biological research – drugs for soldiers. We torched it. Destroyed all their data."

"Spear the bleeding whales." Shadow shook his head tiredly. "As if the Corps can't kill people efficiently enough already." He looked at Maretti, then Raven. "I guess Wiz uncovered it for you. But how did you get involved, Raven?"

"I used to... know someone who worked there." She looked away. "He died."

Shadow inclined his head in sympathy, then asked, "And afterward? What were your plans?"

"I didn't really have any. I just wanted to smash the people who'd murdered Paul. After that... well, I like what the Fist of Peace does. And it's not like there's a shortage of targets. After all, when you come right down to it practically all the megacorps are fair game."

The others shifted uneasily.

"Uh, not that any of us think the Fist of Peace could take down Asgard, for example," Gadger amended.

Raven looked faintly disappointed. Leeth quickly schooled her expression when she saw Shadow had noticed. "Anyway, I didn't really have anything worked out past the first payback."

"Who does?" asked Shadow.

They all fell silent. Leeth watched him, wondering if maybe she and he together could convince the Fist to be a bit less... gentle. That'd be pretty chill.

"So, I guess you have things to do, Shadow," Maretti hinted, an hour later.

"Me? No – done my biz for tonight. A little synthing, met a man about a gun. Afterwards, I thought, as long as I was in the area..."

"Yeah, well, don't feel like you have to hang around."

"Tony, you always make me so welcome! But hey," he went on, injecting a note of concern into his voice, "I'm not keeping you up or anything, am I?"

Maretti just scowled and stood. "We're going to start at dawn tomorrow," he warned the group in general. "Stay and gossip if you like – I'm not your nurse-bot."

He stalked off.

The others watched him go, Gadger looking apologetic. Shadow just grinned.

"So what's new with you, Jack? Still working on the new album?"

"'Power'. Yeah. And still writing for 'Dead Don't Cry'. Did you see my piece on old Sioux tribal law? Some interesting lessons for us there, today."

"Uh, no, it's not really my sort of 'feed."

Chopper sniggered. "Nah – maybe 'Microtronics Now', or 'Mud Wrestling Babes', eh Gadger?"

Gadger threw his empty beer can at Chopper.

The talk drifted on into the small hours. Leeth, gradually coming down from her caffeine high, became absorbed in the discussions. It made her realize how little she knew.

Most of what they said went over her head, as the discussion delved deep into society and politics. It made her feel young, naive, and uneducated. She couldn't ask questions, either, since that'd reveal her ignorance.

The idea of corporations as potentially immortal sociopathic living organisms, created by human beings, struck her as kind of chill, if also creepy. It set her dreaming of ways to kill a Corp, sighing finally when she decided it'd probably need to be done with computers and stuff.

But she paid close attention when the talk delved back into the past, back when the US still had fifty-two states.

"We lost our way," Shadow said, "when we lost sight of a simple truth: a country is a living thing, made up of all its people."

"And the land," Wolf added. "The land is not a resource to be *consumed*."

Shadow nodded. "And when we started treating people as statistics – as socioeconomic groupings, regional bodies, corporate blocs – even people became invisible. Their voices unheard by those they voted for, nor paid for the work they did – only what the corporation doled out. Wealth dribbled down from the top of the pyramid, soaked up as it descended, leached away at each layer, even though the work at the bottom created the wealth for the top. Until work itself was devalued."

Davo agreed. "That, and the corruption of rules designed to benefit the many, into rules that benefited the wealthy few."

With the bots, jobs were drying up even faster. The money flooded to the rich, who owned the bots. For a crazy second, she had the impulse to blurt out that *she'd* helped stop some of that, by killing Mr Xing Deng Zhu.

She bit her lips, instead.

The greatest tragedy of all, Shadow said, had been the lost chance for revitalization. For a few decades, earlier in the century, everything had been in place – country-wide communications, total access, free sharing of knowledge. Even attempts to set up a universal basic income system, to share the wealth built from billions of collective years of effort.

At that, Leeth couldn't help snickering. "Billions!"

They'd all looked at her.

"Do the math, Raven," said Chopper, of all people. "On average, fifty million workers, over even just a hundred years."

She did, and then sat back, clamping her lips shut.

The talk continued: how people had lost faith in the politicians, and how that distrust and disengagement only accelerated the process. While the boldest actions, the biggest investments – reversing climate change, creating Mars Colony, developing Thorium power – had been tackled by business consortiums. Because that's where most of the money was, and money was power. Those bold actions though had helped erode faith in democracy itself. Though big business hadn't helped with eco-destruction. The Brazilian 'war' still festered.

And the truth wars, as Western societies struggled to balance free speech with orchestrated misinformation and lies spread by those trying to tear them down. Both from within and without.

People gave up hope.

"But Hope never dies," Leeth whispered.

Shadow looked at her. "What?"

She just shook her head, increasingly aware of how little she knew and how out of her depth she was. "Nothing."

She went back to listening. Strangely, unlike everyone else she'd ever heard discuss any of this stuff, Shadow said the return of magic – even Melisande d'Artelle's deadly and insidious viruses, and her Second World Storm – had been inconsequential in comparison.

And lots more. Some of the ideas seemed simple – like moving the President's Day holiday to Election Day. Others, more radical. Like replacing Senators by 'juries' of people elected by lottery, the abolition of the role of President, compulsory voting, a thing called MMT that sounded important... she couldn't remember it all.

She just sat back and listened, letting the others do the talking. Trying to look cool and knowing. The strong, silent type.

Eventually, they wound down. One by one they drifted off, exhausted, but charged up with fresh determination.

At last, Gadger too said good night and staggered off to his cot.

Which left just her and Shadow.

CHAPTER 62

Shadow studied her with lazy interest. She could practically hear him mentally changing gears. She'd moved up onto the couch hours ago; and he'd appropriated the battered executive chair Maretti had abandoned before they'd even gotten onto politics.

"Do the shades ever come off?"

She was still framing her answer when he went on.

"Or maybe you have an allergy to bright lights?"

She bristled at the implication she was some sort of Melt victim.

"Or – and this is *my* guess," he drawled, his voice dropping lazily lower, "it's an image thing. You couldn't look half as menacing without them, could you? Or old enough, maybe?" *Early twenties*, he figured.

She didn't answer, just glared at him.

Rising, he came over and knelt in front of her as she sat curled up on the couch. His eyes blazed an intense green. She wanted to move away, stop him digging for secrets.

She wanted him to touch her.

He reached out one hand, slowly, his fingers just resting on her sunglasses.

She didn't move.

He slid them off.

She was lovely, he saw.

He'd half expected some terrible scar across her face, puckering the skin into an ugly mask.... But she had beautiful eyes – a rich amber, deep as an abyss. And she was young. Stars, she was young.

She felt like he'd just stripped her. She saw first appreciation, then surprise steal over his features.

His voice was a whisper. "Damn. I'd say nineteen." His hand reached out, stroking one silken cheek. Traced her small, rounded chin, then up and along the high cheekbone. He ran a fingertip over her very expensive-looking choker, noting how she tensed when he touched it. He eyed the subtle black-on-black engravings. "*This* ever come off?" he teased.

"No. It was a gift from my father. Why? Do you want one, too?"

His warmth felt like a force pulling her closer. And he was so *near*. Her own hand reached out, her fingers snaking through his hair. Drawing his head down to hers, she brought their lips together while thrusting herself up.

A small sound escaped her at the contact.

Suddenly her barriers were gone, burned away by the kiss. Shrugging off the black leather jacket, she dragged him down on top of her.

Much later, the kiss ended.

With his right arm he propped himself up and let his eyes wander, slowly, over the gentle curves emphasized by the soft black material of her figure-hugging top. His gaze was almost tangible, an invisible caress.

His left hand followed the path his eyes had just traced, his fingertips leaving a tingling wake, a wave of pure pleasure shivering over her skin.

He lowered his head again, renewing their kiss. His hand moved, gently pinching a nipple, and he felt it stiffen, eager for his touch. Their tongues danced, dueling together, and he laughed gently in the back of his throat.

She growled a soft warning.

The kiss ended, but their eyes never lost contact, his left hand staying on her breast. She was breathing hard.

"Mutually assured seduction," he murmured.

Her nostrils flared, rejecting the clever words. No. Rejecting *words*.

He watched her hand descend to her crotch. As she pulled the zip down, she raised her hips lasciviously up, then wriggled her tight black jeans off, her eyes watching his.

Her lips parted.

She raised her top, rolling it up over her breasts, baring them to his gaze.

His pupils dilated, but then he grimaced and held up a hand. "Raven... I don't have any protection."

"Don't worry, I can be gentle. I won't hurt you."

She wasn't making a joke. At first he looked a little confused. Then, for the first time since being alone with her, he felt less than utterly self-confident. "Uh, good, but I meant protection against pregnancy."

That earned an eye-roll. "I *have* an implant." For just a second she frowned, before shaking her head.

She stretched, sending soft shadows snaking over copper-gold skin. He licked his lips.

This time *he* growled, his mouth drawn irresistibly to

the tips of her breasts. But even as his lips brushed them and her eyes closed involuntarily at the fresh shock of pleasure, her fingers reached lower, making him gasp. It was her turn to laugh quietly, savoring the feeling of *her* mastery.

He raised himself over her. Her tongue darted across her lips, her smile an open invitation.

He moved, she moved, and he felt himself guided smoothly within. Her eyes, still open, de-focused at the intimate contact, her lids closing to mere slits. When they opened again, her pupils had dilated so wide, her irises seemed eclipsed.

He began with long slow strokes, setting a rhythm, holding himself above her. And her eyes stayed open, fixed on his – sometimes widening, sometimes narrowing. She watched him enjoying her responses. Both of them as aware of the pleasure granted, as that received. A give and take of equals. Not a contest of wills, like with the Doctor. Not a demonstration of dominance, like with Luiz.

Just two souls touching, creating joy. For some reason, she found herself blinking back tears.

At times she had to clench her teeth and bite back her cries; at others, her mouth opened wide in a silent shout; but always she watched him watching her. Made a gift of her responses, her feelings. Let him know exactly how she felt – the pleasure he was giving her. It added amazingly to the intensity of the union. It made her want to cry.

Urgently, quietly – while the others slept – the two fed their passions.

For one night, she could pretend she'd found love.

CHAPTER 63

Slowly, they drifted back to themselves. She reached down, found her sunglasses, and once more veiled her eyes. She found a rag and wiped herself, then him. An oddly fastidious gesture.

He raised himself, one forearm braced on the armrest at the end of the couch, absorbing the sight of her. His other hand softly traced the curving lines of her naked torso. She arched and stretched luxuriously, with a smugly sated smile. But beneath that, he sensed a peculiar vulnerability. Sadness.

He'd met and loved many women, some considerably older than her, who were far less accomplished in their lovemaking. "Full of surprises, aren't you?" he said, softly.

"Mmmm," she agreed.

"Where did you learn to do... all that?" He was genuinely curious.

After a few seconds, she realized he expected an answer. But she knew not to admit to special training.

"I like sex. I read about it, watch movies about it, practice in my spare time." She thought, then quoted the Doctor to him. "Our bodies are instruments. We should learn to play them to the *best* of our ability."

"Mmm."

She took it for agreement. He'd stopped stroking her, now, and they eyed one another. She started to unroll her top, pulling it back down taut over her curves.

His hand reached out to stop her. "Not yet."

"It's getting cool. Maybe you should take a photo?" She finished pulling it down.

He laughed in outraged delight. Shook his head.

She grinned back at him. She liked him, she realized, as she tugged her panties and jeans back up. *Really* liked him. She swallowed. And she'd like to know him better. Small chance of that, though, given the circumstances. For a moment she felt a stab of annoyance at the Department. At how difficult it made parts of her life.

"Hey, can I ask you a question, about some of your lyrics?"

She got the distinct impression he stifled a groan, for reasons she couldn't guess. She *really* wanted to know, though. "Can normal spirits lie to you? To try to get inside you?"

He blinked. Blinked again. "What- *why* would you ask that? And why me, of all people? I'm a minstrel, not a mage." For some reason, though, he shuddered.

"Well, there's that line in Soul Quest," she said, "the spooky whispery bit where you sing 'wo-orld's be-e-looved', when he's being tempted. I... I just thought maybe you knew...."

But from his expression, he very clearly *didn't* know. Probably it'd make more sense to ask Wolf. Though maybe not until after she'd completed her mission, judging by the way Shadow was looking at her. Kind of as if he expected... a ribbon of darkness to unfurl from her mouth and slip inside him. Or something.

She changed the subject. They talked about his work – he even read some lyrics from a new song he was working on. She got the strong impression he did more than just write the words. She sensed he was someone Eagle would consider a danger to society – a society that had turned its back on all the people living in places like the Dumps. She made a sudden promise to herself: not to mention Jack Shadow in her report.

Once again, she imagined her and Shadow together; wondered, even, whether she might achieve more good by joining him, or the Fist, instead of staying with the Department.

"Penny for them?"

She had no idea what he meant, but just gave what she hoped was an inscrutable Raven smile, and shook her head.

It seemed to work. "So, you've been with the Fist of Peace a few days? What do you think of them?"

She thought about it, and smiled. "They're nice."

He blinked, slowly. "'Nice.' Nice isn't the word I would have chosen, myself."

She shrugged. They *were* nice. She looked at him, her head tilted to one side. "Why do you ask?"

"Because you don't seem to fit. You're *with* them, but don't seem fully a *part* of them."

She studied him carefully, reading his posture, the position of his hands, his arms. It all spoke of simple curiosity. Maybe even honesty. She felt she could trust him. A little. More than she could trust *some* people, anyway.

She listened to the breathing of the others, satisfying herself they all still slept. "I guess I don't feel *really* comfortable with them. Except Gadger, I guess. And Don."

He'd started to nod. Started to. Then froze in disbelief. "You feel comfortable with Gadger. And *Don*."

She nodded, puzzled by his reaction.

"You don't feel Don a little... threatening?"

"Mmm," she agreed, a smile playing at the edge of her mouth, her face coming a little more alive.

I may get a chance to try myself against Don. She bit her lower lip. She'd have to wait until after she'd found the leak, of course – unless she was lucky and it *was* Don, after all.

He watched her, and the strange expressions that crossed her face woke a dawning comprehension.

"You *have* killed cops, haven't you, Raven?"

She looked at him, snapped back to the present. *Damn.* Somehow, she knew he'd recognize a lie, and on a hunch, decided to trust him. A little. She shrugged.

"How many?"

He looked very... judgey. "None, actually. They all got Healed, so none died permanently."

He just blinked at her. "And how many who *weren't* cops?"

She thought about that, frowning. The very first person she'd killed, that guy in the park... she shied away from the memory, flushing. *That* one she shouldn't have done. Those guys who'd attacked her in the alley, though, when she'd just been asking directions to the Red Fist Dojo... *they'd* deserved it. One of the muggers, after the opera with James.

She swallowed, remembering the guy on the stairs, when she'd been staying at Emma's place. But that had been kind of an accident – did it count? Maybe not, but she did know it made it wrong, not right. She grimaced.

Then there were those nights she'd snuck out from Emma's to go hunting in the Dumps.

When she'd been on the run in the Dumps, too, there'd been those rapists. Oh: and the whole *nest* of scum she and Tash had cleared out, Club Juzz. And a few more important ones, for the Department: Marc Disten, Shepherd Fox.

Luiz.

Her recent jobs for the Department.... Oh. The six or so mercs who'd kidnapped Marcie, *last night!*

Blood rushed to her face at the belated recollection, pride in her accomplishments collapsing like a sandcastle crushed under a wave.

He was still waiting, though she caught his expression changing, something dark and heavy, challenged by a spark of doubt. She wanted him to understand, she suddenly realized. Jack Shadow, the writer-composer of the Soul Quest saga. She was about to explain most of them had been child rapists, when she pulled back from the brink, gritting her teeth against a powerful urge to slap herself. Those kills were hers, not Raven's. Raven hadn't killed anyone.

Yet. Something inside her stirred, darkly.

But you just spent too long trying to work out the answer to simply say 'none' now, you idiot! "I'm not sure I've *killed* anyone."

"Except those cops – who were magically healed."

"Right," she agreed. Then saw he still looked angry – as if the fact they'd all been healed didn't count! She glowered at him. "Will you tell the others?"

"I don't know. Why shouldn't I?"

"But that's not fair! You know they wouldn't understand."

"You expected fairness?" he asked, his expression strange.

Her own expression darkened. "No. Life isn't fair."

"True. Nature isn't fair, and you can't force people to be fair, either. You can *show* them, however."

She looked back at him, taking hope from the words, but his expression remained more than troubled. Clearly, he was still weighing his decision.

"I thought you'd understand," she said, catching his eye. "I trusted you."

"And they trusted *you*. I've told you no lies, Raven. Can you say the same?"

Damn! Why had she thought she could trust him? She was always doing that! Well, not always... But what should she do now? She wasn't going to kill him. And he was still waiting for a reason.

On a sudden inspiration, she removed her shades. "I *want* to be a part of the group. I like what they do. And I want them to like me, to accept me. But they've got this code against killing. Like now, we're investigating some group that deliberately released poison gas, killing twenty-six innocent people in the Dumps. And we're going to, I dunno, break in and smash their equipment, screw up their computers with viruses or something, and then pat each other on the back and say 'well done'!" She spread her hands, looking up at him earnestly. Widened her eyes, just a little.

Maybe the 'innocent' look worked, since he seemed to relax. But his reply surprised her.

"They *are* a bit inflexible that way. To be truthful, I think they'd be more effective without it. Whoever heard of revolutionaries with a code against killing?" He snorted.

It was her turn to look at him in disbelief. "You don't... mind?"

His stare was suddenly remorseless, demanding. "Vision has always fed on blood. It depends on *why* you kill."

She stared back, though again, something inside her resonated at his words. "What vision? I don't understand."

He looked annoyed. "The only true measure of any vision's worth is blood: what it saves, or what it spills. You may learn that, in time." He brushed all that aside and leaned toward her, his green eyes intense. "Now tell me: why do you kill?"

She still didn't fully understand. But she was sure of her answer, all the same. "I kill *cancers*."

He raised one eyebrow. "Really."

She met his stare.

"And what makes you qualified to decide who is, and isn't, a *cancer*?"

She raised her chin, defiant. "By what they do, who they hurt. By the damage they do to our country. Or to the world." She glared at him, daring him to disagree.

"That's... interesting." He stared into the distance, seemingly lost in thought.

"So. *Will* you tell the others?" she demanded, at last.

He looked back at her. Considered. "No. No, I don't believe I will."

She pulled him back down to her, strangely warmed when his arm slid around her waist. His eyes stared into hers, and she again let herself imagine the two of them, working together. Maybe...? "You said you and Jacob created the Fist of Peace. Don't you think they could be a real force for good, if we could convince them to tackle tougher targets? Be a bit *harder?*"

His eyes moved across her face, and she could tell he was making a decision.

But in the end, he just said "You need to sleep: you guys have a mission tomorrow."

She couldn't work out whether she'd failed, or if he simply wasn't ready to share whatever his secret was, with her. Yet.

CHAPTER 64

A touch on her shoulder brought her awake, hard. She twisted, leaping backward and up off the cot-

To see Chopper, and behind him the others, eyeing her in mild surprise.

"Jumpy this morning?" asked Maretti. "Or just over-tired?"

Scowling, she shouldered between them, wishing it was easier to work out who the traitor was. Surely if one of them had lost a half a million cred deal the night before, they should be real angry?

But what if the holocube *hadn't* come from their last raid? Suppose there'd just been a cupboard or something they'd missed, with cubes in it some scavenger found, and there *was* no sell-out in the Fist of Peace at all?

She wasn't going to kill an innocent person.

In the kitchen alcove, she gulped down a mug of water and grabbed a stale bread and cheese roll. Tearing into it was strangely satisfying. After a quick bathroom break, she trotted down and out onto the chill pre-dawn street. Val and Skinner were already there, tinkering with their bikes. Shadow had left in the early hours.

She rubbed a hand over her face. What was wrong with her? Chit, she could *really* do with another hour's sleep. But having to be shaken awake.... She flushed, embarrassed.

At least she hadn't fragged Chopper, though – that would have blown the mission. All the same, she wondered if she'd been with these gentle people too long. Jumping *away* from the threat, instead of attacking.... Was their softness rubbing off on her?

She scrubbed at her eyes, trying to pull herself together. To focus.

The heavy steps behind her were Thug's.

"Uh, Raven, I thought maybe you'd like a HungerStunner. Zapped it, so it's hot?"

She turned and looked up into his friendly, worried face. She shook her head and took the plastic-wrapped bar.

He grinned. "Brung you a juice, too."

As she peeled the wrapper, the sudden spicy aroma made her realize the stale roll had only distracted her hunger, which returned full force, with a growl. Thug's eyebrows rose comically at the sound from her stomach. Breaking it in half she blew on it, huffing and chewing around a grateful smile up at the giant.

He beamed down at her in delight.

The others approached, Maretti giving final orders. "Davo, you'll be Cyn's driver. Wait for word from us down on the old Embarcadero freeway. Stay back near the edge of the first escarpment to keep out of sight.

"Chopper, I want you maybe two klicks down the freeway, with Val and Skinner. If the truck somehow gets away from Davo and heads that way, just follow it." They were all out on the deserted street now, and after a brief frown at Raven he stopped beside Thug. "Thug, you take Wolf, once he's invoked his city spirit for the accident. I suggest you wait on the top of the west wing of the old hospital. You know, with the new graffiti of that black volcano?"

'Black volcano' made her picture a black glass blade reflecting lava-bright heat and light. Leeth shuddered.

"You should be able to see the truck leaving, from there. That's all you need, Wolf, to set the spirit on it, right?"

The shaman nodded.

"Let it get five minutes or so from the Station, though. They're probably still on alert."

"Don, you'll come with me. We're going to stay central, in case things go wrong, to back up any of the others. Raven, you're with us."

"Any questions?" He looked around.

"That's it, then. Let's boot it up, team."

But after Gadger and Wiz headed back inside, and the bikers purred off on their sleek black beasts, Raven dragged her heels. Some gentle mockery from Maretti teased out that she wanted to see Wolf's spirit ritual.

Wolf had no objection, simply nodding and turning back to the east. Maretti sat on the balustrade of the building's steps, looking on with indulgent good humor. Don stood a short distance behind Raven, silent and patient. She thought maybe he was expecting her to pull something.

Leeth had had time to reflect on her actions. But it had probably worked out for the best – Maretti seemed to have genuinely relaxed in her presence for the first time she could remember. *Happy because I showed a weakness? And why does his relaxation make me feel so good?*

"Does it happen exactly at dawn?" she whispered, half turning to him. "What's he actually doing?"

Maretti shrugged. "Some kind of 'attuning to the world' thing. Exactly at dawn? Pretty much, yes. First few minutes. If he misses or fails the ceremony, it's risky raising any spirits until after sunset."

Raven nodded, soaking it in, not taking her eyes from Wolf.

"So how does he know when to do it?" she whispered. There was no reply. Just the sound of armored cloth shifting. Another shrug.

Almost imperceptibly, it started, with a prickle up her spine. Staring at Wolf, she realized his outline was shifting. Altering.

Her breath sighed out as another shape appeared, overlaying his. Lupine.

The shaman raised his arms in a welcoming gesture, stirring a breeze that blew for a few seconds before dying away. Light seemed to glint brightly in the reflective surfaces littering the area, the air swelling with expectancy, promise....

Wolf lowered his arms, and for a moment, everything fell still.

His next movements held a businesslike sense of purpose, his hands sculpting shapes in the air before him. A wisp of wind spun a nearby pile of leaves, paper, and dust into a tiny vortex that danced in happy circles around the shaman.

"Ohhhh." She was seeing a spirit summoned – *manifesting,* not just moving invisibly through the world. She moved closer. Wolf looked very dignified. Sure of himself, and the world around him. He looked... kind of alive, and *right.*

The sharp planes of his face and his strong features drew her. Leeth wanted to know him better, she realized. Feel him against her. Instead, she forced herself to take a deep breath and just watch. Sometimes it was hard, not being yourself.

The eddy of wind died, plastic wrappers fluttering back

to lie inert on the grimy street. One of them was her breakfast wrapper, she noticed, with an absurd feeling of having helped.

Wolf turned away and his eyes lost their focus. "The wind spirit knows the monitoring station in Hunters Point. It will follow the truck when it leaves, and speak to me the route it takes."

The second spirit he summoned was more subtle. Around the shaman the light darkened as if he stood in shadow. Wisps and strands of smoke-like fog twisted into existence around him, a looming presence with the threatening imminence of a thunder cloud. The shaman stared up into it, his eyes burning an inhuman yellow, his form overlaid by the wolf, fierce and wild. Leeth shuddered, shutting her eyes at a sudden deep feeling of resonance.

When she opened them again, it was gone.

"It will cause the accident, when I command. A burst tire." He looked worn.

Maretti rose from the railing and stretched. "Right. You've had your little show, Raven. Let's go."

Raven nodded, but went to Wolf. Gazing up at him earnestly, she reached up a small hand to touch his face, to trace the outline of a proud cheekbone. Reluctantly, she let the contact break.

"Thank you," she said, her voice husky with emotion.

Stepping away, she squared her shoulders and nodded to Maretti. He quirked an eyebrow at Wolf, who watched the girl, his face unreadable as she moved with animal grace to wait by Maretti's machine. With a shake of his head, Maretti clapped the shaman on the shoulder and moved off. Don followed them.

Wolf stood with Thug as the two bikes turned a corner and vanished from sight, staring at the girl who clung to Maretti's back.

Raven leaned, relaxed, against the wall that had once bounded the landscaped forecourt of an office complex. Twenty years later, its cracking cement now retained the collapsed building itself. She sat up at the distant sound of Maretti's bike. A few minutes later, she tracked his steps as he entered the building opposite, checking in first with Don. From there he came to her, keeping to cover. He passed across her lunch.

"One soymilk, two 'Works'." She took the unappetizing fare without comment, annoyed that she blushed as she accepted it.

The day passed slowly. Maretti probed her about her failed attempt to find housing, asking if she'd stayed the whole time or given up – stuff like that – but he didn't seem real interested in her replies. Not like someone who thought she'd snuck off to ruin his holocube sale.

Not like someone who'd lost half a million creds. That was a lot of money. She considered what that kind of money would mean to the people living so carefully off scraps in the Hunter Point Dumps.

They'd all be going about their lives now, not far from here. Did any of them ever think about her? Barney, and Teef. Miz J, Tricksy. Even grumpy, suspicious Luce. She should definitely go back there.

Just to build up that cover identity.

She sighed, hugging her shins, remembering what it had been like the night after the Fist Fest, how happy everyone had been to see her – even people she'd never spoken to. They hadn't really known her, but they'd still cared, anyway.

She and Maretti now sat on the retaining wall, legs up and facing one another, backs propped against old support columns.

Leeth stared at him, feeling strangely sad. "You don't like me much, do you?"

Maretti raised an eyebrow and considered his answer. She was hunched slightly forward, arms wrapped tightly round her knees. "No," he answered at last, "not much."

She sighed, a small sound. "You're in good company then," she said in a quiet voice, staring at the ground.

"You're not a very... easy person to be with," he offered, at last.

She raised her eyes before dropping them again. "No. I guess not." Her expression soured. Looking down at her Link, checking for messages but finding none, she looked away.

Maretti shifted, feeling a little awkward. The two lapsed into silence again.

CHAPTER 65

The sun hung low on the horizon, painting clouds in light. Raven scowled at the four large men, desperate to be doing something, considering her next argument. She'd just spent a whole day waiting for a truck that had never showed up. With Maretti, and Don.

She'd even fallen asleep, which Maretti had enjoyed needling her over. As well as griping about how the shop she'd recommended to Gadger had sold them faulty gear. Apparently it had been glitching off and on through the day, each time recording about ten minutes of nothing happening.

But *she* knew the supplier the Department had suggested would be solid, so they had to be missing something. She was trying to persuade Maretti to let her go in alone, just scout around – *and listen* – but he wouldn't hear it.

He shook his head. "You're forgetting the air elemental they have watching."

"It's big. For elementals, big takes time, doesn't it?"

"I- Maybe. Hang on, I'll check with Cyn." He called the sorceress.

Leeth looked away, pretending she couldn't hear Cynthia's replies.

"Thanks," Maretti said, turning back to Raven with an expression like he had something sour in his mouth. "Yeah, Cyn says it would have taken someone five or six hours to invoke. She also said the big inorganic beings are even more rigid and less adaptable to our reality than smaller ones. So he wouldn't have tried to instruct it to come and tell him about everyone who came into the area."

Raven smiled. "So if I don't go *too* close to the station, I should be all right."

"Suppose they have human watchers? Snipers?"

She shrugged. "I'll take the risk."

"Look, Raven, sometimes you've just gotta be patient."

"And other times you've got to know when to act. I *know* something's going on."

"Oh? Women's intuition?" he sneered.

"So you've heard of it. Good. That's settled then."

"Come off it!"

"What, you want to wait around until this 'Soul Twister' or whatever crawls out of the sewers? You can't really believe they're just sitting there, doing nothing? Look, this whole thing is falling apart. Can't you *feel it*? You're letting the initiative slip through your fingers. Besides, if they *do* have any watchers or snipers, we can take one and Mindmeld *him*."

When Maretti hesitated, Leeth knew she'd won.

So now Wolf, Thug, Don, Maretti, and Raven stood in a room at the top of the derelict west wing of the old hospital. Leeth had had a strange moment as they'd turned the corner and seen a large fresh mural of an angrily erupting black volcano. Strange, because the volcano had two small blue eyes painted on it.

She'd had to focus on the others. It *wasn't* calling to her.

"There has been no truck," declared Wolf.

"None you've *seen*," she said. "But Gadger said the surveillance gear activated twice today. Each time, for ten minutes. Long enough to load a truck. An *invisible* one."

Maretti answered her. "You can't make things invisible to a camera. To people, yes. To electronics, no. There's no such spell."

The shaman shrugged, dismissing both points. "Perhaps. But my city spirit watches. The truck could not be hidden on the imaginal plane. Nor could a spell, even an invisibility spell."

She stared at them stubbornly, remembering the invisible spirits at the Institute, which all the magic experts had said couldn't exist. Despite 'Lily', one of those spirit things, trying to kill Godsson every year.

She couldn't tell them any of that, obviously, and this did sound different. It wasn't about invisible spirits. But still.... "Look, they're doing weird magical research. Who knows *what* they can or can't do? I just want to go and check it out. If there are no watchers, there's no harm. And if there are, we capture one and Cynthia can Mindmeld them."

"No way," Maretti said. "I don't want you screwing this up."

"Screwing *what* up?" she exploded. "This whole thing is a joke! We've done *nothing*, all day. Just like yesterday! I'm *sure* something is happening out there, each time the camera starts transmitting." Every instinct screamed at her she was right. She spun to the shaman. "At least call your spirit back for a few minutes, and make it manifest so I can talk to it."

Maretti stared at Raven through narrowed eyes. "Do you think it would agree to do that, Wolf?"

The shaman nodded. "I can ask it your questions."

At that moment, Maretti's Link pulsed. "Tony."

"Chop. I'm on my way up."

"What-?" Maretti swore as the line went dead. A few seconds later, they heard steps down the corridor. Raven was already over by the door, Maretti noticed, with her gun out. Just as she had been before Shadow arrived, last night. The girl might be annoying, but she was sharp.

Chopper strode in.

"Burning forests, Chopper, why aren't you with Val and Skinner!"

He shrugged. "I was falling asleep, so I took a wander round to talk to a few people, catch the word. Seems like last night, PeaceCorp made a sweep through the area. Searching for people. They were asking about strangers in the area. *Us.* It was photos of most of *us* they were showing around."

Maretti stared at him. "How the freaking...?"

"They called on Kirkpatrick, too. Showed him the pics. Told 'em he thought he knew me, from years ago, but that's all. They had photos of all of us except Raven. But the only good ones were of you, Gadger, Cyn, Val, and Don." Chopper looked at Don strangely for a moment, but when Don met his eyes, he gulped and decided not to mention the military uniform. "The others were pretty rusty enlargements."

Maretti swore and punched out a connection on his wristcomm. "Gadger? We're blown. No, I mean all of us. PeaceCorp've been showing photos of us around. *I* don't know. But I want you and Wiz to shut down there and shift everything to the backup location. Yeah. Yeah, now. I'll send Thug to help." He gestured for the big man to get going. "No. We'll stay till sunset. Out."

He swore again.

"Uh, I'll head back to Val and Skinner, okay Tony?"

Maretti nodded. "Sure." But as Chopper slouched for the door, he had a thought.

"Chopper?"

"Uh, yeah, Tony?"

"How long did it take you to find that out?"

Chopper looked uncomfortable. "Like, everything was quiet, and Val and Skinner didn't need me, and like I said-"

"How long."

"A... a coupla hours. I guess."

Maretti glared at him.

Chopper ducked his head, and hurried away.

"You should have disciplined the boy," declared Don, heavily.

"Just shut the fuck up, Don. Don't *you* start telling me how to run things."

Don stared at him, expressionless, and the room went very quiet. Maretti wiped a hand over his face. "Look, I'm sorry. I didn't mean that."

"So, can Wolf call his spirit back now?" asked Raven.

Maretti spun round to her, taking hold of himself only with effort. Grinding his teeth he looked at the shaman, then nodded, curtly.

"We will have to go up onto the roof, out of the building."

"Whatever," Maretti grunted. "I'll call Davo, let *him* know what's going down."

They stood on the shaky roof as the light faded toward sunset through a haze of smoke. Wolf looked around, once, then calmly shut his eyes.

Long seconds passed, and a frown creased his brow. "Something is wrong. Wait." Again his eyes closed, and so they all waited, on edge.

No one noticed the shaman's shadow growing, lengthening at his feet, darkening to deepest black. Not until it had swollen and grown to touch them all; not until the air itself had darkened.

Then Maretti looked up, wondering what had blotted out the sun. Wolf stared down and saw himself suspended over a black abyss.

Which erupted in a geyser of ash and air, a nightmare of flailing metal and sand, shredding his armored clothing and lashing his face as it spun itself around him. He cried out, staggering back but somehow staying on his feet.

Don took a half-step closer, gun in hand, then hesitated, knowing it was useless.

Raven lunged straight into the mini tornado, one arm raised high, plunging down as she disappeared into the maelstrom.

Leeth struck, the blow numbing her arm with its solid contact, but she felt something in it tear, the thing collapsing in on itself a little. As it faded she saw the shaman shred spirit tentacles latched to his face, revealing eyes again wolfish and yellow.

The whirlwind folded, shrank to a silvery point, then winked out. They all stood, stunned.

Blood welled from dozens of geometrical razor cuts to the shaman's face, his expression of anger slowly fading to one of shock.

"What in the puking, dying soul of man was *that*!" demanded Maretti.

Wolf turned to him shakily, looking somehow weakened. One hand trembled as it touched the freely-bleeding gashes on his face. He stared at the strange radial patterns printed on his bloody palm, then stared past Tony, unseeing. "My... city spirit?"

Raven swore, stepped to the gaping hole they'd climbed onto the roof by, and jumped down.

Maretti cursed again. "Follow her, Don. We'll be with you... shortly."

The dark-clad man nodded fractionally and jumped heavily down after her.

She moved at a steady jog toward the pollution station. She knew she should probably keep off the road, but urgency had gripped her so strongly she couldn't bear to pick her way over the rubble spilled onto the streets. She didn't know much about spirits, but she *knew* that what she'd just seen should never have happened. It was almost like the creature had become polluted. Just by staying near the monitoring station.

To see something so powerful and natural, warped and twisted into that sick thing.... It struck a deep, angry chord, offending some fundamental part of her. As had the look of shaken faith on the shaman's face.

The wind was getting in her eyes, making them water.

Shutting the thoughts away, she put her head down and ran harder.

Don pounded along, well behind her, his cyber-strengthened muscles bunching and flexing smoothly as his gaze swept the streets with long-drilled military caution.

Unbelievably, she began pulling away from him. Redlining his augments, he increased his pace.

Wounds healed, Wolf sat on his haunches, breathing calmly, trying to regain his center. Maretti stood off to one side, watching, concerned, speaking quietly to Wiz on his Link.

Disconnecting, he eyed Wolf, who looked like his world had just collapsed. Melting chips! And according to Wiz, the camera was active right now. If Raven *was* right.... He stabbed at the wristcomm.

Leeth could see it in the distance now, and with an enormous heaving breath, slowed her pace – and suddenly could hear *nothing*. Nothing except the pounding of her own heart. She couldn't even hear her own gasping breaths.

Her wristcomm pulsed. She took the call, frowning down at Maretti's tiny face mouthing silent words at her. She shook it.

Something was terribly wrong; horribly imminent. And then sound abruptly returned, way down at the lowest ground-shaking register she could hear, building to a screaming, shaking crescendo *right on top of her*.

She flung herself sideways off the street as the world shook and *something* thundered silently past her.

She slid to a stop in the rubble, a rusty spike of rebar tearing through the heavy material of her black jeans, gashing her leg. She stood, shakily, as a tiny voice at her wrist slowly swelled.

She stared down at Maretti's face.

"- okay? Are you okay? What happened?"

She panted down at his worried face, then grinned. "I think I just missed getting run down by an invisible truck. Don't ask *me* how to locate it to grab the driver for a Mindmeld though!"

In the distance, she saw Don turn the corner.

"Get off the ROAD!" she screamed to him. With amazing alacrity he jumped into the rubble.

She stared at the road before her, limping a couple of steps over to study it, then looked back at Maretti's face. "Oh, and there are fresh tire tracks in the ooze on the road. Big, heavy tracks, Tony. How would Wolf feel about invoking a *fresh* city spirit?"

CHAPTER 66

Maretti and Raven stood with Don by his bike. All three watched Wolf, waiting tensely.

Earlier, something inside her had ached, seeing him standing there, his head hanging. Hesitating. She'd gone to him, pressing both palms to his chest as she stared up into those dark eyes, admiring the chiseled cheekbones, *willing* him to believe her. "It's the Soul Twister thing," she'd whispered. "Don't doubt yourself. It's *them*. They've done something awful, something that needs to be *un*done."

He looked kind of bemused, but then relaxed. "Your leg is injured."

His eyes didn't leave hers as he bent down. Her lips fell open, surprised, as his descended, but instead of kissing her, his fingers brushed her thigh. She blushed, but pressed into him as the healing warmth washed into her.

"Raven, you can get a room later, okay?"

She'd rolled her eyes at Maretti's remark and pushed herself back. But letting her hands slide from the muscled chest, she considered the suggestion seriously, and saw Wolf's irises widen. She grinned, putting a wiggle into her backside as she rejoined Maretti and Don, before realizing Raven wouldn't do that, and stopped.

The three of them watched the shaman now as he leaned against his own bike, his eyes looking Elsewhere, into imaginal space.

Finally he straightened, and Leeth felt her own heart lift at his expression of restored certainty. He spoke into his communicator so the others, waiting to start their pursuit – Chopper, Val and Skinner, Davo and Cynthia – could all hear. "The truck became visible once it left the area. It travels north on the old Embarcadero freeway. I feel they head for the Bay Bridge." He lapsed into silence.

Yes! As hoped, the spirit, a part of the city and prowling the area waiting for a truck to appear from thin air, had quickly located it. Leeth wanted to move closer, wanted to see if she could somehow sense the spirit as it came and went, but she *so* didn't want to mess this up.

Several minutes passed. Then Wolf inclined his head as though listening, and spoke again into his Link. "The driver has taken the left exit onto Sixth. He heads toward the Skyway. You are two kilometers behind."

It was a little disturbing to consider how effortlessly the invisible spirit shuttled back and forth between its summoner and the moving truck, even noting the position of Davo's car in passing. Something to file away for future reference.

Maretti was also linked. "Okay, Davo, now it's off the freeway, close up, fast." He turned to Wolf. "Tell your spirit to do it now. Blow out tires one by one until the truck has to stop."

Wolf sat down in the dirt, cross-legged. He looked up. "I will join the spirit and watch imaginally. Just in case."

Maretti nodded, but the shaman's form was already going limp.

Raven gritted her teeth in suspense, continuing to massage her arm half-consciously, where it still ached from killing the twisted spirit.

A few minutes passed before Davo's voice came from their Links. "We've spotted the truck – curbside tire's blown, truck's pulled over. One guy's working on it. I'll go past.... Pulling over not too far ahead.... Right. Cyn's casting her spell... guy's still working – he hasn't even noticed!"

Some minutes passed, then they heard Cyn. "Burn the forests! The man's a soldier. Army corporal."

Maretti looked around in mild surprise. "Okay, everyone. Now we know who's looking for us. Looks like we've got ourselves another head-damned military op. Usual sub-teams for the relocations."

"Relocations?" Raven asked.

Maretti looked at her like she was an idiot. "We're all being hunted by the military: that means grabbing bare essentials and relocating. And I don't want anyone going off on their own, right? Especially you, Chopper."

Chopper tried to look innocent, but couldn't help grinning – until Don cuffed the back of his head.

"Ow! What the-?" But the moment Chopper saw who'd hit him, his mouth clamped shut.

"You can help Gadger, Raven."

Two hours later they regrouped on the outskirts of the slum area. Davo got off his bike, garaging and locking his car once Cyn stepped out. She headed over to Maretti as

Thug rolled up beside the rest of the group.

"Any problems?" Maretti asked her.

"No. I did an imaginal fly-by before Davo and Thug checked out the area on foot. Then we just loaded my stuff into the car and let my 'avatar do the walking' around Virtual New Francisco and found a place. Not as nice as where I was, but it'll do for now."

"Good. What about you, Gadger?"

"Ditto."

"Wiz?"

"Dit."

"Okay, that's everybody's relocated. Let's go."

Conversation died as they powered off on their bikes to the secondary headquarters.

CHAPTER 67

Hanging back, Leeth casually tipped her sunglasses forward to scan the darkened street. They'd stopped by a rusty metal roll-door, half blocking an equally rusted garbage dumpster. From the back of it, Maretti unhooked something and shoved the skip to one side.

Davo stood at one corner of the block, Skinner at the other, checking they weren't being observed. The area seemed dead and deserted. Leeth peered up and around into the shadowed doorways and gaping window frames of decrepit tenements.

Nothing.

Maretti stepped up to the battered fuse box now uncovered and swung open its corroded cover, revealing a Hamamatsu palm scanner. It was very quiet as he pressed his hand to the device.

Idly, Leeth counted the sounds of people breathing. Thug. Chopper. Maretti. Gadger. Wiz. Val. Cynthia. Wolf. Don. The faint hum of the scanner died. Davo, Skinner. Good – they were alone. Or at least, no one was right on top of them.

There was a solid click, and Maretti hauled at the handle of the roll-door. It slid heavily but smoothly upward, belying its rusty exterior. In the dark space beyond, she heard a rat, then saw it dart off into a hole. She pushed her shades back up over her nose.

Maretti stepped aside, letting Gadger peer cautiously in. His thermographic eyes scanned the interior.

"It's okay," he stated, confirming Leeth's private assessment.

"You install the scanner, Gadger?" she asked, flashing him a smile. "Nice work."

He grinned. "Wait till you see the entrance at the docks!"

Maretti frowned. "That's enough, Gadger. Need-to-know only." He inclined his head, gesturing Raven inside.

She bared her teeth in a feral grin and grabbed the frame at the top of the aperture, jumping down and swinging gracefully into the blackness. She vanished into the dark without a sound.

Maretti tensed.

Gadger chuckled, watching her on his thermographics. "Flick, I wish she could teach Thug to move half that quietly!"

"He's not built for it, Gadger," Raven's voice drifted back from the darkness. "Gotta have the bod."

Maretti wheeled his bike down the concrete ramp that took up half the opening, thinking the command that woke dim lights inside. The others followed.

"Pretty sure of yourself, Raven, aren't you?" Maretti growled as Thug rolled the door closed, annoyed afresh by her faint air of superiority.

She didn't respond straight away – instead, just shrugged off her reinforced leather jacket. The Magnum .44 looked enormous in the holster slung from her narrow waist. She sighed in relief, stretching in sheer animal pleasure, her thin black sweatshirt clinging damply to her. The band of mirror-black across her eyes gave her a faintly menacing air as she prowled toward him, stopping only a foot away, hands on hips. Her close-fitting garment didn't leave an enormous amount to the imagination.

"I've got a lot to be sure *about*, Tony."

The others sauntered over from the far side of the large basement, their bikes now parked clear of what was obviously the main living area.

Skinner leered. "You sure have, babe! Should've lost the jacket before now," he said, eyeing her appreciatively.

Val glared and moved in front of him. "Cap it, Skinner! She's too thin for you, and I have a date with a long, warm shower. Wanna soap my back?"

He snorted happily. "Whattya *think*?"

The two of them headed off to one corner of the basement, while over by the roll-door Davo picked up a chain and heaved. The dumpster outside rumbled up noisily, banging into the metal shutter. Maretti brought the lights up fully.

Broken furniture and assorted junk had been cleared away into one corner of the underground area. From the opposite end came the sound of running water as Val and Skinner hit the shower, next to a heating unit and a huge plastic water tank.

"Where's my gear?" demanded Raven, abruptly.

Thug grinned. "S'okay, Raven. I was real careful with it when we moved everything over here." He pointed. "That one there's got your stuff in it."

She headed over to the plastic box he'd indicated, amongst a small row of similar ones, sorting through it quickly. Climbing gear, extra ammo, a few clothes – and the plastic explosives and detonators. She relaxed.

Gadger unpacked some of his own stuff in one corner. A spiderweb antenna opened out, and he hooked it to a tiny comp. "There. That should make us a little safer."

"What is it?" asked Raven.

"Listener-spotter. Scans the airwaves. Decodes what it can into speech and does keyword matches. Also registers local radio transmissions." He shrugged. "You usually can't decrypt 'em, but just knowing there's a point-source local broadcast in a null zone like this'll mean it'll be time for us to flash."

Her lips pursed. "Great." *Rats.* That probably meant she couldn't use her choker to report from here.

Maretti eased himself into a once expensive executive chair, the cracks in its leather patched with duct tape. Gadger collapsed onto a battered couch nearby as Thug headed for the ancient refrigerator.

Pulling out a couple of warm beers, he grimaced as he handed one to Davo. "Sorry, I forgot, before," he said, plugging the cooler into the power-board from the Phasion unit he'd dumped off here earlier.

Cyn took a seat beside Gadger and opened a cheap data reader. With a grimace she plugged in the cube with Scott's published research papers.

Wiz began unpacking electronics stuff, including the trid unit, while Maretti laced his hands together in thought. Leeth began prowling, looking for exits besides the one they'd come in by. No one seemed inclined to bring up the recent events. *They* looked a little depressed at having to flee like scared rabbits into new burrows; it just made her mad.

Leeth considered the noisy roll-up door, and the dumpster on its chain outside. *No way anyone could sneak in that way*, she thought, resuming her search. Gadger, Maretti and Don watched her movements with too-casual disinterest. Chopper's eyes were glued to her too, though in his case watching her figure with frank appraisal.

She was very conscious of their eyes, while pretending not to be, as she tapped walls, considered the disused Exit door, and eyed the ventilation shaft. There were symbols inscribed in the cement floor, inside circles. Probably for Cynthia's use. They reminded her of something she'd seen in a small, disused building back at the Institute for Paranormal Dysfunction.

Hands on hips, she stood thinking. The only places she couldn't see were behind the pile of junk in the far corner – not much good for a quick escape – and the area with the shower cubicle. A sewer exit, maybe? That seemed likely. Maybe the showers, then. She headed over, then stopped just outside. Most people were funny about being seen naked, she'd learned. No point in annoying Skinner or Val.

Thug came over. "Hey, Raven. Wanna Coke?"

"No, I'm okay," she smiled. "But there *is* something you could do for me, when Skinner and Val are done."

"Yeah? What?"

"Show me the secret way out through the showers?"

He nodded fractionally, before turning to Maretti. "Uh, Tony, is it okay if I show Raven?"

Maretti shook his head, acknowledging her score with a resigned smile. "I think you just did, Thug."

Thug looked puzzled, then turned back to Raven.

"Yes, Thug. He means yes, it's okay."

"Oh."

Gadger sniggered his appreciation.

They'd just started discussing food options, when Wiz chuckled. "Hey, Cyn, scan how your idol's coping with the media buzz." A low-res, laser imaged holo blipped into existence, of Marcie Dunkirk battling through a swarm of media drones shouting questions at her. One drone even tried to land and crawl inside her cab, before she flicked it out.

Leeth stifled a groan.

"And get this – I betcha didn' know your Stryker Zaxx was one of the girls rescued from Club Juzz by Sleena and Tash."

Leeth stilled.

"What!" Cyn lurched forward. *"Mar-D was raped?"*

Wiz shrugged, his expression more anticipatory than sympathetic. "No one's saying. But remember that obviously faked vid of the girl, Jane Baker, raging through the hospital where Dunkirk lay, paralyzed? Before forcing a surgeon and 'the hatted mage' to cure her?"

"That vid's not fake-!"

Wiz continued over the top of her. "Wait, look." The holo of Marcie battling the drone swarm vanished, replaced by the vid in question.

A small teen pushed a man in a wheelchair. Both wore floppy hats, obscuring their faces. The girl also dragged a doctor through hospital corridors, casually disarming and stunning security guards as she went.

As relieved as she was to see the end of Marcie's repeated torment, Leeth swallowed, steeling herself for what she guessed would come next.

Wiz zoomed in a little, replaying just the action sequences in a loop. "Don, you tapped a vid of the last Fist Fest. Could-"

"Tapped a vid?" Raven demanded.   "Somebody recorded it?" Despite the Department's searching – which meant Nelson – nothing had turned up on the net, or any undernet. So they'd said.

Maretti frowned, about to ignore her, when Davo answered. "There were some cybers there, sure." At her obvious confusion, he looked almost embarrassed. "Vid gets shared, brain to brain." One hand went to the back of his neck, where she knew he had some I/O ports.

She had the sudden image of these big tough men with a cable jacked from one head into the other's. It seemed a little... intimate.

Davo actually blushed at her expression.

Her eyebrows lifted. *Men were weird.* But it seemed what she'd heard about the Dumps people protecting the privacy of the Fest was true.

"As I was saying," Wiz broke in, "could *that* chick be Sleena, Don?"

No. Please don't do this, Leeth begged. *Not now.*

Don considered. "Moves like Sleena. Same build. Zoom the eyes."

Wiz obliged, finding a brief shot of her face, squashed beneath a stocking and badly pixelated despite the smoothing algorithms.

"Blue eyes. Paler skin. But moves like her." He nodded. "Disguise."

I am so dead. Or they *will be,* Leeth thought, eyes screwed shut, *if the Department hears about this.* She wanted to change the subject, but didn't dare draw attention to herself. Why were they even bothering with this, though?

Wiz rubbed his hands together, making sure everyone was watching him. "Right, so, according to the stories, Jane Baker, with Marcie Dunkirk's help, rescues their entire acting school after they'd all been kidnapped by The Breaker, Marc Disten." He looked around. "Don't you get it? Jane Baker is Sleena!"

It got the reaction he'd hoped for.

To Leeth, the gasps seemed to hold as much delight as horror. It made her want to punch them. *Why's it okay when* Sleena *beats people up, but not* Raven?

She fought to unclench her jaw.

"Think about it," Wiz continued. "During the rescue, Disten cripples Dunkirk. A few days later, bam! – Baker pulls her hospital stunt, and vanishes. A month later, this little blonde sliv appears at the 'Fest, Sleena. She teams up with Tash and the two of them wipe Club Juzz off the map *and* end The Breaker. Then *both* vanish."

Leeth opened her eyes, trying *so* hard to keep her face calm. The entire group watched Wiz, rapt. For a fleeting moment she savored the idea of knocking him out.

"Then this latest thing – Dunkirk's kidnapped, and this silver *killbot* rescues her and slaughters a bunch of mercs. Now look at this."

Wiz set the vid looping now from the hospital fights to the Sybarus one, and then to the few seconds visible of the mall fight. Leeth hoped he might leave it at that, but then he added the creepier stuff at the end, where maybe the dagger *had* been somehow influencing her.

"So, Don, how 'bout this Killer Queen thing? Could it be the same... 'girl', too?"

They all waited for Don's answer.

CHAPTER 68

While Don watched the projected video, Leeth wished she could sink through the floor.

"Yes. Heavily disguised, or augmented, but yes. It could be. Same weird concealed Wolverines as Sleena, too."

"Wolverines?" Leeth asked, noticing Don nodding to Maretti, who stared down at his own hands.

"Retractable blades," Val explained. "Tony had 'em, when he was young. Till his body rejected 'em."

"But... those glowing eyes?" Davo wanted to know.

Yeah, wondered Leeth. *I'd like to know about that.*

"Could be built into the lenses," Wiz said. "Assuming she *isn't* a secret gov gynoid killing machine. Or – my guess – a vamp that's been augmented and turned into a cyber-ninja."

"That makes no sense," Maretti objected. "Nobody'd create a thing like that just to be Marcie Dunkirk's protector."

"And you couldn't augment a vampire," Cyn argued. "They heal far too fast. Their regen would reject any cybernetic implant. Thank God!"

Wiz shrugged. "Maybe somebody's found a way? Maybe it's a secret government experiment that's escaped? All I'm saying is I think they're all the same entity, and Dunkirk is the link."

"Poor kid," Val said. "Imagine having a freak like that as your 'protector'." She shuddered, and the others nodded their own agreement.

The words slid like knives into Leeth's chest. Why were they even talking about this? Why did they care? They had far more important troubles – like being hunted. She wanted to scream at them, but couldn't risk even appearing *uncomfortable*.

She took a long, soft, steadying breath.

"Raven sees well in the dark, too," Don suddenly said.

Chopper pointed dramatically at her, grinning. "That's it, Don! Raven is Jane Baker, Sleena, *and* cyber ninja girl!"

Kill! The urge blazed through her, but somehow she kept her expression neutral, helped by the mask of her shades.

"Uh, guys?" Chopper looked from one to another, his grin cracking.

They'd all turned to her; Maretti ignored him, studying her. "Yeah, and she was off on her own when all this Dunkirk shit went down."

"Guys? Come on! No offense to Raven, that ninja bot was *stacked!*" Chopper, meeting the black gaze of her wraparound shades, was waving both hands as if trying to wipe out his words. "Guys?"

Leeth heard both Wolf and Cyn shift, and glimpsed finger movements from Cyn. *Truth spell*, she guessed, when nothing else happened; and thought very, very carefully about her next words.

Sleena was a role, she told herself. *Jane was a role. They're not me. I'm Raven.* "I had a shitty night that night, Tony. I went to the DPA. Waited. You know how slowly the hours pass, waiting for your number to be called? Only to be told 'accommodation request denied'? I had to spend the night at our headquarters. Cold, and soaked from the rain."

Wiz and Chopper sniggered, Chopper even whispering, "Oh yeah," under his breath.

"You still have that DPA rejection text?" Tony asked.

"Text? They print it on funting *paper!* No, I screwed it up and tossed it."

Maretti didn't look surprised. Like he'd known the DPA used paper.

His question had been a trap. That hurt. It hurt *a lot.*

"Wiz. Howzabout you hack into some street cams, city surveillance? See if you can pick up Raven's movements that night."

"Ah, I already tried, Tony. No dice."

Cynthia gasped. Wolf grunted. "That is a lie," he said.

"What the *fuck,* guys? You're s'pposed to be scanning *her,* not me!"

"She spoke the truth," Wolf said. "You did not."

"Wiz?" Maretti demanded.

"Yeah, yeah, all right, her story checked out."

"Even the wet clothes bit," Chopper blurted.

"Huh? What?" Raven's shades locked first on Chopper, then Wiz. "You have cameras in your HQ? You *recorded* me?"

"Hey, you triggered the infrared sensors! It was my *duty* to review the footage."

"Why, you funting...." But blossoming rage just as quickly died under an awful realization. *I broke in, before I met them- but chilled to the bone! Chattering. Numb. Freaking krek! I pulled that off by sheer dumb luck!*

She still needed a diversion though; needed them off this whole Sleena-Baker-vampire hunt. Carefully, she re-stoked her anger. "Delete the vid."

"Sure. No prob," Wiz agreed.

"That's a lie too," Cyn said.

"*To-ny*" whined Chopper.

All three women stared him down.

Cyn kept her Truth spell running until they'd deleted *all* the copies they'd made.

And then Raven held her breath.

"All the same," Maretti said, "it'll be a good idea to learn what we can about this Sleena character. Find out if she's a cybernetic vampire, an experimental gynoid with a Stryker Zaxx fixation, the Chosen Warrior, or whatever."

Leeth screwed her eyes shut. *The last thing the Fist of Peace should investigate was... Wait, what?* "Chosen Warrior?" she asked.

"Don't worry about it. Though it might be fun to see how *you* felt, if you ever met Sleena face to face."

"Sure, if you arrange it," said Leeth with a shrug. Though she had the impression that if they did try hunting Sleena it'd be to see her locked up, not recruit her.

"Hey, Tony," Wiz asked, "you mind if I head out to a public comms booth? I want to check out the military an-gle of the setup of that place, two and a half years ago."

Maretti looked up. "Yeah, you do that. Davo, go with him and keep him out of trouble."

Davo shrugged. "Sure, Tony. Maybe the beer'll be cold when we get back."

"I will go, too," declared Wolf.

Maretti nodded, checking the newly reactivated security cameras. "Street's clear."

The three men rolled up the door, pushed aside the skip, and drove their bikes up the ramp and out. Thug slid the door back down and casually hauled the chain in, pulling the dumpster back into place.

Skinner, Val, and Chopper volunteered to head off to buy pizzas.

Leeth decided she should probably call in a report, too, now they'd discovered the military connection. It might be important.

"Hey, Tony, I'm going outside. I want to scout out the area a little." *And call Father.*

He shrugged. "Sure. Thug, you go with her."

"I'd rather go alone."

"This isn't a nice neighborhood."

"I can look after myself."

"Good. But Thug goes with you, even if it's just for *my* peace of mind, okay?"

Leeth shrugged, unwilling to push any harder. So it wasn't that he thought she couldn't look after herself – he obviously still didn't really trust her. Staring into his eyes, they suddenly seemed weirdly familiar. *Why?* Straining to work out the reason, she felt a stabbing pain in her temple.

"Come on, Raven," Thug said, interrupting.

She let him take an arm, her answering smile more a grimace. *I guess Father will just have to wait.*

Thug stuck by her like a shadow. She didn't even get a chance to record a message to transmit.

An hour and a half later, they'd all eaten – except Davo, Wolf, and Wiz, who'd just returned, in high excitement. Wiz moved with jerky speed, speaking as soon as Thug shut the entrance behind them.

"You're gonna love this, Tony. I've got the location of the base, confirmation of Scott's link through *military* balance sheets, and – the guy behind it all is our old friend Captain *Bragg.*"

The whole group tensed.

CHAPTER 69

"Bragg?   Fry the raping mages!" Maretti swore, before noticing Wolf and Cynthia's expressions.   "Uh, present company excepted, of course."   He turned back to Wiz. "*Bragg*? Are you sure?"

"Yep," said Wiz, smug.

"Who's Bragg?" asked Raven.

Maretti ignored her. "Continue, Wiz. Dump it all."

"Right.   So, the Red Level pollution event in Hunters Point, two and a half years ago: twenty-six dead, and the clean-up action?"

"Yeah."

"The crews for the evacuation, and the clean-up, came from the small army base down in Vallejo. Commanding officer: Bragg."

That sparked a fresh round of cursing.

"Who is Bragg?" asked Raven, again.

But Wolf addressed the group, not her. "I think Wiz is right. It was Bragg I sensed, underground."

"*Who is Bragg?*" demanded Raven.

But Wiz had more news.   "And *Callahan Scott's* with him! My purchase-profiler gave an eighty percent match to Scott, when I fed it the Vallejo accounts. Just after the pollution event."

Raven slammed a hand on the table.   "I'm going to *punch* someone if you don't tell me who Bragg is right now!"

Gadger turned to her. "He's a killer. A murdering racist who used to be a Colonel, stationed in Vallejo. We faced him three, four years ago.   Jacob had been chasing up someone supplying mil-grade tech to the League of Purity, who were using it to hunt and kill ogres all over New Francisco."

Leeth clenched her jaws, imagining people hunting Teef or his son, Barney. It was weird: before meeting them, she'd have agreed with the League. More and more, it seemed like everything the Doctor had taught her growing up had been lies.

"We traced the leak to Bragg, but he learned about our investigations and set a trap for us. Jacob spotted it, and turned things around so it blew up in Bragg's face. But we didn't have hard enough proof it was Bragg selling the stuff, so he didn't get court-martialed. The thefts stopped, though. And we heard he got demoted."

They all fell silent, eyes staring into the past. At last, Cynthia spoke. "The first disappearances were children of the Melt."

Ogres and trolls, Leeth mentally translated, while Cyn continued.

"If they were planning some sort of magical experimentation on people, it's probably why they chose Bragg for this operation."

There were nods of agreement.

The sorceress's eyes widened in sudden horror. "But in the Dumps – if Kirkpatrick knew of eight people who'd disappeared, wouldn't the real number be higher?"

Chopper nodded. "If they chose their vics cleverly – picked felch-heads no one cared about? Yeah, they could've taken two, three times that many."

"As long as Bragg made his first few victims tell him who wouldn't be missed," said Don.

Chopper grimaced. "Yeah. I c'n scan Bragg doing something like that."

They all looked sickened by the suggestion, Leeth saw. Except Don – he just looked angry. Like she felt. She let her feelings show, too.

"Did you learn the name of the project?" Maretti asked Wiz. "Or who's in charge? Bragg wouldn't have the authority for something like this."

Wiz shrugged. "Sorry, no."

"What about the location?"

Wiz used the trid unit to display a view of a wide expanse of low, flat land by a large body of water. Shabby, but the roads were all intact, like the buildings, most of which still had windows. There were even a good number of trees.

Staring at it, Leeth had the funny feeling she knew the place. Then her mouth fell open as she recognized a bronzed, vertical tower. Her breath hissed out. Hunters Point. So different to the shattered earth and staggered tiers of its current self.

"This is early 2044, just before the Big One wiped out half the city. Notice this twelve-story office block. Okay, I'll mark that spot... and now, here's the same area, today."

The view changed to a familiar pollution station at the

center of a stretch of bare concrete encircled by kudzu. To its east lay rubble and devastation: millennia of mud thrust from the Bay floor, stirred with decades of wind-banked ash. It looked like a scene of nuclear destruction, but represented a mere flexing of Nature's muscle. Earthquake and fire.

"Okay. Building's gone, *but*, the five underground floors of car parking matches pretty well with what Wolf saw, imaginally. And here," a long dotted line appeared at his words, "you see an old spur line of the BART, and here," another line appeared, at an angle to the first, "this one, sewage, intersects the pollution station. And finally, here's the blocked stormwater drain." This crossed over the sewage line, just beside the station.

"That's it for sure, Wiz. Excellent work."

"What address was that?" asked Raven. "What used to go on there?"

Wiz frowned. "Just offices. What does it matter? They're gone. Pulverized." He turned to Maretti. "So, now what?"

"I want to know more about the truck. Cyn, did the driver know what he was carrying? Was he delivering or taking away, or both?"

"He had no idea. He wasn't even the usual driver. His orders were to take the truck afterwards to a warehouse back at the army base in Vallejo, leave it there for fifteen minutes, then shuttle back again to the monitoring station. And to do that till further notice."

"Wolf, did you look inside the truck when you went imaginal?"

"Yes. It held many boxes and some machinery. No emotions attached to them. All would have fitted through the manhole."

Maretti thought for a while. "Sounds to me like they're moving house. Into the army base. Once they're in there we'd be crazy to take them on. Even that damned underground installation would need a small army to dig them out of."

Chopper snorted and bounced to his feet, slamming one fist into his palm. "Nuke 'em!"

The others stared at him for a second. "Sit down, Chopper," Maretti ordered, tiredly.

"Obviously, we have to strike during the relocation. But Bragg'll be expecting that.... They'll have military backup, for sure, covering them during the move." He thought about it. "Our strong point is that we have two mages on our side. On the down side, though, they have Scott, who seems even stronger."

"He won't be too effective if he can't see to target his spells," declared Raven.

Maretti looked at her, then at the two mages. "Is that true?"

Cynthia looked slightly uncomfortable. "Pretty much. Most spells require at least a glimpse of your target's aura. You have to see or touch, roughly speaking, to target your spell. You don't *have* to, but that makes it much rougher on the caster. So yes, if we could blind him, he *should* be pretty harmless."

Maretti grunted. "How come you never mentioned this before?"

"We've never needed to worry about it before. Normally, Wolf and I are more than a match for any mage we've come up against."

"Gotcha!" said Chopper, nodding. "It's part of the secret mage's code. The stuff you don't tell mundos, right, just like in the trids!"

"Frag, Chopper, you just vacuumed your brains?" asked Davo.

Maretti shook his head. Though he did eye the shaman thoughtfully.

Wolf met the look squarely. "We have not needed the tactic in the past, and none like to speak of their own weaknesses. Why do you suddenly doubt us?"

"I don't, man, I don't. I'm just a little tense, is all." He looked at Raven. "How'd you know about that, anyway, if it's something mages don't talk about?"

"They talk about it when they have to."

Maretti stared at her a moment longer. "Yeah. So I see. Well. What exactly do we need to do? Do we have to put a sack over his head, or what? How hard is this going to be?"

For another half hour they discussed tactics.

Raven's suggestion that she be sent in alone on a stealth mission was dismissed out of hand. Which was super annoying, considering she was sure she could kill the mage easily enough. And hide the body or something so they didn't find out after and get upset.

It made her wonder how they planned to make Bragg and Scott pay, or even just shut them down for good, if they weren't prepared to kill any of them? She asked, but wasn't surprised when they had no real answer. *Frickin' amateurs!*

She sat back, frustrated, mostly listening. Would this upcoming attack produce anything the traitor could try to sell, to give her another chance to uncover him – or maybe *her?*

As they talked, she checked her Link for any messages from Marcie. Half hoping, half dreading what she'd find. But there was still nothing. She swallowed. *It's for the best. I keep getting her in danger.*

At least this was all taking her mind off Luiz. That felt long ago, now. With a little surprise, she realized the thought of Luiz didn't hurt any more. She breathed a long sigh, glad that at least *that* wouldn't come back to haunt her.

While she considered her doubts about the Fist's ability to really shut this thing down, and the wisdom of reporting in anyway, Leeth rubbed the back of her neck, surreptitiously setting her choker into record-mode. Eagle wouldn't like the army killing people and experimenting on others. Even if they were CIDless. She was pretty sure. "So, we know this army captain – ex-colonel – Bragg, is involved in this. That the military are probably funding it. That they're moving out from their underground location at map reference H8-05, but we don't know *when* their next invisible truck will arrive at the Hunters Point pollution station for the next load."

She noticed the others were looking at her curiously. She decided she'd better wind up, before they became suspicious, wishing she'd thought of doing this stupid 'detective monologue' thing earlier, when she'd been outside with Thug. *Idiot.* She grimaced. "You said you and Don are going to be out buying munitions, Tony, and Cyn's got hours of Invocation to do – but what about the rest of us?"

"Wiz and Gadger can try and crack the military comms band. The rest of you should check your gear – bikes, night-scopes, the lot. Make sure we've got enough sleep-gun rounds. Buy more if you're low. Otherwise, just get some rest. We should be ready by...?" Maretti looked across at Cyn questioningly.

"Can you give me eight hours?"

He frowned. "Maybe. Yeah. Try for that, but be prepared to break off and move earlier if we have to. The munitions biz'll take four hours or more. So the rest of you should just relax. Sleep if you can."

Leeth rubbed her neck again, to stop recording. "Tony. Okay if Thug and I scout around again, before we all settle down?"

Maretti nodded. "Yeah. Don't be long, though."

"Sure. Come on, Thug."

Outside, away from Gadger's 'Listener-spotter', Leeth touched out the Transmit sequence on her choker. Seconds later, she felt the double pulse against her neck that meant the coded transmission burst had been sent.

She relaxed. "So, what's this about sleeper ammo? That stuff won't penetrate military armor, surely?" she asked later, as they headed back inside.

Maretti, Don, and Cynthia left to perform their own tasks.

CHAPTER 70

Eagle waited patiently while security levels were negotiated, tight-beam transmitters came on line, and maximal encryption facilities exchanged complex single-use handshakes. When the link finally opened, it was limited to two-dimensional black and white video.

As he'd expected from Leeth's revelation, General Weatherburn, in New York, clearly hadn't slept yet.

Eagle's expression was cold. "Intel reports you have moved into damage control on your Scott project."

Weatherburn's face stilled into a poker mask for several seconds, before an expression of confusion formed. "I don't know what-"

"General, I know Bragg reports to you. If my investigations uncover nothing damaging to our nation, no case to hand the President, you have nothing to fear."

Weatherburn stared at him.

"Include the research data itself in the list of expendables, in your cleanup. For your own safety." If he didn't, Nelson's Ghost would quickly find it.

The General's face had set into a rigid mask. "I have no idea what you're talking about."

"I hope so. Because unless your cleanup is perfect, I will send you down. And I mean all the way."

He punched the disconnect.

That would minimize the risk of a leak from within Weatherburn's team. If the fool managed that well enough, he might even be spared. Provided Spinoza, the Bureau agent he'd just ordered to investigate from that end, found nothing. And if Leeth could tidy up her end.

"Thank you, General." Scott terminated the call and turned to Bragg. "A pity Weatherburn wasn't always so co-operative when we needed materiél. It seems your fears about restarting in Vallejo were unwarranted."

But after a quick scan of Bragg's aura, Scott focused his full attention on his security officer. "Problem?"

"Hell yes. Getting all we need at this short notice? The chips of Bureaucracy don't run that hot."

"Your recommendations?"

"Have Schenk do his Overmind melding thing with the Military Planning System. And *you* duck out to the Fort imaginally yourself."

Scott's expression remained as calm and calculating as ever. "Very well."

Twenty minutes later the mage returned to his body. Bragg tried to read his expression, but failed. "Well?"

Scott ignored the question. "What did Schenk learn?"

Bragg scowled. "The base is on silent alert, expecting a small-scale offensive, with a magical defense component. Possibly expecting an attack from Maretti's crew."

"Or from us."

Bragg nodded. "And your imaginal scouting?"

"I am unfamiliar with what is normal there. However, the youngest one of your people...?"

"Ferez."

"Yes. Private Ferez. Distinctive aura. I tracked him down. He and the others from the first delivery are on an eastbound military jet, feeling apprehensive and betrayed."

Bragg's face turned red, his fist slamming down on the table. "That back-stabbing, virus-loading, bastard son of an ogre whore! He's sold us out! It's not the chip-frying Fist of krupping Peace they're waiting for at Vallejo. It's us!"

"You believe we have become an embarrassment?"

"Yeah."

"In that case, I consider my contract with the Military to have been terminated."

"You don't say."

Dr Callahan Scott ignored the sarcasm. "I see no problem. My data cubes are all I absolutely require. Bio-Block are far from the only DNA fabbers in the market. We'll take our existing cultures, and my ritual materials, since they are costly and portable. Money will be our immediate problem, but your men can serve both for our defense, and to acquire what we need by force."

"Aren't you forgetting the watching spy drones and satellites?"

"The improved invisibility matrix does not *require* us to be in a truck. We will simply walk out on foot."

Bragg looked surprised. Then, for the first time in many hours, smiled.

CHAPTER 71

Fifteen minutes after sending her coded transmission, Leeth felt the double pulse that meant a message had arrived for her. Gadger's Listener device beeped, and he got up to check it. "Huh. That's odd. That was a millisec cast, quite strong. Not local, though." Leeth left him muttering worriedly over it as she moved off to the toilet cubicle. She checked the volume was turned all the way down. At that setting, it challenged even *her* hearing.

She activated the Play sequence.

"Be at the shadow-clinic on two-oh-five on Seventh Avenue in nineteen minutes for instructions."

Eagle's voice was followed by two long tones, meaning a twenty minute countdown had started. She blinked in surprise, while repeating the message to herself. Why couldn't they trust the normal encrypted broadcast to her? Though, with the paranoid way Gadger was acting, maybe it was just as well.

She poured water down the toilet and stood, thinking, still repeating the message to herself while refilling the bucket from the grubby plastic hose. For comms that could be intercepted, the Department's protocol was that you added one to all numbers. So it would be three-one-six on Eighth Avenue. She headed back out to the others, after checking out the address on her Link.

"I'm going to go to a street clinic near here. Get some slap patches. Pick up a few gas masks."

Chopper grinned. "Excellent idea, Raver. I'll get some C-Z while we're there."

She glared at him. "It's Ra-*ven*, unless you want to be *Flopper*."

His grin collapsed.

"And what's 'C-Z'?"

"Krek, Raven, where'd you grow up?" He gave his best roguish smile, spreading both hands wide. "C-Z. You know, Combat Zone. Modern combat drug."

Her expression set into icy distaste. "I don't need drugs to perform." She turned her back on him, not seeing Chopper's smile crumble.

"Me either," volunteered Thug. "Wanna lift?"

She hesitated only a moment. "Sure, Thug. Why not?"

She checked the outside security monitor, then hauled up the door, pretending it was heavy. Chopper watched her climb onto Thug's bike, fists clenched at his sides as they left. He looked around as Davo rolled the door shut. Wolf merely turned over on his side, and Wiz and Gadger hadn't even looked up from their radio gear. He thought of Val and Skinner, who'd probably already finished buying the extra sleeper rounds and were probably screwing themselves stupid in a coffin motel somewhere.

He snarled under his breath. They should've just nuked the place from orbit, like he'd suggested. And then, inspiration struck.

The clinic was up a dark, narrow stairway reeking of disinfectant and the vinegary smell of aging plastic. At the top landing an equally narrow corridor led away past rows of identical doors. Halfway down, a red LED glowed faintly.

The place was a death-trap, her instincts screamed. Too confined. She began looking for ways out. But Thug strode confidently to the LED-marked door, peering through the frosted glass before beckoning her up.

Inside, the claustrophobic waiting room was empty except for a derelict with an arm bandaged in rags – and the stench of disinfectant over sweat and blood. The smell was strong enough to count as a second presence in the room. Across from them, an inner door was closed. A programmable adhesive sign, its edges curling back, glowed with the words *Please take a seat.*

From behind the door stabbed the teeth-gritting whine of an ultrasonic drill. The first warning pressure of an incipient headache began to throb behind her ears.

She and Thug took a seat as far from the derelict as possible, who grinned at her. Wrinkling her nose, she turned her head away. But the man lurched to his feet and stumbled over to sit beside her, ignoring the baleful glare she fixed on him.

She pulled away in disgust as the stink of unwashed, sweaty male enveloped her.

"Hey, sister," he croaked, laying a hand familiarly on her shoulder, greasy lank hair falling down into his eyes. "Ya look like-"

It was as far as he got. One hand knocked his arm away while her other flashed around to grip his throat. The urge to kill was almost overpowering.

"Go. Away," she ground out before throwing him forward out of his chair.

Thug stood as the man, massaging his livid neck, staggered to his feet, now angry.

He used his bandaged arm as he got up, Leeth noticed. And moved determinedly back to her, despite Thug's massive interposing form.

The realization of who he must be drenched her like ice water.

"The lady doesn't want to talk to you, fren."

Leeth jumped to her feet. "It's – it's okay. Maybe I was a bit hard on him. Here," she said, taking his injured arm carefully and leading him back to a seat. "Sit down."

Alert, she saw his other hand slip a disposable mini-reader from his shabby coat pocket, and she winced as she turned, presenting a pocket of her own black jacket while shielding his hand from Thug's sight.

He dropped it in even as he pushed her away.

"Frag you, bitch." A stream of far more colorful curses flowed as he staggered to the exit door and slammed out, leaving her and Thug alone. She felt her ears flush red.

There was a short silence.

"Geez, Raven, you oughta, you know, lighten up. Try'n relax."

She tensed, an angry retort on her lips, but hesitated at the uncritical concern on Thug's earnest, open face. Sighing, she forced her hunched shoulders down.

"Maybe you're right."

In her jacket pocket, her searching fingers met a slim mini-screen, and her tension eased. That had been too close. When the Bureau concealing the 'Accounts Department' sent a messenger, they didn't go for half measures. Now she had to find somewhere to read her instructions in private.

The drill had stopped, she realized, as she heard steps approach the inner door. It opened to reveal a small middle-aged man with two obvious cyber eyes, wearing a blood-stained disposable surgeon's apron.

"What's going on out here? What did you do with my other customer?"

"He fell off his chair, then left," Raven snapped.

The man stared at her suspiciously. "What do *you*

want?"

She told him, including the ratings for the medpatches and trauma dampers.

He didn't have gas masks. "I can give you pollution filters." He shut his eyes. Opened them again. "Five hundred, fifty. Stick?"

He held out a hand impatiently.

Leeth winced. That wouldn't leave her much. She repeated the figure to her cashstick and passed it over. *The Fist had better appreciate this*, she vowed. Then wondered if they might pay her back. *And I'd worried about the cost of that steak dinner, with Gadger!*

The street doc tapped her stick to his, eyeing it with a grunt. Handing hers back he moved off, slamming the inner door shut behind him. Leeth raised her eyebrows and looked at Thug, who merely shrugged.

"We're lucky he's seein' us early," Thug said.

The man was back within minutes, shoving a plastic bag into her hands before disappearing once more into the inner room. The door slammed shut again and the drill restarted. She checked the contents of the bag, and they left.

Out on the street Thug inspected his bike, then locked their purchases away in its armored pannier and eyed Raven hesitantly. "Uh, there's a bar near here, I used to go to. Wanna take a break before we head back to the others? Relax a bit?"

She was about to say no, when she realized she'd be able to get some privacy there. "Sure, Thug. But maybe we should call Tony, see if everything's okay?"

"It's chill. They'd call *us* if there was a problem. 'Sides, Wiz'd be angry if you interrupted him."

He started the bike and she slipped on behind him. As they rumbled the short distance down the dark street toward the intersection, a distant, heavy bass-beat steadily built, blending with the sound of the bike's motor.

Thug pulled up alongside several other bikes, visible in the dim light diffusing through the many-times-repatched sheets of plasplex that had replaced the windows long ago. Switching off and planting the kickstand, he swung off the bike and they headed inside.

Eager to read the secret message, she resisted the urge to push Thug inside. *At least this should be simple*, she told herself.

CHAPTER 72

To the left of the entrance a long wooden bar stretched the length of the room. People sat in scattered groups at tables in the dim light, and in one corner a small band of unknowns struggled unsuccessfully with their electroboards and bodysynths.

"Where're the restrooms?"

Thug indicated an archway at the far end of the bar. "Through there, past the pool tables."

"Thanks. Will you get me a tomato juice?"

"Sure! But you sure you don' want-"

"I'm sure. See you in a few minutes. Not too close to the band, okay?" She cringed when the girl in the synth-suit's foot slipped on the beery floor, triggering another off-key note.

The big man grinned. "You got it."

As she turned away, on the projected screen by the bar she glimpsed the front porch of a familiar house. A swarm of media-insignia drones buzzed around it as a voice-over said "... Underworld series, Marcie Dunkirk, still refuses to expand on her earlier, prepared statement." Leeth almost stumbled. Continuing on, she focused on the speaker.

Through the archway, all the pool tables were fully occupied by what looked like the local bike gang. She threaded her way through them, ignoring their leers. From behind, Marcie's recorded voice said, "I don't have answers to your questions: who our abductors were; what they wanted; who or what our rescuer was. It was *not* a promotional stunt. I don't even know if it was the same cyborg or gynoid or whatever that was in the robot fight at Sybarus. Vince and I are innocent victims."

A different voice: "Can you comment on claims that this was the same creature who forced Dr Ranatunga to operate on you at-"

Marcie must not have answered, since the speaker changed. "In other news, jobless figures...."

Inside the 'Chix', with clenched teeth, she chose the cubicle farthest from the couple screwing in the end one. Shutting the door, she fought to calm down. *Thanks to me, Marcie's being hounded by the media.* She wondered what Mother, and Eagle, were thinking. *They know I can't say anything to anyone outside the Department, so at least they won't be worried about security leaks.* And she *hadn't* told Marcie anything. Just her cover story, about working for her mother and father. Admitting to Marcie, ages ago, that she'd killed some unnamed person wouldn't count. Surely?

Her 'love', Luiz.

She waited a heartbeat, for a pain that didn't come, and felt a tiny stab of guilt at that lack. Chewing her lip, she counted. Had it really been six weeks ago?

But she couldn't think about Marcie right now. *Focus on the mission! Don't screw things up even worse.* Pulling out the bead-shaped personal data projector, she tried to lose herself in security protocols. With these things, any secret stuff only displayed as long as the inbuilt scanners recognized the correct – and living – retina looking into it. Aiming it at her right eye, she saw the day's news headline – WARRIORS REACH FINALS. Taking a deep breath, and putting Marcie from her mind with a feeling she should be doing more – like shooting down the drones buzzing around her house – she pressed her thumb to the bead. It read her prints, and retina, and the news cleared to a message that said simply:

'E to L. Sensitivity 13.'

A prickle went up her spine. A direct message from Eagle? And sensitivity thirteen, in red letters. She frowned. Wasn't that the very top code? For National Security? *Uh oh.*

She squeezed it forward, and the image changed. She read, screen one of three:

'L: Dr Scott has broken the Global Moratorium of '38. Global trade sanctions against Scott's ultimate funder is certain if this becomes public knowledge.'

Good! But... wait. Scott's funder was the military. So his ultimate funder was... the government. There'd be global sanctions against the United States? A chill went through her. Swallowing, she read on.

'Your new priorities:

1) Prevent research leaking to Tik Tek.

2) Retire Scott and associates Bragg and Ford.'

Scott, Bragg and Ford. *About frick'n time!*

'3)(a) Destroy and (b) Retire evidence of subject's research.'

She frowned. Destroy the evidence, sure. But what did they mean, *kill* it too? Oh. They meant she had to kill any people who'd been experimented on. She grimaced. What if they were *nice* people? Or kids? Like Barney? She rocked back at the thought. Swallowing, she aimed the bead back at her eye and read on.

'4) Destroy research notes.'

Well, *der*.

'5) Copy research notes.'

How could she do that after she'd-? Oh. Copy them if she could, but destroying them was more important.

'6) Retire FOP leak.'

Like I'd forget. She squeezed for the next screen.

'Estimate 6-7 hrs until Military Intelligence ops active on (3)(a) and (4).'

She squeezed the bead back to the second screen. So Military Intelligence would also be looking for the research notes and other evidence she was supposed to destroy. Okay. She could beat those guys. Squeezing it forward she read on.

'A Bureau agent, Spinoza, is now involved. Keep your distance. Do not let him see you. There must be no hint of our involvement. All further reports will be directly to me. The affair is now strictly need-to-know.'

Savage! She studied the picture of Agent Spinoza.

'Be aware: We believe some of the research contravenes the Moratorium of '38. If the FOP learns that, you may be required to Retire the FOP.
E.'

And just like that, soaring excitement collapsed into a cold, dense lump. They might order her to kill the whole *Fist of Peace*? But some of them were friends!

Shaking her head, she scanned numbly back through the list of priorities one last time. Then squeezed on past that last, terrible screen to one that read Wipe. Squeezing again, the display reverted to the news headline.

She squeezed one more time, to be sure the data was gone. *Nothing*. She crushed the reader and tossed it in the disposal.

Stood, and flushed the toilet.

You may be required to Retire the FOP.
She headed back out to the bar, eyes wide but unseeing.

CHAPTER 73

"Hey, sliv, cruising fine. Catch some smash?"

Half aware of someone leering down at her, blocking her way, she swept his legs from under him and continued into the main bar. In her mind, she saw Thug, and Wolf, and Gadger, all looking at her, betrayed. Cynthia, Davo, Val, and Skinner. *I don't want to kill them.*

Spotting Thug she headed over, frowning when she saw he wasn't alone. Some amazon in the only other chair at the table was leaning in toward him.

"... had ta work for this bod. But *you* – ya look like you've nulled out, beef," she was saying as Leeth approached. The woman wore black, jeans and an exercise singlet that left her shoulders and arms bare, her muscles on show. She had a tattoo of a volcano on her left shoulder. What was it with volcanoes? They seemed to be following her around.

Leeth halted midway between the two chairs, and the woman looked lazily up at her. Thug seemed really uncomfortable. The woman dismissed her with a glance, turning back to Thug. "You still drink Bud?"

"Huh?"

She raised her eyes to heaven as she turned back to Leeth. "Get us another Bud and a Razorback, girl."

A waitress? She thinks I'm a waitress? Leeth's pulse throbbed hard, blood pounding her temple in a black storm of rage. Her vision narrowed to the woman's sinewy neck, rich and ripe. The skull would be more satisfying to crush though. She teetered on the brink of 'Retiring' the woman before remembering where she was. In a room full of people. In front of Thug.

Her teeth ground together.

"Uh, Zonya, this's my teammate. She doesn't *work* here. Raven, this is Zonya. Kinda an old friend."

The woman looked her up and down, her expression raising Leeth's hackles, and tossed a battered cashstick on the table. "Look, howzabout you grab a nice drink at the bar for five, sliv? Go wild. Me an' my old meat need a little comms." She turned back to Thug.

Leeth couldn't believe her ears. This woman had to die.

"Look, Zonya, we have nothin' to talk about. That's all over. I'm here with Raven, and I want to talk to *her*, not you. So howzabout *you* take your cashstick and leave us alone, hey? Howzabout *that*."

The woman lifted her chin, glaring at him for long seconds before thrusting her chair back and standing. "You always were the dumbest man I ever knew, Thug. Can't believe I forgot that." She stormed off.

Thug looked sheepish. "Sorry 'bout that. She just came and dumped on me. I *told* her I was here with a fren', but it didn' make any diff."

Black sunglasses stared flatly back at him. *She looks angry*, he thought. "I mean, she always was pushy. Even back when we were in a, uh, *gang*, when we used to go together. Long time ago, now. But hey, forget about Zonya." He gestured to the chair opposite him.

Leeth sat, but twisted around to see where the woman went. *Maybe I can kill her later.*

The woman disappeared into the pool room.

Thug's hand on hers brought her attention back to him. "Hey, Raven, forget it. We came here to relax, remember? Don't let her coil you up." He searched for something to distract her. "I got you the tomato juice you wanted?"

She took the drink, trying to pull free of the black anger. But it was like it'd taken root, a seed of dark fury now smoldering deep inside. For a moment she imagined slicing into Zonya's over-muscled chest, reaching in.... She took a breath, then a swallow of her drink, and the tart, rich taste soothed her. Actually, she *was* quite thirsty. "Thanks, Thug."

She drained it and sat back, sighing.

Thug beamed back at her, happy again. "So whattya think of this place? Apart from the band, I mean," he added, grimacing.

She looked into his rugged, open face, considering.

You may be required to Retire the FOP.

The reality of her situation closed in on her, and she squeezed her eyes shut. Unless she kept the Fist from finding out anything Eagle considered too serious, she might soon have to decide what to do if he ordered her to kill Thug. And Gadger and Wolf, too.

"Raven? You okay?" He sounded worried.

She screwed her eyes tighter shut. Suddenly she wanted to be out, and away. She didn't have time for this anymore. Suddenly, working for the Department didn't seem like such a good thing. She opened her eyes.

But Thug had tensed and was looking past her. Over the background music she heard several pairs of booted feet heading their way from the pool table room.

"Uh oh," he said.

She rose from her seat, turning to face the approaching group of six bikers who halted in a circle around them. As Leeth stepped away from the table, Zonya and another biker moved up, flanking her.

Zonya smiled a shark's smile. "Come on, sweetbuns, you and me're going to the bar. Ya didn' wanna before, but meb you've changed ya mind now *my* man's here."

Leeth burned. *Sweetbuns?*

Thug stared steadily up, still seated. "Zonya, what're-"

The man mountain with Zonya pushed forward. "Talk to me, deadmeat, not my bitch." Almost troll-sized, he made Thug look small. "You sniffed her too loud already, deadmeat." He, too, was tattooed, but the lurid volcanic eruption used his whole bare chest for its canvas.

More volcanoes? Leeth thought, shaking her head.

"Toa don't like nulls try'n slot his bitch," one of the other massive bikers added.

Taking Leeth by the waist, Zonya dragged her toward the bar, the man on her other side.

"Try your slutting judo tricks now, sluk," he spat.

Leeth wondered what on Earth he was talking about, but let them drag her off to the bar, happy to let their opponents split their forces. Maybe, with a little luck, she could deal with these two without the other four noticing? Even get a surprise attack on the others? Especially if Thug could hold their attention.

She turned back. Thug still sat there, watching her go, serious and calm. He only looked back to the problem looming over him after he saw her safely away.

At the bar, Zonya took the stool on her left, the man perching on the one to her right, the two of them 'encouraging' her onto the bar-stool between them. Her rage felt like lava, boiling inside. They all three watched as Thug faced the giant. The familiar tingle burned along her nerves.

The man's hand closed around her neck, then forced her face around to his, his lips parting. A wave of unexpected lust took her with the suddenness of an attack of vertigo, and she let his mouth close on hers. Her nipples hardened involuntarily, even as he let her go.

She stared at him in horror.

He chuckled. "*Oh* yeah, girl," he promised, before turning back to the scene across the room, confident in his mastery.

What the krek! Why did I just let *him-?* Like fighting her way through molasses, she forced the unwanted reaction aside, and saw Zonya sneering at her. The anger slammed back, full force.

She lifted her chin, then reached into the pocket of her jeans. Drawing her hand out carefully, with thumb and finger pinched together as though holding something small, she pretended to place the thing on the bar top. Nodding down at it, she smiled with razor sharpness at the large woman.

Zonya half turned, peering down at the empty surface.

Leeth's other hand swept up behind her neck, and, in time to the band's next down-beat, abruptly pounded the woman's head onto the bar, hard.

Zonya's eyes glazed over and she collapsed off her seat. "Hey-!"

She pounded a fist into the other biker's groin, fighting to hold her claws contained, a part of her hungering to see blood. She snarled as he doubled over, and went to Thug, finally now standing.

"- your best shot," she heard him say, wincing as the giant raised his fist and smashed a massive haymaker into Thug's face – a blow that should have knocked him across the room.

Unbelievably, it merely rocked him to one side.

His head swung slowly back, blood flowing freely from a torn lip. But he smiled around it. "My turn."

One heavy fist drew back, then slammed into the biker's face, staggering the behemoth backward almost into Leeth's arms.

The punch she hammered into his kidney sounded like gristle tearing. *Oops.* As he went down, Thug ripped the table up, bolts snapping as the legs tore free of the ground to crash into the remaining three. Grabbing her hand he dragged her away, racing for the door.

Out on the street they charged to his bike, Thug scrabbling at one of the panniers. *Finally*, the band had stopped their torture. Behind them, she heard pounding feet from inside the bar.

As the first bikers poured from the doorway, Thug swung to face them. Maybe it was the determination on his face that brought them to a sudden halt. Or maybe it was the Heckler and Koch submachine gun in his hands.

"We don't want any trouble," he said, quietly.

For several long seconds no one moved, then the figures in the doorway melted back inside.

Thug looked down at her, but it was hard for her to read his expression round his badly swelling face. "Sorry 'bout that, Raven. But we'd better go, huh?"

"Sure, Thug," she said, forgiving him for dragging her away. She didn't want to risk getting him hurt. *Oh,* and *I'm not supposed to let them know how well I can fight.* She replayed her part: one head slam and one punch, while Thug's view had been blocked by 'Toa'. One more punch, to Toa, screened by his own massive body.

He started the bike while she swung up easily behind him. As they powered off, she leaned forward to speak into his ear. "Would you *really* have shot them all?"

Thug laughed thickly. "Sure! With sleeper rounds."

Leeth shook her head as they sped into the dark, twisting side streets.

CHAPTER 74

"Rape the slutting whales, Raven," Maretti complained. "I might've known. You go out to buy some band-aids, and manage to get Thug beaten up in a brawl in some sleazy dive."

She blushed.

"No, Tony, it wasn' *her* fault, an' *we* didn'-"

Maretti made a cutting gesture. "I don't want to hear it. Just go and have Wolf Heal that."

Thug hesitated, looked at Raven, then shambled over to the shaman.

"Gadger and Wiz manage to scrounge anything off the military bands?" she asked.

Maretti scowled down at her, his hands clenching and unclenching like he wanted to throttle her. She swallowed, almost taking a step back, then felt a small burn of anger in response. What *was* it about him that kept getting under her skin? Forcing her expression to remain serious and professional, she just waited. At last he took hold of himself.

"Yeah, kind of. We can't make any sense of it though. While you and Thug were *playing*, a whole bunch of personnel from the Vallejo military base were deployed into the area around the monitoring station. No attempt at subtlety. They're there right now. Wiz hacked a camera feed showing them securing the area, but it looks like they're more worried about what might be coming up *out* of the ground there, than 'terrorists' like us attacking and trying to get *in*. We had to cut the link, though. Wiz said we'd have them down on our necks once they got their gear set up."

His jaw muscles worked, but finally he added, "So – *you* make anything of it?"

He actually wants my opinion! She considered his question. The army was moving against their own people? Eagle had said Military Intelligence would be involved in six hours. It probably meant her report earlier had set this whole thing off. He was closing them down. But her job was to make sure the research, whatever it was, either went to Eagle only or was utterly destroyed. And kill Scott, Bragg and Ford.

"Hello? Anybody home?" Maretti waved his hand in front of her face.

She blinked, an urge to punch him making her flush. "I think we made them move out, by disturbing them. And I bet someone back at Vallejo let something slip to someone higher up, and now the project's been discovered. So, I guess their bosses are probably trying to take control of Scott's research."

His eyes narrowed. "That's all just guesswork. Though if you're right, they mustn't've uploaded their research to the cloud, even encrypted."

"Hey, you're not the only one who has good hunches, you know." She looked up into his face, and her pulse accelerated, confusing her. It was his eyes. His jawline, too? They *meant* something. Something important. Had he been a patient, at the Institute...? She winced at a sudden jab of pain, then blinked, scrabbling to remember what her idea had been. "Uh, did any more trucks leave?"

He frowned. "Yeah. There was one about an hour ago. Wolf and Cyn followed it to Vallejo, but couldn't risk tackling the imaginal guards and tipping our hand."

She nodded. "But we know it didn't have everything they wanted in it, otherwise the soldiers wouldn't be attacking the underground base." This was fun! It must be like how Mother and Father worked.

The others had gathered round to join the conversation. It made her feel good – like she and Maretti were leading them, together. Wiz broke in. "So, either Braggs's lot have burrowed in – in which case we let the military dig 'em out, and try to intervene right after – or he's already blipped out. Which we won't know unless we head over there and see what happens. So either way...."

Maretti nodded. "Right. Get your gear. We're moving out."

At last, *some action*, thought Leeth, and ran over to her pack. Maybe she'd even get to use the explosives!

Seconds later, she froze. Someone had been through her stuff. "Tony!"

He looked up from his modified AK-97. "What?"

"All my C4 is gone. And the detonators."

He frowned. "Are you *sure*?"

"Gee. Let me think." Finger and thumb to her chin, she tilted her head to one side. "Did I blow up any buildings in the last couple of days?"

Cynthia looked around. "Has anyone seen Chopper recently?" she asked.

"He pushed off after Thug and Raven went out," offered Davo. "Said he had... said he had something to do. Oh, no."

Cyn nodded. "You remember earlier – he said we should nuke the place."

A chorus of disbelieving groans met that statement.

"How long ago?" Maretti demanded.

"About an hour, now."

"If that idiot's had an idea, we're in trouble. We'd better-"

His wristcomm buzzed, interrupting him. Recognizing Chopper's caller ID, he answered it.

And found himself staring into Bragg's face.

CHAPTER 75

Thirty minutes earlier, from his vantage point in the derelict hospital, Chopper scowled across the expanse of former Bay floor. The buried and encrusted shapes of dumped wrecks made it look like Hell was erupting from below, or like some nightmare infection had escaped into the waking world and was creeping toward the pollution monitoring station.

The trouble was, Raven said her explosives would've collapsed that other building – but would they be enough to break through solid rock? He didn't know as much about explosives as Don, but he knew you needed some way to contain the blast so the force'd go downwards into the underground complex.

Maybe quick-setting cement?

He'd need a krup-load of the stuff, though. Maybe he should go back. Maybe this wasn't such a good idea?

The wind rose, moaning like a creature from a horror trid, and he shivered abruptly. There was something about this place. Looking around the eerie green scene shown by his light intensifiers, he had the uncomfortable feeling something watched him.

And then the air darkened and thickened. The alien face of an air elemental stared incuriously at him as his lungs clawed for breath. He ran, out of the hospital room and down a deserted, decaying corridor, struggling to escape the creature enveloping him. It stayed effortlessly with him, around him, its unblinking eyes watching incuriously. As the blackness flowed from outside to inside, Chopper had time for one last thought.

Shit.

It was time to set the trap, Bragg decided – time to call the Fist of Peace. Scott's ability to extract information from an unconscious brain had once again proved valuable. Pity he refused to share the spell.

Their little rehearsal had gone well, though. "You think you've got that, Corporal?" he asked, "or do you want to run through it again?"

"No sir. It's not too much to remember."

Bragg turned to Scott. "Director?"

Scott nodded. "This will really deceive them? Force them to act tonight?"

"Believe me," Bragg said, baring his teeth, "I know them. They won't abandon their idiot friend, here, and they'll have to assume we can do what we claim."

"Proceed, then."

They headed to the room they'd started setting up as the laboratory, half their equipment already unpacked. Ford, the geneticist, had even dug out some test tubes to hold the implied 'virus'. Strapped into a chair in one corner slumped Chopper, sedated.

Scott stood off to one side as Bragg took a seat at the desk, the corporal at attention before him. "Are we ready?" he asked.

At Scott's nod, Ford crossed over to Chopper and administered the stim, then moved away and began unpacking more vials and shuffling test tubes around. Scott stared off into space, while Bragg glared down at the paper before him, looking impatient and pretending to read as the corporal stood waiting.

At last, Chopper groaned faintly and moved. Scott, watching imaginally, made a hand gesture.

Bragg looked up. "So. Are we ready, Corporal?"

"Yes, sir. We have enough of the cultures to seed into the atmosphere. Early release means we won't get an optimal dispersal, though. It'll take 48 hours to cover New Francisco, and probably two weeks before the contagion is worldwide."

Chopper, staring through slitted eyes, stiffened; then carefully relaxed again, pretending unconsciousness.

"What about the predicted rain?"

"Projections say contamination of the water supply will spread it almost as effectively."

"And we have enough of the vaccine for our own people?"

"Yes, sir. Enough for the period of contagion."

"How long till you can begin dispersal?"

"The cultures are almost thawed. Dr Ford says another hour for them to reach a critical state. After that – just open a window."

"And what about the Fist of Peace?" asked Scott, stepping forward. "Suppose they decide to act quickly?"

Bragg smiled. "Simple. Watch – but don't speak." He moved over to Chopper, unsnapped his wristcomm, and swiped it unlocked.   Chopper remained still.   Bragg touched for redial, and waited.

He smiled as Maretti's face filled the tiny screen. "Maretti? Bragg here. Two things. First off, please tell Raven I've considered her offer, but her price is much too high.

"Second, I have Chopper, and I've had him Mindmelded, luckily for you. You've got the situation all wrong. Why don't we meet somewhere, about midnight, and straighten this out?"

Chopper suddenly came to life, straining at his bonds. "Midnight? Tony! No! In *one hour* they're releasing some kind of virus-"

"He was supposed to be sedated!" swore Bragg before slamming the disconnect button on the Link.

Ford, grimacing theatrically, applied a trank patch to the struggling prisoner, and all waited for his cursing and movements to die away.

"Excellent, people," Bragg said.   "Very convincing. That's it. As of now, we're on full alert."

"What about the prisoner, sir?   Can't they track us through him?" asked the young officer.

"I'm depending on it," declared Bragg.

CHAPTER 76

Every member of the Fist of Peace was staring at her. Every single one. Maretti had his gun out, its muzzle pointed at her like the dead black eye of a shark.

His eyes didn't look kind, now.

She stood, fists on hips, facing them. Furious.

"Well?" demanded Maretti at last.

"What!"

"Explain what he meant by 'Raven's offer'."

She shook her head. "There's nothing *to* explain. *You* work it out."

"You offered to betray us to Bragg, for a price. A price he wasn't willing to pay."

"No."

"No? Then how did he even know your name?"

"Chopper was Mindmelded, you... you *dopestick*." She bit her lip. "Bragg even said so."

The barrel lowered a fraction of an inch. "Why should we believe you?"

Don abruptly spoke. "He sows dissension."

"He seeks to disturb our harmony," added Wolf. "To weaken the Fist's spirit."

"I've never spoken to the slug, Tony," Leeth said. "Never made any kind of offer, or deal. I like being one of you. Being part of what you're doing." *It was all true*, she realized. Being with them, with *him*, a part of a group, fighting for right.... It felt better than just good. It felt... she struggled for the word. Like she *belonged*? "Don't send me away." *Or should I actually hope for that? Might that keep them safe?* Then she realized it'd more likely mean the opposite, winding up with her ordered to hunt them down and kill them. She shivered, and shook her head. *No.*

Maretti lowered the gun. "What do the rest of you think? Was Bragg lying?"

"Raven was telling the truth," declared Cynthia. "I checked."

Raven glared at the mage for a moment, bristling. Then shrugged and turned back to Maretti. "Can we *please* kill Bragg, when we find him?"

Maretti's mouth opened. Closed. Then he sneered. "So you can silence him?"

Why was he being so *difficult?* "Look, Tony, you talk to

him as much as you want. Do Truth detection spells on him, Mindmeld him – write his whole fragging life story for all I care. But can I kill him, afterwards?" She pictured herself carving Bragg's heart from his chest.

Maretti hesitated.

"Oh, come on! Surely you don't let *all* your enemies go free?"

They looked at one another uncomfortably.

"Oh... *fuck!*" *How could a whole group be so stupid?* "I don't believe this! What, is he like your 'nemesis'?"

"We'll talk about it *if* we capture him," Maretti told her. "First we've got to find him."

"You think it's a trap?" asked Davo. "Pretty convenient, Chopper knowing he was lying."

"Yeah, probably. But does it make any difference? We can't take the chance they *aren't* going to release some virus in an hour's time. And we can't abandon Chopper."

"So how do we find them?"

Wiz looked up from his comp. "Give me a few more minutes. I'll tell you what Link cell that call came from. We may not even need Wolf or Cyn to do a Sending on Chopper to locate them."

As the minutes dragged past, though, Wiz began looking increasingly desperate. Cynthia cleared away junk from one of the carved ritual circles, while Wolf fetched Chopper's bedding and a holo of him, passing them to Cynthia.

But they all knew such a ritual casting would take at least an hour.

Gadger had recorded the last part of the call, and was playing it back, trying to isolate the background noises. His face was grim but determined.

Wolf waited a few minutes more, then went Imaginal. He said he'd try to find out what was happening at the underground complex. It was, after all, the most likely location.

But Val and Skinner, Thug, Davo and Maretti could only wait helplessly. Raven paced. "Did Chopper visit the Pollution Station? He'd be on the recording!"

Gadger didn't look up from his electronics gear, but his terse "No" conveyed his annoyance at the interruption.

Raven grimaced and resumed her pacing.

Eagle needed to know about this new development. But she had to report only to him, and even with the choker, she couldn't send a message without Gadger picking up the transmission. Besides, they were so keyed up they'd probably notice her doing it. Especially Maretti, who was keeping a really close eye on her now. And she could hardly just head off and make a call.

Damn Wiz! Nelson might be a complete null as a human being, but by now *he* would've worked out which Link cell Chopper's call came from, and probably have dug up a complete list of all the people he'd contacted in the last month, too. What was taking Wiz so *long*? Should she remind him they had less than an hour? Chit, since Bragg had used Chopper's Link, he even had the originating call ID.

Wolf's spirit returned to his body. Everyone except Cynthia and Wiz stopped what they were doing, but the shaman just shook his head, grim-faced. "The soldiers are moving in. The tunnel was mined, and collapsed after eight of them had gone through, trapping them. I sensed an elemental spirit of the earth moving on them, and heard their death cries.

"Above, there is little activity. They have cordoned off the area."

"But what about below? Didn't you go back into the complex?" demanded Raven.

"The area has had ivy fastened over it. I cannot penetrate a living barrier."

"Bragg will have mined the walls," Don said. "The army will bring in the Earth Corps."

"The Earth Corps?" Maretti asked.

"The army has mages, with elementals, always waiting."

"How'dja know that?" asked Val.

Don ignored her question. "They will send a large elemental in to tear down barriers, trigger traps, and tunnel into the complex."

While Cynthia continued her ritual to locate Chopper, Raven turned to Wolf. "Could you sneak in after the elemental?"

After some thought, the shaman nodded. "I can try. But I will invoke a city spirit to accompany me. Just in case."

Maretti agreed. "Do it."

It felt good, having him listen to her again.

Leeth checked her watch. It was *twenty minutes* now since the call from Bragg. She sat with the others, trying to be calm. Patient. A true Hunter.

She *so* wanted to kill something.

Grinding her teeth together, she glared across at Wiz. He was probably taking this long just to provoke her.

Wolf's recumbent form suddenly shuddered. He sat up. "They've gone. It was empty. Purely a trap."

Groans met this pronouncement. All eyes turned to Wiz as more seconds trickled, dying, into the past.

Gadger stretched back, discreetly unplugging an audio jack from the back of his head. "Listen to this. I've managed to cut out the foreground noises and voices, pretty well." He flicked a switch on his comp.

There was a confused melange of sounds, a murmuring foreground of imperfectly-canceled speech; a background that might have been the rushing sound of traffic. Something that sounded like a safety catch being clicked off. And the adhesive-ripping sound of a med patch being primed. Through it all, far in the background, a deep background pulse.

"Kill the high frequencies and boost the low, Gadger," ordered Raven, staring at the comp.

He obliged and replayed it. "Music?" he suggested.

Raven gnawed her lip. "Do you have any good headphones?"

"Eh? No. I've got a datalink. What would I want with an analog device like that?"

"I have," volunteered Davo.

She waited while he fetched them. After Gadger patched them into his comp's audio output, she fitted them over her ears. "Okay. Again." The sound started up again, but she interrupted him. "Kill the speakers. They're terrible."

Gadger looked offended, but did as she asked. They all watched Raven's tense expression in silence. Her head began rhythmically nodding. She half-closed her eyes, her frown deepening. Which slowly vanished as her lips curved up in a smile.

She removed the 'phones and grinned at them all. "It's Elliptical Compasses 'Summon the Night'."

They looked at her blankly.

"You must've heard it, it's a big dance hit. Retro-mechno. Grubby."

Maretti was looking at her curiously, but Davo nodded, slowly. "I've heard it, yeah. Doesn't sound like Bragg's style." *Or yours*, he thought, but didn't say it.

"They're next to a party, or someone with their radio up loud, or something," she added.

"Maybe," Davo said. "Can I've a listen?"

She handed him back his headphones, and they all waited. But he shook his head. "Could be almost anything. All you get is just the regular 'dum-da dum-da dum-da'."

"No. That's all *you* get. It's Summon the Night."

"Didn' know you were such a big jammer, Raven," Val mused.

Wiz saved her. "Got it! They're Downtown! Near the Oakland Tunnel on-ramp." The trid projector sprang to life, a 3D map of New Francisco materializing in the air above it. With dizzying speed the view zoomed in to a few blocks that included part of the entertainment district, which suddenly stood out as though bathed in red light. "Somewhere in there."

Maretti looked at Wolf. "That's not too big an area. Imaginal scout?" The man nodded. "Cyn! Break that off. I want you to back up Wolf – and his spirit?" Wolf nodded. "Imaginally."

She came over, looking slightly nervous.

"This looks like an above-ground parking station, here," Maretti said, pointing at the hologram. "We'll take a car and bring your bodies with us while you're out, and all meet up right in the Link cell. This time Bragg's screwed up. After blowing up his own people, the army really isn't going to be pleased with him. He'll have zero backup. He's on his own now."

"Except for Scott. And the men with the black aura," reminded Cynthia.

Maretti looked thoughtful. "Yeah. Except for them."

CHAPTER 77

Perched behind Thug on his bike, leaving the hideout, the chaotic churn of her thoughts matched the jolting ride down potholed lanes. At least, until the transition to the sleek, smooth streets of the corptoys' downtown playgrounds.

She had to tell Eagle what was happening: that the people they were hunting *might* be going to release a virus into New Francisco tonight. But if she left to make a secure call, the Fist would never trust her enough to let her rejoin them. If she called on her wristcomm, it wouldn't be secure at all. If she used the transmitter in her choker, Gadger would pick up the signal – he was carrying the chitting Listener thing with him, now.

Her thoughts looped back in tangling circles.

Thug took a message on his transceiver, then angled his head to Raven, not knowing she'd overheard. He raised his voice over the low growl of his bike. "Tony says we'll work from the carpark up ahead!"

She patted his shoulder in acknowledgment. This was it. She had to do something. Suddenly her eyes widened. With Gadger still in Davo's car, might its body shield her for the second she'd need to make a burst transmission?

She took one hand from round his waist but he only muttered 'careful'. Keying the encryption mode on the transceiver, she spoke in a low voice, alert for any sign he heard her. "Message to Eagle direct. Private. MI *targets* have moved downtown. They *claim* they're going to release some virus into the city tonight. In less than forty minutes. Moving in, and hunting now. Out."

She keyed the transmit sequence while Thug turned into the ill-lit concrete structure ahead and gunned the bike up the first ramp.

Nine pm, not far from Union Square. Waiting, on the third level of a carpark. Thirty minutes before Bragg's deadline was due to expire. The Fist stood by the car and bikes, spread protectively around the inert bodies of the two mages whose spirits now hunted ghost-like through nearby buildings.

By the metal rail at the edge of the carpark, Leeth looked out into the city's vivid lights, so bright here, amongst them all. She wondered if she'd survive the night – see Faith's babies; somehow make things right with Marcie; work with James and Emma and Dojo again. She and Wolf had exchanged a look just before he'd closed his eyes and laid down on the back seat of the car

The look had said he was scared.

He'd still gone, of course. But it made her wonder. Something about what was going on had really shaken the Native American warrior. Something about Scott, and the magic he did.

She looked forward to killing the man, for that alone. Her hands tingled at the idea of coming face to face with him.

Another thought brought such a blaze of joy she was glad she was facing away from the group at the time. If Eagle had trusted her on a mission *this* important, he *must* be pleased with her work as an Agent. She'd make him proud of her: kill Bragg, Scott, and Ford, *and* the mystery traitor. Whether the Fist said she could or not.

And she'd stop Scott's research getting to the Fist, and keep them safe, too.

From the level below, a woman's outraged shriek triggered a chorus of laughter before transforming into a strident demand for 'Dan' to wait until they were in the stimsurround. A car horn blared its displeasure, to be answered by more shrieks and laughter from below.

Outside on the building facings, brilliant holograms cycled through garish advertising routines, almost overpowering the streetlights beyond the carpark. There was no wind, just a distant rumble of thunder.

Leeth rejoined the others, hands jammed in pockets. From the ramp of the carpark a vehicle emerged onto their level, its headlights sweeping across them as it corkscrewed its way to the levels above.

They waited.

"I-" Val coughed strangely, almost sounding like she was choking. "I was just thinking, times like this, waiting... Chopper'd wanna go for pizza." She glared at Raven, for some reason, then turned suddenly away and headed to the rail to check the streets.

She's upset, thought Leeth. She looked around. They all were. She hunted for something to snap them out of it.

Distract them. Cheer them up.

"So, Tony. Is now a good time to work out if it's okay to kill Bragg and Scott?"

They all turned to stare at her.

Well. At least I've distracted them. "I mean, we know they've caused at least eight disappearances in Hunters Point, and killed a bunch of soldiers tonight. Plus the twenty-six innocent people they poisoned with nerve gas. And Bragg hates you all. He'll kill you if you give him the slightest chance, right?"

"We can't decide now," declared Maretti. "Not while Cyn and Wolf are 'away'."

"Okay, okay. But when they come back, *then* can we decide?"

Maretti gave a curt nod.

"Dump me, Raven, are you *always* this bloodthirsty?" asked Gadger.

She stared at him, swallowing back one reply after another. "I just want to clear the air, that's all," she offered at last.

Except for Don, they all looked at her doubtfully. Even Thug. It made her feel kind of weird.

"No." Cynthia's hand slashed the air. "Absolutely not. We'd be as bad as they are. And what about our rep – are there *any* other groups like us, who achieve what we do, without taking the easy way out? Without blasting someone as soon as it's expedient? We do it hard, but we do it right."

It was ten minutes later, and the two mages had returned to check that all was well.

Raven stared at Cynthia in frustration. "Okay, let's set aside the fact he's trying to kill you – us. And that he's killed, and will keep on killing." She threw both hands dramatically up. "Funt, as long as we're fantasizing, let's pretend the two of them aren't working on some *really* nasty magical stuff. Like black auras, and shrinking Wolf. *Chip shit*, Wolf had to have his *Totem* guru thing come to him in a dream to fix *that!* We owe it to *society* to stop them. If we don't, they'll just sneak off somewhere, find some raping megacorp to fund them, and we'll have let *everybody* down, not just ourselves. It's our *duty* to stop them! Permanently."

Cynthia looked slightly less adamant.

No one spoke. They all just stood around, avoiding each other's eyes.

On the street below, a single car rushed past, the sound of its tires fading into the distance. In its wake, the air fell still and silent.

And in that momentary silence, muffled by intervening walls and buildings, Leeth heard the faint pulsing bass of a distant dance band. Her head lifted, hunting its direction.

The silence collapsed as the unusual lull in traffic ended, cars once more flowing past below. She turned to Maretti. "I just remembered. There's a place near here, plays the sort of music I heard in the background during Bragg's call. I'm going to see if I can find it."

"We will resume our hunt," declared Wolf.

Raven went to him, looking up into his eyes as she placed one hand flat on his chest. "Can you come back in, say, five minutes instead of fifteen? If my memory's right, I don't think it's far from here. It's in that direction," she added, pointing.

The shaman nodded, and he and Cynthia went back to the car.

"Davo'll go with you," decided Maretti.

"Fine. But let's move."

Then she was off, loping with deceptive speed for the stairwell. Davo raced after her, but by the time he reached the open doorway, she was already out of sight. He could feel the iron handrail vibrating as he put his hand on it, though, then heard a thump from below. He charged down after her.

In the darkness at the bottom a figure lay sprawled at the foot of the stairs, breath rasping. Davo stopped, moving forward slowly, alert for some sort of trap. From one corner he caught the glint of a knife blade lying on the floor of the smelly alcove. As his feet touched the bottom, Raven's head poked in from outside. "Come *on!*"

"What- who's that?"

The figure groaned.

She shrugged. "Who cares? He was just lying there. Come *on.*"

A little later they paused, Davo sucking in deep, raking breaths. Raven was looking around, but something about the way she moved made him think she was listening. She grabbed his arm. "Come on. I remember now. This way." And they were off again.

They hadn't far to go. Maybe three blocks. When a side door opened and people emerged, the music was loud enough to make Davo wonder how much the club paid in bribes to stay in operation. If it was that intense here at the corner of the street, it'd be painful inside. The door closed again, the sound of the music blending into a closer roll of thunder.

They looked at one another. Raven jerked her thumb back in the direction they'd come, and he nodded. Melting back into the shadows, they trotted down the side street, then picked up the pace once they were out of sight of possible watchers.

Wiz had the trid projector on the driver's seat of the car, a 3D map hanging frozen in the air. He was calling up details of the building they'd identified before Davo had recovered his breath.

Raven paced up and down, waiting for the mages' spirits to return to their bodies. "What's keeping them? It's been almost six minutes, now," she asked, checking her Link.

Val answered her. "Chill, Raven. Relax."

"Maybe something's happened to them?"

"We are fine."

She spun round, to see Wolf's eyes open and Cynthia sit up from the back seat of the car. She ran over. "Look, here. This building's a dance-club. Could be what I heard, on the cube."

Wolf nodded, and opened his mouth to speak, but Wiz interrupted. He spoke abstractedly, still jacked into his comp, and a digital pointer was abruptly superimposed on the trid image. "This one."

The building abruptly de-solidified into a wire framework showing its interior floor plan. "It stretches the full length of the block. Leased to Intermedia, whoever they are." The building re-solidified. "Beside it we have a jeweler's – no floor plan on public record, natch. Behind that,

a games parlor. To its right, a restaurant, then a carpark.
Behind that, a stimsense theater. Across the road, a mall."
Each of these buildings faded in turn, wire-frame floor
plans glowing through translucent walls. All except the
jeweler's.

Cynthia cleared her throat. "Wolf and I are pretty sure
it's the jeweler's. Their imaginal security measures are still
in place – a strong Barrier. The weaving was well-made,
and still holds. So imaginal penetration is out. But it felt
like a bad place."

No one spoke.

Wiz's hands still danced, though. "Registered to 'Kas-
par'. Here's the ID." A 2D barcode appeared in mid-air.
Maretti angled his wristcomm toward it and said "Call". A
synthetic female voice responded. "The Link-ID you have
requested is no longer registered."

Maretti smiled. "How about we move to this closer
carpark right now? Looks like Raven might be right after
all." Thug thumped her on the back.

She beamed, but the smile was predatory.

CHAPTER 78

Lightning flailed the sky, thunder crowding its heels – closer this time, the introductory bars of a gigantic celestial movement. A blast of wind gusted through the carpark.

No one was smiling now.

"You sure you can't get a plan for the building, Wiz?" Maretti asked.

"It won't be online, Tony, for security reasons. Same reason the building has protection against imaginal intrusion."

"Fifteen minutes left," intoned Don. "And remember what the old woman said: one, then one, would die. That the Soul Twister would emerge during a storm."

As though responding to his words, lightning sheeted across the sky, followed a second later by a rolling thunderclap.

"And Bragg loves booby traps," Maretti added.

Raven reached into her knapsack, pulling out a sleek gray flare grenade. "I've just thought how we can get in, if we can get onto the roof." Her grin was ferocious.

The Fist of Peace watched, tense, faces craning upwards as Raven climbed. Gadger, thanks to his infra-red cyberoptics, described the progress of the small figure fighting the buffeting winds.

The mages had imaginally scouted the outside of the jewelers. Between them and Gadger's drone, they'd spotted a tiny security camera on the roof. Gadger landed his 'bird drone' right on top of it despite the strong winds.

Wiz now used the drone to record the same view the camera saw, waiting for the next flash of lightning. "Come on, come on," he muttered. At last the heavens obliged, and a small lightfield screen snapped out from the drone and down over the camera's lens. "At fracking last! Right, that'll be seamless."

Gadger transmitted the news. "Roof's clear, Raven."

The wind howled, another flash of lightning strobing the windowless building. She'd paused near the top, but at his words she reached up to the lip.

Just as a savage gust plucked her from the wall and threw her to one side.

"Fuck!" Gadger cried, then, "No, it's okay! She, she somehow belayed herself." Her up-stretched hand had flashed out, almost like she'd only then stabbed a spike into the wall, just below the lip. "Don't know how she did that, but she's recovered nicely."

"I really need to take the time to try to invent some sort of lifting spell," muttered Cyn.

"Yeah, or we could just fork out for a grapple gun," Gadger said. At that moment, the first drops of rain started falling, quickly multiplying into lashing squalls. He swore as it washed out his vision. "She didn't like that, but I think she's made it. Yeah, there's the cord."

The roof assault team charged out across the alley, Don carrying a coil of rope over one shoulder. He tied the rope to the cord she'd lowered, and Raven drew the rope smoothly up the side of the building. Don would ascend next, then help Davo. From there, the two men would start hauling the rest up.

The ground assault group already wore balaclavas, ready for their simultaneous attack on the front door. Gadger turned to them, pulling a hood out from the collar of his jacket and checking his gun one last time. "You ready? We may not be going to do any singing, but it's almost time for rock and roll."

Cyn and Thug looked at him blankly. "You're a strange old man, Gadger," declared the mage, as she took his arm. Thug stepped out behind them, his 'skeleton key' – an assault cannon – and a submachine gun hidden by his long, armored coat.

"Will Wolf be able to do what Raven said?" the big man asked, worried.

"Let's hope, Thug" Cyn answered. "Let's hope."

When Val joined the tense, wet group on the roof, she headed over to Raven. "You okay, girl?" she whispered. All watched the shaman standing in the center of the roof, arms thrust dramatically up into the raging night. "Scrapes, bruises?"

The younger woman's grin was feral. "I'm going closer."

Maretti, who'd followed Val, grabbed her arm. "No you don't, Raven. Wolf said it could be dangerous."

Slender fingers grasped his wrist, plucking his hand loose with a force that tore a curse from him. "So am I, Tony."

The rain battered down on them all as he tried to tug his arm free, disbelieving the strength of her grip. Droplets beaded and ran in streams across the black surface of the shades she *still* wore, and he wished he could see her expression.

Maybe she saw what he was thinking, because she suddenly snarled and snatched them from her face. Two amber eyes glared madly into his before she released him and spun away. But just for a moment he thought he'd seen them flash lapis lazuli blue, sending a stab of ice down his spine. It had to be a trick of the storm light.

Stalking over to the mage, Raven stopped a few paces behind him.

Maretti's steady stream of cursing was drowned by the storm, as a power, a tornado of force and violence, rage and destruction, swelled into existence over the shaman's head.

Wolf stood in a strange place, unsure how he'd come here. He gazed across a barren landscape of narrow spires and gaping canyons – a network of mesa, gorge, and butte, a drunken multiplication of the baddest badlands. On a tower of rock a bare meter across, winds plucked and tore at him with living cunning. Roiling black clouds churned above while lightning forked down into miles-deep abysses surrounding him.

The journey had taken his whole life, he knew, without knowing how he knew – a hard, bitter struggle. But at last, he was here. With feet planted on the sandstone with a solidity and permanence that came from the strength of the Earth itself, he suddenly knew why he was here. Remembered the need. And from that need, made the Call.

Winds stilled and fell away. Thunder rolled into silence. Nothing moved.

But something heard. A presence answered.

One massive crackling bolt struck the pillar on which he stood, its sound a physical blow, its force oppressive. It blasted the rock, searching out weakness. Fear. Self-doubt. Lightning arced and writhed, inches away. Challenging.

Wolf held.

Held, and then lifted his chin, answering it; offering it a

route through him to channel its force into the mundane world. Opening his heart to its rage-filled inspection, revealing his core. And in doing so, he saw himself. Saw himself in utter clarity. He had crossed the Imaginal, and reached Elsewhere.

The lightning vanished, leaving a negative image like cracks in the sky, and the world fell still. Hushed.

Waiting.

And then, pouring from those cracks, a black storm cloud boiled out. It engulfed the spirit that had brought him here, swallowing it as a whale would a tuna. Two lapis lazuli eyes opened, the force of that gaze pressing him down, pinning him in place. "And will you offer blood, Man-of-Wolf? A death, in return for my servant's service?"

Whatever the thing was, it dwarfed the powerful storm spirit Wolf had summoned. But he refused to be cowed. "No! That was not the bargain struck. What are you? *Who* are you?"

The eyes vanished briefly in a lazy blink. There was something sly in the thunderhead face now filling the sky. "No matter. My Herald will provide, if you will not."

With that, the eyes closed. The pressing force eased, like a vast curtain drawing aside, revealing the shaman's storm spirit behind it. Wolf's thoughts stuttered at the sudden change of scale. Both man and spirit took a moment to regain their centers. Then together, they threw themselves into the chasm, falling like stars toward the night.

Slowly, Wolf lowered his arms as the raging vortex before him filled with a spitting web of crackling blue light. He gestured at the only feature of the roof, the small outbuilding with its door. Slowly turning, his arm swept out to include the frail humans standing back, near the building's edge. Turned further, a moment later, to indicate the girl behind him, and finally himself.

For a moment he stood, his eyes white and wide, shocked, then he shook himself. Clenching one hand into a fist, he thrust it skyward, and nodded to Maretti.

Maretti, watching, spoke into his Link. "Now!"

Wolf's fist descended, and with frightening speed lightning blasted from the heavens.

The outbuilding exploded in a ball of light and fury, debris flying past the humans standing or cringing in the lashing rain, their eyes clamped shut and hands over ears. Only the storm spirit's channeling of the force away from them made their gestures more than futile.

Electricity drowned the shaft into the building. And while echoes of thunder crashed outwards into the city, a string of explosions erupted from the now-exposed stairwell, and suddenly the power blacked out for blocks around.

The sound of Thug's assault cannon below signaled that the others had begun their frontal assault, as the group on the roof charged to the gaping hole. Raven grabbed Maretti's arm as they ran.

"I'm deaf," she declared, in a too-loud voice. "But I'm ready."

"Shit. You'd better hang back," he ordered.

She nodded and accelerated to the stairs, drawing her gun and her flare grenade and disappearing into the darkness.

"Fragging, dumb-! After her!"

CHAPTER 79

From somewhere below, the muffled sound of return machine gun fire told them the front entrance was well-defended. "Night-goggles on, now," Maretti ordered, moving down the stairwell.

The iron guard rails were hot, warped, and smoking, the air stinking of ozone and incinerated paint. Sprinklers blasted at full force, mirroring the storm above, charred spiderwebs of melted copper revealing where steps and railing had been wired for electrocution.

Maretti gestured at it. "Careful of more traps, people. That won't be the last."

At the foot of the stairs, Raven kicked the solid fire door's lock fruitlessly. "Tell that to Raven," suggested Davo.

Don shouldered past, leveling his assault cannon at the battered door. They all backed away and Don fired, the sound deafening in the enclosed space.

"Hey, I heard that!" Raven shouted, grinning, and wrenched the door toward her. Don leaped through, gun ready. She darted after him, into an empty corridor between silent glass-walled offices. Around to their right, more stairs angled back and down to the ground floor. Wiz and Wolf, with Davo at the rear, fanned out, alert for traps as Don scanned the wide lacquered rosewood stairs.

Raven crouched, and leaped down the entire flight.

They had only an instant of warning as a glowing pebble curved in a wide spiral up the stairs towards them.

Wolf, guessing what must follow, desperately tried to protect them all as the pebble exploded, a massive spell grounding through it from imaginal space into the physical world. A towering wave of negative force crashed down on them like gas smothering the embers of a fire.

Val, Skinner and Wiz collapsed where they stood, guns falling from nerveless hands. Maretti, Don, and Davo staggered but resisted. Wolf growled as he helped them fight the effects of the stun spell.

Below, out of sight, Raven tossed her flare grenade into the large dark room below her, throwing herself flat on the landing.

Cyn's voice came over their comms. "Front door guard's Stunned! Thug's going in now." She sounded tired. "My first Stun failed utterly. Don't know why."

Wolf reached out into the darkness, searching for the house spirit that must be there, calling the entity to him. Instead he found only a strange, cold emptiness. A flash of actinic light burst from below, and the others leaped down the stairs after Raven.

"Die, Maretti," called a voice thick with hatred. The thunder of a second assault cannon roared from below, the elegant stairs exploding upwards beside the group to spray shrapnel into the air like wasps.

A desperation shot, Maretti realized. Raven must have blinded them with her flash-grenade. Grinning, he bounded down the stairs in the dark, Don in front and Davo a few steps behind.

"Chopper's down here!" Raven called out, a moment before an explosion ripped into the stairwell above him, throwing him down the stairs with Davo's scream echoing behind. Tony flew through the air toward the deadly chatter of an SMG raking the air ahead of him, then he was bouncing off a wall and sprawling onto a carpeted office floor.

Dazed, he absorbed the scene, in the eerie green glow of his light intensifier goggles. Don spun toward an opponent firing through a crudely hacked gap in carved wood paneling. Thug struggled to pull his weapon free from a small man who whipped the giant around like a dancing partner. Gadger coolly pumped shot after shot of sleeper rounds into the same enemy. Raven traded blows with another, in a confusing blur he couldn't follow. The hated figure of Bragg lowered the muzzle of a grenade launcher from a gaping hole in the ceiling, aiming blindly in his general direction.

And Chopper, tied, struggled helplessly, seated in front of the massive overturned table Bragg was using for cover.

Maretti staggered up in a drunken run between the figures as Bragg fired again, the explosion smashing into the landing at the corner of the stairs. He was on Bragg before the man could get off another shot.

On the stairs, Wolf rose to his feet, swaying. Ignoring Davo's broken, bleeding body felt like hooks tearing his flesh. He forced himself on, stumbling past his fallen friend.

Stepping into the darkened room with his gaze tuned to

the Imaginal, he sought the auras of his teammates. And Saw the radiantly cold form of the mage he'd last encountered underground stand up from across the room. He barely had time to reach out once more to Shield his friends from the magical force exploding across the room.

By the Great Spirit! Although weaker than last time – Dr Callahan Scott had limits, after all – it was still enough to stun Don and Tony, despite his help. Raven- his eyes widened. Raven fought a human shape of pitch darkness. And Thug- he was almost unconscious, mottled injuries of sickening size darkening his aura as he, too, struggled against a shape streaked in nightmare darkness.

Thug and Raven fought the two figures who had damaged his astral form, under the pollution station. But while Thug faltered, his opponent strangely impervious to every blow, Raven burned with an assured ferocity that chilled Wolf. Her aura was strange, too, he saw: darkness shivering confusingly through its light, as though she also fought some dark internal force.

Both Raven and her opponent moved with frightening speed. The man punched and jabbed with fists like jackhammers.

But Raven swayed and twisted aside, somehow evading or parrying every strike, pounding him in return with elbows, legs and knees. Each of her blows landed with the ugly sound of a mallet striking meat, but with no visible effect on her enemy. Even his expression didn't change.

Raven's lips parted, her face a feral fury. Her blows *intensified* as she threw herself totally onto the attack.

But Bragg and his assault cannon were the bigger danger.

Tony snarled, grappling with Bragg for control of the weapon, interposing himself as a shield in front of the helpless Chopper.

But Bragg forced him backward over Chopper's form and smiled – and Maretti's eyes widened as though sensing the murderous radio pulse. A monstrous blow from behind hurled him into Bragg, the two of them crashing together on the floor. From across the room, Cynthia screamed in horror at Chopper's now headless body still strapped in its chair.

Don's assault cannon roared into Dr Callahan Scott.

For an instant the glowing shell hung, straining in the air. Then it was through, blasting the still-smirking mage off his feet.

Don swiveled, his barrel tracking Bragg as he hauled himself upright over Maretti's bleeding form, bringing his own weapon to bear. Don fired first, staggering as the weapon punched back into his heavy armor. The front of Bragg's armor ruptured, tortured past its limits.

Don fired again.

Bragg's torso exploded like a balloon, his body crashing backwards in a shower of blood and flesh to the ground.

Cynthia wailed. "No, *Don*, no!"

A hammer blow tore Thug's night goggles from his face, plunging him into blackness. Another pile-driver impacted his side, something rupturing deep inside. Teeth gritted, vision swimming, he ignored the agony of broken ribs to smash down a double-handed blow on the smaller man who was somehow killing him. He felt rather than heard the crack of bones. And *finally* the man collapsed.

Thug stood, swaying in pain, on the borders of consciousness, hardly daring believe he'd won.

He turned, to see Raven punch up into the left side of her opponent's chest, her whole body behind the blow. The man left the ground with a sickening noise of rupturing flesh, crashing down to lay unmoving on the floor.

And suddenly all was quiet, except for gasping, raking breaths.

Wolf, after a grim glance at Chopper's body, staggered back up the stairs to focus a desperate healing spell on Davo, calling for Cynthia's help.

Maretti crawled over and stared down at the mage. Dr Callahan Scott. The man whose research had started all this. Don's assault cannon had torn apart his chest, spreading it open like some obscenely-butchered cut of meat. Half a palm comp had spilled out of the shredded jacket. Picking up the other half, he popped out a translucent orange data cube. At last Maretti allowed himself to look away. Back aching, he pushed himself to his feet. They must've used a shaped charge to kill poor Chopper, or he'd be dead too, armor or no armor.

Raven moved past him to a door at the far side of the

room. "I saw someone else. He ran through here," she said over her shoulder, matter of fact, before disappearing into the blackness. He groaned, and spoke into his communicator.

"Gadger. Bring the car round the back. We won't have long before the cops arrive. It's been almost a minute since the blackout." He looked around, and heard Raven kick a door open. "Thug, go with her."

He shook. They'd come close to being wiped out tonight. Grabbing stim-patches from his pocket, he lurched back up the stairs to revive Val, Skinner, and Wiz. With luck, they might only've been stunned by the damned mage's spell. If being hit by a force like a wall of bricks could be called lucky.

On the first landing, Wolf and Cyn crouched by Davo, setting broken bones straight and struggling to force the healing patterns through his bleeding body against the resistance of his cyberware. Maretti paused, relief washing through him when it looked like Davo was responding, and squeezed past. The last one, the one Raven had seen run, must've been Ford, the geneticist. Surely *he'd* be a pushover?

Maretti knelt beside Wiz to check his pulse.

Her hearing was returning. At least, she hoped that was what the ringing in her ears meant. She'd checked the rest of the place, and now faced the massive steel door before her. The darkness deepened, making her whirl round, only to see Thug's large form step into the small room behind her. He looked like crap.

"I think he's locked himself in here." She gestured at the electronic lock. "And I still can't hear properly. Will you get Gadger to come in, see if he can crack this? And maybe Wolf could take a look inside."

Thug's lips moved, before he turned slowly to limp off. "Hey! Thug! I meant, talk to them on your Link." In the dark, she saw him nod and stop.

She shivered, her rain-drenched clothes cooling, dripping water on the carpeted floor. She still had to get or destroy the pay-data from Scott's research. She *had* to keep it out of the Fist's hands. She had to! The seconds were counting down.

But she was getting ahead of herself.

A wavering torch beam made her blink, interrupting her thoughts. Pulling her shades from an inner pocket, she slipped them on as Wiz, Gadger, and Maretti crowded into the room. It was unsettling, not being able to hear people coming. Gadger pulled an instrument from his pocket and moved to the lock, and she stepped back to give him room.

A tap on her shoulder made her spin around, to see Maretti's mouth working. She waited for him to stop, then shrugged. "I still can't hear. Don't worry. I'll wait here until we crack this door." Maretti scowled and shook his head, his lips moving some more. She stared at him, her head tilted to one side, until he stopped. "No problem. I'll wait. I wouldn't miss this for anything."

He glared at her before saying something to Thug, who moved off awkwardly. In the diffuse light of the torch, Thug looked *terrible,* like he'd been run over by a truck. She rubbed her own bruised arms in unconscious sympathy. The guy she'd fought could've broken her in half if his punches had really landed. His strength reminded her of Marc Disten.

As had his disinterested expression too, come to think of it. She was surprised Thug wasn't a slab of meat on the floor. She wondered how Davo was doing.

Her gun was out, as were Gadger's and Maretti's, while Wiz pulled the door open, staying behind it like it was a shield.

The guy inside looked scared, and after a glance at how many people faced him, tossed a gun on the floor. She recognized Dr Jeremy Ford from the pics Wiz had shown them all, and a wave of hope flooded in. Maretti patted him down and confiscated a comp.

There was a roaring in her ears now, but over it she thought she could hear voices. They marched the thin-faced man out at gun point. Leeth turned and followed Maretti out while the others finished ransacking the room. They exited via the back door, where Davo sat hunched palely at the wheel of his car. Half the group staggered into the vehicle, forcing the thin captive in between Gadger and Don, while Wolf tiredly invoked a spirit. To conceal them in their getaway, she assumed.

Just then the streetlights came back on.

Val, Skinner, Maretti, Wolf and Thug – who looked a little better – started jogging to the carpark. Leeth followed Maretti. There was no way she'd let the recovered comp out of her sight.

Leeth perched behind Maretti on his bike, holding his waist as they cruised out of the area of the hue and cry. She hadn't given him a choice, just gotten up behind him despite his angry glare, explaining she didn't want Thug worrying about her as well as trying to cope with his injuries. Around the time she thought she heard a siren, he stopped arguing and they left.

She could even hear the purr of the bike's motor now, a little. All she had to do next was steal or destroy the data, and find and kill the traitor. Remembering Maretti standing between Bragg and Chopper, trying to save the young idiot, she held his waist a little tighter. Hoping that, somehow, the traitor was none of them. Maybe not even Wiz.

CHAPTER 80

In the war zone that had once been an office, Dr Callahan Scott's flesh finished knitting back together. As the programmed healing spell completed, he climbed back to his feet, his last wounds vanishing, then stood swaying, his body shaking and clothes in tatters. The spell construct had worked perfectly, but his limbs still spasmed and quivered from the astonishing pain. Nor had he expected the hunger. His torso looked starved, his ribs prominent in his chest.

His research computer lay on the floor, split in two. No data cube though, when he searched.

Moving unsteadily through the wreckage, he noted fragments of keyboards, shrapnel he recognized as screens, and the ruptured cases of computing units. He paused by Bragg's body. From the extent of the wounds, Bragg had been killed by the same cannon used on him. One hand went to his own chest, his gaze distant as he estimated lost body mass, frowning at the final figure.

That had been a near thing.

He eyed Bragg. Could the man be of any further use to him, alive? But the time it would require, and the sound of approaching sirens, decided for him.

Pacing through the carnage, he stared down at his two creations, Schenk and Sommers. Unfortunately, they could not be Healed. A minor down-side to the alteration. As the sirens' wail increased, he headed for the strongroom.

Seeing the open door, for a full second he allowed a curl of anger to grow, before ending it. Stepping in, he stared at the empty place where the serum supply and his own research cubes should have rested. How had they breached the strongroom? There was no sign of damage. But also, no sign of Ford's body.

Returning to the main room, he saw they'd removed the captive, 'Chopper'. Or rather, the body, he deduced from the blood and gore on the overturned chair and desk. With economical movements he collected tissue samples. Assuming they planned some typical funeral observance, this could still work out very well. Ford's input to the research had followed a very straightforward line, after all: searching for a gene complex that could be used to bring the limbic system and other parts of the brain under conscious control. Such a pity the last serum had never reached them. He would very much like to know who had intercepted it. And why.

Still, perhaps being forced to a simpler, purely magical approach would prove beneficial in the long term. He nodded slowly, seeing a path forward. There was no need for all that distracting, unnecessary clutter. In truth, even the genetic manipulation and DNA analyzers had been a diversion. Caging the reptile brain. Still....

The sirens were very loud, now. He poked through the discarded equipment until he found an empty syringe. Bending over Schenk's body he extracted blood through the large carotid artery – with surprising difficulty. Just outside, the sirens' wail rose to a fever pitch then stopped. He paused in sudden thought, staring down at Schenk's body and the meager pool of blood he lay in.

What had the girl in black done to Schenk? Come to that, how had a mere girl bested *Schenk*, of all people? That the human gorilla had beaten Sommers, he could barely accept. The man had absorbed blows from Sommers that had surely broken bones. But *Schenk* should have crushed the girl like a mosquito.

The same girl who had intrigued him with the sense of something deeper, hidden within. He remembered her from the day the Wolf shaman had penetrated his complex. He'd hovered over her – until he'd seen her intent to attack, even though he was astral at the time – while the shaman and mage had watched him in fear.

Under Schenk's left arm, several parallel puncture wounds cut straight through the armor jacket to penetrate deep into the lungs. His eyes slitted. The injury somehow suggested blades, of exquisite keenness.

But hadn't she been fighting barehanded? Closing his eyes he checked the memory. *Yes.*

Rolling the body over, he confirmed the wound under the armpit as the source of the blood flow. But why so little? Especially considering how difficult it had been to draw his sample just now? Was she some kind of vampire? Had she crouched there, drinking Schenk while he himself lay an arm's length away, the countdown to his Bound healing spell silently underway?

Spotlights flared into brilliance outside, spilling in

through the smashed front door. He straightened and made himself broad-spectrum invisible, then inaudible. As he hurried past the plasglass security wall and down the short corridor to the front entrance, he shifted the spells out of phase. It was conceivable the metropolice team included a mage. He didn't want the spells seen.

Two heavily armored figures were edging along the front wall from either side as he stepped out the front entrance. Shading his eyes from the intense light, he assessed the situation. Mundane idiots with large guns and heavy armor performed their well-rehearsed but pointless maneuvers. Two commonplace mages, who he ignored. But the water could be a problem, he realized, and began slowly crossing the brilliantly lit area, careful not to splash in any puddles. Fortunately the storm had eased. He moved off down the street.

Several blocks away, striding toward the brighter lights of Market, he checked his Link and ordered a ride. As he waited, he considered again the opening of the strongroom. Only himself, Bragg, and Ford had had the access codes, and Ford's body wasn't here. He vaguely remembered Ford running from the fight even before the big weapons had opened up. He must have unlocked it for them, or tried hiding there. Scott considered. Ford was of no further use – could even be an embarrassment. Then there were his own research notes, taken.

He needed those.

As the car pulled up, he checked the paper-wrapped remains in his top pocket. Getting into the vehicle and closing the door, he proceeded to book the necessary thaumaturgic equipment for a Sending, paying for a priority place at Outer Circles, then leaned back into the soft synth-leather seats, turning his mind to Schenk, and his death, while staring out at the rain-slick streets.

Perhaps the girl could make a suitable replacement.

CHAPTER 81

The bikes reached the rendezvous point, in a badly polluted part of the Potrero Dumps, in three quarters of an hour. Not too far from their secondary hideout. Less populated than Hunters Point – less stripped clean – it hadn't taken long for Wolf to scrounge enough material to build a small campfire.

By its light they waited for Davo and the others to arrive.

Leeth dismounted, watching Maretti intently.

Wolf seemed to be in some kind of trance, or communing with spirits or something. But she spared only glances for anyone except Maretti, watching for someone to 'borrow' the comp from him. She still didn't know who the traitor was, and now the stakes were way higher. Her skin prickled, hyper conscious of her orders to kill anyone the illegal genetic research data leaked to.

I need to make sure it doesn't.

Thug limped over, slumping by her side with a drained grin. One large hand fell to her thigh, reassuring, and after a moment she leaned in against him.

Eventually Davo and the others arrived, having worked the car into the rubbled streets as close as they could before hiking the remaining distance.

Wolf sat cross-legged, resting against his bike. He didn't look as tired as Cyn, Leeth thought. With a murmured word to Thug and a pat of *his* thigh, she headed over to the seated shaman, positioning herself so she could keep an eye on Maretti and those near him.

"My ears are hurting, still, from the thunderclap, and I can't hear properly. Will you try a healing spell?"

He frowned up at her impassively for long seconds, like he was considering something deeper than her simple request. She had the feeling she might've somehow revealed too much of herself. During the fight, maybe. And she realized she wasn't being Raven. She stilled.

Cool. Serious. Patient.

There was something different about him, too, she realized. More than just having his confidence back. He looked more... certain. More solid, or something. Like he'd come through an ordeal successfully. Like he was seeing things more clearly.

At last he nodded, and stood.

His warm, strong hands cradling her head made her feel suddenly protected. She forced the illusion away. The healing began.

If the cessation of pain was a cool breeze, the return of sound was a deep ocean wave bringing her back to herself. Joy surged as she settled properly back into the world again. Closing her eyes she savored the lifting of the mental fog as objects reappeared. The distant city took its place, then the wind; the crackle of the fire, Wolf's breath as his hands rested against her head... the floodgates parted, and the living, moving, *noising* presences took up positions around her. She exhaled, the sigh drawn from the depths of her heart.

She heard Maretti shift his stance, the sleeves of his jacket folding as crossed his arms, standing across from her. Not knowing what was nearby, around her, had been uncomfortable. Almost unnerving. *That must be what most people are like*, she realized, shuddering. She heard the faint rattle of datacubes in their storage box and knew, even with her eyes shut, that Maretti hadn't unpacked them. She felt the muscles in her neck relaxing. She hadn't even known they'd been tense.

She opened her eyes and faced Wolf's steady look. She nodded, and he lowered his hands from her head, taking a pace back to his bike, and half sat on it, also with arms crossed, still appraising her.

Something about the posture rang a jarring note. She fought to recall the Doctor's boring lectures on body language... She couldn't remember, though. Other than that it wasn't good. He looked tense, too.

Had she said something wrong? Done something?

"Thanks, W-" She stopped herself, remembering they had a stranger present. Their prisoner. "Thanks, man." She turned, seeing Maretti standing exactly as she'd expected, then saw some of the others were watching her strangely, too.

Even Cyn – who'd been crouching over Thug, for an incredibly long time now, looking like she was forcing him to heal by sheer willpower – even Cyn watched her. Their captive stood between Val and Skinner, half defiant and half nervous, but wholly like he'd much rather be somewhere else. Hoping to distract them, she nodded to the man and looked at Maretti, who was scowling at her, fists clenched.

"So who is this guy?"

Maretti just looked at her, not answering. "All business, eh Raven? How convenient."

Blinking, glad of her shades, she glanced around at the others. Val, Skinner, ... most of them were watching her, their expressions cold.

She bit back on her first response.

"What's wrong? Why do you all look so angry?" They did, apart from Thug – and even his eyes slid away.

"Really?" demanded Maretti. "You've got no idea?"

She shook her head.

"We just lost someone."

It took her a moment to work out what he meant. "Chopper?" She frowned. "That's sad, but how's it *my* fault?"

At that, they all stirred, Val snarling in disbelief. "'Coz he charged off to impress *you*, Raven."

"What? No, no way! That's ridiculous." But looking around, it seemed like she was the only one who thought so. "He spent most of his time spamming me!"

No one spoke. Then Val groaned and rubbed her face with both hands, muttering, "Dumb 'bliv half-deck."

Maretti's anger, though, only seemed to deepen. "Wolf, why wasn't Raven protected from the thunderclap on the roof?"

"She was. The Spirit of the Storm vowed to shield us all from the damage it called forth."

Maretti's eyes hadn't shifted from Raven's face. "And how *is* it you can see in the dark? Both mages swear you've got no cyberware. And you sure don't *look* like you have any Altered genes."

Be Raven, she told herself. *Be Raven*. He's needling you. Trying to make you lose your temper. This wasn't about Chopper, she somehow knew.

So *why* was he doing it? And why did it *hurt*?

Should she just could come clean? But she still had to get Scott's research, and find and kill the traitor. That'd get much harder if they discovered what she could do. Swallowing, she said nothing.

"And on the roof, when I tried to stop you interfering with Wolf's invocation – you pulled out of my grip like it was nothing. Practically crushed my wrist."

Ahh. That *must've been the final straw*, she realized. *I screwed up.*

"*What are you?*" he whispered.

They were all watching her now. Shit.

Shit, shit. Not *now*. She kept her face impassive and stared right back.

"I'm nothing you've ever seen before." For a moment she fought the crazy urge to declare herself, strip away the disguise and show them her real self, tell them her true name. But in the heavy silence that greeted her outburst, inspiration suddenly welled. "I'll tell you one thing, though," she said, reaching up to her shades. "I'm on your side."

She was, too. She'd find and kill the traitor and keep the poisonous data from the rest of them. She *would*.

Pulling off the dark glasses she stepped up, then couldn't resist brushing fingertips along Maretti's stubbled jawline. A thrill of strange hope ran through her, and she found she was bouncing on the balls of her feet, nervous but unable to stop.

She spun away from him, coming to a stop by the camp-fire in the middle of the group.

"I'm on all your sides."

Squatting by the flames, she looked up and around at them. "Yes, I can see in the dark. And yes, I'm strong. And the storm spirit hurt me, but none of you.

"But so what? It's nothing to do with you. I'm here to help you all!" Her thoughts swam, veering onto dangerous ground – and out of her hands as she remembered her mission, and the Doctor's controls began to cut in. "I DON'T WANT TO TALK ABOUT IT!" she shouted, before the gray could crash down and silence her. She sprang to her feet. "Can't you *see* that?" She stopped, panting.

"I'm on all your sides."

She turned, slowly, until she faced their prisoner. "But not his. Who is he? Why-" *didn't you kill him*, she almost asked. "Why is he here?" She rested her fists on her hips, as if confident her answers had been enough and they could now get back to the matter at hand.

Maretti, studying her unexpectedly youthful face, looked a little off balance. Unsatisfied. Like this wasn't the end of the matter. But he answered her.

"Dr Jeremy Ford. Degrees in Genetics and Magic, but unlike Scott, not a mage. Number two on our list, if you remember. Supposed to have died in '60. A genius, and expert on the Melt virus. So they say."

Leeth eyed the man, wondering how she could carry out Eagle's orders given the Fist's crazy reluctance to kill people. Though Don had, tonight. Twice. "An expert on the Melt virus. Does that mean he was one of the creeps who helped create it, for Melisande d'Artelle?"

Everyone flinched. It took several seconds before their captive, his mouth open in horror, collected himself enough to stutter a denial.

Maretti turned from her to face the man, looking for a significant moment at Wolf, who nodded, then at Cyn, obviously tired too, but *still* crouched over Thug, healing him. How could a human being have taken *so much* damage and stayed conscious?

Maretti walked over to Ford, circling behind him, before stopping there. After a hesitation, the man turned to face him. And away from Wolf, who quietly cast a spell on himself before focusing his attention on their captive, nodding then to Maretti. Ah. A truth spell, Leeth realized.

"Doctor Ford," Tony began, "it's time for you to convince us we don't have to kill you."

Ford glanced nervously at the guns trained on him by Val and Skinner.

Leeth raised her eyes to the night sky. The guns were loaded with stun rounds, and if the Fist of Peace could work themselves up to kill the man in cold blood, she'd eat her underwear. She sighed. This was going to take a long time, she could tell. They'd probably end up letting him go, and she'd have to sneak off to kill him.

She shook her head, but said nothing.

Maretti still stared at Ford, not speaking. Perhaps he'd been hoping it would increase the researcher's nervousness, but as far as Leeth could tell, it seemed to be having the opposite effect.

Tony must have thought so, too. "What were you doing? What was the project?"

The man looked really coolly back at Maretti, almost as if he was considering not answering. A glance at the guns apparently decided him, though. Maybe they held a real threat, if he'd seen Don blast Bragg and Scott.

"It was called Clarity," he answered. "We were looking into ways to produce more effective soldiers."

It was suddenly very quiet.

"How?"

"Well, it was based on Scott's earlier work. What he called his 'Calculus of Rationality'." Ford's eyes went distant, and he shivered.

Whatever he was remembering made him more uneasy than the guns had. That reaction brought them all alert.

"Were the two... *people* who beat up on..." Maretti pointed to Thug, then Raven, frowning as he compared the huge man's terrible injuries to Raven's mere bruising, "my people here, products of this 'effective soldier' project?"

Ford visibly shuddered. "Yes."

"How did it work?"

Ford shivered again, swallowing. "Some magical editing of the, of the mind." *There would have been genetic editing, too, if their order from Bio-Block hadn't been hijacked by persons unknown.* But he was already in enough shit, no need to dig his hole deeper. "Scott called it 'The Process'. He made some breakthrough just a few months back, when we found a, ah, mentally damaged man and woman from the local area. Victims of some kind of trauma. They were creepy as fuck."

Tony slipped the case of data cubes into his jacket, and took the researcher's comp out. Ford's eyes followed every movement in helpless expectation. Tony slid back a panel in the unit, tapping out two data cubes into the palm of his hand.

Leeth watched, tensely. The traitor *had* to make their move, now.

Maretti held up one cube between thumb and forefinger, staring at Ford. "So all your data, all your research, is here?"

Ford started to nod, then shook his head. "Yes and no. That's our main comp. It holds most of it, but Scott kept much of his research, including his Calculus of Rationality, on his own comp. And his magical notes are something else. I, uh, looked at them once or twice." He shut his mouth, hoping he'd given them enough, until an appreciation for just how remarkable Scott and his research had been, washed over him.

Feeling a sudden need to learn what had happened to Scott's comp, he found himself eager to tell them more. "Lots of it used his new 'mental calculus' notations, but some used other notations I couldn't find a key for. And not just the notations other mages use to write down the metaphysics behind their spells. His own stuff. I think he'd come up with some new way of thinking about magic. That stuff isn't limited to military applications. It would make any mage super effective. Scott could design whole new spells in hours – spells that others needed weeks or months to invent. He could do things I don't think anyone else could. His notes would be worth a fortune."

"But *you* don't know how Scott did it, since you're no mage." Maretti held up the other cube. "The stuff in *his* cubes, unlike these, is beyond you." He popped the cubes back into the computer and put it away. Reaching into his pocket he brought out the orange data cube he'd taken from Scott's ruined Databrarian, his eyes never leaving Ford's.

As he held the orange crystalline cube, Leeth felt a peculiar disorientation. The memory of Marc Disten's hand pinning her head to a marble benchtop flashed into her mind, paired with Maretti staring at his fingertips where his cyber blades had once been. She suddenly felt nauseous, her stomach falling away, but had no idea why.

Wolf, who'd been watching Ford exclusively, looked up, then around, before catching Cynthia's eye. "Did you sense something?"

She looked tiredly back at him. With a heavy sigh, Cyn forced her perception to the imaginal and looked carefully around. At last she shook her head. "Nothing." But as she glanced towards Ford, she suddenly gasped, and scrabbled away from him. "Look out!"

Ford's eyes went vacant. For several seconds he swayed, then simply collapsed like a robot that'd lost power.

"What the fuck?"

Everyone froze for a moment. Then Don, Raven and

Davo drew guns. Val and Skinner dived for cover.

They all looked to Cynthia, who stared in sick fascination at the unmoving body.

Wolf's eyes widened, his nostrils flaring, and he took a step back.

"What? What's going on?" demanded Maretti, looking from one to the other. "What's wrong with him?"

"I think he's... dead, Tony." There was something unnerving about the way Cyn spoke the words.

"Well quickly, heal him! What happened?"

Cynthia blinked. Looked at Wolf, doubtfully. "I'm... not sure we should touch him. I Saw something... it was like, like one of those 3D wire-frame models people use, only black. It just suddenly appeared, like spider's legs erupting from inside him! It poked out through his skin then folded back inside like it was grabbing him. Right before he dropped."

"Yeah?" asked Skinner, crouching down to take his pulse. He looked up, dropping his hand. "He's still alive."

"Good." Maretti said, then registered the two mages' horror-stricken faces.

"No, it's very far from good," Cyn whispered. "It's horrible. His whole aura is *gone*. Like it's just been drained off, leaving this- leaving some... I don't know, a hole?" Her whole body shuddered.

She looked to Wolf, but he looked as lost as her.

"Well, can you get it back?"

"Get it *back?* From where? No! There's no way. I wouldn't even know how to start trying. And he'll die, Tony. Without his aura, the body will sicken and die. In just a few hours. The process has already started."

"What caused it? That magical wire frame thing?"

Cyn nodded. "It had to be."

"Was *that* Mad Betty's 'Soul Twister' thing?"

"Maybe? But that doesn't feel right." She shook her head. "What we saw... felt more like some kind of trap?"

"But what triggered it? Can it affect *us?*" Maretti rubbed his head at an unexpected stab of pain. About to suggest studying Scott's notes, instead he said nothing.

"I hope to God not. I suggest we burn everything, now. I'll use my Spirit Fire spell to immolate everything we took – and pray *we* can't be targeted."

"But we might be?"

Spots of color rose in Cynthia's cheeks. "Yes. Maybe. I'm not even sure it was magical. Maybe it was some kind of inorganic being, planted inside him."

Maretti made a soothing gesture. "Okay. Let me think about this." He stared down at his feet, playing idly with Scott's orange gem-like data cube.

For long minutes no one spoke.

"Right. Pile everything on the body. We'll burn it all and maybe get you to do a Kill Disease on each of us, just in case."

He looks pleased, Leeth thought, watching him finger the data cube. Scott's data cube. "We'll have to do something about him, too," he murmured, the data cube pinched between finger and thumb, before finally flicking it down onto the still-breathing researcher.

And all at once, Leeth knew. A scream boiled up inside her.

CHAPTER 82

She was back on the tilted slab of marble in Candlestick Tower, Marc Disten's fingers clamped around her head as the thing inside him tried to worm its way into her mind.

Maretti was interfacing with the chips through his fingertips.

It was pure intuition, but she felt certain. *I've done it. I've found the traitor. Maretti.* But the revelation didn't thrill her. Instead she found herself panting. Even as she stood shaking her head in denial, part of her kept implacably on. *He must have some sort of interface adapters.* She'd read of people with removable fingertips. Maretti's probably extruded through retractable dermal covering. *Maybe his body never* had *rejected his cyber implanted blades?* Tik Tek had probably given him excellent quality brainware memory capacity and the smoothest data transfer and copying facilities, too. Undoubtedly, sparing no expense.

And *that* was why she'd kept having that same dream. Why couldn't her stupid subconscious just have *told* her?

He was working his way through the other data cubes they'd taken. As he flicked another chip onto the body and took the next, she moved up beside him, staring down at Ford's empty husk, feeling sickened, dreading what she had to do. Like the moment before killing Luiz, all over again. She flushed cold and hot, and felt her Raven persona fall away, its comforting, warm cloak abandoning her. *Unless... maybe I'm wrong?*

From the corner of her eye she judged the angle and focused. *Please let me be wrong.* With speed that could snatch a fly from the air, her fingers flashed to Maretti's, pincering the cube. She twisted it sideways.

The click of breaking contacts shivered through her fingertips, and she actually *heard* the tiny 'snick' as his dermal covering snapped shut over metal and optical circuitry.

She stared up into his face. His eyes, the very shape of his jaw, somehow wrapped around her heart. Yet he was the traitor, the forbidden data inside him now. Locked inside, but maybe only for a few more seconds. Something deep inside her wailed, begging her to stop. She clamped down hard on it. To save the Fist, she had to kill him. *Now*, before he could upload the data.

She wanted to scream. It felt like bands of iron tightened in her chest. Her vision blurred.

And she had to kill him properly. There would be blood.

A darker part of her surged at the thought, exultant. *Yes! Blood!*

As his hand shot to his holstered weapon her breath exploded outward, her right hand stabbing forward, slicing through the kevlar of his armor jacket, through flesh and bone, straight into his heart. In, then out.

Blood geysered.

She stepped back, both of them staring in disbelief at what she'd just done. Then he fell forward.

There was an appalled silence. And somehow, behind it, a massive pressure of anger hovered in the air, pressing down on her, watching.

He could still be healed, she knew – and then there was the hypothetical memoryware holding copies of the cubes he'd handled already.

She was already dropping to one knee, the familiar sharp tingle hardening her hand as she scythed down in total concentration. For some reason, weeping.

A sickening crack as she carved through the skull and plunged her hand into the soft pink convolutions, blinded by tears as she felt for the cyberware memory chips.

Numb, she tried to tell herself this was the Doctor's doing, that somehow he'd conditioned her, like with Luiz. But he hadn't. She squeezed her eyes shut, tears falling. He hadn't.

It hurt so much, though. Like she dug through her own flesh and blood.

Her eyes opened wide, and time stopped.

Was Maretti- did I just kill my own father? She tried to wrap her mind around the concept. *Who* was *my father? My* mother? *Where did I come from, before the Doctor?*

Around her, time resumed. All hell broke loose.

Cynthia was screaming. Don thundered forward as she felt a spell explode against her, its coercive pattern smashing into her psyche. Which bent and then lashed back upright, resisting, resilient as a sapling.

Don's foot lashed out to kick her aside, but she twisted, deflecting and grabbing his leg then thrusting it up and sideways, one-handed.

Got it!

Her other hand plucked a foreign object free. Crushing its central node, she turned and rose to face Val. A spell clawed weakly at her iron determination. She could feel Cynthia's tiredness through it – then a stronger wave of will-force crashed over her.

It found no purchase, no area of weakness. Wolf growled.

Dropping the shattered cyberware behind her, she raised both hands and backed away, feeling for the 'ware under her boot. She crushed it into pieces.

She felt cold. Drained. Distant from her own body, staring down at Maretti's. Her father's? She felt numb. "Sorry."

Her earliest memories were of the Institute for Paranormal Dysfunction. But there had to be stuff before that. Unless her mother had been one of the inmates? Why had she never thought about that, before? Was *that* something the Doctor had done to her, too? She'd find out, she vowed.

Val halted protectively over Maretti's body. Davo and Skinner had their guns trained on her, as did Wiz. But her eyes were drawn to the weapon in Don's hands, the assault cannon that had blown away Bragg and Scott... and then higher, to Don's eyes, hungry to use it.

This time, Cynthia wasn't screaming for him not to shoot.

His finger tightened. "You shouldn't have-"

She didn't wait for him to finish, digging in the toes of her boots to launch herself diagonally forward. The muzzle swung, tracking her as she dipped sideways, touching earth. Claws stabbed deep, anchoring her as she pivoted and kicked out, smashing the barrel up into his chest.

Don toppled. She thrust against the earth, erupting upward. Grabbing the barrel she rode his body to the ground. "I don't want to hurt you!"

"Holy fuck!" swore Davo.

Snarling, still gripping his cannon, Don's cyber muscles whined in ultrasonic registers as he in turn flipped back to his feet. She came with him.

He thrust his weapon out, then wrenched it suddenly

back.

Raven came with it, her grip implacable, her small body slamming into his front.

She should have looked silly, even cartoonish, dangling from the long black barrel, her feet clean off the ground.

But as Don continued to struggle, a sense of the uncanny grew. Raven released one hand, which blurred forward, the heel of her hand striking his forehead with the sound of a home run.

Don swayed, and Raven's hand dropped back to the barrel. Planting both feet against his chest she thrust, tearing the gun free and somersaulting backward to land on her feet.

"Halt the funting show," breathed Val.

Don, staggering, shook his head.

Raven, looking around at gaping faces, tossed the weapon aside. "Look...."

I can explain, she wanted to say. But how could she?

Gadger stared at her in disbelief – they all did – and she stared back, drawing a deep breath.

I've done it, she realized. *Killed the traitor before he could pass the data to anyone else. They're safe!*

So why do I feel like shit? "I'm sorry," she said again.

"Sorry?" Davo growled.

Don scowled, looking from her to his assault cannon, his hands opening and closing doubtfully as strain meters fed a digital stream of damage reports into his peripheral vision.

Cyn and Wolf knelt beside Val, crouching over their fallen leader, mouths open. Thug stared in shock, his face that of someone who'd just seen his best friend murder a hero. His white face, crumpled in anguish, suddenly seemed a fragile mask. She had to look away.

She swayed on her feet, wanting to scream, feeling everything falling apart.

Cynthia crouched on the ground, shoulders heaving and hands cradling the halves of Tony's skull, shaking her head, trying to force a miracle. Wolf took her hands, pulling her away, drawing her in against his chest, holding her. His dark eyes burned into Leeth's.

She swayed, again. *Am I in shock? Why? Because Tony Maretti was my father, and I just killed him? Did the Department lie about his daughter dying? But he looks nothing like me! Except maybe the shape of his eyes.* Or was it some magical conditioning the Doctor had done, secretly somehow? But from bitter experience she knew *exactly* what that felt like. Or had she fooled herself into thinking that? Without consciously knowing she'd been doing it.

Wolf frowned. "Raven is distressed," she heard him growl to Cynthia, who stiffened. Hissing, she pulled free of his arms, her face ugly with fury. Until it softened, just a degree, into a kind of baffled rage.

She's seeing my pain, Leeth realized, gritting her teeth. *Seeing* me. She shook her head, taking hold of herself. Now pinned by a bunch of angry and shocked gazes.

In the end, it was Gadger who asked the question, his voice strained. "Why, Raven? Why did you...?" His voice cracked.

What could she tell them? That the leader they'd trusted, who they were all mourning, had been copying the data to sell to Tik Tek? That he'd done it for *every salable secret* they thought they'd destroyed, from the day he'd taken charge? They might still work it out, if they found the headware she'd torn from him.

Eagle had said to be gentle with the Fist of Peace – to avoid 'ruining the group's cohesion'. She felt sick, seeing just how badly she'd wounded them.

Thug's expression in particular hurt like a knife between her ribs. Even now, she avoided his eyes.

Could I have delayed? But even a minute would've been enough for Maretti to upload all the data to the net. Wireless was only a thousand times slower than optical hardlink – she remembered *that* much from Nelson's stupid lessons. And with the data escaped, there'd have been *no* way to prove none of the others had gotten a copy.

Of course she couldn't tell *them* any of that. She wracked her brain for a plausible excuse... then gave up. Wolf would know if she lied. She hung her head. "I had to do it." That was true. But then... maybe she *could* tell the truth. "I felt I had to. The data cubes... he kept touching them, and I knew something was going from them into him. Into his head."

Cynthia bristled, facing the younger woman.   "And

that's why you smashed it open and- and *groped* around in his *brain* like it was a pudding? Are you *mad*?"

"No. Something went into him." *Copied files.*

Cynthia's eyes unfocused as she furiously percepted the girl's aura, reading her emotions. The horrifying joy that had briefly blossomed had died completely, leaving just sadness, and certainty – and soul-wrenching regret. No real enmity, either. Cyn shook her head.

"Wolf, is she telling us the truth?" asked Wiz.

The shaman nodded. "She believes her words."

"Could it be *true*?"

Wolf shrugged. "Who knows? 'Blast' failed on her."

"Tony told us to burn everything," said Gadger, tonelessly. Stunned. Looking almost as devastated by her actions as Thug did. "And we still don't know how Ford was targeted, remember. And he *was* handling all that stuff we took. Maybe it had some kind of spirit guardian? Or curse?"

Davo stepped forward. "Raven. How about you ease your gun out and just toss it on the ground over there. Right now."

The words sliced like razors – the pain came seconds after the fact. Of *course* she'd lost their trust. What else had she expected? *But, so what?* she told herself, ignoring a pressure in her chest that was making it hard to breathe. She kept her face expressionless.

At last she shrugged.

They all watched tensely as she drew the gun, then tossed it away.

Cyn spoke again, her tone numb. "Have her drag Tony's body over next to Ford's. Then have her take every vial, and pile them on the bodies. Then all the cubes from the rack, there, that Tony dropped; and find the one that was in his hand when you killed him. Put them all in one pile."

They all noticed how little trouble Raven had in shifting the two bodies. Or in finding the data cubes in the dark. How she cracked the orange one in two with finger and thumb before dropping it onto the bodies.

There was deathly silence as she scooped up the obscene severed mess that had been the top of Tony's head and placed it – strangely reverently – with everything else. For her part, she saw Don had retrieved his assault cannon.

Davo borrowed Wiz's flashlight and had her move back while he and Wolf checked out the still-steaming remains. They played the beam over the blood-soaked armor jacket, then the cleaved skull.

Davo shook his head, staring down. *Strike three.*

With a grim expression he knelt by the case containing the med-lab and opened it. Tugging on a pair of surgical gloves he looked up at Wolf, shrugging. "I want to check something, and I already carried it here from the car." Straightening up, he went back to Raven. "Hold out your hands."

She hesitated only a moment before obeying. Davo turned to Wolf and Cynthia. "Come and look imaginally. But don't touch her."

For a long time, they did just that, but at last shook their heads and stepped away. "No cyberware, Davo. Nothing odd," declared Cynthia.

Wolf, frowning, said nothing.

Davo finally took Raven's hands in his, prodding and probing their supple softness, feeling their warmth. Turning them over, he bent and straightened each finger. At last, baffled, he too stepped back. Stripping off the gloves he threw them onto Ford's body.

"How did you do that? How did you slice through an armor jacket with your bare hands? Cut through ribs. Through a *skull* bone?"

She shrugged. "I just can."

"Whenever you want?"

She stared at him for several seconds, aware of the still-ness of the whole group. Then nodded.

Davo stared. "Shit, Raven. Or should I say, *Sleena.*"

She heard several gasps.

"You really are her, aren't you? Just what are you? Are you also that silver slayer-bot?"

She didn't answer, and Davo turned away in disgust. "Okay, Cyn. We've put this off too long already. Burn it up."

The female mage nodded bleakly.

"Chit!" swore Leeth. "I don't believe this. You're going to burn Ford alive? At least kill him properly first. His body's still breathing!"

Cynthia looked ill at the thought of what she'd almost done.

"Okay," conceded Davo. He motioned her to one side, then stepped up, aiming his own gun.

Something inside Leeth leaped, like a voice inside urging her to volunteer to do the killing for him. She fought down the weird *eagerness*.

The muscles in Davo's jaw worked, making the scar across his face whiten, then he squeezed the trigger.

The explosion was shockingly loud in the silence.

"Okay, Cyn. Do it now."

Cynthia nodded. Spreading her arms, she stepped up to the pyre. A faint, luminous globe formed between her arms, enclosing it all. She backed away, jaw clenching in pain as she channeled the destructive imaginal pattern into a searing, cauterizing ball of intense heat.

For a moment, Wolf thought he sensed a pulse of fury in the air around them. Lifting his head, he looked around carefully. Then imaginally. Still nothing.

At last he turned his attention back to the cremation, ready to support Cynthia physically. The spell required a terrible effort, he knew.

Ford's clothes smoked, then burst into fire.

The wind had died, and the smell driven them all back. The somber group now stood by Davo's car. Everyone was still watching her.

"Look, Raven, *Sleena...*" Davo said, "maybe you really thought you were doing the right thing by killing Tony, but we *can't* just forget it. And there's obviously a lot more to you than you're willing to trust us knowing. Unless you've changed your mind?"

He stopped, giving her one last chance.

She stared around, stunned, realizing that even after all she'd done they might still be willing to accept her, let her be one of them. Trust her.

If *she* would just trust them. Tell them the truth.

Suddenly, meeting their eyes, her own filled with tears. She *wanted* to speak; desperately. The need was so very, very strong. In Thug's eyes, the way he leaned toward her, she saw hope in every straining muscle of his body, and ached to fulfill that hope.

His faith felt like a lifeline thrown to her, his eyes *begging* her to take hold and pull. So unlike the Doctor, with all his ways of tormenting her, right under Eagle's eyes. So unlike Mother's sneering disdain, or Father's distance. But Emma and James were like her, fighting for something bigger than individual people. And Dojo – the idea of diminishing herself in his eyes filled her with dismay.

Besides, the Department was making a difference. Fighting far bigger problems than the Fist could tackle.

Wasn't it?

But she *liked* these people, she suddenly realized. They cared about the innocent – just like Superman did. Heck, they even had a dopey code against killing, just like him! And if she joined them, with Maretti gone, maybe she could persuade Jack Shadow to rejoin the group? Even lead them? How awesome would *that* be? Together, maybe he and she could make the Fist see that sometimes you *had* to kill the bad guys? She'd even do the killing for them, let them keep their hands clean.

"Well?" Davo asked. "You gonna tell us who you really are? Trust us?"

She blinked and swallowed, a strange shiver running through her. Feeling her eyes widen, she realized she'd decided, in this instant, to throw her old life away and join them. *Maybe we can even still do the occasional job for Eagle? If I decide it's for a good cause.*

Warmth surged through her with the decision. It felt *right*. It'd let her protect people like Marcie, or Barney, or Teef, rescue more kids like she and Tash had at Club Juzz. All those little people too insignificant for the Department to care about.

The *'sheep'*.

She relaxed, feeling a burden lift, one she hadn't known she carried. Opening her mouth, she felt her lips curve up in a smile.

My name is Leeth, and I-

The words didn't come. She tried again.

I work for these people-

Her mouth working, her smile vanished. *What-?*

Her eyes widened in dismay: the Doctor's magical conditioning! *No!* No, she wouldn't let him do this to her, steal this chance from her! Glaring, hands shaking, she fought the mental bonds.

But Val didn't give her time. "Drop the act, drama queen," she sneered. "You've lied to us from the felching start, and just killed Tony fucking Maretti in front of us. That's it. You probably *are* that silver slaughter-bot, too. I've had a bellyful. I'm calling for a vote of expulsion from the Fist of Peace, right now. Out."

No. This couldn't *be happening. Not now! She could explain....*

Skinner wouldn't look at her. "Out."

Don stared blackly at her. "Out."

Wiz looked smug. "Out."

Cynthia sighed. "I just don't... oh, out."

Davo's expression was complex. She saw his shoulders slump faintly. He looked sad as his eyes met hers. "Out."

Somehow, the words began to cut, each rejection a slice of pain.

Gadger wrung his hands before staring down at his feet. "Out."

Thug looked around at the others. "But Tony got infected, guys! Raven had to do what she did! In! Keep her!"

The rejections had hurt. But Thug's simple-minded loyalty made her eyes burn, her face screwing up in torment, tears welling up again. Through them, she tried to return his encouraging, damaged smile, but couldn't seem to make her face work properly.

She tried to thank him, but her voice wouldn't work. So she was out, there was no question of that, and Wolf had saved his vote till last. She braced herself for the words she sensed coming. She didn't want to, but forced herself to meet his eyes. He stared at her unblinkingly for a long time. In some ways she liked Wolf best of all. She respected the shaman. They were alike, she sensed.

"If we meet again, I will kill you."

Her face froze, while he stared in scorn at her tears, dismissing them. Dismissing *her*.

It *hurt*. Far worse than she'd expected. She swayed on her feet, feeling strangely small, and *wrong*. For a second, the night sky swamped her, and she imagined strong hands in her armpits, lifting her and then lowering her into a strange boat, a billowing white sail snapping in the darkness, urging it away. A face, older than Wolf's staring up at her with a mixture of horror and regret.

Cast out.

She spun around so they wouldn't see. *She didn't need them. She didn't even care.*

Blindly, she walked away.

Shoulders hunched, Raven disappeared into the darkness, into the Dumps.

In silence, the Fist of Peace watched her leave.

CHAPTER 83

Tears still falling as she stumbled through the rubble, she relived the terrible moment she'd realized Maretti was the traitor. Could she have done anything differently? Killed him secretly instead of right in front of them all?

But there'd been no time. No time at all. He might have already been uploading the data, about to share it.

Killing him instantly had been the only way to stop the leak and guarantee the others knew nothing. To keep them safe.

From *her*.

Part of me thought he was my father, but I killed him anyway! What sort of monster am I?

And what about the Fist of Peace? Would she have done it? Killed them, if ordered? *No*, she decided. But even as she thought that, a part of her still wondered. Something inside seemed to whisper: spilling their blood would end the pain you're feeling. Pay it back.

In her mind's eye, she could picture the Fist of Peace all around her. Herself in their midst, invisible claws extended as never before, a black dagger in her other hand, geysers of blood feeding the soil.

She stopped, horror-struck by the image, pressing her hands to her face to block it out. *How could I even* imagine *that?*

She swallowed, forcing the vision away, focusing on reality. What did she need to do right now? Were the Fist safe, really?

Wiping her eyes, she considered. *I need to return to the Department. Report in. 'Mission accomplished.' And speak to the Doctor about... something.* That last thought slipped away, and she grasped for it. Oh, yes. Her report.

She hiccuped, a choking laugh. Then stopped. Would her written words be enough?

No. She couldn't leave it at that: she needed proof there were no loose ends. To really keep the Fist safe, she had to go back, rake through the ashes and make sure all the data cubes had been destroyed.

The Fist *should* have left, but if they *had* lingered, that just made it more important to go back. If some scrap remained, and they found it....

You may be required to Retire the Fist of Peace.

For a moment, she felt the order leap up inside her, felt

again the urge to strike back at them and hurt them like they'd hurt her. But the memory of Thug's bewildered expression of pain was enough to quench the urge. No: she'd finish her mission properly, thoroughly, and prove the Fist couldn't have gotten any of the data.

For a moment, anger at Eagle himself welled up. *How dare he suggest I might have to kill the Fist of Peace? I should kill all of* them*!* If instead she took the dagger, she could break the Doctor's conditioning-

She clutched at her head, shaking it. *What is* wrong *with me? No! The Department's not that bad!*

The sound of powerful electric blades thrashing the night sky snapped her back to the present. Hadn't Eagle said he was sending a Bureau agent to investigate? Not to mention Military Intelligence. She had to go back and make sure all the data cubes were fully destroyed. Now.

Shoving her worries aside, she circled back as quickly as she dared. Ahead, the unseen rotors slowed and stopped. But creeping through the dark, trying to be silent yet fast, she started feeling a prickling between her shoulder blades, like she was being watched. She stopped, listening... but there was nothing.

The feeling still rode her shoulders as she approached the funeral pyre of Tony Maretti and the scientist. But peering cautiously through the broken shopfront of a decaying Seven Eleven, that feeling vanished in shock.

The pyre had almost burned out, though the smell of burnt flesh was stronger than ever. The Fist were still there, which somehow didn't surprise her. But what she couldn't understand – what chilled her with the horror that she'd killed the wrong person after all – was seeing Davo talking to a guy in a military uniform. No doubt from the helicopter.

Was this the Bureau agent Eagle had warned her would be investigating, in disguise? It might be, but it might not. She had to get closer, get a better look at his face. Work her way round to the side. *Maybe* work out what the funt was going on here.

Davo leaned back against the bike, trying to look casual and in control. Unworried. Trying to match the sheer audacity of this man with the ice-blue stare. Trying to work out just how deeply in the crap they were. "How do I know I can trust your offer?"

The man's reply was cool, assured. "I'm trusting you. I sent my men away, as you demanded. I'm here alone. I'm not asking you to betray any of your people. All I'm telling you is that some people acted without authority, on a project of their own. If you tell me what you learned about it, and who was behind it, it will help me track them all down. A goal I'm in a better position to achieve than you."

Davo, seeming to mull the proposition over, glanced across at Wolf. Who looked surprised by the complete truth he'd detected in the man's words, and nodded that message to Davo. "And this is off the record?"

The soldier inclined his head. "Yes."

Again, Wolf nodded.

Davo met the eyes of each member of the group, seeking agreement before answering the soldier. "All right. We think the project started in September 2059. Colonel Bragg, from Vallejo, was working with them, but we think his boss was Dr Callahan Scott – a heavy duty mage and mathematician. Used to work for the University of Illinois. But he was dismissed from there for human experiments, then disappeared. Who organized *that* – the person actually running the program – we don't know. But Bragg and Scott are dead – killed in a firefight, I heard. So you can't ask them. The other researcher was Dr Jeremy Ford. Expert on medicine, magic, and the Melt retrovirus." He jerked a thumb at the almost burned-out fire. "His ashes are over there. Along with one of our own people."

There was a short silence.

"They both died here?"

Davo nodded.

"How?"

Davo shifted, uncomfortable. "Ford died really strangely. Just dropped, like a puppet with its strings cut. Our mages said his spirit just – disappeared."

"He was a mage?"

Wolf answered. "The man was not magically active. My people speak of things that steal souls. I think something ate his soul."

The night seemed suddenly colder, more hostile. The large man stood silent for a long time. "And your person?

He died the same way?"

Davo looked still more uncomfortable. "No."

He's trying to protect me! Leeth realized in wonder, feeling her eyes well up again.

"What killed him?"

Wiz spoke up. "Raven did. She used to be one of us."

Thug swore and lumbered to his feet, pointing an angry finger down at the hacker. "She only did it cause she thought something went into his head. Thought he wuz infected."

"Then she should have given Cyn and Wolf a chance to cure the infection, shouldn't she?"

Thug's mouth gaped open, then his shoulders sagged, his voice dying to a whisper. "Oh. I never thought of that."

"Well, the rest of us did."

"How did she kill him? You have mages – you could have healed him."

Wiz seemed suddenly unsure of himself. As though he couldn't properly believe what he was about to say. "She-she stabbed him through the heart then smashed open his skull and- and mashed up his brains."

The man blinked. "Uh huh. Where's her body?"

"We didn't kill her! We just kicked her out."

He studied Davo's face, then checked the others' expressions. "And?"

Cynthia answered. "Nothing. *We're* not killers."

The man just looked at her. "You let a murderer walk free." His gaze pinned her. "Will you give me a description so my men can look for her? Bring her to justice? Or do you condone her actions?"

"You wouldn't bring her to *justice*," Cyn snarled. "You'd bring her to the *courts*. If those courts dispensed justice we wouldn't need to do what we do."

The man shook his head. "Will anyone give me a description of her?" He looked from one member to the next.

Leeth, watching and listening, squeezed her eyes shut even as she felt her heart swell like it would burst. They were *still* protecting her, now with their silence.

But she'd think about that another time. Right now the military was after her. *That's all I need.* Eagle *would* be pleased. The man turned, looking at Skinner, facing her direction at last. She didn't know him. It wasn't Agent Spinoza.

Frowning, she kept watching.

"All right. I'd like to call our truce to an end. I'm going to order my men into the area to search for this Raven. To avoid bloodshed, I'm prepared to escort you beyond the search perimeter. So there'll be no excuse for trigger happiness. Acceptable?"

"No fraggin' way," swore Skinner. "You expect us to lead you-"

"Yank it, Skinner," cut in Davo. "He'll go back in when we get to the edge of the Dumps. And if he doesn't – then there *will* be blood." He looked around at the others. "Unless anyone has a better suggestion?"

One by one, they had to shake their heads.

Leeth watched them, waiting till they left so she could slide out, collect her gun, and rake through the ashes. While she waited, she worked out her next steps. Maybe she'd follow behind them, at least to start with. They'd probably figure she was somewhere ahead of them. Looking around, she spotted a rusting dish rack.

Finally, some luck!

She crept forward, picking up her gun from where Davo had made her drop it, then began sieving layers of still-hot ash and... more dense stuff, with the rack. Fully conscious of time running out, of the soldiers searching for her. But she had to be certain no data cubes had survived Cyn's inferno.

From their shapes and the way the pieces were piled, she recognized the fragments of Maretti's skull, before they crumbled at the touch of the dish-rack. A silvery blob of melted metal was all that remained of the cyberware in his head. Bones crumbled – *wow, Cyn's spell was* super *hot* – and she recognized the charred onion layer remnants of solid state memory cubes. *There* was a blob of fused glass that had been a syringe, and here was what looked like bubbled gray threads, metal wires heated until they'd burned. A few small droplets of fused orange crystal.

She stuffed it all – everything inorganic – into a fold-out pouch, her hands soon filthy.

At last she stepped back from the stomach-turning ash pit. Fingering her choker, she wondered whether she should report in. Then she remembered Nelson's lessons, and thought of the military out there surrounding her, undoubtedly with all sorts of electronic sensing devices.

The feeling of being watched returned. She darted to the rusted shell of an overturned delivery van, and from there into the shadows of a fallen power pole. Then waited.

Nothing.

But her instincts were screaming that she wasn't alone. Staying under cover, she headed as swiftly as she could in the direction the others had taken.

Well past the cordon, she paused, assessing. With most of the buildings collapsed, spilled into the street, she had to stay out in the open. Padding softly, she followed the edges of the fallen bricks and concrete, crouching low but still exposed.

Freeze. Listen.

Nothing. She scanned the dark, blocked street ahead, then behind, back the way she'd come. Clean. She checked the skies, again, and again saw nothing.

The military hadn't been too hard to avoid, despite their night scopes, drones, and electronic detectors – they made so much *noise*.

She studied the night sky, the skin at the back of her neck still crawling. Whatever watched her, wasn't military. It was something elusive. Careful. The same thing she'd felt watching her while she was deepest in the Dumps, even before she'd headed back to the pyre to search it. The feeling had faded while she'd eavesdropped on the peculiar meeting back there. But as soon as everyone had done their fades, it had returned stronger than ever. She *knew* she was being followed.

One last look, then she moved again, around the burnt and rusting shells of what must have been a pile-up of massive proportions. It had cost her time, but she didn't regret going back to the pyre. When Eagle asked, as she knew he would, she could honestly tell him she was *certain* all the data cubes, and Maretti's internal copy, had been destroyed. She pictured tossing the ashy pouch down on his gleaming white desk.

The bad feeling had been with her a long time, now. At least she had her gun again. She kept the weapon out.

She just wished she knew what was following her. And why she couldn't hear it. Something was niggling at the back of her brain.

Something she should remember.

PART III

Blood

Although the feeling of being watched had eased, she stayed alert. She'd almost reached the far side of the ruined shopping plaza when movement from behind froze her. Listening, she built a mental picture of the threat: three people; each one, big. But with none of the ultrasonics she'd come to associate with cybered opponents. So perhaps not soldiers?

They were still fifty meters from her when they split up, moving to flank her as if they knew where she was. Frowning, staying under cover, she headed for the one to her left. *So they want to hunt* me, *do they?*

Despite their size, they moved well. They made little sound, as if they saw as well as she did in the so-called dark. She scowled up at the blanket of cloud that reflected city lights from the night sky.

The other two weren't in sight when she stepped out in front of the first. He reared up, then leered down. An ogre. But unlike her friend Teef, this one was filthy and dressed in rags, with broken teeth crowding a diseased mouth.

Delight blossomed in his face as he saw her, one meaty hand dropping below his waist. She watched, disgusted when he pulled his erection free of his ripped jeans. She looked back up into predatory eyes, his arms reaching out for her.

Rapists. Another filthy rape gang! Stepping forward, turning, she hammered his heart with her right while her left palm struck up into his chin, snapping his neck.

Catching the two meter tall dead-weight before it collapsed, she lowered it quietly to the ground.

In the darkened plaza, empty shells of broken shops loomed on every side. Listening for the other two, she heard them creeping closer.

But something felt *off* about the whole situation. They'd approached from behind her, well beyond the range of even her own hearing. Emerging from the dark. Hunting *her,* she was somehow sure.

Again the sense of being observed prickled down her spine, and her eyes narrowed. Her head lifted, scanning all around, especially the sky, but still hearing and seeing nothing.

A faint movement to her right snapped her attention

back. *Okay, you can be next.*

Crouching low, she ghosted between squat concrete boxes whose purpose she couldn't guess. Another ogre, she saw, at the same moment he saw her. Healthier looking than the first and better dressed, but the same mad hunger in his eyes.

She ran forward to meet him.

This one knew how to fight. Ducking his haymaker, she blocked his left jab, keeping her hands on his arm, deflecting it down. Gripping it to leverage a knee strike into his side, she slammed a fist into well-padded kidneys while deflecting a returning elbow strike.

He grunted and kicked out at her.

Rolling over his leg, she let herself fall, grabbing his thick ankle and springing up, sending him airborne. Snatching a flapping trouser leg she hauled herself close, mid-flight, snapping a knee between his legs as his back hit the ground.

He cried out, kicking, but she pulled her legs up to land crouched on his belly. Fists blurred, pile drivers cracking ribs like green wood. For a moment he lay stunned. Gripping his jaw and head she twisted, hard.

Crack.

She sprang back to her feet and to one side, panting, then controlled her breathing to listen.

Why didn't I use my claws? Or just shoot him? While anger scoured through her and part of her cried out to spill blood, she let the truth wash through her.

Because you really *needed to punch something,* really *hard,* she answered herself. She felt lighter. Then her neck prickled, the sense of being watched returning stronger than ever. *A drone?* She listened, intent on her invisible watcher, again scanning the skies, listening for the ultrasonic whine of motors or the whirring of lift-blades; even a heartbeat.

Still nothing – nearby. But moving closer, faster now, heavy steps pounded her way.

Well, yeah, that last fight hadn't exactly been silent.

The footsteps slid to a stop, and she spun, diving sideways as a third ogre pulled out a gun. She drew her own, time slowing as he aimed and fired. She squeezed off two shots, nicely grouped on his heart – thinking, incongruously, of her SHUTZ training, and how pleased Father would be by that accuracy – and then she was rolling in the rubble, listening for more enemies, her heart pounding.

Silence.

Letting her head fall back against the dirty, cracked paving of the plaza, she felt rainwater seeping into her clothes. She smiled up in the dark before springing once more to her feet.

The trouble was, those shots would surely attract the soldiers out hunting her. Holstering her gun, she slid back into cover. *They'd* be using light intensifiers or heat vision, too.

At last, with the still expanding cordon far behind her she paused, stretching, satisfied. Time to head back to the Department. Report in: Mission accomplished. She used her Link to call a cab, judging it safe enough now. She'd just lowered her wrist when it chimed, with Marcie's tone.

Marcie? She flushed hot, then cold. It'd been two days since... Why was she calling now? *Has she made a decision? Is she forgiving me, or calling to tell me to stay away?* Worse, she had a sudden sense that Marcie's younger sister, Amanda, was in trouble.

"Jane."

At Marcie's flat tone, she knew something had driven her to call. "It's Amanda, isn't it?" she blurted.

There was a second or two of silence. Leeth's heart raced, her fears confirmed.

"Um, yeah, it was."

Was? Leeth felt her eyes widen in the dark.

But Marcie was shushing someone. Then her voice fell, muffled. "She knew it was you, kiddo," Leeth overheard. "Is this some dumb prank you and she've cooked up? To get the two of us back together?"

What? Despite Marcie covering her Link's mic, Leeth, listening, heard Amanda's voice. "No. I just had this bad dream, that Jane's in big trouble and needs our help, *right now*. She isn't? She's okay?"

The volume jumped as Marcie uncovered her mic. "So, Jane. Are you okay? Sprout here had a bad dream, and insisted I call."

Leeth sagged. "Amanda's okay? I thought you were

calling me because *she* was in trouble!"

"No, she's fine. We're both fine."

Leeth sighed into her Link. "You have no idea how glad I am to hear that." Then wondered why Marcie's younger sister was dreaming she was in trouble?

For several seconds, Marcie said nothing. Then, "I notice you haven't answered my question." She paused, but when she spoke again, a trace of warmth had returned to her voice. "Are you okay? You sound a little... like you've had a rough night?"

Leeth made a small choking noise. Then shook her head. "No, I'm okay. I think. Everything's okay, actually: I've fixed it." She took a breath, and plowed on. "Look, Marcie, I'm so sorry. I never meant-"

The first spell struck.

CHAPTER 85

A shiver ran up Dr Callahan Scott's spine. It had taken four attempts before the girl fell truly unconscious. And if he hadn't been targeting her with imaginal sight, he might have been lured into her trap when she'd collapsed – clearly unconscious – on his third casting.

She'd proven remarkably resilient. But then, he'd half suspected she would, having just seen how easily she'd dealt with the three ogres he'd set on her.

He'd followed her, watching – invisible, flying, and magically silenced – yet she had *still* somehow sensed him. Had even looked directly at him once or twice, chilling him.

Observing her performance as she fought, the curious alteration to her aura, he'd seen for the first time that, yes, here perhaps was someone who might have overcome Schenk.

A good thing he'd cast the Shock spell from fifty meters, too. He landed beside her body. She looked only slightly damaged from the final blast. A moment of uncertainty gripped him. Suppose she was still play-acting? Involuntarily, he Percepted her again. Certainly unconscious, he saw, annoyed at his own instant sense of relief.

Turning her over, he ended her call, then removed her Link and tossed it aside. Curiously, she had one hand gripping her throat. He peeled her fingers away from the black neck ornament. Feeling the cool metal surface, he hunted for a release clasp to examine it more closely. After a few seconds though he gave up. He was wasting time. From his coat pocket he drew a pair of wire-framed lenses and began a close imaginal examination of her unconscious form.

At first, she appeared depressingly mundane. But through the special lenses he began sensing interesting finer structure to her aura. He looked more deeply.

Fascinating. There was something very like magic bonded right throughout her skeleton, nerves, muscles... and also her eyes and ears. A little calculation suggested it might let her go beyond normal physical limits, just as the Process did for Schenk and the others. Like the two illuminating victims they'd found in the Dumps three months ago. He wondered, again, about their stories of the 'robot-like man', Marc Disten, whose psychological torture had changed them. And how that change – that 'perfection', they had called it – had so closely matched what he had achieved, over the course of the last two years.

Interestingly, her alterations, cluttered with their messy organic frills and inefficiencies, appeared not to interrupt magical transactions. Unlike the Process.

Her mind, too, looked as though it had been tampered with, over a long period of time. He saw evidence of layer upon layer of artificial blocks and conditioning. Controls and triggers. Some of them deep in the pleasure and pain centers, others in areas whose purpose he didn't know. Quite impressive workmanship really.

He dug down, and down, as he always did, seeking the seed from which the magic had sprung. Deeper. Ever deeper. Until he found himself at a point of stillness, seeing... nothing. Nothing magical, anyway. Instead, a self-reinforcing structure, purely mundane, yet from it, somehow, emergent magic.

It took his breath away. *That* would mean magic, like consciousness itself, was not a static *thing*, but something dynamic. A *process!*

He needed to study this. Determine how this revelation could be fitted into and modeled by his own calculus. Perhaps a scan of her memories first, however.

He cast the spell, settling its multiplying filaments into her brain, and waited for the first mental constructs to begin flowing. Working from the raw physical encodings of memory, it did not require her consciousness.

The information began... but in odd dribbles. As if something choked the flow. She was part of a group. But *not* the annoying Fist of Peace. Something... governmental?

Kill Callahan Scott.

While he reeled from this second revelation – that his work's destruction had been something planned, not chance, and that this girl had specific orders to kill *him* – faces tried to form. One man's, a second, oriental... but each refused to resolve. For one, he sensed merely command, and the certainty that the other was a warrior, or teacher. Perhaps both.

Then the face of a young woman, replaced in turn by a...

dog? With cybernetic eyes? Both, loved. Then, behind them, surfacing like a shadowy leviathan, an older male face with deep set, hooded eyes. Pain. Ah. That one, linked to the pain.

He tried to steer the memories back to the government group, only to feel the trickle vanish, twisting sideways. Instead, he saw a very aged man's face. A wheelchair. A mansion, and the viewpoint dropping toward it from the sky. A confusion of wood paneled corridors and intense heat, then he was sucked into a vortex of gray chains or whips, flailing and lashing, tearing and feasting in a treasure vault of magic, feeding...

Then something within the memory saw him. An obsidian blade.

Pure instinct had him thrust the spell from him, an instant before a dark spike of the imaginal pierced it, sucking in its magical energy like an inhaled bubble.

He found his heart thumping in his chest, his body attempting to panic, telling him to flee. Instead, he fought the urge, acknowledged his body's reactions, then with an effort set them to one side. Not for the first time, he wished he could apply the Process to himself. But to do so would cost him his magic.

So. The government had ordered this girl to kill him. And something *within* her, in some sense, had just reached out and very nearly done so. Possession?

Perhaps I should just kill her. Yet even as one part of his mind considered methods – a spell, or simply cutting her throat – his fascination made him focus his imaginal gaze on her again.

Tighter. Deeper.

Oh. Like he himself, she *resonated*. Connected to something in those depths below reality. The *same* thing. The feeling of a transparent gossamer strand.

Then he sensed strands, plural. Three? Four?

How was that even possible? It suggested multiple connections to the collective unconscious, to archetypes. More than one.

Just what *was* this girl?

He straightened, sighing, the ache in his back abruptly making him aware he had become so engrossed in the examination of this creature that he'd spent longer than he should, and far too much effort.

He stretched, painfully, tired. It had been a long day.

Still, he should have a good half-hour before she would start to recover, so.... With dismay, he realized the Shock damage had faded even more swiftly than he'd anticipated. He'd been too engrossed.

He stepped back, and recast the stun spell.

But, with his new tiredness, he couldn't focus the force with the precision he needed.

Even unconscious, he watched her somehow fight back, the spell not achieving its full effect. A tiny tendril of something like fear wrapped around the base of his spine. She was recovering faster than he was.

He considered.

Bending down, plucking her gun from where she'd dropped it, he smashed its butt heavily against her skull. There was a cracking sound, and he realized he'd struck too hard. He shrugged. From his examination, he knew her body was accustomed to responding to healing magic.

For fifteen minutes he rested, restoring his reserves and designing a modification to his memory scanning spell, to protect himself. After a quick trial of it, he levitated her, the two of them drifting up into the night sky.

They flew, invisible, away from a cordon of searchers in military uniforms, still searching.

Scott deposited his 'injured daughter' on the rotting couch of the slum building's self-appointed landlord. "I need a quiet place to nurse her back to health."

The man scarcely looked up, even at the post-midnight check-in. Just held out his cashstick. "Twenty creds a night." He flicked a disinterested glance at the girl on the couch, his eyes returning to a net-bead.

At least the man would be able to tell any investigators nothing useful. Scott paid for two nights, then picked up the girl and left. The man did not even glance up.

Human beings were scum. Until they were Processed.

Floating up the last flight of stairs he skimmed over the landing, sensing wood so badly eaten by termites the boards now sank under their own weight. Absolutely perfect. There was no way anyone could climb those last few flights, guaranteeing him both safety and privacy. And the rent had been laughably low.

The fumes of the cheap liquor stank on his clothes, so after depositing the girl on the dust-covered couch, he stripped off the stolen overcoat.

Still levitating, he checked her pulse, finding it weak. But he wouldn't be gone long, and even if she died, he could heal her. He let his weight descend to the flooring of the room. One foot went through the second board he tested, but the joists were still relatively solid.

Thoughtful, he floated up from the couch and pocketed his wireframe spectacles. Drifting over to a window he considered his next steps. He'd need restraints for the Process, as usual.

Before he flew off, he set a Ward against prying eyes, and created a watcher-construct to cover the unlikely possibility of a miraculous recovery. He even took a lock of hair, slicing it off with a sliver of broken window glass and carefully pocketing it. Just in case she had further surprises up her sleeve.

From what he'd just read from her memories, he'd need to be very careful indeed. Fortunately, those memories also offered a solution to his current predicament.

CHAPTER 86

James and Emma retreated to the limousine, defeated by the building's rotten stairs. Harmon lowered the bullet-proof smoked glass of the passenger window at their return.

"That's the location all right," James declared, leaning against the car and eyeing the building warily. "One good storm could probably blow the top floors away. Anyway, after a small donation to the building fund, the caretaker remembered a gentleman down on his luck who rented the whole top floor to look after his sick daughter just now. He must have used magic to get her up there though – the stairs are eaten away past the fourth floor, and there are no tracks in the dust on the steps after the third. Can you-"

Harmon interrupted, pointing up through the car window at dirty wooden shutters, paint peeled off. "That corner room, top floor. The only one impenetrable to astral visitors. There was an unusual imaginal creature on watch, which I dispatched. I have no idea what lies inside or I would have sent the elementals in. But go *now*. The link to Leeth is fading. And tread carefully – that whole floor is made of rotting wood. I'll follow you astrally, and bring the Air elemental."

Emma took James's arm. "Fire escape. That at least should be bolted into the brickwork."

Harmon nodded, and the two moved swiftly off as the car's dark window slid slowly closed. Shaking his head, he wondered what Leeth had gotten involved in now; who had brought her here. It was three-quarters of an hour since Marcie Dunkirk's panicked message to 'Jane's mother' had woken him from sleep and brought the Department to the alert. Not the use he had expected when he had created the contact, but it would nicely build trust he could exploit later....

Eagle himself had organized Leeth's rescue, locating her through her choker and insisting Harmon take the Air and Fire elementals on permanent readiness for magical attack, elementals he himself had summoned into service so many months ago. Along with James and Emma, 'for contingency'. He felt sure there were other measures Eagle had taken, but not thought fit to share.

In fact, Eagle had been singularly uninformative, and it had also been quite obvious that neither Mother nor Father were fully cognizant of the details of this mission.

Harmon left the large Fire elemental guarding his body, the Air elemental following his imaginal form as he flashed across to James and Emma ascending the flimsy rusting steps.

The two agents seemed to take forever to get in via the window and kick down the Ward, but in reality it was only a few minutes. Once inside, they picked their way from joist to joist to reach the room where Leeth lay unconscious on a moldy couch, but the flimsy door presented no obstacle at all.

She groaned as the Air elemental lifted her from the sagging sofa while James and Emma retreated to the external fire stair.

But all went smoothly, the elemental placing Leeth's unconscious body in the limousine beside Harmon's as he sat up.

She looked worse, even in the short time it had taken to bring her down. Immediately, he cast Healing. As the restorative patterns infused her, the pallor began leaving her skin, and her breathing eased.

It finished, but she did not become conscious.

He frowned, taking the time to sense her injuries more carefully – and found a subdural bleed. There had already been a considerable build-up of blood. He grimaced. That would be consistent with an injury at the moment her conversation with Marcie Dunkirk had abruptly terminated. Nor did he know any safe way, magically, to quickly drain that blood. She needed to be returned to the Department, *now*, so the auto-surgeon could drill in to relieve the pressure.

But instead of giving permission to return, Eagle demanded they wait there – in fact, ordered him to lie in wait in the room in which Leeth had been left, and disable or capture her abductor *when* he returned.

"Wait? For how long? She needs surgery. She may die!"

"Then keep her alive, Doctor," Eagle said.

"I've stopped the bleeding, but I *cannot* ease the pressure without surgery!"

From his Link, Eagle's face stared at him as if he were

an idiot. "I'm sure you could find a way, Doctor, if you could think as creatively as your former ward. We *cannot* send her to a hospital, as the situation there would be far too... unconstrained." He disconnected.

Damn him.

So instead, Harmon eased his spirit from his body. Ordering the two elementals to follow him, he returned with them to the room from which they'd just rescued Leeth.

And waited, while she inched closer to death.

The moment the intruder flew in physically through the window, Harmon's elemental attacked. But before he had time to speculate as to why James and Emma had not shot the fellow on his way in, the room erupted in some kind of imaginal storm.

It only took seconds to regroup and issue new orders – but the man was gone.

While the limousine hummed at the nominated location, Harmon sat slumped on the back seat. James waited, alert for threats, while Emma did what she could for the still, pale girl on the back seat. The car's large power-plant idled with an almost silent vibration, minutes piling up like water against a dam wall. In the limo, neither spoke as it sat on the deserted street, facing the concealed garage door that could admit them back to the Department. *Provided* Harmon returned to his body and gave the all clear.

When he at last sat up, both James and Emma released their breath.

"Clear, Doctor?" asked James, waiting to put the car into gear.

Harmon stared at him a little wildly, James thought, before nodding.

"The elementals will stick with the car? We wouldn't want them locked outside, eh?"

Instead of answering, Harmon just looked away.

James exchanged a look with Emma. She raised her eyebrows. «Civilians,» she silently messaged him, then relayed Eagle's instructions for the Doctor's benefit. "We're to drive forward onto the turning plate. A car elevator will take us down."

The concealed door rolled up as James eased the limo forward. The garage door closed behind them, plunging the disused mechanic's workshop into deeper darkness until the car's headlights came on.

After an initial shudder, the platform descended steadily, headlights illuminating smoothly bored stone on all sides. But then the downward motion stopped, while a faint rumble came from overhead. Followed by silence.

This time, Eagle spoke through the car's console. "Doctor, instruct your elementals to search the immediate area for spells, or astral presences. Assist them. Order them into the vehicle when you're done, if all is clear."

The check took little time, Harmon sitting up as the air in the car *thickened* around its occupants. "Clear."

"A pity," Eagle said.

The moment he finished speaking, sprays of water blasted the car from all sides, jets crisscrossing the air, centimeters apart. It battered them for minutes, Harmon's eyes widening as he imagined those streams dicing any astral entity trapped in it.

When the jets stopped, the car's paintwork had been stripped, bare metal gleaming.

The limousine resumed its descent.

Harmon, Percepting the two agents, found them as perplexed as himself.

Emma and James watched from the medbay door as the robo-surgeon folded itself away and began its sterilization procedures. *Finally!* Harmon thought, and cast the simple Healing spell. Still shaken from his recent whirlwind encounter with Leeth's attacker, he was unprepared for the surge of emotion he felt when her eyes flickered open.

Her uncle's face swam into focus above her, but that moment of traitorous relief was instantly eclipsed by shame. She remembered collapsing in the street, clinging to consciousness in a slimy puddle, hoping to lure whatever was magically shocking her, close enough to kill. It hadn't worked. She remembered her arm falling, Marcie's desperate voice fading, her other hand scrabbling at her choker, trying to remember the code to call for help.

To call for help!

Her expression froze into stony defiance, and she saw the no-doubt superior smile on the Doctor's face evaporate to reveal the distaste he felt at having to rescue her.

She swallowed, turning her head away, refusing to even acknowledge the healing he was pouring into her body – only to see Emma's worried face, and then James's. Her face blushed bright red, her jaw clenching.

Who else would be invited to witness my failure? Dojo? Eagle? She forced herself up out of Harmon's lap, ignoring the stabbing pain in her head that made her vision blur.

Shutting her eyes, she clamped her lips and waited for the healing to run its course.

CHAPTER 87

All four were called straight from the medbay to a private debriefing wth Eagle.

"You were watching imaginally when the man *flew* in the window, Doctor. Unseen by Emma and James, waiting below. Invisible? Think: in the moment before the attack, you saw active spells running?"

Harmon's expression changed slowly to shock. "No."

Eagle merely nodded. "And his ability to react instantly to an attack which one would assume had surprised him?"

Harmon drummed his fingers on the armrest of his seat, staring down, unseeing. He answered slowly. "I had the impression the response was instantaneous. Even... automatic."

"I see. Thank you Doctor. Perhaps you will spare some time from your research to give the matter some attention." It was not a request. "Doctor, James, Emma – dismissed. Please keep your written reports concise."

James and Emma grimaced but said nothing, and the three rose to leave.

"Oh, Doctor, one last thing." His finger stabbed a button on his desk and an image sprang into existence in the air between them. "Is this the man you saw?" Leeth drew in her breath, recognizing Scott.

Harmon hesitated. "I couldn't say – I saw only his aura. It could be him."

"But we killed him!" swore Leeth.

"That will be all."

Leeth clamped her lips shut. James, Emma and Harmon exchanged looks, then left the room. Eagle's eyes burned into Leeth's. She braced herself for a reprimand, or worse.

"It appears Scott is still alive. Did you achieve any of the objectives I set?"

Her chin went up at his tone, angry. "I made sure the data from his research was destroyed, and didn't leak. I worked out who the leak was – Maretti – and killed him." *Despite feeling he was my father.* Something she needed to grill the Doctor about. "We killed the two weird guys he must have been experimenting on. And Bragg. The other researcher, Ford, collapsed strangely, right in front of us all, but Davo shot him and his body was cremated, along with all the research. The Fist of Peace bought my explanation for why I killed Maretti, and actually seemed to be pulled together by it, despite the fact they'd just lost Chopper, too."

She continued, Eagle listening without expression.

"... and that's it. I woke up in our medbay."

Giving the report settled her nerves. Eagle had even agreed that, if Scott's wound had been as obviously fatal as she'd described, then her actions could hardly be held against her. Her thoughts returned to that point. "I still can't believe he's not dead. I mean-"

"Scott's body was not there when the military police arrived at the scene."

Her mouth fell open, her thoughts racing.

"It appears Scott has mastered several magical capabilities not seen since Melisande d'Artelle's passing. Either being able to create illusory injuries capable of passing close inspection, or being able to heal *automatically* after an otherwise deadly injury. Being able to somehow elude imaginal sight, and hide spells from it. Automatic magical defenses. Draining auras. And of course being able to cast far stronger spells than most magicians without exhausting or damaging himself. Coupled with the direction his research interests lie, I'm afraid he could pose a threat to national security. But until he resurfaces, there is little we can do."

"Uh, Ford also said Scott had this magical math stuff, that let him invent spells real fast."

She expected him to comment, but he said nothing. "Maybe we should ask Mr Abrams about that," she added.

Eagle slowly nodded.

She stared down at her hands, considering her next question.

"Yes?" he prompted.

"Uh. What will happen to the Fist of Peace?"

"That depends on you. If it leaks out that government funding was used in contravention of the world-wide Moratorium against human genetic alterations, the consequences will be disastrous. After the Incident of '38... global sanctions against *us* would be the most optimistic outcome. At worst, the Corporations might gather sufficient sympathy to instigate a no-confidence motion in the government and force a snap election. And believe me, with the state of things in Washington right now, the repercussions of that could spiral into global calamity within years." Eagle stared at Leeth, considering once again his hope that here sat the key to ending that insidiously spreading rot.

"Emma and James recovered your bag of incinerated objects from the tenement. Based on that, and what you have said so far, it appears the evidence of this research project has been destroyed."

"Yeah, except for Scott. But what about their underground headquarters? The military moved in. They might've gathered evidence."

Eagle smiled slightly. "No, the military are quite keen on cleansing this record. The only remaining threats are Scott himself, and the Fist of Peace. Scott we will be actively watching for and hunting. As for the Fist? If the group were to reveal what they knew of the matter, they might be able to force a public inquiry. How likely do you estimate that probability?"

I could get back at them for kicking me out, she realized. She couldn't be *sure* they wouldn't say anything. But she still respected them. Still liked them. And she'd never forget how they'd given her a last chance to join them, despite everything. They'd even refused to give her description to her military hunter.

She shook her head, very definite. "Nuh-uh. They wouldn't do that. For one thing, a few of them are almost patriotic. Besides, as far as they're concerned the thing is over and they won."

"But might they not take the opportunity to generate negative publicity for the military?"

"Uh, publicity's not their style. They're more the direct action types, you know?"

"That is also my own assessment. However, we'll keep them under observation all the same."

She beamed. He'd actually asked her opinion, and was going to trust it! She asked about Spinoza – who she hadn't seen – and the blue-eyed guy. Eagle showed her a picture of Military Intelligence's operative, which matched the guy who'd been questioning Davo. She sighed. "I guess I'd better go and do my report, then."

"Please."

She stopped at the door, about to leave. "Eagle? Did I do okay?"

He considered. "Your performance was acceptable."

She nodded, coolly professional, and stepped out, then waited for the door to whisper shut.

Once upon a time, she would've felt excited and happy – praise from Eagle, a mission accomplished. But she'd needed help, had to be rescued, and the worst bad guy was still out there. On top of that, she'd been kicked out of the Fist, and still wasn't sure if Marcie had forgiven her. She wasn't sure it was even *safe* for Marcie to be friends with her.

And of course, in the doorway of the rec room, the Doctor stood waiting. She slowed her pace, trying to read the expression on his face. He wasn't smiling. Her stomach clenched, and for a moment she thought about turning back, avoiding him.

Instead she stopped. *Wasn't there something she'd been going to ask him?*

"Well, Leeth? Was Eagle pleased with your work?"

She nodded curtly. "He said it was okay."

"Good. And how do you feel? I would have brought you back at once, but Eagle's orders were to lie in ambush for Scott instead. And 'Eagle always wins', eh?"

She just narrowed her eyes.

"James and Emma and I were quite worried, when we rescued you."

He waited. *'Again,'* his eyebrow twitch signified. She clenched her fists, and saw him not-quite smile, giving a slow and satisfied blink at her reaction. She unclenched her fists, forcing herself to calm down.

"How did you end things with your new 'colleagues'? Shall we be planning future team-ups with them for you, or did they reject you?"

'As will everyone except I' was there in his eyes. She clamped her lips.

"You should visit your friend Marcie. It was lucky for you she called when she did."

True. As if Amanda had somehow known...

But the Doctor gave her no time to think about that.

"Lucky that Mother had given her a contact number, in case she grew worried about... you. You should thank Miss Dunkirk for her part in your rescue."

Heat burned through her. That was twice now he'd needled her about his rescue. Surely he wasn't expecting her to *thank* him?

"No?" His chin lifted. "Ah. Or perhaps you worry that your friendship endangers her? Makes her a target for your enemies? Still, she knows the risks. If she chooses to put herself and her family in harm's way, what can we do?" He shrugged.

She took a step forward, at that.

But he didn't move at all, just kept smiling his terrible, superior smile. "I shall ask Mother if there is a way we can warn Marcie about Dr Callahan Scott, without breaching security."

She was scarcely aware of him walking past her, as horrifying new possibilities swarmed her.

She rammed her door shut with satisfying violence, hearing servo-motors whining in protest, then stared round the so-familiar space. So vacant. No sound of Chopper joking around, annoying everyone. No Thug, enjoying her company, offering her food, drink. Patting her leg.

The desk she called her 'study', Toby sitting in pride of place. Her bed and wardrobe just past it. Her bathroom, and to its right her kitchenette. Empty, dim and bare. The short hallway leading to the lounge she'd never used. The air, still, and antiseptically clean.

She found herself blinking, rapidly.

A faint scent of ozone was the only evidence that a housebot had recently attended to the rooms. That, and the sterile cleanliness.

Welcome back, Leeth, she told herself. *Home, sweet home.*

She had to talk to Marcie. Let her know her call had saved her. She flushed, gritting her teeth at that truth. Remembering Emma's concerned face hovering over her. *Again.*

Her hand went to her Link. '*Hi Marcie, there's a superpowerful mage probably targeting you, Amanda, or your father, just to get at me.*' Her heart quailed. *And I need to do it before the Department says I can't.*

But what do I say? How can they protect themselves against Scott, how can I protect them, when I couldn't even protect myself?

She touched her Link anyway, with a gulp. "Call Marcie," she told it, and let herself fall into the seat at her desk, biting her lip. Two a.m. Would she still be awake?

Marcie's worried face appeared straight away. "Jane! My God, you're okay! I was so worried! What happened? Can you tell me?"

Leeth blinked, then flushed. "Uh, not really. But I'm good. Uh... listen..." *you're all in danger.* Her mind flashed through possibilities. But for each idea, she could see how Scott could counter it.

"Jane? You alright?"

Despite the weight still hanging over both of them – her killing of Marcie's abductors, a few days ago – Leeth saw her friend wasn't going to bring it up now. Not till she knew 'Jane' was okay. Not wanting to add more burdens. *She's too good for me. I don't deserve a friend like her.* She blinked more rapidly.

But how to answer her question? Leeth looked at her helplessly. "I'm fine," she said at last. "Your call – Amanda's warning – saved me." Her mouth worked. What did Superman do, when his enemies hunted his friends? Her eyes narrowed. *He protected them. And went hunting.*

She swallowed. "You guys, take care, okay? I mean that. Stay alert for, uh, *trouble.* I'm on it." She swallowed. *Maybe I don't* need *to tell her?* She cringed at the thought of Graham Dunkirk's reaction to such news.

Don't be a coward.

Gritting her teeth, she found and shared a pic of Dr Callahan Scott and explained, not entirely sure that what she was doing was wise. She finished the call quickly, feeling a little sick at Marcie's final expression at being told of the evil 'super mage'. Clearly aware their friendship was *again* putting her in danger. And not just her: her whole family too, this time. But she'd *still* tried to hide her fear from 'Jane'.

I have to see Eagle. Killing Scott has to be my next mission!

CHAPTER 88

In a dark corner of a 'nut and gift' shop in Sacramento, Dr Callahan Scott sat nursing a coffee, planning. Not only had the girl and her witless allies ruined Project Clarity, they had also destroyed the only copy of over twenty years of groundbreaking magical research. As well as his even more significant philosophical research.

Not for the first time, he wondered if Melisande d'Artelle had made the same discovery he had. Perhaps it was just as well he'd not published his magical research. 'Power corrupts; absolute power corrupts absolutely.' Were the gods of old, like those who had tried to return to power in India, simply practitioners who had found that same path? Would he himself have fallen into that trap had he not first made his philosophical breakthrough?

He took a sip of coffee, staring out the window at the wide, empty street, idly considering ways to put a so-called god under his microscope.

Whatever happened, recreating and publishing his Calculus of Rationality should be high on his priority list. Now, more than ever, mankind needed freeing from the emotional bondage of its animal nature. It had been five long years since his epiphany. Four and a half since his dismissal from the Beckman Institute for Advanced Mental Science. Now, once again, he found himself alone and unfunded, ousted due to animalistic fears.

A great pity he had missed his chance to meet 'The Breaker', Marc Disten. From the accounts of the two subjects Disten himself had created, a discussion would have been fruitful. How odd that they had both been working toward the same goals, within walking distance of one another. Could that be mere chance?

But as ever, the first imperative had to be survival. At least now he knew he was being hunted by a creature capable of single-handedly dealing with Schenk, acting under orders of a government agency determined to kill him.

That was problem one. He spent several minutes transcribing its essence onto paper, then the required alternative outcome, and sketching out the first few steps in the solution, seeing what was required.

Turning to a fresh page, he set out a second problem – how to acquire resources – and again, began calculating.

Casting the spell he'd humorously named 'Powerpoint',

he projected the girl's memory of the treasure vault mansion onto the surface of the table and photographed it. A short Earth Map image search provided the target's location: a two-hour journey from New Francisco. Returning to the first problem, he listed several new spells he would need to develop, to remain safe. Staying invisible was not a long term solution.

The calculations showed he needed replacements for Schenk. Four would be the optimal number, given the time constraints imposed by his other problems.

Two days later, watching his reflection, he cast the first of his new spells. By degrees, he made his face younger; squared the jaw and added definition to the cheekbones; lightened the hair and added a beard. The spell would of course be detectable. He could hide it, but based as it was on a common one, if he made his face moderately attractive, any observing mage would simply take it for mere vanity. Only careful study would reveal that unlike the common spell, it altered the appearance *optically*, not just in the minds of observers.

The second step was equally simple. Floating invisibly in the West Oakland Dumps, a day of observation identified a source of healthy subjects, unlikely to be missed. The gang's own den offered an isolated and unfrequented location suitable for the Process.

In contrast to his peculiar female enemy, a single strong Sleep spell rendered them all unconscious. Cable ties secured them, and the inaudibility spell kept them ignorant as he Processed them one by one. It wouldn't do for those not yet Processed to hear the screams.

Their leader died of heart failure. Indeed, the overall success rate proved lower than with the subjects taken in the Hunters Point area. And despite one swift success with a female member – who achieved full rationality in mere hours – another two, after Processing, opted not to assist him.

Those, he followed and terminated, regretting the waste. Secrecy however was needed for now.

In all, three full days yielded just four Processed individuals. They had names, of course, but none objected to being referred to as One through Four. He looked forward to comparing his new female subject's development, to that of the huntress who had escaped.

Most of his attempts to locate that one, using the lock of her hair to target a Sending, failed. Apparently she spent most of her time either underground, underwater, or behind Wards. On two occasions he succeeded, briefly clairvoying her undertaking insignificant social or transactional activities.

The evening of the third day, after a final look around the den, and terminating the surplus surviving members of the gang – by mutual agreement – he ended the inaudibility spell and the five walked to an area where cabs accepted calls. From there, their destination lay just two hours north.

In the cab, Scott shared what he knew of their target. Large parts of the journey passed in silence – one of the benefits of working with Processed humanity.

But closing the final distance, Percepting the enormous Barrier looming up, he decoded a pattern of warning barely in time. "Car: brake!" he yelled.

The car juddered to a halt, a meter from the Ward.

"Why do you stop?" asked Two.

"There's a Barrier ahead," he told them. "Wait here."

He exited the car to examine the massive construct. It towered up and away, enclosing the target and much of its grounds.

The longer he studied it, the more impressed he grew. Reading his group's hostile intent, it would have hardened the air itself into a shield lattice. Striking that at speed would have been like driving into a rock wall. He himself would have auto-Healed, but spells, even healing, did not work on the Processed.

He sent the four off to buy supplies while he continued studying the magical construct.

But an hour later, parts of it remained beyond his analytical tools. Since their destination lay at the center of it however, the construct was probably created by the aged man of the girl's memories: Abrams.

That one would likely have to die: a person with the experience and strength to produce such a construct was too great an unknown to allow to survive. Especially on his own territory, with who-knew-what spells in his repertoire and defenses in his home.

The truly astonishing thing, however, was that he saw no evidence Abrams had used a systematic magical calculus like his own to weave this Barrier – several subtle inefficiencies indicated otherwise. No, somehow the old mage had fashioned it by art alone, not science. Art, and a stronger magical index than his own.

Remarkable.

Finishing his analysis, he contacted One to add a few items to the list of supplies. While he waited for their return, he began modifying his memory access spell. It should be possible to read much from the old man's brain before cellular degeneration ended the information flow. The vault of magical treasures might even prove the *lesser* prize – if they could bypass Abrams's Ward.

Even Abrams, however, could not craft a Barrier that penetrated living earth.

When the others returned, the tunneling began.

And at night, on the seventh day after the girl had destroyed his life's work, the five walked the final distance to the mansion's double doors.

CHAPTER 89

'Leeth, we need to speak. Come soon; come alone. Tell *no one.'* Excitement flared through her at the terse text. She'd never had a message directly from Mr Abrams before!

The only worrying part about that was the last bit. She texted back, 'Not even E?'

'Definitely not,' came the swift response.

But could she be sure this was Mr Abrams? Her Link said he was the originator, but still.... She texted back, 'Come where?'

'My house. Ankhet will meet you at the door.'

Ankhet? Oh! Anne Ket! She flushed, feeling she might've called the woman Anne. Oh, well. It was *her* fault for having a weird name.

'Should I bring anything?'

'Just yourself.'

She checked the time – ten pm – and logged on to the Department's calendar system, as Mother had drummed into her at length. She noted her plan to go out, but left the return time open. It was chill being an actual Agent, trusted to come and go as she pleased.

It only took a few minutes to select a suitable outfit. She even remembered to take a cashstick to pay for the cab fare. And a snack or two. The ride would apparently take a couple of hours.

'Is it okay if I arrive around midnight?' she texted.

'Ideal,' Mr Abrams replied.

A funny shiver ran through her. She just *knew* this involved the obsidian dagger. Not that it called to her, or anything.

She just *knew.*

She told the car to stop before it left the woods, then instructed and paid it to wait for an hour, just in case. Standing beside it as it sighed into sleep mode, she peered through the trees at the broad expanse of well-lit lawn ahead. Through it, a spotless asphalt road snaked up to the house.

Why was she even *thinking* of trying to sneak up on the mansion? *Mr Abrams* had called her here, himself. There was nothing to worry about!

With a shake of her head, she began walking.

Emerging from the trees, she squinted into the flood-lights. Another defensive point. Closing her eyes, she listened. Maybe for the sound of a gun mount on the roof swiveling to target her; maybe for the sound of an alien, scaly Ginsu machine grinding through the soil beneath the road.

Wow, you're in a weird mood. All the same, she kept her eyes mostly shut and trod a straight line to the mansion's double front doors. Her pulse accelerated as she crossed the open grounds.

The trees stood silent watch, encircling the house in the still night. Small animals moved, beetles rustling through fallen leaves on their nightly quests, moths flying. No sound from the house, though. Not until she was perhaps fifty paces from the front doors, when she heard their handles twist. Opening her eyes as the oak doors swung wide, she saw Ankhet.

With them open, she could hear the woman breathing. With a smile and a wave, she jogged forward.

Ankhet stared for a second before lifting a hand to wave back, the sides of her mouth curving upward.

Leeth's heart thumped hard, once, a shiver flashing through her. Something felt *off*. Had the alien thing come back?

"Uh, hi *Ankhet*. What's up?"

The woman was dressed in a simple but elegant white robe that flattered her figure, though she wore no makeup. Her eyes looked a little red, as if she'd been crying, but right now she looked composed. *Very* composed.

"Best if you see Mr Abrams. He is inside, waiting." As Leeth started up the front steps, Ankhet looked past her and then around the empty stretch of lawn. "Where is your cab? Did you come alone, as Mr Abrams requested?"

She was getting a *really* bad feeling about this. Why hadn't she heard Ankhet approaching the door? It's not like she would've just been standing inside, waiting for her to arrive.

Once at the top of the steps, at the entrance, she looked past the other woman into the entry lobby and the hallways running off from it. All well-lit. Empty.

Silent.

For some reason, she hesitated to actually step inside.

"Mr Abrams?" she called. "Are you okay?"

Ankhet studied her. "He cannot hear you from out here. Won't you come in?"

Leeth, keeping one eye on the woman, called again, louder. "Mr Abrams!"

"You appear tense, Leeth."

"And you appear weird."

Ankhet looked her over, carefully.

"Mr Abrams!"

"I told you, he cannot hear you from here. He waits for you inside." Ankhet stepped back from the door. "Are you remembering your injuries, the last time he called you here to help?"

"How about you go and fetch him?"

"He is occupied. You need to go to him. Or are you afraid to enter?"

Leeth bristled. "No." She shut her eyes, *listening*. She heard nothing but the sound of Ankhet breathing, and far more faintly, the calm beat of the woman's heart. No one else, lurking out of sight.

Nothing odd.

All the same, she dived in, eyes darting right and then left, past Ankhet, wishing she'd brought a gun. *Stupid.*

The taller woman merely closed the front doors, and turned away. "Follow me," she said, moving off down the same hallway they'd used last time.

Leeth padded swiftly after her and grabbed her arm, tugging her to a stop. "Why are you acting so weird?"

For just a moment, Ankhet resisted, almost pulling her arm free before relaxing and turning. Her eyes once again ran up and down Leeth. "You are the one behaving strangely," she said. "Your breathing is fast, your pupils dilated. Your right fist is clenched, and your weight rests on the balls of your feet. You appear frightened." She nodded. "Yes. Perhaps you fear you have been called back to face danger and pain again. Your imagination floods your mind with possible scenarios, triggering the 'fight or flight' instinct. You are so scared, you are close to panic."

Ankhet's lip curled up, her eyes narrowing, and suddenly Leeth realized she was being sneered at.

But it all felt wrong. Wrong, and creepily familiar in a

way she couldn't quite pin down. One thing she knew, though, she no longer trusted Ankhet, and wasn't going to meekly follow her into some trap.

She plunged past the woman, slamming open doors, her fingers tingling, invisible claws ready to slice. Alert to danger, she strained to remember the route she'd followed the last time she'd come here. *Listening* ahead, aware of Ankhet further behind her, following with a calm and measured tread.

Something was screaming at her that that calmness was important.

Muffled by the solid door ahead of her, she heard the quiet hum and pulse of Mr Abrams's life support wheelchair thing, and threw the door open.

Two men stood at his sides, a hand on each shoulder. His head struggled to lift, his eyes blinking sleepily before burning into hers, warning-

"Freeze!" someone from inside ordered her. "Down on the ground."

From each side of the doorway, a man and a woman stepped into view, guns raised.

She charged to the side, twisting. Bullets slammed into her as she tore out the man's throat, sliding an arm around him and turning, holding him as a shield. The woman stepped further back, still firing.

The men beside Mr Abrams raised their guns and fired as they retreated, drawing him back and out of her reach. Bullets hammered into her leg, her exposed arm. Shifting her human shield, she grabbed the gun from his dangling arm.

Something slammed her chest like she'd been hit by a bus, and she *felt* her heart stop beating. *No!* She *refused* to fall. She swayed, her balance failing her. She struggled to lift the gun, while her human shield slid from her hand...

And that was all.

CHAPTER 90

At the restarting of her heart, blood hammered a wall of pain through her, shocking her awake. She tensed, but kept her eyes shut, listening, trying to understand as the familiar soothing, restorative warmth of a healing spell flowed through her.

She was upright, seated. She tried slumping forward, but ties at her wrists held her up. She tried to shift her ankles slightly, but they were bound, too. *Of course they were.* Furious at being captured and tied up *again,* she fought for calm. Better than the alternative, though.

Without moving, she identified the sounds of Mr Abrams's life-chair; his breathing, and her own pained breaths; and those of a second person, too, someone who was touching her, unmoving and calm. Male, by his smell. Straining, she heard more: the very soft breathing of two men near Mr Abrams; Ankhet's lighter breath; and the woman who'd shot her.

Her nostril twitched at the copper-iron smell of blood. Mr Abrams moaned, slurring something that sounded like 'Wha'r theess th'ngs?'

The healing stopped, but pain remained, burning in her chest, arms and legs.

"No need to restore you to full health."

The voice at her side her was male, and calm. Not one she'd heard before.

For several seconds there was only the sound of Mr Abrams's life support chair, and people breathing.

"I can explain just as well while you pretend to be unconscious, Leeth."

Her name on a stranger's lips struck like a slap to the face. But he hadn't finished.

"That is an odd name. Especially for a girl originally called Sara."

She flinched.

"Or perhaps I should say, Happy Mouth?"

If 'Sara' had felt like a punch to the gut, the *other* name struck with terrifying force: it felt like he'd stabbed her mind. Her jaws clamped, trapping a scream, tears springing forth for no reason she knew. As if mourning someone she'd loved, and lost.

Panting, through slitted eyes she saw she was indeed bound, by nylon ropes. At least that was a change. She tested one, felt its lack of give, and growled, opening her eyes and shaking the tears from them before turning to glare up at the man taunting her.

Tall and bearded, with sandy hair and a strong jaw, he watched her with mild interest. Mr Abrams's head rocked up, his eyes seeking hers, but blinking, drooping, struggling to stay open.

"You and your... acquaintance, Mr Abrams, are alive because you both have some value to me, and I have a little time to try to realize that value."

His face bugged her. Was he the *brother* of someone she knew? Someone she'd met, with the Fist of Peace?

The two men by Mr Abrams's sides watched her, each with a hand clamped to a thin shoulder. *Why wasn't he casting spells, wiping them all out? Why wasn't Ankhet? What was wrong with her?*

She twisted, staring at Abrams's student. Had Mr Abrams, secretly, treated her like, like the Doctor had *her?* Was this revenge?

But Ankhet merely stared back, incurious. As *all* the armed people did. Belatedly, she noted the man she'd taken down. He lay in a spreading pool of blood, his head connected to his torso by just a scrap of flesh. No one had moved him. No one had attempted to heal him. As if none of them cared.

"Why are you doing this? What do you even *want?*"

"Initially, simply my life: something you have been illegally ordered to end."

"Huh? I don't think I've ever even *met* you, let alone been ordered to kill you." His face seemed vaguely familiar, but something about his calm tone was *really* ringing bells. "And of course killing people is against the law," she added.

He knew her real name, though, and knew she killed people – which was a big secret. *Who* was *he? Had Mr Abrams told him about her? Had* Marcie? That thought sent a chill through her. *Or was he somebody who knew about the Department?* Somehow, none of those guesses felt right. After all, he'd known... those *other* names....

Maybe she could taunt him? That's what you did with evil villains, after all. "You're nuts. I'm just-"

"Wasting time is foolish. I brought you here to end your

threat to me. Here specifically, because it is somewhere you could be drawn, with the correct message, and because the contents of the vault will redress some of the losses you have caused."

Why were bad guys so hard to understand? Redress? She shook her head, concentrating on the rest of what he'd said. *He'd* been the one to send the message from Mr Abrams? She'd been *lured* here? She ground her teeth in anger. *Of* course *that's why the message said to tell no one!* Swallowing down that piece of gullible stupidity, she felt her choker, still comfortingly around her neck. Which probably meant he *wasn't* someone connected with the Department. Not that she could reach it to send an SOS. Like the other night...

"But if you think I've been ordered to kill you, why would you bring me to you? That's just dumb."

She stared at the man. Who...? *Dr Callahan Scott!* her instincts shouted. The super-mage who'd stunned her and captured her, apparently. But... he looked really different. A spell?

Though if this *was* him, it was actually kind of convenient, considering she *had* convinced Eagle she should kill him and all. She gnawed her lip. *I just need to work out how to do it. Before he can kill* me.

At that moment, a Link chimed. Scott looked first at his left wrist, then his right, and she saw him pause. Then he waved his people – and Ankhet – back from her, and away from Mr Abrams. "Release him and move away, just while I cast this."

The two men let go of Mr Abrams's shoulders and stepped back while Scott reached out and took the older man by the throat, closing his eyes for a moment. Then he removed his hand and stepped away, gesturing the men to return. Turning toward her, one finger sketched a quick circle.

He took the call. "Abrams."

Leeth felt her mouth fall open. He sounded *exactly* like Mr Abrams.

And joy blossomed as she heard Eagle's voice.

"Are you all right?"

"No!" she shouted. "Dr Callahan Scott's here, he's captured us both!" Though she ground her teeth in shame at the admission.

Scott barely glanced at her. No one else reacted at all.

"All is well here. Is there some reason to think otherwise?"

"Eee-"*agle!* she started to call, but instead choked on the name. She fought past it to the rest of her warning. "It's Scott! He's right here!" she screamed. "You're talking to *Scott*, not Mr Abrams!"

Eagle ignored her, as if he hadn't heard her at all. "We register Leeth at your location."

Scott, in his Abrams voice, sounded amused. "I am well aware of that, I assure you."

Again she tried to scream Eagle's name, and again her throat closed up instead. She saw Scott notice.

"Did she try for the sacrificial blade?" Eagle's voice sounded heavy with regret.

"What? No! Can't you hear me? Ee-" Once again her throat seized up.

"In a sense," Scott said, still in Abrams's voice, "but *I* called her here. We're discussing it now. She should stay overnight, however. I'll call you in the morning."

Uncle's conditioning, she finally realized: 'You won't be able to speak of the Department....' She lunged forward against her ties, wrists straining against the nylon ropes, fingers slashing futilely against air. Throwing her weight forward, she moved the chair a step. Another. For the first time, Scott looked worried, and she suddenly remembered the *silent* truck that had almost run her down. He'd silenced *her!* Struggling and jerking, she managed to tilt forward, still tied to the chair but balancing now on the tips of her toes. She waddled forward, desperate to escape the circular zone he'd drawn – the silence? – before Eagle's call ended.

Scott gestured Ankhet and the other woman toward her, but instantly changed his mind, instead frantically waving them back and away from her.

"Very well," Eagle was saying. "But keep her safe. Especially from herself. I believe in her: I won't have even you sell her short."

Scott blinked at her, lazily. "I won't."

"It's a trap! You're talking to *Scott, Dr Callahan Scott!*" she screamed, her head tilted so far forward she faced the ground.

"I shall. Goodnight." Scott ended the call, just before her chair crashed down beside the dead man, half in its pool of coagulating blood.

A tiny finger gesture, and Scott's voice was his own once more. "I do believe you were calling my name. You have worked out who I am? You're quite resourceful, aren't you? Who is 'Eeeee'?"

"Suck my pussy," she spat at him.

"Now you're angry. Continue shouting insults if you wish to end this conversation."

His bored tone made her want to scream, but with a supreme effort she mastered herself. Panting, she felt her bullet wounds burning with renewed pain from her exertions.

"Five, right her chair."

Ankhet stepped forward, lifting and setting her and the chair upright with one hand. *Five?* Leeth blinked at Ankhet's casual display of strength, noting her uninterested expression. Like she was watching a bug.

And the name. *Five. Why had he called her Five?*

Oh, fuck. Crazy strength. No emotions. Like the guy she'd fought and killed last week. Like *Marc Disten*, before him. Remembering the awful clarity of his near successful attempt to 'Perfect' her, a sense of chill washed through her.

Clarity? Project Clarity! She almost groaned aloud. Was Callahan Scott behind *all* of that? Was he the one who'd created Marc Disten in the first place?

Could this night get any worse?

"Tell me about this sacrificial blade which 'E' thought you had come here for," Scott asked.

CHAPTER 91

Her eyes darted around the room, re-evaluating her situation. They came to rest on Scott's two henchmen holding Mr Abrams. She remembered Marc Disten touching Tash and the vampire collapsing, and suddenly realized why they held him. The same reason Scott had madly waved the other two away from *her* when she was escaping his silence spell: because their touch ruined magic. They weren't just drugging Mr Abrams: the two goons were gripping his shoulders to suppress his magic!

She filed the insight away.

Though she wasn't picking up Marc Disten's creepy vibe quite as strongly from these guys. She lifted her chin. "I beat Marc Disten. You don't scare me."

Scott gestured negligently. "*You* dealt with Marc Disten? Interesting." He stared at her.

Uh oh. Maybe I should have kept that to myself?

"We should proceed. She can be questioned after."

It was the woman who'd shot her. She spoke in a dull monotone like Marc Disten's, her expression equally untroubled.

"True," said Scott, though still watching her, tied up in the chair, like she was a puzzle he planned to solve. "Explain about the sacrificial blade now, or you will be Processed, and you can explain then."

Leeth sneered, despite the pain burning from her wounds, and being tied helpless. "Oh, is that what *you* call 'Perfecting'?"

"Enough. You will be Processed, or I will read the information from your decaying brain."

"My brain isn't decaying."

"It will be, if you die during the Process. Or if your progress is too slow."

"And what about Mr Abrams? What are you planning to do to him?"

She considered adding, 'he's just a helpless old man,' but the way Scott had his anti-magic hench-goons holding him, she knew they weren't going to fall for that. She *was* worried about him, though. He *was* old. Just, not helpless. When he wasn't drugged. *How were they doing that?* Then she realized his humming life support chair probably provided the perfect means.

"You misunderstand who asks the questions, and who

provides the answers."

And you misunderstand I've already smashed the thing you're working for into a million pieces, once before. She bit back on that reply, however. Why *was* this happening again, anyway? It was just plain *unfair!*

Scott did *something,* stretching out a hand toward her head, and it was like being back with Marc Disten, battered and cold and lying on a slab in a deserted, tilted building as winds whistled through it.

Instead of trying to dodge aside, however, she closed her eyes and focused inwards, gathering her resolve.

Just in time, too. The sensation was exactly as she remembered: an invisible touch worming through her mind, seeking her anger, her fear. She rejected it, rejecting the soulless clarity she knew lay at the end of that path.

It slithered around her thoughts and feelings. But quietly sure of herself, she stayed calm. Mentally withdrawing, she opened her eyes.

Scott's had narrowed. The worm in her head pressed tighter. She allowed herself a small, tight-lipped smile.

They all watched her with a peculiar intensity they hadn't shown until now. Like spectators waiting for a surprise they knew was coming. All except Mr Abrams. *He* was blinking and squinting, like he was struggling to focus but sleep kept dragging him away.

Apart from Mr Abrams, they'd *all* been Processed. She knew it. Ankhet, too. Probably tonight.

They watched, waiting to see her suffer the same ordeal. But she knew it couldn't get in if she didn't let it. You had to open the door a crack.

Scott kept trying, and she kept him out, increasingly confident but waiting for some clever counter-move, hoping she wasn't falling for a trap. But five minutes passed, then ten, twenty, and nothing changed.

"I don't understand," Scott finally said. "You are so complementary, this should be trivial."

"Complimentary? Untie me, douchenozzle, and I'll *show* you how complimentary I can be," she growled.

He ignored her. "You match. You match perfectly. Your Processing should be easy. Perhaps even painless."

She could have explained, could have told him she'd already been through it – but knew that would be stupid.

One of the men holding Mr Abrams spoke. "She cannot be Processed, so it is time to kill her."

"True." Scott agreed. "I will read the information from her brain afterward."

The two men, and the other woman, raised their guns, sighting.

"Aim for her heart," Scott said. "Don't damage her brain."

CHAPTER 92

"Wait, okay! I'll tell you about the dagger."

"She is desperate. She attempts to delay her end." That was bitch number two.

But no one shot.

"No, she gave the dagger to Abrams." That was Ankhet, her voice toneless. It took Leeth a moment to realize she was speaking in her favor. "She obtained it from her lover, an Asgard magic researcher."

Luiz. His name no longer hurt. Somehow, that lack of pain felt shameful.

Scott seemed to read something from her reaction.

"She wielded it during an...." Ankhet stopped, hunting for words.

Good luck with that, thought Leeth, shuddering at her own memory, confused as it was. But she still had three unwavering guns pointing at her. And if these people were like Marc Disten, they'd hold them till their arms dropped off.

Remembering she and Thug fighting Scott's other 'Processed' people, she recalled how they hadn't felt pain, or fatigue. Not until they had nothing left.

So she kept her mouth shut. Holding onto Emma's words, that even a tiny advantage sometimes meant the difference between life and death.

"Continue, Five," Scott told Ankhet. "Why have you stopped? Information is needed for effective action."

"The incident is difficult to describe.... Thirty-nine days ago, the day after Abrams put the sacrificial Aztec dagger in the vault, something appeared inside. It began consuming artifacts and growing. It generated a... heat-generating barrier that affected only manufactured objects. The barrier could not be passed. It was on this occasion, while Abrams contacted someone for help, that the code he used to unlock the vault was observed. A helicopter soon arrived, carrying Leeth, a mage, and a cybernetically augmented man. Leeth stripped and was able to pass the heat barrier and enter. On the security camera, she was seen to grab the dagger and use it to cut apart and kill the... thing. She is deadly. She was very badly injured, but before Abrams and... Abrams and...."

She swayed, and Leeth saw her confusion. For a moment, even, felt hope.

"Abrams and Ankhet," Scott supplied.

Ankhet nodded and continued.   "Before Abrams, Ankhet and the other mage, a Dr Harmon, worked to heal her, Ankhet saw her imaginally. Ankhet was terrified: the girl is Death.   She also mended unnaturally quickly. Ankhet thought the girl would die, she was so badly injured. Large amounts of flesh regrew. Bone, too. Ankhet was disturbed."

Scott looked unimpressed. "Leeth has been healed between four hundred and four hundred fifty times. It is merely the Spencer Effect. Continue."

Leeth glared at her captors while Ankhet continued blabbing the details to Scott.

"But after the attack, after examining it, Abrams put the dagger back on a shelf in the vault by hand. He said its potency had been drained."

Ankhet stopped talking.   Leeth expected Scott to say something, but he gazed into the distance, apparently thinking. *That* couldn't be good.

"Why'd you wait until they were about to shoot me, to explain all that?" she asked Ankhet.

"Scott asked Leeth, not Five. Five merely corrected the false suggestion that Leeth begged for her life."

Despite the circumstances, Leeth rolled her eyes. *There it was: the trademark, annoying avoidance of 'I' and 'me'. Just like Marc Disten.* Oh! She looked at Scott, who obviously could still do magic. That must mean he hadn't been through his own Process. And just being *near* them didn't seem to cause him problems. Maybe they had to touch you? She filed that away for future reference, too.

But he appeared to have come to a decision. "So Leeth may have been the only one who could safely use the sacrificial dagger, but it is now drained of magic and worthless." He looked at her dismissively. "The dagger was of marginal interest. The other, undamaged items will provide sufficient funds. Since you are incapable of being Processed, you are a threat and nothing more."

"The dagger is *still* important! There are bad guys, really bad guys, we won't be able to defeat without that – *if* it hadn't been drained of thousands of years of, of *stored* magic. But I can recharge it!"

I can? She'd blurted the words without thinking, but

she *could* recharge it. It charged up by blood. *That* was part of the terrible secret she'd killed Luiz to bury: that blood – or death, really – could be used to make super powerful magic. Blood like Dr Scott's. She pictured her hand holding the gold hilt, the black edge slicing sweetly into his chest, carving out his heart. Joy thrilled through her. He was a powerful mage. That would make the sacrifice even better. *She knew.*

The image was clear, vivid. Exciting. Her breath sped up. She *had* to get the blade. With it, she'd kill them all. She'd win yet.

She saw Mr Abrams, despite his heavy-lidded stupor, react with dismay. But so what? Who cared what Mr Abrams... Mr Abrams....

Ohhhh.

She stared, stunned, seeing the elderly man with new eyes. It was like he glowed with honeyed light, from all the power locked up and hidden deep inside him. Vast power, power that dwarfed Scott's. Her heart pounded harder as she stared at him, mesmerized by the sight, straining against the ties binding her.

It inspired her, as she remembered her situation. The need to persuade them. "Mr Abrams is old. *So* old. Much older than he looks – that's just a disguise within a disguise. Don't you know who he *really* is?"

She was making this all up. Or was she dreaming? She felt strange. But Mr Abrams looked *really* good. She *needed* him. His blood.

Except, at her words, his eyes opened wide despite the drugs, this time in clear horror. And she knew, with a sudden shock, that every word she'd just spoken was true. She remembered a simple, carved stone bowl slipping toward the consuming coils of the alien *thing*, and a burst of absolute anguish shivering through the air. Anguish which had come from Mr Abrams, she'd somehow known, filling her with the necessity to save something unutterably precious.

She blinked, a hunger centuries deep surging through her, the hunger both inside and outside her. Somewhere quite close, her blade waited patiently on a shelf – a ravenous, hibernating bear smelling food nearby.

Dr Scott tilted his head, his gaze distant, as if once more calculating. "Five, fetch the blade. I have an idea for a valuable experiment."

Anticipation surged so fiercely her heart tried to leap from her chest.

Mr Abrams stared at her in horror, shocked into alertness.

Shaking his head.

CHAPTER 93

By the time Ankhet returned, frowning, with the dagger, and offered it to Scott, Mr Abrams had slumped back into his struggling daze.

The weapon wasn't dead. Just... weakened. *Hungry.* Leeth felt it, its mere presence setting her skin prickling. She watched it, hoping it was playing possum, waiting to drain Scott the moment he touched it.

Maybe he had the same thought. Instead of taking it, he gestured Ankhet to stop, while he examined it with that odd sort of unfocused mage stare.

She watched its two blue lapis lazuli eyes as if she could feel them staring back into his. She imagined it whispering to him, sharing its secrets. He looked from it to her, as if it had asked him to, and she felt a throb of pain as his eyes probed deep. She'd felt that ache before, a few times: from Godsson's gaze, and that handsome shaman, when she was little. And from Mr Abrams.

Scott's expression changed from doubt to interest. "You are a very physical person, aren't you?" he said. "So it would be foolish in the extreme to hand you a mystical weapon of unknown power and not expect you to use it to attack, yes?"

Bending to the floor, he picked up a shell casing. Taking out a pocketknife, he moved around behind her, and she felt two fingers probing gently against her spine through the seat's open back. "If you don't wish to be paralyzed, remain perfectly still."

Sharp pain sliced between his fingers and she sucked in a breath. She felt something pushed in against her spine, agony spearing from it. Then a steady pressure of fingertips and the warmth of healing.

At her first movement she froze, feeling something sharp inside her, jammed against her spine. Even a tiny change to her posture fired red hot barbs stabbing out from it.

He stepped back in front of her. "That will limit your physicality," he told her, then moved to the far side of the room. "You are accustomed to pain. You deal with it. The pain you feel now is different, however. It's your body telling you one wrong movement, one wrong twist, will sever nerves that will paralyze you from the waist down."

He looked smug. "Ankhet, loosen her left wrist and toss

her the weapon."

The other three still held their guns trained on her.

"No."

Surprised by Ankhet's refusal, Leeth started to turn, stopping instantly as agony flared from her spine.

Scott and the others, however, did turn.

Ankhet stepped into view. "That would be foolish. She is too deadly."

"You worry unnecessarily, Five," Scott said. "She will have difficulty merely walking. One wrong movement and she will collapse, crippled."

"No. You are not thinking clearly. You should kill her. Instead you seek excuses to keep her alive. She will do something unexpected."

"Your thinking is colored by memories of your fears, Five. I have just rendered her harmless. She can barely move. We have guns, and I have spells."

"No. You do not understand. You are Unprocessed. Unprocessed people desire her. She fascinates. Ankhet was Abrams's student for over three years. Yet Abrams saw more value in her than in Ankhet. You learned she has been ordered to kill you. You correctly planned to end her threat by killing her, or by Processing her so she might aid you.

"Yet after she refused to surrender, and had to be shot, and died, you healed her: to Process her. That was rational: it is true she would be a formidable tool. But you could not Process her. And now you plan to put a mystical weapon in her hand, because she says she can recharge it. She will recharge it through your death. You do not need the artifact. There are sufficient others to sell. Your thinking is irrational."

Scott didn't respond.

"Wiser to sacrifice her, then Abrams."

Scott appeared to consider her words.

"You don't have all the information you need," Leeth broke in, knowing she argued for her life. "Without that obsidian blade, that thing the other night would have consumed every artifact here, and after that, probably you and Mr Abrams and all of us. And then just kept on growing. We don't know who created it, or how many more there are. We *need* the dagger for next time. And you need *me* to wield the dagger."

"Those are mere assertions," Ankhet said. "Other wielders might be found. Other weapons might work."

"*Might*. But would you gamble the fate of the whole world on that?"

She saw Scott cast some spell, felt the tickle around the edge of her thoughts so familiar from her childhood, and effortlessly split her attention, focusing the surface on what she saw, how she felt. Hiding her thoughts. He blinked, slowly, dismissed the spell, and cast a second.

"You believe the fate of the world rests with this blade?" he asked.

She started to nod, then froze at the stab of pain from her spine. "Yes. Probably. But it needs recharging."

"And sacrificing Abrams to it will do so?"

Mr Abrams's face held an expression of sick dismay.

"Oh, yes," she replied, the hunger to feed, swelling. *Abrams... Abrams would be a feast.*

Knowledge held in the matrix of volcanic black glass washed back into her, of the other foes waiting; how they could be overcome with ease, together. Blue stone eyes stared into hers, filling with dark life. She sensed a strange kind of movement, underneath everything. Something slow but unstoppable. A behemoth stirring.

Once again she felt the golden warmth of nourishment held just out of reach.

'*Tezcatlipoca.*'

"What? What did you say?"

She blinked, confused for a moment by Scott's question.

Mr Abrams's eyes had gone wide and white, staring like something had just badly scared him. "No. Leeth. Aztec... Death...." Then his eyes dropped shut, his head lolling forward.

She had trouble focusing, his shape no longer making sense. What was inside him overwhelmed it. And she was dying, literally *dying* from hunger. The food looked *so good*. Far better than Scott. The others... ugh. She needed to feed! Her head turned toward her dagger. Why weren't they feeding her? Banked fury roiled.

"This plan is reckless," Ankhet said. "Time is short. If the dagger is important, this one should sacrifice Leeth, then Abrams. The group should then take all the artifacts and leave."

Leeth felt strange, like she'd just missed something. She shook herself and froze again, the pain making her blink. Ankhet had been saying something about 'this one.' The words reminded her how much she'd learned to hate Marc Disten speaking like that.

"No," Scott was saying, "it would be unwise for a Processed to perform a sacrifice."

A sacrifice, yes. She screwed her eyes shut, then open again. Had she dozed off? She replayed his words, sure he'd just revealed something important. *Ah ha! I was right, they do screw up magic!* She kept her expression neutral though, as Scott glanced at her.

"Then you should perform the sacrifices," Ankhet told Scott.

"It would be foolish to risk myself, when we know Leeth can wield it. You worry unnecessarily," he said, indicating the three guns trained on her. "We will deal with her if she tries to get creative. Especially since one aggressive move will cripple her. Your logic is clouded. Loosen her left wrist and toss the dagger to her."

"No. You said you would Process her, or kill her. You, too, have been seduced by her. Your logic is flawed. She will kill everyone here. This life holds value. Two's idea holds value."

Ankhet tossed the dagger, hilt first, into Abrams's lap.

As it fell, the scalloped razor edge turned, slicing through the dark linen of his trousers to draw blood. The elderly man cried out, rigid with a pain far beyond what the cut should have caused. The hilt stood vertical, its blue stone eyes gleaming wickedly as it teetered, before falling, as if reluctant. The chunky gold hilt lay glinting between his legs, its eyes staring hungrily.

Leeth saw the path, finally, to freedom, and let the golden warmth fill her.

Yes!

She was hardly aware of Ankhet turning and walking from the room. Of Scott watching her go, saying nothing.

The woman's footsteps faded.

"Two, loosen Leeth's left wrist and stand well back."

Leeth felt a thrill. It would make more sense to order one of the men to do that. That way they could take her in a crossfire if she tried anything. It meant that even drugged, they thought Mr Abrams was a bigger threat than her.

She was barely aware of the woman fumbling at her wrist. Instead she focused on Mr Abrams slumped in his chair, so rich and full, death's dagger in his aged lap. Visible through sliced cloth, blood welled up and shrank away, pulsing stark and livid against his pale and papery thigh, in time with his heart.

Mr Abrams swelled in her eyes, as if he grew closer. He smelled of alder and earth, looming until he was the only thing in the room, filling her vision. She noted the wispy threads of wires running to monitoring points, heard the surge and hum of pumps and oxygenators. Traced the tubing running toward his back.

"Well? Do what you promised."

She blinked, the room snapping back into view, Mr Abrams suddenly normal size, but shaking his head, trying to work his lips, his expression one of dread.

Feverish, she worked her left wrist free, quickly, holding her spine rigid and unmoving. With her left hand she untied her right, even as she felt the yearning to simply *cut* instead, burning at her fingertips.

But when she tried to bend enough to untie an ankle, shooting pain froze her. Very gingerly, she eased back in her chair, panting. Looked up at Scott.

"I can't reach down to untie myself."

Scott stared at her. "We do have time, but not for games. Remove the ropes within... ten seconds, or I will have Two, Three and Four shoot you."

"But I can't bend down to untie them!"

He said nothing.

Dammit. Did he know? Stretching out her invisible claws, she gingerly lowered her hand, and sliced. The ankle ropes fall away.

He didn't look surprised. "Now the sacrifice. If what you said was true, you can console yourself it is for the greater good."

I think I hate him even more than Marc Disten. Calming her breathing, she focused inward on her body, on her center of balance. Then, millimeter by millimeter, managing each movement more carefully than if she walked a tightrope, she stood.

It took a full minute, tears running down her cheeks from the pain of each microscopic mistake.

Then she began the even more Herculean task of taking the twenty shuffling steps separating her from Mr Abrams. While the blade yearned and urged her forward, and Mr Abrams gaped in horror.

CHAPTER 94

If she'd thought simply standing had been an ordeal, the journey to Mr Abrams was a nightmare. Sweat ran down her forehead, half blinding her. Though she learned she could wipe it away if she kept her arm close to her body and moved it slowly enough.

The closer she came to Mr Abrams, the larger the dagger in his lap swelled in her vision, until finally, it filled it entirely. But crouching to take it would be as hard as descending a rain-slick building with numb and freezing hands.

She swallowed.

Keeping her back perfectly straight, she sank first to her haunches – an exercise in silent agony. From there, she reached out, finally, to the armrests of his chair, laying her arms over each of his. They quivered.

She refused to meet his eyes.

Steadying herself, she paused, panting, collecting her reserves.

Behind her, keeping out of her sight and no doubt watching imaginally, stood Dr Scott. At last, prepared, she raised her head, meeting old eyes dazed with drugs but still jerking open in terror. She slid her right hand down to his thigh, stopping just short of the blade now screaming at her to wrap her fingers around it.

"I'm sorry," she told him. Picturing where each captor stood, their sight lines, she *stretched,* fighting the stab of pain. One flick of a fingertip sliced tubing while others stabbed down, piercing his skin for distraction.

Mr Abrams cried out, his chair urgently beeping, before a wrinkled hand spasmed and pressed the control to cut the warning off. His eyes widened in shock.

"Sorry, I'm sorry," she cried, bracing herself on his lap, taking her weight. Gathering herself for the final blow. Knowing Scott watched, she embraced the agony of her tortured body, allowing herself to sob from the pain.

She half expected him to berate her, to ask why she delayed. That he didn't, confirmed he was watching imaginally, and had Seen what her short journey had cost her. Maybe he even sensed how the dagger filled her mind's eye, its blue orbs trying to snare hers, its hilt already warmed and calling for her hand. Her child, begging for food.

It waited for the sacrifice, life yielded for life, death providing life for those who followed. The eternal cycle.

But Leeth waited for more. Still panting, focusing on the pain from her spine, she kept her eyes on Mr Abrams's, rolling hers and letting her lids droop in exaggerated mimicry of his, hoping he'd take her cue. She welcomed the yearning for her weapon, letting it fill her and dominate her thoughts. She fought the torture of her body, using it to mask the flicker of hope hiding beneath.

As she was now, she couldn't defeat Scott and his three Marc Disten clones. But if she could just deal with *them*, she'd bet on Mr Abrams over Scott, any day.

Hope never dies.

But she would. She doubted Mr Abrams would heal her, after this.

Sliding her left hand from his arm, she lowered it to his lap, and then somehow her fingers were curling around the golden hilt, unbidden.

Hunger roared through her in an ecstasy of triumph. She fought to ride the wave, holding her spine rigid as she slowly stood, small noises of pain escaping clenched teeth.

Both men at Mr Abrams's shoulders had pulled back as far as they could while still gripping him. One gun pointed at her head, the other at her heart.

The dagger in her left hand tugged forward, as though Mr Abrams had a powerful magnet buried in his chest. She raised it high.

"Goodbye, Mr Abrams."

She'd *intended* to drop the dagger. But found she *couldn't.*

Both hands sliced up and out, her back shrieking as agony tore through her, her legs failing. As the two men crumpled, blood geysering from severed throats, she snatched one falling pistol while the woman at her back began firing.

From behind, a truly massive sleep spell detonated. Her eyes rolled back in her head.

Abrams, reading its pattern, shielded himself a moment before it inundated him. Frantically, he burned the last of the sedative from his bloodstream, fear flooding through him. He gazed up at Scott, shaking his head. "That was a mistake. You've knocked *Leeth* unconscious." Percepting the dark thundercloud riding her aura, he saw his worst fears realized.

On the ground, her body dragged itself around on its forearms while Scott's last remaining ally, the female, coolly fired into it, again and again, tracking up the body. Leeth's head jerked suddenly aside, the last shot passing through the space it had occupied. Then the arm holding Leeth's gun rose and shot the woman between the eyes.

Scott, now behind his own shield spell, disagreed. "She doesn't look unconscious to me, old man." With a gesture, a wave of force rippled the air, splintering floorboards as it flashed across the room.

It washed over Abrams, outlining a protective sphere.

"That's not Leeth," the old mage told him.

Leeth, her eyes now fixed on Scott, dropped the gun as the woman toppled. Unprotected by Abrams's shield, Leeth remained strangely untouched amidst the destruction wreaked by his blast.

Scott, frowning, saw her eyes had changed, both iris and pupil solid black, the sclera changing from white to sky blue, the color intensifying. *Glowing.* Both eyes stared into his. And she still held the dagger.

And then, impossibly, she floated up off the floor, facing him, her legs dangling.

He vanished.

Moments later a fireball exploded around her, setting the room ablaze. Abrams, mind racing, sent his electric chair into reverse, backing from the room. Imaginally, Leeth's aura was a fiery ravenous black. It swallowed the fireball like a storm extinguishing a match. He Saw Scott's invisibility spell, a moment before it too faded from his other-worldly gaze. His eyebrows lifted, impressed, even while mentally cursing the clever but unwise magician.

Abrams silently thanked the mage as he hammered spell after spell at Leeth's body, shaking the room and drawing its Host's attention. He quietly inched out.

It had to be exhausted, surely? The 'alien' incursion had weakened the blade, and the entity tied to it had been quiescent a thousand years. Five and a half centuries ago it had stirred, at the last moment falling back into slumber. He winced at the certainty that here, tonight, it would soon be feeding. And after that, coming for *him*.

Finally reaching the doorway, he spun his chair to make his escape – and the room behind fell silent.

He froze, not daring to turn to look behind. Shaking, heart racing, with blood pressure soaring from the disconnected drip, he could only wait, to see which prey the thing chose.

He *prayed*.

Then sagged, when the wave of oppressive presence faded. Hunting Scott.

Concentrating, with a not quite malicious pleasure – and a single Word – he Sealed his house. From every side came the slamming of shutters, reinforced by the strongest physical bindings he knew. He felt the energy flood from the house's heartstone, powering up the spell – and neatly removing one more food source from play.

Accelerating away, he retreated into his mansion, heading for the vault. He had to find some way to deal with this latest catastrophe. The moment Leeth had severed his drip, his chair had summoned emergency help. That meant innocent medical personnel were already scrambling for a chopper – lambs summoned to slaughter. He needed a way to stop her.

Hopefully, too, before his house burned down.

CHAPTER 95

Scott needed the wealth of the artifacts his team had collected, that lay packed and ready for removal almost within arm's reach – but he needed to stay alive even more.

Feeling an uncharacteristic sense of apprehension, he retreated, invisible, inaudible, and airborne, to the front doors. All while his mind worked to fit the unexpected new data into his world model. *Well, you wanted a god to study.* But he had not – as yet – worked out the protocols needed to safely trap one.

He calculated, groaning as he saw that the better tactic would have been to do nothing, rather than blast it with spells. It would have fed on Abrams first.

The front door in sight, he considered. Once he had escaped, once the god-ridden girl had devoured Abrams, he saw little chance it would simply vacate the premises and leave the treasures for him to return and collect.

Even for him, it might take days to design constructs sufficient to bind the force he'd just confronted. Melisande d'Artelle had done something of that order to produce the Second World Storm, though, so it *was* possible.

He reached the front door, its lock broken by One when they had entered earlier, and grasped the handle. It should have turned, the door opened. Instead, it refused to budge, a carving in a rock wall.

He frowned and tried again, tugging harder.

Behind him, he felt a dark intensity building. Ignoring it, he shifted his gaze to the Imaginal to examine the stubborn mechanism.

Eyes widening at what he saw, his gaze rose, following the intricate tracery of potency now woven through doors, windows... every outer surface.

He spun, silent in his inaudibility construct, to see the girl floating down the corridor straight toward him, her unnerving blue-on-black eyes still alight, locked on him. To the Sight, she sat at the center of an obsidian storm cloud, dark spiral arms reaching out to him.

Holding his nerve, he recalculated quickly. But the unknowns in his formulae highlighted how little he knew of the layout of the large house, and the danger of being cornered. Left, or right?

Time had run out – she was on him. He had to guess. He darted left.

Behind him, he heard harsh snuffles, huffed out then sniffed back in. They softened into a sound halfway between a long, drawn out croak and a shutter slowly ratcheting open. Then silence, creeping closer... until a sudden full-throated animal's snarl. For the first time in years he felt his pulse race.

He'd entered a spacious kitchen. Copper saucepans and Japanese blades hung displayed for ease of use, incongruous beside the gleaming sleek curves of a late model chefbot, one aqua light blinking in standby mode. Flying past the long central food preparation counter he wrenched open the far door, glad for his silence spell, hands shaking. Behind him the feeling of black pressure gathered, relentless.

Without turning to look back, he rushed through the door and slammed it shut. It should grant him an extra second; perhaps as many as five. Heart hammering, to his right a passage led to a back door with narrow, stained glass panes.

Floodlights outside still burned across the mansion's lawns, holding the encroaching darkness at bay. But across those panes too, he saw the deceptively fine tracery of Abrams's reinforcing magic. A physical shield spell, but taken to an extreme degree. The glass looked old though, and thin.

Concentrating, he focused a massive blast of force on a single pane. Corridor walls cracked as the spell arrowed down it, and only his noise canceling spell protected him from the rebounding shock wave. But when it was over, the glass remained unbroken.

Automatically, he recalculated his earlier threat assessment of the older man, including this fresh datum, sucking in his breath at the index score produced.

It did however present a simple solution to his problem: lead his hunter back toward what must be a far more tempting – if challenging – target than he himself.

The corridor ahead led to the unyielding back door, then turned to the right. He moved in that direction.

Or tried to.

Looking down, he saw a ribbon of black smoke curled around his invisible feet. He felt his face flush as he turned in the air, heart thumping now in his chest like a drumbeat of doom.

The girl licked her lips, and then spoke, syllables that popped and spat, her voice throatier, raw with hunger. Instinctively, he recast the spell he'd tried to spear through the back door, this time targeting her. His skin chilled at the speed her arm moved.

The energies vanished, sucked into her hand, this time not even damaging the corridor it raced down.

She smiled, and he felt himself tugged closer, as though he were nothing more than a worm on a hook.

Desperately, he tried the simple sleep spell, pouring everything he had into it.

Imaginal spiral arms swallowed that spell, too, as she floated closer, purring. Her legs dangled uselessly below her, blood dripping toward the floor from multiple bullet wounds... and disappearing, somehow swallowed before reaching the ground. But her teeth were bared now, her upper lip pulled back and her mouth opening wide.

Then she was on him, and he had nowhere to run.

One small hand lashed out to his throat, pinning him up against a wood-paneled wall with a strength beyond that of any of his creations. Kicking and punching, he grabbed her arm as she raised the obsidian dagger.

With his free hand he struck a face as unyielding as leather, punched a side of rigid muscles. The banked glow of her eyes rekindled, blazing in delight.

Grabbing her wrist with both hands, he pushed back against the approaching weapon with all his strength.

For all the effect it had, he might have been *helping* her slide the black blade into his heart.

His vision flared white.

In his vault, Abrams heard the death scream. It rose and fell, echoing and re-echoing through every room and corridor of the house.

And then there was only silence.

CHAPTER 96

A dream of floating. She was beyond ravenous, and some-one had hidden her meal. Drifting down wooden tunnels she pushed through tissue-thin walls that blocked her way, pulling them apart as she closed on her food.

At a large circular iron door she came to a halt. Behind it, in a metal chamber, her offering waited. She studied the heavy door, looking inside its structure: iron encasing a material like limestone. She traced massive metal rods, locked in place by a clever mechanism of gears and cogs, in turn held frozen by magnetism born from tightly-twisted spirals of controlled lightning. Ingenious. With a touch, she swallowed the lightning, killing the magnetic forces, then pushed apart the heavy puzzle pieces with her mind.

Spinning the circular handle unlocked the massive door.

She pulled it open. Then blinked in surprise.

Inside, the space still reverberated, reality itself bruised from some Greater Working a mere heartbeat ago – less than two lunar cycles. Coincidence? Surely not. Such timing suggested a trap for her. She paused to sense more deeply.

A recent attempt had been made, using sheer force, to reverse a slightly older Working. Breathtaking in its magnitude – a *billion* human deaths? – yet delicate. Performed the year this body had been born. But unlike the subtlety of that decades-old surgery, this recent assault had been brutal, leaving Reality weakened.

A billion deaths. Did this new world hold so many people, now? How was that possible? But of more interest was the one who had worked Reality.

She searched the brain she used, finding a name and a strange concept – Melisande d'Artelle, and 'aliens' – bound up in images of succulent power. The desire to feed roared over her, until the memories showed that one had died years before, a delicacy lost.

All past, now.

This was not a trap.

On the threshold she paused, whispers of other memories drawing her attention. A wolf; dreams of a dragon; one man she named Uncle, and hated; and another, Gods-son. Another named Eagle. But closer still sat the ancient now before her, in his clever chair that moved. Revived by his blood she would hunt down the other death cheaters. And feed.

After them, the priests of the feeble Christ god would follow. Five hundred extra solar cycles her exile had lasted, thanks to those cowards and fools. Their reward would be her vengeance, a feast of extinction.

She stepped in. The sacrifice waited in his cunning wheeled chair, surrounded by shelves holding a scattering of objects of power. One, the strongest and gentlest, rested in its lap. His lap.

He was a magnificent creature. She had never seen his like, not in thousands of cycles. His sacrifice would replenish her, restarting the proper rituals of death and life.

His eyes held fear. Like so many before him, he would not go lightly into her vast dark. He had evaded his ending far beyond what was right. Although this one seemed strangely unsullied by his stolen centuries, still she felt a burn of anger.

One tiny, foreign part of her, her unconscious host, begged to allow him to continue. But her need was both greater, and for the greater good.

She drifted to the ancient to harvest him, raising the delicate claw made of her own frozen black blood.

But unlike her last offering, who had gifted her with a hunt, this one, though fearful, did not flee. With reverence, he lifted the truly elegant working of potency from his lap, frozen in its form of a stone chalice.

Ready to harvest him, she paused once more, alert.

He fashioned a shaping, which he held out for her study. A simple Healing, she saw. Inclining her head, she accepted the offering as her right.

He spoke words of sad regret in a tongue she did not know. A part of her recognized the words: a farewell.

Unexpectedly, he poured the regeneration through the raised stone cup – but it only multiplied and deepened it. Still no traps. Reaching out, she absorbed the offering, letting it flow through her unfiltered. The wave of swift repair roared through her body, the fiery pain recalling the heat of the Mother.

From the waist down, sensation returned. She felt her legs – but more, felt that tiny foreign part of her awaken.

"Goodbye, Leeth. I'm so sorry."

The ancient man, Mr Abrams, touched her black claw, and via that bond pulled apart the world, the lines of his face sketching hope and regret.

Leeth felt Mr Abrams do *something*. A massive force grabbed the dagger and flung it through the tear in space. But the dagger was her.

She saw his eyes widen in shock as she fell with it.

CHAPTER 97

She stood in a realm of featureless gray, unsure of distance, uncertain if she was even really seeing.

"Oh man, not again!"

She *thought* she was standing, but on what, she couldn't say, or see.

As she turned her head, a now-familiar agony stabbed up through her spine. She remembered Scott bending down and picking up a bullet casing, cutting her open and healing it inside to press against the nerve.

I need to cut it out. At the thought, she realized she still held the obsidian dagger in her left hand. Her muscles twitched it toward her spine.

"Oh, no. Not using *that!*"

'*Oh, yes.*'

She stilled. Staring down past her nose, she tried to see her own lips. Knowing *she'd* been the one who'd spoken those words.

'*Dedicate yourself to me.*'

Instead of arguing, she reached around to her back, gently probing until she felt the hard edge of the metal casing beneath her skin. Stretching her claws, she delicately cut, digging out the cartridge with fingers soon slick with blood, and tossed it away.

'*Unwise.*'

A ribbon of night spiraled out from her to the bloody object, furling around it like a frog's tongue. That is, if a frog's tongue was meters long and made of black smoke.

It curled back in toward her, dropping the casing back on the ground, with no sound. At her feet, the steel gleamed like silver, scoured clean.

She spun around, but found no one there. Looked down, but saw no shadow. Looked up, and saw no light source.

'*Here, your Will shapes reality,*' her own voice advised her.

It had to be the black dagger. She held it before her, shifting her grip so the hilt was upmost, its molded face and two lapis lazuli eyes staring back into hers.

It smiled, and she flinched and almost dropped it.

"*You're* the one talking to me, aren't you?"

She felt herself laugh, and say '*No, I am.*'

Which would be a touch too creepy at the best of times.

Which this wasn't.

"Marcie!" she screamed, remembering how her friend had heard her, once before, the last time this had happened, and helped her back to... back to the real world. Then she remembered Mr Abrams saying goodbye just before sending her here. Somehow. He'd been sad. And scared.

Of her.

She closed her eyes, working it out. *Because I'm possessed, aren't I?*

'*I would say, Hosting. Let us go back, so I may take nourishment.*'

And there it was. The reason she couldn't go back.

The hand holding the gold weapon sliced the air. She felt space itself part, with a kind of rubbery tugging that satisfied like picking at an old scab.

Instinctively, she wrestled back control of her limb and reversed the cut, *willing* the tear closed, remembering what it had told her earlier about shaping reality.

She laughed, which only got creepier each time it happened. '*You are a quick study. But when you shape, you also Call those who dwell here.*'

She felt a weird kind of twitching and tugging. Looking around her, she saw three, no, four, wispy... strands...? threading off into the nothingness.

'*Oh.*'

She got the distinct impression she'd surprised her... hitchhiker. "*Oh*? What does 'Oh' mean?"

It didn't answer, and she concentrated, trying to see again the pale, or maybe *translucent* strands she'd seen a moment before. Choosing one, she reached out to it. At its touch she felt a surge of confidence and an urge to reach inside and tear the intruder from her.

I can probably actually do *that here, too!*

'*I wouldn't.*'

"Oh yeah? Why not? Because it'd *work*, and you're scared."

She chuckled, then outright laughed. '*No, little Huntress: because you might slay yourself. Making you perhaps the briefest Archetype to have ever flickered into existence. Know that I am Tezcatlipoca, mightiest of all gods. God of many things – from the night sky to the earth, from beauty to war, from sorcery to the storms that lay all to waste.'*

"Don't forget, god of boasting." She felt a kind of surge of anger, felt it fuming, but she – it – said nothing.

She reached out to another of the faint strands, and... her thoughts steadied, focused into crystal clarity, and re-arranged themselves. One: she was possessed by an Aztec deity. Two: ejected here by Abrams, because... three: because she had been about to kill him and feed him to Tezcatlipoca. Four: she could use the deity to go back. Five: its power would be useful. Question: cost?

"How many sacrifices per day do you require?" she asked.

The translucent strand she held swelled between her fingers. Something vast, industrious and relentless surged down it. The twist of air changed in her grip, taking on a metallic, segmented form. It was coming for her, coming to join-

Her hand opened, jerking free of the quicksilver twist of air.

'By the Five Suns, what foul thing was that?'

"Uh..." She stared into the gray, her thoughts tumbling out of their horrid cold clarity, the passionless calculations that had passed for thought.

'Bring them, then!' it ranted. *'Call your Deep Kin – your Huntress, your Machine, your Seductress – I will slay them all!'*

It was *inside* her, speaking through her. Which was how she knew she'd somehow scared the ancient thing. Or, *she* hadn't – rather, the thing she'd sensed coming for her had. "Okay, I get it: don't touch. Don't 'call' things to me from the vasty deep. *Juice* dude, chill out."

Inside, she felt... really peculiar. She could still sense 'things' approaching, juggernauts fumbling blindly toward her from somewhere deep inside the gray. She sensed time was running out, and that she really shouldn't stay here. Despite all that, she felt herself relax; then realized she was feeling the thing inside her unruffle its feathers.

"You live here, don't you? This is your 'place'. I want you out of me. What do you even *want* with me?"

'We can help one another. Help the world. Restore the natural order. Defeat your enemies.'

"Yeah, right. You were going to eat Mr Abrams."

Anger surged, but inside her, not *from* her. She was starting to get the feel of when it was the thing inside her, rather than she herself. Hmm. If she could *feel* it, could she somehow get a *grip* on it? Just *force* it out?

'No. We have killed, and are bonded. And you owe me a debt: you drained my conduit.'

Something about that seemed suspicious. She looked at the dagger. It didn't seem quite as... empty, as before. With a growl, and from long practice, she split her attention, hiding her inner thoughts from it. "I'm not helping you eat Mr Abrams."

Again a pulse of anger. *'It would balance the debt.'*

"Too bad. No. I won't allow it. He's needed." She wouldn't budge on that.

'Do you think him your friend? *It was* he *who sent you here. He is one of those who cheat death. His, longer overdue than most. Such kind are schemers and plotters.'*

Her skin prickled, as if a storm was building, or maybe *approaching*. A stillness filled the world, imminent and oppressive in its weight. And then she felt a change, and knew she was suddenly moving – not that she understood *how* she knew that. Maybe, from the way the pressure eased. Feeling something wet trickling down her upper lip, she dabbed at her nose, her fingertip coming away bloody. She frowned at it.

"Yes, he *is* a friend. And unless you promise me you won't eat him, or harm him, I won't even *try* to go back... there. Out. Home. Whatever. Not ever."

She felt it think about that. While it did, she wiped her upper lip again. "Why am I bleeding?"

'Because you are a weak vessel, and hard to move at this speed.'

About to snap back at it – *'We're running away from something?'* – she intuited it was trying to distract her. "I need your promise," she said, instead.

Her mouth growled. *'I give my word not to eat or harm your Mr Abrams unless he tries to harm me.'*

In its grudging anger, she sensed honesty. "I guess that will do."

'I will need other sacrifices. But you are a killer – it is one reason we fit. Dedicate those deaths to me.'

She knew who she *would* like to sacrifice: the Doctor. But something about this whole deal made her hesitate. "Ah, I think we need to talk about that properly, first. Come out of me, so I can see your face."

'No. *If I leave you, I will not speak your tongue; nor you, mine. Why do you hesitate? Has mankind forgotten that the circle must turn? All die. Death feeds life. Each death feeds those who follow.'*

"I guess. But you'll get out of me when we go back? *Can* you take us back?"

'Yes. *You can be sent back to your proper place.'*

"And then you'll leave me."

'No. *You face terrible, subtle foes. You* need *me. If I leave you, we could not speak.'*

"Yeah, well, you can teach me to speak your language, then we can." She sensed anger, but it didn't respond. Not through her mouth. Which *still* had a kind of, 'out to lunch, gone mad' feeling to it. "Agreed? You take *us* back, then leave me?"

'Yes. *And in turn I have your promise: you will gift your kills to me.'*

"Look, I'm not so sure about that part. Mr Abrams sent you away for a reason."

'Simply *because he fears me. He is not your friend. He hides truth from you. Abrams is not even his name. He has lived far, far beyond his span. As with all such, his fear of death has grown with each passing century. I have been gone too long. Mankind needs to unlearn its fear of death.'*

"Ah, I guess. Maybe." People sure did seem scared of dying.

'You kill. *Do you kill for good cause?'*

"Of course! But not everyone kills. In fact, hardly any-one does. I'm kind of unusual." It was true. And hardly anybody *appreciated* her killing, either. Even James and Emma didn't seem to always approve.

'Life *is* built *on death! All* life kills! *All* life eats! *You know this.'*

"Plants don't."

She sensed anger. 'All life that moves.'

"Hngh. I guess."

'Yet you are judged for this. Rejected. Feared.'

She couldn't deny it. Even in the Department... Would anyone *ever* understand her?

'*Your people don't understand you. They care not for you. To them, you are merely a tool. But I understand you. I see the darkness in your soul. An echo of my own.*

'*Return with me. Together, we will restore Mankind to truth. Help them face their fears. They will grow as they should have, relearning the nobility of sacrifice. Re-earning the gifts of the gods. I saw little of your world, yet I felt its pain. Felt its air weeping, its oceans, choking. Felt the echoes of untold deaths, squandered. Untold lives, yet so* many *merely existing, not living.*

'*Besides, child, you need my help.*' She felt her shoulders shrug. '*You are special, a worthy Host, but you face enemies who will challenge us both, even joined.*'

"Yeah, well, E... *people I respect* think I might be able to do that on my own."

'*Might. You need me, not those others. They do not care for you. They should not decide who lives and who dies. You* should. *There is much I can teach you. How to shatter any wall. How to expand your reach with essence weavings. How to summon spirits and command them. Together, we will be stronger, faster. Wiser. Better. You would no longer be alone. I would no longer be alone. Together, we can cleanse the world of evil. None could stand against us.*

'*Leeth: will you be my partner?*'

She felt the potency behind the promise. Its power sang through her blood and bones. Utter confidence, certain of itself. But that belief, even some of the words... she'd heard them before.

"No." *I am so over people telling me what I need.*

For long seconds the air rang with a kind of a shocked and silent stillness. Then a storm of anger thundered through the gray. 'No*?!*'

"No. I have a hunch that... people I trust, kind of work to *stop* gods returning to the world."

'A hunch*? You reject the gift of a* god, *on a* hunch*?*'

"Yeah, well, I have real good intuition."

For a while, nothing happened. But she wasn't kidding. Her mind was made up. Maybe it sensed that.

'Then you will stay here until you are consumed. I end my protection of you. I will not send you back.'

From her mouth and eyes, from every pore of her skin, furious black ribbons of molten obsidian and darkest storm clouds spiraled out. Whipping and spinning in angry arcs, they coalesced finally into a raging hurricane that towered over her.

Maybe she should have been terrified, but it was actually a relief just to see *something* again in all the unrelieved gray. The thing also reminded her of that other leviathan, the one hidden behind Marc Disten. She'd smashed *that* into a million pieces. She could do it with this one, too.

She hoped.

With a thrill, she let her claws unfurl. '*What you Will here, is*', *it had said. And it'd be pretty chill to kill a death god.* She swallowed, feeling her pulse accelerate.

Knowing it had been so desperate for her help to return, made her certain she'd made the right decision. Which gave her another idea.

"Hey, how about a different deal?" She lifted her left hand, still holding its obsidian blade, up into the 'sky'.

This time the sound came from outside her.

"SPEAK."

That wasn't what it *said* – the meaning kind of flowed into her mind like an echo, from the dagger. She winced at the sheer volume, then rolled her eyes. "If you send me back, I *will* take your dagger with me. At least that way, you have a chance someone might make offerings to you, right?"

"YOU DARE SET TERMS FOR *ME*?"

"Ah, yeah, I do." She shrugged. "Look, I found my way out of this place once before." Even as she said that, she had a weird memory of talking to Godsson in a small room that somehow reminded her of here. She shrugged it aside. Probably just some dream. "I'll figure out how to do it again." *I hope.*

"YOU *DARE?* I HAVE TASTED YOUR *BLOOD*, GIRL!"

"Yeah, well... and *I* know you like to shrink down and hide inside girls!"

"ENOUGH! I NEED NOT YOUR AGREEMENT!"

Something wrapped around her, coiled through her, and she felt a shifting, felt it sliding inside, rejoining her.

"No!" Her right hand flashed to her chest, directly over her heart, pressing down with her invisible blades, drawing blood. She *would* die rather than let this thing back into the world.

A pity no one would ever know.

She prepared to kill herself.

The grip released with a howl of frustration. A hurricane exploded around her, but this time with physical force, ripping the blade from her hand. She let it go, gladly, and prepared to dive into that storm, her claws stretching out, already seeking its heart. She could almost taste how to do it. Feeling a surge of glee, her spirit soared, anticipating the Hunt.

This time, its weird shouty syllables meant nothing at all to her, though she sensed surprised approval.

The wind spun her away. She landed, crouching, feet spread, ready to launch herself back up into it.

Instead, from the sky, two small blue eyes in a hilt of gold, a cruel black obsidian shard with an edge as sharp as her own, spun down and fell at her feet. The dagger.

More too-loud foreign words boomed out, but somehow she knew it had agreed.

"You don't have to shout, you know," she said. But then, instead of bending down, she *willed* the sacrificial dagger to float up into her hand. Wanting to jump in delight when it did exactly that.

"I WHISPER, LEETH, JUST FOR YOU."

"Hnh. Well, I'm ready when you are. But no tricks,"

she warned it. "We have a deal, right? You help me get back, in return for me taking your dagger with me."

"AGREED."

The hurricane swept around her, bringing her into its eerie heart, but staying outside her this time.

She felt a weird sense of the world *pushing* in on her, remembered Marcie's voice calling to her, a rope to pull her up, and shut her eyes and *willed* herself away.

Hoping she wasn't, somehow, still being tricked.

CHAPTER 99

"And then she vanished?" Although Harmon's tone dripped with sarcasm, he appeared distracted, his attention elsewhere.

"Yes," Abrams said, "and while I helped, I suspect it's partly your fault, Doctor."

That earned a glare, Harmon turning to face him. "*My* fault?"

Abrams shrugged. "You sought to connect her, at some fundamental level, to an Archetype? Well, I judge your experiment a success." He held back the rest of it, however: that there was more than a single connection.

Little Brother, the third person in the room, finished repairing the life-chair tubing that Leeth had severed to end Mr Abrams's sedation, and looked up. For several seconds he glowered at the Doctor, before remembering what Leeth had said about mind reading. He schooled his expression. "She's really gone? Will she be coming back?"

Neither the Doctor nor Mr Abrams even glanced his way. They just faced one another, the older man pensive. "A better question is, how to deal with her if she *does* return. Our worst fears have been realized. I tried to send away just the Aztec deity; but it had indeed bonded to her, and took her with it. Which means Leeth remains a stepping stone back, for it."

The EMTs and fire brigade had finished their work. Agents Drexler and Havoc of the Bureau for Internal Development were somewhere nearby. They seemed hopeful they'd been able to forestall the police investigation that should have been triggered after the EMTs had called in a multiple homicide. *Five* counts of death by violent causes.

Abrams, facing the doorway, made a warning gesture, and Harmon and Little Brother fell silent.

Drexler, the male agent, re-entered the room. Despite having his evening's entertainment ruined, hauled out here by helicopter, the tall, well-dressed man radiated composure. "Okay, all five bodies're bagged and loaded into the ambulances," he said. "Your front door bolt *had* been snapped, Mr Abrams. But we've found no sign of the sword you said was used for the three decapitations in here. And I've seen some shit in my time, but I have *no* idea what kind of weapon was used to kill the guy who'd run. Scott. From what little blood spray there was, someone short held him up against the wall to do it, though. Someone short, and inhumanly strong. Haven't found the heart, yet, either. Sliced out of him.

"Your student, 'Ankhet', has been brought in. She's a queer one. She in shock? Traumatized? Anyway, she confirmed the break-in and robbery, but claims a girl the intruders lured here probably killed *the other four* of them: she says she saw her kill one. She said the girl's called 'Leeth'. Weird names: Ankhet; Leeth. These chicks foreign?" He looked around. "And where is this Leeth? We need to question her."

"I'm afraid my student suffered a psychotic episode, Agent Drexler. I'm unsure what Dr Scott did to her, exactly, but this 'Leeth' is a mere figment of her imagination. As I said, there was a sixth member of their group, an augmented individual who had a change of heart-"

The *room* flickered, a thin line appearing, like the lightning bolt of a migraine's aura. Harmon, his eyes wide in shock, stared from it, to Abrams, as his Sending gripped his heart and yanked. "It's her! Bring her back, Abrams!"

Little Brother, wide-eyed, nodded.

Abrams shook his head.

"Curse you, old man!" Harmon demanded. *"Bring her back!"* He remembered James's description of Leeth's previous 'unvanishing', and Marcie Dunkirk's role in that. Slumping to the ground, he projected himself from his body, determined to help.

Abrams swore. A single gesture, and Drexler's eyes rolled up in his head and he crumpled to the floor. That done, Abrams's own head lolled to the side as he threw himself from his spindly body, determined to stop the situation devolving back into disaster. Not willing to see defeat snatched from the jaws of victory ever again.

Drexler's female partner, Agent Havoc, yanked from sleep, her hair still wild, stepped into the room. "What in the seven hells is going on here?"

Seeing the widening fissure in the middle of the room, she drew her gun.

-

The god, Tezcatlipoca, sending the girl *back*, felt another reach for her, helping. Smiling in delight, he continued to *push* her. Now, she was at the Door, bearing his token.

Now, passing through. But she had not worded their bargain to demand he remain behind, and she could not stop him now. He grasped the other who had reached through to assist her return, and began his own transference, following the girl back into her world.

But as he rose, rainbow coils far older than him snaked around him. Holding him, effortlessly. For just a heartbeat.

Just long enough to break the link.

Below her, Leeth felt a sound that tore the air and shook her bones, and knew it as a hurricane's roar of fury. Looking back, she saw for just an instant a furious black cyclone looped in vast jewel-colored coils. They seemed oddly familiar.

Then the gray was gone and she *squeezed* back out into Mr Abrams's room, where a woman with bed hair stood with a gun trained on her, braced on her forearm. She was wearing a jacket over the top of pajamas.

"Freeze! Drop the weapon!"

Weapon? Oh. She still held the black dagger. Little Brother crouched by Mr Abrams's fancy wheelchair, staring up at her in shock but saying nothing. Her Uncle, nearby, stirred, sat up, and smiled at her.

Yes, the dagger seemed to say. *You can.*

His eyes widened in dismay – as if she'd already stabbed him and torn out his heart, not just pictured herself doing it.

"Drop the weapon!" the woman practically screamed.

She *knew* – speed coursing through her as the room stilled – what flick of her wrist would send the obsidian shard razoring into that heart. Saw the dive that would pluck it free, the simple spin needed to plant it in the Doctor's chest. She felt the blade's essence slide around the bonds in her mind and offer to cut her free.

Mr Abrams's opened his eyes, his gaze other-worldly.

The Doctor stared at her in horror.

But her instincts....

"Oh, all *right.*" With a sigh, she crouched, slowly. "It's an antique, though, so I'm putting it down real gently, okay?"

The barrel tracked her all the way down as she bent to

place it on the scorched lacquered floorboards, and all the way up as she slowly stood, her spine twinging, and suppressed a groan. Sniffing, she looked around, at stretches of charred wood. Had Mr Abrams lit a fire in here? She could feel the cut in her back bleeding, along with several sharp stabs from places where, she knew, bullets still rested, lodged inside her under recently healed wounds. It might not be a good idea to mention them just yet, or ask for them to be removed.

"Agent Havoc, Bureau of Internal Development," the woman said, barrel still trained on her, introducing herself.

"Uh, hi. Nice to meet you? I like your pajamas."

A man lay stretched out on the floor, a pistol a short distance from his out-flung hand. The woman took a single step closer. She kicked him, then stepped back. The man groaned.

"And Agent Drexler," the woman added.

Drexler wasn't one of her kills. Raising one eyebrow at Mr Abrams, she angled her head in the direction of the woman and man, curling up one side of her mouth for added emphasis. *What're* they *doing here?*

Mr Abrams just bent his head forward and closed his eyes, liver-spotted fingers massaging the bridge of his nose.

"Wha-?" The man on the ground dived for his gun, rolling and staggering to his feet.

"Glad you could join us, Drex. Nice nap?" his partner drawled.

Mr Abrams's eyes screwed tighter shut. From the corner of her eye, she saw the Doctor give a tiny shake of his head, his expression complex as he stared at her. Like he wasn't quite sure *what* he felt.

The dazed man, Drex, wore an expensive, tailored suit that would have looked much sharper without the huge bloodstain painting its front. It looked like he'd been lying right where she'd last seen the two hench-goons holding Mr Abrams. Or spraying blood as they collapsed, to be more accurate.

Their bodies were gone.

She looked around, frowning. *All* the bodies were gone. *That* pool of blood back by the door was where the guy who'd been shooting at her had fallen: the one she'd kind of cut the head off when she'd first charged into the room. So, they'd removed the bodies but hadn't had time to completely clean up?

"And where the fuck did she just come from?" said the angry, bed-haired woman.

Havoc, had she said? *Cool name!*

"That wasn't an invisibility spell dropping. Let me guess: Leeth, right?"

Leeth pursed her lips, looking from the Doctor to Mr Abrams – waved to LB, who blushed – and wondered if she'd get in more trouble from the two strangers knowing her real name, or from killing them to cover it up. She took a guess. "Uh, no, it's, Tanya Denison." She just barely kept the question out of her tone. That *was* her most recent ID, wasn't it?

"That's right!" nodded Little Brother.

"I was just bringing Mr Abrams's antique dagger back for him." She smiled innocently.

The smile would have been more convincing had her hair not been matted with dried blood and her arms not gore-stained to her elbows.

Mr Abrams just groaned.

"Um, can I ask how come two Bureau of Internal Development agents..." Her head lifted, at a heavy tread coming softly down the corridor. A very heavy tread.

"Uh..." Putting a finger to her lips, she pointed urgently to the doorway behind the two agents, mouthing 'Someone's coming' as clearly as she could. The two frowned, clearly suspecting a ploy, but they stepped away from the door, half turning so they could cover both it and her.

She realized there was also a lighter set of footsteps accompanying the ominous one, and held up two fingers in warning.

A familiar, grossly overweight figure swayed into the room, service revolver in one hand and ID badge raised in the other. Behind him came a small, ferrety man. *Oh, no way!*

"Detectives Berlusconi and Franks, NFPD." His eyes locked on her, running up and down her body and noting every bloodstain, she was sure, while a hungry smile pushed up his cheeks. "Well, well, well. Sara the vampire. I *thought* the report sounded like your handiwork." He scanned the floor, pausing at each drying pool of blood. "Wasteful. But I guess five bodies are a little too much even for you to drain, huh?"

Everyone started talking at once.

Ignored by the others, Mr Abrams leaned forward and gripped her upper arm. "What was that, just as you returned?" he whispered.

"You *saw*?" She grimaced and shrugged. "Some god. Tezsh Catlick Poker, or something like that."

"Not that. The other. *Restraining* Tezcatlipoca."

"Oh, the big, pretty one? Dunno." Or did she? For some reason, she pictured a small room, with her and Godsson and *it* in it. Probably best not to admit that, though.

Mr Abrams jerked and gaped at her, and she felt the whispers of another's thoughts in hers. *Dammit!* He'd cast Mindmeld and she hadn't noticed.

She pushed him out.

Harmon looked around. Abrams's aged head was shaking slowly from side to side, bowed. The two BID agents were trying to pull rank, pointing out the NFPD had been specifically ordered *not* to attend, as this was a BID matter. The loud and angry police mage, the same one who had questioned he and Leeth in the Golden Gate Park about her very first, most unexpected kill, was having none of it and getting more and more worked up. Leeth herself seemed aware, for once, she'd caused a major problem. Again. Perhaps she was, finally, growing up?

Four guns half-consciously tracked her, despite the furious argument, as she stretched, then, hands on hips, strolled over to him and Abrams before crouching between them to whisper so only they and Little Brother could hear her.

"Wouldn't these four make great additions to the Department?"

Or maybe not, Harmon thought.

But even as she suggested it, Leeth remembered her time with the Fist of Peace. The unfamiliar but exhilarating sense of freedom, despite the restrictions of having to play a role. What would it be like if she left the Department and just worked on her own? Seized the freedom to just be herself?

That thought sent a weird shiver through her, when she remembered Scott calling her Happy Mouth. Again, the name set her heart racing. What was that all about? *Should I ask the Doctor?* She glanced across at him, but something warned her to hold her mouth shut. The shiver shaded into a deep uneasiness, and a sharper ache in her head. *Yeah, I'll need to dig into that. Just, not right now.*

If she did leave, would she someday find a group who could accept her for herself, instead of rejecting her like the Fist had? Like the Doctor had predicted. Was it true – would everyone reject her? Except him?

She refused to believe that.

Maybe she didn't need anyone. She could fight for justice and what was right, on her own.

But the thought of being alone again made her heart ache. *I guess I can stay with the Department for now.*

After all, there were still those aliens, that she was sure were on their way. Not to mention the thing that scared the Department itself.

Yeah. After all, how tough could they be?

AFTERWORD

I hope you enjoyed the fourth episode in Leeth's saga.

It's March 2019 as I write this. I aim to complete #5 in 2020. I provide progress reports on twitter, and also on my web site *AToeInTheOceanOfBooks.com*, where I discuss this series, writing, and self-publishing.

Over half a million new books are published each year in English alone. That makes it hard for Indie authors to be noticed by readers, and for readers to discover books they'll enjoy. Word of mouth can solve both problems.

So if you did enjoy this, rating and/or reviewing it would be wonderful thanks. (A review doesn't need to be a 'literary critique' – you can just say what you thought of it.)

To the first 50 people who publish a substantive (say, 50 words or more) and honest review of *Violent Causes* – good or bad, I read them all – and the first 20 people to find a previously-undetected error in this book: email me at my address below to receive a free electronic copy of either the sequel when it's ready, or any of the earlier books, at your choice. I keep email addresses strictly private, and *only* use them to send the free ebook.

https://www.goodreads.com/review/edit/44660072 is the link you'd use on Goodreads – a great site, incidentally. (You'd need to sign in to your account.)

Finally, for a sneak peek of what's in store for Leeth, I've included the current draft of an early chapter of The Leeth Dossier Vol. 5, *Lost Girl*.

luke.kendall@gmail.com, Mar 2019. @LukeJKendall

Go deeper.

The shock of chill water paralyzed her, the warmth she'd won suddenly punctured, leaking fast. But she'd be too visible at the surface if they shone that searchlight her way. Adrenaline surged, demanding action; but a deeper memory triggered. A finely muscled man, tattooed. Not much taller than her.

Pause. Assess. Then Act. Do not let panic drive you.

She'd taken those words to heart. Learned them. Now she recalled them, and *paused: assessed,* while fear flailed at her, the waters below deep and black and silent. Anything could be down there, hunting. Hungry.

She pushed those thoughts aside, deliberately, wrapping her arms around her waist, already cold. Her legs dangled, only her head above water, the occasional wave washing over her as she bobbed, her mouth at sea level. *Wasn't I floatier before?* Not that it mattered, with the rebreather. Another wave crested over her, washing through her long hair like a lover's fingers. The pain in her head pounded dully, now. The cold seemed to be actually helping with that. Or maybe it was just numbing her through.

Hugging herself wasn't doing anything to keep her warm. Time to move. Calm now, arms outstretched as if to in welcome, she gently windmilled them, pointing her toes and slipping beneath the surface. Air with a metallic tang hissed in as she drew on the rebreather. She blew back into the mouthpiece, keeping her lips sealed tight around its molded flange. *I wonder where I learned that?* She frowned, the pain in her head sharpening until she let the question fall away.

As she sank down, the darker shapes of the boats receded in the water above her, the hull of the new one larger and shark-like. The smaller boat, the one she'd left, glowed like Hope, haloed by the light focused on it. From its front and back, two dark lines arced in gentle curves into the depths. The anchor ropes.

The light faded quickly as she 'rowed' herself deeper, her head tilted up, watching the fading light. The darkness made the cold feel worse.

Warmth was just a memory as the light shrank and dwindled.

Suddenly angry at herself for clinging to the sight, she growled, spinning in the water and turning her back on it. Mouth gripping the breathing apparatus, strong thrusts of her arms and legs drew her into the inky deeps.

Fear sang her nerves alight, the darkness tugging at her, a precipice urging her to fling herself over it.

Parts of her tingled, aroused. *Why am I so turned on?* She fought for control. Breathing hard, a cloud of bubbles escaped her mouth. She concentrated on that. *Bubbles could be a problem, if anyone saw them.* Pausing, stirring the water with her hands, she turned over to look upward in case anything had changed. She couldn't see her hands now. Nothing. *Nothing.* Just pitch blackness. Dismay spiked through her. Honest fear surged in its wake, seeking to drown her, break her. She fought back with sheer stubbornness, *refusing* it.

No. Never.

A dim glow rotated into view, its wan light shivering through her like a physical joy. She'd just been pointed the wrong way. She exhaled gustily in relief, faster than the rebreather could absorb, and more bubbles escaped, ghostly outlines wobbling upward. *Calm. Let the mind be at peace, even in the midst of motion.* The remembered words let her center herself, and soon she was breathing more gently into the mouthpiece.

What if they shone a light straight at her? She needed to go deeper, but it'd be too easy to lose her bearings completely.

Again she paused, stilling her mind as she'd been taught – aware of the dull head pain retreating even further, but refusing to let even that relief distract her. Making out the faint dark line of the anchor rope above her, a solution appeared – follow it. Too dark down here though to see where the rope passed her, too easy to miss if she simply swam blindly for it. She probably only had nine minutes of air left, too: no time to waste. She began swimming up to the anchor line, putting aside the urge to curse herself for the wasted time. *The past is past. Let it be.*

How long would the searchers stay? How quickly could, could *someone*, someone *male*, up above, get rid of them?

Sudden confusion, the pain in her head returning as she swam up toward the man who waited. *Something's wrong.* She struggled to remember. Why was she in the water? *Hiding.* Who waited for her, in the boat?

No answer came.

She couldn't remember. Just that it was a man. She was sure of that much. A firm jaw-line; stubble. The pain returned, stabbing deep, the cold gripping tighter.

She swam angrily, the burn of exercise a relief, but the effort came hard, her muscles not responding as they should. *You're near exhaustion,* that annoyingly detached voice in her head offered. *Too bad,* she told it.

She pictured her *self* and forced that essence into her muscles; imagined spirit wires charging them like batteries. Deep acid pain burned, and a sudden vision of her peeling her own flesh to feed into the fiery engine of her body flooded her, summoning an image sharp as memory, of watching strips of her own skin flensed from her. The spike through her brain twisted, as if the appalling memory, deeper and crueler than the burn in her muscles, triggered the pain.

Clenching her jaw she forced the image away, forced her muscles to her will, burning them up. *Too bad. I'll* never *give in.* The acid burn ate at her, but it only made her set her teeth more firmly. *Never.* Never *give up.*

The beam of light abruptly swung down from the boat above, spearing into the waters, probing the depths. Probing for her.

Looking up into its light she saw two dark shapes with flippered feet plunge into the water beside the shark-shaped hull.

Confusion vanished, and she felt a fierce grin form in response to the new threat. Especially when the beam flashed past overhead to briefly illuminate a dark line angling from *her* boat into the depths. Hah! For seconds, she paused, fighting the lure of the scuba figures – the need to approach, to *hunt*, intense and urgent – but finally she forced herself to turn away, swimming instead for the so-helpfully revealed rope. Her guide into the depths. Into the darkness.

The strange tingling she'd felt earlier, the arousal, returned with sudden force at the thought of surrendering to the blackness below. It washed through her and over her in a wave that rode the acid burn to bring every part of her awake. Each nerve-ending felt as if it *unfurled* from her in a strange way, until she wasn't sure where *she* ended and the water began.

And in return, the water came *alive.*

As if in response.

As if she'd called to it, as *it* now called fluidly to her.

Tendrils of strange power coiled around her, questing over her skin like the kisses of curious butterflies, attuning to the spirit lines she'd threaded through her muscles. She gasped as pleasure first flooded her whole body, then swept on into her mind. Twisting and twining through her, flowing into her, tasting the consuming fires.

Her hand struck the heavy anchor rope even as her body flared with life. Excited, *eager.* She clasped the rope. Pulling herself swiftly deeper, hand over hand, all restraint swept away by a sudden, urgent hunger. Down. Down!

www.ingramcontent.com/pod-product-compliance
Lightning Source LLC
Chambersburg PA
CBHW030655190726
48286CB00001B/35